FOR TWO DECADES,
THE KINSALES RULED . . .

Hub—the one-legged family patriarch. He liked to bed the orchard girls, and hated the oil that flowed from his rich cattle land.

Kyle—polished, elegant, he took what he wanted from men, and was given it gladly by women. Now, with the dark power of Kinsale oil, his desires would become insatiable.

Troy—the oil seeker, tough and gifted. He would build a town in the dunes of California—and breed a new generation from the Kinsale dynasty.

Luanna—Troy's half-Cherokee wife. Her jealousy would become a tool she would use to her own ends—even when it meant sleeping with the wrong brother.

CONTINENT'S EDGE

Continent's Edge

Niven Busch

PUBLISHED BY POCKET BOOKS NEW YORK

POCKET BOOKS, a Simon & Schuster division of
GULF & WESTERN CORPORATION
1230 Avenue of the Americas, New York, N.Y. 10020

Published by arrangement with Simon and Schuster
Library of Congress Catalog Card Number: 79-21784

ISBN: 0-671-81998-4

First Pocket Books printing December, 1981

10 9 8 7 6 5 4 3 2 1

POCKET and colophon are trademarks of Simon & Schuster.

Printed in the U.S.A.

For Suzanne

Acknowledgments

I wish to give high and special thanks to my friend and editor, John Dodds, for his optimistic but relentless grasp of all matters, great and small, related to this book, and above all for his patience.

And here also I would like to record a few of the many people who have also given generous help: R. W. (Johnny) Apple, Alvah Bessie, John Black, Dr. Briton C. Busch, Noel Busch, Dr. Terence Busch, Gordon Buskirk, Herb Caen, Henry Carlisle, Ernestine Carpenter, Ken Chew, Ninive Clements, Richard D. Collins, Barnaby Conrad, Frederick Drost, Paul Erdman, Bill Fields, Dr. Alexander Gansa, Dr. Armand Hammer, William Hart, Cornelius Hill, Steven Hulett, Chandler Ide, Matthew Kelly, Maryon Davies Lewis, Anne Giannini McWilliams, Walter Morris, Diane Mulligan, Ruth and Scott Newhall, George Nickel, Bill Pearson, Eric Pedley, Bernard Petrie, Bert Picard, John Renshaw, Juan Reynal, William Rintoul, John Rosenkrans, Jr., Dr. Robert Schwantes, Avery Shope, Rouse Simmons, John Sutro, Derk TeRoller, Lucille TeRoller, Clem Whittaker, Potter Wickware, David Wilson, Tom Wright.

PART ONE

PART ONE

CHAPTER ONE

A Family Gathering

1

We lived, then, in an age of heroes. One war had just ended and another stirred its muscles, over the horizon, but in this space between the two we turned for assurance to the doers of great deeds, we pelted them with flowers and money, we asked of them only that they confirm, with so much in flux, the notion that the individual could still prevail. We needed them, we needed them a lot, and for the citizens of Altemira, California—a pleasant northern country seat which no one had ever heard of—the Kinsales fulfilled that need. They had come through. They had put themselves among the odd, hypnotic myths which enchanted us at that time—Lindbergh and Ederle, Valentino and Dempsey, Fitzgerald and Harlow and Hemingway. Mind, the Kinsales were not sporting or literary figures—by no means, although Kyle, the most dashing of them, admitted to some sport proclivities. The Kinsales had their own game, but it was enough, indeed it was so much that an Altemiran, traveling, could identify his town to non-Californians by saying that the Kinsales came from there. They didn't really, but their headquarters ranch was only forty miles away. It wasn't much of a lie.

What seems odd now, on reflection, is not that we admired them but that we knew so little about them. We just had the hometown data. We knew which of the men were the womanizers, which the wanderers, which the stay-at-homes; we knew the family's kindnesses and meannesses, their tastes and their vices; we had gone to school with some of them; we had competed with them for girls and ridden against them in roping contests; some of us had been confirmed and taken Communion with them. That was another thing: the Kinsales were Catholics. Most of us weren't, in Altemira, but we didn't hold that against them. They did their shopping with us when they could just as easily have taken it to King City or Coalinga. We appreciated that. We liked to see their carriages and fine matched teams and later their automobiles (I'm speaking now of the first quarter of the twentieth century) moving through our streets or waiting outside our stores and banks and lawyers' offices; we enjoyed the vicarious importance of having the family members around. They were good-looking people, most all of them, except Hub: tall with a nice proportion of flesh and bone. They were dark-brown- or rufous-haired men and women (Kyle was the only black-haired one), but whether red or darkish, all had a certain glisten to them, a certain way of moving and of holding their heads, particularly when talking to each other—an angle, a slant, not superior necessarily but private—and all, without exception, had the Kinsale skin or some substance covering them which wasn't really skin but a stuff similar to it and performing the same function, only better—paler and tougher than ordinary skin and proof against the skin troubles that might affect less favored folk: sunburn and poison oak and chiggers, perhaps even heat and cold.

They were ours. At least for a long time they were ours, then at some point there was a breakthrough. We heard about the first oil well, the dramatic one, and then the winds of family change, the hurricane of money which some of them rode so dashingly, so conspicuously, onto the front pages of the world's newspapers. Not that we read newspapers all that much. (The *Literary Digest* or *American Magazine*, which praised famous people, or *The American Mercury* or *Mc-Clure's*, which ripped them up.) We read the *Altemira Free Lance*, but even the *Free Lance* mentioned these developments. Then again, some of us traveled; we took note, along the great pale highways, of the neat green-and-gold KinOil stations and their newfangled glass-windowed pumps, and we filled up with KinOil gas, partly out of loyalty and partly because it was the best gas going and the price was right.

Gabe Evans, the saddlemaker (he had turned out hand-crafted rigs for three generations of Kinsales), sold his shop when he was ready to retire and he and the wife took a trip to Chicago and brought back word about the KinOil Building there, sixty stories on State Street. There was another, smaller building on Bush, in San Francisco.

We saw the start of it, the Kinsale legend. We had no real idea of how far, how fast it had moved, though we were given hints from time to time. One such—of an unusual kind—occurred at the end of the thirties when a team of Secret Service men arrived in town. They inspected the railroad station and conferred with a Southern Pacific maintenance detail as to the condition of the tracks from the S.P. station in Altemira out to the Kinsale ranch. The S.P. had recently acquired that line but for many years it had been a private holding. Calvin Kinsale, the founding grandfather, had built it before the turn of the century. He'd wanted a way to ship his cattle to market without taking weight off them. (To any Kinsale, taking weight off cattle was the worst thing you could do.) One wonders how much of an economy the railroad had proved to be; still, there was something grand about it—and about a family that *owned* a railroad line, no matter how short, no matter in *what* condition.

The Secret Service said it was all right. They were orderly, uncommunicative men with the indoor faces of prisoners or house servants; they wore dark suits with baggy, pleated pants. After inspecting the track they took on guard duty at the ranch. They were responsible for the safety of someone coming down to the Kinsales'—the Vice President of the United States, for God's sake! And he—well, he was going to be on hand in his capacity as an official government welcomer to someone else, someone even more important, who would be there: the Emperor of Turkey! Such was the gossip at the post office until someone remembered that Turkey wasn't an empire, it was a republic. Nor was the head of it coming. That was ascertained later. Not the headman but the number two man and he not by train, it seemed, but by automobile, by three automobiles in fact, black Lincolns—what we'd once called bootleggers' cars—he riding in the middle one. The motorcade stopped at the KinOil station across from the State Theater and the number two man got out and went to the gents'. He was a stooped, no-longer-young individual with a mustache-beard, as you might call it—a ring of black hair which tightly circled his mouth. Since he was being accorded

head-of-state status, one of the Secret Service men stood
outside the door while the Turk relieved himself.

CONSORTIUM BACKS FOREIGN LOAN

The *San Francisco Chronicle* and the *Altemira Free Lance*
both used the same studhorse head, but the *Chronicle* had it
on the second section. The loaning entities were listed as
KinOil of California, Pacific Refineries, Piru Pipe and Drilling, and the Bank of America. Pacific Refineries, a partially
owned Kinsale subsidiary, distributed KinOil products na-
tionally. Piru Pipe and Drilling was the KinOil exploration
branch. The Bank of America, KinOil's "lead bank" in
California, had underwritten the loan in conjunction with
Lazard Frères of New York and Paris, an international
banking house.

What the deal amounted to, behind the corporate fronts,
was that the Kinsales were privately lending twenty million
dollars to a foreign government. They got six percent bonds
and an oil concession in return.

The New York Times felt they'd achieved a coup: the oil
concession, close to the proven fields of Royal Dutch Shell
and British Petroleum, could have great value.

Twenty million dollars—well, it was a risk. A huge sum for
those days (KinOil had "gone public" in 1931). What other
family, above all what other California family, could deal
with a needy nation as if it, the family, were *another nation?*
That was something to think about. And not only as if it were
another nation, but clearly the more powerful as well as the
richer of the two, since the Kinsale nation, if it could be so
called, had made the Turkish nation send its man, that pisser
with the round black beard on his mouth, over land and sea,
clear to the headquarters ranch to sign up for the money.

It made you proud to be neighbors with a family like that!

We have leaped way ahead. There was no sign, earlier on,
of such glory in the offing. There they were with us, these
extraordinary people, but how were you to tell they were
extraordinary? They had seemed so long to be like any other
dullish, landed California family, rooted to the earth as we to
our town by birth and necessity, by taste and tradition, and
above all by their stubborn, rawhide innocence.

The truth is that, but for the grace of God, they might
never have made the first move, they might have missed the

whole exercise—in fact, through the mouth of Hubbard W. Kinsale, titular head of the clan at that time, son of Calvin, husband of Emilia de Baca Kinsale, father of Mildred, Kyle and Troy Kinsale, they actually made the decision to do so, made it officially and passed it by resolution and read it into the minutes of the Kinsale Land and Cattle Company, the basic company of all, which is not and has never been a public company, in the course of a stockholders' meeting.

That meeting was not the first at which oil was discussed but it was the most critical.

There was a strict protocol about Kinsale Land and Cattle Company meetings. They included lunch. Some of the people had to come a hundred miles, and a few farther; they couldn't go too long without food. Hub well knew that shareholders, like other folk, were easier to deal with when they were properly fed and provided with a few shots of well-aged grog. The shareholders had been getting frisky. You could not order them around the way old Cal had done. Cal had incorporated the family business in 1910, under the laws of the state of California. He'd kept a controlling stock majority for himself, but on his death a new distribution had been made. Hub held more shares than any other single person— not enough, however, to prevail should all unite against him. So far this had never happened and to make sure it never would Hub had, on reaching sixty-five, stepped down from the presidency, handing that duty over to Kyle, his eldest son. Kyle was his favorite. They understood each other. Kyle was a well-educated person, a special person, and Hub had need, in the pressure of new ways, new times, of Kyle's education, his brilliance and charm and tact. Being so special, Kyle also had special needs, and Hub had seen that these were satisfied. A fair exchange! It would be a cold day in hell before Kyle moved against him. On the other hand, Kyle would not be at today's meeting. He was in England, riding in a point-to-point (whatever that might be!). There was a rumor that Troy had been in touch with him—that Kyle, if that could be believed, had written a letter supporting Troy's demand.

Troy himself would be on hand. That was assured, but for once the meeting started without him.

He was late.

Troy had presented a drilling program the year before, and the stockholders had approved it. It had been a modest program. Troy was convinced that there were oil deposits on the remote Piru ranch, one of the family's holdings in the southern part of the state. He had drawn a map on the blackboard used at the meetings for detailing propositions and for writing columns of figures showing profits and losses. By no means all of the projected figures went into the profit column in those days. There were good years and bad ones. There were years when much rain fell and the range was rich, and there were years on the other hand when a critter could walk all day and hardly find a blade to eat. Though you might hold, in the aggregate, close to half a million acres, there could be marketing problems. The cattle business, even in the best cattle country God ever made, was chancy. It was chancy as hell.

Troy was aware of all this. He took note of it in his presentation. He had grown up with cattle but his real interest had always been oil. There were places on the homeranch where it oozed out of the ground—perhaps not real oil, but a gummy asphaltlike substance closely related to real oil, and smelling even worse. Troy, as a little boy, had several times got himself covered with it from head to toe. He and Kyle had made a canvas canoe and waterproofed it with the gummy stuff; it had not been the best of canoes, but it had been waterproof all right. Later Troy, all alone, had found a black seepage under a ledge, down by the San Benito River, and had dug a well there with a hand auger. Paul Shanley, the chemistry teacher at Altemira High, had certified the product as petroleum. Troy had casked almost a barrel of oil before Hub forbade further drilling.

Hub had sealed off the tiny well, but not his son's fascination with what had come out of it. In Stanford University, Troy had concentrated on geology and chemistry. He had left after two years to go to sea on a Norwegian tanker, jumping ship in Valparaiso to work in the oil fields. For the next several years, in California and Texas, in Mexico, San Salvador and Venezuela, he had labored as a roustabout, then a driller, and finally—with little help from his family, and less favor—as a tool pusher with his own rig and a crew working for him and money in the bank. He had married an oilman's daughter, Luanna Keleher of Pawhuska, Oklahoma, and had two children of his own and lively hope for more. He had made his mark, and when he said there was oil on the Piru ranch he knew whereof he spoke, or certainly seemed to. To that date it had been the most worthless chunk in all the

family's holdings. Like the homeranch, the southern appendages, or floats as they were originally called, had been
Spanish or—later—Mexican land grants. Calvin Kinsale had
picked up a number of them in the seventies and eighties, the
drought years when the Californios, in debt to Yankee loan
sharks, were desperate for money; sometimes they hadn't
even read the deeds by which they signed away their grand
estates. By their traditions it was not mannerly to show
concern for legal language once a deal had been agreed upon.
A glass of *aguardiente* and a handshake between *caballeros*
was enough.

In the stretch of properties, reaching from Altemira almost
to the Mexican border on the south, and from the ocean on
the west to the Sierras on the east, the homeranch was the
earliest and best but not the largest. If you considered the
homeranch as a kite, these appendages were the tail of it,
odd-shaped and sometimes unproductive pieces strung down
toward the southern portion of the state, but they were land
just the same—and land was what had interested the Kinsales.

Troy had been drilling at Piru now for almost a year. He
had begun with a couple of dry holes, then moved onto a site
that promised better. A few weeks before this 1923 meeting
he had run through the last of the money allotted for the job
and had driven north all night in an Overland pickup to ask
Hub for more.

Hub had been loading cattle at the ranch railroad siding.
They'd argued for more than an hour, both of them tense and
angry, before Hub gave in. He was doing it, he stated, only
because the talk was costing money—his critters were sweating fat off there in the sun. He'd held a check against the
blistering side of a boxcar and scribbled his name on it. "But
that's the fucking last," he said. "And you know I mean it."

If he could unite the shareholders behind him, Troy might
reverse his father's dictum. That was his task, that September
day in 1923. It was his only chance.

As a rule the meeting was called to order in the parlor, but
today, being unusually hot, Millie Kinsale Braden, who
functioned as company secretary as well as official hostess,
decided it should be out on the lawn; she had also served
lunch out there, now just ending. Sweet Millie! Openhearted
Millie! She had invited not just stockholders but *everyone*.
That was her way, her openheartedness—or was it, Hub had
wondered, a way of forcing his hand, or trying to, by sheer

force of numbers? She and Troy had always been close! And with Kyle away, Millie's husband, Doc Braden, would be sitting as chairman *pro tempore*. Dr. Carl Winston Braden, graduate of Stanford Medical School, respected throughout San Benito County and wherever else he chose to go.

"It gets so stuffy," she'd insisted, "if it's only *us* . . ."

They'd been coming in all morning, the dim Kinsale yeomanry of parched valley towns and mountain aeries and foggy Mendocino seaports, people seldom seen outside their own bailiwicks but brought in this one day to rub elbows and clink glasses with the family core, the power echelon, as well as with those certain foot soldiers and retainers who had served with honor and been doled out a few shares of stock to secure their loyalty: lawyers, priests, accountants, suppliers, managers, administrators, politicians, cattle buyers and commodity brokers, clerks and insurance salesmen, and so forth and so on.

In front of the huge, fancifully carpentered and turreted and glassed old house, in the softly moving air, in the shadow of the great trees, a card table had been set out for the chairman with a pitcher of water and a pad and pencil and a gavel on it, but Dr. Braden had not yet taken his place there; the Mexican girls were still collecting plates and passing coffee, everyone chattering and casting glances at the driveway, waiting for Troy. But where was he? It was certainly the question of the hour and as it passed from group to group a special look went round.

Family resemblances inevitably appear more pronounced when the people who share them are gathered for a tribal rite. In the Kinsales there was, of course, the skin, the toughness of it, the glaze of it, but along with the skin, or even without it, there were the upthrust Kinsale cheekbones and the eyebrows which could be dark or pale or gingery but which were nearly always thick, sometimes extruding like little snouts, sometimes brushed elegantly upward from beneath, like mustaches. No one individual had all the imprimaturs but all had some: the protective low ridges of bone over the eyes, the long, sorrowful upper lips. Something! Still, such things were just features. They were not The Look. That . . . well, it was a code. It was a manner of pitching the shoulders slightly forward, of holding the head in a special way, above all when speaking to someone else who pitched the shoulders, who held the head that way. It was a bold and impatient movement of the eyes, begging you to get on with whatever you were saying so that one could pass to more interesting subjects; it was a slouch, or not exactly a *slouch* but . . . a placement of the legs so that in case of an unexpected attack one could spring onto a horse or into the bushes. It was The Look and today you saw it everywhere; it moved and rippled among the people, young and old, male or female, Kinsale kith or Kinsale kin, like the wind on a stock-water pond.

Today it seemed especially pronounced, possibly because nerves were on edge, tempers—always to be reckoned with among Kinsales—pulling at the curb. This oil business! Where did one stand on it? Troy was in trouble with the well: that much was known. It had seemed like a good thing when he'd talked about it, but a frightful expense, as Hub had pointed out when they first voted. Now another go-round, a year gone by and all that money spent. Sheer waste possibly, but yet . . . if it came in after all, what a godsend! The decision could go either way. It would depend on what Troy had to say. He'd telephoned earlier, using the phone in Percy Yountman's service station. He should be arriving now most any time.

2

The road was the loneliest in the whole wide brown land. It sprang out of a clutch of low hills to the southeast and charged fiercely at the mountains to the northwest as if bent on slicing them in half. It was a good road, narrow but well engineered in spite of having been constructed of three different materials spaced on loosely alternating sections—macadam and gravel and plain packed earth; it was also very straight, but its straightness, while impressive, was no virtue, since at this hour of the day, with even the few drivers pulling off into the shade to eat, and no one to be seen, the empty road, disappearing into the horizon, appeared useless, an expensive artifact tossed down for show and left there to mystify future generations.

Only on one of the earthen sections was there some stir of life—the movement of a car which pushed on purposefully, absurdly in that huge landscape, bouncing quixotic reflections from its slanting windshield and its brass trim and bright paint, dragging a wedge-shaped cloud of dust behind it: the brand-new, left-hand-drive Pierce-Arrow, Model 48, which had recently replaced Troy's battered Overland as the implement of family transportation.

They had been traveling since 4 A.M.—Troy Kinsale, his wife, Luanna, his son, Cliff, and his daughter, Helene. Heat smashed down from the immense golden sky. But in the car it wasn't hot, only pleasantly warm. The top was up but the isinglass window panels had been taken down for the summer.

Helene, not quite three, slept in her mother's arms and Luanna herself was more than three-quarters asleep; she had nudged over toward Troy the way she did in bed until she rested against him. Cliff, aged seven, had started out in the front seat with his parents but had wriggled and chattered so much he had finally been relegated to the back. Here he slept peacefully, his head on Troy's folded jacket, his legs jack-knifed on the seat.

Troy drove. He did this, as he did everything, with complete attention. He enjoyed driving, above all, in such a car as this!

Luanna, though she liked the new car as much as he, had called it an extravagance. It was not an extravagance. He'd financed it on his confidence that he could persuade the Land and Cattle idiots—force them by sheer logic—to let him keep drilling. Soon he'd be able to afford anything, ten such cars if he wanted them. With the same faith he had refused to close down the rig; when Hub's most recent handout was exhausted he'd used his own savings to keep the crew on the job and the bit chewing at the earth, nearly a mile down under the surface. What was down there couldn't be seen, but the car—a visible, advance token of the splendors to come—was in truth a beauty, perfect in every detail: the burnished russet of its paint, the high rounded hood, the spare tires up forward in their brown canvas covers, in their deep fender wells, and the headlights, those great powerful lamps, not tucked down in front of the grille but spread apart for wider coverage, spaced out on the curves of the fenders themselves. Perce Yountman had never even serviced such a car. Troy had had to show him where the gas intake valve was, craftily placed behind the trunk—a trunk as big as a boxcar.

Troy held his hands high on the wheel, aiming the large brass radiator cap exactly down the center of the road, the hypothetical meeting point of the parallel sides.

He lacked something of the traditional Kinsale height, but

not of the glary skin or the looseness of bone—a brown-eyed man with big-knuckled hands and a nose slightly flattened at the bridge. He was thirty-five years old and had a lively competent air about him even when, as now, he sat perfectly still. His apparent equanimity and good nature, however, were deceptive; he was a brooder as well as a doer and demanded much, often too much, from the people around him. Before Luanna calmed him down he would drink and get into fights. He still drank, though now more moderately. He was a passionate lover, a good husband and a tender father, very loving with his children. He was thinking now how glad he was that young Cliff, even under stressful circumstances, was to have this visit to the ranch. Cliff loved to go there. To any boy the place was a paradise to explore and pull around him. It was an enormous and fascinating schoolroom in which he could learn how to live. He would find out things he would never learn in a thousand years in a grubby oil town. Luanna always said this, and it was true. She had grown up in oil towns, but she hated them.

The road grew narrower. All macadam now, it descended into little draws, then charged up the other side like a cornered outlaw; it hairpinned around outcroppings of lonely, crumbling granite and flung itself head on at shaly slopes hung with streaks of alkali and bewigged with tumbling wire fences, their sagging redwood pickets wearing suits of moss like fur on their north sides, where the sun never reached. Climbing steadily upward, bending perilously around curves, it kept company for a time with a gas line engaged in the same struggle but better fitted for it since the pipe, elevated on trestles, could stab its way straight across gullies and gashes that the road could negotiate only with elaborate, defensive tactics.

Troy knew all about that pipeline. It was a twelve-inch line, the sort which oilmen were calling a "spaghetti line" in contrast to the twenty-four-inch lines which were now coming into use. It carried gas from the Coalinga-McKittrick oil fields 150 miles straight north to fuel the stoves and furnaces and factories of San Francisco. It was one more proof of the long reach of oil and oil products, of the need for them, the thrust of them.

The pipeline took off by itself as the road, still buckling heavily, made for the crest before beginning its descent into Dead Eagle Valley. Spanish names left on the California land were mostly monuments to long-departed undernourished

men and women who had suffered such deprivations and
tortures while alive that some restitution had to be made to
them in death: San Geronimo, San Luis the Bishop, San
Ysidro, the friend of farmers; San Marcos, San Francisco,
Santa Teresa, San Domingo and the like. American names,
on the other hand, products of a more pragmatic demonol-
ogy, tended to identify locations with the folk who had lived
in the region or with small, specific happenings there: Whore
Creek, Shirt Tale Slough, Bad Bear Crossing, Hangtown
Gulch, Whiskey Hill, Fremont's Peak, Wild Horse Lane, etc.

Dead Eagle Valley drew its name from a bird found
impaled on a stake and placed at the entrance to the principal
valley trail by the Mexican owner of the land when he
evacuated it and returned home. Apparently he meant to
convey to his successors the idea that the valley was not a
good place to settle in.

He was correct. The Americans ignored the dead eagle, but
its sinister message had been confirmed through the years by
the sort of living that was done there in the valley named for
it. There was not too much, even of that. Here and there,
tucked into hill shoulders or balanced perilously above
washes which could, and did, regularly overflow, were meager ranches consisting of a few pole corrals and a weather-
beaten house with junk machinery around it and a sag-roof
barn painted with a Mail Pouch Tobacco sign. In contrast to
the profligate wealth and fecundity of the Kinsale spread in
the mountains, less than fifty miles away, the fields of Dead
Eagle Valley were flinty and arid, and at the least suspicion of
neglect the banished sagebrush and jimson and manzanita
and the pale impudent plumes of yucca would reclaim their
imperatives. The cattle that fed in the higher slopes got
hipshot climbing for a bite of filaree; deer bred down to the
size of rabbits and jackrabbits bred up to the size of goats;
hawks killed the quail and there wasn't enough water for
dove; when hunters tried to have a go at a buck they
discovered, instead of game signs, the bleached droppings of
the mountain lions which had thinned the herds and the bones
of the fawns and does they had left to mark the kill.

The people of Dead Eagle Valley had, like the animals,
suffered genetic damage. They had interbred, crossbred and
counterbred and formed ignoble but productive alliances
unrecognized in area genealogies. They had sad eyes and
pigeon chests, skinny arms and legs, and long heads and long,
pale faces. You could tell them anywhere. There weren't

many of them, so they stuck together. First cousins married first cousins and nieces married uncles and nephews married aunts and there were situations even closer than that, a lot closer, which nobody talked about. Possibly as a result of all this, the immunizing capability of Dead Eagle Valley bodies weakened so that now they were coming down with diseases modern medicine had long ignored, believing them extinct.

Dr. Carl Winston Braden looked upon Dead Eagle Valley as a challenge. He felt he had been called by destiny to take on its pathology, largely in single combat. The doctors in Altemira would not have set foot in Dead Eagle Valley for a year's fees. In accepting this type of practice Doc had shown courage but at the shareholders' meetings little of that spirit was visible; he was extremely conservative, especially when acting as chairman *pro tempore*. Doc, who had experienced hard times as a younger man, working his way through medical school, showed no appetite where money was concerned. He collected readily if patients paid him, but if they failed to pay he never sued them.

Suing was against his principles.

"They needed the care" was all he'd say.

Doc most generally voted with Hub on company matters. He let Hub tromp all over him, much to his wife's annoyance. Hub had moved for a Land and Cattle Company loan for Doc—presenting it as a wedding present, this shylock handout which paid the company three and a half percent! With the money thus acquired, in the form of a first trust deed, Doc had built his house, office and clinic, three buildings economically sandwiched into one—but only on condition, entered in the escrow, that Doc would forever treat all Kinsales without charge.

"But of course he'll do that, Father," Millie had stormed. "You don't have to put it in writing. Don't you know what kind of *man* he is?"

But Hub had insisted on the legal clause.

"People can switch on you," he said philosophically.

Troy hoped Millie had been talking to Doc about the well. If the two of them divided their vote they would nullify each other: they held equal amounts of stock, Millie having shared hers with her husband.

Troy turned off the county highway onto a private ten-mile strip into the ranch, topped with asphalt from the ranch deposits he had mucked around in as a boy.

Night or day, he could have driven this road with his eyes

closed, so often had he traveled it, in cars and in carriages and
spring wagons, on horseback, on bicycles and on foot.
Whether he was asleep or awake, the road was always
there—*his* road—softly unfurling in his mind. He knew
without thinking the road's dips and hollows and level
stretches; he could tell from the feel of the tires or the pull of
the wheel what part of it lay under his progress. Some eight
miles in, for instance, a mile or two past the first cattle guard,
was a railroad warning sign, then another cattle guard, then
the tracks themselves, then a third cattle guard before the
road bore on again, down into a dip and up the other side,
across Cal Kinsale's railroad.

His grandfather had even put in a station, a building
conceived for ornament only, not much bigger than a doll-
house but constructed in faithful imitation of the official S.P.
stations. Here, when Kyle Kinsale had been in college and
sometimes later, at his order, chartered engines had chuffed
up and stopped, pulling chartered parlor cars. And from the
cars had descended Kyle's guests, young men in white
flannels and blazers, some wearing derbies, some boater
straws—also attractive young women in lacy summer dresses,
with parasols and garden hats (Kyle's parties, needless to say,
were always in summer). Kyle had met his guests with flatbed
wagons turned into charabancs by bolting seats onto them.
Four- and six-horse teams pulled the wagons here and there,
and after their tour of the ranch's more noteworthy features
the guests gathered on the front lawn where Chun Wuk had
the barbecue fires going and Mexican girls handed round
glasses of whiskey and champagne, real stuff, brought in from
Canada.

Troy had attended some of these parties. Kyle had introduced him to everyone and he had flirted with the girls and
gone through the motions of having a good time but he had
never fitted in. It was strange how Kyle could be, besides his
brother, his best friend in the goddamn world, but at the same
time talk the language these guests talked, which was like a
foreign tongue.

"How did you learn all that?" he'd asked Kyle once.

"All what?"

"All that hoopla."

Kyle laughed.

"It's silly, isn't it?" But then a sharp, intense look jumped
into his handsome face. He took Troy by the arms and

gripped him hard. "But it's jim-dandy, too, you know. Isn't it really *the thing?*"

Troy could also have used the railroad. He could also have given parties. Hub told him so.

"Have your friends down, boy. Have 'em anytime."

Troy had thanked his father but never availed himself of his invitation. He hadn't had many friends, not at that time. Later he had more, but they were not the kind you would load onto a drawing-room car or ride around in flatbed wagons draped with bunting. None of them had boater straws or blue flannel blazers. They all smelled of oil.

3

The car had now reached a place where the road divided. One part continued on to the corrals, service shops and barns while another section became the front driveway of the main house. Surfaced with pea gravel, lined on both sides with enormous eucalyptus trees, the drive ran for a mile from the fork to the big old mansion set square at the end of it. Troy could see the people moving around on the lawn and smell the smoke from the barbecue fires. He gently detached his wife's head from his shoulder; she woke up at once and wakened Helene, who whimpered.

"She's hungry," said Luanna.

"I'll see if Millie can get us some food. Maybe we still have time to eat before they begin."

Troy reached into the back seat to rouse little Cliff.

Cliff's first act, on reaching the ranch, was always the same: he would grab something to eat—today a large broiled rib, so hot he could hardly hold it—and be off to the company street, the service headquarters which was the nerve center of the big spread's multiple, diversified activities. Here was the carpenter shop, with its marvelous smells of pine, cedar and redwood, the sounds of planing and sawing, the shavings which were swept up twice a day but still clumped, rustling, before a footstep, thick as leaves after a forest wind. Here the wonder of the treadle saw, which worked on a pedal and would eat through a thick hardwood plank like a knife through cheese; here was the lean-to that housed the blacksmith, T-bone Winnick, a tiny Welshman, and his huge, mean

son Rondo, who hated kids around and would lay Cliff on his
ass if he caught him near the forge. Here were the racks of
muleshoes and horseshoes, some to be put on cold, some hot;
the kegs of nails, the implements for stretching, shaping,
cutting, and threading metal into anything desired—axles or
hasps, tools or weather vanes or stove fittings. Here was the
commissary where workers could buy clothes or food with
company script—a private currency so well backed it could
even be used, at a slight discount, in Altemira. Here the
wagon and equipment sheds, with trained men to repair and
maintain the vehicles, whether horse-drawn or motor-
propelled; the tack room, always kept locked (riders who
would rather have cut their throats than be known as thieves
would sometimes filch one of the beautiful ranch saddles, a
cowhand's basic piece of equipment). At the end of the street
was the feedlot, a ten-acre square, elaborately fenced and
cross-fenced, notched with loading chutes and water troughs
and serviced with a steam-operated conveyor that brought
feed from the mill on the hill behind it—one of Hub's
innovations. The mill worked by electricity. It would grind
any kind of mix you wanted, coarse or fine, alfalfa or oats or
bran, cottonseed or wheat or corn—and not only mill it but
funnel it into sacks which required only one attendant to lift
them off the conveyor and sew them up. Hub always swore
the mill made money for him, Kyle suspected that it lost; but
there it was, an alchemist's dusty laboratory, humming with a
secret, electrical song: a triumph of farm science.

The street had not been quite so fascinating when Troy, as
a boy himself, had haunted it, but he well understood its
magic. He watched with a sort of envy as his son headed off
on the road that led to it. He would have given a good deal at
that moment to change places with him, but he had business
in hand.

Already, while he and Luanna finished their plates of
cooling, rather unappetizing food, salvaged from the left-
overs of lunch, Doc had taken his place at the chairman's
table, about to call for order. A tap of his gavel accomplished
this. Talk died down on the lawn; people moved chairs and
redwood benches closer, for better hearing. Doc called on
Millie for the minutes of the last meeting and she promptly
obliged, reading somewhat too rapidly in her oddly inflected,
countrified voice, so different from Doc's confident, professional way of speaking.

The first item on the agenda was consideration of refencing

one of the company's lesser holdings—a piece in the Sierra foothills, used mostly for summer pasture. The ranch manager, one Quincy Ortega, a Mexican-American whose grandfather had worked on the homeranch when Cal Kinsale purchased it, favored accepting an outside contract to put in fence by the mile, with a motor-turned post-hole digger. The contractors could do it cheaper than the company could with hand labor, though the posts were more costly. While the pros and cons of this were being debated Troy took from his pocket once more and read over Kyle's letter of support. He wanted to have it clearly in mind so that he would have no trouble when it came to reading aloud. It was a good letter. It might do the trick. But oh, if Kyle had only been here himself! How much better that would have been . . . how easily then could the opposition had been brought into line!

The letter was handwritten on very thin, aristocratic-looking paper. Though it had arrived only in the nick of time to be read here it was already three weeks old, having taken that long to cross the Atlantic and the spread of the continent, even with the fast trains and boats which now carried the mail. It was dated at Craven Lodge, Melton Mowbray, and it read as follows:

To the Shareholders of the Kinsale Land and Cattle Company:

Greetings!

I regret that business in England keeps me from attending this year's meeting—the first annual meeting I have missed in a long time. Looking back, I can say—and I'm sure you will agree—what a fine growth this span has brought to the Kinsale Land and Cattle Company! The next decade will, and must, be as good or better and with this conviction I respectfully direct the attention of the shareholders to my brother Troy's operations on our Piru ranch.

Troy and I have been in close and constant touch and I am fully informed both on the progress made so far and the difficulties recently encountered. He will expose these matters fully to you all and I have asked him to read this letter, assuring you of my unqualified support for his proposals. I hereby delegate Mildred Kinsale Braden to vote my shares in favor of any motion for further funding which he may see fit to bring to the attention of the meeting and I urge you all to vote the same way. A show of confidence in Troy may well be the best investment that the company has ever made.

Sincerely,
Kyle Kinsale, Pres.

Kyle had enclosed this missive in another, less formal communication:

Savoy Hotel
London
30 August 1923

Dear Horsethief,

I feel sure this will do the trick. Even our fellow shareholders, stupid as most of them are, must see the advantages to be gained from your adventure, and the low risk.

Over here the most important oilman is an Armenian, Mr. Calouste Gulbenkian. He's been negotiating for oil concessions in the Persian Gulf, then selling them off. "Mr. Five Percent" he's called, since in each deal he keeps that override for himself. Not bad, eh? He's the richest man in the world at this moment, *not* excluding the Aga Khan or John D. Rockefeller. He keeps to himself, mostly in Paris, where he has a huge place on the Boulevard Haussmann but sleeps in a suite at the Ritz. I've met his son, Nubar, a pain in the ass, but if you can put up with his affectations—the orchid in the buttonhole, the monocle, et cetera—you find he's smart as the devil. He invited me to hunt with him (translation: Fox hunt. On jumping horses). Here I gave the natives a treat—turned out in ten-gallon hat, California stockman's boots and Chihuahua spurs with three-inch guthooks. Got my picture in *The Illustrated London News*, by God—for whatever that's worth.

Yes, I'm good at social gambits like the above, but how I wish they weren't necessary, how I wish I could negotiate with Gulbenkian as an equal instead of trying, as I am now, for a piece of his business. Even he can use American dollars and I just may know where I can find him some, from friends of mine. Were it not for this deal I would have come home for the meeting with our redneck cousins. Anyway, never fear. They'll give you the money. Then you'll be on your own.

The well must come in, Troy-boy. It must! Everything, everything depends on it.

Good luck!

K. K.

On the homeranch lawn, Troy listened to the discussion about the fence. Yes, these dear and loyal friends and relatives were certainly rednecks, but they were rednecks out of whose purses, today, he would somehow have to squeeze forty-two thousand dollars.

"Motion: That Salinas Valley Fence be requested to submit a bid, within thirty days, for work and materials on that property owned by the Kinsale Land and Cattle Company and located at [blah blah blah and so forth]."

Motion proposed, seconded and carried. Doc Braden tapped the card table with his gavel. He glanced, smiling, in Troy's direction.

"Our agenda now calls for a report from Troy Kinsale with respect to petroleum drilling operations on the company's property in Piru, Los Angeles County . . ."

4

Troy stood up, smiling and nodding at those assembled, showing a confidence he did not feel. Although he tried to conceal it, he always experienced some awkwardness when called on to address a group; he had none of Kyle's flair for the dramatic. Once he began speaking, however, the facts of the matter in hand took first place in his mind; he would concentrate on them, forgetting all else. This was a friendly audience and the commitment he needed from them was, after all, greatly to their advantage.

"We haven't got what we want yet," he said, "but we're close. We're pretty sure of that. If you ask why, I'd have to come up with a lot of technical jargon that might only be confusing—half the time I don't know what it means myself. [Mild laughter.] We could talk about stratigraphy, which is of course the study of strata in the earth—the Cenozoic, the Mesozoic, the Paleozoic. And then the subdivisions: the Quanternary, the Tertiary, the Cretaceous, Jurassic, Triassic and so forth, all the layers of the various geologic formations we look at and take samples from—corings—as we drill down for oil. In some parts of the world we find oil in the structures near the surface. California has a lot of surface oil, usually not the best. Sometimes the strata are shallow and you go through a lot of geologic time with very little drilling. Sometimes, on the other hand, we go five thousand feet to get through the Miocene level, which in another place might be less than a thousand feet in depth. The same is true of the deeper strata where the better grades of oil are usually found. And the biggest wells.

"Now there are two ways to drill. I mentioned them to you last year, when I first asked the shareholders for money to start operations at Piru. The safest way is to go down in the parameters of a proven field or offset a producing well. You have the data from other drillings to check with, and if you don't encounter more or less the same structures and bring your well in at approximately the same depth you can figure you've got a dry hole. So then you walk away and try somewhere else. Well, we're not doing that. We're not playing it safe. This well, Cliff Kinsale Number One—named after my son, and I call it a well because I'm sure it's going to produce—this well is a wildcat. There's not a producing field within forty miles of it. We can't use other people's data; we have to rely on our own. And here's an interesting thing: Cliff Kinsale Number One is turning up corings that tally almost exactly with the stratigraphy of the best fields to the north— the McKittrick and Bakersfield and Coalinga formations—but with this difference, that our layers are thicker, a lot thicker. So what does that do? Well, it makes our well deeper than those northern wells and deep, my friends, is where the good oil is, the high-gravity stuff. In the last month we've brought up fossil indications that we're close to a strike. I was even hopeful that we'd meet our deadline, stay within the budget, and that I could come to this meeting and tell you we'd proven up. Unfortunately, I can't do that. Not yet."

Troy looked around. The faces turned to him were attentive, friendly—the ovals of burnished skin, the dabs of dark or reddish or bone-colored hair blended into a receptive audience, one which had previously gone along with his intentions. As he spoke he had been moving from his seat at an outlying table, where Luanna still remained—the only places open to them as they hurried in late; he had strolled down toward the chairman's station, under the largest of the elm trees. He now leaned over, with a smile which asked permission, and poured water from the chairman's pitcher into a glass which Doc had immediately pushed toward him. As he sipped, relaxing for a few seconds before the next, the crucial, portion of his talk, he glanced over at his father—the danger point from which, if there was opposition, it would come.

Hub Kinsale had angled his chair sideways. This was a practice of his at the annual meetings, which he found boring—the angle in itself, though hardly courteous, was not necessarily to be construed as hostile. Less encouraging was what Hub was doing with his hands. From a little pile of sticks, stacked to provide starters for the barbecue fires, Hub had selected a chunk of pine. This he was whittling, his head bent to the job, the long, sharp blade of his jacknife flicking tiny shavings on the grass. Hub was a consummate whittler. He liked to keep soft, clear-grained bits of pine or redwood around to work on. He would pick one up and start on it, sometimes to avoid a conversation, sometimes simply to compose his thoughts, as a woman might pick up a piece of needlepoint or knitting; the blade would flick, the shavings fall, and when you looked at the wood again it would have turned into something else—a spoon or a pot handle or an animal. When his children were small he had whittled toys for them, wonderful little objects which they had collected and treasured and traded—proofs of his love for them. (And he had loved them! Of that somehow, in spite of his moodiness, his sudden streaks of meanness and even cruelty, they had always been sure!)

But assuredly, when Hub whittled he was not giving you his entire attention. He could be thinking of ways to impress his will on you.

". . . what we have run into," Troy was saying, "is a hard structure. So doggone hard that the bits we've been using on our drill stem won't go through it. But there's a solution for that, which I'll describe to you . . ."

He went on to tell his plan: to have, if necessary, a special bit made to order. There was a firm in Texas which specialized in just such orders. It could be done. Then again, the matter of the hard formation: several oilmen he'd talked to had run up against this bitterly resistant mineral, or something much like it, in Mexican and Venezuelan drillings which had later developed big wells.

"We think, on the basis of the best information we can get,

that it may be the roof, or dome, of a fantastic oil deposit . . ."

Hub was still whittling. Troy, though he was speaking now explicitly and confidently, deeply concerned with his presentation, kept turning back to his father, trying to see how he was taking it. And still there was no way to tell . . .

Hub Kinsale was a big man, like most of the Kinsale men, but narrow and thick. Seen from the side, his current exposure, he was more imposing than when seen from the front. Though extremely powerful, he had a big belly, like many old-time hands who like the fat of a good steak better than the lean of it, and his big nose, in its opulent curve, matched his belly.

Sometimes a nose lends dominance and order to an otherwise insignificant face, but such was not the case with Hub's. His nose narrowed at the top so that his eyes, the color of nailheads, seemed to be looking at you out of the same hole. His head also narrowed above where it was circled, tonsure-like, with a scruffy halo of soiled gray hair. All he had of the true Kinsale look was the enamel-hard white skin and the slanty way of holding his head when talking.

In Hub's case the slant extended through the whole body, the accommodation of a basic physical deficiency. Hub had only one leg, the right. The left was artificial, the latest product of its kind.

Hub had once sported a wooden leg. It had been made of a nice chunk of hickory. Hub claimed to have whittled it himself. There's little doubt but that he did. The hickory leg, however, had been crude. It gave Hub a jerky motion when he walked; his whole body, compensating for the stiff wooden piece, lurched and tilted wildly. Also it was hard to keep the peg leg in a stirrup even though Hub made a special cup for it. He needed two good stirrups. He rode rough stock.

Stories differed on the manner in which Hub had lost his leg. Some people said he'd had it ripped off by cannon fire. So Hub had hinted, bellying up to the bar, as he occasionally liked to do, in Ross Swindell's speakeasy in Paicines—the hamlet between the Kinsale ranch and Altemira—the only bar to which Hub could conveniently get on horseback. Cannon fire! All right, but in which war? It would have had to be the Spanish-American. Hub was the right age to have fought in that one though there was no record of his having joined the colors. A likelier version had him losing the leg due to gangrene, when a horse fell on him. Even the family never knew which account was true. Nobody much cared. His three offspring had gone together to buy him the new leg—a Christmas gift, several years earlier. Hub had learned to use it perfectly. He could even bulldog with it, and the prosthetic member, heavier than a real leg, actually helped him, he claimed, acting as an anchor as it dragged behind him in the corral after he had slid from the saddle to grab a calf by the horns.

Not many men in their sixties—even with two good legs—still did that. Not even in San Benito County.

". . . our purpose is to punch through the formation as quickly as possible and with the least possible expense. We don't know how thick it is, there really is no way to tell, but from all that I've been able to find out about comparative situations we doubt if it's more than a few hundred feet. Having special tools designed, of course, comes high. To see us through, even anticipating difficulties, and allowing almost twice the time I feel will be enough, I'm estimating an additional investment of forty-two thousand dollars. I've communicated that figure to Kyle, our president, in England, and he has replied as follows."

Here Troy read Kyle's letter, which brought an unexpected spatter of clapping. It was clear that the mood of the meeting, whatever it had been at first, had turned in his favor. Dr. Braden inquired, in the pause that followed, whether Troy wished the shareholders to consider a motion for the sum requested, and when Troy indicated that he did, the chairman presented the motion.

"Has anyone," he added, "any remarks to make before we vote?"

Troy was grateful for the way Doc phrased his question. Doc, whose position hadn't been clear before, seemed to be on his side. He was trying to push the appropriation through. But Hub had stopped whittling. He held up the shiny blade of his knife to demand attention.

"The Chair," said Dr. Braden, "recognizes the chairman of our board, Mr. Hubbard W. Kinsale."

5

"I rise to my foot to oppose this motion."

Hub "rose to his foot" at every meeting. This was, as he sometimes said, his "standing joke" and could be relied on for a polite titter. This time, for some reason, no one laughed. The meeting had just about made up its mind to give Troy what he asked, frightening though this sum might be on top of all they'd given him already. They wanted to vote, recklessly, impulsively, not like a staid family corporation but like racetrack gamblers: they wanted to rush on without scruples to embrace sudden wealth.

Hub glared around at everyone. He was always at his most formidable when agitated about something at a meeting—and it did not take much to agitate him. What bothered him now was his deep affection for his son Troy versus his hatred for oil. His eyes bulged on each side of their narrow divider so that, appearing to merge, they gave his one-legged body a one-eyed look as well—Cyclopean and threatening.

Hub pulled at his nose as if to rid it of the reek of oil; he worked his lips around as if to clean his mouth of its taste.

Slyly he peered at his audience. He could sense their frame of mind. A mad dream had them in its clutches. Very well—he would fix that. As holder of twenty-one percent of the total company stock, he was used to manipulating these people as he liked. He could order rather than persuade. But if strategy was needed he could use that too. And he would. He branched quickly into a religious pitch, usually a crowd-pleaser: piety was big with the small shareholders.

"If the good Lord had meant for us to have petroleum, he'd of put it where we could get at it—not to hell an' gone down underfoot. That's devil's territory there, friends. That's Satan's south forty."

"Oh, come on, Grandpa," said a youngish male voice from the rear. "We're growed up now!" And another, a woman's this time, chimed in: "Who you tryin' to kid?"

The old man flinched. They were riding his ass, something that had never happened in the whole history of annual meetings, clear back to his own father's time.

Hub hunched his thick, narrow shoulders. He sucked in a deep breath and let fly at them.

26

"I guess if you're so smart back there, whoever you are, you should be smart enough to know when I'm funnin'. But there's still deviltry in it just the same—and that's not a joke. There's always some of us tempted by an easy dollar. I worked hard for every one I got. I din't need oil. I din't need Mesozoic and Paleozoic and the rest of it. What we all needed we had handy—*this!*"

And now balancing on his artificial leg he kicked at the lawn with the real one, his booted heel knocking loose a clod of turf. He picked up the clod, passing the earth through his thick, gnarled fingers.

"Land. Land, my friends! We got some beef stock and we put it on the land and fed it and it multiplied, yes it did. Has anyone here at this meeting ever been hungry, that he can remember? Anybody ever needed a roof over his head or a cayuse to throw a leg over?"

Voices, mostly of the older men, with a few women joining in: "No, Hub." . . . "No, Poppa." . . . "Never." . . . "It couldn't happen."

Hub grinned.

"That's what I thought!"

He silenced a spatter of clapping with a chopping motion of his hand. And Troy, listening with some embarrassment, so out of touch with current fashions and feelings did Hub's deliberately dated, deliberately exaggerated "country style" seem to him, realized that the old man was taking over.

". . . forty thousand dollars. Pardon me, forty-*two* thousand dollars. Rainbow gold! It's sweet, it's dandy. Only, we got two businesses here—the oil business and the cattle business, and they don't mix. Put just one dab of oil in a water trough an' stock won't drink it. Ooze it outa the ground and they get mired down! . . . Did you ever figure how many stout, chunky yearling calves the Kinsale Land and Cattle Company could buy with *forty-two thousand* dollars? Kinsale Land and Cattle Company, it ain't failed you. No, by God, the checks come in, the dividend checks we all depend on. You run up a little bill at Baughman's store—Easter bonnet and a few glad rags. Little old checks take care of it and more too, like the new hot-water heater that's been such a comfort, eh, Aunt Angelica?"

And with this, braving the gawking of those around and the giggles of some, a gaunt, big-boned countrywoman rose from her seat and blew the orator a kiss.

"They sure did, Hub, bless your heart."

Hub motioned sternly for silence. His glance roved round. "Yes, siree, Bob. Those little blue checks. Pay for a weddin' ring now and then, eh, Danny? And medicine for Uncle Follis and laundry soap for Mel and Brig even if they don't use much of it. [Laughter.] Oh, yes, we been lucky so far, but we could of been luckier and that's the truth. Now—any of you ever stop to figure what's gonna happen to the dividends *if* there ain't no oil under that hard stuff Troy mentioned? Well, I'll tell you, there just *might not be no dividends!* That, or the rate will fall like a turd from a tall ox. Alkali and seashells, friends, that's what comes out of them dusters—"

The order of the meeting, never very stable, had broken down; shareholders were leaving their places in the rear, moving down toward the card table to make sure they heard everything. They were jotting down notes and comparing these. Doc's gavel whacked. Troy was called on to answer questions. Why did the new equipment cost so much? How long would it take to drill? What were the real chances of finding oil under that subterranean barrier, if he *did* poke through it? They wanted facts now, where earlier, guesses had been enough; they demanded assurances he couldn't give them. He stood before them like a man on trial, answering as best he could, trying to explain enough to swing the vote his way.

It had not been—indeed, by no means—enough. Millie had tallied the names. She did not have to look in the registry of stock to see what each vote counted. She knew the allotment by heart; her father, on the day she was elected secretary, had explained how the company worked.

Grandfather Calvin had set up certain checks and balances. His last will and testament had given his own rules for frugal living:

No coffee, tea, sugar, whiskey nor tobaccer
No vests, socks, undershirts, no drawers
No high-heeled boots, gold-headed canes nor
    jingling watch chains
No IOU's

The auction business had taught him the ways of human avarice; he had vested his estate in the Land and Cattle Company, of which, at the time the articles of incorporation were filed, Cal Kinsale owned one hundred percent. Twelve thousand shares had been issued (a figure later expanded by many split-ups but never by an additional issue, though the wealth it represented eventually came to be measured in billions).

Hub could overrule his own progeny. But the three children, on the other hand, could prevail against their father if supported by enough other stockholders.

Millie took note of today's voting. She put down the total in her neat figures, to be typed when she did up the minutes. She looked over at Hub, straddling a bench, sipping a cup of bourbon whiskey, and she hated him for his stinginess. Since the death of her mother—now so long ago—Hub had tried to crush her with that, the clinching argument against trying anything new or daring. She had refused to be crushed. The only woman in an all-male household, she had quietly gone her own way. She had lived her life, she had found her own man, she had her own house, she kept the minutes of the meetings. She still came over to look after Hub when he needed her and she had loved him once, but the place in her heart where the love had been was closed. Hub was so tough. He could lie on you like such a weight, he and his land and his stinginess. It would have been such fun to be really rich, with money to prove it, instead of just the notion that you had the land and that the land was worth money. Troy had been dreaming of this well all his life. Now because some stupid little thing had gone wrong and the hard stuff had been there he might never have another chance.

Troy was standing a few yards away, waiting, his hand on his wife's shoulder; Millie Braden could feel his eyes on her as she went over the figures a last time, as if a new addition would change them. It didn't. She drew a line under them and broke the point of her pencil and dropped the pencil in the grass.

"The shareholders," she said in a matter-of-fact voice, "have rejected the motion brought by Troy Kinsale to continue drilling for petroleum on the company's Piru ranch."

CHAPTER TWO

The Cutting Shed

1

Emilia de Baca Kinsale, wife of Hub, mother of Kyle, Millie and Troy Kinsale, had been an heiress in her own right. The De Baca land grant, later incorporated as a holding of the Land and Cattle Company, comprised a great sweep of foothill country on both sides of the Coast Range, south of Monterey, as well as the separate piece which later became the Kinsale homeranch. By the size of its herds and the quality of its people, the family had made its brand famous— the steer's head ("De Baca"), a series of curlicues looped onto the animals' hide with a running iron: what the gringo cowboys called a Mex brand. The De Baca grant in fact was Mexican, not Spanish: it had been deeded after the Mexican colonies declared their independence, but the family lost no prestige on this account, its members stood high among the *gente de raza*. Their gardens, irrigated with water pumped by Indian labor through terra-cotta subsoil pipe, could have rivaled the Duke of Alba's; the De Bacas were skilled in all kinds of crafts, orcharding, winemaking and weaving, for instance, in addition to beef raising. Their women, so delight-fully indolent when in the parlor, so accomplished at their grand piano (the only one in northern California, except that of General Vallejo), also quite publicly smoked cornshuck cigarettes and thought nothing of riding all day, sidesaddle, on spirited horses. Emilia's grandfather and one of her seven uncles had stood to be counted in the Californio regiment which, without guns, played hell with General Stephen Watts Kearny's cavalry at San Pasqual, pulling the blue-coated troopers off their mounts with rawhide lariats and piercing them, as in medieval jousts, with fourteen-foot cottonwood lances tipped with steel.

Many suitors had come courting Emilia de Baca. Some, according to family gossip, had been men of renown. Others were probably just country Romeos, excited at the prospect of bedding a lovely girl who was also extremely rich. Hub fell into neither category. As a cattleman he belonged to a genre which of all gringo types the *gente de raza* found least acceptable. He was crude. He ran after women and got into fights in the little *bodegas* which the California villages, now Americanized, had inherited from their Spanish and Mexican founders. It hardly improved his eligibility that Cal Kinsale, the future father-in-law, had rolled up a fortune buying cargoes, sight unseen, from incoming vessels, which he then auctioned, at shylock prices, on the San Francisco waterfront. Hub himself was never an auctioneer. He had the voice but not the temperament for the job; his habitat was the range. He won Emilia's hand and her love. He took care of her while she lived with a slavish and dedicated passion and after her death he manfully assumed the job of bringing up their sons and daughter.

Loss pushed the family together. For some years Hub became gentler in his ways. He'd never understood the complicated mores of the elegant, fading world to which his wife had belonged but he did sense the new values that were creeping into his own; he'd seen to it that his offspring got the education he himself had lacked and encouraged and paid for this up to and through the college level—by no means a general practice in those days. He'd been a stern but observant father and what he lacked in nurturing zeal he made up for in reasonableness. He knew the danger of favoritism in a two-boy, one-girl equation—the father would be expected to lean toward the girl. Hub guarded against this by making Millie work as hard as the two boys combined; in addition to the managerial skills demanded of a woman supervising a big household copiously supplied with low-paid female help, he also put her on outdoor duty. She team-roped with him; she castrated and branded and dehorned stock with him when the cattle were gathered at spring and fall roundups. With a poncho and bedroll on her saddle she rode fenceline like the men, sleeping out in the tules when need be. By the time she was seventeen she could have run the ranch, inside and out, with no assistance except the regular kitchen help and range hands; this included keeping the accounts—a job she enjoyed more than any other and which she later took over both for the Land and Cattle Company and for her physician husband.

"I treat them all alike"—Hub's boast when child-rearing came up for discussion—was thus obviously untrue in Millie's case. It was equally false with regard to Kyle, whom Hub indulged at every turn, even sending him (apparently at Kyle's whim, though the idea might have been implanted by Emilia—Kyle, as the oldest, had been closer to her than the others) to an eastern boarding school and then to Yale. Troy, for a wonder, had taken all this in stride. He had not been in the least put out either by Millie's accumulation of authority or the money lavished on his brother. He had never wanted fancy trimmings for his life; he had been perfectly satisfied with the ordinary spin of it and with his own stature as the in-between person, the second son. He wanted that and also, as a clincher, the knowledge that Hub accepted him: that Hub did not and would not discriminate against him. A father's recognition is important to a boy at any age but above all to one who sees himself as less gifted than others in the family. Troy saw himself in that way. He was not worried about it but as he grew toward his teens he had formed the habit of watching his father, trying to detect ways in which he could attract his attention, to prove himself to him. He did this successfully for a long time—or at least with the small measure of favor which was all he required. By twelve years old he was a manly, attractive boy, easy to get on with, and well set in his ways and interests, chiefly this freaky fellowship with oil. He reasoned with small-boy logic that his mother, who had loved everyone, had loved him more (this was why he could never be jealous of Millie or Kyle). He had been allowed his necessary and proper status and his satisfaction with this enabled him to withstand rebuffs. Millie, long afterward, remembered one which, as she described it, had seemed cruel to her at the time although it had little apparent effect on Troy.

Hub's birthday, which fell in March, was always an important family feast. No outsiders were invited. It was strictly family but there was a solemn pomp to the occasion. The house was cleaned and spruced up as if for Christmas—or the call of the bishop of the Catholic Diocese of Northern California, stopping around for the yearly diocesan donation. Millie had a cake baked and decorated and a special meal prepared, a goose or a suckling pig (beef, no matter how select, had an ordinariness about it on a ranch where a steer a week was butchered for the household and the outside hands, and one a month for the dogs).

Presents were given after supper. You had to think a long time to decide on something Hub wanted. Millie, who had formal sewing among her many accomplishments, stitched personal articles for him: shaving towels with his name on them, pillow covers and so forth—once a sampler which Hub framed, a front view of the homeranch itself, in colored thread, under the motto "God Bless Our Home." Before this particular birthday Hub had dropped a hint. He'd broken his shaving mug. Each of the boys decided to supply a replacement, neither revealing his intention to the other.

Troy made a mug out of wood. He'd never seen one like it, he just felt it could be done. He'd cut a burl of persimmon wood, then seasoned it and hollowed it with auger holes. He whittled out the wood remaining, polishing and sanding the shell until it had a perfect finish. It was the right shape, shallow and hard, a perfect bowl for holding the round slabs of barber's soap Hub used for his badger-hair brush. The making took Troy many secret evening hours; when it was done Troy and Millie both felt he had crafted a beautiful thing.

Kyle took no such trouble. He went to town at the last minute and for a dollar bought an imitation German beer mug, a painted-up store trifle.

Hub opened Troy's present first. He shook hands with his son and patted him on the head. Very nice, he said. Thank you, son. Made it yourself, eh? Pretty good, you know. Then he opened Kyle's gift. He beamed as if he'd been handed a thousand dollars. He hugged the boy and lifted his feet off the floor. Remembered your ole dad, did you? Well, it's beautiful. Several times he mentioned what a great present Kyle had given him. What was more, he used Kyle's mug every day thereafter. He put Troy's away in a drawer.

"He's stupid," Millie said indignantly to Troy. "Yours is so much better."

"No, it's not," Troy said. "Kyle had more sense. Who

wants an old scoop of wood? I should have bought him something."

One privilege, however, was Troy's alone—he was the keeper of Hub's memories. He had acquired this position by the default of others: Millie busying herself, even after supper, with house chores, and Kyle off on his own affairs. There were winter evenings with the northeast storms pounding on the house and Hub whittling by the fire, whittling and talking; summer nights also, the long day fading at last and Hub on a wicker stretch-out on the porch, puffing his pipe and slapping at the heel flies and midges which settled on his skin, though they lacked strength to puncture its enamel.

". . . had this dumbass Injun ridin' partner, Hector Bearmeat. Never hobbled his horse at night, jest left a rope on him, the loop trailin' on the ground. Dumbass trick, you better never do it, you git to ridin' herd with the kind of stuff we trailed in those days . . ."

Hub in his youth had made many trips into Mexico to buy cattle stock. He had taken pride even then in his reputation as a sharp and ruthless bargainer. Trailing was both easier and less expensive than shipping by the newly built southern spur of the S.P. Also, you avoided travel fever contracted in dirty railroad cars.

This was the period—the early and middle eighties—which lived most vividly in Hub's mind. Having a boy to listen to him brought it into focus, although there were times when the narrative faded off into reverie and Hub required prompting.

"But what did Bearmeat *do*, Pops?"

"Do? Why, nothin'. Them Injuns never *did* a pissant worth of work, outside of stink. And ride around . . ."

"But you said—that dumbass trick with the rope."

"Oh, that. . . . Well, let me tell you somethin'. Stock like that, you don't find a whiteface or a cherry red in the whole goddamn bunch. They'd be Chihuahua runts with more sags than a shithouse door and horns like hay hooks. Either that or they'd be mossbacks, swamp angels—spooky, hell, you had to stalk 'em like deer. We were camped down in a bend of the Colorado River, place called Alamanitos, near the railroad bridge. We was bedded down, the stock belchin' and blowin' off, full of good grass and all, and then about midnight the ground starts shakin', the train lets out a whistle for the river crossin', and I mean two thousand head is off like corncrib rats, headin' for home with their tails over their heads. I hear

Bearmeat yell. There he is in the moonlight, sittin' on the ground. His horse had drug him far enough so he woke up, reachin' for his foot where the boogered horse has pulled the loop up tight. But every time he moves . . . ha. That was a shit of a night, boy. And don't forgit it."

"But what happened? I mean, did he get loose?"

"Did who git loose?"

"Bearmeat. You said the horse was dragging him and he—"

"Sure it was draggin' him. Boogered, that's all. Dumbass trick, leavin' a loop where it could . . . Shit, son. I should of been out after the stock but goddamn if I could move. Just set there, laughin' my ass off. You see what I mean? He couldn't unlatch hisself, and that's the truth. That horse is boogered but not so boogered he ain't watchin', and each time that Injun makes a reach for the rope he's off agin, draggin' that Bearmeat by the foot. Could of killed him, of course . . ."

"Did you get him out of it?"

"Hell, no. How could I do that?"

"Did he die then?"

"Hell, no, he didn't die. Not that it would of been a loss, because it wouldn't. Only if he had, my dad would of blamed me, just like I blame you if you pull some dumbass trick. Only one way out. I had a gun on the saddle. Savage thirty-thirty carbine, sweetest saddle gun ever made. Best fuckin' shot I ever made, too, dropped that horse in his tracks. Hated to do it though, he was worth six Injuns, anytime—leave alone a dumbass one."

The herders—the point riders, the flank guard and the tailmen—pushed through the Sonora wastes, across the international line, into the dry southern tip of California. They had stayed near the rails they would not pay to use, watering at the railroad tanks. Hub had other train stories: shoot-outs with S.P. line patrollers; cowmen giving aid to stricken passengers after a trestle wreck; four flank riders coming on an engine stalled for lack of boiler water, hitching their ropes to the piston housings, pulling along, the tough steeldust ponies strained sideways, till the big iron beast started downgrade to the next station.

". . . engineer says, I'm grateful, boys. Here's two dollars apiece. Give them hides a feed of oats. They deserve it. Well, they did. Wouldn't you figure?"

"Sure would, Pops."

"Well, they didn't git it. We spend that money for squirrel whiskey. Got piss-eyed drunk. You'd of done the same now, wouldn't you?"

"I guess so, Pops."

"Well, don't you ever try it. I'll beat your bottom raw."

Because of the stories, Troy knew Hub better than anyone else did. They had lived a secret life together, sharing adventures from which others in the family had been excluded; they had been companions in the great dry arroyos where a foolish deed could mean death. He understood Hub. His father had brought into a gentle time, a quiet place, certain qualities not needed there, acquired by him in quite different circumstances. He had not, as some said, outlived his time. He had merely continued living his true life in that other period, which suited him better. He charged into each day as if into an unexplored landscape of mesquite and rattlesnakes, strewn with bones. That was what gave him his loneliness and harshness. But there was bigness in him. There was that slow, saturnine laughter and that wariness of people that only the lonely have. He bedded down alone every night under stars which, because of the thin air of his world, burned more brightly and dangerously than in softer skies. Naturally he was lonely. Why wouldn't he be? He had been separated out, cut off not only from that world of thirsty earth and dangerous heavens but from the person he had loved, the woman who had died. He tried to replace the happiness he'd known with her with random assignations, not always wisely chosen. Troy had heard all about that. Even before he'd gone to Altemira High he'd been in contact with the gossip of the town. He paid it little heed. It was okay with him if Hub had a woman or two. That was his right. Nor did he hold it against him, after the 1923 shareholders' meeting, that he had blocked drilling for oil. Hub didn't understand oil—never had. There was no way you could pound its potential into his head. Troy had about given up on that, but not on the Piru well. Never! His deepest instincts, as well as the skills picked up in ten years' work in various oil fields—that "nose for oil" which even geologists respected, and acknowledged as a true capacity, though there was no explaining it—convinced him more than ever that the Piru location would prove up. Thus he fought the feelings of discouragement that followed the meeting, the notion that if he had been more persuasive, not made a mistake, somehow he could have swung the vote his way. It didn't matter. He would get another chance. Somehow, someday he would raise the necessary money. He would take another whack at it.

He had no way of knowing that his chance was close at hand.

Millie was at the homeranch at the time; she'd chanced to stop by to leave off some home-canned preserves for Hub. Old Aunt Marty put up preserves too, but not like Millie's. Aunt Marty would put up hers in the fall, like the eastern women who prepared then for winter, whereas any California woman knew, who really made preserves, the picking season was the time, from the early picking of the apricot trees, always the best fruit, the first to take on color.

Millie hadn't been in the house more than a few minutes when Chun Wuk, the cook, found Hub and came running in and he and Millie by themselves raised him up and brought him to the house—apparently they never thought of calling for help, though there was plenty of it around. Millie rang up her husband at once, at his office, and he arrived within the hour.

Dr. Braden was optimistic. Hub had lost a lot of blood, but he was tough. Once he'd had something that looked like a heart attack but had proved not to be; his heart was really in excellent shape now and Doc felt strongly that he would make it. It wasn't until twenty-four hours later that the complications developed and Millie tried to reach her brothers.

She didn't supply particulars. She didn't have them to impart—although there was another woman, possibly still on the ranch when Hub was found, who could have filled her in.

2

Maria Candelaria Felipe Sanchez had worked at the ranch the previous summer and helped her mother pick, though not officially on the payroll, the summer before that. She enjoyed the picking, she was strong enough to do it; she could pick as well as any man. She was seventeen and had been mature since she was eleven. The arithmetic of her beauty, measured in inches, pounds and feet, had been published in the *Altemira Free Lance* when she had been nominated as a contestant for a public honor—Queen of the Altemira Rodeo and Saddle Horse Show. Her picture had also been published, both in a group which included the other five contestants and by itself. However, due to her father's old-fashioned ideas as to what was seemly for a young woman, she'd had to withdraw her name. She'd cried a little over it but had not, in the long run, been particularly upset by it. She was accustomed to obeying her father, an employee of the Altemira Packing Company. She had five brothers, Manuel, Lope, Luis, Mauricio and Aguirre, all older than herself, and all working in various paid capacities in San Benito County. They had approved their father's decision. They, too, had been brought up to accept Juan Sanchez' ideas. They were loving but stern in their attitudes toward their sister, the only female in the second generation of the family. They were glad her beauty had been recognized, but for it to be used for display or in competition with others, that was stupid! It might interfere with her making a good marriage.

Laria Sanchez was a communicant of the Roman Catholic Church, in the parish of St. Francis Xavier, Altemira, and as of that morning, July 10, 1925, she was a virgin.

Laria hadn't made the first bus. She'd been late getting to Monterey and Fourth Street, where the Peerless buses provided by the ranch waited in the blueness before dawn to convey pickers to the Kinsale orchards. She got on the second bus and went quickly to take a place near a window. She liked to look out and watch the wash of light move across the valley as the sun got higher. Some distance to the southeast, where the Santa Anas broke their orderly march from north to south, rose up some craggy peaks—the gateway to the Kinsale stronghold, facing the Gabilan range, which enclosed the valley to the west. Sometimes, when the land below lay clear, the crags were dark, ringed with clouds like iron bands; at other times, with overcast below, you could see a ring of polished light up there, catered in, as it were, by special order, bright as a blessing from the Pope. Thus the Kinsales, who had so selectively set their domain apart, seemed to have imported their own weather for it, perhaps not better weather than in town, but different. Their own!

Today, as always, Laria Sanchez felt a sense of elation, of excitement at the day ahead. The ranch was a special place. She had picked at other ranches, for summer work was plentiful; the roads to the south and east of town were lined with small fruit farms and they all needed pickers. But the

Kinsale orchards were the best and biggest, as might be expected. She was glad that the ranch, which serviced itself in so many ways, still had to bring in men and women for the picking.

The special climate and the beauty of the place made the work almost like a holiday.

It was deliciously cool in the orchards and the first apricots pulled off the trees by the pickers' fingers made a drumming sound as they dropped into the empty pails; soon all the orchards were full of this low, pleasant tinny drumming overlaid with the voices of the pickers talking to each other from tree to tree and with snatches of singing. The songs were never complete but bits and pieces recalled to fit a passing mood, refrains handed down from the Mexican people's great sad treasury of singing: marching songs, love songs, feast songs, homesick songs, execution songs. There was applause and hooting, mingled, when the first woman filled her bucket and ran to a checker's bin with it. The glimmering secret tunnels of the trees were full of the golden fruit and the warm flesh of the girls working and flashes of the brightly colored, much-washed clothes they wore. The chocolate-colored adobe earth, rolled smooth for the picking, showed the prints of shoes and sandals and of broad bare feet and the marks of the ladders as the workers moved them from tree to tree. Now and then some fruit that had become too ripe fell out of a tree and was mashed on the ground, adding its acid sweet smell to the damp smell of the ground and of the moist sheltering leaves and of the women's bodies.

In the orchard calligraphy of earth markings could be observed also the marks of a man's tread—prints of an unusual kind. The right print was normal but the left, as it slogged along, made a sweeping, circular pattern on the ground. These were the footprints of Hub Kinsale. He had come into the orchards promptly at 6 A.M. as he always did, to see how things were going. He would stay all day. Though the nearest orchard was only half a mile from his house, he had ridden out on a fine sorrel stock horse; this mount, with saddle, bridle and saddle blanket removed and placed neatly under a tree, nibbled the rich grass growing around the edges of the orchard. Hub would not have dreamed of walking out to the orchards; like most cattlemen, he deemed walking a social humiliation. It was also one of the less easy things he did.

His walk was almost perfect. All he did was swing the artificial leg out and around a little, leaving those scoop marks when the going was soft.

The heavyset, one-legged man stood under a tree. His stockman's hat was pushed back on his forehead, his heeled hand-tooled boots planted firmly in the earth—his earth. He was watching one of the checkers. There was always the possibility of collusion between the checkers and the girls coming in with their buckets full of ripe, heavy fruit. That was what he had come to look out for. He knew how they did it. The checkers could punch out more than one square on the tickets when the girls brought their buckets in. Later the girls would split the added pay. That was how they worked it, but you had to look sharp to catch them.

Hub covered his watchfulness by pretending to fuss with his leg. He would turn the leg this way and that, as though it were hurting him, or feel around through his pants as if adjusting the straps that attached it to his body.

Few checkers became aware of this strategy, but there had been an instance when one did. Hub had gathered quite a group around him as he gave the man a dressing down. He had enlarged at some length, vigorously and profanely, on the fellow's general worthlessness.

The checker waited until Hub was through. Then he had delivered his own valedictory.

"Mr. Kinsale," he said, "for you I wish only one thing. I hope your fucking leg grows back."

It was getting on toward noon, and the sun was hotter than ever. Some of the pickers were settling down among the trees, alone or in groups, to eat the lunches they had brought along; others, determined to draw maximum pay, were staying on the job, but there weren't many of these. A leafy, steamy quiet settled over the orchards. Only at the south end was there any activity, the place where the mule-drawn flatbed wagons worked their way in, stopping at the check stands to pick up the bins.

Laria Sanchez laid down her ladder. She took her last bucket to a checker and he punched her ticket. He was a young Mexican from Jalisco and all morning he had been freshing up to her, trying to flirt. He was a well-built fellow with regular but not Indian-looking features and curly hair. He had joking, overfriendly, overknowing eyes. She liked his looks but she was in no mood for flirting, even an orchard flirt which would not count anyway. These checkers, young or old, thought they could fuck the picking girls and some of them did; if you gave them the slightest encouragement they lost their heads. One of them had even inquired where she lived and had come to look for her at her parents' house. Her brother Mauricio had to take him aside and explain the facts of life to him.

Laria was not particularly hungry; she thought she would eat a little later, after she'd had a rest. She'd put the paper bag in one of the cutting sheds. Her mother had written her name on it in large, uneven letters. Her mother's writing was childish, but she was very proud of it. She had never been to school. Her husband, Juan, the *carnadero* of the packing company, had taught her to write. Juan could do anything; paint houses, break horses, and drive a car. Above all, he could kill steers for the packing company. He didn't kill them like American slaughterers, by hitting them with a sledge. He put them away with the *puntillo*—a blow in the back of the neck, with a short, thick dagger.

Laria peeked into her lunch bag. She knew the lunch would be good, it always was. Sure enough, there was a feast inside. Her mother had seen to that. There was even a piece of cactus candy. Laria sat down in the shade with her back against the wall of the shed and ate the candy. She always liked to start her lunch with the sweet instead of ending with it. She spoiled herself that way when she was working; any kind of small indulgence, even stopping for a drink of water or to listen to a song, made the day go better. After the candy her appetite picked up and she rapidly ate the rest of the lunch. She decided to rest a while before going back to work. During the morning she'd been bothered slightly by menstrual pains; she knew they would be worse in the afternoon if she didn't rest. Her periods were seldom painful, only a little on the first day. She hadn't expected this one so soon; if it really came on fully she would have to go and put something on.

There was a place to rest, all right. Many of the women used it from time to time. It was in a partially dismantled cutting shed now used for storing trays and sacks. No one seemed to mind if a girl went in there and made a temporary bed by spreading a few sacks on the dirt floor. They all worked on a piece basis, so the ranch lost nothing by this. Some of the workers, in a bygone year, had even rigged up a shower. They'd hoisted an old bathtub on a frame made of pipes and run a hose to it from the cutting shed hose bib. For privacy they'd put four trays around it, clewing them together with wire, with a latch and wire hinges on one to form a door. The shower head was a lard can with holes in it, attached under the bathtub vent. This contraption was used mostly by those pickers who instead of coming and going in the buses elected to sleep at night in the orchards. There was always a certain number who did this. They brought blankets with them. They brought food with them and cooked it over fires. There were gay times around those fires, then sleep, and in the morning this place to wash up. But the shower was seldom used during the day.

Laria, half dozing, noticed with surprise that someone had gone in there now. Water was splashing down and the trays that formed the shower walls were bumping as the person moved around inside; after a while the water was turned off and the bather came out. It was Hub Kinsale. He reached out, wet as he was, for his pants, where he had hung them on a nail, and put them on. Then he came into the part of the shed where Laria was resting. He was drying the upper part of his body with his undershirt, leaning against the shed wall to balance himself, somewhat precariously, since he had taken off his leg with the rest of his stuff. He had shed it just as if it had been another article of clothing—hung it up by its straps! Laria, her eyes wide open now, could see where he had put it; probably getting it wet would have been bad for it.

Hub dried his arms and face and his foolish little circlet of scalp with the shirt and then, shifting himself against the wall, he turned and looked at Laria.

She quickly closed her eyes again. Just as well for him to think she was asleep. It was obviously not right, and in fact ridiculous, for him to be bathing in the pickers' shower in the middle of the day. If he'd wanted to take a shower he could have got on his horse and ridden down to his own place where no doubt there were showers ten times as good as this one and probably bathtubs as well. His action was puzzling and also, because of his nearness, disturbing.

She kept her eyes closed and willed for him to go away.

Hub took several steps, hippity-hop, along the wall, moving toward her, putting out his hand between each step to balance himself. He stood looking down at her for several seconds. Then he said, "What's your name, girl?"

At these words, a deadly, sickening fear went through Laria. She was familiar with this fear. A really beautiful woman learns more about men at an early age than some women find out in a lifetime. She had come to understand, almost before she could understand anything else, the substance of male desire. She had to deal with several parts of this situation in turn, as fast as she could. She raised herself on her elbows and gazed calmly and with utter scorn at the big maimed man balancing there before her.

"Please go away," she said.

"Take it easy, honey," Hub said. "You know you don't want me to do that!"

And with this he dropped his pants. He hopped out of them and with the next hop he was onto her. She bit him and they rolled on the sacks, she with a basic advantage, two legs to his one, knowing if she could just get his big-gutted weight off her she would be up and there would be no way in the world he could come after her. But there was also no way she could get up. Thus the struggle was joined, a contest which consisted in thrashing around on the sacks. She wished she was out of this but her anger was in full operation now and the strength-sapping fear was fading.

She turned this way and that, with her legs tightly locked, and the ill-balanced weight of the man on top. Gradually her fear thinned away until it was no more than a wisp of fog hanging in the back of her brain, soon to dissolve entirely.

She didn't yet have control, but she was close. Unless he hit her, which she was sure he wouldn't do, there was just no way he could get into her, push and pry as he might with his hands and rub as he might with his stubby sawed-off thing, well up now, wet on the end and red as a wagon lamp. His weight was tilted sideways, resting partly on her and partly on his good leg, with the stump of the gone leg flapping on her thighs. She'd got a good look at the stump when he dropped his pants and it was really bad; the doctor who sawed off his leg must have bungled.

They messed around, meshed together like a single body, partly at least, but thank God not completely, which they never would be, on the dusty, grain-smelling, mouse-infested walnut sacks.

She could have laughed then, for there had been a change, a tremendous alteration in the struggle in her favor.

At first it was hardly anything. It was like a tiny movement, like the faintest stir of coolness on a stifling day when far back, in a house standing breathless with all the windows open, gasping for air, or far up in the leaves of a green tree motionless and deathlike in the heat, there comes this ghost of a breeze, this tiny, incredible promise of relief, of renewed life.

The movement spread, gained strength. It became delicious, it increased like a wave, it rippled from the tip of her brain down into her loins and pelvis and began to surge and tingle, and the last of her fear was gone. She could have laughed, and did . . . only it came out less of a laugh than a moan. For this was not relief, it wasn't happening because it couldn't happen, or if it could then not to her, only to someone else . . . an accident of this kind because . . . she was coming, and the feeling swelled, it took over the nerves in her back and belly as she moved, trying to stop it but only bringing it on stronger until she climaxed, shuddering, her eyes going blank, her mouth falling open as she lost control of her jaw muscles and her legs, so tightly clamped together, coming apart like cotton.

Hub was ready. He had not expected this but he knew what it was. In that moment when she opened up he was into her. With a series of slow, then harder, hurting thrusts he ejaculated, wasting no time, during which he felt her come again. He pulled out of her and gallantly rearranged her clothes. Then, with a groan, he pushed himself up. He reached for the wall to brace himself and went hippity-hop along it, back to where he'd hung his leg on a nail. He strapped on his leg, dressed quickly, and went out.

The entire exercise had lasted about fifteen minutes.

Laria lay still. She felt neither anger nor remorse, she was incapable of such refinement of emotion. She was done for—that was all she knew. This was the end of her as a person. She could, of course, pretend as she had in her throes that the individual involved had not been really her, but now there was physical evidence to the contrary.

She could not get married now. Any self-respecting bridegroom, finding on his wedding night that he had been cheated, would send her back to her parents. She was an evil person, a real *puta*. Even detesting the man, as in confession one might declare to a priest, as required to, that one detested one's own sins, she had given way to her feelings.

That put her beyond the reach of confession. No priest could keep to himself such evil as this. It would not be fair to expect him to. It would come out. People would know. What had happened must remain forever locked inside her until purged eventually in the only way it could be, by the fires of hell.

She could have revenge, of course. That would be easy. One word to any of her brothers would be enough; he would know what to do. Or her father. Only if any of them did what they would do, that would be the end of the family her father had put together with so much labor, with so much love. She would be the destroyer. She thought about that for a while, until she perceived a way out. So far the only person destroyed was herself. All right. What she wanted done now must be done by herself and no one else.

She lay in the shed for a long time, turning the proposition over in her mind. Her own evil, which Hub had now disclosed, would be the end of him. She intended to go on living. Why not? In spite of what had happened life was sweet. The problem was different. It consisted in this—that she was unwilling to live in a world which also contained such a man as Hub. She thought of the stump of his leg slapping against her. Her goal now was to eliminate him as one would eliminate anything unseemly and dangerous to other people. She made up her mind to kill him, and the thought brought comfort to her—such lean comfort as she was to have that day.

She lay still a little while longer. Then she got up and cleaned herself and went back to picking in the orchard.

3

Millie had done the right thing. She wouldn't have known about the phone at the rig (where there was one), or had the number even if she'd known. She'd realized that telegraphing was the only way she could reach Troy.

"Sinking." The word had a doomful significance. Millie would not have used such a word unless the situation was bad.

Seven words in all. Troy had written them down as he heard them, so when the operator asked him if he wanted a copy of the wire he'd said no, he didn't need it. He didn't want the goddamn words. He wished he could have wiped them away before he'd heard them, obliterated them forever, if by so doing he could have nullified whatever it was had happened to Hub or was even now happening to him. *Sinking!*

It sounded as if Hub were out alone in a leaky boat. Or not even in a boat. In the water, in a stormy sea, with huge dark waves rising round him like glass mountains, sliding out from under him, sucking him down, and he struggling, thrashing with his arms and leg and . . . yelling . . . but no one there to hear him or to help.

Millie could maybe have used three more words. She could have told what in hell was *wrong* with Hub. Three would have done it and she would still have been within the limit of ten and no extra charge.

Troy knew Millie. Cost would have been a consideration with her. Yet, there was also another consideration, her firm characteristic reluctance to reveal information, even of the most routine kind, about herself or any member of the family. That was the way she was and she'd be the same way if he delayed and tried to put a call through on the ranch line, privately owned and strung along trees and fences here and there, to save poles, so that it wasn't the best of lines, and also a tri-party line which meant that every long-eared housewife on it would be easing up the receiver and clamping it to her head when she heard the ranch ring, one long, two shorts.

It would have made a lot more sense if Doc had called him instead of Millie. But if Hub was sick, Doc was undoubtedly attending him. Doc might have been too busy to call.

Better just to take off, he decided. Which was what he'd done. He went out and spoke to Charlie Ott, number two man on the rig. He gave him his instructions for the next two days.

It would take about that long, he thought. Maybe three. Charlie would know what to do. He didn't need to be told. He'd been around since Jim and Jonathan Elwood drilled the first oil well on the Kern River, on Tom Means's ranch, in 1898.

Charlie drove him home. Troy could have driven himself but then he would have been idling a company truck by leaving it at the house while he was away. He got the children and Luanna into the Pierce Arrow as fast as he could and they took off. When he stopped at Percy Yountman's station, a hundred miles from the ranch, Perce had a message for him: "Could he pick up Dr. Braden at the clinic?"

Troy drove like a demon up the Dead Eagle Valley road, the tires of the big car squealing on the switchback curves.

Doc was standing in front of the house. He had his black medical bag in his hand and was attired in his regulation summer costume—army pants and leather leggings combined with a linen Norfolk jacket. He had removed the stiff collar which usually topped off this ensemble; his long, gold collar button peeped out of clustering gray hairs at the base of his throat.

The usually bouncy, optimistic man was tired. His eyes, behind his pince-nez, looked like bundles of red worms. He insisted on sitting in the back seat so as not to disturb Luanna, but when Luanna wanted to change places with him he pulled down one of the jump seats and sat on that, to make conversation easier. He leaned over the front seat to talk about how much Helene had grown since he'd last seen her.

"Wonderful, wonderful!" he said. "Another beauty in the family. Young lives coming up, coming up!"

That's Doc, thought Troy. Looking for something cheerful so we won't ask him what's really happening.

"How's my father?"

Doc cleared his throat. "He has a good chance, a fighting chance. Yes. I think so. I really think he may make it."

"What the hell does that mean?"

"It means just what I say," said Doc with a slight edge to his voice. "It's still a little too—I mean too soon to tell. Early this morning his life signs were . . . not stable."

"Millie said . . ."

"Yes," said Doc, "we all thought so at that time. Not good at all. Then he rallied. Blood pressure, heart action—both much better. That's how these things go sometimes. I left at half past eight."

"You mean there's no doctor with him now?"

"There most certainly is," snapped Doc. "I called Dr. Shelton in Fresno, and he came right over. That was last night."

"I never heard of him."

"Well, you don't have to worry about Prentis Shelton. He's a top man, wonderful with respiratory situations. We'd been trying to reach your brother in Burlingame and when we got through to him he . . ."

Dr. Braden's cough was the only indication he permitted that the influx of nonlocal medical opinion had not been necessary. Or not to his taste. Doc allowed neither implication.

"Kyle wanted Keeler. San Francisco. Made the call himself. Donald Francis Keeler. I didn't know him, but—"

"He didn't come?"

"He most certainly did. Promptly. Excellent man. We had a consultation at six. Millie can tell you, she sat in on it at my request. Family witness to . . . Yes. Then a patient came for me, rancher over in the Bitterwater. Wife in labor. I delivered her by caesarean section. Husband returned me to the office, so—"

"What's this about a respiratory—"

"That's the basic problem now. Pneumonia. He'd been lying there quite a while, you see. An hour, perhaps more. Night coming on and . . . Well, let me put it this way. If a horse goes down, the lungs fill up. It's not precisely the same, of course, but similar when—"

"Lying *where?*"

"In the tack room."

"What was he doing in the tack room, for Christ's sake!"

"Take it easy, Troy," said Doc Braden calmly, but his voice sharpened once more. "You mean, Millie didn't tell you—"

"I never talked to Millie. She sent me a wire. You mean, he *fell* in the tack room or—"

"Troy, your father was stabbed."

"In the *tack room?*"

"In the tack room. Someone was waiting for him there."

"That room is always kept locked."

"The person entering found that out. There is evidence that he or she worked on the hasp of the padlock, trying to loosen the screws. The wood is old and splintery, of course, but that didn't work. The person finally obtained entry by the window, which was covered only by a piece of quarter-inch steel mesh held on by fence staples. It may have been no great problem to dig out the staples."

"It's a damn small window."

"It is. So we know the person was not large. We also know that Friday night, late afternoon, your father came back from the orchard. He took the tack off his horse and turned the horse into the corral and he walked into the tack room carrying the saddle and someone in there came for him. Stabbed him from behind, not once but several times. Not enough penetration to sever the spinal nerves, but enough to put him into shock. Chun Wuk went looking for him. Your father had lost considerable blood. Blood pressure plummeted. Pulse hardly detectable by the time I took the call."

"All right, all right, Doc. Go on. Go *on.*"

"Very well. I transfused. This is a relatively new process.

Started in the Great War. Blood loss from battle wounds. Last resort, of course, but . . . Millie was the donor. Hub reacted beautifully. Then, it seems—"

"Wait a minute. When was this?"

Dr. Braden took off his pince-nez. He rubbed his eyes delicately with his thin fingers. It was clear that in his fatigued state the divisions of time were blurred for him.

"Friday night. Yes, Friday."

"Millie didn't send the wire until *last night*. Sunday."

"My wife notified you when I told her to," said Doc peremptorily. "It was not necessary earlier."

"When was Kyle notified?"

Always, in relation to his father, Troy thought of his brother: it was almost as if, in his mind, his diagram for the family was a triangle, he and Kyle the sides, Hub the base, Millie a vertical line in the middle.

"You were both notified at the same time."

"I'm sure they were, Doc," said Luanna, entering the conversation. She felt that Troy was pressing Doc too hard. She touched Troy's leg, letting him know she was not taking Doc's part against him but merely wished the talk to go a little easier. She kept on addressing Doc. "We're all most grateful to you for what you've done. I don't know what would have happened without you there to take care of things."

"Thank you," said Dr. Braden. He moved from the jump seat into the back seat and closed his eyes.

"Is Granpa going to die?"

Cliff brought this out academically, addressing no one in particular. The adults suddenly seemed tired of talking. He had to repeat the question before Luanna undertook an answer.

"Doc was just saying he doesn't think so, dear. Doc thinks he has a very good chance, or at least a *chance*. Isn't that what you said, Doc?"

"Yes, I did," said Dr. Braden.

Troy was turning off the county highway onto the private road into the ranch.

"When you talked to Millie?"

"That's right. When I talked to Millie," said the doctor. He spoke without opening his eyes. As the motion of the car changed in response to the narrower but better-maintained private road his head tilted sideways against the seat.

"Doc's asleep," said Cliff.

"Hush," said Luanna.

"Why should he hush?" said Troy. "Let those sleep who can."

Luanna moved close to her husband on the seat. She spoke in a low, urgent tone, her head close to his.

"Please, honey. Don't be annoyed with Doc. I'm sure he notified us the minute he thought proper. I'm sure he's done all he can. He's very fond of Hub. And Millie is devoted to your father. She would have called you without his telling her to if she'd thought that—"

"Shit," said Troy. "What were the cops doing all this time, if he'd been attacked? He's knifed in the neck, and nobody gives a damn. That's what gets me. That Altemira sheriff, old pork belly—"

"Dudley Polls?"

"Yeah, Duddy. What was he doing? I'd like to know some of those things."

"Well, Doc has nothing to do with *those* things certainly. He's worn out. Right now he's asleep back there. Anyway, the important thing isn't the law. All that. It can come later. What's important is your father's chance of recovery. Doc just got through saying—"

"I know what he said. You've got to read between the lines."

Troy's jaw muscles flexed. To cover his slipping control he leaned forward and turned on the headlights. Their broad, splendid beams, twice the width of any other car's lights, swept the road and the rolling land on each side of it. The fragile but lucent twilight suddenly seemed much darker.

The long summer day was over at last. All that was left of it now was a thin slash of crimson, high in the sky, in which a few wisps of cloud floated timidly, rapidly shredding apart. Rich damp smells filled the air and insects smashed against the windshield and the lamps of the car.

The house blazed with light from every window as if a feast or a ball rather than an old man's dying was what its people had in hand this night.

Troy drove in and parked in the curve of the drive. Half a dozen other cars were parked there, including a county car with a sheriff's star painted on both doors.

Millie Braden looked as tired as her husband. She had been putting on weight recently but was still a pretty woman with her luxuriant piles of red hair and her burnished Kinsale skin. She greeted the kids and kissed Luanna. The two women were obviously glad to be together again.

Troy got the hamper and suitcase out of the car. He looked in the back seat for his coat and put it on. Somehow it would not seem right to walk into the house in his shirt sleeves. Cliff carried the hamper, Luanna the suitcase; with Millie leading they set off on the path that traversed the south part of the three-acre lawn. They would be staying in their usual place, a separate dwelling known as the Spring House; they preferred this, for its privacy, to the guest rooms in the main house. The Spring House was a small, classic Spanish adobe, built by the De Bacas. It had been the first structure on the ranch property.

Troy went into the main house. The air, so long familiar to him with its proprietary indoor odors, in all seasons and changes, had a new smell now: in addition to its customary blend of floor polish, the churchly smell of seasoned, lived-in wood, the smells of cigar smoke, cooking, carpets and bygone days, it had the grievous smell of medicine and death.

Troy went through the hall into the big parlor to the left and sat down in the first chair he saw—a small, oaken, upright chair set against a screen.

The room was full of people. Here the new smell was at its worst, as might be expected, since Hub's room, the sickroom, opened off it. Hub, even in Cal Kinsale's time, had always used this downstairs bedroom, the biggest bedroom in the house. It was reached by three doors, one from the hall opening into an alcove, one from the living room, and one from outside. Along the walls, frescoed on top with hand-painted designs, Hub had placed a cherrywood armoire for his clothes, his teakwood gunrack and marble-topped oak chest of drawers, and his canopy-topped four-poster bed. The room was heated by two fireplaces, one for real logs and one for gas logs. Cal had introduced electricity at the turn of the century but had kept the original gas lighting fixtures and gas piping, serviced by a home gas-making plant, as a reserve energy source. Tonight both types of lighting were in use throughout the house, as if someone had decided that sufficient disclosure of the earthly scene would keep Hub among the living. Even the heavy silver candelabra in the dining room were burning, as were the candles on the mahogany tables around the sides of the room.

A young nurse, carrying a thermometer, came out of the kitchen, crossed the hall and entered the bedroom. The people sitting in the family room watched her with great attention; her appearance might provide some clue to what would happen next. The minute she was gone, however, they relaxed once more into their overlighted torpor.

Troy sat bolt upright in the stiff little chair. He held himself in the posture of a caller in an unfamiliar house, his knees pressed together and his broad, powerful hands resting on his thighs. He felt weary from the long drive and at the same time self-conscious and ill at ease.

Nothing here was the way he had imagined it would be. He had thought that nobody would be present except the family and the medical people and yet here were all these intruders, some of them ranch employees, others complete strangers, distributed helter-skelter around the downstairs rooms. All these rooms had been built without doors. They were connected with high pointed arches of polished wood ornamented at the sides with intricate spindle-and-saw work and above with varishaped panels of colored glass fashioned in the glowing, brilliant tones perfected by the turn-of-the-century glassmakers. The glass shades of table lamps and hanging lamps, with which the rooms abounded, reflected the same colors so that the whole windless, closed-in space, pulled together rather than separated by the arches, twinkled like some kind of spectacular, indoor glass garden.

For once, the California night had brought no coolness. Now and then there was a sizzle as some bug burned itself up in a gas jet.

Troy couldn't stand the look of things. Usually, in spite of the glut of stuff around, there had been a harmony about these rooms, as if each object had been bought to go exactly where it was—as perhaps it had. This order and beauty had been the work of his mother. Hub had respected what she'd done. Now and then he or Millie had tried to change the arrangement but the experiments never worked out and soon they would put everything back the way it had been before.

All was different now. Chairs and side tables were pushed against the walls. Rugs lay off-angled on the polished oak floors, lamps were lumped together tastelessly, small objects were disarranged, cups and saucers and plates with coffee dregs or particles of food clinging to them were dumped down carelessly, anywhere at all.

The whole place looked as if it had been jerked from its roots and junked out for the moving men to take away. He felt sick looking at it.

Was there some law, unknown to him, that death sent disorder, like a scout, to ride ahead of it?

His uneasiness turned to irritation. He wondered what was going on back in the bedroom. And why didn't Doc tell him to come in?

He turned his head cautiously to examine the other people, these strangers who had jammed in here, uninvited, as far as he could tell, to partake of the deathwatch. He'd seen only one of them ever before—Sheriff Polls of San Benito County, a prototypical satchel-assed sheriff, his knife-clench features swathed in rolls of flesh, his gun and gun belt hanging on the chair behind him. Next to Polls, smoking a cigarette which he held cupped in his hand, as if it were against the rules to smoke, was a deputy, and catty-corner to the deputy two men in clerical collars, a young one with a blue beard coming through his tightly shaven chin and an older, hound-faced one, flabby and gentle, with a huge cross on a red ribbon: a bishop, Troy judged.

Two fellows in unseasonable business suits, with vests and gold watch chains, had pulled a delicate drop-leaf table between them and spread papers out on it.

The room was very quiet. Its stillness was amazing for a place with so many people in it. Troy's eyes closed for a minute but, almost immediately, the decent and welcome silence was aborted. Somebody's stomach was rumbling, stertorously, obscenely—an ill-bred, absurd rebellion of trapped gas. Troy's eyes jerked open angrily. Heads were turning. He realized that the stomach making the noise was his own. He closed his eyes again. Why shouldn't his god-damn stomach rumble, he hadn't put anything in it since a sandwich lunch, eaten in the car! He considered going back to the kitchen to see what he could find in the icebox. That was what others had been doing, judging by the plates and cups around.

He had reached the hall when the bedroom door opened

and there was Doc, his Norfolk jacket now replaced by a white surgical coat, beckoning him to come in.

Troy turned and went rapidly into the bedroom.

Here, in contrast to the glare in the outer rooms, it was quite dark. The only light came from a kerosene lamp burning on the mantelpiece of one of the fireplaces and a small electric night light beside the bed. Hub lay on a hospital cot that had been brought in and placed in front of a window. On one side of the cot stood a steel flask of oxygen. This had hoses and a face mask attached to it which the nurse was taking off; she had just been giving Hub a treatment. On the other side, perched on a stool, sat Martha Kinsale, ninety, sister of Hub's father, Cal. She was the oldest living Kinsale and as a child in San Francisco had been lifted up by a bystander to see vigilantes hang a man in Portsmouth Square. She remembered a great span of history with considerable accuracy and possessed also the ability, which she had proven, of communicating with famous people who had passed on. One such was Colonel (later General) John C. Frémont, with whom she had had a love affair when he lived on Las Mariposas ranch. So close had been this relationship with him that he sometimes returned as a spirit and inhabited her body, enabling her to speak in his voice on subjects to which she brought an amazing wealth of detail. This verbal surrogateship had delighted her grandniece and grandnephews as children and when bored with their games they would beg her to "talk funny." Aunt Marty always professed not to know what they meant and if they kept after her she would fly into a rage and chase them around, trying to spank them—a performance almost as entertaining as her funny talk.

Marty Kinsale could never get along with Hub. She criticized his slovenly table manners and made him take baths; she washed his dirty clothes and forced him to leave his muddy boots outside the house. Above all she upbraided him for bringing up the children as heathens.

"Hell, I never been baptized," she would say when he argued her own lack of piety against her. "They *have*. That makes a difference. Do you want them to roast in hellfire?"

In spite of the trouble she gave Hub when he was well, Aunt Marty took beautiful care of him when he was sick. She now sat with a bowl of ice water in her lap, dipping a shaving towel in the water and wiping his face and his narrow, fleshy chest; when she saw Troy she stood up at once and motioned him to take her place. He refused, but the old woman, ignoring this, moved quietly to another part of the room. Troy pulled the stool slightly away from the cot and sat down on it. He leaned forward, listening to his father's rapid breathing and staring fixedly into his face.

Hub had changed, but not as much as one might have expected. The biggest change was in his nose. This had already become thin and waxy, the way dead men's noses are. For the rest, his face looked as it always did except for an expression round the mouth which Troy did not remember ever having seen there before—a look of calmness and determination. It was the look of a man gathering his forces for a major effort of some kind—to deliver an important speech or assume command of troops cornered in some doomed and vulnerable redoubt. Whatever energy Hub had left over from this secret and imperious task of his soul he used for breathing, a feat that presented difficulties. Hub had to get the air in and out very fast. His chest heaved with the work and his huge body trembled with it. As the air passed through his tubes it made a bubbling, rasping sound.

Dying, if that was what he was doing, shouldn't be as hard as it now seemed.

Troy looked around for Doc Braden. Doc was standing near the door that led to the patio—the door through which Hub, in happier times, would bring his women; he was talking there in low tones with another doctor who had just come in, a rosy-faced, well-scrubbed-looking man with gold spectacles and a flame of brushed-back blond hair. The new arrival kept glancing sideways at the chart the nurse was holding for him to see. As Troy moved up to him he offered his hand and said in a normal conversational tone, "I'm Dr. Keeler. You're Troy, I believe? We're so glad you could get here."

Not waiting a reply, he took a stethoscope out of his pocket and bent over Hub, listening to his chest in several places; then he had the nurse help him roll Hub over and did the same thing to his back. They rolled him carefully right side up again, the nurse holding his head to keep stress off his wounded neck. After this, the doctor smiled at Troy again and went out of the room.

The nurse put the oxygen mask over Hub's mouth and nose and adjusted the gauges on the tank. She turned on the oxygen and Hub's breathing became easier. He opened his eyes for the first time and winked at Troy.

"Hello, Dad," Troy said.

Hub winked again. Then he closed his eyes and resumed the business of getting the air in and out. He was absolutely determined about this business, he would tolerate no interference with it, though Troy felt sure, in view of the trouble it caused, that Hub would really have preferred to stop it. But he couldn't. He was bound to it by some implacable commitment. Whether taking oxygen or not taking oxygen he would open his eyes from time to time as if listening, even turning his head so as to hear better, and when he did so the pull of the same powerful purpose that Troy had observed before was visible in his father's face.

He's waiting for something, Troy thought.

Troy's stomach rumbled again. He was getting sleepy. Now that his father had recognized him there seemed no point in sitting on the small, uncomfortable stool staring at him. He could go and eat something and come back. Nevertheless, he didn't move. He wanted to put out his hand and take hold of his father's hand which lay outside the covers, only a few inches away, like a bony, big old frigging yellow turkey claw.

He wanted to know what Hub was waiting for. He concentrated on this question, thinking about it intently for several minutes during which he watched Hub turn his head, listening . . . in fact almost lift himself up when there was some sound in the house or out there beyond the window screen where the big summer stars were painted on the fathomless night sky.

And then he knew!

It's Kyle, he said to himself, *that's what he's hanging on for . . . to see Kyle, one more time, the one son-of-a-bitching person in the world he's ever cared about. He'll stay in there, he'll hang on for that, no matter what. I'd bet my last dollar on it.*

So sure was he that he too took on the vigil, as if sharing it would make it easier for Hub. He too began to listen, he too became conscious of the slightest sound or whisper, the rattle of a plate in the kitchen, the shift of a chair where the people were holding the deathwatch, the satchel-assed sheriff with his shoulder holster and the bishop with his big gold cross and his bag of unctions and forgiveness that Hub would surely never let him use. He could hear the squeak far off in the dark where a night creature hunting on wings quiet as cruelty sliced down and made its kill. He could hear the stir of insects in the charged and waiting air. He could hear, he thought absurdly, the pass of time itself. And then the real sound became audible, at first no sound at all, but the premonitory ghost of one, then a rustle like the hum of a bluebottle's wings and then, in reality, an approaching motor on the drive.

5

Kyle parked his car beside the sheriff's. He got out slowly and stood with his head tilted back, looking at the house as if he had never seen it before. He was preparing himself to deal with the problems shut up inside it.

There were always problems. They might be more pressing now than usual, perhaps, but certainly nothing that he could not deal with. He was in control here. He had always to some extent had this control, enforcing it since he had been very young by means of his ability to make decisions, to take chances and to charm people, but for the last few years by legal order and right as president and general manager of the Kinsale Land and Cattle Company, Hub having then moved up voluntarily to the post of chairman of the board.

Like everything about him—his clothes, his height and strength, and his lean, bony, dark good looks—the car was a proper extension of his personality. It was a Rolls-Royce Silver Ghost—there were only four others of this model in the state of California. Troy had waited until almost middle life before buying an expensive car but Kyle had had his Rolls a long time—and another before it, just as good. The first one had come with an English chauffeur and a mechanic from the Rolls-Royce company to show how it should be driven, repaired and cared for; Kyle had learned everything the mechanic had to teach and had soon discharged the chauffeur. He loved to drive at reckless speeds over even the worst of roads and he had taken this particular car on his horse-buying trips all over the state, to the most ridiculous, out-of-the-way places. Once, when a bridge had washed out, he'd hired twenty mules to pull the car across a fording on the Feather River, then in flood. Bystanders had predicted the ruination of the Rolls, but on the other side Kyle, who had never moved from the wheel, steering behind the animals, started it up and after a sputter or two the engine had taken hold and he'd promptly gone on to his destination.

Horse buying was a minor pastime of his life but a pleasure, just the same: he had respect for horses. They were instruments to him, a means of enlarging his sense of aliveness and his need for motion and urgency. California horses! They were fine, grand; all you had to do was find the right stock and breed them properly. The breeding part was new for him, he hadn't really had time—nor, the truth was, money enough—to go into it the way he meant to.

Kyle had become proficient in eastern-style horsemanship at New Haven but he was annoyed when the Meadow Brook and Aiken and Tidewater people ranted about their kind of hides as if there were no others. Stupid! He knew something about California horses, he'd been riding bucking stock in rodeos when he was fifteen years old. Not that you wanted broncs on the polo field—hardly. But breed a home-state steeldust mare with a thoroughbred stud or vice versa and you had a polo mount that would go with the best anywhere, even the Argentine.

Fiercely, argumentatively, Kyle Kinsale was a Californian.

At eleven he had done a curious thing. Sent east to a famous boarding school, exiled and lonely there, finding to his amazement that being a Californian wasn't something you bragged about, that it was considered somewhat freaky by snot-nosed people around you just because they happened to be born and raised in the pissass colonies George Washington had staked out—longing bitterly for home he had written to Troy to send him a box of dirt, of California earth. He wanted to keep it in his room. And Troy had done it.

In the blaze from the banks of lighted windows Kyle's tall shape threw an enormous shadow which stalked after him, dodging among the trees, as he walked toward the house. Kyle knew that Hub lay ill in there and he felt much affection for Hub, he was going to do right by him, but for the present he was not thinking about him. He was noting that the north side of the house needed painting. That side had been skipped, last time around, because the south side needed painting more. Have to attend to that. Probably it *should* have been attended to last time around, but Kyle's conscience didn't bother him that it hadn't nor did he reproach himself for setting up, at the last Land and Cattle Company meeting, the maintenance and repair budget which had precluded, that year, that particular expense.

Troy had his drilling rig. Hub had his orchards, his women and his cattle. Hub would have observed quickly enough if a corral fence had needed whitewash or a shed roof was leaking or there was a dicey belt or leaky gasket in the machinery of the mill where he ground up the grain mixes for the feedlot. Troy and Hub each had areas of interest—Millie and Doc likewise—but *his* interest was the whole family business, this ranch and the railroad and the Piru and the Orange County ranches, it was the whole company. And if the money he took out of the company meant a tight budget here and there, if it meant more than the company could afford, it was also a hell of a lot less than he personally needed—a minimal addition to his private income.

He had been good for the ranches—a good manager, better than Hub had ever been. He had got rid of thieving superintendents and accountants, hired new lawyers, put an end to the practice of paying help with goods instead of cash—a perpetual invitation to steal. He had introduced modern methods of seeding and harvesting and baling hay and bought machinery to do it with; he'd brought bulls from Scotland and Holland to improve the stock. No beef in the state had better ratings than Kinsale meat; no stock sold for such prices at the county fair. Where was there ground for complaint? His private life was his own affair; he wanted something more out of it than his father and grandfather had extracted from theirs. Boarding school and then Yale and then, by the grace of God, and the favors of a rich and appreciative woman or two, Europe, had taught him the uses of . . . elegance? Grace might be a better word for it, the thing he valued. It was more than the accoutrement of pleasure, a lot more: it was a sort of investiture, the uniform of power. Once you had it, whatever it was—a way of getting done circumspectly what you wanted done, a certain disciplined approach to social relationships—well, having that didn't mean, of course, that you had power, the real purpose of the game. Not at all! But if, on the other hand, you lacked that style, that class, there was then little likelihood that you would achieve power, ever . . . and if you did, through blind luck and the use of your grubby peasant instincts, manage to wangle just a trickle, a mere soupçon of it, what you got was still unlikely to do you any good.

Kyle stood still for several moments, his eyes straying off to the Gabilans, vaguely sinister against the luminous night sky. He was less than entirely engrossed in what he saw. He had glanced, just in passing, at what could be seen through the living-room windows and it was clear from the behavior of the people there that his arrival had not gone unnoticed. They'd been waiting for him. Well, all right. Troy was in there somewhere, Troy who would be stricken to the heart by this sad business. Troy whom he loved. Perhaps now they could even things up, set the odds right, those odds which had always been framed against Troy somehow. Kyle wondered sometimes how he would have felt if their situations had been reversed and Hub had always found money for Troy's slightest whim, for his games, his travels, his professors, his flirtations, at the expense of his, Kyle's basic rights. Not too happy, he thought. A bit jealous, he thought, and more than a bit angry. And the wonderful thing about Troy was that he didn't have a jealous bone in his body or an angry feeling in his simple, open heart. Oh, there had been unfairness, of course there had. High time it was ended and the brotherhood closeness invited back.

High time and past time the score was evened up!

Kyle moved around a corner of the house. At a place where a big acacia, planted by the first owner, screened him from the windows he bent down and dusted off his footwear with his pocket handkerchief. The shoes were hand-tooled kangaroo-hide starboots, stockman's boots you could wear to rope in, with their three-inch heels, or loaf in if you liked in a Paris drawing room—perhaps most suitable of all. Kyle wore them with a lightweight suit turned out for him by Henry Poole of 789 Savile Row, London, who made clothes for the Prince of Wales. Kyle saw nothing wrong in combining the two styles, the western and the sophisticated European: in such blends there was interest, there was character. No one knew better than he how to put the two together or when to come crashing on with the western alone. That theme, properly presented, swept all before it. It was precisely why, as someone had told him, the English had taken him up. He was so American, above all so Californian, as he had proved by turning out in western attire to ride with the Quorn Hunt. Kyle remembered Hub's comment when he had shown him the picture in *The Illustrated London News,* explaining that the members of that hunt had been impressed by his costume.

Hub had been puzzled.

"But son, what the hell would they *expect* you to wear?"

Hub had been even more bewildered by Kyle's interest in polo, a game Kyle had started playing in college and at which he rapidly came to excel. And when Kyle confessed that he had paid a thousand dollars apiece for four polo ponies, Hub had been furious.

"*Ponies*, son? If yore ridin' them things, yore ass is halfway to the ground before you get fair started."

There would be people in the house who knew Kyle and people who didn't. Those who didn't always were the easiest to deal with. As a rule they accepted the stereotype that had been pasted on him in most parts of the state, though not in Altemira. They regarded as appropriate the catchall epithet "sportsman," or sometimes, more opulently, "international sportsman," suffixed automatically to his name when it appeared in newsprint—oftener in the society columns than on the business page. Such people approached him with their guard lowered, expecting to deal with a dilettante, mistaking for harmless gregariousness the facade under which he chose to disguise his social acuity and his thrusting ambitions. For such people he had contempt, for the rustic entrepreneurs who tried to lure him into their petty schemes, for the conniving country tradesmen and thieving contractors as much as for the "hicks," the "rednecks"—the cattle barons of San Benito, Hub's cronies and drinking companions, who had watched with suspicion and uneasiness but quite without envy as he grew away from them, acquiring new friends, new interests, new tastes.

Those with clearer sight, or who had dealt with him before, recognized him as a serious businessman, knowledgeable and suspicious. He could meet these head on. He could even find pleasure in according them a temporary equality, an assumption of which, when it came down to trading, they would soon be disabused. He enjoyed getting his hooks into them. He had become expert in making people feel that their interests were more important to him than his own—at the very moment when he was making them do precisely what he wanted. The process was, for him, merely another exercise in . . . style . . . the evasive but heady quality which he valued above all and forever disciplined himself to polish, to perfect . . . and if his adversaries, especially the nice ones, suffered from such confrontations, they had no one but themselves to blame. In a way he was doing them a favor— teaching them a lesson. They had been stupid to move out of their own class.

The acacia no longer screened him off. He was out in the clear now, in full view of them all. He mounted the steps, watching with amusement as the seating arrangements in the overlighted room began to fragment. The bill collectors—for there was nothing else for those people to be with the uneasy faces primed with secret resolutions, in the suits which looked as if they had been bespoke in a prison tailor shop—started edging toward him; the two at the ormolu table, not wishing to be among the early clamorers, backed against the wall; the bishop raised his hand in greeting, then lowered it; the sheriff, feeling he was unobserved, spat on the floor. Kyle himself looked neither right nor left. He crossed quickly to the bedroom door, politely but firmly moving aside the nurse who, not knowing who he was, tried to bar his way. He went straight to Troy, who had risen from his stool, and embraced him.

Troy whispered, "He's bad off, Kyle."

"I know."

"Where the hell were you?"

"In L.A."

Troy felt his body expand. The breath, squeezed out of it all evening, suddenly came rushing in and filled him from head to toe, easily, buoyantly.

"L.A.!"

Between the brothers, "Going to L.A." was a running joke. It was like saying you'd gone silly—something no one did unless he'd lost his senses.

"Sweet Jesus!" whispered Troy. "L.A. Sheee-it."

He peered at Kyle with all the warmth of his soul, squinting eagerly from the jutting ridges of bone that protected his gentle, gleaming brown eyes. Troy's bones were seamed in vagrant fleshy lines, the scars left by the random fist fights of his rather wandering life. Schoolyard fights, oil-field fights, shipboard fights under alien skies. Standing close to his taller, extraordinarily handsome brother, so much like him in stance and skin, and yet so different, Troy seemed reduced, as if his natural warmth and confidence suppressed themselves in the careless, superior presence of Kyle.

Life had left no scars on Kyle. True, he might, and did, have a few broken bones, from polo and jumping contests, stowed away here and there under his elegant clothes, but if they took spring out of him anywhere, put stiffness into back or knee or turn of his tall muscularity, their presence merely perfected him, individualizing his hawky force.

Kyle turned aside briefly to speak to Doc Braden, who had approached him, and Troy took the opportunity to leave the room. He didn't want to see the meeting between Kyle and Hub.

Dr. Keeler joined the low-voiced conversation with Kyle and Braden. He confirmed Braden's estimate of Hub's condition: the old man had improved after the transfusion but was weakening again. It was doubtful whether he would last the night.

Nodding his dark, shapely head, digesting what the doctors were saying, Kyle seemed remote from the emotional tensions in the room. He too, from his manner, might have been a professional of some sort, called in to make an independent diagnosis. He moved back to the cot where his father was sleeping. From the moment when—and it was long before anyone else—Hub had detected the sound of the Rolls-Royce's tires, he had fallen asleep. His breathing was easier, slower. Lying on his back he still aimed his nose at the ceiling like a fieldpiece elevated for a very long range shot; he still clutched the sheet to him with turkey-foot fists, but he was calmer. There was no doubt in anyone's mind—he knew of Kyle's arrival. He had been strengthening himself by his little nap for the exertion of welcoming his favorite son.

The sheet covering Hub dumped into a trough below the stump of his amputation; the prosthetic leg, its straps looped over a coat hanger, hung against the armoire, as if ready to walk off by itself.

Kyle sat down beside him, at which Hub acknowledged his presence by opening his eyes. He kept them open—one more so than the other—only for a second or two; during this time, in the corner of the lesser-opened eye, a pool of moisture formed. It turned into a tear and rolled down toward the cot. Kyle took a corner of the sheet and wiped it away.

"Take it easy, Dad."

Kyle chuckled gently, in the way he liked to do—not a laugh but the kind of easy, throaty sound that might come before a laugh, that might just *make* things easy, as he'd said, even if he had to bring a laugh clean up into the air.

". . . a . . . rr . . . ttt," said Hub.

"Sure you're all right. Anyone can see that."

Hub's eyes snapped wide open now.

"The hell I am," he said clearly.

"The hell you're not. Aren't you the mingey son of a bitch to get yourself into a shape like this, though? . . . Now don't start beefing," he ordered, as Hub's chest heaved again and the mean lines bunched around his sunken mouth. "You just rest for a while, so you can get better."

It was the old bullshit again, the crap you talked to people who were dying and knew they were dying and knew you knew it but you said it anyway because someday you would be in the same fix and people would say it to you and you would be grateful.

Hub's chest heaved five or six times, as hard as he could heave it. He was again having a terrible time making terms with dying; once more his breath had turned into a rapacious antagonist and resisted his best efforts to drag it in and out. The nurse gave him more oxygen and Kyle held his hand until Hub went to sleep again.

A few minutes earlier he had been hoping his father would live and had been half confident, in spite of what Millie had said on the telephone, that he would. Now he was by no means sure that life would be the best thing for his father. The wasted and helpless person on the cot bore little resemblance to the Hub he had always known, the man whose shadow had laid so heavily on him and on all of them, whom he had sometimes deeply hated and even wanted to kill, so willful he had been, so grasping and terrifying. And at the same time Hub had been the giver of all. He had been as big as the sky.

How could Hub go back to life when he had already become estranged from living and when the effort to get on with it took such terrible toll of him?

Kyle had never reproached himself for not loving his father more. He was not in the habit of looking for faults in himself. He was no monster, no ungrateful son. He had loved Hub enough to get on with him while he lived and to wish him well now that he was going somewhere else. Certainly, Hub had heaped favors on him but almost everyone showed him special attentions of one kind or another. There was nothing so wonderful about that. Hub might have spent too much money on him, to the detriment of Troy and even of Millie—he might have selected him for glory just because he couldn't stand having a person around him who resisted him, whom he couldn't enslave and who saw him for exactly what he was, an ornery redneck son of a bitch. Hub might have figured he could buy his love. Well, he hadn't—not quite. Affection, well, that had always been there. What Hub had bought was something else: a working relationship that had been to everyone's advantage.

Kyle walked to the center of the family room. He took his place in front of the big fireplace, now empty and cold. Aunt Marty, recently ejected from the bedroom, was sitting on the fire stool, holding her body stiffly and staring straight in front of her. Kyle knew the signal—she was going into one of her fits. Her lips moved and a man's voice came out, low at first, deep and musical.

"Men! All this will pass. Take heart, all of you. It will soon be over. I give you my word on it. We have already passed the crest of these mountains; we shall now begin our descent into the valley."

Kyle spoke into her ear.

"Please be quiet, Auntie."

The old lady didn't hear him. She pressed both hands against her incredibly wrinkled cheeks and the voice came out stronger than ever, now with a strange, sad urgency.

"We will leave our hardships behind. We will rest in the peace of the valley; we will be made welcome at the fort."

Kyle looked around the room. Once more, at his entrance, there had been a drift, a rearrangement of people and faces. But . . . what were they all doing here? He noticed, as Troy had previously, the disorder in the room, the furniture moved higgledy-piggledy and the plates and cups around, the stuffy smell in the air, the bids for his attention. Very well, if they wanted action, he'd give it to them. He motioned to the bishop and that dignitary got out of his chair at once and trotted over like a bellboy.

"He's sleeping, Father. But if you could administer the . . . ah . . ."

"Without waking him? I could!"

"Then go ahead."

"Thank you, Mr. Kinsale. God's will be done!"

"All right."

Have to send him a check later, I suppose, Kyle thought, watching the bishop and his curate, their heads together, taking religious stuff out of the little black bag. Sheriff Polls, next in order of precedence, started to get up, but Kyle signed to him "Not yet."

He dealt in turn with the other members of the deathwatch just to get them out, to get them out of the house: the contractors with back bills—even when Hub had had cash in hand for ranch debts he often used for other matters; a lawyer who had a title dispute only Hub, he said, could settle; the accountants, shop craftsmen and foremen who had come ostensibly to show concern for the stricken man but really to find if they would be able to stay on, should Hub go. And so forth and so on. Kyle handled each matter with subtle differences of technique—and sometimes with a check; he got the people moving along, satisfied or not, sent them on their way with nods of understanding and inquiries about their families and peremptory yet friendly pats and flicks of his big hands. Only when the last of them was gone did he turn his attention to Sheriff Polls. They walked out to the parked Rolls-Royce and Kyle opened the door of the back seat and motioned the sheriff in. He took an alligator cigar case out of his jacket pocket and cut the end off a small cigar. He lit the cigar. He did not offer a cigar to Sheriff Polls.

"Yes, Sheriff?"

"We have a suspect, Mr. Kinsale."

"Aha."

"But we don't have a case. We'll need a little help from you."

"You'll get it. What do you need?"

"We'd like to come on the ranch and talk to some of your help here—"

"You don't need my permission to talk to our help."

"We didn't want to interfere with your operations."

"That's kind of you."

He was impressed with this consideration on the part of the sheriff; at the same time he knew he was *supposed* to be impressed. It was a calculated gambit, laid on for openers.

"This is with reference to the day Mr. Kinsale Senior was—"

"I understand."

"The orchard help. The checkers at the bins. The wagon drivers. They're permanent hands?"

"More or less. You want to ask them about someone who was working here that day?"

"Yes, sir."

"You'd also want to talk to the bus drivers—the ones who bring the pickers out."

"We already talked to them, sir. They come in town. They remembered, all right. They know who gets on and off those buses."

"Then I'm assuming that this person, the one we're concerned with, is a woman? I'm surprised, Sheriff."

"It being a woman?"

"I would have thought that . . . Well, let me stick my oar in, may I? You know more about this sort of thing than I do,

Sheriff. It's your bread and butter, you might say. You've been sheriff of San Benito County a long time, haven't you?"

"Seven years."

"That's quite long, I'd say."

"For an elective office it is, sir," said the sheriff. The key word was "elective." Kyle nodded. Sheriff Polls was getting to something, he felt, that had not yet been brought out. He waited, but since the sheriff chose not to amplify, he went on.

"One would usually expect a man, wouldn't you say? A crime of violence . . ."

"Check. A man with a grudge. That's how we figured in the Sheriff's Office."

"Then why a woman? He paid women off."

"I never heard that, sir."

"Look, Polls, of course you've heard it. And it's true, I personally hope I never have to do it, for myself, but I also hope that if I'm single at his age I have occasion to do it. Have you talked to the woman you suspect?"

"No, sir. To do that we'd have to bring her in."

There was silence for a beat or two as Kyle reflected and the sheriff watched him, his eyes returning the glow of the house lights.

"May I ask what evidence you're going on so far?"

"One girl came out on a bus. Boarded it in Altemira, four-thirty A.M. Monterey and Fourth Street. But she didn't go back on the bus that night."

"Is that so unusual?"

"No, sir. Some of them sleep in the orchards. We know that. But this particular girl did not sleep in the orchards. We know that too. We know quite a little. We have the knife, the one she used. Or that whoever did it used. A cutting knife. Taken from one of the cutting sheds and found in the tack room."

"Christ, we buy those knives by the gross. The blades are only two and a half inches long. Not much of a murder weapon."

"A man can be killed with a blade only one inch long. In the right place."

"I'll be goddamned if I ever heard that."

"It's true."

"Possibly. Yes, I suppose so, though I doubt it. But, yes. With two and a half inches, and he wasn't killed, as we know.

But to go on. So you have the knife. And you have fingerprints. I see what you're getting to."

"No, sir."

"What do you mean?"

"We don't have fingerprints. We have no way to take fingerprint impressions in Altemira. We wouldn't have a use for it. Once in a while, but it's just something we don't do. When there's a reason for it we send the object up to the city. To San Francisco. There's a feller there does it for three counties, San Benito, Kings and Monterey. He used to be in the San Francisco Police Department, retired now. Homicide. It don't take much handling to wipe out fingerprints. Overlay them. You need a whole print to have anything. Otherwise it could be anybody's print. And on a small object—this knife, now. Every son of a bitch that went near that tack room handled the knife, pardon my language. Your Chinese cook. Mrs. Braden. Others. No, we don't have prints."

"You don't have prints. And you don't have positive identification of the woman, putting her in that tack room, at that time? I can see why you don't have a case."

"Maybe," said Sheriff Polls quietly. "Maybe we can put it together. She came on the bus. She worked in the morning. She didn't go home on the bus. Maybe she got to a telephone. Someone came and picked her up. Maybe she just started walking. And walked."

"Thirty-seven *miles?*"

"They'll do it. Mexicans. Do a lot of things a white person wouldn't. The women as well as the men. The fact is, Mr. Kinsale, we don't care how she got home. She got there. We're not interested in that. We're interested in what she did during certain hours. She worked in the A.M. there in the orchard. Not much in the P.M. There was a gap there. She went into a shed. This is something to be verified. Strictly a rumor, but it could . . . I guess you know how it is. These women are always big-eyeing each other. Especially they're big-eyeing the pretty ones. Watching for some kind of shit flying. And there's word going round that Mr. Kinsale Senior, that he was in that certain shed during some corresponding period of time. That would have to be checked out. It could be like I say, bullshit of the first order. But in case it could be checked out and an incident of some kind, you understand, if it took place in there, then there might be a possibility . . ." Sheriff Polls stopped in mid-sentence, apparently worn out by the effort of his long speech—possibly the longest consecutively worded speech of his life.

"I see," said Kyle slowly.

"Thank you, sir," said Sheriff Polls.

Kyle extinguished the butt of his cigar and lit another. This time, with the alligator case halfway to his pocket, he offered the sheriff a smoke; Polls declined but lit a cigarette. The two men smoked in silence. Well, thought Kyle, he finally got it out, he got to the point.

The woman had got in somehow. She had waited there in the small unlighted room. When Hub cane through the door, burdened down with a thirty-five-pound saddle, she was on him, she came for him like a train. It all made sense, it could all be put together quite logically provided one thing, provided there existed what this tactful mannikin, this wide-assed and well-experienced lawman, has now been kind enough to provide, a motive.

Sheriff Polls, by his silence, was serving him. He was asking him a question which now had to be answered, and to obtain that answer the sheriff had waited patiently. Namely, what did the Kinsale family want him to do? The sheriff had gone above and beyond the call of duty, a wide-assed sheriff, to be sure, but a keen one, this seven-year incumbent of an elective office, as he'd emphasized. Oho! The eighth year, then, was coming up—and that was the election year.

So there was room here to move.

"I can see, Sheriff," he said after a pause, "why you want a solid case. Witnesses. Good substantial testimony. Nothing else would be any good. It would be stupid and it would accomplish nothing to bring this girl in, whoever she is, and then have to let her go."

"Yes, sir. But I got this other problem, Mr. Kinsale. The girl might leave town."

The sheriff's voice had changed slightly with the last sentence, but his face was expressionless.

"I hadn't thought of that."

"It could happen."

"It certainly could."

Kyle stretched. He leaned forward and opened the car door.

"Let's get some air," he said.

It was then half past two in the morning.

The bishop was leaving. The house smelled of incense. The

last rites had been administered. Troy was asleep in the porch swing. Kyle found a light blanket and laid it over him. Chun Wuk was still moving in the kitchen. He prepared a chicken sandwich and some hot homemade soup for Kyle. Doc Braden had replaced Dr. Keeler on the living-room couch. He was snoring peacefully as Kyle passed him, going back into his father's bedroom. Kyle and the nurse, Mrs. Emery, and Dr. Shelton were the people with Hubbard Wingate Kinsale when, at 4:52 A.M., he died; his breath, due to the congestion in the lungs, literally expired in a rattle over which could be heard Aunt Marty's rocking chair, thumping in the next room. Aunt Marty felt the approach of her spectral lover. Her face knotted and she sat up straight. A clear young voice pealed from her mouth, the voice of a cultured, educated man.

"We have raised our colors but . . . an attack is coming. I am determined to . . . fight . . . to the last extremity!"

Cliff and Helene and their mother slept peacefully in the Spring House. The place had its own kitchen, and Luanna had made dinner there for all three of them. Millie left for a while, then came back with a pitcher of lemonade.

She and Luanna had sat up late talking. There seemed to be so much to say, these rare times when they got together, they just had to keep on till they were talked out. Each had something in her hands to work with, as countrywomen do—Millie working a piece of cross-stitch, Luanna sewing on a jacket of Cliff's, where he had chewed the sleeve.

". . . I don't know," Millie was saying. "I really don't know how Troy stood it, it went on so long."

"Well, he left, after all," said Luanna. "He got away."

"Yes, he surely did—he ran straight to you!"

Millie's glistening red head cocked for laughing. But she didn't laugh. She was always very delicate, very softly probing in her fondness for her sister-in-law. She stopped short of saying that Hub's severity had driven Troy away from home, to go adventuring in the world—then marry early. It might not be true anyway.

Luanna was the one who laughed. She held up the ragged sleeve so she could see how the stitches were going.

"It didn't hurt a bit!"

She went on with her work but Millie let her hands rest in her lap.

"He was always such a wonderful little boy. He was always so sweet to me."

"Was Kyle mean?"

"I don't know. Kyle had his own way of *not* being mean. He was just—Kyle, I suppose. One or two jumps ahead of you all the time. I'm sorry," she added quickly. "That doesn't sound right. But you know what I'm saying."

"Yes, that's how he is, I guess. But he seems to fascinate most people. Even me."

"Of course, you. Because Troy talks about him?"

"Partly. And because of what I've seen. But Troy does talk about him. He misses him, working so far away and all. They're really such—brothers. I don't know many brothers like that."

"That's true. I know Troy loves Kyle."

"Yes."

"And Kyle reciprocates. Which may be the nicest thing one can say about my elder brother, the Yale man. A Yaley! Don't you love that expression? It seems to fit him so well. A polo player. Did you know that Troy was the star of the Altemira football team for two years? Fullback. And Hub never went to a single game."

"Troy did tell me that. That he played, not that Hub didn't go. I think he always wanted to be closer to his father. He felt it would happen somehow, though of course it never did. If only Hub hadn't swung the meeting against Troy two years ago. Made him stop drilling . . ."

"But it *was* a dry hole, wasn't it?"

Luanna's small-featured, countrified face, so relaxed till now, took on a different expression. Red patches appeared in her cheeks. She remembered the excitement around the derrick, the conviction of the crew, one and all, that this would be the big one.

That had been the first and only time she'd seen Troy turn against his father. He'd driven home silent and shaking, too furious to talk. Nor had they ever discussed later the impact which the decision of the meeting had produced on their lives. What could you say? As for her, she'd hated Hub passionately from then on. Tonight she'd thought: *If this is the end of that mean old man, will we get another chance at the well?*

She didn't finish the thought. But even leaving it not quite finished she joined the now considerable group of women who in the last few days had felt that benefits could be derived from the demise of Hubbard W. Kinsale.

"It wasn't a dry hole at all," she said. "We all had great hopes for it."

6

A Requiem Mass for the repose of Hub's soul was celebrated two days later in St. Francis Xavier Church, Altemira, a place of worship which he hadn't entered since his confirmation there some sixty years previously. Rt. Rev. Brendan O'Melveny, Bishop of the Northern California Diocese, celebrant, Rev. Mons. Fr. Amancio Rodriguez, VGPA, assisting. The Mass was preceded, Saturday night, by a Rosary in the Holy Spirit Chapel of the Oratorian Community of St. Philip Neri, Fr. Emeric Kieffer, Orat. More than three hundred persons signed the Rosary book, being at least a hundred more than capacity for the Holy Spirit Chapel, and since no crush was observed outside at any time, it must be concluded that a number who wrote down their names took leave again without actually attending the Oratorian offerings, inspiring though these may have been.

On the Monday following the Mass, the *Altemira Free Lance* reproduced, in part, Bishop O'Melveny's tribute to Hub, ". . . member of a pioneer family . . . outstanding cattleman and . . . long enough to possess and enjoy the blessings of . . . and beloved by . . . *requiescat in pace*. Amen."

Troy and Kyle both served as pallbearers together with a cousin, Rodman Kinsale of the Wineglass Ranch, Salinas, and Dr. Braden of Dead Eagle Valley. The remaining two of the six pallbearers were professionals, members of the St. Francis Xavier parish who regularly augmented their incomes by the six-dollar fees which they received for this type of work when it was available: Lloyd Homan Wilkins, automobile repairman, and Juan Sanchez, an employee of the Altemira Packing Company.

Members of the board of the Kinsale Land and Cattle Company served as honorary pallbearers, the burial party breaking up immediately after the interment. Troy and Kyle went back to the homeranch where Kyle, with an elder brother's prerogative, broke out a bottle of bourbon whiskey —solid hooch laid down by Hub before Prohibition, in charred oak casks, so old now that a faint mist of charcoal sediment floated in its clear depths like sand in the turn of an amber wave.

Troy held his glass up to the light. He'd needed the whiskey. In addition to the little matter of the drilling money there had been another question he'd wanted an answer to; he'd been feeling, that afternoon, for a way to ease into it. It was not the sort of question you put to a brother who was close to you and who had just set you up in the most important venture of your life. *Didn't Kyle care?*

Somewhere, probably not far away, the person who had attacked Hub was walking around free, not called to account, not even apparently in danger of being called to account! How could Kyle live with this?

They must act! Jesus, didn't Kyle see that? The cops . . . what had they done so far? Instead of questions, Troy found himself issuing protests, uttering queer jerky demands, only half thought out but deeply felt and far, far from his usual manner of speech with Kyle. And Kyle had nodded and sipped the whiskey, looking off at the mountains that ringed their stronghold and encompassed their lives. He did see. He did agree.

Only—something hadn't been explained.

"Now hold on. This will set you back. I gave Polls two thousand dollars. One thousand for his campaign chest; he's up for re-election, as you may know. Very well. He'd helped. He isn't stupid, this is something that he was entitled to. The other thousand dollars was for the girl."

"Jesus Christ. I don't think I'm hearing this right."

"It isn't all that complicated. Polls said she might leave town. He laid it on the line to me. Or enough so I could read what he was saying. If he opened up the case there was going to be the hell of a stink, I mean one of dimension. You know how Hub was with the orchard women. And others. He got worse. Maybe a person does, an individual of his type, as time gets shorter. He was a great person, a wonderful man but . . . just so you won't think the lady in the tack room was some kind of nut."

"A person who tries to kill an old man with a two-and-a-half-inch cot-cutting knife isn't a nut?"

"She might just be a very angry person. But she also, if I may say so, had a head on her. I'd passed her the money through the sheriff but she knew it didn't come from him. When she decided to give it back she figured whom to give it to. She gave it to me."

"I'll be a son of a bitch."

"So will I. Two sons of bitches. But we won't have our old man defamed in death by a well-meant but stupid police action because no one had sense enough to protect him."

"Oh, Jesus Christ. Quit harping on it."

Kyle gave his brother a quick, hard look. This look passed and in its place, as his eyes remained on Troy, appeared a quality of tenderness.

"I figured you'd understand—eventually. Keep this in mind—*the woman didn't kill him*. The death certificate said he died, quote, of lung congestion following an accident, unquote. I had a hand in writing that one too. *No crime.* Hence no charges. If there'd been a proven crime then nothing Polls or anyone else could have done would have hushed it up. But as it was . . ."

Silence fell. Troy got up. He reached into Kyle's jacket, laid over a chair, and extracted Kyle's cigar case from an inside pocket. He sat on the porch rail, speaking through eddies of gray smoke.

"You *saw* this girl?"

"Right after the Rosary."

"But I was with you then. We all were."

"We were in the front pew, right? And no one moved until we'd gone up the aisle, going out—Millie and Doc, Luanna and Cliff. Then you. Then me. Well, she was waiting. She stopped me."

"Outside?"

"Inside. Beside the font. She shoved this envelope into my hand. Didn't say a goddamn thing. Just shoved it at me and walked out."

"But you got a look at her—"

"I did. Not much of a look, but enough. Tall. Really tall for a chili-bean woman. Stacked but they're all stacked, the chili-bean types. Good-looking, I'd say—what I saw. And here's another part. This is the goddamnedest part. I called Polls on the telephone right away. Told him she'd given the money back, and he was *surprised*. He thought she'd keep it. So he checked, himself, and she *has* left town. Now figure that one out."

Troy studied the end of his cigar.

"It might figure," he said. "I mean, if something of the sort you're hinting at took place—before the tack-room thing."

"Yes," said Kyle. "Before the tack room."

CHAPTER THREE

In the Dunes

1

Two years, here in this lonely place, the seasons changing and time working its will. The grass had grown back, the road through the dunes had all but disappeared, no more now than a vague, wavy line in the sage and mesquite. Troy stood on the rise and looked south along the diminishing slant of the desert, streaky gray in the early-morning light. He'd come back so often in his imagination he'd stopped believing there was such a place, or if there was, that he could ever find it again.

Maybe the road would do. It had been well tramped in the old days by the vehicles moving in and out. Maybe the wheels that came now would just settle by some natural law into the old ruts and the road would redefine itself. Already he could see something moving out there, the first of the big trucks loaded with bright pine lumber for the new derrick and behind them the pickups carrying the boss carpenter and the construction crew.

Troy had brought Charlie Ott out in his own pickup and old Charlie was nosing around the site in a hapless, disgusted way, as if looking for some evidence that would prove it could never be any good. Charlie hated all jobs the first few days. Sometimes he hated them clear through to the end. He'd never been on a good one yet, to hear him tell it. He hadn't said a word all the way out. He'd been on a tear for days in Jerd McConihe's cathouse in Taft and had heated himself up, in the truck, drinking hot coffee from a thermos. The reek of booze he was sweating out came through his clothes.

"How deep was you when you pulled out?"

"Four thousand two hundred and eighty feet."

"You saved yourself some money."

Troy let this go by.

"Wednesday," he said, "we'll have the wagon out and pour the slab."

"Wagon never goin' to make it through them weeds and potholes. How much pipe you leave in the hole?"

"A thousand feet."

Charlie spat, the angle of his jaw projecting his contempt for anyone insane enough to leave that much steel casing in an uncompleted well, though he well knew there would have been no way to get it out, a state law requiring that the well be cemented. Another law required that if a drilling was to be abandoned the hole must first be plugged with concrete. It was a good law. It prevented seepages of oil or connate (fossil) water which might pollute other oil-bearing structures or render surface areas unfit for agriculture. An excellent law, and one copied in most other states, but a law which, nevertheless, made problems if you tried, later, to go down near the same spot. Troy got a camp ax out of the pickup and drove stakes to show where he wanted the derrick to go. Then the trucks pulled in and he shook hands with the boss carpenter and showed the Mexicans where to put the lumber. Once the derrick was up and the slab poured, the engine in place and the casing pipe and drill stem stacked, ready for use, he would build a bunkhouse and a cookhouse for the crew and put in a tank for drinking water. There was water enough on the site for drilling mud but it had too much boron in it to be drinkable.

He'd taken two weeks to put a crew together, the best he could get—twenty-one men in all, most of whom he'd worked with before. Actually there were four complete crews, five skilled workers in each—a driller, a derrickman, and three floormen, or "roustabouts." Each crew would work an eight-hour shift, or tour, as it's called in the oil fields (pronounced to rhyme with hour); the fourth crew would be split to relieve individuals in the other crews on their days off.

He himself, the tool pusher, would have no days off, but Charlie Ott, who'd pushed tool on many jobs, with a rig of his own in the cable-tool days, would stand in for him nights.

He laid on a cook and an Indian swamper.

It was a good outfit. It would get the job done.

He'd made arrangements for Luanna and Cliff and Helene to live in Piru. He could get home there most nights, it wasn't far.

It wouldn't be easy—any of it. It would be hard, exhausting, endless but it would also be joyous, glorious, just as today, the gray fall weather and the stir and voices of the men working, the smell of the new timbers and crushed vegetation of the desert, all was joyous, glorious because he was back here and the well was going to happen; this time he had money enough. This time he had all the drill stem he needed plus a special bit that would cut through the hard stuff they'd hit before, the stuff that had stopped them. They would find a way to get through that fucking stuff when they hit it again. They would go down, if they had to, as far as anyone had ever drilled in California.

Troy could not have said why he thought the oil would be a mile down. He'd pulled that figure out of the air. He'd put it in the prospectus because that was as far as you could go and he'd wanted the maximum, but as time passed and the figure kept being repeated and people kept asking him about it he came to believe it himself. That's where the oil would be. A mile down there, waiting—the immense black, still, thick reef formed by the droplets pushed upward by the pressure of the gas below, up and up through one or four or however many million years, through the dark, subterranean night of time, in permeable (not to be confused with porous) rock. Up and up those droplets had come, tadpoles of fortune, fighting for their lives every inch of the way, never stopping, yielding to the shoving of the gas and water below, up to the hard stuff where, with resistance met, they bellied against the geologic dome for an appointment with a drill bit.

Work at the rig was going well. The cement truck, in spite of Charlie's predictions, had got in over the washouts in the desert's gray hide, but the first rains of October turned the cracks and seams into arroyos and the surface to slippery ooze. Troy had the road macadamized. That would pay off before they were through.

Long before Christmas (his theoretical deadline) the bunk-

houses and the cookhouse were finished and the raw pine
tower of the new derrick stood high in the sky, on its lunar
hill, darkening from yellow to brown in the dry desert air.

Cliff Kinsale #1.

So said the sign where the private macadam branched off
the county road over which now came the drill pipes. One
silly roughneck, half smashed probably, rode the last load,
doing handstands like a circus clown when the big vehicle, too
long to make a right angle at close quarters, had to back and
turn in the little desert hamlet, and the people came out of
the stores to stare.

On spudding-in day, Troy let Cliff stay out of school. Since
the kid had a well named after him, he should have the honor
of pulling the switch. That was customary, Troy explained to
Luanna—quite unnecessarily: as an oilman's daughter as well
as an oilman's wife she already knew it. She stood between
husband and son in her best dress and hat, under the gray,
tumbling skies. The engine was in place, bolted down. Steam
was up, the chain on the block, the block greased and ready
to turn, and an eighteen-inch bit slotted into the first section
of the stem. Cliff put both hands on the lever, looking
confidently at his father, as if this was something that could
happen any old day, why not? It was good fun. Troy gave him
the go signal and Cliff pulled the lever. The engine coughed
and took hold, the chain groaned, the huge rotary table
turned and—whap!—under the derrick floor the bit chewed
out its first bite of the long trip down.

One by one the crewmen came up to Cliff and shook hands
with him. They did the same with Troy and Luanna, as if the
entire family had just achieved some notable distinction.

Down there the earth in its inscrutable layers had lain for
millions of years, composed and heavy, compressed by
aeon-long alternations of fire, ice and shifting geologic plates,
and above all by the weight of time. Now for some insane
reason the somber and contained march of centuries considered as millennia had speeded up so that time had no longer
worth or dignity; now hours developed individual crises, even
seconds shrilled their importunities, and the derrick blazed all
night, lighting the land for miles around, hung from top to
bottom with electric bulbs like some monstrous, aberrant
Christmas tree.

Troy pressed on as fast as possible. He wanted to get done
before the heavy winter rains and he wasn't sure what

difficulties he would meet. He was using a new kind of bit, rented to him on terms many times higher than those for an ordinary drilling tool. During the summer he'd gone to the Hughes Tool Company of Houston, Texas, to discuss his problem—how to drill the hard stuff that had slowed him up the first time around.

Noah Dietrich, Hughes's vice president, had expounded on the new bit.

For some twenty years in California and elsewhere, the only drill bit in general use had been the old standard fishtail—a holdover from cable-tool drilling; since the fishtail's two cutting edges quickly grew dull in rock formations, tool designers changed to bits with three, then four cutting edges. They improved the temper of the steel. Tungsten-carbide bits, the new rage, cut better in both hard and soft formations but Troy still was not satisfied with them. He'd heard that Hughes Tool had perfected a bit with industrial diamonds—the hardest substance known—folded into sixteen tungsten-carbide edges. The rumor proved true—Dietrich showed him the bit, which had been tried only in a few selected situations which presented problems like that of Cliff Kinsale #1.

Dietrich offered an agreement—if the bit didn't do everything required of it there would be no charge, but if it did, then Hughes Tool would have five percent of the action. Troy turned this down. His instinct was against sharing the well with anyone. He took the Hughes bit on a straight rental. It went through the hard stuff just fine.

Color was coming up now in the cuttings as the drilling mud shoved them to the surface.

Troy laid on tankage. On concrete slabs, in notches dug into the dunes, a special crew riveted steel plates and the paint crew painted them the brindle color that the L&CC used for its railroad station, its buildings and wagons, and the buses for the orchard girls. Now Cliff Kinsale #1 had three ten-thousand-barrel tanks, each about enough to handle the first splutter or two of that well, if it was what he thought it might be.

Troy ordered drilling stopped while he sent into Bakersfield for blowout prevention equipment—BOPE: the biggest casinghead manufactured, weighing fifteen tons and secured to a hundred-ton concrete slab. He brought in seventy-five Mexicans to dig a trench for a pipeline and put up tents for them and a special cook tent and laid down the pipeline and welded it and hitched it to the tanks and the tanks to the casing-head.

He wired Kyle in Del Monte, where Kyle had gone for a polo game, and told him to get his ass down to the rig.

". . . Monday is the day we give babies away."

CHAPTER FOUR

A Life That Would Do

1

"I'm sorry, sir. That line is still busy."

"All right, operator. I'll try later."

Kyle hung up. He knew that Troy, to avoid the delays that had occurred during the crisis with Hub, had installed telephones in his house as well as at the rig, both ringing on the same number. Must be a busy day down there—that was understandable if the well was really coming in, as Troy seemed to be saying. He wondered if they were still drilling or if, in Troy's judgment, they were now so close to results (*Monday?* They could pick a *day?*) that they'd stopped temporarily. They could do that. Troy had once explained the process. They could stop and then later bail the well to renew activity when they were ready for it.

Propping the telegram against the room-service coffeepot he read it again. Wild, wonderful news to wake up to! He felt well rested yet somewhat out of himself, as he always felt after a night that combined not quite enough sleep with a slight excess of lovemaking. It was the way he liked to feel under any circumstances, but particularly on the day of a game. Ha—the game! But that had suddenly receded in importance. If Troy had said to come today instead of Monday Kyle was sure he would have chucked it all. He

81

would have told Gordie Moore to find a substitute player for him. He would have jumped in his car and driven straight to Piru.

He poured a second cup of the strong, clear coffee, smiling at his brother's choice of words. That bit about babies brought back a summer day when he'd been fourteen, Troy eleven, and they'd gone with Hub to the California State Fair at Sacramento, their first trip there. Later they'd become State Fair sophisticates but then it had all been new to them: the flags wagging on top of the grandstand, the calliope music brassy on the midway, the horses running, the livestock in the corrals, and the geese and ducks and chickens in their cages in the long sheds, and the crusty pies and fancy cakes and jarred fruit and glistening table settings in the household-exhibit tents. The barkers yammered at the lazy, slow-moving crowd, pulling the marks in to play the concessions, and both boys took a crack at the baseball-throwing game that dumped a black man into a barrel of water if you hit a target lever; they tried the shell game, the marble game, the bingo game, the car crash, the airplane ride, the tunnel of love, the carrousel and the Ferris wheel which, that day, kept getting stuck; you could see the trapped passengers gesticulating angrily from their seats, hung high up against the bald-headed sky.

A fine day indeed, but Troy had brought a hand-raised steer, a pet, to the auction—brought it unwillingly, at his father's orders, knowing that after it had been judged it would be auctioned to some packinghouse or restaurant for meat. His gentle friend! Such was Troy's misery that Kyle, to distract him, took him to play the races. In no time at all they were out of money but then came salvation—a gnome in a high stand-up collar and a tiny Irish cap, a mystery person who promised a miracle. He could recoup their losses. It was simple. Bring him a hundred simoleons and he'd fix the last race. He knew all the jocks, by Jesus—and he'd proved it, freely passing in and out of the jocks' room that had a state marshal outside to guard the door. Hub wouldn't put up a penny but the brothers had scurried around, borrowing from Altemira storekeepers, watchful and pale in the trade exhibits, and from the stockmen, Hub's drinking pals, around the barns. The miracle man chose a horse, Fire Extinguisher. He'd bet the hundred for them, and the jock on Fire Extinguisher, seeing them with the gnome, standing beside the gate that led from the saddling enclosure to the track, had raised his whip significantly, pointing right at them—the agreed signal!

"Did you see, now?" said the gnome. "Lads, this is the day they give babies away."

It had all come true, almost. Fire Extinguisher had won by ten lengths. What did it matter that the gnome had disappeared with all the money? They'd had a winner!

Very well. This time they'd have another. Kyle felt he could go down to Piru on Monday and force oil out of the ground, if need be, by the action of his will alone.

He dressed quickly in a pair of jeans with an open-neck mesh shirt and stockman's boots; his polo clothes were in his locker at the club, where he would change before the game. He telephoned the garage at the Del Monte Hotel to have his car brought round.

2

Tip Morrisey, his groom, was cleaning tack as Kyle drove up to the barn. Tip had a Hermes saddle over a rail, working soap into the cheek flaps, smoking a stubby briar pipe. Kyle decided not to show annoyance at the smoking—it was just no good around a barn. As a rule Tip obeyed orders about this but made an exception of game days, as if these were specially licensed. Well, thought Kyle, they're not—and the irritation he'd been holding back came out with a rush when he checked Warren G., a gelding that he'd just brought in from the ranch. Warren G. could make a hole in the wind. He'd planned to use him in the first chukker, and the last as well, if the game went overtime.

"What happened there?"

The gelding had a cut on his right foreleg, a noticeable swelling below it.

"Got a breath of a tiny kick there, he did—gettin' in the trailer."

"I told you not to load him with another horse."

"Can't get him in without anither; Kyle, now—you know it yoursel'."

"You could put a twitch on him."

"Won't load with a twitch, won't load with nothin', but put anither hide in there, now, and he walks in like a judge."

With delicate pressure of his thumbs Kyle palpated the flesh around the swelling.

"I been working him over, like," Tip said. "Put blue ointment on the cut. He's sound as a bell o' brass."

"Well, I want to find out."

"Right now, sir?"

Tip always became respectful when confronted with an order he didn't like.

"Right now."

Warren G. stood docilely while he was made ready, Kyle himself wrapping his legs with soft wool bandages laid over cotton pads. When he worked a horse he always liked to hit a few balls, to stop and turn in an approximation of playing conditions. The big, fast horse worked smoothly; as Tip had said, he seemed sound, showing the bruised leg no favor. Kyle signaled for a ball and the groom, who had walked to the sideboards of the practice field, flipped one out to him; Kyle hit some backshots, then took a half-circle turn and smashed a long, high drive upfield. Instantly the gelding, with a surge of power, stretched out to follow the shot.

He was ready all right. Kyle checked his run and turned him lightly—his mouth was so sensitive that he played in a rubber bit—returning him to Tip. He had the saddle switched to Trixie, a stick-and-ball horse. He picked up a mallet and climbed onto the mare, cantering along the sideboards, dribbling a ball in front of him.

Another rider, easily recognizable, was working at the far end of the field: a woman wearing cowboy chaps, her blond hair pulled back so tight it could have passed for one of the new, short haircuts. She had broad shoulders and a tiny waist, and when she stood up in the stirrups to hit, she turned, in elegant form, in a complete right angle, following through powerfully like the best of male players. She had been practicing penalty shots at the goal but when Kyle rode up she backed the ball to him and for a while they passed to each other, riding in half circles and figure eights, holding both horses well in hand. They kept at it until Kyle let a pass go untouched and reined up to her.

"You're out early," she said.

She pulled a knee across the pommel and slid down, holding up her face to be kissed.

"So are you."

"I didn't try to outlast the music."

"What do you mean? I was asleep by midnight."

"Then how was it that your friend Marjory, as I happen to know, didn't get in till two A.M.?"

"Can't answer that, Your Honor."

"You may leave the witness box. I can't stand men who kiss and refuse to tell."

"Vicky," said Kyle, keeping his tone carefully light, "if anything needs telling you'll take care of it. That's what I love about you."

"Thanks so much."

"Don't mention it."

"I won't. But may I mention something else? You're a real prick."

She turned to remount, jerking her horse around. The animal shied away from her. Kyle reached for the bridle, steadying him.

"Stupid to get angry."

"I don't exactly enjoy being called the town crier."

"That's not what I said."

"It's what you implied."

"All right. I apologize."

"Go fuck yourself."

She touched heels to her horse.

"Goodbye, Vicky," he called after her.

But she was already too far away to hear.

Kyle felt a momentary pang. He'd meant to convey a tactful warning, rather than infuriate: there'd been gossip, and he suspected most of it had come from her. She had, just as he'd told her, a reputation for tattling all she knew, and much that she merely suspected; aside from this trait, he liked her. He had long admired her abilities as an athlete, a range of physical talent which rumor—again possibly set going by herself—had suggested as not being limited to the polo field.

Victoria Schuyler von Hagen had come to Del Monte for several winters in a row, bringing a string of horses with her. She was in her middle forties, widowed by one husband, divorced by another—both extremely rich; in a group of horse-oriented women, mostly from Meadow Brook and Aiken, who had got into California polo, she was the only one who carried a man's handicap and played in the otherwise all-male, midweek practice games. Too bad, probably, to put her nose out of joint; she could be counted on, in some devious female way, to make him pay for it. But was she really all that angry? He noticed, as he went on with his practice, that she'd put up her horse and was circling the field in her car, a light-colored Wills St. Clair, heading toward his section of the south stable. She sat in the car, waiting, as he rode in.

"You silly ass."

He turned on her his most charming smile. "I tried to apologize."

"And as before I refuse to accept it. But I'll buy you a drink."

"Not till after the game."

She looked put out.

"At least, stop by the cottage. Marge gave me something for you."

"Don't I get a clue?"

"Something you'll need this afternoon. Will you come?"

"All right—in a while. I have some things to do here first."

She put the car in gear.

Kyle delayed half an hour, checking the other mounts he planned to use and instructing Tip as to the order in which he would ride them and the way he wanted them equipped. The groom knew all this as well as he and could have supplied the same instructions, word for word, without prompting; however, the dialogue was a ritual established for game days, and must not be changed. And on such days Kyle left nothing to chance.

Vicky von Hagen's "cottage" was a large stone house, rented yearly through an agent, in the pine hills near the hotel. Built by a mining magnate at the turn of the century, it had a tennis court, an elaborate steam bath and other amenities which Vicky liked to have about her, wherever she happened to be. Kyle left his car in a stone courtyard and passed through a second court, hot as a greenhouse, with a fountain and tropical shrubs in it, together with some kind of recording which played birdsongs. At the front door a Japanese servant said that Mrs. von Hagen was at the pool. Would he go out?

Vicky lifted a wet brown arm from the water.

"There it is, honey. On the table."

She was pointing to a polo helmet, a type recently introduced by C. T. I. Roark and some of the other internationalists. It differed from the ordinary kind in that the rim swooped down in a flange that protected the back of the neck. It was held on by an exceptionally broad, strong strap. The helmet rested on the table with its inside up and in the crown of it was a card in the handwriting of Marjory Laufer.

> Darling: I borrowed this from Glenn so you could try it out. Please wear it! So much safer!
>
> XXX Marge

Kyle dropped the card on the table. He had no need to test the helmet for size. It would fit. He'd used Glenn Laufer's tack before. Glenn had come into polo well supplied with everything he needed, except possibly ability. Just a little lacking there. Not much. He would not, for instance, ever quite make an international team, the one ambition of his life.

Now and then in the past Kyle, whose horses were the best that he could get in California, had borrowed a horse or two from Glenn Laufer, whose horses were the best he could get in the world. Recently, however, Kyle had stopped this practice, it had no longer seemed good form to him and he was a stickler about form. One had to be. He had learned that during the course of his travel and education even though not, perhaps, as one might say, in the course of his up-bringing.

The helmet, well! He'd have to think about the helmet. Probably should wear it to please Marjory, so nice of her to be concerned. Safety was a bugger, of course. That might have passed through her mind, but it was not the point. The point was that she must show her feelings at all times, even if she had left him only a few hours previously; Marjory, who was giving a lunch party, wouldn't be seeing him before the game, but since Vicky would, then Vicky had been delegated to convey from her this touching gift or loan, which-ever it might be, and above all this anxious concern for his safety.

Her knight! With her magic gift to protect him, going into action. What was it that ladies gave real knights to wear, the warriors who flopped around in iron suits on Percheron-type chargers? Scarves or something. So why not a helmet from Thresher & Glenny's?

Well, he might wear it. And then again he might not.

There was a pencil on the table, and Kyle picked it up. He began to make notations on the back of Marjory's card:

500 barrels a day @ $2 per bb. = $1,000
1,000 bb. a day   " " " " =

How many barrels of oil had Troy said was a reasonable projection? Maybe he hadn't said. Maybe he, Kyle, had made it all up. But . . . hell, no, one thing Troy *had* said was that the importance of this well was discovery: if it was any good at all it could be, almost had to be, an arrow pointing straight at further deposits, large ones, perhaps a field . . .

He felt an irresistible need to talk to Troy at once. Surely the goddamn line wouldn't be busy now. He looked around. A telephone—the magneto type—was in a niche of the house wall behind him. He went to it, cranked the bell handle impatiently and gave the operator the Piru number. Again the buggering buzz-buzz-buzz.

"Operator, that line has been busy now for more than an hour. Can you see if there's a conversation on it or—"

"I'll check it for you, sir."

He leaned against the wall, watching Vicky's smooth foamy wake as she churned up the pool.

"The line is out of order, sir. Do you wish me to report it?"

"Please do. It's very important. Tell them to fix it immediately. Can you do that?"

"They won't fix it immediately, sir. I'm not supposed to say that. But as long as it's important—"

"It is important. Urgent. Could I talk to someone else about it?"

"You can talk to my supervisor, sir. Do you wish to talk to my supervisor?"

"I just wish to know why they can't fix the telephone, if it's out of goddamn order."

"It's Sunday, sir. Repair. That department doesn't work on Sunday. I know that for a fact. Not in a country district, and the district you were calling is country. Nor in city districts either, unless it's an emergency."

"It is an emergency."

"I'll connect you with my supervisor, sir."

3

The pool grew quiet, then ripped open at a corner. Vicky was coming out.

Vicky did things her way. Not many women swam without a cap, fewer still without a suit. Kyle had observed his hostess's informality on his arrival, but he had not been quite sure it went all the way. His doubts were beautifully resolved as Vicky jackknifed her smoothly muscled body in one strong, shiny heave over the side of the pool, finishing on her feet. She reached for a cotton robe and picked up a towel.

The chaise creaked as she sat down beside Kyle.

"Did you like it?"

"Loved it. Would you do it again?"

"The helmet, smarty."

"It's a nice idea."

"Marge's. She has lots of nice ideas."

"Yes, she does. I'm undecided, though."

"Whether to wear it?"

"Yes."

"I think you should."

"Sweet of you to be interested."

"Oh, come off it, Kyle. I adore Marge. I just hope you love her as much as I do. But I want to talk to you about her. About the two of you. So come on back—" She gestured toward the rear of the pool area. "Just give me five minutes to make myself decent."

Her robe pulled open more than decency—thus modestly invoked—might have required as she put up her hands to squeeze her hair. She pulled the hair into a knot behind her head and tied it with a piece of ribbon; the tightness of the golden hair, now dark with water, drew up the skin of her face, making her look sly, tough, and virginal.

"All right?"

"Wonderful."

She touched him lightly with water-cool fingers, carefully unflirtatious, and moved off toward the house.

Kyle settled back to enjoy the sun. In a few minutes he would move, the only question being, in which direction? Vicky had made her intentions clear, in a nice way: a modest, maidenly declaration. You could take it that she wanted to get laid and you would not be wrong.

The helmet, now. She and Marjory had, no doubt, cooked that one up together—though on analysis it looked more like Vicky's work than Marjory's. Marjory's mind didn't work that way. She wasn't a sporting figure, she didn't calculate sporting odds or tricky, hidden gambits. Marjory was a private person. She had feelings, and they could be hurt. She was gayer than Vicky, richer than Vicky, smarter than Vicky—but she was exposed. She had become exposed by loving him, and this was dangerous for her. It threatened the arrangements she had worked out with Glenn Laufer and he with her, whatever these might be. So far the arrangements, apparently, had worked out very well. Glenn could be as rich as suited him, with her money, and she could be as private as she wanted, without Glenn. There was no strain on either party except during those months when Glenn took leave of absence from his duties as a paid executive of her family's steel business in some Middle Western city to play polo in California. At such times the arrangement was in trouble. There were times indeed when it seemed undone. Both Laufers, however, in their respective styles, had become, with practice, very good at pulling it through.

Kyle decided he would have the drink that Vicky had suggested earlier. He went to the bar and mixed himself a small one. A small one would clear his head for the moment and, later, tend to make him drowsy. On game days a light workout was recommended, following which he liked to take a nap. He might do that today. It would be agreeable, perhaps even beneficial, but one had to weigh its value against other possibilities. There was also the knowledge that back there, under the eaves, in an angle of the long, rambling house of the dead mining magnate was a bedroom, no doubt opening directly on the pool. It would be cool back there, sheltered against the sun by summer curtains through or around which air could pass. Kyle had an impression of a shower going in the bathroom, visions of hard-hitting jets of water sluicing down between Vickey's long, long legs and through the now probably soapy and certainly surprisingly black swab of pubic hair which Vicky, despite all due and proper modesty, had so much trouble hiding in the robe.

Odd, that Vicky and Marjory were such good friends; they were nothing alike except in one sense—they were both talkative. Both also liked to sit up late, and he could imagine them, after Marjory had left his bed, gabbing away last night, perhaps beside this very pool; Marjory's house (owned, not rented, though she occupied it only a few weeks a year) shouldered the next piny knob of hillside. Marjory might have seen a light on and gone in for a chat. Or Vicky might have gone over the ridge between. It could have been either way. And Vicky, who rose early to ride, had been pleased to bring the helmet and the message. Being a gossip, she was jealous—she probably gossiped *because* she was jealous—and the helmet, an excuse to ask him up, gave her a chance to provoke an answer: was he "serious" about Marjory?

Kyle sipped his drink, considering the deviousness of women. He didn't have to provide answers for them. It was enough that he had some answers for himself. If by "serious" one meant "marital intention," then no, he was not serious about Marjory; he was getting tired, in fact, of having that particular question put to him, in one way or another. As long as Marjory remained in the protective custody of the arrangement he could be—and was—happy with her. Not otherwise. She was part of a life that would serve him only until his real life began, the life which would come with the fulfillment of the Plan.

Kyle was not sure how the Plan had been born. Sometimes he thought it had started with polo, but on analysis had decided this was wrong. He'd turned to polo originally because the game appealed to him and because the horse-manship which gave him proficiency in its refinements was the one instrument he could use to emerge from his loneliness at Yale; by means of it he had at last made himself accepted there in terms which the young men of the Eastern Establish-ment could respect. It hadn't been easy but in his last year he'd been tapped, somewhat to his own surprise, for a senior society; he'd even had the temerity to graduate with honors—an act of daring so unfashionable that only a person very sure of his position would risk it. He'd been, if not a big man on campus, certainly one who had made his presence felt. He would be remembered by the men who, as cliquey, casual freshmen, had rejected him, and then been won over as friends and equals. They would be waiting. They would be standing with faces turned toward him, their hands raised in welcome when he arrived in his own good time at those clubs, those banks, those certain small, warm, leathery offices where, by virtue of some obscure but adamantine franchise, they manipulated power, ordering the economic and political affairs of the nation.

Polo had helped. There was no doubt of it. And then as if by accident, after he'd become so good at it, polo had moved west for its winter quarters and he'd gone on playing it, joyously, for the game itself, the only game in the world in which your physical potential was enhanced by the muscles and intelligence of a thousand-pound animal, and in which a mistake could cost your life. Unluckily, the fevers developed on the field did not end with the game; they passed on into the people whose lives eddied in changing and decorative patterns around its margins, setting up a second arena there, as interesting as the first and perhaps more dangerous, but no longer real. He might just be through with polo. He would never stop liking it, never stop missing it; it had long been a way of life, but it was wearing thin. It was only part of the Plan.

No, the sources of the Plan went back farther than that. Maybe clear back to his mother. Was it absurd to relate her to something which only a man—experienced and ambitious— could have conceived—such a man as himself? Far from it! Because when you said "such a man as himself" you were talking about a synthetic creature, a person put together in bits and pieces of skin and bone, of marrow and love juices, of secret twitches of the soul and stolen tilts of the eyes. And no one—even discounting genetics—had contributed as much to the shaping of Kyle Kinsale as this woman, Emilia de Baca Kinsale, who had died when he was seven years old.

Troy had hardly known her.

Hub had never understood her.

Yet Hub, for all his crudity, had idolized her; he had followed her suggestions, had stood meekly before her, shivering with love, when she gave him, in her sweet and gentle way, her imperious orders. Aristocratic, opinionated and wise, she had helped him carry out not only her designs but his own as well; when she died he had been totally unable to replace her, even perhaps to think of it: he'd settled, instead, for mistresses in town or chased after orchard girls, running the ranch with such a heavy hand that he'd made enemies right and left.

Troy's case was different.

Kyle knew how his brother felt. He and Troy had talked a

lot about their mother; in bed at the homeranch as little boys, in the room they'd shared so long, they'd frequently started talking about her the moment lights were out. Emilia's fascination, as an after-hours topic, never flagged despite the fact that Kyle had never properly satisfied the interminable question: "But where did Mommy *go?*" Later Troy seemed prodded by a fierce curiosity to know what sort of person she had been—to bring into clearer focus his baby conception of her as a tender, fragrant disembodiment from which blessings, since removed, had flowed. He wanted a brother's share in Kyle's experiences: what she had said, how she had looked, why she had done this or that, the Christmas parties she'd given—what were they like? How had she known just where Millie would go, the time Millie ran away from home? He had to hear about the quail whose broken leg she'd fixed and which had survived in a cage on the front porch, long after her own death. What about the Chinese cook, predecessor of Chun Wuk, who had gone crazy and threatened to kill her with a meat knife, and she had taken the knife away from him and cut off his pigtail with it and then sent him packing! Was that true?

Troy wanted to know everything. And Kyle had told him. He had told him all of it, all except about the day he had gone into her room to find her for some boyish need and she hadn't been there but the door of her closet had been slightly open and he looked in and found her hanging from a silk cord tied to a hook she herself had screwed high up in the wall above the clumps of soft dresses, full of the sweetness of her bath powder and her person, among which the boys had loved to burrow, playing hide-and-seek.

Kyle hadn't talked about this part. He felt too awful when he even thought about it. A queer coldness would creep into his body, chilling him—especially for some reason around the lips. The cold would settle there. His lips felt stiff. They felt like ice. It was impossible to talk with lips in such condition.

They hadn't found the note until the next day: *"I want no one blamed for this."*

Kyle loosed his shirt, letting the full blaze of the sun onto the glittery glazed skin of arms and chest, the Kinsale skin which never burned. The skin was his legacy from Hub but the dark hair and eyes came from his mother. Sometimes, growing up, he had stood in front of mirrors, looking at photographs, comparing himself to her. She had said not to blame and he hadn't blamed—the black-hearted mystery of it was too terrible for such a simple thing as blame—but he had found out early that when he demanded anything from Hub he got it.

He had demanded much. He had traveled and he had learned. He had put the Plan together and somewhere in the Plan was a frame, measured and prepared, which would contain a wife; her impeccable image would fill it precisely, but her qualifications must be without flaw. He could never settle, as Troy had, for an affectionate, friendly woman who would share his interests, bear his children, love, honor and cherish him as wives were supposed to do. Mrs. Kinsale would be all that, do all that, of course, but she would also be, would also do, so much, much more. She would not necessarily be like his mother. That might be asking too much. She would, however, like his mother, possess an innate superiority or aristocracy, the knowledge of better ways to live and to do things. She would not be as vulnerable as his mother had been. She would have enough dross mixed with her elegance to make her strong. She might not be beautiful, she might not even be rich, but she would have been bred to understand what a very rich man needed. And above all, she could never have been divorced.

Kyle set down his glass beside the chaise. He took off the shirt he had previously unbuttoned and laid it on a chair, took off his hand-tooled boots, stood them together, took off his socks and dropped them into the boots. He had made a decision which had nothing to do with the Plan but which stemmed in part from the stimulation Vicky had supplied so inconsequentially, in the take-it-or-leave-it-my-friend manner that became her so well.

Pleasure guaranteed. It was also secure. It was not, however, proof against gossip, the polo-world chatter of which, as he'd told her, Vicky was the main purveyor. For her to gossip at this point would mean sacrificing the best-friend status with Marjory—something Vicky would not want to do but would do, out of habit, and because she could not help herself. The real indiscretion, to be sure, would not be Vicky's. It would be his own. Rather an amazing piece of indiscretion, too, since he preferred to be discreet. What made the difference, he decided, was the telegram, Troy's news about the well, the well that would set him free. If it was true, if the well was coming in, he would not need other people. He would not need Vicky. He would not need Marjory. He might not even need polo, much as he had loved it. He would be off and running in a new direction, perhaps several new directions.

Kyle found a glass and poured it half full of Scotch: enough for two persons—a love potion, as it were. No ice. Ice made cold fingers, which would never do. And what did fucking make? Fucking made weak backshots, his polo coach at Yale used to say. But when one player had persisted, demanding to know if it was really ruled out before games, the coach had temporized.

"Not always. But *never* in the half time!"

Scotch in hand, he stood still, thinking about Vicky in the bedroom. Some women showered, getting out of a pool. Most, probably. Some, again, didn't. Best if they did, washing off the chlorine. But not if they put on more perfume. Much nicer if there was just a ghost of the perfume they'd had on before they went in the water in the first place hidden away secretly in the skin. Skin, when you came down to it, was the main thing.

His timing seemed right. If there had been a shower it was over. Vicky lay on the bed, naked and shapely, reading a book, the book resting on her strong horsewoman's thighs, the ribbon gone from her hair, which, still dark with water, she was rubbing bemusedly with a small towel. She looked up lazily, noting the brown glass in his hand.

"Is some of that for me?"

"It's all for you, if you want it."

"Good lord, no! I don't even *need* it. Look . . ."

She took the glass and handed him the book, open at an erotic drawing of two women ministering to the enormous whang of a bewigged middle-aged man in eighteenth-century costume, one astride its base, the other trying, with marked lack of success, to get its engorged tip into her mouth. No wonder Vicky was horny, prepping herself with this crap. She now had his britches open, working on him, her wet hair falling forward, wrapped around him so that it contributed a delicious roughness to what she was doing. She stopped momentarily to drink out of the glass, giving him time to lift the ratchet of the silver trophy buckle he'd won in a bucking contest when he was sixteen years old and which he had unbuckled numerous times before in similar circumstances. He went into her easily, but less easily than he expected,

rather put off than stimulated by the noises she was making—
enough to bring up the house detective if they'd been in a
hotel; very quickly though, and with no change of position, a
feeling built in him which he experienced only in the rarest of
times, a sense as if his cock had somehow become welded,
way back inside, to his backbone, the two together forming a
shank on which this moaning, jerking stretch of female body,
no longer quite recognizable as Vicky or anyone else, would
flop forever. She orgasmed suddenly, violently, in absolute
silence, immediately after which, with no perceptible alteration in what was going on, everything changed: the harsh,
salty, squirmy fuck had smoothed inexplicably into real
lovemaking, an elaborate structure of caring and giving,
aimed at mutual destruction, after which it subsided into
childish, gentle sleep. At least Kyle slept. Vicky must have
been doing something else. She woke him with just enough
time to get ready for the game.

They drove to the field in the silver Rolls-Royce, she
holding the borrowed helmet in her lap.

She had her answer about him and Marjory. It was an
answer she would keep to herself.

Kyle had already put both women out of his mind. He was
concentrating on the game ahead.

Earlier in the day it had seemed just another game, with
better teams than usual, but the main thing, looking forward,
had been to enjoy it, ride hard, do as well as possible. Now,
with only minutes to go before it started, all this was changed.
Now the California team had to win, it was impossible to say
why but a reason must be found if only to leg himself up. If we
win, he thought, the well will come in. That's it—a good-luck
sign!

It was ridiculous, but he knew that was how it had to be.

4

Lunch parties were breaking up—the merry little gatherings
that preceded Sunday games. Players were well advised to
stay away from them.

The best party would be George Gordon Moore's at his
place up in the Carmel Valley. Great patron of polo, Gordie
Moore. All the money in the world. Said to be an illegitimate
son of Edward VII, late king of England. Gordie always had a

mount or two to spare for friends. He might have a good one to stand by in case Warren G.'s leg went bad.

Well, too late for that now. Have to make do with what he had.

They passed Marjory's house; people on the terrace were getting up to leave. Sounds of piano music. Marjory liked to have musical people visit; she played the piano herself with frantic and impressive virtuosity—jazz, classical, anything. Lately, she'd had a thin-necked, slick-haired fellow, George Gershwin, visiting—wrote scores for New York musicals. Sometimes he and Marge played duets on her two grand pianos, and when they did, the crashing chords did not sound like New York musicals, they sounded a lot better. But Gershwin, apart from that, was a bore. He couldn't ride, he slept till noon every day, and he left lighted cigarettes around. Marjory liked him.

Kyle dropped Vicky at the grandstand. He continued around to the club, bucking a line of cars already leaving, starting for the game. Late! He was late, goddamn it. Why had he been so stupid? He parked the car carelessly, askew at the front door. Drew stares from people coming out as he rushed inside.

Just as he'd thought—the locker room was empty.

Mac, the steward, perceiving the fix he was in, came over to help him dress.

"They cain't start till yawl git there, Cap'n."

Kyle grinned at him and slowed down. Mac handed him the borrowed helmet and he took it without glancing at it, though he'd half made up his mind to leave it and wear one of his own.

Back to the field. Usually he liked to walk down, get himself in hand—but no time for that now. And to make it worse, he was sleepy! Jesus!

Kyle well knew this sleepiness before a game. It had nothing to do with his bout with Vicky, though making love to her might not turn out to be the smartest thing he'd ever done. The sleepiness came from being scared shitless. A thickness of the brain. And his fucking stomach churning worse than ever. If he'd eaten even one bite of something he'd be upchucking it now. But he hadn't eaten. So why did he want to puke? Sheer funk!

"Here you are, sir."

Iced oatmeal water in the milk bottle, a wet towel around

the bottle to keep it cool. God bless Tip Morrisey, best groom he'd ever had. It seemed impossible that he'd been angry enough to kill him this morning.

Kyle forced down a few swallows. He felt the gruelly stuff spreading inside, settling his gut. He sat down in a canvas chair, a wave of lovely black sleep washing over him; he fought it off, forced his eyes open, kept them that way by staring at his mallets, spread out fanwise near the sideboards. He looked at his horses, all properly saddled, bridled and bandaged, the hot-walkers holding them on lead lines, the cooling sheets folded and laid aside, to walk them in after each chukker.

"Give me a rammer."

"No, sir," said Tip.

Tip had a half-pint of brandy on his hip. It was for emergencies—a spill or an overtime chukker—nothing else. Such was their understanding.

Kyle spat. He'd known Tip would refuse. Tip was quite right, of course.

Kyle submitted quietly to the refusal.

In front of the center boxes, Tommy Hitchcock, the team captain, was chatting with the umpires. Hitchcock, a handsome, powerfully built man, was always up on his game, ready to play. Catch him asking for a rammer! Why should he? He was, by most estimates, the greatest polo player in the world, had played twice for America against England for the Westchester Cup. There was no cup for this game though it was, nonetheless, in essence, an international event.

The Argentine flag flew alternately with the Stars and Stripes from the poles along the back of the stands.

White team against Blue!

Actually it was California versus Argentina; that would have seemed a lot more impressive, but the game could not formally be considered that way. Alfredo Harrington had not yet arrived, so the Argentines were short a man. California was lending them Glenn Laufer to play One. The California team would be Hitchcock at Four, Pedley at Three, Boeseke Two, and himself at One. A thirty-six-goal team. At handicap, they'd have to give the Blues three pops. That could be managed, but the Argentines rode like devils and their pampas-bred thoroughbreds could fly. They might fool you. The main thing would be to cover Manuel Andrada, their big Number Four, stick on him tight, keep him from turning the play. If he, Kyle, could do that on defense he'd be doing all that anyone could ask, other than not miss his tries for goal when one of White's long hitters set him up.

The Argentine players were mounting. Jorge Pelayo, scarfaced general, rich from the blood of others, heavy-shouldered, beautifully mounted, getting the leg up on a lovely gray thoroughbred, a long hitter, a dirty rider. Watch him for fouls. Juan Reynal, merry, spoiled by women, but a sportsman through and through; Manuel Andrada, their captain and Number Four—a heavy Indian face, evil till he smiled, then a prince of charm. Conservative on the field, but when he let out he could be as tough as Hitchcock. Probably an underrated player, even at nine goals.

Last but not least, the U.S. loan-out—Glenn Laufer. Glenn's horses were at the remount station next to Kyle's, and Glenn, like Kyle, sat trying to relax. He'd looked over once and nodded and Kyle nodded in return. That had been all. Was there usually more? Kyle tried to remember. He wondered what Vicky, earlier, had been about to tell him about Glenn and Marjory or Glenn and himself. They'd never got around to that but Kyle suspected what it was. Have to find out later—one hoped not in the course of the game.

Glenn was a hunk of good solid American flesh chopped out in sharp but muscular angles, as if he had been put together by an armorer. He was riding his best horse, Sacramento, in the first chukker.

Would the game never begin?

Ah, there it was—Hitchcock mounting at last!

Impassive, with the mahogany faces of idols, wearing embroidered shirts, with daggers in their belts, the Argentine grooms put their masters up on the matchless horses they had shipped in to play and then, when the tour was over, to sell.

The band from Monterey Presidio struck up "Dixie"! Christ, did they think Argentina was a southern *state?* Warren G., far from a music lover, clawed at the sky. Kyle pulled him down roughly, spun him, mounted. Just the first sign of a limp out of you, old pal, and you go back to the barn.

The teams lined up, number for number, man for man. They rode, banging, and bumping, toward the umpire, who lifted the ball up to toss it but then decided there was something wrong; he blew his whistle, made them turn back and come on again. This time it worked. Everyone cantering in lockstep toward the umpire and crack! the ball was in, Pedley had it, was away, with Kyle racing to midfield to get his pass. A beautiful off-side forehand arched over Kyle's head.

"Leave it!"

Pedley hit almost to goal. But Andrada was on it, backing to Pelayo, who crossed Kyle to take the shot on his off side. A foul, you Indian pissant; but the whistle didn't blow and Kyle bumped, Warren G. bearing in with all his weight. Pelayo was the heavier man and his pampas-bred gray the bigger horse but screw you, amigo—Kyle had his knee where it would do the most good and the general was losing his seat, was out of the play.

"Ride the man, Kyle."

Shit. There was no one else he *could* ride.

Boeseke's low curving smash just missed goal. The umpire dropped a new white willow ball for the knock-in and Andrada cantered back. He stood for a second as if turned to stone, mallet raised, stiff as an equestrian statue in a town square; then with three or four loose loping strides he cantered to the line, stood in his stirrups and—crunch! a seventy-yard shot to Reynal—the dangerous option across his own goal instead of to the boards. Off again, everyone wide open—Reynal to the general, the general to Glenn and Glenn, playing beautifully, pulling Sacramento to the left, taking the ball as it passed diagonally in front of him, scoring the first goal with a lovely nearside neck shot, the most difficult shot in polo.

Cheers, Blasts from the band. Warren G. rearing in the melee—the ball under his belly and Glenn off with it before Kyle could bring him down.

What's that? The goal judge with his flag wigwagging again! Another Argentine score. Then another. Glenn again, on one of Andrada's long ones. That gaucho could hit. Why hadn't somebody warned them? Three to nothing!

Ha! Andrada angry, changing things around. *Mi général* liked to score the goals himself, his executioner's face was full of storm clouds. Glenn, a gringo, had been getting too many shots. They changed positions, Andrada now at One, Glenn at Four.

"Ride the *man!*"

Kyle could feel hate exuding from Glenn's body. It came out of his pores, out of his marrow, it churned in the juices of his balls. When they bumped, Glenn wasn't trying to ride him off, he was trying to kill him. Once, with Kyle on the ball, Glenn came in at such a bad angle that Kyle's mare, Juanita, went down, wedging Kyle under her, Kyle taking out two sections of the sideboards, one with his head and one with his horse. He blacked out, woke with the ambulance on the field, a doctor called out of the stands.

"Are you all right, Mr. Kinsale?"

"How the fuck would I know?"

Everyone laughed as if this were very funny. Tip, lovely Tip Morrisey, there with a rammer. And after as long a time out as the umpires would allow, Kyle up again, this time on Chollar, Tip leading Juanita to the sidelines, going on three legs.

Much applause for Kyle's gameness. Brassy salutes from the band. The umpires on the field consulting the judge in the stands. Yes, indeed! Penalty Number 1, a free goal for California. One more to go for a tie.

He knows, Kyle thought. Either it's the gossip or Marjory has said something. But he knows for sure.

"Back it."

Hitchcock to Pedley, Pedley to Boeseke, Boeseke to Hitchcock. Such hitting, such riding as was seldom seen, even with these men at their best. And he, Kyle, in position, hooking Glenn's mallet as he raised it to back the try for goal, Glenn crashing through a goalpost, his head twisted round so he could and must have seen the tail shot with which Kyle made the score.

Funny, though, Kyle thought, as the two teams loped toward center field, the helmet staying on when I went through the boards. The broad strap did it. Marvelous of Marjory to give it to me. Might have saved my life, or a concussion anyway. Have to thank her. Glenn's helmet, though. Maybe ought to thank him too. He's fouling, the son of a bitch, but he's playing way above himself, best day he's ever had. Too bad it won't count, he's going to lose—both ways.

The goal judge was helping a maintenance man put the post back up.

Kyle's mind soared in the madness of well-being, the glory that combined the game, himself, his horse and fate itself. But now, in the last chukker, the lift was gone, a sudden, awful weariness engulfed him, drained him dry: not funk now, just plain exhaustion. He could hardly sit upright, couldn't hold a mallet straight, had to lean it back against his shoulder like a frigging shotgun. All this came over him in the wink of an eye, after he'd scored the goal. He would have to go to Hitchcock, tell him he was through. The whistle saved him.

Chukker! Tip stuck a piece of ice into Kyle's pants. Another rammer now, another drink of oatmeal water. But—what horse to play? They'd all gone one chukker each, full tilt.

Tip had the cooling sheet off Warren G.

"Can he make it?"

"He's all you got, sir."

"All right then."

Foot in stirrup, he hopped around one-legged, lacking the strength to mount. Tip had to put a hand under his ass. They were all waiting. In came the ball. He laid back, not out of caginess but because he wanted to save motion. Mallets and hooves milled around, the ball suddenly squirting out of the melee, right to his feet. Off he went, out alone, free of everyone, nobody now to yell fucking "Leave it," goal to go and this was sudden death, the first team to score would win the game. His downfield shot was the hardest he'd hit all day, the ball starting low, curving, climbing, rolling straight on for a dribble, a fleck of the wrist that would put it through, and then . . . and then he was tilting, pulled out of the saddle. What the hell? Hooked? No. But he was losing his seat, going over, he was on the ground, Warren G. had spilled. The goddamn front leg from the trailer kick. It had stiffened—gone out at last. Tip was running out with Rinky Dink, the chestnut gelding Kyle had played in the third chukker. Kyle waved him away. Rinky Dink would never do. No heart for a clutch moment—and far from enough foot. He needed a flyer, a wind ripper. Like Glenn's Sacramento. So? So there was the lovely thoroughbred Sacramento himself, short-coupled sorrel with hindquarters like a rabbit and the speed of the *Superchief,* there he was, a few yards away, through for the day—relaxing. Without a word, in a flash of decision, Kyle took Sacramento's bridle from the hot-walker holding him; the man gave him a puzzled, startled look but obediently stripped off Sacramento's cooling sheet. Kyle tightened the cinch himself, rammed two fingers under it to test it, mounted and was into the lineup, his arm up to show the umpire he was back in play. Thirty seconds later Pedley passed to Boeseke from the sideboard, Boeseke bashed it through and the game was over.

Handshakes across horses' necks, each man to his opposite number, only Glenn abstaining.

Clean up a little. Pull on coats, line up on foot!

With towels round their necks they stood in front of Sam Morse's box and had their pictures taken. Then a tall green-eyed girl in a camel's hair coat handed out individual trophies. The coat was the wraparound kind which let you be fully aware of the tiny waist and the full breasts and curvy hips it covered. Her blond hair wasn't cut in the current flapper mode but was tied behind her neck with a ribbon, flaring out behind, and when Kyle put his hand on the cup she was giving him, she laid her own hand over his and said, "Oh, my goodness!" Then she laughed and kissed him on the chin. The kiss would have landed on his mouth except that he saw it coming and turned his head slightly. Lady, he thought, you could be a combination of Miss Isadora Duncan and Miss Greta Gouzis, and you could be standing here naked as a jaybird and I wouldn't notice, the way I feel now.

After the cup presentation they all had their picture taken again. Kyle could see Vicky and Marjory, those dear friends, standing up in the box where they'd been sitting together, clapping.

Kyle rode to the club in a jaunting-cart with Elmer Boeseke. Elmer was as tough as Tommy. Nothing fazed him. Elmer handled the reins of the hackney pulling the cart, with Kyle sitting sideways on the bench seat next to him.

"You played damn well, you know, Kinsale," Elmer said.

And in the locker room Hitchcock himself, with a bath towel round his middle, put his arm over Kyle's shoulders.

"You'd better come back east with me, we need you there. Will you do that, will you do it for sure?"

Kyle told him he'd try. He couldn't lift the arm he'd fallen on. His whole side there was one big charley horse. Aside from some hot towels there was nothing much that he could do for it. The pain would come later, when the bruises stiffened. Kyle didn't care. He sat on the edge of a rubbing table with a telephone in his hand, trying once more to put a call through to the rig, but the line still hadn't been repaired.

"I made a bet with myself," he said to Mac, the steward. "If we won this game I'd hit an oil well, my brother and I. Do you think that was foolish?"

"You got a good sign goin' for you, Mistah Kyle," said Mac.

Kyle leaned back against the locker, laughing.

The steamy room exuded goodwill. Pelayo had brought in a

magnum of vile Argentine champagne and after the glasses
were full Andrada took the bottle into the shower and poured
a baptism over Pedley's brow, getting dunked in return.
Reynal was face down on the rubbing table, sucking champagne through a straw while the rubber worked on his back.

Kyle had almost finished dressing when Glenn Laufer came
into the room, naked. He'd drunk his share of the general's
wine but otherwise participated minimally in the celebration.
He liked to tub instead of shower, and sometimes—as he had
today—called in a private masseur to attend to him. His body
glistened with the masseur's cold cream or whatever he used,
the surface shine accentuating the muscles, which, one felt,
were set into his bones by springs and bolts and activated by
machinery. His wedge-shaped torso tapered to a tiny waist
below which swelled thighs powerful enough to crush a
horse's ribs, should Glenn apply them for that purpose. From
the end of the aisle where both had their lockers he addressed
Kyle.

"Ready to go, I see."

"I'm in no hurry."

"Good. Then perhaps if you have time you'd stop by to
look at that horse of mine. Just make sure he's all right."

"What horse is that, Glenn?" said Kyle quietly.

"The one you borrowed, I suppose you'd call it. I'd call it
appropriating. Taking without permission."

The edge in Glenn Laufer's voice was not loud but it was
not conversational either; it cut a corridor of quiet through
the cheerful hubbub of the room.

"I'm sorry about that. I hoped you wouldn't mind."

"I minded. I don't like having personal possessions of mine
used by other people. Even by people I like. And I don't like
you."

"Oh, come on, Glenn," said a new voice. "We're all
friends here."

George Gordon Moore, patron of polo, possible bastard of
royalty, had risen from a locker bench. Glass in hand, he
challenged the icy silence through which could be heard the
splashing of a distant shower and the voice of someone
singing off-key.

George Gordon Moore detested quarrels. They were bad
for the sport he loved. He picked up General Pelayo's
champagne bottle and advanced with it toward Glenn.

"Let's have a splash of bubbly, old boy," he said in his

deep, pleasant voice. "And then let's forget this nonsense, shall we? I see you have a glass—"

"Yes," said Glenn. "I have. Thank you very much. I'm very glad to drink with you, Gordie. I'll drink with you anytime. But I want it understood that I'm not drinking with *him*. You do understand that, don't you?" he said to Kyle.

"I do indeed," said Kyle.

He knows all right, he thought. He knows, and for some Christ-forsaken reason he wants to make it public. All right. Let him. Let him take a swing at me if he wants to. But I'm not going to proclaim, for his justification, that I've been screwing his wife.

"I'm sorry about the horse," he said. "Had no right to him, you're perfectly correct. And I do apologize."

Mac helped him on with his jacket and Kyle turned, putting the last articles away in the locker. Tape. Liniment. His helmet. Moore, leaving Glenn, flashed Kyle a look of gratitude.

"One for the road?"

"Thanks but no thanks, Gordie. Good night. Good night all. Great game. And thanks again."

"Just a minute." Glenn worked his lips as if to get enough moisture behind them to speak. "Does your apology include that too?" He was pointing at something—the helmet Kyle still held in his hand. "Which, as I seem to recognize, is also mine. And which you've also grabbed without by-your-leave. Where did you get it?"

"I don't know."

Glenn put down his champagne glass. The oiled, machine-like naked body started down the locker aisle toward Kyle, a caricature strong man, but with noncaricature killing in him.

"Really now. You don't know! . . . Goddamn hard to believe that, isn't it?" he said to the room at large. "Has it, but he doesn't know where he got it. Well, by Christ, I'd like to check on that. I'd just like to know if there's anything *else* of mine he might care to make use of. Or might not remember. I'd like to know. Is that clear? *I'd just like to be informed.* TO BE INFORMED!"

"All right, I'm informing you," said Kyle. "I *don't remember*. And here's your goddamn helmet!"

With a hard underhand throw he sent the helmet flying straight at Glenn. Then, without looking to see where it landed, he turned on his heel and walked out of the room.

"You didn't have to black his eyes, you know."

"I didn't black his eyes."

"Well, you threw the helmet at him."

"I tossed it to him. He just didn't catch it."

"Oh, no. He caught it. He caught it all right—right on the bridge of his nose. The skin is all off. And there's a bruise."

"You must have inspected him pretty carefully."

"I did. He made me."

"I thought you were through letting him make you do things."

"I have to let him make me do a few things," she said. And she added, "If I'm going to go on living with him."

This left a pause, which lasted longer than it should have. She measured it by swirling ice in her glass. The barman, who had carefully stationed himself out of earshot, looked over to see if she was signaling for a refill. She shook her head.

Kyle took a sip of cognac. It was the first drink he'd had since the Argentine champagne, and he was feeling it. He'd been asleep in his hotel cottage when her call came through, saying she'd like to meet him in the bar. There would be no one there, she said, when he suggested the cottage instead.

She'd been right. There was no one, unless you counted the piano player with the slicked-down hair and the long, skinny neck who had arrived with her but immediately moved over to the piano and proceeded to fill the air with odd-sounding chords.

"And besides," she said, "I'm afraid we may be all through with my coming to your place, nice as it's been and all . . ."

She not only had the message, Kyle thought, but she was feeding it back to him!

"He must have blown his nose."

"Would that do it to his *eyes?*"

"Oh, every time. After a punch or anything. Pushes the blood up into the tubes or something. So it settles there and—"

"Turns black."

"Definitely."

She sighed. This time, when the bartender looked over, she nodded.

"Well, at least I'm glad it wasn't a *punch*. If you're sure it wasn't."

"I was goddamn careful for it not to be."

The barman poured her gin and dropped the twist in it. When he was gone she said in a different tone, "I'm grateful for that, Kyle."

"You don't have to be. I don't like that type of action any better than you do. It stinks."

"Maybe we do too," she said.

He put his hand over hers where it lay on the bar.

"Marge, I got all the flagellation I'm ever going to need out there this afternoon."

"But not self-administered. Is that what you're saying?"

"Right. Nor by an individual as wonderful as you."

"Don't worry. I wasn't going to get into it."

"Oh, yes, you were."

"Maybe just a little. Because maybe I'm a little down. I hate to lose choices, and now we've lost one. I mean," she said, "the choice of staying the way we were. Naturally, we couldn't have had that forever, but it was nice to pretend we could."

Suddenly the flesh around her eyes seemed to puff up. She purse-rummaged for a handkerchief. Kyle handed her his.

"What the hell difference does it make?" she said. "I made my deal. Little Marge Rintoul, the music phenom of Winnetka, Illinois, moves into the sporting world. Time for a change, I felt—and there it was. The organ music and the trust fund and the arch of swords. Did I tell you that we had an arch of swords? We did, when we came out of the church. Glenn was a captain in the National Guard, by crickety. Arch of swords, ring of steel. Both for the price of one. How's that for a bargain?"

"Marjory," Kyle said carefully, "I'm just not up to it tonight. Do you mind?"

"Hell, no, I don't mind. You played beautifully. I forgot to tell you, but you did. So did Glenn, don't you think? I never saw him so . . . spiffy. On the field and in the locker room, a champ. Lovely to look at, isn't he? Nude when he went for you, I hear from Gordie. Was that true?"

"Well, he didn't exactly go for me. He—"

"Never mind. He likes to be nude in such situations. Did you ever wonder where he got his muscles? I'll tell you—he got them beating up women. Fact. Beat up his first wife. She was a Dodge, Dodge Motors, and she *got it*. That's why she divorced him. I don't even have *part* of an automobile company, and I should get less? He's promised, laid it on the line, he'll do it to me if I so much as speak to you or glance at you again as long as I live, so help me God."

"I wouldn't let him."

Marjory Laufer finished what was in her glass. She returned Kyle's handkerchief and made motions to the skinny-necked piano player, indicating it was time to go.

"Kyle, darling," she said, "I don't give a shit if he divorces me. I really don't. He claims he's had a . . . surveillance on us or something. He has all the grounds he needs. To hell with it. All that hurts is that our choices are so limited now, like one or . . . nothing. I hoped that would never happen, but it has. Him and his black eyes. Blacked? Whatever. I just thought you ought to know."

The piano player had now come over and was standing quietly at her side. Seen close up he was, in spite of his skinniness, quite a handsome fellow.

"Call me," Kyle said.

"I don't think so, darling," she said, "I'll have to see. Maybe I ought to stick to my own kind"—she smiled at the piano player—"my own kind of music. You know George, don't you, Kyle? I'm sure you two have met. Kyle Kinsale, George Gershwin, America's favorite songwriter. George was sweet enough to drive me over, and now he's going to take me home."

Kyle put out his hand.

"Yes, indeed," he said. "We all know George."

Standing at the bar, he lit a cigar, watching them leave.

When he got back to his room the telephone was ringing. It was Troy, calling from a pay phone in Piru.

CHAPTER FIVE

The Plan

1

Nothing disgusted Troy more than seeing a new well blow out. The waste was terrible when that happened. Nine times out of ten the surging spume caught fire. An automobile would backfire or some idiot would light a smoke. Even the spark caused by a drive chain falling on the block would do it. In a few seconds the derrick and everything around would be incinerated. Men you had been working with moments earlier would turn into torches. Enormous flames, architected by black smoke into towers, spires and gargoyles, piled into the sky like beautiful, evil cathedrals. You wanted to run, to get far away, as fast as you could, but you had to stay, you had to save the goddamn oil somehow.

He'd been through it. Once a well standing cemented at two thousand feet had broken loose, and he'd lost that one entirely. For another blowout he'd got in a team of fire fighters from Taft. Wearing asbestos suits they'd walked right up to the wild well and put a rack there. They laid out two hundred pounds of dynamite on the rack and ran wires back to a detonator. By exploding the charge they'd created a vacuum and snuffed out the fire. They'd saved that well. But you couldn't always do it.

His determination to keep Cliff Kinsale #1 under control

had slowed the final weeks of drilling. From two hundred feet a day he'd cut progress down to a hundred, then to fifty. Showings continued in the mud pushed up by the hollow drill stem but the critical zone, if it was there, lay deeper. How far down? Could he reach it with the tools he had, or would the earth itself frustrate him now, the way Hub's meanness had before? Such questions plagued him night and day; he slept jerkily, sometimes getting up in the night to drive out to the derrick.

The crew felt his tension. They too were edgy and nervous, pulled tight by the isolation of the job and the pressure of the long tours. A derrickman, grabbing the lines to twist the blocks around, had his hand mutilated, caught between the blocks and the sheaves. Another brought booze on the job. Troy fired him along with his buddy who had shared the bottle. Quarrels broke out. Charlie Ott, who had been sober and sensible up to that time, picked up a derrick hatchet and chased Bill Gardine, a hillbilly roustabout, around the bunkhouse, trying to part his hair. Such things could happen, but they made Troy wild to have them clump up at the end of the job, just when everything had been going so luckily.

Suddenly afraid his telegram to Kyle had been premature, he ran more tests. These restored his assurance. He was using a new device, a heavy rubber packer, conical in form, run on the end of the drill pipe. With this the drilling mud above the packer could be separated from the oil and gas entering the perforated pipe below. At the start of the test the weight of the mud contracted the pressure of the formation but this would alter as the packer was pulled back up the hole. There was gas down there, a lot of it; the mud wagon (as they called the on-site laboratory) showed a high level of hydrocarbons. There was no doubt now in Troy's mind that he had a working well, possibly a monster down there in the sandy shale, deeper than he had ever gone before.

He talked to Luanna about it and she agreed, why not celebrate? Ordinarily no secret in the oil business was guarded like the results of a drill-stem test, but Troy threw caution away. He telephoned the *Bakersfield Californian* and invited a reporter down; he invited the mayors of Bakersfield and Coalinga and the executives of the equipment companies that had been supplying the job; he wanted them all to see, for once, what an oil well really looked like coming in under control. He had the rig carpenter build some picnic tables out of redwood planks and put them in a sheltered dip in the dunes and he got hold of the best booze to be obtained from Carlo "The Rat" Giovanelli, who supplied all the blind pigs for fifty miles around. Luanna baked some hams and chickens and made a huge bowl of potato salad; she bought tin cups to serve the booze in and tin plates for the pie-wagon pies—she had no time for pastry making, for God's sake.

Everything was ready for the well to start producing—a day and an hour now predetermined.

Kyle drove in early in the Silver Ghost, local dignitaries arriving soon after. It was a pleasant, soft misty day, warm for March; wildflowers patched the dunes with sudden spurts of color, and spicy odors rose from the sage and mesquite. The rig crew had washed up and put on their best clothes. Faces which had not been shaved for weeks emerged in shiny, unexpected contours. Everyone had a go at the booze and then tucked into the good viands; while the guests were eating and drinking, Troy put some men back on the derrick and began pulling stem and for a while Cliff Kinsale #1 seemed to share the spirit of the occasion. Gas forced the packer up the hole. There were rattles and groans in the casing and then a whistle and a belch came out and then a lot more gas with a rumble like a volcano. The noise and the gas production lasted more than an hour but gradually tapered off and quiet ensued. The people waited. Troy poured more of the Giovanelli redeye and some conversation was attempted, largely consisting of guesses as to what was causing the delay. The mayor of Bakersfield, tin cup in hand, had a stab at delivering the felicitous remarks he had come prepared with but his nice-mannered, chubby wife, seeing that he was drunk, made him sit down. All waited some more. The crew was embarrassed, mostly for Troy though for themselves also. They would never share the riches of the well, should there be any, but so far it had been a mutual project: why had Troy jinxed it with his stinking picnic? He was an oilman, he should have known better. Some slipped off into the scrub to sleep; others got cards out and started a lowball game on one of the picnic tables. The tints of the bright and lovely sky deserted the high arch of it and bunched behind the hills to the west; lizards left the rocks where they had been sunning themselves and jackrabbits came out to romp and feed. The reporter for the *Californian* was the first to go, the civic officials following; the equipment people, hopeful to the end, shook hands all around and departed with a show of cheerfulness which on their part was perfectly genuine: they got paid whether a well came in or not.

At the last minute, no one could find Cliff. His mother finally located him, alone in the derrick shack; as he led him out they could be seen arguing. Cliff hung back, refusing to move toward the car.

Luanna approached her husband.

"Honey, he won't give up. He says it's his well, named for him, and he knows it will come in."

"I wish he was right."

"You're sure there's no chance now?"

"Not a chance in the world. Cliff had just better learn to obey when we give him an order."

"You'd better talk to him then. He won't pay any attention to me."

Troy's mouth set. He crossed to where his son was standing, skinny and frightened but defiant.

"It will come in, Dad. I know it."

"Some other well, some other time. Not this one. Now you get in the car as your mother told you to."

"Can't we wait just a little longer?"

"No, son. I'm sorry. Come on now."

But Cliff pulled back when Troy reached for him.

"I'm staying here, Dad."

"I told you to come on."

"Well, I won't. I don't care. It's my well. I'm staying here until it comes in."

Troy slapped him. Then he picked him up and shoved him in the car. It was one of the few times he had ever hit his son. Cliff didn't cry. When they reached the house in Piru he got out silently and went to his room. Later he approached his father, who was mixing drinks in the kitchen.

"I'm sorry for your trouble, Dad," he said.

Troy, drinks in hand, stared at him, then walked off without a word. Cliff turned pale. He feels bad, he thought, he feels awful bad.

That night Troy and Kyle sat up with a bottle of Kinsale bourbon, long after Luanna had gone to bed; they talked on and on and the talk, sometimes aimless and half drunken, softened gradually into the special tone of talks in times past, the dialogue in the big upstairs bedroom at the ranch. Even then they had sometimes talked about oil—those places on the ranch where it oozed out into plain sight. And of the possibility of drilling a well. To this idea they'd had different approaches. Troy had been concerned with oil as a fascinating phenomenon in itself whereas Kyle had thought of it as a means to an end. Kyle had always been *dead sure* that he would someday possess, if not oil, then some other resource or substance that would make him a rich son of a bitch.

It was amazing. Troy had no such convictions. Not then and not now. The debacle of the day had left him feeling drained and foolish, Cliff Kinsale #1 having thinned out to a fiction as devoid of substance as the Rover Boys Series, those twenty-five-cent novels which they'd read so avidly, winter evenings at the ranch. Time stood still for a long stretch there, and then, unexpectedly, the window blinds changed color; it was getting on toward sunup. Troy could see that Kyle was drunk. Kyle's face had stretched so long it seemed to have a second pair of eyes in it. Troy made a determined effort to help him over to the couch, where he was supposed to sleep. Kyle opposed this. He put on a pot of coffee. His proposition was that they share it, after which he would drive back up north and take Troy with him. Voices rose, bringing Luanna inquiringly out of the bedroom, very pretty in a flimsy cotton nightgown. She took over the coffee detail. She had the pot in her hand and the three cups set out when the floor jolted and the scalding coffee spilled all over the table. The kitchen walls sucked in, then expanded; she had just time to put the pot down before there was another spasm of the air, then another jolt. Troy let out a yell. He yanked the door open and ran out onto the scruffy patch of lawn, all tamped down where Cliff, though forbidden to, had been riding his bicycle. There, way over to the east, where on clear days you could see the top of the derrick, there was no derrick any longer but a black monument that rose, phalluslike, into the sky. The black column quickly bushed out at the top, shredding apart, ugly and shapeless now, as big a blowout as you'd ever want to see.

The disturbance had wakened the children. Luanna got blankets around them and put them in the car. Wearing a coat over her nightgown, she got in too and the men put pants and jackets on and all drove out onto the desert, all of them, together with the car and the landscape, drenched with oil within half a mile of where the rig had been.

Once more Cliff Kinsale #1 had shown its unruly temperament. It had shucked off the blowout prevention equipment with a toss of its mighty power, tossing the hundred-ton concrete slab and the casing head straight up through the derrick, making splinters of the twelve-by-twelve timbers. The cookhouse and bunkhouse were intact and no one had been hurt, but for three days the well deposited an estimated ten thousand barrels of oil a day onto the dunes of Piru, then caught fire, predictably, and burned up the same daily ration for a week more before fire fighters brought it under control. Production, in the first pipeline run, toned down to 7,953 barrels. Cliff Kinsale #1 was not as big as had been first rumored, but it was a good one.

That first morning, all of them groggy with lack of sleep and drunk with elation, the Troy Kinsales and Kyle had gone back to the Piru house. Troy slumped in a living-room chair and was snoring in thirty seconds. Luanna put the children to bed. She was too tired to clean them up. The oil had gone through their clothes; their bodies were smeared and slippery with it as was hers. Past caring, she threw an old sheet on her own bed and lay down on it. The sun was high in the sky, the little frame house, shut while they were gone, hotter than a depot stove; she lay on her back, hoping Troy would come in or that she would sleep but she could still hear him snoring in his chair and sleep would not come. Kyle was fussing around in the kitchen, breaking loose an ice tray, fixing himself a drink—as if he needed it! She knew she ought to shut the door but she was just too tired to move; she looked for a towel to pull over herself but there was nothing she could reach and he was standing in the doorway, fully dressed, covered with oil from head to foot. He grinned at her—the disgusting, prying son of a bitch; she'd never been able to stand him, if the truth were known, him and his big spending and his high-flown ways.

"Jesus Christ," she said, "if your polo-playing friends could see you now!"

Stockholders in the Kinsale Land and Cattle Company soon received the following letter:

Dear Uncle [Aunt, Cousin (first name)] de Baca [or Kinsale or (married name); or in the rare instances when the recipients, though working for the company, were not family members, then simply Mr., Miss or Mrs. (last name)]:

As you may have heard, a drilling crew in the charge of our Vice President, Troy Kinsale, funded by the

Kinsale Land and Cattle Company, has made a petroleum discovery on the company's Piru ranch in the area denoted on the map in Section 15, T8N-R7W. Explorations in this area are continuing. A full report on the entire petroleum situation together with statistics of the discovery well will be submitted to the shareholders at a special meeting to be held at the homeranch May 15, 1926, at ten o'clock in the morning, after which lunch will be served.

I am looking forward to seeing you all then.

Sincerely,

Kyle Kinsale, Pres.

2

"Have you noticed something odd about us all today?"

Millie Braden put this question to her husband as the meal was ending. Each, as co-hosts with Kyle, Troy and Luanna, had presided at separate tables, but Millie had come over to join Doc as the Mexican girls cleared away.

"Of course. We're scared to death."

Millie was used to Doc's jokes but this one took her by surprise. She looked at him vaguely, then put back her head and laughed. She said, "I just meant—well, we all knew what we were going to be told. More or less, that is. I would have expected everyone to be gay. And we're so serious."

"I'm serious too," said Dr. Braden. "There's nothing more terrifying for the average person than to find he's just come into a large sum of money. At first it sounds grand, but he soon realizes he hasn't the least notion what to do about it. New demands will be made on him which he doesn't know how to meet; he may have to make changes in his personality and dress in order to conform to new standards. Also improve his table manners and so forth—in all likelihood give up a way of life which may have been perfectly satisfactory to him. What will the new one hold? The unknown always gives you goose pimples. Isn't that what we're talking about?"

Millie pondered this. It was hard to keep up with Doc when he was in a mocking mood. Shadows of leaves stirred across her glistening skin and made ripples in the piles and puffs of her rich red hair.

"You *are* joking, and I don't think it's very nice of you. We were rich before. We've always been rich."

"You should have told me."

"I don't mean *you and me*. I mean the whole family. After all, we're not tenement people who just came up winners in the Irish Sweepstakes."

She made this statement with considerable hauteur. Now it was Dr. Braden's turn to laugh.

"Excuse me, dear. I wasn't casting aspersion on your background. I've long recognized the Kinsales as superior."

"And a good thing for you we are, you slob."

"Exactly. Otherwise I wouldn't have my clinic. And your relatives wouldn't be getting free professional services, as per the terms of my contract."

Millie put her fingers up to her eyes, stretching her eyes wider so as to parody amazement.

"Am I hearing right? We're now supposed to be *grateful* for those services—which, incidentally, I've seldom heard of you supplying?"

"If you weren't," said Doc complacently, "could that be called biting the hand that bleeds you?"

"Such a slob," said Millie. "It's going to be horrible, now that you're a rich slob."

She rose to take away a platter of steaks on which flies were settling. Regardless of new wealth, the steaks would make another meal, cold or in hash.

It had been nice to have such a lovely day for the meeting. There were such days at this time of year, plenty of them. Millie had been ready, in case they'd had to eat inside, but it had been so much easier to feed everyone on the lawn. Pleasanter too, though any way you looked at them, the shareholders' gatherings were trouble.

Millie had been coming to the homeranch two or three days a week. She had to make sure there was food in the kitchen cupboards and to see that Serafina, the girl she'd hired to look after Aunt Marty, dusted the downstairs rooms and cleaned the one bathroom still in use. There was no sense laying on additional help with no one but Marty living at home. Millie had even considered closing the big house and moving Marty into the Spring House. This, however, seemed a drastic step; the big house hadn't ever been closed—not since it had been built, she thought. Troy wouldn't like it; Kyle might not either. Millie knew how they felt. Though her own roots were more transplantable, she too wanted the continuance that the homeranch, with its box of childhood secrets, seemed to guarantee. And an old house, once empty, quickly fell apart.

There would be plenty of time later to discuss the problem of closing up, if that were to happen.

They had turned out in force to hear the tidings of good fortune. They knew, naturally, much in advance; the news had gone out over the party lines, it had even been printed in the *Bakersfield Californian* and the *Los Angeles Examiner*, and the *San Francisco Chronicle* in its stuffy way had said that the facts "were waiting verification." *Verification*—when the desert for a mile around the well had been a foot deep in oil? What they had wanted, what they had to have, were details, lots of them, as quickly as possible, and that morning Kyle and Troy had supplied them generously, marvelously, to all present—the shareholders summoned by Kyle's letter and all those others who did not exactly hold shares but were people just the same. And there they were, trying to assess what had happened to them.

All right, fourteen thousand dollars a day, or a hundred and fifty thousand dollars a month, more or less. Not bad. No matter how you split it up it wasn't bad. There would be some costs, he'd said. Well, you expected costs. Nothing very much. What was there to cost? The beautiful gas shoved the oil up to the top, he'd said. You didn't have to pump it. People talked about a well "pumping" but that was a misnomer, a mistake common to the naïve or the uninitiated. Already the stockholders knew better. Troy had explained the true process. This well flowed. Gas, not suction, pushed up the oil. By the hour, the day, the month, the year. The well never rested. What did that one well deliver *by the year*? At seven thousand barrels a day, a year's production would be two million, two hundred and fifty-five thousand barrels. Suppose you had two wells . . . or a hundred . . . or a thousand?

But wait a minute. Hold on there. What *had* he said, precisely? People at the tables, even while attacking the barbecued steak, the yams and the canned peas, even while swilling down the good brown booze, had fished in their pockets for envelopes or just taken paper napkins and located pencils or pens and tried, eager to get it all straight, to reproduce the diagram Troy had drawn on the blackboard.

He'd made an X to start with. That was the discovery well. He had added squiggly lines to represent the duny, scrawny dry-gulch country around Piru and other marks to indicate the explorations he'd completed so far, X's for the test holes he was sure would be producing wells and O's for the dry holes. The formation was down there. It was known—proven! All that was required now was to determine its outlines, and in addition to the test holes there was a new and more sophisticated way to go about this, a technique perfected by an American named Everett E. DeGolyer. He set off dynamite charges and recorded, on delicate instruments, there in the field, the speed with which the shocks traveled underground. Oil, Troy explained, lay in structures through which the shocks of the explosions traveled faster than through ordinary earth or sand. Troy had been using the DeGolyer method on the Piru ranch. Since the discovery well had come in he'd done several weeks of most intensive work, not only on Kinsale land but on adjacent ranches that the company had leased. He'd stood there this morning at the blackboard and he'd drawn a sweeping spheroid, starting at the big well and embracing a good-sized hunk of land, east and west, north and south, miles in extent. *Miles!*

"Ladies and gentlemen, we have a well—this one here!" And he'd hammered with his chalk on the X. "It's a fine well, a big producing well. But what we are talking about isn't one well. What we're talking about here, ladies and gentlemen, is an oil *field!*"

Jesus! It boggled the mind.

Kyle was still seated at one of the tables talking with a scoop-faced man who had come in late. He motioned to Troy to join him, introducing his companion—a Mr. H. Lamar Custis, *"of Texas,"* Kyle added portentously. The scoop-faced man puffed up at the introduction; like all Texans, he regarded the mention of his home state as a flattery. He was small and meagerly built except for a sudden little potbelly of which he seemed proud since he had adorned it with a big gold watch chain. He wore a pepper-and-salt suit and a bow tie. He had a very sharp, attentive look around the eyes.

"A new breed," Kyle told Troy when Custis, as if by prearrangement, moved away. "He's a petroleum engineer. They've started giving that degree now, in a few universities. Plus which he has a master's in business administration from the University of Basel, Switzerland. He's published a paper on petroleum merchandising."

"How were you thinking of using him?"

"Maybe we could work him into that committee we were talking about."

Kyle's voice was casual, but Troy was startled. True, they'd mentioned a committee or executive body of some sort to be set up within the Land and Cattle Company specifically to handle oil operations. Troy had by no means been sure that it was such a good idea.

"You really want to go ahead with that?"

"I do. I've given it a lot of thought. I'd like to suggest it to the shareholders, now that we've got 'em here. Save us the trouble of calling a special meeting later."

"But we've adjourned."

Kyle knotted a big fist. He playfully knuckled Troy on the jaw.

"Trust me, Troy-boy," he said, using his brother's childhood nickname. "We need this committee. You'll see how it will work out. And li'l ole Lamar Custis may jes' be sent from heaven to help us run it." He caricatured Custis' accent, making Troy smile in spite of himself.

Troy looked around for the Texan, wondering whether Custis, with his odd combination of skills, could also read lips. But at the moment he was standing off by himself, twirling the big watch chain, his gaze aimed at the distant hills.

Kyle picked up a glass and knocked on it with a spoon. As talk died out he moved toward the center of the lawn, a poised and attractive figure in a polo shirt and English riding coat with which today, as if to emphasize the informal note he wanted, he wore stockman's pants and western boots. Smiling at everyone, he turned slowly on his heels, an actor in complete command of his audience.

"Hasn't it been, I should say, isn't it being, a marvelous day? Just wonderful?" And then, stilling the immediate spatter of handclapping and the "hear hears" of certain family voices, often raised at company meetings and ready at the least opportunity to launch into speeches of their own: "I honestly believe we've just held the most memorable meeting in the history of the Kinsale Land and Cattle Company." This brought real applause and he let it run. "I can promise you," he said, "that the meeting *has* adjourned; we aren't going back inside. But before we break up"—and he made the snuffling, infectious sounds of a laugh which he wanted to share with them, out of sheer lightheartedness, had he not a more serious purpose in mind—"I think we should drink a toast to Millicent Braden [applause], who arranged this delightful lunch, and . . . *and* . . . *to my brother, Troy, for striking oil* [shouts and handclapping, quickly stilled by Kyle], a toast which I hereby resolve to drink each day of my life from now on and suggest that we all do the same." Laughter, more clapping, clinking of glasses.

Kyle turned to Troy, raising the toast with the same oratorical gesture he had used for the toast to Millie:

"To Troy Kinsale!"

Only now did he drink, thus forcing everyone, not at all to their distaste, to drink again, while he himself crossed to Troy and put his arm around him. He peered affectionately into his eyes, finally freeing him only to lead off another round of clapping.

Troy, taken by surprise, was content to wave to the assemblage and call out, "Thank you all. Thank you very much."

"And now," said Kyle, as the ruckus subsided, "one thing more. We plan, Troy and I, with your consent, to set up a committee to handle the new activities the Land and Cattle Company will now be engaged in. We'll cook up a name for this body—the Executive Committee for Petroleum Operations or some such lofty title. You will all shortly receive in the mail a description of the committee and a definition of what it will be supposed to do, together with a ballot which you can mail back to Millie, our secretary as well as our hostess, by which you can indicate whether or not you want such a committee set up. And the members—at least the initial members, I may say—shall be Troy Kinsale and probably also myself, unless someone better can be found. That makes two, and we need three, even to start. I'm therefore proposing as the third committeeman a person who is here today, not a family member but a professional in this type of work, a qualified outsider."

With this he introduced Custis, then had him come out and stand with him while he filled in the details of his background.

People soon began to leave. Kyle drifted around, joining Millie and Doc Braden in farewells to their guests, clannish little rituals in which Troy did not participate. He sat down in a wicker chair on the porch, watching his brother's maneuvers with the people, the handshakes, the cousinly pats and kisses and reassurances—all the architecture of Kyle's family caucusing; he himself could not have behaved like that to save his life! . . . But hadn't he too become a victim of the same process? Something had gone wrong: the main outcome of this day of celebration had been an arrangement which, if it went through as outlined, would give Kyle sole control of the oil.

That was it, and no mistake about it: the creation of a committee.

Perfectly proper. Obviously useful and sensible. But that was exactly how it would work.

Troy tilted back his chair and put his feet on the porch railing, watching from between the toes of his hand-stitched boots as Kyle walked toward him.

Kyle climbed the porch steps slowly. He'd shed the actorish look he put on when he was charming people. His bony, sunburned face was gentle and serious—his big-brotherly look. Well, that wouldn't work this time. Troy wanted to get up and yell at him, "What are you trying to pull off? Do you think you can get away with this?" He was as angry with Kyle as he'd ever been but the words would not come out; there had always been a closeness, there had always been love. If there was a quarrel now, with so much at stake, the division might never be mended. He stared up at his brother while Kyle smiled amiably down at him.

"So you don't think much of my idea."

"No, I don't."

"I'm sorry. It seemed such a good time to present it."

"Bullshit!"

Kyle lit one of his cigars. He spun out small gray smoke rings.

"Let's take a ride."

"Now?"

"Yes. Up in the top flats, maybe to the Peak? We can talk up there."

"Too much trouble to saddle up."

"We can send Cliff to cut out a couple of horses. Maybe he'll come with us."

What I have to say to you, Troy thought, had best be said alone, but once more he remained silent. He spat over the rail.

Kyle was trying to make up with him. Well, he could resist that too.

"Okay. You tell him."

He rose, holding his anger inside him like a treasure, and went to get dressed for riding.

Certainly it was a good late afternoon to be out—and a good time of year. The wet winter that had caused trouble at the drill site had been kind to the hills, painting them with wildflowers, streaks of blue and purple lupine, the sunset colors of poppies and the secret yellow, black-centered sparks of wild violets. Mustard was starting. By June it would be as high as a horseman's head; its pollen would tear the lining out of your nose.

The horses made their own trail, switchbacking up the shoulders of the hills. Kyle had ridden Snake Eyes, the sorrel gelding Hub had taken to the orchards the day he was stabbed; Troy, on a mare just in from pasture, struggled to keep up. Each time he lifted his eyes he saw Kyle a turn or two ahead of him, moving effortlessly, propelled as it were by some self-generated power. It was as if Kyle were staging an equestrian tableau illustrating the relationship that had endured all their lives—big brother out in front, little brother puffing along in the rear. Well, it might be time to alter that.

Kyle was waiting for him at the Peak, their boyhood meeting ground where six huge weather-polished rocks, jammed in a circle, formed the knob that could be seen from Altemira. Kyle already had the rig off the sorrel, letting him nibble the few blades of grass to be found at this level. With the saddle for a backrest he sprawled on the biggest of the rocks, smoking contentedly as he looked out at the lovely land below. Troy took care of his own horse. Not finding a convenient place to sit he remained standing, glaring at his brother, groping for words to express the rage that had been building in him ever since the meeting.

Kyle sat up, smiling. He held out his cigar case.

"Light up and cool off."

"No thanks."

"All right then, let me have it. Tell me what a bastard I am."

"You're not a bastard. But you might just be a cheat."

"Might. Only I'm not. Oh, I know you're mad all right. Your eyes look like piss holes in the snow. Only one other time I ever saw you look like you do now. I'll bet you don't remember when that was."

"Can't say I do."

"That birthday of Pop's when we doubled on the shaving mugs: me with that trashy china thing, you with your persimmon carving. Well, I was as disgusted as you, the way Hub acted that day. You felt like you'd been kicked in the balls, isn't that right?"

"I got over it."

"You sure did. You never held it against me, never even mentioned it. I couldn't believe it."

"This isn't the same situation, is it?"

"It's close. I wasn't trying to take advantage then and I'm not trying to now."

"You're not? Christ, how stupid do you think I am?"

"The day I call you stupid you can kick the shit out of me. I'll deserve it. What's wrong?"

"Two votes to one on this committee is what's wrong. You and your man Custis. Where do I come in?"

"You don't want a committee?"

"Not one that's rigged against me."

"Rigged! So you think we'll oppose each other?"

"I didn't, until you showed me you did."

Kyle tamped out his cigar against the rock.

"I see what's bugging you. I never thought of it that way."

"Like hell you didn't."

"All right, can I tell you how to fix it?"

"I'd be delighted."

"I'm not married to Mr. Lamar Custis. I happen to think he's qualified—that he can be useful."

"To you."

"To all of us. Let him serve on the committee but you nominate a man of your own choice to serve with him and let the two of them nominate a third person. That way we'll have a committee of five instead of three, which is better anyway; the fifth man, the neutral nominee, will be the swing vote. How will that suit you?"

Troy stared at his brother.

"It's better than what we've got now, that's for sure!" The heavy, bemused set of his face lightened. "Could be it will work, at least until you think up another fast one."

"Which I'll do, of course," said Kyle happily.

"I'll be waiting."

"Don't you worry. I'll think up a real sockdolager. I'll whiff one right on your beak; you'll never know what hit you."

"Go ahead."

"But for now we have a deal?"

"Whatever you say."

"I say it's a deal," Kyle said, his smiling, relaxed face and his whole long, bony, loafing body stirring with excitement, with tenderness and affection for this brother who had come to him briefly as an enemy and was now once more a friend.

Tension drained out of Troy also. The danger past, he

wanted to forget it had ever existed—his terror of a break between them; he wanted to lie down on the sun-warmed rock and go to sleep. But there was no chance to rest. Kyle got up. With solemn, mock ceremoniousness he held out his hand; as Troy took hold to shake, Kyle whooped with laughter, jerking at their locked hands, trying for a wrestling throw, but Troy, downhill, had the leverage, and pulled him over. Both fell, got up again, fell again. They rolled over and over in the loose, shaly soil, puffing and grunting, pummeling each other with simulated fury, all in fun, now that peace was restored, but somehow not all that much fun either— somehow pantomiming something new to their relationship, something harsh and evasive, bypassed for the present but not to be completely forgotten or thus playfully dismissed.

Young Cliff, chugging up to the crest on a winded palomino, found them gathering sticks to build a fire. Off to the west the ocean sucked down the last daylight; the fire gathered brightness, a frivolous dab of light, mysterious and lonely in that high country. Later Cliff dozed on a saddle blanket and Troy smoked a pipe while Kyle, lazing in the warmth, talked about money.

"Most people don't have one true notion about it, Troy-boy. May I tell you this? They don't have a clue. You don't have one either. I've been studying this thing. I know about it; it's not figures on a page, it's not papers in a vault. That's just the backup. That's where you start. Not one person in ten million knows what happens after that, after you've got the start. You know what I mean? Ten million, fifty million. That's openers. That's where it stops being white chips. Now, if you understand its properties, you make it *self-create*. Hell, I'm not saying this right . . . you're a long way from real figures yet—a hundred, two hundred million. The *real* openers, you see. You're not there but you're close, before long you *understand* and then you've got the secret. You're about to experience the wildest thing that can happen to a human being, you're in the movement, all laws suspended, natural and man-made—do you know what I'm talking about?"

"Not yet," said Troy.

He was long to remember this conversation—many times— to go over it, trying to pin down the words, the elliptical meanings, as Kyle expressed for the first and only time this concept, this thing he lived by.

"Californians!" he said. "Did you ever hear of one who knew one thing about money? Christ, and here is where money *started*, the gold lying there in the stream beds, waiting to be picked up. So they panned it. Californians! They hacked it out of rocks, they blew each other's brains out for it and they spent it on whores. A few hoarded it. That's true, but they had no use of it. They might as well have hoarded marbles or cigarette flags. Some built railroads and stuff but never knew the real nature of what they had and most of them ended up broke."

"They bought land."

"Yup, they bought land. Like Henry Miller. He has a million acres or two million. Who cares? Granpa Calvin, how much did he leave to Hub? How much do *we* have? Half a million, three-quarters? With that much land in Europe you wouldn't just live like a king, you would *be* a king. You would screw princesses and ballet dancers. Hub screwed orchard girls and got stabbed by one of them. He was a redneck like the rest of them."

"Wouldn't that make us rednecks too?"

"It would and it does. Oh, we've got plenty of company!" Kyle held up four fingers. He pressed them down one by one. "Huntington, Stanford, Hopkins, Crocker. Rednecks all! Storekeepers, penny traders—"

"They also laid a lot of track."

"Californians have always performed great deeds."

"In a country sort of way?"

"No. One made it—William Randolph Hearst. Got out of California as fast as he could. The first newspaper he bought was in New York. I'd say W. R. can move a few pieces around. And you and I will move some pieces around, Troy-boy, and don't you forget it."

"I hope you know how."

"Oh, I think so. Give it a whirl anyway."

"Is that what you learned at Yale?"

Troy knew instantly his tone had been wrong. He hadn't meant to mock. Wild as this concept or plan of Kyle's might seem, it was not a disclosure to be shrugged off lightly.

His brother looked at him sternly.

"I was shit at Yale. I was the lonesomest asshole who ever cried into his beer in Morey's and I was the same in boarding school. That's why I had you send me that box of California earth, so I could remember where I came from. Now we're going to show people something. I didn't have the do-re-mi before, but now I've got it and we're going to take that money and move a few pieces around with it. You and me, old buddy. That's where the fun is. You just punch some more wells and keep them pumping, pardon me, *producing,* and you'll see stuff start to happen around here."

Kyle had said more, but Troy hadn't followed all of it. Driving south with Luanna next day, he tried to tell her what Kyle had said.

"He thinks that from now on we'll be living in a private world where rules no longer apply. Or if there are rules, you just make a phone call and have them changed. Do you know he always believed he'd be really rich—felt somehow he *had* to be? And he made plans for that day. Or *a* plan. He has it all worked out."

"Did he say what it was?"

"Not specifically. I gather it's some kind of power game, his version of Monopoly. He calls it moving a few pieces around. That's what excites him. The money is just the start of it. Money puts you into the real game. After that it's not important."

"Not important to Kyle? That's silly. But I can certainly understand why he had to be rich and knew it; I can't imagine anyone who would need to be rich more than your dear brother, the way he spends. He needs money because it's *money* and don't ever let him fool you."

"He isn't like other people."

"That's true too but not necessarily to be admired, though he'd be most willing to have it that way. It's queer, seeing the two of you together. You seem to shrink several inches when you're with him. I don't want that to sound nasty."

"It does though."

"All right, I'm sorry. I like Kyle. Really I do. He's extraordinarily attractive. He's clever and he's . . . interesting. Romantic? I know lots of people would think he's romantic, a romantic figure with his looks and his education and all, but I don't. He's a tough person, his fancy ways are just froth on the top. Plans! Purposes! Yes, he has them, obviously. I always felt his main purpose was to have you make him rich. And now you've done it. More than anyone could have believed, you've done it. So what comes next for Kyle Kinsale?"

Troy did not answer at once. He continued driving in his methodical way, aiming the long hood of the car down the middle of the highway; now between his knuckles, which he held high on the wheel, appeared the outlines of Percy Yountman's service station. While he didn't actually need any more gas it would be pleasant to stop and get some. He and Perce could cut up a few touches and the kids could go to the john. He could treat them to a Moxie out of Perce's cooler.

The truth was, if he was starting a new kind of life, as Kyle said, it didn't seem much different from the old one.

"Well, honey," he said, "I guess we'll just have to wait and see."

PART TWO

PART TWO

CHAPTER SIX

The Coup

1

There was a heater in the 1934 Rolls Phantom (which had replaced Kyle's 1923 Silver Ghost) but though the December morning was cool, Kyle had not turned it on. It wasn't needed. The shut-in, leathery climate of the car derived its heat from an animal rather than a mechanical source. Kyle had noticed the phenomenon at other times—this personal heat, hypnotic and sensual.

No ordinary woman was endowed with such a force; no ordinary woman would be able as Alma was to project it even without wishing to and, indeed, being powerless to turn it off.

But Alma Paris was no ordinary woman. She was in fact two delightful and perfectly healthy but quite separate people; the private Alma, who, late at night, using the key he'd given her, would come to his cottage at the Ambassador Hotel and get in bed with him, and the public Alma, who insisted that after any sort of social gathering, particularly when they planned to be together later, they should be seen saying goodnight to each other.

He touched her hand lightly where it lay, shapely and ringless, on the folds of her mink coat.

"What are you going to do now, sweetheart?"

"I'm going to the beach."

"Good God!"

"What do you mean?"

"I'd think it would be too cold."

"I like it when it's cold."

"Then it will be all right."

"Of course it's all right. I used to do it a lot. Before."

This use of the adverb *before* was peculiar to the vocabulary of the private Alma: the code reference to that stretch of time which had existed prior to their love affair.

"I used," she said, "to go there a lot in the winter. The Beach Club stays open all year round. That's one of the nice things about it. I have this big, fluffy sweater in my locker and I put it on. I walk in the edge of the waves and if a big one comes I dare it to get me. They have a special lunch there too, at the club on Sundays. Do you think you'll be very long?"

"I'm not sure."

"Do you want me to call and check? You don't *usually,*" she said, reproachfully rather than jealously, though Alma could be jealous. "You don't usually work on Sundays *at all.*"

"This time I have to. But I'll be thinking about you."

As he said this, he could see her, bare-legged, bright-thighed, running from the white slash of a breaker, heading toward the special lunch. And, at the prospect of eating his own lunch alone or in company with the KinOil staffers whom he saw and lunched with every day, his decision wavered; it would be so much nicer to be with Alma.

"I'll be through at two o'clock or thereabouts. Could you meet me then or would you rather stay at the club?"

"Well, let me think . . ." Alma pantomimed a lady in deep thought. "What have you to offer, my good fellow?"

"We could have a snack."

"Not enough. I want a *meal.*"

"All right."

"And then?"

"Then we'll see!"

"I accept."

"Good. Then it's settled."

Mort, his driver, had his arm out, making a left turn into the parking lot of the KinOil Building. Few instructions were needed with Mort, a man of experience and discretion. He would take Alma where she needed to go, then return to resume the business of the day. Almost before the car had stopped, it seemed, Mort was on the pavement, opening the door.

Kyle got out. Alma, at the side window, blew him kisses; she held up two fingers. Her pretty mouth, daubed with the heavy red lipstick obligatory at that time for women of all ages, at all hours, shaped the words, "Two o'clock." Then she twined the fingers together. Kyle laughed at the sensuality of the signal code. He stood tall in the parking lot, his dark head thrown back, watching as Mort wheeled the Rolls into the traffic on Wilshire Boulevard, light at this hour of a Sunday morning.

2

The KinOil Building shone as if made of ice. Its many windows, sparkling clean, its towering walls of polished stone, its sharply angled setbacks and terraces, drew to themselves whatever light there was in this mild, waiting air. At the summit glinted a spire of stainless steel, visible for miles. It was, in truth, a beautiful building—a masterpiece of architecture. Kyle never looked at it without enjoyment, but on the other hand, he never flattered himself that he had designed it, as some businessmen did when they put up a skyscraper. They would hire the world's best architects and then brag that they'd told them what to do. Well, he'd hired Eric Mendelsohn and let Mendelsohn tell *him* what to do.

The KinOil Building represented the work of talented men, accomplished at their trades. Kyle always stressed this when he talked about it, minimizing his share in its creation. Still, it did embody a dream of his own. He had wanted it to be beautiful, unique, and it was. He was proud of that—also that he had chosen the right place for it. He had planned for the building to stand apart, just as KinOil stood apart, a strong young company making new paths among the heavy, ruthless dynasties of oil. Not for the world would he have built downtown, though land was available there: on Main Street, near Mobil, or over on Broadway, near Texaco. There the men of the old-line firms could hobnob, meeting in The California Club or the Jonathan Club or walking the few blocks that separated one office from another; there they drank toasts of brotherhood and made solemn covenants of friendship while they poked into each other's plans and projects, each trying to hold on to his own secrets but obtain those of his rivals. Kyle wanted to stay away from their whole sorry game. He had felt that the placement of the KinOil

Building in the Wilshire section known as "The Miracle Mile," halfway between downtown Los Angeles and Beverly Hills, put the company in the proper perspective.

Entering his office after hours, or on a holiday, Kyle's actions were different from those of a weekday. On a weekday his coffee would have been ready. Rose Brady, his secretary, would have brewed it, would have had it warming in its glass flask, ready to drink and to serve to callers. Rose would have pulled back the curtains which screened the great panorama of the city's sprawl to the west, the MGM sign in Culver City and beyond, along the ocean's edge, the oil fields of Inglewood and Playa Del Rey. But today Rose, inevitably, was at Mass; he could see her in his mind's eye, kneeling in the Good Shepherd, clutching a missal from which holy medals, blessed by the Pope, dripped on wilted ribbons like defeated hopes. Let her pray for KinOil then, he thought. We might need some prayers this day.

Kyle started his own coffee. Then, having shed his jacket, he went to a receptacle on his desk and fished in it for a slip of paper. Rose was supposed to have this memo with its laconic notation ready for him daily—the last available quotation of KinOil Common (designated on the ticker as KinCom) on the New York Stock Exchange.

The receptacle itself was unusual. It didn't fit the elegant decor of the office—the rose-quartz chandeliers, the Coromandel screens, the Oriental rugs. Even the desk on which it rested was not actually a desk at all but a refectory table, laid on from Joseph Duveen's London gallery at a price which Kyle's grandfather would have refused to pay for a fine cattle ranch. The receptacle was the butt section of a rusty drill bit, stained with petroleum, as if it had just been recovered from a deep encounter with a rock. It was the bit which had been at the end of the drill stem when Troy had struck oil, nine years earlier, in the dunes of Piru. Troy had saved it as a souvenir but Kyle had begged it from him to use as decor. There was power and dignity in the old bit. It reminded visitors not to be misled by the room's fancy trappings. It suggested the nature of the business to be transacted.

Kyle put his hand into the pipe end of the bit. The memo slip was there. Even before he unfolded it Kyle knew what it was going to say. He could feel it in his fingers, in the skin of his soul.

The stock had gone down again.

That was how it had been for days now, stretching into

weeks. No big drop, no distress signals—nothing like that at all. Up a few, down a few—the sort of trading which on a graph looked like a wobbly, slowly descending line. "Mild activity," a stock analyst would have called it. But the trend had been established: more downs than ups, from close to 80 down to 70, and then into the 60's—the danger zone.

Kyle laid the memo on the desk. He sat down and glared at it as if by sheer concentration he could change what it said. How could a company with a billion dollars' worth of untapped assets stored in a vault of prehistoric rock be threatened by a stock quotation? Yet that was exactly what was happening.

Until now, the stock had served him well. The public offering, put out by its eminent underwriters in the depths of the Depression (reluctantly and rather despairingly, because business must go on even though the woods were burning), had been fully subscribed within a few weeks.

Possibly investors had been tired of the hard times. They no longer believed in them, just as in '29 they had no longer believed in prosperity. They were bargain hunters, they had money put aside in cracked teakettles and sequestered under mattresses—money which the magic of California oil could lure out. Issued at fifty dollars, with a million shares authorized (twenty-six percent being retained by the Kinsale Land and Cattle Company, the parent entity), the stock had risen nearly 30 points.

Here was money to spend—the cash flow he'd needed to expand KinOil. Kyle had used it well. He'd shopped for new facilities he'd needed—picked up a fleet of tankers from a bankrupt Belgian company, a string of Midwestern filling stations from a Texas corporation which had marketing position but lacked oil. Above all, he had acquired other companies; KinOil had taken over four smaller but potentially valuable California outfits which had fallen on hard times. Every trade had involved stock as well as cash and in most, as the essence of the deal, KinOil had guaranteed a price below which its tendered Common would not be allowed to fall. There was, for instance, the operation planned for today—the biggest takeover of all, so formidable that just the announcement of its consummation might turn the market around. And if it didn't? Well, he would face that when he came to it.

Under the edge of the refectory table was the office

intercom with its rows of initialed buttons. Kyle started punching these. As usual, he rang Lamar Custis first; when the Texan, always peaked and sour-looking in the morning, appeared before him, Kyle pushed Rose Brady's slip across the desk.

"How are we going to stop this shit?"

3

Lamar Custis smoothed the scrap of paper in his bony, liver-spotted hands. His scooped-out face was troubled, and his eyes, under their shaggy brows, serious and bloodshot. He had turned into a dandy these days, indulging himself in high-collared shirts and loud, garish suits with padded shoulders, silk socks with arrows stitched along the inseams and narrow-toed two-toned shoes. The haberdashery came from the best suppliers, but in combination with the wearer's shrunken frame and small, prominent potbelly, it gave Custis the air of a racetracker in the chips rather than the treasurer of a responsible company.

"I don't know," he said quietly, "but I got some ideas."

Lamar Custis always had ideas. That was one of his great assets to KinOil and to Kyle Kinsale; he had proved himself a tireless innovator, agile under pressure, and aggressive even when the going was toughest. His experience as a negotiator and his excellent connections had helped the company in many ways, particularly in the matter of its acquisitions.

"Well, if you have, I'd like to hear them."

"All right. For starters, there's been selling in KinOil—big action. Did you ever wonder who might be doing that?"

"A stock can't drop nineteen points in five weeks without people selling. Is that the best you can come up with?"

Custis shook his head.

"I don't mean public sales. I mean some private party unloading in *big blocks*—little by little. Not like they're trying to knock the quote down, you hear? More like trying to hold it up, best way they can, while they ease out of their holdings."

Lamar's devious mind had seized on something Kyle had never thought of.

"Are you talking about one or two people or a combine of some kind?"

"No combine," said Custis succinctly.

"Then I don't get it, Lamar. No outside person has that kind of holding—you know that as well as I do. And even if the big holders, such as there are, wanted to get out, and did, it wouldn't affect the market that much. A few points maybe—then it would be all over."

"Right."

"Then what's your point?"

"You said outside person. There's others."

"No one but *family*."

"Kyle," said Custis firmly, "you just think about it. If you had KinOil and you wanted to get liquid, with the rise we had, this might look like a good time to do it. Wouldn't it? Most of all ifen you hadn't paid for the stock in the first place."

"Then you do mean family, by God. Members of the Land and Cattle who had KinCom *prorated* to them."

"I said think about it."

"Well, my friend, I may not *care* to think about it."

"You said you wanted my ideas. I gave one to you."

"You did. But this . . ."

He broke off. Custis watched as Kyle, as if to contain his disturbance, crossed to the coffee urn to refill his cup.

"No offense intended, boss," said Custis dryly. And then as Kyle, stirring his brew, made no reply, he added: "Maybe this is the last of the bad news, anyway. Maybe the Atlass deal will straighten us out."

Kyle set down his cup. With his right hand he made a queer, chopping gesture, as if attacking some unseen enemy. "Yes," he said. "That's what I'm hoping. Let's get on with Atlass. That's what we're here for, isn't it? But you hear this, Lamar, I refuse to consider your insinuation that my brother or my sister or any family member might be liquidating their holdings. I just can't believe it. Don't ever mention this idea of yours to anybody else. No one, is that understood?"

"Understood, boss," said Lamar Custis compliantly. "It's goin' no further. Just a notion, came to me in passing."

His bony fingers, plunging into the vest pocket of his high-toned suit, produced his Phi Beta Kappa key; this, on its thick gold chain, he twirled absently, watching with a scoopy, undershot look as Kyle, back at his desk again, pressed the buttons summoning Reeves Thurmond, head of KinOil's legal staff, and Dan Shannon, Vice President, Sales, to the presidential suite.

4

Waiting for the men to appear, Kyle passed the time impatiently. He shifted in his chair. He picked up small objects and arranged them in new but aimless patterns. He doodled on his desk pad. He was never really at ease in an office, even his own—easily bored with the administrative detail necessary to any large-scale enterprise. The meetings, reports, and planning sessions had to be got through somehow, and Kyle got through them, but he was happiest in action—confronting adversaries, probing for their weaknesses or for some area of common interest; squaring off with them man-to-man and in the end, in his urbane, easy way—flattering and disdainful at the same time—molding them to his will. This he understood. The confrontations appealed to his gamesmanship. And to prepare the ground for the game and to mop up afterward he had this team—the three men with whom he would be meeting now. Each, in experience and competence, was a talented, forceful person, qualified to head an enterprise of his own (and two of them once had). They had signed with KinOil for the opportunity it offered; a small company on the prod for power, moving fast and hard for a top place in the world's most lucrative industry.

They were Kyle's men—extensions of himself. He paid them big salaries and he put around them the magic of his charm and the force of his wealth, creating a special climate in which each could function at his best. There was only one condition: these men were on call. They were required to leave relay numbers with the KinOil round-the-clock switchboard, designating where they could be reached at any moment Kyle might need them.

Kyle's hours were unpredictable. He might not be seen in the KinOil Building for a week or more: he might go slamming off to Europe or New York in chase of a deal; he might—and did—disappear from time to time with a woman, not always the same woman. He might leave business in abeyance while he involved himself with a family reunion or a week at the Bohemian Grove or the performance of a new horse at the stud farm on which he was spending half a million a year. But sooner or later, usually at some outrageous, unthinkable hour, the operator would be there, getting the poor bastard on the line, and then would come the sniffle, the snuffle of the laugh that never quite became a laugh, and the warm, vibrant voice saying, "Hey, I know this is crazy, but do you suppose you could come over? Just for a few minutes?" . . . Or "God, were you really asleep? I'm sorry, but look . . . here's what I've been thinking . . ."

This time Kyle hadn't made the calls personally. One of the night operators had put them through between 2 and 2:30 A.M., Pacific Coast time. Would Thurmond, would Custis, would Shannon mind meeting with Mr. Kinsale that morning, in the office?

No one had to be told why Kyle wanted him there. The meeting would concern the Atlass deal, a critical transaction by any standard and one which could still easily go wrong.

Kyle marched up and down the carpet, under the heavy, glittering chandeliers, preoccupied with his thoughts. Eager, a few minutes earlier, for the conference to start, he now seemed to have forgotten all about it; he hardly noticed when first Shannon, then Thurmond, got out of the private elevator and crossed to the comfortable chairs grouped by the south window. His talk with Custis had upset him; he had not been able, as he usually did, to screen off personal feelings, move on to other concerns.

Disloyalty in the family! Somebody close to him, liquidating stock! It was a sickening notion. Might it not be better to ignore Custis' suggestion and his own suspicions, now thoroughly roused, better just to bullass through and pretend or pray that the family had not produced a Judas, that some other explanation would be found for the fall of Kin-Common?

Custis joined Shannon and Thurmond by the window. Kyle now took his usual place there. He lit a cigar and began the conference but for several moments could not concentrate on what was being said.

Who could it be but Troy?

Not that there was any division between them. Not really. Both had been careful not to let that happen. Points of view could differ, tempers could rise—and had—but the only serious quarrel Kyle could remember had been the time he'd brought in Lamar Custis without giving Troy the due and proper notice which his dignity demanded, or some such issue—that time when Troy had been so angry they'd almost come to blows but had cooled off later, up on the Peak. The old feeling had been there, and it had saved them; the friendship, the brotherhood, had all come back, so warmly, so wonderfully.

Troy was no fool. He would know what heavy selling would do to the stock. He also damn well knew what shape the company was in, with KinCommon pledged far and wide as collateral and pegged at 62.

But if Troy had wanted to liquidate, why hadn't he said so? And what would he need money for? He was already drawing the company's second-biggest salary. Did he want the *biggest* salary? He could have it: he would have known that too. All he had to do was ask!

Kyle felt like calling off the meeting. He felt like going straight to the telephone and ringing Troy, seeing what he had to say. For several moments he contemplated this, but slowly canceled the idea. The call would reveal suspicions, for which Troy, if he wasn't guilty, would never forgive him.

Stick to realities. The Atlass deal was the solution.

"All right," he said, still partly absorbed in his calculations, "what have the wire-room people been doing? Have we been getting anywhere?"

Dan Shannon pulled out a notebook. He was a tall Irishman with a priestly bald spot and hard, predatory eyes. The staff had nicknamed him "The Blade"—he was so thin that it was said if you looked at him sideways you couldn't see him. His health was bad, his manners sensitive and formal. He was primarily a lobbyist and fixer, invaluable to KinOil in these capacities, but also because, like a casting director, he could produce a man for any job, from staffing a rig to running a company division. It was he who had recruited the wire-room staff from the flotsam talent of Depression salesmanship: brokerage men, advertising account executives, bookmakers' clerks and such—good men down on their luck and willing to work around the clock for meager pay, just to keep going.

"Sixty-two thousand shares in the last fourteen hours. That's as of nine A.M. this morning . . ."

"Pretty good."

"Better'n that, Kyle, and you know it," said Custis. "I'd say, just wonnerful." He swiveled around in his deep chair to beam at Shannon. The Texan always wanted it known that, when it came to rewards or censure, his endorsements carried an independent importance.

"So now we have a leverage of what—eleven, eleven and a half percent?"

Shannon didn't have the figure on this. Thurmond did.

"Sorry, fellows. Nine and three-quarters. Maybe ten. That would be tops."

The statement dampened the spurt of optimism which Shannon's report had stimulated. All present knew that, even relying on the lowest estimate, control of Atlass International would require seventeen percent of the voting common. The job of the wire-room operators had been to acquire stock by submitting private offers, by telephone, to certain individual shareowners. Only those holding a thousand shares or more were being solicited. The selection had been made possible by scrutiny of Atlass' registry of stockholders, acquired through Shannon's connections.

"However," Thurmond went on in his gravelly voice, "we're not hurting. Nine or ten percent would still be a strong hand to go in with if we got down to a proxy fight. And by that time, going the way we are, we might pick off three, four percent more."

Thurmond had been over the route before. From a steamy, dusty office in Bakersfield, where he had hung out his shingle soon after the Great War, he had moved rapidly into the top levels of petroleum litigation; he had played every side of the table in his day, representing oil companies in lease and franchise suits against each other and landowners in class-action suits against oil companies. A criminal case, until he joined KinOil, had been as welcome in his practice as a corporate one: he had become famous as part of a team defending the oilman Edward L. Doheny in the removal of two billion dollars' worth of U.S. Navy petroleum from the Elk Hills reserves. The case had produced a unique split verdict: Albert B. Fall, former Secretary of the Interior, had been sentenced to jail for accepting a bribe from Doheny's group, but Thurmond got Doheny acquitted on the charge of paying it.

A heavyset man with a leonine face and a head of bushy white hair to match, he looked at Kyle for approval.

Kyle shook his head.

"We're in sixteen million now; a proxy fight would cost too much. No way to tell, and anyway"—his glance moved around—"a proxy fight is out. Don't forget, Mobil and British Petroleum, to name just two, have been looking. Lord Hector Mellis of BP is in San Francisco right now. He didn't come across the pond to see us pick up Atlass at bargain rates."

"Maybe not," said Custis. "But I don't notice BP making tender offers of their own."

"Right, Lamar," said Thurmond. "That's a point I mentioned to Kaplan, Atlass' attorney, when he called last week. I'll stress it again when I see him."

Kyle swung around to face Thurmond.

"You haven't seen Kaplan? I thought you were meeting with him yesterday."

"He canceled, and we reset the date."

"Why?"

"I don't know."

Kyle glared at Thurmond.

"Shit, Reeves. He's stalling us!"

"We have no proof of that."

"What the hell do you mean, proof? This deal is close to the rocks. Sure, the wire room has done a job, but if you want to know, I didn't want ten percent of the stock by now, I wanted maybe like twelve, thirteen, and it's going to get more expensive every fucking day, every minute. I want to go out and see H. H. Atlass today. I want to get some answers. Is that all right with you?"

Shannon looked at Custis, who made a subdued signal of disavowal: this new tactic was nothing he'd started.

Thurmond said, "I know Harry Atlass. He's not that easy to see."

"Meaning, we can't get to him?"

"Oh, we can get to him all right. Only, uh, possibly we might pause to reflect . . ."

"What do you think, Lamar?"

And Custis, feeling he had the support of Thurmond and Shannon, said, "Seems like short notice to me."

"Is short bad? The only better kind of notice would be *no* notice." Kyle sniffled and snuffled and then, belatedly, came out with an actual laugh. He quoted a saying of Hub's: "If you want to skin a catfish, nail him to a board."

"Do you know where to reach him, Reeves?" said Custis.

"I can call Herb Kaplan. He'll know."

He took a telephone from a side table. There was desultory conversation while he placed the call, which required little time. Thurmond hung up.

"H. H. Atlass is playing golf. He won't talk business on Sundays."

"Where does he play?"

"I doubt if Kaplan will tell us."

"So why do we need Kaplan? Here are some clubs: Bel Air, Wilshire, Los Angeles Country Club, you think of some more. Call all of them. And when you find out what we want to know, step into the wire room; I'll be there with the fellas. They might need a few words of encouragement."

And so saying, followed by his honor guard—now minus Thurmond—Kyle exited to the elevator.

5

During the drive from Los Angeles to the Lakeside Golf Club in North Hollywood, Kyle, Shannon, Custis and Thurmond rode together in the Rolls.

The journey took less than half an hour but this was long enough for a tactical approach to be outlined, the principal ingredient of which was shock. It was to prove effective.

The Lakeside golf course occupies a green corner of the San Fernando Valley, between the dry bed of the Los Angeles River and a large, weedy pond. It is a pleasant course, drawing a medium-elite membership: part downtown business, part motion-picture people. The latter element, in preponderance at the time, underwent some harassment from the Lakeside caddies, most of them notorious snobs. From behind the hedge which screened them off from the front entryway the corps of bag packers kept vigilant watch, according each famous arrival his signature greeting: for James Cagney, murmurs of "Take that, ya dirty raat"; for Adolphe Menjou, falsetto "French"; for Bogart, orally produced machine-gun fire; for Clark Gable, shouts of "Hey, *King,*" "How are ya, *King?*" followed by lip farts (Gable not being identified as an extravagant tipper).

Strangers, unless political or stage figures, the caddies ignored: quiet prevailed as the KinOil group made its way inside.

It was nearly noon. The club bar and the dining room were filling up as players, making the turn, came in for a bite and a drink before starting the second nine; the cardroom was busy and in the adjacent lounge a small fire provided cheer to those members who studied form sheets, working the Sunday wires to the Mexican racetracks.

Kyle approached the reception desk. He smiled at the young lady there and she smiled back at him.

"Is Mr. Atlass in the club?"

"No, sir. He's playing golf. Did you wish to leave a message for him?"

"No, ma'am. We would like to talk to him personally."

"Then perhaps you could leave a note, sir. Or come back a little later?"

"It would be better if we could see him right away."

In the eyes of the receptionist, it was now clear that the gentleman inquiring for H. H. Atlass belonged to a type seldom encountered at Lakeside—the type who would be a nuisance.

His next question confirmed this.

"Does the club have a manager?"

"Yes, sir. But he's not in his office today."

"Do you suppose I could reach him at home?"

"He's in the club," said the reception lady, "but I'm not supposed to bother him."

"I'd consider it a great personal favor," said Kyle. "I don't really think he'd mind, this time. I'm Kyle Kinsale, of the KinOil Corporation."

And so saying, Kyle presented this young woman with his card. She looked at it dubiously, but her bearing eased. Either the name had registered—a name that one had heard somewhere or read in the papers—or the word "oil" carried its own force, a power to change rules. She returned to her desk and dialed a number, apparently part of a club inter-com system. She was heard talking over this system in a voice too low for the words to be distinguishable but with the result that after a few moments—actually a surprisingly short period—a small, slight man wearing a cashmere sweater and expensive slacks entered the office from a door behind the switchboard. The reception lady handed him Kyle's card; he was still holding it as he stepped around the counter to confront the four men waiting there. It took him no time at all to decide which of the four was Kyle.

"Marty Zahn," he said. He put out his hand and Kyle took it.

"Kyle Kinsale, Mr. Zahn," Kyle said.

"I know," said Zahn.

He looked at the card again.

"Would you say," he said, "that this matter is an emergency, Mr. Kinsale? The matter about which you wish to see Mr. H. H. Atlass?"

"Yes," said Kyle.

Both he and Mr. Zahn experienced relief in having arrived at an operational term.

"Because in a case of emergency, we *can* send out on the course. That is if the situation—if it is such that could come under the head of—"

"It is."

"Then in that case you might like to speak to Mr. Atlass privately?"

"That's very kind of you."

"If you will follow me . . ."

With the visitors queued up behind, Mr. Zahn led the way down a carpeted hall to a door which he unlocked. The room beyond, evidently used for meetings of a more formal nature, had as its principal furniture a table with seats at it for a dozen or more persons. There was also a small pantry bar, unused at the moment, and a large plate-glass window through which, a few moments later, a pickup truck could be seen heading out onto the greenery beyond.

The truck returned shortly at a faster clip with a stout man in golf clothes seated beside the driver and another golfer (the vehicle was too narrow to accommodate three in front) bouncing precariously on a load of leaves, tools, and grass clippings behind.

The truck stopped. The stout man and the one sitting on the junk got out quickly, appearing immediately thereafter— like actors making a stage entrance from the audience—in the committee room. Kyle, Custis, Shannon and Thurmond stood up.

"For Christ's sake—" said Harry Atlass.

"Kyle Kinsale," said Kyle.

"I know you," said Harry Atlass, "I've seen you before. But what the hell . . ." He looked around him, somewhat wildly. Seen closer, he did not seem so stout—just squarely built. He had on a cross-striped sports shirt and white woolen plus fours, both of which accentuated his squareness. His companion, also stylishly outfitted, was taller. His enormous hands, held slightly in front of him, drooped from the wrists, their angle paralleling that of the Scotch flaps on his golf shoes. He held out one of his hands to Lamar Custis.

"I'm Jack Taraway, the dancer."

Custis smiled but ignored the hand. Taraway put it in his pants pocket.

"What the shit is going on here!" said Atlass. "They sent word it was about my daughter. My daughter Dede."

"We wish to talk to you about another matter, sir," put in Thurmond.

"Shit!" said Harry Atlass. He shook his round, oversize head confusedly. His face had no blotches in it, it was blazing red all over. He shook his head like a fighter taking a count, pulling his wits together. He spun around, facing Kyle.

"Sit down, please, Mr. Atlass," Kyle said soothingly. "I'm sorry there's been this confusion, that you took this personally. What we have to talk about—"

"What you have to talk about you can stick up your ass," said Atlass. He turned to his companion. "Come on, Jack. Let's get back on the course."

"Five minutes of your time today," said Kyle quietly, "will save you many millions of dollars. It may also result in savings for KinOil. You are correct, I think, in identifying this as a takeover; we have a position in Atlass International, ten percent as of this morning, nine A.M."

"You're lying," said Atlass. He looked around for a chair.

"He's not lying, Mr. Atlass. That I can assure you," said Thurmond. He got up courteously, yielding his seat to Atlass.

"I don't know," said Atlass. "I never ran into anything like this. You don't have ten percent, you prick. You don't even have two percent or one percent. What kind of crap are you giving me?"

Kyle turned to Custis.

"Do you have a makeready copy of that advertising, Lamar?"

"Yes, sir. I do." Custis opened his briefcase, producing a proof sheet. This, struck from a double-truck newspaper insert, he handed to Kyle, who, in turn, passed it on to Atlass.

"This is scheduled to run Wednesday, Mr. Atlass. In your good friend Mr. Chandler's *Los Angeles Times*. Also in W.R. Hearst's *Examiner*. We can cancel, but not later than tomorrow noon. The decision rests with you."

Harry Atlass stared desolately at the sheet of paper. Though the type was large, he was obviously unable to read it. He also seemed to have difficulty drawing his breath.

"I don't have my glasses," he said. "Here, Jack, you read it."

Taraway took the sheet.

"Aha," he said, "Taraway gets *lines*. This is one for the book."

He read in a stilted, self-conscious manner: "To Holders of

Common Stock of Atlass International: KinOil Corporation, a California corporation (KinOil), hereby offers to purchase any number of validly tendered between one hundred and seven-two thousand zero zero zero and four hundred and sixteen thousand zero zero zero shares of the outstanding Common Stock, fifty dollars par value, of Atlass International Corporation, a California corporation, hereinafter known as The Company, at fifty-eight dollars a share net to the seller in cash. Tendering shareholders will not be obligated to pay brokerage commissions, fees or . . ."

The voice droned on, reading the lengthy and involved legal language of the tender offer while the listeners sat in a torpor as thick as if they had been poured into a mold of Jello. Finishing, Taraway looked at Atlass as if for some comment on his performance. Atlass paid no attention to him. He turned to face Kyle, his head down on his chest and his lips pulled back in a queer way.

"I see what you're trying to do," he said. "Well, all right. Go ahead. You won't get away with it—never! Not in a thousand years."

He seemed to speak out of a great weariness, to someone at a far distance.

"Mr. Atlass," said Kyle, "we aren't trying to get away with anything. The intention here is the purchase of your company, at terms greatly to your advantage."

"Crazy terms!" said Thurmond. "I opposed them."

Kyle, his eyes on Atlass, wiggled a finger and Thurmond subsided.

Harry Atlass sat hunched over, glaring sadly at Kyle with his lidless eyes. Thrashing in the toils of his sudden, awful weariness he once more forced his voice out, hopeless and harsh.

"Never! . . . You'll see . . ."

"Mr. Atlass," said Kyle, "how would a proxy contest serve any of us? It's a stupid way to go. If you choose that way, KinOil might have to withdraw something I haven't mentioned but I think should appeal to you—a seat on the board of the combined companies for you, Harry Atlass. Probably an officership as well. I'd be inclined to favor it. Wouldn't you, Lamar?"

Custis nodded vigorously.

"I most certainly would. A real oilman! How long you been in business, Harry?"

Said Atlass, in his strange, new low voice, "Okay, then.

I've been in business forty years, forty fucking years, eighteen ninety-four I started, Coalinga. A cable-tool man. And today I lose my company in half an hour, in the middle of a golf game. Is that the idea now, is that what's on the schedule?" He looked around at all present. "You know," he said, "when they told me an emergency, I thought it must be my daughter Dede. Planes! I hate the damn things, but she's always flying. East, west, all over. I asked her to travel some other way . . ."

6

"He'll go like a gentleman," said Thurmond. "He'll have his shower and his rub, and then he'll roll over and play dead."

"He might fool you," said Shannon. "He might go back on the golf course."

Custis disagreed. "Not him. Odds are he was losing there too."

Kyle smiled.

"He didn't look like a golfer to me."

"He didn't look like an oilman to me," said Custis.

"Said he was, though," put in Shannon. "Said he started in the cable-tool days. You ever hear of him, Reeves?"

Thurmond shook his head.

"Most of those cable riggers died out like the dinosaurs in the La Brea tar pits. They couldn't keep up."

"Atlass sure as hell could. Or how did he get smart enough to buy the cracking plants and steamboats? And the French and Italian setups?"

"He has smart lawyers."

"And he's on the phone with them right now," said Shannon.

Custis laughed, but Thurmond said judiciously, "I doubt if he'll make trouble. Did you see his face get red, then dead white? I thought he was going to have a heart attack. Oh, he'll cuss and stomp around some, but he'll fold. They most always do, in a takeover. Christ, we're paying him fifteen, twenty percent more than his company is worth. He'll be a very rich man."

"And his golf game will get better," said Shannon.

"One thing is for sure," said Custis: "he'll have that club manager fired. Can you imagine that son of a bitch disturbing a member when he's out on the course?"

For some reason, this seemed to all present an immensely funny remark.

The big burnished car rolled north on Black Canyon Road, then west; it moved noiselessly through the quiet Sunday streets and the men in it enjoyed themselves, relaxing in the jocularity of an assault group returning from a successful strike. Kyle was at peace. It had turned out to be a wonderful day. He recognized from the past this combination of elation and calmness, this affection for others; he had experienced it before in special situations, after certain sexual encounters and sometimes after polo games, the high-goal games he had loved so much and now played so seldom. He corrected this: only when he had been a winner. That was the truth of it. Winning was . . . the *thing*. Not an action, but a way of life.

Wasn't that what he had always wanted? Even back in the party days of the special trains to the ranch from San Francisco and the girls in the big hats and the lacy summer dresses and the men in the blazers and the boater hats.

The thing.

He lounged in a corner of the back seat, his long legs crossed, smoking one of his little cigars. No longer did he feel concerned about the drop in KinOil stock; even the notion that some family member had been secretly unloading it did not upset him. He would give his attention to that. He would get to the bottom of it. Now it was enough to enjoy his peacefulness. It was enough to let his mind roam free and to look forward to his rendezvous with Alma.

CHAPTER SEVEN

Cottage 17

1

Even if they had been together the night before, the afternoon appointments with Alma were special occasions, different from the evening rendezvous.

In the evenings, Kyle and Alma would come back to Cottage 17, his rooms at the Ambassador, like a married couple. They would already be slightly sated with each other. They would have been together at dinner and perhaps later for dancing, or at a party; they would have been anticipating lovemaking but would often be a little sleepy for it by the time the door was firmly locked and the DO NOT DISTURB sign hung on the knob. Also, in the ordinary course of such evenings, one drank a certain amount—not enough perhaps to dull delight but enough to reduce awareness of just whom one was having it with.

The DO NOT DISTURB sign, in itself, was silly—meaningless except for that first half hour or so when they were actually in each other's arms. Kyle would be disturbed, as in fact he demanded to be, by his regular morning call, coming through at seven or, if he was going out to watch his horses work, much earlier; as for Alma, she carried a tiny gold alarm clock in her purse and would set it so that she could get up and go home sometime in the early-morning hours if she had not fashioned an excuse for staying out overnight.

In short, there were stresses connected with love in the evening which were removed from love in the afternoon.

In the afternoons the day had as yet made no inroads on desire. In fact, the day might almost be beginning. There was no hurry about anything, and through the window blinds, which were ordinary pale-green blinds of the sort supplied by any hotel, even the best, and the voile curtains, also very plain, came a special shade of light, delicate and naked as skin; also like skin, although one knew this was not literally so, the light seemed to contain a secret smell, fragile and erotic.

There was no hurry. You could have lunch first. Kyle always took care of this, ordering it sent over well in advance of her arrival to keep warm in the room-service ovens, heated by spirit lamps. He ordered the foods which Alma liked—no problem since their tastes were so much the same. He and Alma had found to their surprise and pleasure that this taste coincidence held good in many categories besides food, namely, automobiles, people and popular tunes.

He liked Alma Paris. He liked her very much, although he did not express his feelings to himself in just this way; it seemed too crude a way to put them. The best thing you could do with such feelings was leave them alone—but as their affair progressed that was not always possible: he sometimes even put it to himself that he was "passionately fond" of Alma. That seemed right—if anything, it was an understatement. All very well to say to yourself that she was just a friendly, available girl who would do *for now*. Kyle had taken this stance with a number of women in the past—with nearly all women, in fact; it was surprising to discover, on rechecking, how many belonged in this category. Recently, however, he had come to suspect that the practice of categorizing women had, in itself, worn thin—that it had become stupid and meaningless; it wouldn't do at all for Alma.

True, of course, that a fuss had always been raised, through the centuries, about virginity. This was nonsense. Alma's goddamn virginity had almost wrecked their affair. But then, on the other hand, you didn't put a girl *down* because of virginity. From a certain standpoint, it had been a plus.

Kyle looked at his watch. Half past one! The trip to the golf club had taken more time than he'd expected—nor had he known, when he'd suggested two o'clock for his appointment with Alma, that he would have such a busy morning. Alma would be on time. She was always on time, though she did not necessarily expect you to be. That was one of the nice things about Alma; it was a natural part of her, like the seriousness of her dark eyes, which could, in a flash, light up with laughter—or with fury.

There was no hurry but just the same it was high time he ordered; this he now did, directing that with the food his waiter should bring, as always on these special afternoons, a champagne bucket full of ice, but without champagne: the wine Kyle kept in his pantry was far superior to what the hotel could supply, after the long attrition of Prohibition. He lay down on his couch, one of those lamentable imitation *fin-de-siècle* couches with which luxury hotels at that time equipped their suites.

A nap? It would be nice, but noises were issuing from Cottage 15, across the walkway—laughter, of a mixed company, dominated by the nasal bray of the celebrated actor John Barrymore. Mr. Barrymore retained an Ambassador suite permanently against times of marital agitation or to serve his impulse for partying. The crash of a heavy object falling—could it be a body?—ended the merriment.

Kyle closed the window, then lay down again. He wanted to review a sound he had heard in the skim of shallow sleep from which he had been roused: a telephone ringing. This had not been an actual sound, like those emanating from Cottage 15, but part of a dream; he had been thinking of something about Alma and the sound had been the cue: for some time she had been no more than a background person, one more blurred, attractive face and body in the shift of pretty women who came and went in the uneasy mix of film and "society" people at the parties given by Los Angeles hostesses. She had not flirted with him. She stood her own ground and made her own judgments—sharp but not uncharitable ones, as he was to find later. Neither her values nor her sense of being her own person had been damaged by the climate of her parents' genteel, stuffy home or what she described as her "art deco" education at Marlborough.

Alma had refused to conform at Marlborough.

"I wouldn't take showers in the gym. I was terribly shy about my body."

"You like it better now," Kyle had said.

(This conversation had happened further on in their relationship.)

Alma had smiled.

"Much better. You changed me."

"You would have changed anyway."

"Perhaps, but I want you to have the credit. That makes it more personal, like a gift."

The ringing of the telephone cued his memory of that earlier call which had set them both in motion.

She called him at his office. Her manner had been casual and charming, but little in accord with the shyness she attributed to herself. She had invited him to take her to a concert at the Hollywood Bowl.

Someone was knocking on the door of Cottage 17. Kyle let in Feliciano, the waiter, with the rolling tray, the spirit-lamp ovens, the champagne bucket without champagne. He let Feliciano decide where to put everything, not wanting to interrupt the spin of memory.

It had been a pleasant evening. Of that he was sure. All the evenings of those summer days of their courtship had been that way, long twilights stirring with cool airs and a sense of ease. He had gone to her house straight from work, wearing a cotton business suit, looking forward to a martini poured, in the fashion of the times, from a large silver shaker.

There had been no martinis. Instead, Alma had a bottle of white wine open and some sandwiches packed in a basket. After they'd each had two glasses of the wine she fetched another bottle—for the basket. They would get to the Bowl early and picnic while waiting for the orchestra to get there. Alma explained this to him gently, but as something he should have expected. He didn't know much about concerts. The seersucker suit! You could wear anything to the Bowl, anything at all except a business suit and a cotton one at that. It got chilly at night in the Bowl. She made him trade his suit coat for a heavy hacking jacket of her father's. To his surprise, the jacket almost fitted.

"Oh, yes," she'd said, answering a question he had not asked, "he rides. Not the way you do, of course, but he likes it and it's good for him. A groom from Dubrock's brings a horse to the Sunset bridle trail and he goes along there, between the houses."

"But you don't go with him?"

"I'm a beach girl. I was born in Santa Monica."

"That would make you grass-roots California—in a sandy sort of way." Kyle had said, but she had answered seriously,

"I am, I'm afraid—on both sides. But not sandy—citified. Town planning and orange groves and stuff too dull to mention. We're not the hardy souls who came round the Horn and stole land from the Mexicans."

"I see you've heard about the Kinsales."

"I didn't mean *that*."

"It's all right. We were thieves indeed, early on. I try to get by now as a Yale man."

"You're nothing at all like a Yale man."

"What would I be, if I were like one?"

Alma thought about this. She took his arm as they walked out to the car—her car. Kyle had given Mort the night off. He had driven himself, but when they left her house Alma had ignored the big pale Rolls. She was carrying the basket, and she put it in a small Dodge coupé. She handed Kyle the keys.

"Suave. I don't think you're terribly suave."

"I haven't been trying."

"Good, I'm glad. I detest suave people. Also you're very well known. Famous. I think that's nice."

"I'm not sure about that."

"Oh, yes. The oil and all. And the horses. I've never been out with a celebrated person before."

"You'll probably find a lot of them at the Bowl."

"Wearing other people's hacking jackets?"

"Exactly. That's how we turn out, it's sort of a code."

"Have you some way of communicating with one another?"

"Of course. We bang out a signal on our picnic baskets."

"If you don't stop making fun of me," said Alma Paris happily, "I shall get very angry. And then our date will be ruined."

Evening had already settled in the scoops of the hills and there, on the tallest, raggedest hill of all, giant letters braced themselves in queer, spent attitudes against the lovely sky, as if about to fall down, as indeed they were:

HOLLYWOO LAN

With plump brown hands, the knuckles of which bent inward instead of out, souvenirs of prize-ring days, Feliciano, the room-service waiter, arranged the table, the terrapin soup, the watercress salad, the creamed chicken in its chafing dish. There would be strong coffee in the heavy nickel pot and winter strawberries in a bed of ice. Feliciano handed Kyle the check.

"Is there real turtle in that soup, Feliciano?"

"*Sí,* señor, I catch him myself this morning."

"I thought you went to confession this morning."

"I go to confession at Christmas, señor."

"Will you confess how you butted Fidel Labarba in the eye?"

"Fidel, he hit me in the balls, señor."

"That's not what the referee said."

"The referee is married to Fidel's cousin, señor."

"You should pick better referees."

"*Sí,* señor. Enjoy your lunch."

And off went Feliciano with the tray.

Living in a hotel you had such conversations: with Mrs. Kindred, the housekeeper; with Dennis, the head bellman, who owned a quarter interest in a racing car and raced it at the Ascot track; with Rudolpho, maître d' in the Cocoanut Grove, where the name bands played and where, occasionally, you might drop in for a dance or to catch Benny Goodman or Tommy Dorsey or Paul Whiteman.

The conversations were an effort at community—momentary treaties against loneliness, the common enemy, entered into by people without homes.

Kyle had never thought of himself as a homeless person. Home was the ranch. That would never change. You could go back and it would be there; then, renewed by the touch of your mother, the earth, you could rise refreshed and go about your business.

Kyle was sure that Troy and Millie had this feeling too. Troy had recently gone back there to live. He was using the ranch as his permanent headquarters, putting Luanna in charge and Helene in school in Altemira. He commuted to his job by plane—an open-cockpit, tandem-seated Waco. Kyle had warmly approved of this idea when it had come up at the last meeting of the Land and Cattle Company. It would be fine to see the old place as a center of activity once more—far better for Troy, also, than bringing up teen-agers in an oil town.

Millie's situation and Troy's, naturally, were different from his own—Kyle was keenly conscious of this. They had their families, whereas he was still alone. He had sold his house in Burlingame; he'd found that, as KinOil expanded, he was there less and less. Los Angeles was central, and the Ambassador convenient to the office: he had moved into the cottage, planning to stay a month at most and had remained longer than he liked to think. You had a choice, a house or a hotel, and for a house you needed a woman to put in it—and in this context he had been thinking about Alma.

HOLLYWOO LAN had originally been HOLLYWOOD-LAND. Possibly the D's, with their unbalanced curve, had been harder to brace against the slipping, shaly earth up there. Nobody could remember when both were standing, although once, of course, they had been, and in those days a girl had jumped off one of the letters. She had climbed up the studding at the back of the sign, planning to kill herself because she could not get roles as a movie actress. The jump, unfortunately, hadn't gone any better than the acting; she had fallen into the gorge far below and lain there apparently a long time before she had been found.

It was not a pleasant story and Kyle, though he thought of it (as everyone did who knew it, when they looked at the cramped, straggly letters), made no mention of it as he drove along in the small car with Alma Paris, out on their first date.

There was a crush on Highland Avenue. People carrying blankets and cushions (and some, like Alma, baskets) were crossing the street and turning up the paths toward the stadium; carts and buses queued to get into the parking lots. The sky blazed with big summer stars. At first the proscenium shell was dark; then the lights came on and there was a spatter of applause. From the big houses on the crests above the Bowl the rich left their dinner tables and strolled out onto the lawns, stretching out in deck chairs to enjoy the music from afar.

Alma had seats in the reserved section; here she and Kyle ate the sandwiches and drank the wine. People were hurrying in now from all directions, but it seemed impossible that the enormous amphitheater could ever be full. Then suddenly it was. The musicians, hardly noticed, had taken their seats; the audience lights went out and across the furnace opening of the shell a tiny man with a brown face and bushy silver hair dashed in, ignoring the applause which his entry occasioned, and whacked on a music rack with his baton. With three somber, crashing chords the concert began.

3

The three chords. They, or the piece they had introduced, had been the theme of the next three months, the months of his courtship. Perhaps there was no other term for it, just as there was no name, or none known to him, for the musical composition itself.

Well, if it had been a courtship, certainly Alma, rather than he, had been running it; she enjoyed watching polo, when he had time to play, and she took an interest in his racing stable, but when he talked about his oil deals her attention wandered. Money, in her eyes, was a convenience—not much more. Its availability could be taken for granted, hence its acquisition held no fascination. Not large amounts of money: that was something different—she had never considered money in the terms in which he thought of it, as a tool, a means to power. He could not explain this to her and after one or two attempts he stopped trying. There was no reason for him to drag her into an alien world when she shared her own, pleasanter one so bountifully: the books she liked (even if Kyle had only time to leaf through them); the people she found interesting (even if he found them less so); the openings of new films (she frequently knew people in the cast, though not the stars); the performances of aging Broadway hits, effectively staged at the Pasadena Community Playhouse. Now and then they went to parties—the queer Los Angeles mixes of ages and professions, of good styles and bad: generally her friends' parties, seldom his, but in either case the type of gathering in which cordiality between strangers is stimulated by the hope that one will not see these people again—combined with the conviction that somehow one will.

"I'd like you to meet the girl who's giving this," Alma

would say. "She's heard about you . . ." or "It will be boring, but we'll just stop in for a drink . . ."

At most of the parties there would be a sprinkling of well-known people, in or out of the arts. Such was the nature of the city—the famous would be on hand, whether you wanted them or not. But even when they were around in profusion Kyle's presence had an impact that amused Alma. She liked to make a grand entrance on his arm, then take him away before the hostess could exploit his celebrity.

"They don't know what to make of you," she said with satisfaction.

In her own home his status was equally equivocal, but this was changing. He had been accepted on a conditional basis. If, at his age and with his conspicuity, he had been a foreigner, with or without title, or a Texan—even an Easterner, unless one with impeccable credentials—he would have met little favor. But he was a Californian, and a notable one, and somehow thus to be judged on merit and performance. No longer did Alma rush to the front door in person to answer his ring, ready on the dot, checking her handbag for comb, key, lipstick and mad money, calling goodbye over her shoulder to invisible stay-at-homes. On his third visit Kyle had met Gallatin Paris, her father, proprietor of the hacking jacket, a massive, preoccupied man who wore an eyeshade while reading financial papers in a small, stuffy room between the living room and a porchlike enclosure known in the family (erroneously) as the arboretum. Plants grew there, not trees. There were a lot of plants there and several birds in cages. The birds were silent but from the plants came rustlings and a sound of gently spraying water. It was in the arboretum that Kyle first kissed Alma Paris. He took his time, getting around to this, but with Alma, in the rush of his own life, he had the feeling that it was well to take all the time he wanted.

The Parises' house stood on a valuable corner lot in a midtown residential district. Mrs. Paris' father had given it to Ernestine Paris as a dower. It was a stout, gloomy house, planted firmly in the middle of its huge lot. Perhaps when first built, before the city, which in those days lay to the east, had caught up with it, the house might have seemed large, a mansion, but it had diminished, it had pulled in on itself, conserving its stubborn strength to defy the apartment houses which had reared up around it like titanic gravestones.

The rooms of the house had shrunk also. They had

clustered together. Mrs. Paris had them cleaned constantly but she did not allow the curtains to be opened, so the rooms were dark, lightened only by the intense tiny beam of the light by which Mr. Paris, with his eyeshade, sat reading. Every day, after riding his horse, he read the financial papers, then he listened to the radio. He did not drink or smoke and he kept himself very quiet in the compact dark house, reading about what was happening in the world he had left.

He had retired too soon, Alma said. He had been a developer of certain areas east of the city, very good ones. There was a Paris Boulevard in Burbank and a Paris Park in Glendale, and if people imagined that the name referred to the French city rather than to a native individual, that was their mistake; it took nothing from him. He chatted with Kyle about the market, tactfully omitting reference to the fall in KinOil Common. Kyle appreciated his consideration. Mr. Paris was accepting him on the basis of his daughter's interest, and Kyle appreciated this also. After the first few meetings, and one rather uncomfortable, probably unnecessary family dinner of four (". . . at least *that's* over with" was Alma's summation), Kyle found a bottle of Chivas Regal and one glass set out for him when he brought Alma home. There was no glass for Alma. She could of course go out to the pantry and get what she wanted but her father did not encourage her to drink at home, or anywhere else, for that matter.

But he trusted her judgment.

Mrs. Paris was a different sort. She was medium-sized with a humorous look to her and a bold scratchy voice. Now and then she looked at Kyle as if to say, "Well, my lad, if I were a few years younger I could give my daughter a run for it, make no mistake!" She had Alma's coloring and must have been a beauty in her day, and as if in memory of that lost era she still had a man or two hanging around—"to pay compliments," Alma said: an obliging young chap, son of her husband's former business partner, who owned a theatrical makeup business, and a plump little man who lectured on travel. Thus a small swirl of activity moved around Mrs. Paris; all true life in the house centered in Alma. She came and went with her light step, with her flashing eyes; she made her parents no major concessions, yielded up no privacy, but she never put them down; she was kind to them without being patronizing, and gay when she could be. Her own rooms were the best in the house, the only ones with light in them: she had taken over the suite of a sister who had left to get married; she had redecorated it, making the drapes herself, and stuffed it with books, pictures and musical instruments, several of which she could play. She had been of marriageable age now—for how long? Well, five years, if the first milestone was eighteen. Yet it was easy to see why, though marriage bound by all the conventions of her upbringing and her times, she had failed to find a husband among the men on her club beach or the Spring Street bachelors with their padded-shoulder suits and polite bleached faces with whom her mother had been trying to match her. She would have been too much for them on every count as they and she well knew; even the stupidest of them would have been able to penetrate the role with which, out of modesty or desperation, she would have had to camouflage her quick, mocking intelligence, her impatience with shams and her excitement about life in all forms, life itself:

"I'm a beach girl."

Kyle had not been deluded. He recognized her early on as an exceptional person, a delight to be with and—if you were to accept her professed lack of sexual experience—a challenge. Perhaps no more but . . . certainly that! He was also in her debt for redirecting him to cultural pastimes that he had responded to at Yale but never seemed to have had time for, the books and the shows and the concerts. The concerts appealed to him most, he could not have said why. He began to watch the papers for announcements and would always choose the Bowl as against any other proposal, if a concert were on.

This had pleased Alma.

"How could you have missed music till now, when it means so much to you?"

"I like it. But I don't think you're right, that it means anything."

"But it does. You *listen,* so few people do."

"I can't very well turn my ears off."

"Your *ear,* you mean. The other night, when I couldn't remember the Ravel, you whistled it for me."

"What's so remarkable about that?"

"I've heard it half a dozen times, and I couldn't whistle it—though my ear isn't bad. I couldn't even work it out on the piano. And you'd only heard it once!"

Kyle puffed his cigar.

"Do you suppose an ear, as you call it, could be inherited? Because I suspect that one branch of my family was musical. Or at least could have been; there's evidence to that effect."

And he told her about the De Bacas' grand piano.

". . . it wasn't the only one in California, though we claimed it was. General Vallejo had one, in Sonoma. But I don't think the De Bacas knew it. They didn't get on with the Vallejos; they regarded them as upstarts and troublemakers."

In bits and pieces he told her about the De Bacas. And about the Kinsales, Millie and Troy, and about Hub, and the manner of his dying, and Cal Kinsale and the Embarcadero auction business. But most importantly, somewhat later, about his mother, and how he had gone into the closet that day, among the clothes that carried her presence in their smell and feel, the dresses on their hangers like frail loving versions of herself, alive, but she hanging there dead. And no explanation for it.

He had more or less blocked all this out of his mind, and still could not remember most of it with clarity. There was something blurred—too bad to be otherwise. And as he spoke, this memory he had never been able to share forced itself up so that the woman with him could plumb this depth, understand this part of him, the coldness he had experienced before, in connection with this memory, spread over him— his skin, his lips. Why his lips?

Telling it to Alma, he had chosen an unlikely place—sitting in Montmartre, a private nightclub on Hollywood Boulevard, where a conventional band alternated with a Brazilian combo playing the rumbas and sambas then coming into vogue.

Alma had sat quietly, holding his hand below the table. Alma had said: "The reason might just have been madness. That happens to some people, especially Spanish and Mexican people. I've read about that and I've seen it too, that mournfulness beyond words. You can hear it in their songs."

"Yes . . ."

"A black mournfulness that could also be a kind of madness. It might come out of history, their history is so awful, such terrible suffering in it. No other countries have it that way, that kind of dark madness."

"Except maybe the Russians," Kyle had said.

He had never thought of it this way before—the tragedy of his mother being part of a larger ethnic tragedy, impersonal and hence more acceptable.

"Yes," he said, thinking about it, "a Dostoevskian thing, that kind of thing. Terrible. And speaking of inheritances and so forth, there was that inheritance too, specifically. She had a sister who killed herself. She jumped overboard from a ship at sea. The captain stopped the ship and put out a boat and saved her. This was another family story. We heard it much later. She was saved, but it didn't do any good; later on she killed herself some other way."

Alma nodded.

"So you see, it could have been that way. Not impossible to understand, even if it doesn't bear thinking about."

Kyle had been grateful for those words. No longer as shaken as he had been when he dredged up the memory from the dark of boyhood sorrow he had sat at the table finishing his drink and restoring order to his feelings; presently the orchestra or the combo had begun playing again and he and Alma had got up to dance and he felt the warmth of her go through him like a dark swift wave.

4

That had been one of their evenings. There had been many others, not all so easily remembered but all making a total of a time that was memorable overall, a leisured stretch of good living and of slowly coming together. The evenings were long and easy, with huge, dusty sunsets tumbling into them from the unseen Pacific and the stiff parade of tufted palm trees stretching to catch the last of the light, high overhead, along the avenues where they walked or drove.

Alma liked to dance. She liked being with people also and Kyle understood that since people and the enjoyment of them were so much a part of his own life; he understood also that people were not easy for her to reach. Because of his different placement in life, his growing fame for *something* (though just what, at that point, no one seemed sure), his grand wealth and, above all, his age, they were easiest when alone. The separateness which enclosed each during the day, holding them apart, formed a field of force that locked them fast the moment they were together.

There was no hurry about anything. Above all there was no hurry about going to bed together. This was something just over the horizon, held in abeyance in the float of the wide yellow evenings—a predictable event, but as yet uncharted, and resistant to examination.

There were certain times and rooms, certain restaurants and situations, when its inevitability seemed more pronounced than at other times, other places. One of the good situations was the dancing. For this they went sometimes to the chic and famous places along the Sunset Strip: the Trocadero, with its crush of celebrities; the Clover Club, which provided a small, delightful dancing room carefully walled off from the gambling rooms adjacent. There were also the little clubs, springing up on the side streets, some quite expensive, with excellent bands or combos. Kyle learned new steps. Hitherto he had looked upon dancing, as Clausewitz upon war, as a continuation of policy by other means. Alma changed all that. With her, dancing was a commitment, like eating or breathing. It was also the exercise of a talent; she was extraordinarily good at it. When she stood up for the Latin dances she rippled with the secret pulse of clitoral lust; when you put your arm around her for a fox-trot her body became air, you levitated with it as if you were dancing on the ceiling.

Alma and Kyle danced, that summer of 1934, two or three times a week. They had taken to going out almost every night, except on those nights, welcome as a change, when her parents had an engagement elsewhere and she fixed him dinner at home. Her cooking was as bad as her dancing was good, but Kyle ate up everything, even the most atrocious dishes, with an appetite that was far from assumed. There was no hurry. A day would pass in this or that activity, removed from Alma, but the day would be over finally and the gulfs of dusty light would widen in the sky. He would take a shower at his hotel and get out of the business suit and into the kind of clothes which were acceptable to Alma, the slacks and open shirts, the blazers with the fake yacht club patch on the left pocket. He would park the Rolls a block from her house; she had told him, after his second visit, that she didn't want it parked in front. The edict was a product of her "shyness." Kyle understood. He did everything the way Alma wanted. It was easier that way. He just wanted everything to take its course.

It never occurred to him that he was cheating. This notion popped up much later. It was ridiculous, but he could see how it applied. By the standards of that time, if you were out with an "eligible" girl, you tried, immediately, to hustle her into bed. That was the honest way. It proved you had no serious intentions. If she took you up, the risk was hers. You had declared yourself. This was for fun, regardless of what twists and turns the matter might take later on. But if, on the other hand, with a girl like Alma, if you were headed down a different path, then you did exactly what he had been doing. You went slowly. You went out in the yellow evening light and let a mood build up; you sat late at little tables, talking, touching, and the field of force took hold of you and squeezed you together till your lips mashed in, till your veins turned blue. Ha, old boy, where were you then? What was the next move, old pal? Make no mistake about it, you were in deadly peril or in line for a great prize, depending upon how you looked at it.

Kyle suggested to Alma one day that they drive down to Mexico for the weekend, and she, in the same offhand manner, accepted.

For her family, she arranged some acceptable alibi.

5

They drove south through an overcast which cleared as they reached the Coast Highway; they passed Signal Hill, with its tangled mop of derricks, like a wig of iron hair, to the clarinet licks of Benny Goodman's "Stompin' at the Savoy" on the car radio; at Balboa fierce little sailboats jockeyed in the harbor mouth and the Goodman band did "Sing, Sing, Sing"; somewhere along the way they lunched on cucumbers and fresh abalone which turned out to be as tough as rubber. Alma moved over in the front seat and laid her head on Kyle's shoulder, not waking until they were through Tijuana.

Forty miles south of the border an old truck lay on its side. Three Mexicans leaned against it. Hay had spilled onto the road. The three *compañeros* waved happily as Kyle slowed down.

"Hi, señor . . . you got a rope? Help us, señor . . ."

Kyle stopped, studied the hay with care, then backed up and punched it aside with the grille and bumper of the Dodge. The Rolls would have done it better, but he managed with the headlights intact. The *compañeros* at the roadside might indeed have been in trouble but he doubted it. They had seemed disturbed as he drove off.

You did not stop, and above all you did not get out of your car, on a Mexican road, that year, if you could help it.

La Playa Hotel at Ensenada was a large arrangement of Moorish-Spanish masonry wedged into a cliff above the sea. A card in the suite advised the hotel guests that games of chance were conducted nightly in the lounge.

This delighted Alma.

"Oh, I've never gambled."

"You could have done it anytime, in the Clover Club."

"That's different. It's illegal, and I've heard they cheat. It's nicer here!"

"I'm sure it's quite all right."

"I'm going to gamble like mad," Alma said firmly.

She had brought two large suitcases with her. Kyle wondered whether she intended extending the weekend to further travel, possibly around the world. She unpacked systematically, producing a "travel set" of toilet articles, obviously never used before, which she arranged on the dresser; she also had tissue paper and she lined a drawer with it—the drawer for her underthings.

"Do people dress for dinner here?" she aksed with sudden suspicion.

"Well, not black tie or anything."

"Heavens, I don't mean that. Just dress, to look nice."

"A lot of them, probably."

"Most of them?"

"I suppose so."

"Well, I'm going to," said Alma.

"Fine. Then I will too."

Alma went into the bathroom and turned on the water in the black marble tub. When she came back she kissed Kyle passionately but refused to be drawn over to the bed—a huge Spanish four-poster.

"I just thought we might relax a little."

"Later, sweetheart. Do you mind? I'm so icky from the trip and all."

"Of course. I'll have them bring up some margaritas."

"Tell them to bring wine for me."

The drinks came up. Kyle tried to take Alma's in to her but found the bathroom door locked; when she came out she had on a most becoming robe of heavy, clinging silk. She put on garments from the drawer lined with tissue paper without taking off the robe.

Kyle lay on the bed and took a short nap before going in for his own bath. He left the door slightly open but nothing came of that so he dozed some more in the bath water. He didn't feel as easy with Alma as he had in the early times of their courtship on the sunset-dusted avenues and later in the little dancing clubs but he was glad they'd come to Ensenada and he was looking forward to the evening very much.

Dinner was wonderful. The service might have been a little slow but that made no difference since the food was so good. They ate in a high-ceilinged room with intricately carved wood paneling; mariachi singers strolled among the tables and through the stalls. The restaurant interior had obviously once been part of a church and the ecclesiastic atmosphere was carried out in the pewlike squares in which the tables were enclosed. Candles supplied the only light. Something had gone wrong with the electricity. *Roto!* It would be fixed in the morning, the waiter said, but the barman, possibly better informed, suggested that the trouble was not in the fuses but nonpayment of the bill. It was a matter of no importance since one could see to eat and drink perfectly well without electric light, and to gamble also.

Alma played twenty-one. She bought her own chips, paying for them with a hundred-dollar bill she produced from her bra. She did not understand the game and kept standing on the wrong cards; when the hundred was gone she borrowed another from Kyle and lost most of that too.

A Mexican lady sitting next to her at the table tried to give advice. She was a wiry little lady with prominent small breasts. She had gold paint on her fingernails and a good command of English.

"*Diecisiete, querida*—that is the number seventeen. If you have seventeen, you do not ask for the next card. Is right, señor?"

The lady touched Kyle's hand and smiled at him brightly, seeking his support.

"Absolutely."

"At least seventeen," said the lady. "I am playing every night, always winning. *Más o menos*. If not seventeen, I do not ask. Otherwise I lose."

"I know all that," said Alma.

Holding a ten and a six, she rapped for a card, drew a five and made twenty-one. She had recouped her losses and made a profit besides, ignoring the lady's rule.

"Thank you for your advice, señora," she said acidly to the

wiry lady. She took Kyle's arm possessively. "Shall we go, darling?" As they walked back to their suite, their arms around each other, she said, "That bitch was trying to flirt with you."

"I think she plays for the house. She knew that if you didn't win a little you'd get bored and quit."

"Darling," said Alma, "she was flirting. A woman knows these things. I should have slapped her face. She is a complete bitch and a whore as well."

"Times are tough everywhere," Kyle said mildly.

"You shouldn't joke about it."

In the living room of the suite an oil lamp was burning on the desk and candles on the smaller tables; the windows were open and the air smelled of flowers, wax and damp grass.

Alma looked around the sitting room like a hostess wondering how to seat a dinner party.

"Darling, would you mind waiting here for a minute?"

"Whatever you say."

Alma kissed him lightly. She smiled at him with strained, unfamiliar lips and disappeared into the bedroom.

Kyle lit a cigar and looked out the window. What am I doing here with this virgin? he thought. He wanted a drink in the worst way but the Chivas he had brought was in his suitcase in the bedroom. He stood looking across the patio at the shadowy figures of the people standing and sitting at the gaming tables in the candlelight.

"Darling . . ."

Alma had come in soundlessly. She had put on fresh makeup and redone her hair. She had on several yards of diaphanous dry goods which, when he came closer, were seen to consist of two pieces, an underneath thing that was probably a nightgown and an overthing, made to be part of it, that was a robe. Her huge black eyes were blazing with excitement and torment.

"Do you like it?"

"Love it!"

"I bought it specially for the trip."

With a lovely, perhaps precalculated motion, she let herself slip down his body. She knelt at his feet with her arms around his thighs.

"Make love to me."

"Well, not in here."

"Oh, I didn't mean *here* . . ."

"Come on, then."

He drew her up. He wondered whether he was supposed to carry her into the bedroom, in the romantic style which seemed to have taken over, but it was not all that easy to carry a girl as big as Alma. So he half carried her. He undressed quickly and jumped into bed beside her. Still wrapped in the bridal layers of filmy stuff, she kissed him. He could feel her shivering.

"Darling, I love you."

"I love you too."

"Then hold me."

"I am holding you."

"Then kiss me some more."

Kyle kissed her. Her lips felt like rubber bands. The lovely warmth which was her body's best gift turned itself off. He kissed her again and she moaned. Her hand plunged recklessly down and she took hold of his penis. She manipulated it a little, then clutched it as if she would never let go. After a while, he disengaged her fingers; he was a long way from having an erection.

Silence fell. Through the windows, mixed with the soft tropical odors, he could hear the people at the gambling tables and the singing of the mariachis in the rooms beyond. Presently from Alma's side of the bed came a light snore, then a harsher one, and then more and more regular breathing of a healthy young woman in the first sleep of her night.

Heat sprang back into Alma's body. It radiated from her, a dark, soft current, through the wedding-night negligee and stuff.

Kyle began to sweat. Easing himself quietly off the bed, he took a shower, then put his clothes back on. He stood beside the bed, listening to Alma's breathing. Little chance of its changing, he thought, for some time. No harm in stirring around a bit.

He went to the gambling rooms and played for three hours, winning at every game he tried—five straight passes at the crap table, a dull stretch at roulette (two zeros on the wheel, as against the single zero at European tables), then a cleanup at twenty-one. Dawn, behind the eastern hills, was as cold as a diceman's smile when he let himself back into the suite.

The bedroom was a blazing box of light—electric light!

A miracle! Either that or sometime in the last few hours,

unknown as yet in the public rooms of the hotel, a repair had been made or a computation entered that allowed the current to flow, that forced it into bulbs above washstands, into wall sockets, and into table and standing lamps, several of which now lay on the floor, mangled, destroyed. Drawers had been dumped, a mirror broken, chairs upset, bedclothes ripped. The place looked like a hideout where a fugitive had been captured after a long battle and the scene left untouched to provide the news photographers with pictures.

"Alma!" Kyle yelled in horror. "What's happened?"

"Go on back to her!" she said.

"Christ, what's wrong?"

"You've been screwing her, you bastard. Don't come sniffing around *me."*

Alma's bosom heaved, her breath jerked in and out in hopeless gasps.

"What woman? What the hell are you talking about?"

"DON'T LIE!"

"I swear before Christ, Alma, you've lost your mind."

"Oh, yes? Well, I *know,* so don't give me any of your lying filth."

She swung at him with amazing speed, hitting him on the nose with the heel of her hand.

"Get out of here, you son of a bitch!"

"All right, I'll get out. But you'd better understand—*there is no woman.* It's all some insanity."

"Of course there's a woman!" She rolled over onto her face. Her words came up half muffled. "That's why you didn't get an erection. You . . . . *didn't want to!* You were saving it for her!"

"Jesus Christ . . . ."

"You made me go to sleep . . . and then . . . you went back to find her . . ."

Kyle seized her by the shoulders. He rolled her right side up. His nose was bleeding, the blood dripping onto her body.

"What goddamn woman? *Just answer that one question: What woman do you mean?"*

Alma's throat had contracted. She gulped; she could not utter a sound. When her voice at last came out it was a thready whisper, like a voice from the grave.

"The woman with the gold fingernails. The whore at the . . . twenty-one table . . ."

"So that's it!"

"Yes . . . and you know it . . . so don't pretend any more . . ."

"Alma!"

"All your *pretending* . . . you should have been an actor . . . you could have *been paid* for it . . ."

"Alma, look!"

From the pockets of his jacket—now a ruin—from his pants, his shirt, his wallet, as he discarded these, he pulled the money he'd won—pesos, pesos in denominations of tens, of hundreds, and one bunch of thousands, pesos loose, pesos wrinkled and crumpled, pesos in bundles, bound neatly with rubber bands. He threw them at her, at the bed, into the air, he spilled them onto the floor.

"That's why I went back . . . I couldn't sleep and I . . . went back to gamble . . ."

"Oh, my God!"

"There was no woman. I never saw that fool again. I went back to *pass the time* . . . That was all, but—"

"Oh, dearest, sweetheart . . ."

"I won . . ."

He dropped his shorts. His erection was unexpected, but it was notable and getting more so.

"Honey . . . she was flirting with you and . . . oh, God . . ."

"Forget it."

"Oh, darling . . . go inside me . . ."

Alma's body, which had been moving on the bed with a rhythm all its own, became still, as if in a seizure. Her legs strained apart. She hunched forward, guiding him into her with both hands. On her face, twisted sideways on the bare mattress, was an expression of savage, childish glee.

"Way up . . . inside of me . . . way up . . . oh, sweetheart, that's good, oh, darling . . . keep on . . . oh, that's so good . . . that's so wonderful . . ."

Her vaginal muscles, unused, unbeloved, closed around him tighter and tighter as her orgasm approached, clasping him with inexpressible hunger. And for Kyle, the long day, the long drive, the embarrassment of his impotency, the elation of his gambling coups, all smoked away . . . the only reality was this woman, so unremarkable and yet unique, this person whom he desired above all others. He had a momentary thought that he might just . . . might not make it, since it meant too much . . . but this passed also and he knew that everything was as it ought to be. Alma, at this point, was saying something, probably what a girl was supposed to say in that era, an untouched, expensively educated girl, highly protected and presumed to be fertile, something about *pulling out* . . . but bugger to that, there had been no maidenly obstruction, no physical certification of the blue-ribbon virginity that was supposed to be delivered with Alma, and which could nevertheless still be a fact. They'd come a long, rocky road to this encounter which he now proposed to enjoy without let or hindrance or, above all, Jesus! interruptus, and he drove on into the beautiful bigness and tightness of Alma until his sperm exploded and he felt it sloshing into her in long, heavy spurts.

6

"Nobody," she said later with feeling, "nobody ever had such a wonderful trip."

There was always, in her reminiscence of that trip to Ensenada, the peculiar emphasis on the word "trip," as if in the private lexicon of Alma it had been enlarged to mean something more, to expand in rubrics until it became "wedding trip."

Now the word "love," which had been banned, came into currency; both used it—Kyle sparingly (he was still, in his own phraseology, "passionately fond" of her); Alma more freely. Even today, in Cottage 17, in the winter light with its patinalike skin, filtered through the voile curtains, the hotel window blinds, after the good lunch and a certain amount of the excellent champagne, "lovemaking" was the accepted term for what they were doing. It was appropriate; there was a new conjugality about them now, something wifely in the way she undressed, paying dues to the banished shyness only for a second or two, that moment when she slipped out of the last thing, turning her back, the wifely curve of her buttocks, the submissiveness of her neck to his view, stepping out of the thing, deliciously, before lying down to embrace him.

She was filling out—and this too became her. She was still the Santa Monica beach girl who could take her hundred-pound pine surfboard from the section of surfboard lockers at the Beach Club and carry it down to the waves as lightly as if it had been a paddle or a parasol; her waist was still tiny for so big a girl, her thighs arched without a trace of extra fat on them—only her breasts were bigger now, stronger in their uprightness and the nipples darker. "That's because I'm happy," she said with a smashing smile when he commented, in a carefully understated fashion, on her improved proportions. "It's another benefit of being with you."

Today Alma left early. Her mother wanted her to attend some party for a titled European person, the sort of party that Kyle would be sure to find fault with. Alma would do as her mother asked unless he, Kyle, wanted her to stay with him, and he did not want this; they'd had a fine Sunday, but he had other things to think about. However, since it was expected of him, Kyle found fault with the party in advance. He suspected that the titled person was a Nazi. He lectured Alma sternly about this. The new Hitler regime, in power almost two years, was sending out these Prussian nobles, when it could get hold of them, as public relations people. Hitler thought they might persuade the Western nations that Germany was a proper field for investments. He had proselyted capitalists in Spain, in England and even in France to put money into German industry.

Kyle directed Alma to check the guest of honor out. Her father might know about him. If he was a Nazi or a Nazi sympathizer, she was to stay away from the party. Alma consented. She was quite surprised at his stern tone. To make up for it, Kyle was very tender, very loving with her as he walked with her from the cottage to the parking lot where she had left the Dodge.

7

All day, in spite of his sense of well-being, his satisfaction in the interview with H. H. Atlass, he had kept turning back to the early-morning scene with Custis, heard again his suggestion that someone in the family had been liquidating KinOil stock. He could not, would not sleep until he had looked into this.

He called Millie in Dead Eagle Valley and relayed his fears to her.

". . . and Lamar thinks the selling is all coming from the West Coast."

"Oh, my God. But who could it be?"

"Someone with big holdings."

"What about the aunts and cousins, a few thousand shares here, a few more there—"

"Possible. But only if a lot of them—nearly all—wanted immediate cash, or if they lost faith in company operations and acted together. Have you had wind of anything like that?"

"Never!"

"All right. You could still make some inquiries in that direction. You can do it more easily than I could from here. But the main thing I want you to do is this, and I don't want it done on the telephone. Go to the San Francisco office tomorrow and talk to the stock transfer agent for KinOil. As secretary for the parent entity, Kinsale Land and Cattle, you have access to his books."

"Scott Stanfus . . ."

"Yes."

"But of course. Scott and I are the best of friends."

"So you've been poking around KinOil," Kyle said easily. But there was an edge to his voice.

"Poking around! Well, I like that! I like figures, remember? I can read them. I poke around anywhere that I can find them."

"Good."

There was a pause, with static from the northern farm line heavy on the wire: a reminder that ears other than their own might be listening to the conversation. But in spite of this likelihood Millie burst out: "Kyle, you fool, are you suspecting *us*? Doc and *me*?"

"I'm not suspecting anyone. I'm just trying to arrive at some facts."

"Well, it's not us. We don't need money. Even if there was no KinOil we wouldn't need money. Doc is a physician, for Christ's sake. He has a *practice*."

"I know that."

"And even if we did need money, we would never, under any circumstances—"

"I told you, I'm not thinking anything, I'm—"

"Yes, you are. *You are!* Oh, Kyle . . ."

"I'm checking out all the angles."

"*Not Troy!* But if you called, if you so much as hinted that you—"

"I'm taking that into consideration."

"He loves you; he loves all of us. And there he is, stuck out there in the dunes, while you wheel and deal. Don't you see how he would react?"

"Millie," said Kyle, "I'm going to call Troy. I'm not an idiot. I'll know what to say."

Millie sighed. Or perhaps the rustle that came to Kyle's ear was just a murmur of the sagging, squirrely wire, or the scrape of some eavesdropper, bored now, hanging up a receiver. Then she said: "All right. Now tell me what I'm supposed to do when I see Scott Stanfus."

CHAPTER EIGHT

The Doctor's Wife

1

Stanfus investigated, as ordered, but nothing came of it, and Millie's fears of division between her brothers lessened. There was other evidence also that the two were on good terms.

Kyle planned to give a party at the ranch later in the month. He needed Troy's consent for this since Troy, having gone back there to live, was now much more than a sharer in the old place, he was its proprietor, and the ranch, which since Hub's death had been used mostly as a center for VIP gatherings and the yearly Land and Cattle Company meetings, was once more, handsomely and appropriately, a family home.

Kyle loved what had come to be known as his "conquest parties." He made elaborate plans for them. He chartered limousines and airplanes and ran private railroad cars to the ranch station as in the blazer-and-boater celebrations of his youth. The festivities had been getting fancier with each company KinOil took over—Brookshire Petroleum, then Trigg-Liggett, and, in that order, Coachella Drilling, Hull Exploration, and Jack Rabbit Mountain.

This one—to celebrate the acquisition of Atlass International—was to be the biggest, brassiest wingding of all.

"*. . . KinOil honors its new board member and Vice President for Research and Development, Mr. Henry Harmon Atlass . . .*"

So said the engraved invitations—crap, of course.

Kyle pretended he was extending the hand of friendship to the victims of his takeovers when he was really parading them in chains, Roman style, under what Doc called an "Arc de Rawhide."

A conquest party in December! It could hardly have come at a worse time. There was more than the usual run of winter sickness loose in Dead Eagle Valley; Doc was working much too hard. Millie was worried about him. She could ill afford just now to be away from the clinic, using her energies for a purely frivolous purpose. Rich people did that, of course, and she was now rich; there was no doubt of it. She was very rich indeed, but in some strange way the new richness had given her more to do than she'd had before it happened, just as the new medical facilities, the sophisticated equipment and the bright assistants, Dr. Wilde and Dr. Sotomayer, had trapped Doc into doing more and relaxing less. Not that she would have gone back to the old days. You lived with what you had, but Millie privately wished Kyle weren't set on giving an Arc de Rawhide a week before Christmas.

The one comfort this time was Luanna. As the hostess in residence she could have refused to give the party, in which case Millie could have begged off the preparations. Not that either would have acted in this manner, not for the world. It would have been impractical.

Kyle always got what he wanted.

At least Luanna was on hand to help; Millie felt grateful for this. She liked her sister-in-law and got on well with her, and when it popped into her mind, as it had from time to time, that she would have preferred to see Troy with a more stylish wife, she put the thought aside as unworthy. She herself was not stylish, heaven forbid; she was a country doctor's wife, she knew her job, but she appreciated style in others, particularly in men, and she recognized that a woman, the right sort of woman, extended a man's style and set it off. Kyle's style, of course, was superb—one did not have to be his sister to see that. He would have trouble finding a woman to match it, let alone one who could adorn it—which might be the reason, or one of the reasons, that he'd never married. Troy, on the other hand—well, Troy was quieter; he might have done with a calmer woman, a less restless woman than this person with the Cherokee red in her eyes above the high Indian cheekbones.

Such had been Millie's estimate of Luanna—until Luanna had moved to the ranch; from which time on Millie had changed her opinion considerably.

Luanna possessed skills never learned in a wickiup or needed, for that matter, in the Oklahoma, Texas and California oil towns where the couple had lived when first married.

She had not changed the basic look of the house. Nobody would have stood for that, as she must have known; the open feeling of it was still there, the glint of old wood and the stir of air through the big downstairs rooms, the diffusion of light in the evenings through panels of colored glass surrounding or surmounting doorway spaces without doors; the morning smells of coffee and of cleaning wax and brass polish and of apricot and eucalyptus firewood even when no fires were alight. Basically, it was the same house but there were changes now, significant ones and all to the good. New carpets, new wallpapers, new kitchen; a dab of alteration here and there, nothing much. Such furniture as had been added was suitably chosen. Millie found it difficult, in renovated bedrooms, to be sure which pieces had always been there and which were additions. There was a new north wing with a library in it and a lovely sitting room. There were servants' quarters and new bathrooms and a big new guesthouse Kyle had put in for business entertaining, pulling out part of a prune orchard to make room for it. The house, in its new guise, would have different functions to perform than it had had before, and it was ready.

The servants were the biggest change of all. You might still walk in with horseshit on your boots, as in Hub's time, and you might take the boots off in the front room, if you were that kind of redneck; you might stand them by the fireplace, but if you did that now, in the house, someone would come along, unseen by you, and take them away and clean them and return them upstairs, to your closet, where they belonged.

This was now, for example, the sort of house which would never run out of towels. They would be available, no matter what—fluffy piles of them, all sizes and colors, in every bathroom, placed on racks through which heat ran to keep them warm—but you would never see the people who put them there or took them away after you had used them.

The old headquarters house was now the sort of house

which Millie's, on its ledge above Dead Eagle Valley, would never be—a place in which the rich could live.

"You've done a wonderful job," she told Luanna. "I never knew it *could* be done in just this way."

"Oh, it wasn't my job, not my doing at all," said Luanna. "But thank you, it's so nice of you to say that. Everyone says it, so I guess it's all right."

She smiled, but in a hesitant way, her lips pulled down as if she were embarrassed by the compliment.

"But of course it was your doing. Who else would have managed it? Not Troy; you could say he had but I wouldn't believe you. Troy wouldn't have known where to begin."

The two women were in the silver closet, checking the services to be used at the party—the heavy Spanish silver handed down in the De Baca line, with the old steer's head marking on it, and the lighter plate bought later by Millie's mother or given as wedding presents when she married Hub. Two sets—far from the most pretentious—belonged to the Bradens, left here partly for safekeeping and partly because Millie, after all, had scant use for them.

"He did know where to begin, though," said Luanna quietly. "He hired someone."

Millie stared at her.

"Are you funnin' me?"

"No, of course not. Why should I? It's true."

"Well, I never heard of that."

"He might not want me to tell you. But he never said—"

"Troy? Oh, my goodness!" Millie's fleshy body shook with delight at this revelation. "I just never *thought* of such a thing. But of course he wouldn't mind. If Troy does something he doesn't care who knows. Above all, family."

"That's why I told you. Somebody from San Francisco. A very wonderful woman. She recommended an architect, Mr. Maybeck. That was for the new part; he drew the plans and all. But Mrs. Crocker did the rest. She didn't have to tell us what she bought. She just ordered everything and had it sent down. One armoire wouldn't go upstairs. The men had to take a window out and drag it up on ropes."

"Crocker is a famous San Francisco name."

"Troy knew that. She comes from that family too, but not the main branch. So she does this work. Troy heard of her through the bank. She is an old-fashioned person and at first I didn't like her but I finally did."

"Did she hire the servants too?"

"She picked them out. I'm going to fire some of them."

"They seem to do very well."

"I can get others. That butler. Every time I walk into the dining room he stares at my ass. He'll be the first out! Just the minute this party is over."

Luanna's full, rough-looking lips flattened and the red lights glinted in her eyes.

Millie nodded gravely. "I don't blame you." She paused, then went on: "You wouldn't really need a serving man, unless you plan to entertain. Just a good cook would do."

"You have Doc, Millie," said Luanna quietly; "you have your own life. It's different for you. I've lived in oil towns all my life, I'm sick of oil towns. I wanted Troy to move back here long before he did. This is his home, he belongs here and so do we. He can go to Kinsalem all he needs to, in the plane, and be here the rest of the time. He's not so busy anyway, now with production cut back. Helene will have a decent place to grow up in. She can go to Altemira High. I don't want her in school back east, like Cliff."

"I thought possibly you put him there because Kyle went east to college."

"No," said Luanna firmly, "we would much rather have had him at Berkeley or Stanford. We're not copying Kyle in anything. And I'll tell you something else, Millie"—Luanna touched her sister-in-law's hand softly, looking at her with a vague girlishness, asking for her understanding—"Troy is all through taking a back seat to Kyle. Those days are past."

Oho, thought Millie, so that's how the wind is blowing! But she said nothing, and in the tall, shadowy closet, shelved with the oak and mahogany silver chests, and with glass, china and pewter imagined or known to be precious, the women went on sorting the tableware. Millie watched, as the day went by, how Luanna's small, strong hands moved among the silver pieces, touching them so deferentially yet so possessively, sometimes picking up a serving spoon or a great gold-plated cake knife to heft it or clean it on her apron. *Those days are past*, Millie thought, ho-hum.

She left at four o'clock in a squall of dark rain. She had to be home in time to fix Doc his dinner.

2

Rain bucked hard against the windshield of the Chevy station wagon; it marched in spirals and banshee twists across the range, wiggled down the highway like a roadrunner, cutting out potholes.

Millie switched the headlights on. No doubt of it. Luanna was a good wife to Troy and had been, lo, these many years. Luanna had given birth to Cliff and Helene and cleaned the oil out of Troy's Ajax work pants and J. C. Penney shirts, cooked two meals a day for him and fixed the box lunches and watered the parched grass in the yards of the little oil-town houses and kept herself trim and sexy-looking so he wouldn't run after other women. Had the game been worth the candle? You bet your sweet life it had; the Cherokee kid with the tilted varmint eyes and the long, bony legs was now the lady of a large manor, with an aristocratic person, temporarily running in hard luck, paid to furnish it for her and explain how to run it and the great and famous people of the land ready and eager to come to her table, as they were now about to demonstrate.

Already Luanna had racked up some scores. Millie smiled, spinning the steering wheel to avoid a churning sluice of rainwater with a head of foam on it like San Francisco steam beer. She was thinking how Luanna had bragged, in that vaguely girlish way of hers that was so appealing and at the same time so tough, of how the housewives in Altemira had come out to call. Luanna had run tally on them. Mrs. Polls had called—the wife of the state assemblyman, formerly the county sheriff. Mrs. Gabriel Evans had called—Gabe owned a store, retired now; and Mrs. August Hayflick, wife of the superintendent of the Altemira High School. Mrs. Gaston Crock, the judge's wife. And Bishop O'Melveny, such an old man, so saintly, with a young priest to drive him.

"And many others, also," Luanna had said primly, winding up her gazette. "I know it's the custom to stop by when a new family moves into a neighborhood, but since they all knew Troy I felt as if they'd come to see *me*. It must have been like it was once, way back, when your *mother* came to live here. Do you think that's possible?"

"I'm sure," said Millie.

She did not add that, as far as she knew, no one from Altemira, with the exception of clergy, bill collectors or candidates for public office, had *ever* called on her mother; if they had they would have come again, and she, Millie, would have taken note of them, and they never had. The reason they hadn't would have required explanation. Emilia de Baca Kinsale had come to the ranch from the elite world of landed grant-deed people on whom, in the California of her day, town ladies were not up to calling. They called on Luanna out of sheer curiosity and because the word had come north on the oil-field grapevine that Luanna was a small-town housewife like themselves.

Luanna might not have liked that.

The squall had built into a true storm—a real range-soaker. Millie took a cattlewoman's satisfaction in it, always her reaction to the first tempests of the season, before she remembered the hell such storms raised for a doctor trying to get around on his calls. Doc had gone down into the valley today; he might be late—but then so might his dinner.

Cautiously, she eased the wagon out of the ranch driveway, onto the highway, then swerved over farther than she meant to, slipping almost off the road as she let a pickup pulling a home-built horse trailer go by. Two young men rode in the pickup, two fine stock horses in the trailer; the ranch brand on the sides of both vehicles read "Rafter Lazy S."

That would be the Slater brothers, Mel and Ott, homeward bound after gathering cattle for the last of that year's shipments. They waved and Millie waved, then the Slaters slowed down, one of them, his head out the side window, peering back to make sure Millie was all right. She signaled "Okay," motioning him on, wishing the weather were nicer, in which case, instead of merely checking her well-being, those boys would have stopped to pass the time of day. Such was the nature of the country, a friendly country; people gossiped and connived, as they did everywhere, but they also helped, they also hung together. If a cowman fell ill, neighbors rounded up for him, wired his fences, fixed his roof; if an orchardist tumbled off a ladder and broke bones, friends picked for him and pruned and fertilized his trees. A prosperous country. Folks were healthy hereabouts as well as nice and if they fell ill they usually suffered some illness you could recognize and treat. Why, she thought, couldn't Doc have practiced around Altemira instead of down in the valley with its outlawed diseases and kinky people who would as soon cut a doctor's throat as pay his bill? They rendered little thanks for services even though no outside physician would venture into their doom-hung land to take their calls.

Doc hadn't asked for it. Not really, though with time he'd come to feel himself responsible for the whole witch's gaggle of slanty-eyed, knob-headed patients. She, Millie, had brought him into the county by an act of seizure, as it were, and then, to top off her guilt, had married him and planted him there permanently.

She turned down the valley road. Daylight ebbed fast as the storm closed in. Hard little hailstones were now mixing with the rain, bouncing on the hood and windshield of the Chevy like rice at a wedding send-off: her own wedding. She'd never thought that she was heading for that—hardly!—the night she went out to get Doc; a hell of a worse night than this, she remembered, she herself not knowing whom she was fixing to meet, but sure that when she headed home she'd have a doctor with her.

Hub had needed one. That had been the night of his first bad spell. He'd come back from one of his two-day wingdings in town badly hung over and had slammed around as usual, waking everybody, but this time he'd left his lights on all night, something he never did, and when she'd gone in with a cup of tea at 5 A.M. he said he hadn't slept and cursed her for disturbing him. He had refused food, ordering a mustard plaster for pains in his chest, drinking whiskey to ease them and breathing with a rasp you could hear out in the yard, when he breathed at all.

Millie had been terrified. Hub might not have been the best father in the world, but with Troy recently married and gone and Kyle mostly away, he was all the family she had and, whether he liked it or not, she wasn't going to let him die.

The storm had been going on for thirty-six hours without letup when Hub made the trip from town, a feat only a drunken man who was also a superb horseman could have managed; by the following afternoon, when she'd started her quest, the banks of gullys that had stood for thirty years were caving in like flour in a cake bowl. The Paicines creek, dry for three-quarters of the year, was running twenty feet deep from bank to bank, pushing along chicken coops and bales of hay, chunks of fence, ripped-up outhouses, drowned things and swimming things, and sections of the bridge between town and the ranch. No sense even trying to get Dr. Willabaugh from Altemira. He couldn't have made it out and wouldn't have tried—also, by the time Millie decided to defy Hub's orders and call him, the phone lines were down.

Millie left the ranch at 1 P.M., riding her best horse, a strong short-coupled Appaloosa, and leading a no-name, half-broke, wall-eyed bronc which had been shoved into the corral to get healed of some wire cuts. The bronc led better than he rode, but she figured by the time she got to the Forestry post on the summit grade, he would be tired and would come down the hill without breaking in half.

The doctor could ride the Appaloosa.

There was a light in the post. She saw it from two miles away, working up the grade. With Chuck Roop or any of his fellows there she was all right. She could borrow one of the Forestry cars for the drive down the west side of the Gabilans and across the Salinas Valley to the Southern Pacific whistle-stop at Tuolumne Flats.

She beat on the door till she awakened Chuck, who gave her a cup of coffee with a knock of greasewood whiskey in it. He wanted to come with her, but she pointed out that if he did, there would have been no place for the doctor.

Chuck's personal pickup—the loaner he occasionally made available—was narrow and high and it rode like a mule-drawn buckboard but it got her to the Flats in plenty of time.

Hogue Denish, the Tuolumne Flats freight agent, was eating breakfast. He had to get up early to put out milk cans for the southbound local at 4 A.M. He had no proper rain clothes but he stuck his head through a tarp and went out to set the signal that would stop the northbound *Lark*—the Southern Pacific's night express between Los Angeles and San Francisco.

Hogue was a jockey-sized man with a mean disposition who raised rabbits as a hobby. His thick brown beard was so long he braided the end of it and stuck it in his pants. A lifelong bachelor, he cooked for himself, his breakfast that morning consisting of buttermilk pancakes, jam, syrup, fried eggs, reheated venison steak, stewed quail, and several kinds of pickles. This he shared with Millie. She ate ravenously, forgetting what she had come for till a sudden quivering of the shack which served both as freight office and Hogue's dwelling made clear that the big train was approaching. She ran outside. Far down the track, scorching through the wraiths of the rain, loomed the train's huge yellow headlight, its beam prodding ahead, carving a cave of brilliance in the wet, black air. It came on fast, scornful, unstoppable, its noise roaring through the gorges, its weight shaking the earth, the rails in its path humming like banjo strings. The huge train, dark except for its running lights, once the headlight had gone by, and one lonely car which was lighted, pounded on past the station—*had the engineer gone mad, hadn't he seen the signal?* Millie ran hopelessly toward the single lighted car. She reached it just as the express, with a huge hissing followed by a delicate shudder, like a woman sneezing, drew up, and she climbed the high step of the car with tiny Hogue, dripping wet, following her, carrying a bull's-eye lantern.

"Is there a doctor on this train?"

All the time she had been riding her horse up the mountain trail, which no car or wagon could negotiate, all the time she had been in the car, crossing the valley, bucking the storm, she had been planning these words. She brought them out breathlessly at first, then loudly and forcefully.

That was what you said in a situation like this: a simple question, but a cry for help, a cry that must be heeded—an emergency.

No one paid her the slightest attention.

The car was full of men. Men of all ages, all sizes, all white-faced and respectable-looking—though what they were doing was not all that respectable. They were playing cards and boozing it up! Some stood around a bar counter at the far end of the car; others had pulled the varnished railroad chairs together, messing up the car to suit their convenience; they were all smoking. She could hardly see through the smoke, she gagged on it, furious now, helplessly, angrily, trying her careful, ignored appeal:

"Is there . . . a doctor . . . a doctor . . ."

"WHAT?"

A loose-limbed redheaded man, large and handsome, rose from a bench beside the door, a little red plush seat on which he had been lounging. He was elegantly dressed but he had taken off his coat, like most of the others, and his striped galluses, such as a farmhand would wear, showed under his open vest. He had an impish, ruddy face, masquerading with an exaggerated attentiveness as he cupped his ear, bending from his great height toward Millie.

"Gentlemen." He turned to face the body of the car. "GENTLEMEN! MAY I HAVE YOUR ATTENTION? This little lady"—and here he reached over and put his arm around Millie, moving her forward—"this little lady wants to know IF THERE'S A DOCTOR ON THIS TRAIN."

Someone let out a bawling laugh and others joined; the men stopped their games; in a few seconds the whole carful of men was howling and stomping with mirth.

"She wants a—doctor!"

The passengers rocked and stomped, the card hands getting mixed up, glasses spilling. Several of the merrymakers moved down front to get a better look at Millie.

The redheaded man took pity on her.

"We're *all* doctors, honey," he said kindly. "You hit the right train; every sombitch aboard here is a doctor, and back in the sleepers too. We're going to a convention in Monterey. What do you think of that?"

As if in answer, the engineer cut loose with a fearful blast on his whistle and the conductor, who had probably been sleeping, bullassed his way into the car. He was a slab-jawed man with a voice like a broken brake.

"Two minutes is the limit for a stop at this station."

The redheaded man raised his arms for quiet. "Now, gentlemen," he said rapidly, in a serious, businesslike tone, "time's short. Who's going with this sweet young person?"

"We'll draw!" came a voice.

The conductor grabbed Millie by the elbow.

"Off, miss. Get off my train!"

Hogue whacked his tiny shoulder into the conductor's belly. His braided beard jerked out of his pants.

"Take your fucking hands off her!"

"Stop all this fussing!"

The new voice was a quiet one, high-pitched but manly all the same.

He wore one of the new, fashionably low starched collars, above which his Adam's apple bulged like a pulpit. He had very clear, intense blue eyes.

"No need for any more nonsense. I'll go."

He jumped on a seat to fetch down his bowler hat, medical satchel and a small canvas haversack from the luggage rack.

"I'm Carl Braden," he told Millie, standing on the platform in the downpour. "Where's the patient?"

And so saying, he reached out his large, warm, bony hand and took hold of Millie's small, cold one and smiled at her. His blue gaze jolted through her like a lightning bolt. She fell in love with him then and there.

3

Driving home now in the rain, so many years later, Millie could see the new clinic on its shrubby ledge. Doc was so proud of it! And in truth it was a fine "facility," as Doc liked to call it, small of course, but provided with the most modern equipment—an X-ray unit, a biochemical laboratory for blood and bacteria studies, and an operating room as good as any on the Coast. Doc himself didn't operate except in an emergency but some of the foremost surgeons in the state had worked in that room when specifically needed: Roger Keesling of Stanford, Bernard Frohman of Los Angeles, to name just two. If the patient could not pay for such eminence, the clinic did; none was better endowed. KinOil picked up the yearly deficit, no matter how large, and had permanently funded ten hospital beds for those who needed them, free of charge.

Doc wasn't home yet: if he had been she would have seen his car, a brown Auburn, parked in the first of the three parking spaces labeled STAFF. She would have time to get his dinner ready before he arrived and she was glad of this, but bothered by his lateness nonetheless. He was so resilient —he thought he could stand anything; he overlooked the fact that he was fifty-four years old and had available two younger assistants, either one of whom could have been helping with the outpatient work that day instead of cuddling up to the Dutch stove in the staff lounge. One of them was in there now, Kirk Sotomayer, bright as a button and lazy as a cockroach, visible through the big window. He was a handsome, athletic young man of twenty-eight with a vaguely Continental air about him. He had wide cheekbones, a high forehead and a well-cropped, curly brown beard. He had his feet up on the coal scuttle and he was reading something—probably one of the French novels he would slip into a copy of the AMA *Journal*. Millie was wise to his tricks. He'd had a year of premed at the Sorbonne before going on to Johns Hopkins, where he'd been an honor graduate.

Kirk was young to have the type of credentials he'd acquired—but if he hadn't been young, as Dr. Braden sometimes pointed out, he would not have succumbed to the challenge of a country practice.

"I did the same thing when you pulled me off that train. I saw myself with a whole frontier to conquer and with no one to compete or to criticize—a rural Alex Carrel."

"Also," Millie had reminded him, "I was laying snares for you. And you liked girls."

"So will he, if we can find the right one."

Kirk Sotomayer was good-looking—a wild dancer who set the heads of Kinsale cousins reeling at the Rodeo Ball. Millie didn't think the clinic would long retain his services.

He's too smart for his own good, she thought, irritated by the sight of him there, taking his ease, while Doc, twice his age, and twice the man, chugged around the valley in the year's first nor'wester.

Millie parked the Chevy at her own back door. She entered her kitchen, where she rushed around, getting supper started, a lamb roast she'd partially cooked before going out that morning. She put potatoes to bake around the meat and laid two places for dinner, all without taking off her coat and hat; she knocked back a short one from a bottle of Golden Wedding, kept in the icebox, coughed on it, but felt better.

Umbrella in hand, she crossed the quadrangle separating residence from clinic. She banged on the emergency door. Kirk, the fool, had left it locked.

"Doc called about five," he said as he let her in. "He was still at Cooney Frake's."

"I thought he wanted the Frake child brought in here."

"He did, but we decided not to move her. There's a new case—Mrs. Cosmo, the feedstore lady. Wilde went over to look at that. Doc said, tell you he'd be home, only later."

"This *is* later."

"I know," said Kirk Sotomayer, without sympathy, "but that's what he said. He sounded fine."

Millie snorted. Kirk always appended, when delivering Doc's messages, that Doc had sounded fine, which conveyed nothing at all. Doc would sound fine up to and perhaps several minutes after the moment he lay down to die. He was that kind of man.

Millie could do without Kirk's judgments and without his executive "we," as in "we decided not to move her." But all she said was, "There's always a new case, somewhere."

She moved around, straightening the room.

Kirk Sotomayer resettled himself in his chair.

"Did you ever speculate why that's true only in Dead Eagle Valley, not in the general population?"

"There's meningitis in the general population too, I'm sure."

"Yes, there is, Millie," said the young doctor in his pleasant, superior manner, "there is indeed. Only the incidence is approximately one in two hundred thousand. Perhaps five hundred, seven hundred cases in the whole United States. In the valley, with a population under five thousand, we've had twenty-eight cases in a year. Yet Doc seems to look on this as normal."

"Has he said that to you—that he looks on it as normal?"

"Not in so many words. We haven't discussed it, but . . . his attitude . . ."

"We're not talking about attitudes," said Millie, "we're talking about meningitis. I can tell you that Doc does not consider the incidence here as normal. Only he happens to have more interest in treating the disease than talking about it."

"Why are you annoyed?"

"Perhaps it's *your* attitude that annoys me."

"It's more than that. When is your birthday?"

"Let's not drag in astrology."

"Astrology comes into all relationships. Aren't you a Gemini?"

"I don't know."

"I happen to remember—yes, you are. I'm Cancer. We have utterly no chance to get along."

"Oh, go to hell and give me some coffee."

"I did have a point, you know."

"You didn't make it."

"You didn't let me."

He handed her the coffee.

"I'm not sure that I want to talk about this any more."

"That seems to be the rule in this practice, Millie. We're free to discuss any subject except the work. *That's* taboo—things have always been done in a certain way and they will continue to be done that way, even when we are confronted with an epidemic."

"We are confronted with nothing of the kind."

"Excuse me?"

"Doc feels this is endemic, not epidemic."

"A point on which he and I disagree. Some strains can be epidemic, even though dormant in an area for a number of years. They survive indefinitely in places of a certain kind: garrisons, prisons, orphanages, camps. Places where crowding occurs. 'The workhouse disease.' That's what it was called in Glasgow, in the eighteenth century, where it was first identified.''

"This isn't Glasgow."

"Oh, I know—and Dead Eagle Valley isn't exactly a workhouse either. Rather the contrary, hardly anybody works at all; the bounty of the land—or the Lord—provides. That's the toughest poverty of all.''

"People aren't poorer in Dead Eagle Valley than anywhere else, they're just a mite more shiftless.''

"And dirty.''

"That they are. But you might as well say tetanus, for God's sake, is epidemic because it runs high down there. Well, if you want to know, when *this* came along, that's how Doc diagnosed the first two cases: tetanus. He'd never tell you but he did; it's nothing to be ashamed of.''

"I wouldn't put him down for it, Millie.''

"Oh, yes, you would. When the time came, or the chance. You began this discussion, which I am about to end, by putting him down.''

"Which I withdrew. And you misunderstood. Onset symptoms of tetanus closely resemble meningitis: headache, stiff neck and jaws, the vomiting . . .''

"Good of you to say so!''

"But my point, *not* a medical one, is this: there will always be meningitis down there. Or if not, then something else. Maybe the Mexicans knew something when they spiked that bird beside the trail.''

"It was a trick, of course. They were full of tricks.''

"It could have been more. They could have been making a statement that I, personally, believe—there are places on this earth where people weren't meant to live. There's evidence that some real horror took place in Dead Eagle Valley.''

"Of course there is. Two thousand Indians died of the plague there. They also died in many other places of the plague. They died of syphilis, measles and tuberculosis—all gifts of their conquerors, the Spanish. There was nothing mysterious about it.''

"Wasn't there? I've checked this out. Some of those Indians, the ones in the crypt, were almost mummified and their skin didn't indicate either bubonic plague *or* smallpox; I examined them carefully and I examined the skeletons, which told me more. I found half a dozen spines, the spines of children, bent backward, locked there like the bows one sees

in the last stages of cerebrospinal meningitis. The ailment that
made off with your two thousand Indians is the same that's
killing people down there now."

"Are you saying that the meningococci hibernated for two
hundred years in order to pop up again in the twentieth
century? If you're going to research that, Doctor, you'll have
trouble getting a grant for it."

"I'm not saying that at all. More like the reverse. Look, we
don't understand the origins of life, and grants are given for
studying that all the time. What about the origins of disease?
I'm saying there are places on this planet where certain
unknown factors, not within the scope of current knowledge,
act as counterrevolutionary agents, incubating destruction
instead of life. That could be what's happening in Dead Eagle
Valley."

"You don't really believe that, do you?"

Kirk Sotomayer weighed this solemnly, then smiled—a
sunburst of charm in his ruddy, sullen face.

"No, but it's an interesting concept."

Millie smiled too—still depressed and vaguely annoyed but
also bewitched.

"Like something out of your Madame Blavatsky," she said,
laughing.

He laughed with her, delighted as a boy to have her interest
at last—as if all his talk had been show-off, just to have that.

"Madame Blavatsky is a funny old lady, lively and all—
that's why I read her; I read anyone who's lively. She's a
theosophist, though; she explores the continuity of souls.
But . . . all right. I'll bring my science up to her conjecturing.
A place that harbors influences baleful for the flesh could be
baleful for the spirit too. People would do bad things, terrible
things, and they wouldn't know why. Evil isn't always a
matter of choice."

"Is that still being debated?" Millie asked lightly, still not
losing her good humor—floating in it, rather, and unwilling to
leave.

"Endlessly. Around the world."

"But in monasteries and seminaries, not in the *real* world.
Not in laboratories."

"I never heard that laboratories were any realer than
monasteries. What's more, I doubt that those two thousand
redskin corpses were the real horror. Mission Indians often
died off. They also sometimes revolted, which they also did in
Dead Eagle Valley. They destroyed the mission. What's odd

isn't that it was destroyed, but that the Spanish never rebuilt it. They just went away and left it. Whatever happened there was bad enough to keep them from going back. And you know something? There are Dead Eagle Valleyites who swear they know what it was."

"They'll swear to anything."

"Of course. But I'm not through checking. I just may come up with some answers."

"If you do, don't mention them to Doc. Will you promise me that? He's . . . well, he's working very hard, too hard, in fact—you know how it is, and I don't want him bothered. Do you mind?"

Millie leaned forward, the glow of the lamp on her face and some kind of fear that Sotomayer could not read.

"Whatever you say. But I must tell you . . . Doc was the one who first mentioned it to me. The people in touch with the dead. *That's* occultism, if you like, and I'm not sure Doc entirely discounts it."

"He does, he most certainly does. Why do you say that? He's a doctor, a man with twenty years' experience, not a . . . dreamy young person full of weird ideas . . ."

Millie's voice trailed off. She sat with bowed shoulders, in a chair too small for her, an aging person, a doctor's wife; her body jerked, and the saucer of her coffee cup clattered to the tiled clinic floor.

"I don't want him bothered at a time like this," she said. "He gets upset about the children . . . those longheaded, sad-faced little ones down there, all bent the way they get . . . Listen to me. I don't want you mentioning any of your kooky notions to the doctor. Keep your big mouth shut. You just stay away from him and do your work and let's hope that everything will be all right."

4

Sometime in the course of that afternoon, while Millie was still on her way home in the rain from the headquarters ranch, her husband, Dr. Carl Braden, on his rounds in a small house in Dead Eagle Valley, had given Georgiana Frake, aged eleven, one-quarter grain of morphine, injected intravenously, then waited quietly until she died. The injection was precisely equivalent in dosage to the others which the child had received, on the doctor's orders, every four hours, or as needed, for the last twenty-four hours; it was as far from being a lethal dose as it was from being curative, but it was enough to control the spasms, which was all that could be done.

Dr. Braden had known what would happen. He had been aware of it since his first visit of the day, early that morning. The pustules had appeared, the small clear vessels erupting in the skin. Few patients lived more than twenty-four hours after this stage of the disease was reached, most of them less than twelve. The fatality rate had been running more than seventy percent for children, slightly more than eighty percent for adults. There were no cures. Those who survived did so by brute strength alone. The doctor had once read a theory, put forward in a medical journal, that the convulsions rather than the lesions of the cerebrospinal system were the terminal factor, but autopsy had convinced him otherwise. The morphia helped. He would not have wanted to be without it, but for long-range effect he might as well have been prescribing extract of ergot, as doctors did in the nineteenth century.

Doc hated death. That was perhaps what gave him joy in his profession, that he hated death and loved life. He wanted life to prevail, even if it lost out in the end, and he knew a lot of ways to make it prevail. He was good at that. He felt triumphant when he could accomplish it just as, often wrongly, he felt stupid and helpless when he couldn't. Next to death he hated, then, diseases which could not be cured—and this disease, which medicine seemed to have forgotten or ignored, he hated above all: a disease which lay in wait, in dirty places, where it developed a crooked spirochetelike microbe, to be pushed out against the flow of health and the body's natural immune system, and to attack, above all, children and young adults, who had hardly lived at all.

Get away from me, Death, you mangy, gutless bastard, he thought.

He wrapped the small shrunken body in a sheet that was as near to being clean as any he could find and carried it into the room which had been the child's, Georgiana's, in life—a tiny room and, yes, dirty, to be sure. Cooney, the father, worked as a sack sewer in the barley and walnut seasons, idled the rest of the time, and took snuff. He had a patch of vegetables behind the house which his wife tended, off and on. He trapped some, poached some—they all poached, in the valley. He was a shambling man with melancholy eyes and brown stains around his nose from his habit. When Doc came downstairs he was sitting in the front room at a table where his wife was folded over, sound asleep, with her head down on her arms. Cooney Frake got up the minute he saw Doc. He knew what had happened because Doc had told him that it would.

"She went peaceful," he said convincedly, as if he rather than Doc were the news bearer. He nodded, to impress his statement on Doc; then he put out his hand, not to shake, but because he had something in it, and Doc put out his own hand and took it.

"I'll call Mrs. Williams," Doc said.

Mrs. Williams, a practical nurse, went to valley people when the doctor summoned her; she would instruct and help people like the Frakes, who did not wish or could not afford the services of Digger Carew, the Altemira undertaker.

But Cooney shook his head.

"No need," he said. "We'll tend to it. We won't have no more children."

He walked out onto the porch with Doc, holding Doc's elbow to steer him around a loose board where he might have gone through.

The two men stood together, looking at the rain.

"No more now," said Cooney. "Wife's into the minipause; no more for us. That's what hit her so hard."

"I understand."

The Frakes had three other daughters, all of them off on their own. Cooney had always been proud that they'd left Dead Eagle Valley. Not many young people did, anymore. He pulled out a can of Copenhagen, then thought better about indulging, and put it back. He held out his hand again, and this time he shook. Driving away, Doc could still see him there, still on the porch, with the light behind him, as disheveled as some old carrion-picking bird, shoving snuff under his lip.

Dr. Braden, driving, raised to the dash light the bill Cooney Frake had pushed into his hand. Five dollars! Five dollars for seven house calls, one of them lasting most of a night, three visits from a practical nurse, and a series of morphine injections. A pretty good five dollars' worth. That was the doctor's side of it. He had done a job and he was entitled to his fee. He respected Cooney Frake as a man who recognized an obligation; he was also aware that five dollars might well be the only money in the Frake house that night. But he had taken it, just the same, and if Cooney had not offered it (unsolicited fees were not usual in Dead Eagle Valley!), then he, Doc, would have sent him, and might still send him, a bill for a sum more commensurate with the work put out. The bill might be paid or it might not, but by sending it, as by accepting the money, the obligation would be established, the value of the service.

Millie could not understand this. She had suggested more than once that Doc only required and accepted payment out of habit. He was like old pickle-face Coolidge, saying, "They hired the money, didn't they?" All right: that habit had once been all to the good. It had been necessary, not so long ago, but since the oil had come in Millie couldn't see the point of continued small levies on poor people.

"It's not as if we needed it."

"I don't base my charges on what we need. I base them on what I do for the patients."

"But it seems so unfair."

"Do you want me to work for them free?"

"Not for those who could afford to pay, but—"

"All right. You keep the books, so you know the answer to this, and I don't. How much do we carry forward each year?"

"A lot. But you're only proving my point. The accounts are uncollectable, many of them. So why do you bother to run up new ones and give up on them too?"

"I bother, honey, because I'm a doctor, not a social worker. If those people in the valley knew that they could pay nothing for my work that's just what they'd feel it was worth. They'd send to Altemira for old Willabaugh or to King City for Pringle—not that those gentlemen would come. No. The Valleyites may not pay but they respect me for putting them in debt. They know an effort has been made."

Doc stuck the five dollars in his pocket, then clamped his hand down on the wheel as the car skidded, slipping in the rutted lane. His lips moved, talking to the car as if it were a person or an animal. Watch yourself there, you silly bugger. It was a silly bugger too, this boat-backed Auburn with its slanty windshield, its chrome fittings and high-speed engine, a fine car for concrete parkways or city streets, out of place here. Parked, as it was half the time, in the yard of some mossy, slab-sided little ranch, it looked like the vehicle of some stranger who had got lost in the valley and just stopped to ask the way.

So—all right! The car hadn't been his idea. It had been a present from Millie, like so many other luxuries in their current life. A slicker's car. He drove it but he wondered if it was really such a hell of an improvement over the days when he'd moved along these roads on horseback or in a creaky, unstoppable Model T and the world had been young. Not that he'd lost his ambition, as people were so quick to say of country doctors; he had plenty of ambition, too much maybe —the nature of it had changed, that was all. He still had in his files the paper, "Hypothyroidism as Related to Diseases of the Skin," which he'd planned to read at the convention in Monterey, before Millie took him off the train.

Not a bad paper at all. With some updating he might still get it published; on the other hand, one had to concede that thyroid research had crashed ahead since the twenties. That meant more study, and it was hard with his practice to find time either for study or for writing. He still went to conventions now and then, more for a change of scene than anything else, but he had never volunteered to read the paper, which he had once thought would make his reputation. That laborious contribution to science now occupied about the same importance in his life as, say, the stub of a ticket to a forgotten football game or the collar tabs for his mothballed 1917 uniform. A souvenir . . .

The practice. That was where his interest lay. Dealing with these outlanders, these sequestered people with their queer genetic patterns and their isolated way of life. This was his laboratory, this starved-out backcountry, alternately furnace-hot or exuberant with floods, the bitter acres where once, unrecorded, something so bad had happened that the Spanish, who never gave up anywhere, had gone away and never come back. Why? He'd refused to accept young Sotomayer's notion about occult powers, spirit projections affecting human behavior and . . . disease . . . but he also wondered whether he hadn't been wrong—whether in fact evidence might not ultimately come to light confirming the existence of influences which science still rejected and even derided but which medieval scholars had considered too well proven to admit of doubt, lumping them under a catchall phrase, "the forces of evil."

Something bad *had* happened in the valley. This Doc knew

of his own knowledge, not from research. He had undergone a unique experience—a psychic adventure, as he preferred to think of it. Later he had tried to talk to Millie about it but she had immediately become disturbed; she had rushed to the conclusion that he'd been working too hard (as he had, of course, and still was, as if that had any bearing on the subject!). He was not, never had been, a candidate for a nervous breakdown; he took care of himself, he lived life as he found it, he did not take drugs, he did not hallucinate. Hallucination! There was another catchall, the handiest of all when you needed a term to describe a phenomenon not easily explained. He knew what he'd seen. He'd written careful notes after the encounter—several pages of them, recording everything while it was still fresh in mind.

A mile or two ahead now, on the rainy road, was the place: the hill behind the straggling fieldstone and adobe wall, falling apart, which had once enclosed the entire mission grounds. He had ridden up that hill later, through the sage, *and he had located the seven Stations just as they had been revealed to him that night.*

Wasn't that in itself proof of a sort?

He'd had no prior information about the Stations, nor had he ever run across them, although he had ridden up that hillside several times before, collecting leaves and blossoms. He was an old sagebrusher and among his neglected projects was a field book on California range flora with emphasis on the hilly shrubs: the black-leafed greasewood, which streaked gray when ruffled by the wind—heavy from May to July with strong wild honey; the silver sage, always first to flower after a drought or a burnout, ocean-green and aromatic; the button sage, the badge of land that would be fertile if cleared; and the deer brush, where a buck would lie sleeping in broad daylight till you were almost on top of him, then heave himself up and take off with a few incredible bounds; the wild cherry, sticky and sour; the gin-smelling junipers, packed with purple berries.

He'd found the first stopping place fifty yards up, the rest strung along in a zigzag pattern for a quarter mile or so. The paths joining them had long been overgrown but his horse, an old sagebrusher like himself, had found them with no trouble.

The Stations of the Cross.

The event had taken place in August, the previous summer. It had been about midnight, maybe a little past. Doc had been coming home from a house call, one of the first meningitis cases, when he'd seen the lights; at first he'd thought they were sparks or burning branches—the lightning-originated brush fires of summer's end. They began that way, they slithered along the ground; you hardly had a glimpse of them till a branch lighted up or a dead pine exploded in flames, like a Fourth of July pinwheel. Doc had pulled over and got out to look and then he'd heard the voices, the wild screeching and the chanting. Well, the moon had been up, a picker's moon, almost full, laying down silver like a glaze of ice, plenty of light to see the procession going up the hill.

Indians were still coming out of the mission gates, naked as jaybirds, in a steady stream, screeching "heesoo cree, heesoo cree." It took some listening to catch on that this was their monk-taught version of "Jesus Christ," but they weren't saying it the way the monks had taught it; they had made it into a mockery or a war cry, as if to say, What about Him, that Jesus whom we slaved for, whom we got flogged and castrated for? Let's see Him help you now . . .

The Indians farther up the hill weren't naked like the mission slaves. These were liberators, people from the Sierra tribes and the river tribes. They had on deer-hide loincloths and warrior paint, and the medicine men in charge of the operation, one old screaming, chanting daddy in particular, wore the wolf and bear headdresses and the prayer paint of the old gods, the Banished Ones.

The medicine men were directing the crucifixions.

They had stuck up one old white man already. He must have been a priest, not a monk, since his head wasn't tonsured; the squaws had him up on the poles, his hands were nailed and they were nailing his feet. They had done something to his genitals and the blood was running down his legs. The other two for crucifixion were younger; both were lugging along heavy crosses of peeled cottonwood logs. They still had on their robes and when they reached one of the Stations they would stop. The Indians had them kneel. Then they would beat them with medicine sticks.

"Heeesooocreee . . . heeesooocreee . . . heeesooocreee . . . heeesooocreee . . . heeesooocreee . . ."

The brush kept catching fire. It would be touched off by the pitch-pine torches but where the flames sprang up the squaws beat them out. This was the night of the long nails and they let nothing interfere with their task. They must have piled pine in the mission too, in the main building and the outbuildings; the granary went up first, then the chapel, after which there was more light, as if the moon were not enough.

"Heeesooocreeeheeesooocreeeheeesooocreee . . ."

They had one of the young monks on his cross now and they were piling brush around his feet. Doc was shivering. The dumb sons of bitches will burn the Gabilans from end to end, he thought; I'd better get a call through to Chuck Roop to move a Forestry crew down here before we're all homeless —realizing even while he struggled with this thought that there was no danger, that his timewarp had come unsprung; what he was watching had happened a hundred and fifty years ago. He was ill of course, he was aware of that, although he did not think he had been ill when he first got out of the car.

Doc had stayed out of the office for a week. He lost weight, he was weak and tottery. It was during his recuperation that he divulged his experience to Millie—wrongly, as it turned out; she had been sure he was having a breakdown. Doc did not agree. Even the disagreement, as he knew, could be a symptom of irrationality, but he had to take exception to this too. This land they lived in was a wild land, a very old land, and from the time when glacier action had ripped it out of the ooze and pushed the ocean back so that men could use the strip between the mountains and the coast more than a few "inexplicable" events had taken place. Was the reappearance of a disease that had lain hidden somewhere, perhaps in an old grave for more than a century—or the finding of a billion dollars' worth of oil located by poking a hole in some dunes—really less fanciful that the pageant he had seen enacted or reenacted?

Doc did not think so, but he kept his mouth shut. He should have done that from the start, in which case everyone would have been better off.

Someday, he decided, he was going to look into the records. He was going to Mexico or Spain, if he had to, and find out whether Indians *had* ever crucified two monks and a priest on a Gabilan mountainside before they burned down the mission.

That would be worth doing. It might not prove anything, but it would be interesting. He would do it just as soon as he and Millie could take time off from the practice to attend to it.

Doc wheeled the Auburn onto the country road. He turned on the car radio and beguiled himself with music. The rain had stopped but it had left long sleeves of water in the dips, which had to be carefully negotiated. Doc took his time. The depression that had afflicted him in the house of Cooney Frake was lessening. Millie, he knew, would have something on the stove. He was ready for his dinner. In the suddenly clear and burnished sky the stars were those of any winter evening, Orion rising, Altair and Vega going west, over the spine of the humpbacked mountains.

CHAPTER NINE

Arc de Rawhide

1

The day of the conquest party was brilliant and clear—one of those sunburst days, full of bright colors and sweet smells which make mock of the short California winters. The ranch station was decked out in bunting and a band was on hand to welcome the chartered railroad car bringing in H. H. Atlass and his party. Several planes, owned by other companies KinOil had bought, were parked on the new airstrip; cars rolled up and down the drive all day, meeting trains or coming from them, hauling in guests. A pavilion for dancing had been put up on the lawn and charcoal braziers installed in and around it in case the weather turned cold again; Anson Weeks and his orchestra had been booked in from the Mark Hopkins Hotel. Luanna rushed from the house to the lawn, overseeing everything, giving firm, unexcited orders; she had a billeting list in her hand and as the guests arrived she gave them maps showing the location of their rooms and printed menus of what they were to eat at dinner as prepared by Victor Hirtzel, famous head chef of the St. Francis, borrowed from the hotel for the occasion.

Kyle and Alma had left Los Angeles the day before to drive up in the Rolls, with Kyle at the wheel. Alma looked fetching in a brown fitted suit and a cloche hat with a tiny veil extending no farther than the tip of her nose—the latest thing. At the last minute, afraid she was overdressed, she wanted to discard the hat—perhaps just wrap her head in a scarf? Kyle reassured her.

"They won't care what you wear, honey."

"But I want them to care!"

She was worried about meeting his family. Not about the men. She had already met Troy on several occasions and liked him. There was also a son, Cliff, she understood, in that branch of the Kinsales—he was a sophomore at Berkeley. He might be home for the holidays or he might not. Kyle was casual about Cliff: "Real Huck Finn sort of kid; you'll like him."

There was some overtone in the affection with which Kyle spoke of his nephew. Envy? That could be—here was his brother Troy, younger than he, with a son already eighteen, with Kyle himself without chick or child. Well, that could be remedied.

No, she would be all right with the men. With them she had the confidence of any beautiful woman dealing with the opposite sex. They would like her. That would be enough. The women were different. They were carpers and gossips. They would go over her, looking for flaws.

"What's Millie like? Is she . . . very critical?"

"Millie's a sport. She's just a great gal."

"What does that mean? Tell me about her."

Kyle narrowed his eyes, trying to think what to say about his sister.

"For one thing, she's a good roper. She and old Hub, my father, won the father-daughter team-rope in the Altemira horse show three years straight. Started when she was sixteen."

"Well, she won't be roping this weekend, will she?"

"Hell, no. She hasn't done that for years, I don't suppose. It just popped into my mind."

"Well, what I want to know is, what's she like *now*. I mean, is she terribly straitlaced?"

Kyle, for once somewhat slow on the uptake, saw which way the wind was blowing.

"She's a doctor's wife, baby. A country doctor's wife learns too much and knows too much to be straitlaced. That is, if you mean picky."

"Picky, yes. Like about us."

"She doesn't know anything about us."

"She'd be able to imagine. To a picky person that's even worse."

"Set your mind at rest. She's not that way. She'll love you."

"I don't expect that. If she just gives me a chance to know her, that's all I want."

"She will. Don't worry."

"And Luanna, is she the same kind?"

"Entirely different. She's an oil-town gal from Oklahoma. I wouldn't know for sure what kind of person Luanna is, now that she's made the big time. She might give herself a few airs but don't let that fool you. Underneath she's rough as a corncob, but nice. She'll be more afraid of you than you'd ever have need to be of her."

"I'm not afraid of any of them. I just want to know about them, so I won't make an idiot of myself. Will we sleep together?"

"We'll have adjoining rooms."

"That's much better. I'd hate being in the same room. If they put us like that I wouldn't stay."

"They'd never do it, 'they' in this case being Luanna. She's the hostess, that's something you should remember."

"I *am* remembering it. Did she ask you about the rooms?"

"She didn't have to. She'll know, but if she has to ask someone she'll ask Millie; Millie will tell her."

"I thought you said Millie wasn't straitlaced."

"She's straitlaced enough for that."

"I like her already. Unless that was *the rule.*"

"Rule?"

"That you always had adjoining rooms when you brought girls home."

"You're the first girl I've brought home," he said as convincingly as he could.

"I'm glad. I don't mean I believe you, but I'm glad you said that. It makes me feel better, about everything."

"Good. They'll love you!"

She complained of car sickness on the Conejo Pass.

By sheer luck, arrival at the ranch occurred in a manner greatly to Alma's advantage, in terms of making an impression. She and Kyle drove in just as day was ending. A few minutes earlier the sky had been full of light. Suddenly a shimmering, lucent grayness sprang out of the ground and formed pools around the big trees. Clouds tilted from their roots and fell upon the hills. In this moment, without lights, the Rolls was seen to cross the private railroad trestle.

Helene, who had been keeping watch on the porch, ran into the house yelling, "They're coming, they're coming." Luanna verified this from an upstairs bedroom, then hurried down. Millie, who had noticed leaves on the drive and gone out, in the absence of the paid help, to rake them, stopped her work. She took off her heavy gardening gloves and straightened her hair. Troy had arrived only a few minutes earlier. He was in the pantry of the main house, building himself a drink. He strolled out the front door with the glass in his hand just as the big car pulled under the porte cochere. Thus the family was set up, as it were, in tableau, each locked in some characteristic posture. To Alma, seeing them all in a whirling glance as the car pulled up, it seemed as if they had all bunched there in the streaky gray air to judge her and perhaps, if they had their will, to order her off the property. She looked in terror at Kyle, who was, as she expected, perfectly at ease. He already had the door open and was extending his hand to help her out. She took his hand. She stretched out first one long, shapely leg, then the other. She stood firmly planted on the ground and faced them; keeping a tight grip on Kyle's hand she advanced toward the house. Kyle seemed to sense the solemnity of the moment, in her scale of values; playing up to her, or his relatives—she was not sure which—he made a ceremony of the short walk. He held her hand high. He kept his eyes fixed on her admiringly; he took slow, elegant steps, plonk plonk plonk, as if he were leading her up the aisle of a . . . *church* or something, for God's sake! Step, pause, step, pause, Jesus! And no one *said* anything! Couldn't these people *talk?* Probably they just communicated in code, in sign language, like . . . pulling a finger across the throat . . .

Plonk . . . plonk . . . Each step was a rounded, calculated experience, a beautiful thing, probably, to watch. But . . . *What was wrong with Kyle?*

PLONK!

"Luanna! Millie! Helene! I want you to meet . . ."

He was introducing her en masse, as it were. She faced them with her eyes flashing and a radiant smile.

". . . *Alma Paris!"*

"Pleased to meet you all . . ."

As she said these words a gust of wind whipped off her hat, the small hat with the veil which she had known from the first she shouldn't have worn. The hat spurted onto the drive, then rolled across the lawn with Helene racing after it. Kyle laughed. Luanna came down the steps and embraced her. Troy shook hands with her, then helped Kyle get the luggage out of the car. Helene brought back the hat and Millie took her arm, leading her into the house, insisting that she have tea. Or if not tea, then a drink. Alma said tea would be fine.

So the worst of *that* was over . . .

Early next morning—the day on the evening of which the real conquest party would take place—Alma was seen *in swimming*. No one had swum in the pool since October, and even then it had been chilly. But Alma just went crunching up and down with a proficient freestyle stroke. Helene had watched her from her parents' room, the big front room which had been Troy's and Kyle's when they were boys. Helene studied Alma's figure as Alma sat on the edge of the pool drying her hair; she had decided that her own breasts would never be as big as Alma's no matter how much she massaged them with cold cream to enlarge them, as she had been doing for some time.

"She has no skirt on her bathing suit and she has no cap on," Helene reported to her mother, who was still in bed.

"She's probably used to swimming in the ocean where you don't need a cap."

"Well, I bet she left hairs in the pool, plenty of them—big black dirty ones. Only nuts swim in the winter anyway."

"Get away from that window this minute and get dressed," said Luanna, "and don't say anything to her about the bathing suit or the cap either. She can swim when she likes."

"I'm proud of Kyle," Millie told her husband. "I didn't know he had that much sense."

"Meaning, you approve his choice? She seems very nice—if she *is* his choice, which I'm inclined to doubt."

"Well, at least he's trying her out—on us. He's kept most of his rich ladies at a distance."

"At such a distance," Doc said, "that you have no way of knowing whether they were ladies or not. Or even whether they were rich."

"I have ears."

"I didn't know that social niceties could be identified by sound."

"I'm serious," said Millie; "I like this girl. By the looks of her she's a real woman. Young and intelligent, and she hasn't slept around much, if at all. It's high time he settled down. There's only one thing I'm wondering about—"

"That she might be too intelligent to marry him?"

"Yes, that too. But—she asked me what she should take for car sickness. Do you have car sickness *after* you get out of the car?"

Millie clasped the lower portions of her stomach, pantomiming an enlargement there.

"Dear," said Doc, "you have an absolutely filthy mind."

"After nineteen years with you it should be clean?"

"After nineteen years with me you should know that I don't substitute guesswork for diagnosis."

"So you miss a lot of fun," said Millie Braden.

There would be room enough for everyone to eat and drink and dance and flirt but not to stay the night—no way in the world to arrange that, not even with the remodeling or the building of the cottages and the new guesthouse. Putting such an influx of guests on mattresses was like billeting an allied force composed entirely of general officers and their women. Millie called on neighbors for help, commandeered all the better guest rooms in a twenty-mile radius—from the Somavias, the Selby McCreerys, the Hawkinses, the Breens. To complicate the problem, William Randolph Hearst, the great newspaper publisher, who seldom went anywhere (he operated several huge, castlelike domains of his own!), had decided at the last minute to accept his invitation. He would be on his way down from Wyntoon, his fief on the McCloud River, to San Simeon, his castle on the coast. He would have some people with him.

"How many?" Luanna had moaned in panic, and the firm voice on the telephone, self-identified as Joseph Willicombe, Mr. Hearst's secretary, had said, "Not more than sixteen."

"Sixteen . . ." Luanna had repeated, staring at Millie, and Millie nodded vigorously, yes, yes, any number.

"Miss Davies," said the voice, "wishes to know whether it will be a costume party."

"Who's Miss Davies?" asked Luanna, with her hand over the mouthpiece.

"His mistress. Marion Davies, the movie actress, for God's sake."

Millie took the telephone and spoke into it.

"We hadn't been planning a *costume* party, but we're going to have masks and wigs. Will that be all right?"

"Yes, of course," said the voice. There was a pause, then Mr. Willicombe had added, "Mr. Hearst is very fond of costume parties."

And with this he hung up.

"Why in hell did you say that about the masks and wigs?"

"He might not come if we didn't have *something*."

"Who cares if he comes?"

"Kyle. He wants him very much to come. Don't ask me why. We'll need about a hundred masks. Not so many people will wear the wigs. Probably only half as many."

"I hope you know where to get them."

"I don't, but I'll find out."

"Probably someday I'll learn how things are done around here," said Luanna with some bitterness.

The masks and wigs, ordered from a costume company in San Francisco, had arrived by bus the day before. They had been stored in an oak chest, generally used for linen, at the pavilion door. Helene could hand them out to people as they came in to dance.

Cliff, expected home from college for his Christmas holiday, had not yet arrived.

Luanna, like Millie, understood that, odd as it seemed, the masks and wigs, like the expected coming of Mr. Hearst, and, in fact, the whole event, the party itself, had to do with business, the oil business. To that end they stood in accord. Even during the evening of Kyle and Alma's arrival, business had made its presence felt. The family had eaten together, the only outsiders being Alma and an individual whom Kyle had ordered down from San Francisco. Scott Stanfus, the KinOil stock transfer agent, was a plump, baldish and well-mannered man. He brought with him several heavy, bank-type ledgers. Then, just as the barbecued ribs were being served, a car drove up and Kyle himself went out to welcome the person in it and show him into the living room.

"It's Lamar," he said when he returned.

Troy looked up in surprise.

"What's he doing here?"

Kyle said, "I asked him to drop by. We're going to meet with him later."

Luanna said, "Do you suppose the poor man has had anything to eat?"

Kyle motioned her to remain seated.

"He'll be all right where he is, for now. Lawrence," he

said, addressing the butler, trained in San Francisco, recommended by Mrs. Crocker, "perhaps you'd take some coffee inside. The gentleman there might like a cup. We can finish here and take our time," he said to the group at large. "There's no rush about this."

"Whatever it may be," said Troy, rather heavily.

Kyle gave his sniffling, snorting prelude to no laugh.

"Oh, you'll be interested, that I'll guarantee."

Luanna looked at him in puzzlement, but he paid her no heed. The meal went on to completion, conversation during the last phase of it, however, being obviously less easy than before. When it was over Kyle got up at once; although he had been so hostly in seeing that his visitor received coffee, he himself took none and allowed no time for Troy or Stanfus to have any. Leaving the women still at table, he led the way into the room adjacent to the front room, the same high-ceilinged chamber with two fireplaces and an outside entrance which had been Hub's bedroom but was now converted into a sort of sitting room-office; it was useful since it alone in the wide, gleaming, winking spaces of the downstairs floor had a door on it.

Stanfus set down his ledgers. He placed himself in a leather chair at the central table, choosing—in response to a gesture from Kyle—a seat next to Lamar Custis. As for the latter, he might have had no better notion than anyone else, except Kyle, as to what the meeting was about, but if he experienced uncertainty he did not show it; he pushed back the cuffs of his brindle-plaid racetracker's suit as if about to play a poker hand. He had brought his coffee cup in with him, still half full.

Kyle put the proceedings in motion.

"Well, Lamar, it's kind of you to drop in. I think it's time we counseled together, as you Texans say."

He reached over to a side table, stocked with cordials, and picked up a bottle of French brandy.

"I see you got your coffee all right. Here, let me charge it for you."

He pushed the Courvoisier in Custis' direction.

And Custis, who'd had coffee and nothing else, while the others present had been dining handsomely, shook his head. He looked warily around the group, priming himself for whatever might come next.

"All right," said Kyle, "now you remember a few weeks

ago, the day we went out to see Atlass at the club. You and I talked about the drop in KinCommon, this goddamn decline that's imperiling our loans. We talked in the office, it was on a Sunday morning, and you had a theory—something that hadn't come into my mind. You thought someone in the family had been selling stock. Wasn't that the gist of our conversation that day?"

"That's right." Custis' eyes seemed to shrink. "So what got all this started, if you don't mind my asking. What's he here for?" he said, eyeing Stanfus. "I'd like to be cued in."

Troy looked up sharply.

"So would I if you don't mind," he said. "Has something been going on that I'm not supposed to know?"

"Not at all, brother," said Kyle. "I knew if *you* had wanted to unload you'd have come to me and said so. You and I haven't always agreed on company policy but we haven't crossed each other up. We never will."

"I hope not," said Troy. His hands were on the table and he rubbed his palms along his flattened knuckles. "I'm still in the dark as to the purpose of this meeting." His glance went around the table.

Kyle turned to Custis.

"You want to tell him, Lamar?"

The Texan shrugged. He reached for the brandy bottle.

"Turkey shoot," he said.

Kyle nodded.

"That's pretty close."

"We run 'em different where I come from," said Custis. "The shooters know what they got to do and the turkey knows why he's there too. If I'd been notified I'm 'spose to be the turkey, I could have stayed where I was."

"You were kind to drive up," Kyle said.

"You're welcome, sir," said Custis. "Since it appears this meeting has been called to order, I'll put this on the agenda."

He tossed an envelope onto the table. Kyle picked it up. The flap had not been sealed, and he glanced briefly at the contents before laying the envelope aside.

"I've always respected your intelligence, Lamar," he said; "that's what made you valuable to KinOil. Where you went wrong was taking a pool in with you. The transactions got so big that Scott Stanfus here"—he nodded at the transfer agent—"traced the short action right back to you. Never mind, Scott," he interjected, staving off Stanfus, who, with finger in ledger, was preparing to read. "We won't need that now. KinOil has just accepted Mr. Custis' resignation. What annoyed me most, though," he went on, once more turning to Custis, "is that, as treasurer, you borrowed stock from the company to cover your short sales while you made money from the decline that was wrecking our credit."

"And drawing his salary," put in Stanfus, who had been bouncing in his seat, barely able to contain himself.

"Exactly," said Kyle in the same placid tone. "Lamar, you are a crooked son of a bitch."

Troy leaned forward.

"Is it legal, what this bastard has been doing?"

"Unfortunately, yes. There's no law against it. I expect someday there will be. Kicking his ass is about all we can do, I presume," he said, turning to Custis, who was sitting with his underlip stuck out and a blank look on his face, as if the talk concerned someone else. "I hear you're going to Shell. Could that be true?"

"No, sir," said Custis promptly, "but I have a place to light."

He rose, stuffing the watch chain with which he had been fiddling into his vest pocket, tight about his little paunch.

"Y'all are wrong on a couple of points, Kyle. I didn't have a pool, I went alone. The stock was under plenty of pressure, Mr. President; news just somehow leaked that you were ass-deep in oil and new acquisitions and nowheres to go with either of them. That about my borrowing KinOil stock is right, but what was in the treasury is back there now, as our young buddy here will tell you." His glance traveled to Scott Stanfus, and he smiled at him. "I recommend you put him at my desk. It's all cleaned out an' waiting for him. And if he needs instruction in the job, send him to me and I'll tell him how I operated, so he kin avoid it, ha ha."

"Goodbye, Lamar," said Kyle.

For the first time his voice betrayed some impatience.

"Goodbye to you too, Mr. President. It's been a pleasure doin' business with y'all."

He walked to the door, closing it carefully behind him.

From the lawn, through the open window, came the sounds of workmen putting the dance floor into the pavilion.

Neither Troy nor Kyle changed position at the table, but Stanfus, feeling tension in the air, looked at Kyle for instructions.

"Will you be needing me any further, Mr. Kinsale?"

"No, I think not, Scott. Having you here was enough, it seems."

"Oh, we had the evidence. That's for sure." He tapped the ledgers under his arm, then hesitated. "I'm sorry he said that, sir, about my appointment, the thought that I might become the . . . new treasurer. I am happy to serve in my present capacity."

"You've been doing fine."

"Thank you, Mr. Kinsale. But I wish to say . . . if there were the possibility of my moving up, I would be happy with that also. I believe I could handle the job."

"We'll take that under consideration."

"I'm very grateful."

He left. Troy, pouring whiskey, looked after him with distaste.

"Why don't we make a clean sweep and get rid of him too?"

"He's all right, for where he's at."

"That's what you said about Custis."

"Custis made a lot of money for us, for a while."

"And cost us the same later, didn't he? I disliked the son of a bitch on sight. The nearest I ever came to breaking your ass was the day you sprung him at the meeting without telling me."

"I well remember," said Kyle good-naturedly.

Troy shrugged his heavy shoulders. He had aged more than Kyle; there was gray at the temples and the sideburns of his reddish-gold hair but he looked fit and strong. He had an authority now that he hadn't had before.

"One thing he said made sense. Here we are tonight, giving a hoedown costing ten or fifteen thousand clams to celebrate what? The acquisition of a company as piss-poor as we are when it comes to marketing position—"

"A company with ships," Kyle interrupted, "a company with two refineries, a company with—"

"With outhouses instead of service stations and cigar coupons instead of money in the bank. Don't get me started, brother, old pal. We're going for a new deal. Either you and I work this out between us or I'm going for your pecker at the Land and Cattle meeting. And don't get the idea that I'm kidding!"

Kyle sighed. He reached for a cigar and lit it.

"Suppose," he said, "I told you I had a way out of all this? What would you say to that?"

"I'd suggest if you have a brainstorm you'd better come up with it pretty fast."

"I intend to. And there's a gentleman coming to this house tomorrow who'll help us put it over. W. R. Hearst."

"You've been talking to him about this?"

"No, but I intend to. He'll go along with us because what I'm proposing is right in line with his policies—"

"He despises the oil business."

"He's also a great Californian. And he helps Californians. When I talk to him I want you right there with me. All right? And have a little patience."

Kyle reached his hand across the table. He smiled at his brother, his bony face lit with an affection quick and boyish—a hark-back to an older time, as if Troy were still the ranch-raised, happy boy to whom Kyle had written from an eastern boarding school, ". . . send me some California dirt . . ." and Troy had sent it, a shoe box full, by mail.

But now Troy hesitated. When he finally stuck out his own thick paw and shook, his expression was still surly.

"I'll have patience," he said, "until June."

"Which is all I ask," said Kyle.

2

H. H. Atlass with his wife, Jenny, and other Atlass International executives, several already tiddly, with their ladies and a jolly crowd of other corporate people from KinOil's captured companies arrived at the ranch station in midafternoon and were given a rousing welcome. Some had made the trip before, having been principals at prior Arc de Rawhide parties, but none had traveled in more splendor. The private car *Geronimo*, a classic in rolling varnish, complete with wicker furniture, brass cuspidors, red plush curtains and cut-crystal highball glasses, rolled in somewhat shakily behind a mammoth freight engine, the only steam engine the Southern Pacific could detach from other duties for this service. Troy was nowhere to be seen. He had saddled a horse and gone off riding in the hills, but with the rest of the family on hand to do the honors his presence was hardly missed.

Luanna remembered everyone's name, she greeted them all in just the right way. Now and then she handed the list to Millie and dashed off to the kitchen, forestalling some disaster or repairing one that had already taken place. Three men in bloody aprons stood there slicing up animals in murderous silence, but in the annex, where the stoves were, the two huge gas burners and the one for coal, a voice was screeching. The pastry dough, it hadn't been iced. Iced! The pastry chef, Hirtzel's number two man, had sent the dough on ahead, in wicker hampers—you couldn't make pastry with warm dough. He'd said to ice it. Luanna calmed him down. A Czech person with a harelip had cut himself opening the mussels for the soup. She got him a bandage—would Czech blood spoil mussels?

Two distinguished people, down on the billeting chart as members of the Atlass party, were not accounted for: Lord Hector Mellis, of The Lilacs, East Riding, Devon, England, did not climb down, when others did, from the high steel lip of the *Geronimo*. Nor did his secretary, with whom he was reputed to be traveling.

Millie doubted the accuracy of the chart.

"Are you sure they were to be with the Atlasses? They don't sound like Mr. Atlass' style."

Luanna, who had made the chart from Kyle's typed invitation list, conceded that a mistake might have occurred.

"Perhaps they were coming with Mr. Hearst."

"That seems more like it."

Later checking revealed, however, that the English couple were indeed an Atlass connection. They had missed the special car's departure time and were coming up by rented limousine.

The imperial Mr. Hearst and his entourage drove in at sundown, a motorcade of five vehicles, the Hearst Mercedes leading. In addition to Miss Davies and his son George and George's wife, the publisher's fellow travelers were the same mixed bag of motion-picture and newspaper people he had taken to Europe with him earlier in the year: Harry Crocker, a gossip columnist who also functioned as troubleshooter and had charge of Mr. Hearst's dachshund; the actress Dorothy Macaill (Miss Davies' confidante); Arthur Lake and William

Collier, Jr., youthful actors, along to make the jokes; and a saturnine man named Edgar Hatrick, who, soon after the party's installation in its quarters, was seen doing calisthenics on the lawn.

Luanna took a quick dislike to the dachshund, which, when she tried to make friends with it, snapped at her hand.

A hundred and twenty people sat down to dinner in the downstairs rooms that night—the largest company ever assembled for a meal at the ranch, even in the days of the De Bacas. Twenty-five catering waiters sent by Mrs. Crocker served the seven-course meal; ten others poured the wine. Once more—as on the night of Hub Kinsale's death—gaslight and candles laid yellow gleams and bluish shadows over the movement of bodies and faces and the surfaces of the colored glass screens and panels of the downstairs rooms.

Mr. Hearst refused a cocktail. He turned his glass down when the dinner wines were served but accepted some champagne when toasts were made; he responded handsomely, in a squeaky, testy voice, to Kyle's words of welcome —he saluted Kyle and Troy as "members of one of our state's greatest families, now in the forefront of our business community . . ."

Dancing began sharp at ten. Helene stood at the door of the pavilion, handing out the masks and wigs; nearly everyone took the masks. Anson Weeks tinkled out "The Old Ox Road" and Mr. Hearst led off with Miss Davies, hoofing it like crazy. Both were excellent dancers and though years apart in age they looked well together. Mr. Hearst was quite amenable when younger men such as Dr. Sotomayer and Scott Stanfus asked his lady to dance; however, whether himself dancing or sitting out, he watched her, watched her, his huge head swinging like a spectator's at a tennis match, and his tough old eyes, bright as a buffalo's and cold as charity, seldom diverting from her charming figure.

Mr. William Randolph Hearst, then seventy-one years old, was a formidable person, his height topping Kyle's six foot three, and heavily built; he had sloping shoulders, big feet and a big belly, none of which impaired his looks as much as they would have a lesser man's, due to his carriage—the sense of personage he always conveyed. Clearly he enjoyed life, his lightness of foot, his great cumbersome body, and his sense of power. He had a three-story face, with a high, peeled forehead and a chin like a cornerstone; in between he wore a permanent grin, fixed as if by house paint on his shark-fish mouth.

Mr. Hearst was winding up a wretched year. Profits from his newspapers had fallen off; he was hard put to find the eight or ten million dollars he was accustomed to spend annually on his houses, his travels and his hobbies—collecting antiques and producing movies starring Miss Davies. He had enjoyed, as usual, his European summer, but his image as an old Jeffersonian Democrat had blurred. He'd had a meeting with Hitler; he'd been photographed with Dr. Alfred Rosenberg and other Nazis. He admired Mussolini. He had criticized the unions, urged the readers of his San Francisco newspapers to stand fast against the general strike, to vote against Upton Sinclair when Sinclair had run for governor on a scheme to end poverty in California. Did the old bastard think poverty was good? that the unions, which he'd once supported, had no rights? Was he, who had defended Tom Mooney, the so-called anarchist, now plotting to destroy liberty? Was he a fascist, making common ground with the slick-talking, Jew-heckling radio priest Father Coughlin?

Kyle was not sure. He had met the great man only a few times before—first when he had been invited, like most Californians who were making news, to spend a weekend at San Simeon. One thing Kyle knew for certain: with his sixty-one newspapers, his radio stations and the rest, Hearst could still shape public opinion; he still manipulated certain state and national legislators, eager enough to do whatever he wanted.

During a break in the music, Kyle took Alma over to the table where Hearst was sitting with Miss Davies and his actor jokesters, drinking mineral water; when the women got up to dance again there was a chance to talk. Kyle came out with his doubts: what about the Hitler meeting, had that really happened? And the old man said yes, it had; a Nazi hanger-on, Putzi Hanfstaengl, formerly an art dealer in New York, had arranged it. Hearst had been curious about Hitler, but had gone to the meeting only because his friend L. B. Mayer had asked him to—Mayer had wanted him to intercede for the Jews. And he had done so. He had done that, not just for Mayer. He had wanted to find out the truth about it for himself. The German treatment of the Jews was awful—a horrible business. It had been getting worse all the time. He had told Hitler that. Yes, he had, he insisted, and Hitler had said the oppression would soon be over. It wasn't important, not a permanent part of his policy . . .

Christ, Kyle thought, does he really believe that? From what he'd heard himself it was bullshit. He didn't altogether trust the old man but he thought that on the whole, even if deluded, he was not in the fascist camp. Not yet, anyway.

Once he'd started talking, Hearst went on and on in his queer, squeaky voice, his head swinging, his eyes following his mistress's pretty backside: no, he said, he did not regard Hitler as a war threat, but England and France were arming. There was smoke in the air all right . . .

"Can we stay out of the next one?" Kyle said with a show of anxiety, knowing this to be a theme dear to the great man's heart.

"We must, and we shall. The continental fortress, protected by two oceans . . ."

Hearst was launching into a Hearst-Brisbane editorial on national defense when Miss Davies came up on the arm of Scott Stanfus.

"Come on, Pops, let's d-dance," she said to Hearst.

Her stammer always seemed most irresistible when she was making a demand.

"I'm having a serious discussion with Mr. Kinsale."

"Well, foo to that. Come on, and I'll give you a b-big k-k-kiss."

Hearst hoisted himself up. His submission to a pretty woman seemed to emphasize rather than take away from his macabre power. Kyle, standing aside, suggested that they continue their discussion at a later time. The publisher nodded.

"I like noon meetings. I am not an early riser."

He pranced off nimbly, steering Miss Davies' body with the bulge of his belly.

Bubble lights, like false money, bounced through the air from a hand-operated mixer; the Anson Weeks band played "By a Waterfall." The air in the pavilion was stifling; Luanna had the braziers taken out, cold drinks brought in. She sent Doc to order the men drinking in the house to join the party. Lord Mellis of Burmah Oil arrived late; his hired driver had got lost in the Gabilans. He was hungry. Luanna went to the kitchen and brought him a plate of warmed-over food. His Lordship oozed a prickly, counterfeit kindliness which deceived no one. He said to Kyle, "Build cracking plants. That's the future. Octanes, octanes! The higher the better. Aviation gasoline. I'm sure you understand."

He walked away, sitting down with H. H. Atlass at a side table.

"What does he mean by that?" said Doc, who had been standing with Kyle.

"War, I suppose. The British are hipped on the subject."

"Do you think it will happen?"

"Go and talk to Hearst."

Mr. Atlass had adjusted to the acquisition of his company by KinOil—or else did not realize he was being exhibited as an item of spoils. He seemed to enjoy himself increasingly as the evening wore on. In a dinner jacket, with a costume mask pushed up on his forehead, he drank whiskey and water copiously, staring at the dancers with his lidless eyes and applauding at the end of every number. At midnight, during a music break, he rapped on his glass to introduce, ". . . a celebrity here with us, whom I'm sure you will all recognize from his movies . . ."

At this a loose-jointed, drunken man rose from an adjacent table and, without the band, performed an acrobatic tap dance, finishing with a perfect back somersault, which brought down the house. Kyle recognized the performer as Atlass' golfing companion from the Lakeside club.

Lord Mellis leaned forward.

"Extraordinary. Should I know his name?"

"You'd know Fred Astaire's name wooden you?" Atlass inquired.

"I would indeed."

"Well, that is not Astaire. Jack Taraway is this man's name."

"I shall remember that."

"Astaire's got the reputation," said Atlass disgustedly. "Taraway's got the talent . . . Okay, Jack," he added, shouting at Taraway, who had been about to start another set, "you did fine. Now go siddown."

At 1 A.M. a supper of Mumm's champagne and broiled calves' testicles in patty shells was served. A Mexican combo played Latin numbers, after which Anson returned with "Love in Bloom." Kyle, who had missed Alma at supper, was about to go in search of her when a woman's voice near him said gently, "If you're looking for Miss Paris, I can tell you where she is."

"You can? I'd like that."

"She sent you a message—she's gone to lie down. She'll be back soon."

"What's wrong with her?"

"Upset tummy, I believe. She and I met in the ladies'. I'm Dede Atlass."

"And where have you been all evening? We were expecting you on the *Geronimo*."

"I came with Hector Mellis. I telegraphed you about that."

"We had word he was traveling with his secretary."

"I'm his secretary."

"Sorry. I didn't know."

Moving out of the scruff by the entrance, they had, without either being specifically conscious of it, begun dancing.

She said, "You shouldn't get the idea that I was part of Daddy's deal—I'd been working with Hector long before he began investing in American oil companies. But when he decided Burmah Oil needed backup, as he called it, I sort of steered him to Atlass—only to have you gobble it up first, you ruthless man."

"It's becoming clear."

"Wonderful! If you need anything more I'll look in the files."

"The more interesting information wouldn't be there, would it?"

She stepped on his foot.

"I wasn't being critical," Kyle said. "His Lordship is charming."

"No he's not. But he knows a lot about oil."

They danced for a while in silence. Miss Atlass was not, like Alma, a full-bodied girl who became light when she danced; she was a slender, falsely thin woman who whacked herself bang-up against him. Her shoulders were broad, thin and beautiful, making her narrow body in the low-cut spangled dress look better than it was. She was tall, her blond head just under his chin, which was tall for a woman. Her hair was pulled back harshly and it had no shampoo smell. She had small features and a small, rough-looking mouth.

"Lord Mellis," Kyle said, "is a lucky fellow."

"Come, come," said Miss Atlass, "I thought you were going to look after Miss Paris."

"You said that there was nothing wrong with her."

"I said her tummy was upset. That can happen when a person is pregnant. I didn't mean to disturb you, have I?"

"Not at all," said Kyle stiffly.

Oh, no, not in the least. First of all, it couldn't be true—wasn't true, by any means. No chance. But then again, if it just happened to be true, absurd as that might be, one did not need some damned blond stranger, secretary-mistress to a jolly British lord, telling him about it with a suppressed smirk, as if she might be mentioning, *en passant,* that his fly was open.

He twirled, looking for a place to set Miss Atlass down.

The music, fortunately, was stopping; they were close to her father's table. He gave the lady his arm . . .

Atlass and Lord Mellis had their heads together, deep in conversation.

3

Mellis was enjoying himself. He had been drinking, but not more than usual. He had been attended through the evening by a manservant whom he had brought with him in his car, a person who understood His Lordship's needs and was indispensable to his comfort. One of his duties was to oversee the food placed before his employer and make sure that it did not contain anything Mellis found hard to digest, such as fowl, entrails, nuts, mushrooms, cinnamon or certain types of fish. He was also instructed to bring around a light Scotch and soda every forty-five minutes.

Lord Mellis was a small, chubby man with an underslung jaw and very bleak blue eyes. He was one of the richest peers in England. He had gone out as a young engineer to Mexico during the early years of the century to work for a Yorkshire contractor, Weetman Pearson (later Lord Cowdray), who was building a harbor at Veracruz. Excited by the oil discoveries at Spindletop, Texas, which took place about that time, Pearson sent Mellis through Mexico to look for likely places to drill. They put together a clump of concessions and the two men, now partners, organized the Mexican Eagle (Aguila) company. They negotiated contracts with the British Admiralty and in fact supplied the Royal Navy with most of its petrol through the Great War. Soon thereafter Cowdray's name appeared on the King's Honor's List. Mellis, a lord by birth, had to be content with the money he'd made.

Lord Mellis had a deceptive personality. Though he

seemed a typical caste snob, with his beautiful clothes, his self-indulgence and his old-maidish ways, he had lived all his life in the heat of action. In spite of his age he could still make rapid, accurate decisions. By nature and training he was ruthless but there was also his softer, even religious side. He enjoyed churchgoing, especially the singing of the grand hymns of the Church of England, many of which he knew by heart; he had contributed a font and a chancel window to St. Martin's-in-the-Green and he kept a pew there for years with his plate on it, though he lived in the country and seldom went up to London.

There were other monuments to his name, several of them cast as historical events. When it had seemed advisable in the interests of Aguila to dump Madero as president of Mexico and put in Huerta, Mellis had trooped off to Whitehall and brought back a suitcase containing money to pay for the coup. Later it had been he who, after joining BP, reached an agreement with the Reza Shah, the restless ruler of Iran, extending BP's concessions from 1933 to 1993.

Iranian oil! Mexican and Venezuelan and Burmese oil! All very well in their way—but Mellis had seen early their vulnerability as supply sources for the military and naval needs of his country. The one passion of his life was England —her greatness, her sovereign future: the contributions he had made to these ends were his true and lasting satisfactions. It was incidental that in bringing them about he had also acquired power and wealth. It was not his business if the Reza Shah, rich in a starving country, punished thieves by cutting off their hands, or if Huerta, the Indian-faced executioner, had his enemies, the great fighting liberals of Mexico, dragged off to a quarry and machine-gunned in the night. The world must go on and the quest of securing oil for the Empire, vigorously pursued, did not involve righting every wrong encountered along the way or correcting the social ineptitudes of wogs and aborigines.

Lord Mellis sat hunched in his chair, gazing icily through his monocle at Dede Atlass, who had just danced by in the arms of a redheaded, broad-shouldered young man. This person had come late. They had met at the door. Her partner, though extremely handsome, was not the best of dancers; Dede was gently, laughingly instructing him in a rumba step; then, the music changing, she left off teaching and fastened herself against her partner in her special way, the way which

Hector Mellis knew so well. He was not jealous of Dede's flirtations. She was a splendid secretary and an interesting woman, good-looking, sophisticated and adaptable. You could take her anywhere and he had found by experience that having Dede on his arm and occasionally in his bed was far more agreeable than knocking about alone. She had grown up in the oil business and her instinct for its subtleties had often served him handily; he had become used to depending on her judgment, and when she had directed his attention to her father's company, he had looked into the proposition and ultimately recommended an investment by BP.

Atlass was a tiny outfit by world standards, but Mellis liked it for the same reasons that later appealed to Kyle—its transportation and marketing facilities. He was well disposed toward H. H. Atlass and kind to him for Dede's sake; he enjoyed his stories of the cable-tool days in California, the strikes and riots, the fires and the whoring and the struggles with the Ku Klux Klan; however, he considered that in terms of executive usefulness the old man was well over the hill, and he had shown little sympathy when Atlass, shaken by his interview with Kyle at the golf club, had come to him seeking a defensive merger with BP to stave off a takeover by KinOil.

Mellis had sent him packing. "Take the tender offer," he directed. "Consider yourself a lucky man."

He had watched Kyle's career and met him briefly several times; the best thing that could happen to Atlass International, in his opinion, was to become a part of the domain Kyle had been putting together.

Once the offer had been accepted, Mellis had enlarged his own position in the overall venture by buying more KinOil stock. These purchases, coming on top of the acquisition news, had done much to steady the market.

Harry Atlass had opened his shirt collar for greater comfort. His tie was askew and so was the farm-boy wig which Helene, with a tender smile, had handed him as he entered the pavilion. He was drawing with a pencil on one of Luanna's damask napkins while his wife, an ample-bodied lady with a shy, sweet face and the arms of a lumberjack, leaned forward to study the results.

"A pipeline," he was saying, "right here. Nice, easy gravity flow straight to the ocean."

"To San Pedro?" said Mellis sharply. "That would be three hundred miles."

"To hell with San Pedro, Your Lordship," said Atlass. "Build our own port at Coos Bay or close by. Any one of these fishing harbors here . . ." He made check marks on the napkin. "We might even get a bill into the state legislature to preempt a right-of-way as a public utility. The gas!"

Mellis adjusted his monocle.

"How deep is the water?"

"Shallow, and the bottom is loaded with rock."

"Sounds like a bugger then."

"Wrong, Your Lordship. We dredge out the fucking rocks, build a breakwater with 'em. For like three, four million bucks we could do the whole bit. Put a valve on the end of a pier and bring the tankers bang up to it. Get back the cost in three, four years . . . I'll have one more of those," Atlass added as a waiter slanted past with a tray of drinks.

"Please, honey," said Mrs. Atlass.

Atlass patted her hand.

"Well," he said to Mellis, "how does it look to you, Hector?"

Mellis passed a frigid glance over the napkin.

"Get some estimates," he said; "that would be my suggestion. You're the board member, my dear fellow, not I."

"But it's interesting, eh?"

"All your ideas are interesting, my dear boy," said Mellis.

"That's all I wanted to hear, Mellis," said Harry Atlass. He knocked back the rest of his drink and signaled for another.

"Please, dear," said Mrs. Atlass, "you promised."

He folded the napkin and put it in his pocket.

Mellis seemed to have forgotten him. Once more he was peering through the dancing throng at the big, ruffle-headed boy with Dede. Now which one would that be, he wondered; I don't believe I've seen him before. By "which one" he automatically placed the young man in a certain category; without having to think about it he had recognized, even at some distance, the hair, the stance, the angle of the head—

The Kinsale look!

Outside, in the damp night air, Kyle hurried toward the Spring House. His one purpose was to find Alma. Mostly he just wanted to be with her. That above all. Only then would he get to the bottom of this . . . a story concocted out of whole cloth by the blond lady while she pushed her flat body up against him, flattered to perceive she could excite him physically while she worked at upsetting him emotionally.

Devious indeed—but she was obviously the devious kind.

Tall and powerful, with head high and his thoughts in shambles, he rushed along, hardly noticing where he was going, and suddenly, there in the path where it turned at the corner of the main house, he almost knocked someone down—a girl with her shoulders wrapped in a fur coat, coming in the opposite direction.

"Darling . . ."

"Alma!"

They embraced.

"Were you looking for me?"

"Yes . . . I heard you weren't feeling well. The blond woman said—"

"You met her? She's nice. I did feel badly, miserable—but then it passed. I must have eaten something that—"

Ha! So that's it?

"What's the matter, darling?"

"Nothing. I was . . . a little worried."

"Let's dance. I've hardly danced with you at all. Don't you want to go back for a while?"

And it was true, this was exactly what he wanted, to go back where the air was hot and the music ripping along, the catering waiters weaving in and out of the people dancing or clustered in groups, the waiters holding the trays of whiskey and champagne high in the air, the chefs in the serving pantry preparing the ices and the frosted cakes and cookies. It was a glorious evening, all of it—everything that happened, every plate of food eaten and sip of wine drunk, and every word spoken—all of it was proof of something vitally necessary for him to prove to himself, though its exact nature also was not clear. Not success. Success was a game for newspapers, for *The American Magazine* and *The Wall Street Journal*. This was something much bigger. It was a demonstration of . . . his aliveness. Of his existence in the world. What difference did it make if Alma was pregnant or not? He'd had certain suspicions about her condition—yes, damn it all, it was not exactly a surprise—but . . . was one supposed to be upset? Women had been pregnant before; they got that way daily, in droves, in millions; every son of a bitch walking around on earth was a testimony that a woman had been made pregnant at one time or another. A simple matter of an ovum and a sperm.

He'd have to think about it!

5

The party picked up speed.

Troy Kinsale, after a roll of drums, announced the contest for the door prizes, a diversion concocted by Luanna at the last minute—a prize for the man or woman likeliest to succeed, for the most appropriate wig, for the best male and female dancers, for the most Latin rumba couple and for the best-matched waltz couple. Hearst and Miss Davies won for the waltz and Jack Taraway and a flame-haired De Baca cousin from Gonzales for Latin dances. Taraway was promptly disqualified on the ground that he was a professional but was awarded a consolation prize, a live ranch-raised turkey.

Dr. Sotomayer, who never left the floor, romped off with Alma. The youthful doctor was really an excellent dancer. He was the only man in the room with a beard and this gave him a distinguished appearance combined with his slimness, his straight features and wavy hair, and his fierce concentration on the work in hand. Sometimes he would move very slowly and soulfully, hardly touching his partner, transported into some distant world by the music; then again, in the Latin numbers, holding his back absolutely straight, he would set his handsome face into an Inca mask and send his legs flying out in weird loops and struts and jiggles as if they were made of rubber. Other dancers, put in the shade by his performance, would pull over to watch him. Alma winked at Kyle over the doctor's shoulder but she was obviously having a good time. Kyle abstained from cutting in. He was bored, waiting for her to come to his table and join him. He was impatient to go to bed with her and then, well, have a talk, clear up his thoughts about certain matters. He drank several brandies.

Cliff Kinsale, home from Berkeley for the Christmas holidays, danced again with Dede Atlass.

Anson Weeks packed up at two o'clock and the Mexicans, Los Alamitos, replaced him. There was still a handful of late-stayers cutting up when Alma and Kyle left at three. The apricot-wood fire in her bedroom had sunk into a bed of coals; Alma undressed in front of it. She did this with marked lack of artfulness, her one purpose being to get her clothes off quickly so she could make love, but the net effect was innocently, urgently erotic. Kyle's undressing was too slow to suit her; she reached for him, pulling out his rising cock and wiggling to get under him, squeezing and rubbing him as if urgent contact with his member had been ordered as the only means of saving her life.

"No rubber?"

"No, no, we don't need one."

Her vaginal muscles gripped him, small preliminary shudders circulated through her body.

From long, passionate habit Kyle could usually tell the exact moment—sometimes when he was entering her—when she would first spasm. Earlier in their relationship this quick climax had embarrassed her. She would say, "This one doesn't count," or "That's an accident, go on, go on." She felt somehow that the velocity of her pleasure might put him off; she didn't want to seem ill-bred. She had read about the trouble women had about climaxes, how they were supposed to require something called foreplay—supposed to educate men in its techniques, to be slow and to rate themselves along, struggling toward the blessings hidden at the end of the long road. He'd had some difficulty in convincing Alma she was not a biological freak. She was grateful for his assurances but she kept the feeling that she never quite believed him.

Seldom had he loved Alma or wanted her more than tonight; seldom had he been farther from her emotionally, more vexed with her, feeling with complete lack of logic that if she were indeed pregnant the fault was hers. It had nothing to do with him at all.

Tonight was not the night for encores or experiments. Kyle and Alma made love warmly and separated civilly and later they lay together in the glow of the firelight and he brought the subject up.

"How do you feel?"

It was a loaded question, a mood breaker. Alma seemed startled.

"Why, just fine, dear. Wonderful. Why?"

"Well, in the car driving up, you weren't too happy. Remember, on the Conejo grade? And then after dinner, the Atlass woman—"

"Dede, yes . . ."

"She said you were sick, and I wondered—"

"Darling, are you really trying to find out something, like am I pregnant? I thought you knew."

"How would I know?"

"There are ways to tell."

"You could have mentioned it."

"I am mentioning it. So let's talk about something else."

"How long is it since you menstruated?"

"I detest that word. I never paid much attention."

"You don't have any idea?"

"A long time after Ensenada. We were usually careful."

"We were always careful."

"I can remember some times when we weren't. You weren't."

"Try to think. It does have some bearing on this situation."

"How did it get to be a situation? It's not a situation to me. If you want it to be, have it that way for yourself, but don't drag me into it. All I want to know is how long this goddamn morning sickness or whatever is going to last. Otherwise I don't think about it because if I do it spoils everything."

Alma's voice rose slightly and her body heat, seldom low, along with it; Kyle, lying on one elbow, with his free arm touching her, felt the warmth strike through him—the warmth that was Alma herself.

In some queer reversal of their positions, he was now on the defensive.

"It's nothing to be upset about. We just have to be logical, that's all."

"All right, be logical. One and one make three. That's logical because it can be proved."

"Then it's time we talked about—"

"All three people? No it's not, because the third person has not shown up yet and the second person, *you,* is not involved, not unless you want to be. I'm the one who's pregnant. It's a private affair—mine. If we talk about it, then it's going to get grim, when there is nothing grim about it."

"I merely said—"

"I know what you said, Kyle, and I think you're being sweet in a grim way. You haven't said one word that makes me feel you love me and if you keep on I'm going to yoop right here and now. Before you started talking I was happy and I'd like to be happy again, so will you please shut up? Good night."

So saying she turned on her side; within seconds, it seemed—so quickly that it would have appeared a put-on had he not known her better—her breathing became sleep-breathing. Kyle could well remember the first occasion when he'd listened to that sort of breathing from Alma: in Ensenada. She'd had several periods since then, of course, but that was not the point: the point was that when she stopped she hadn't mentioned it. Therefore one had to assume that she had made some unilateral decision. She was leaving him free to do as he liked. What strength she had!

Unable to sleep, he slipped on his clothes and a thick coat and walked out onto the peace of the great lawns. Dawn, which he hadn't seen come to this house since the night his father died, was a tight-looking corner of the sky, behind hilltop oaks; he turned his back on it, preferring the darkness, the mystery of the Gabilans. The guesthouse and most of the cottages were dark, but in the cottage assigned to Lord Mellis and his staff a light was burning.

He took deep breaths of the damp, spicy air. In the luminous sky a flight of Canada geese moved south, so high that the dark, uneven V appeared like a tatter of cloud or mist. Winter was setting in at last, and he was glad of it. He would marry Alma as soon as possible—by New Year's at the latest. He would tell her tomorrow. It was what she wanted anyway—why, she'd been telling him, in effect, that if he didn't rise to the occasion she would have the baby alone. As if he would stand for that! She would be a perfect wife, a fantastic mother! How he loved her! How happy they would be together! The decision brought instant peace. When he went back to his room he fell asleep at once.

Looking back later, to account for what happened, he realized, as he often had before, the terrifying force of time. He and Alma had had little chance to talk. They did not breakfast together, as they often did: she was still sleeping when he went off to his appointment with Mr. Hearst.

The Hearst meeting had enlarged to include Lord Mellis, who had stayed over for it; Mr. Hearst appeared delighted to find that an oil internationalist saw eye to eye with him on current issues.

"You may not know this, Hector," he said, slashing at a plate of scrambled eggs and venison sausage, "you may not even care, but I am launching the most powerful antiwar movement ever staged anywhere. It's called 'Mothers of America.' I am urging mothers to rise up, all mothers. Can you conceive the force they will exert? I am telling them to put a stop to war because they alone can do it, and they will. They will forbid their sons to fight. They will forbid their legislators to declare a war or That Man in Washington to recommend one. Within one year I shall have sixty, seventy million mothers enrolled. The United States must not, cannot again become involved in a war in Europe. What do you think of that?"

"Splendid."

"Mothers united for peace. A Niagara of opinion, never before harnessed in such a cause."

"Lovely," said His Lordship, "I wish them all sorts of luck, you know."

Mellis' manservant had prepared a proper English breakfast but His Lordship refused to eat anything except a sweet roll, which he broke into small pieces and consumed bit by bit, an ironic smile playing around his lips. He said softly, "You feel that Europe is arming?"

"To the hilt, and as fast as possible."

"Precisely. And what is the critical point?"

"France," said Hearst without hesitation. "The French are politically bankrupt and economically rich. They invite slaughter."

Hearst detested the French, who had picked up his passport and ejected him from Paris because of revelations about secret treaties published in his newspapers. He had never forgotten the incident, but always pretended that his hatred of France was based on its failure to pay war debts.

"Do you know the average age of the French general staff, sir?" Mellis demanded. "Close to eighty! Old, old fellows from the last war—they don't need to be slaughtered; they will drop dead of sheer senility."

"Or fright," said Hearst, with his fleeting smile.

"Fright—certainly. They think Hitler will protect them from the Communists. That is like putting a gorilla in your bedroom to protect your wife from burglars."

Hearst's eyes gleamed. The sacredness of the American home, the sanctity of matrimonial bonds, were among his pet themes. Miss Davies, the only woman present—she had crashed the meeting at the last minute—leaned forward to remove a speck of jam from the publisher's chin.

Kyle looked at Troy across Miss Davies' bent head. He could see that Troy was bored—probably wondering what all this about foreign nations had to do with KinOil's marketing problems or the new oil acquisitions which, at Mellis' suggestion, KinOil was considering in Mexico. Catching his brother's glance, Troy looked up and Kyle nodded as if to say, "You're right, but wait a minute . . ."

Hearst was going on about the horrors of the next war, should it take place.

". . . depopulation, Mellis. And merry England won't be exempt. I said this to Max and Winston last summer; they know England won't fight for the League any more than we will. Why? Because terror will rain from the skies, bombs will destroy cities, devastate nations . . . slaughter children . . . and the mothers who would otherwise bear future generations . . . and annihilating death rays—"

"Surely, not rays . . ."

"*Rays!*" yelled Hearst, his squeaky voice climbing even higher. "The race of man could perish . . . and leave the world to the less stupid wild animals." The old man was becoming excited. "The Channel," he piped. "I suppose you're still counting on the Channel—well, it's no help anymore. You can't mount antiaircraft batteries on water."

"Take it easy, Pops," said Miss Davies.

Hearst patted her knee but went right on spieling.

"Let France go down, Mellis," he said fiercely. "Nothing can save her now, why bother? Planes, you must build planes. I said this to Chamberlain. You can do it; you have the best technicians in the world. A German hegemony in Europe does not mean the end of the British Empire if you have planes. We can't help you again, sir."

Several people clapped.

All the houseguests invited for the party were now in the living room or the dining room, many waiting for their luggage to be brought in, ready for departure by plane, car or the private train already waiting for them on the ranch siding; they pressed in around the table, turning the invitation-only brunch into a public forum.

So much the better, Kyle thought: the old man loves to be on stage.

The flotsam remnants of the Arc de Rawhide party, many of them hung over, might not be an ideal audience, but he was stuck with them, it seemed, and in some ways he felt their presence helped to sway Hearst to his views. The temporary glut of oil was insignificant—a tie-up due to laws against selling to belligerents. Actually there was far from enough current reserve for the nation's needs if Army and Navy requirements were lifted to the size demanded by the world situation. National defense: a tremendous theme. Certainly a cause which the Hearst chain, cautious about it so far, could champion. Oil as a weapon, an arsenal in the ground: payments made to keep it there till needed and to encourage the producers to more exploration. Kyle's solution: a consortium of independent companies put under government contract to produce, refine and store an adequate and stable supply ready for instant use in home emergency regardless of what course the majors, with their world marketing facilities and policies, might choose to follow.

"Hold on now," said Hearst, his hard, close-set eyes suspicious, "what are we talking about here, a socialistic kind of thing?"

"I'm talking, sir, about a weapon to protect this land of ours. If we don't have it—and we lack it now!—the predator nations will think we're up for grabs."

The old man wagged his big dome. The predators! His headline-building instincts fastened on the word. Kyle's plan —there could be complications, but he wanted to hear more about it.

"Not here, though. We've enjoyed your hospitality—now to work. We'll drive to San Simeon, that's where I do my thinking. Can you come with us, can you give me a day or two? We'll thrash this out . . ."

His bony hand fastened on Kyle's arm. Even before Kyle could assure him that he'd give whatever time was necessary, his consent had been assumed. Others, the staffers, must be summoned: they must listen and give their opinions. J. F. Neylan from San Francisco; Ray Van Ettisch, the famous editor of the *Los Angeles Examiner;* Arthur Brisbane from New York or wherever he happened to be. ". . . and if he has a cold, just tell him to come anyway. The poor devil is a hypochondriac, always ailing or thinks he is."

Orders flew right and left. Willicombe must make the calls, could come along later. Meanwhile, the cars were brought around, Mellis alone declining the junket to the Castle; he had appointments elsewhere. That night, in the largest of three big, towered buildings, flanked by swimming pools, a block of tennis courts, stables, corrals, gardens, picture galleries, a museum and a zoo, they sat down to McCloud River steel-head, venison steaks, wild boar and huge cuts of prime rib beef, with which their host's chosen beverages were milk, orange juice, Bevo, and tea.

Miss Davies beckoned Kyle aside, slipped him some brandy from a silver flask she took out of her purse. Seldom had a drink tasted so good. He had heard of the nonalcoholic tradition at San Simeon but had neglected, as more experienced guests never did, to bring his own bottle.

For the next two days, from the four points of the compass, Hearst executives arrived as summoned; wary, highly paid men in dark suits and button-down shirts and wing-tip brogues, reporters who had become editors, editors who had become administrators, youngish still, but tipping into middle age, living beyond their means in the expensive suburbs of large cities, heckled by wives of whom they had grown tired, worried about their investments, their alimony, their mistresses, the costs of private schools for children living abroad. They tested the wind before arguing with the boss. Had he called them here to agree with him or talk him out of something? No way to tell, really—he was so crafty and so changeable and he had a mean temper. No one could handle him except Brisbane, the thunderer, the editorial writer who spoke for him on the front page of every Hearst paper, even those which were losing money hand over fist. Brisbane hadn't come. He was suffering, as expected. Something wrong with his nose, the long beak which could sniff out a statesman's turpitude or a corporation's rascality from a thousand miles away.

The Hearsters liked Kyle's plan, with reservations. They lauded its ingenuity, the neat conception of government guarantees to an industry which, in spite of the hard times, was still making huge profits. Have to walk on tiptoe, though. W. H. had been ever vigilant to condemn the doles dished out to business by the new agencies. Hard to get Congressional approval for bonuses to the majors' competitors, the wildcatters—even such rich and respectable ones as KinOil. Watching the old man, seeing the glint in the arctic eyes under the peaked sockets, like matching outhouse roofs, the conferees sought a way out of the dilemma. Possibly Congress could be bypassed. The Army and Navy managed their own oil reserves. Could new arrangements concerning them be weighed by the Cabinet? The funds needed might already be at hand, lumped in departmental budgets . . .

An issue—that was the meat of it. Hearst's comments, often dead on, fell off sometimes into vagueness, yet the occasions when he rambled were the very moments when the Hearsters paid him closest attention.

During a break, Kyle remarked on this to Ray Van Ettisch.

"He doesn't always stick to the subject, does he?"

"That depends on what you regard as the subject."

"It began by being oil."

"Never. The subject is newspaper circulation—in this instance, how your plan can be used to sell papers. On that topic W. R. is the world's leading authority."

"For a world authority he seems to need a lot of advice. Or what are you fellows doing here?"

"So he can test our reactions. He'll mull these over, then act all alone, out of some gut instinct. Nine times out of ten he'll be right. When he's wrong, he can be horribly wrong—but he'll blame no one but himself. Frankly, I think he'll take you on; he just hasn't made up his mind yet."

They turned back to the table. Hearst was pointing a long finger at Fred Eldridge, famous for his raid on the files at Standard Oil's offices in New York.

"What do you think, Fred? Will readers buy it? Or are they too worried about what's happening in their own back yards?"

"I like it," said Eldridge. "It has stature—your kind of importance. It's not new thinking, of course, but it's timely. You can move people around with it."

"Real Brisbane stuff," said Harry Crocker, the court jester, behind his hand.

Hearst chose not to hear him. He went on at some length, improvising an approach that would bring in the Secretary of the Interior, Harold Ickes. If Ickes favored the plan, a great obstacle would be removed. An hour passed. A servant entered and replenished the fire.

Tonight, for the first time, they had continued the policy parleys after dinner. Suddenly Hearst broke off. He patted Miss Davies on the knee.

"Well, dear. Enough business for tonight, don't you think?"

He rose, drawing her up with him, his long, bony arm around her pretty waist. God, thought Kyle, is he going to walk out again without making a commitment? But in the middle of his exit, with his queen beside him, W. R. looked back. "All right, boys," he said, "let's try it. I'll talk to Arthur, tell him what we've decided. You might call him too, Fred. He has faith in your judgment; he gets tired of listening to me."

"Yes, sir," said Eldridge.

Hearst turned to Van Ettisch.

"You lead off, Van, in the *Examiner*. Find news items if you can, hang a lead on them. Storage of military oil. The United States in dire peril. Arson! Sabotage! . . . If you can't find them, make them up. Give people the facts. Nothing else counts."

"I know what you mean, sir," said Van Ettisch.

"See what kind of heat we can develop," said Hearst. "Once it starts we can go all out, bring in the whole chain, nationwide. This can have size, as Fred says."

"I'm sure it can," said Van Ettisch. He was making notes.

Hearst had already turned his back.

"Good night all," he called over his shoulder. Still with his arm around his lady, he stalked ponderously out of the hall.

Kyle sat up for a while, chatting with the Hearsters. Some were genuinely pleased with the decision that had been taken, feeling the campaign for oil could be a circulation builder; others were not too happy, but their comments on the whole were flattering to Kyle Kinsale personally.

These newsmen knew what he was up to. He was manipulating Hearst with all his world fame and far-flung powers into backing a strategy which, whatever its benefits to the United States or its defense, would certainly result in profits for KinOil. The crude would once more start moving through the pipelines. The refineries, now closed down or working at half potential, would give off steam and stench; the tankers would slip in behind the breakwaters. On the New York Stock Exchange, if all worked out, KinCommon would move back where it belonged. Much had been done in three brief days. Yet underneath all, intruded, lay a decision on which Kyle must act without a moment's further postponement—the joining of his life with Alma's.

CHAPTER TEN

A Woman to His Measure

1

For half an hour the lake had been visible, the color of steel, shaped like the print of a big, bare foot smashed down between the mountains. Day was already ending down there among the pines, above the boat docks, the big summer houses packed away in folds of snow until spring set them free.

The plane tilted down, a flake of darkness in a bonfire sky.

It was a queer sort of plane. It had wide but clumsy wings and a thick, deep-bellied body, like a trough or a suitcase. Graceful when airborne, it became clumsy, almost helpless, as it drew near the surface of the water on which its pilot, driven by some madness, was obviously intending to land it; in spite of its weight it jerked around, this way and that, in the air currents rising from the water; it wiggled like a wing-shot duck about to splash in the tules. It could now be seen that it was made of wood. Wheels dangled under its hull and behind, under its tail, was a huge iron hook, designed to brake its speed if it put down on land, where it belonged. It seemed done for, finished—but at the last minute its nose came up, it touched the water, pulled clear, then settled, splitting the wrinkled skin of the lake in a fine clean furrow. The lake rose to engulf it but then fell away. The plane floated. It squatted placidly, as if resting, on the surface of the water which had failed somehow to destroy it. Then the propellers began slowly to turn again.

The plane headed toward the shore.

Kyle bunched the papers on which he had been working. He shoved them into his briefcase. He had enjoyed the trip, though it had taken longer than he had expected.

It would have been far longer, he knew—perhaps been impossible by air—without the Sikorsky. He had Hearst to thank for that. The old man had heard from Willicombe that Kyle needed transport; he'd suggested the Fokker at first, but changed his offer when he learned Kyle's destination.

". . . no, no. The amphibian's the ticket for you; it's pressurized. The Fokker isn't; you could black out flying those high passes. The Sikorsky can pop you down on Tahoe; you'll enjoy it . . ."

Pilot Brad Kohlenberg cut his engines. A gasoline launch with two men in it had pulled out from the jetty just ahead. One was at the tiller. The one amidships reached a hand to steady Kyle as he stepped from the high-bellied hull of the plane into the boat.

Seated, Kyle flipped off a farewell salute to Kohlenberg, who returned it with a wave and a smile.

The launch headed toward shore.

"Welcome to Nevada, Mr. Kinsale," said the man who had steadied him aboard. "Thank you," said Kyle.

2

It was a fine welcome, the only trouble with it being that Nevada was the last place he had wanted or intended to visit, at least as of eight o'clock that morning, the point at which everything had changed.

Possibly it had been his own fault. He was ready to admit that. He had left for San Simeon in a rush, to accommodate W. R.'s whim: he knew this much about the old son of a bitch, you accommodated his whims or you got nowhere with him.

Alma hadn't wanted to go. She'd had, she said, other plans. She still didn't feel very well and she thought she'd rest for a day or two; she could do this and still help Luanna and Millie clean up after the party. She could explore the ranch, the beautiful and unfamiliar territory where Kyle had grown up and where she, until now, had never been. It all sounded perfectly reasonable, and Alma had seemed gay and content when he called her from The Castle, after his first day of conference, to report his progress. The second day he'd been too busy to call, and when he tried again, on the third day, Luanna told him Alma had gone up to San Francisco with Millie for some sightseeing. Dr. Sotomayer was driving them. They would be staying at the Fairmont. Kyle rang the hotel and left his number, but Alma, though registered, hadn't called back. That had been the last day of his talks at The Castle, when the conferees all sat so late. Wakened early, as usual, by the screams of peacocks and other bizarre birds and the roars of the zoo animals demanding to be fed, Kyle put in another call. He asked for Alma's suite number, but was told that calls to that suite were being transferred to another room, where the line was in use. Did he wish to call back? He said he'd wait. Several minutes passed; when he finally got through he had trouble hearing due to background noises, one of which sounded like a cocktail shaker working.

Cocktails at eight in the morning? Kyle wasn't sure he had the right room. But the low-pitched, warm voice was Alma's.

"I'm so glad you called. We were just leaving. We're going to Reno."

"You have to be kidding."

To his own distaste, he sounded ponderous, suspicious—like a surly husband.

"I most certainly am not. We're all up in Kirk's suite—Kirk Sotomayer. You know? The doctor who helps your brother-in-law. We're with some people from Texas we met last night. They're going with us."

Texas people! Impossible! . . . And this Sotomayer, the dance-floor prancer, how had he appeared on the scene?

"Alma," said Kyle, "let me talk to Millie."

"She went back last night, honey. Dr. Braden is so busy you know. Kirk should go back too, but I'm persuading him to drive us. You don't mind, do you?"

"I'll take you to Reno. To hell with those other people."

But she was going on, "It would be so much more fun, dear, to go there with you; I just wish we'd thought of it, only we didn't. And I know you're so busy! I'll be back tomorrow, the day after at the latest. Hold on—What?" Alma had her hand over the mouthpiece, talking to someone in the room with her. "Kirk even has a place where we can stay, where I'll be chaperoned. Isn't that nice?"

And Alma giggled—also unlike her.

"Listen, Alma," Kyle said firmly, "stay in San Francisco. I'm coming up. I have to talk to you."

"Later, darling," said Alma. "Give my regards to Mr. Hearst; he's such a sweet old thing. I adore him and I hope he makes a lot of money for you. We can talk when I get back."

"Alma—"

"Kyle," said Alma, "I hate to rush, but the bellboy is here for the bags."

"What's to do in Reno?"

"Well, for one thing I can gamble," said Alma; "everyone gambles in Reno. You remember what fun we had with gambling in Ensenada, and everything. So wish me luck . . ."

"Listen, Alma—"

"Goodbye, darling."

A sound which might or might not have been a kiss perked over the line, which then went silent.

Kyle called Millie in Dead Eagle Valley.

"I leave you in charge of my girl," he said, "and you desert her. You should take your duties more seriously."

"Perhaps you should take your girl more seriously."

"What do you mean?"

"I have a feeling she's not too happy."

"I can't imagine why."

"Then your imagination isn't very good."

"Tell me what you have in mind."

"When a girl is in a certain condition it doesn't take much to upset her. Where are you calling from?"

God—another woman telling him about Alma's condition! Was it as obvious as that?

"San Simeon. Listen, Millie—"

"On a party line?"

"Nobody's listening in, Millie."

There was silence on the line as Millie shaped her thoughts. "I am not going to discuss this on the telephone, Kyle. I have some discretion, even if you don't. But I wish you'd think about Alma."

"Millie, are you trying to tell me that she went to Reno with this doctor because she intended to—Christ! What kind of a doctor is he, anyway?"

"Kyle," said his sister, "I've never heard you talking so

stupidly. There are just two places where a girl might go if she wanted a certain thing to happen. Tijuana is one and Reno is the other. Do you follow me? Because that is absolutely all I'm going to say. Goodbye for now."

Kyle's head was spinning. Alma in Reno to get an abortion? It was unbelievable! Yet—was it? That was what Millie thought, and Millie was no fool. If a girl "wanted a certain thing to happen" . . .

It couldn't happen, it must be stopped. At once! Surely there would be time. Such an operation couldn't be set up in a minute, even in Reno.

He would get there. He would put an end to it.

He called Millie back.

"Alma said this Dr. Sotomayer had a place where she was going to stay. Do you know where that was?"

"No, I don't, Kyle. I didn't hear the name of it. I'm sorry."

"Some friend of Dr. Sotomayer's . . ."

"Relative, I think. Brother-in-law or something."

"And you don't remember his name either?" said Kyle in a fury.

"I wasn't taking notes," snapped Millie. "It was a resort. That I did hear. Not in the main part of town, outside somewhere. Surely there can't be too many places of that type; you could check around."

"Or check clinics, perhaps?"

"You don't have to be sarcastic. I didn't realize you'd need to know."

"All right," said Kyle more gently. "I'll locate her somehow."

He began to make calls . . .

He'd thought at first of using the Rolls, but when Hearst heard where he was going the old man instantly put the Sikorsky at his disposal. "Flies like a lead balloon but it will get you there. Only aircraft in my garage that can manage it this time of year . . ."

3

"I'm Deputy Leban, sir," said the man who had helped him aboard the launch. He indicated the steersman. "This is Deputy Tannen. Sheriff Cliff went out on a case, otherwise he'd of come in person. Sheriff Biscaluz of Los Angeles phoned us your E.T.A."

"That was kind of Sheriff Biscaluz," said Kyle.

"Sheriff Biscaluz and Sheriff Cliff are good friends," said Leban. "We have a vehicle ashore."

"Watch your step now, sir," said Tannen from the rear.

The launch had pulled up to the jetty. Here the men secured it fast fore and aft. Tannen unshipped the outboard and handed it up to Leban, who had climbed onto the float at the end of the jetty. Kyle got out, and a boatman in an elk-skin jacket and a cowman's hat got into the launch and began to fit on a canvas storm cover. The breathing of all present made gray plumes of mist in the darkening air, which was so cold that it hurt to breathe and smelled deliciously of snow and of the pines which surrounded the shore and clumped around the clearing between the road and the place where the jetty ended. The trees held up their boughs, burdened with thick loads of whiteness, as if marveling at the strange antics of the men and their concern for the stubby plane which had disturbed the winter dream of the great silent lake.

In the clearing, in the twilight, stood a county car with a driver at the wheel and its parking lights turned on.

Leban stowed the outboard in the trunk of the car. Then he got in the back with Kyle. Tannen sat in front with the deputy who was driving. The car moved off through ice-stiff ruts, heading toward the paved highway which led to Reno.

"Sheriff Biscaluz described your problem," said Leban, "to locate these certain friends of yours. We've been on it all day. We're still trying."

Kyle nodded. The knot in his gut, which had relaxed somewhat during the trip, tightened again.

"We got word," said Tannen, "it wouldn't be one of the downtown places, as far as you knew."

"That's right."

"The downtown places, they'll register their guests according to state law. Them road places, they'd just as soon the Sheriff's office don't double-O the books, the register, the reason being that the guests don't like it. Some of them guests in plain language is hoods."

"I see."

Deputy Leban fished through the open front of his fleece jacket and produced a piece of paper. He snapped on the car's courtesy light. The paper, a lined Sheriff's Office report blank, had two names written on it in pencil.

Miss Alma Paris.

Dr. Kirk Sotomayer.

"Did we get the names right?"

"You did."

"Just checking, Mr. Kinsale. I'm going off duty, but Tannen here is staying with it. He'll have another deputy working with him; they'll call you at your hotel whether they get anything or not. You'll be at the Riverside?"

"That's right."

"The Riverside, Jerry," said Leban. "We still got two places we want to see, Ace High Gardens and the wop's place."

"I appreciate what you're doing. Please tell Sheriff Cliff how much I appreciate it."

In the Riverside Kyle showered and changed his clothes. Now in place of a suit he put on a Pendleton shirt and whipcord riding pants, a costume more in keeping with the frontier feel of the town. While he was dressing the room telephone rang and he rushed to it, hoping for news about Alma, but the caller was the hotel manager, a Mr. Goberlin.

Mr. Goberlin had been studying the register. He was fired with eagerness to welcome Mr. Kinsale to the Riverside.

Kyle thanked the manager. The call did not displease him. During recent years he had grown accustomed to having his name recognized and the recognition generally proved a convenience. In the present instance he used it to cash, at the desk, a check for several thousand dollars. Mr. Goberlin even apologized for not having the money instantly available; there would be a slight delay while he got it from a gambling house a few blocks away—the High Sierra. Kyle said he'd go there himself and pick it up. He might as well go to the tables for a while, he decided: it would pass the time. It would also serve to distract him from the sickening thought which, though it had been responsible for all his actions this day, he had refused to allow headroom in his consciousness; that something bad could happen or be happening right then to Alma. He looked around the large room, more than half empty at this early hour, deciding where to play.

A blond woman with a handbag hanging open hurried past him. She wore some whorehouse perfume that billowed sickeningly from her clothes and body. She went straight to the roulette table. Several other players—mostly garish, elderly people—followed her, the sort seen in Nevada gambling houses and probably nowhere else. They bunched around her, some just watching, others following her bets. Her movements were erratic and her eyes jerky. She had evidently been winning heavily. She pulled chips out of her bag and arranged them in stacks, pushing out one stack on red without counting it or seeming to know what she had done. The red came up. The woman let the bet ride. She did this three more times, winning each time. When she took her winnings out the black came up. The people who had been following had pulled out when she did. All had made money. But now the woman's luck changed. She started playing individual numbers and silly combinations. She lost. Her entourage became disgusted with her and wandered off. The woman was not conscious of this. In her queer, strained position, hunched at the table, she was gathering her forces for a major effort. Her hands no longer twitched and her strained eyes were quiet. Their gaze turned inward. She was sweating. Beads of moisture soaked her dress under the arms and the reek of her became stronger. She played with increasing boldness, pushing chips all over.

Kyle watched her with amazement. He could see that the woman was playing some homemade system which was very complicated and had absolutely no chance in the long run but which just now worked marvelously. Kyle bet along with her as the others had; soon he doubled the stake he had brought in, then tripled it. The table sent for more chips, which were brought; then a new wheelman came on.

"Oh, no, you don't," said the blond lady. "You don't do that to me."

Though it was against table rules to touch a stake after you had laid it down, she immediately dismantled all her bets, dumping the chips into her bag.

"Something wrong, Mrs. Bracken?" asked the wheelman.

"Yes—you, you goniff," said Mrs. Bracken. "Watch out you don't burn your foot with that battery you got taped to it."

The wheelman ignored this.

"Ladies and gentlemen," he said to the table at large, "place your wagers."

Kyle followed Mrs. Bracken to the cashier's window.

"They try that on me," she said when Kyle had obtained his money; "they give me the foot when I'm ahead. Do you want to go to Perinchio's?"

"Where's that?"

"Wop's place, out the Truckee Road," said Mrs. Bracken. "They got an honest wheel there. Honest as some, anyway."

"All right, but wait a minute."

Kyle went to the desk and left word that if a call came for him it was to be relayed to Perinchio's Paradise House, Mrs. Bracken supplying this nomenclature. They shared a cab, the lady nattering along about her gaming prowess. The road was icy and the trip longer than Kyle had expected. A snowstorm had begun. The air became speckled with tiny flakes which drifted horizontally, as if fearful of touching down; they would approach the earth and then veer away, whirling upward in an indecisive, hopeless attempt to go back where they'd come from.

"I'm a dice shooter, first and last," said Mrs. Bracken. "I can make forty, fifty thousand clams a month with the bones alone. I shouldn't bother with the fucking wheel."

Kyle kept nodding, letting her gab away. He could not have said why he had left the Riverside, where he should probably have stayed. He must have been mad to sign on for a freezing ride with this boring woman to a place he'd never heard of! But . . . Deputy Leban had mentioned some resort, "the wop's place." Could this be it?

Mrs. Bracken, after all, had brought him gambling luck. She might bring him luck in finding Alma. She had reminded him—if only because they had met in a casino—of the Mexican *chica* who had made Alma so jealous in Ensenada.

Perinchio's resort was a huge, rambling structure, set back from the road in a clump of trees. It was flanked with a scatter of hotel cottages and topped by a large neon sign. A security guard with an elaborate armament slung and buckled onto him checked arrivals; he looked at Kyle suspiciously, then said "Can I help you, sir?"

"He's with me, dear," said Mrs. Bracken.

The guard's glum, half-frozen face lit up with a smile.

"How's it going, Gilda?"

"I'm sharp as jailhouse coffee," said Mrs. Bracken. "I'll clean Rudy out tonight."

"Wait till tomorrow," said the guard. "Tonight's payroll night."

He motioned to Kyle to go on in.

The cabdriver, who had not been paid, was standing by his cab. Kyle had his money out but Mrs. Bracken would not let him use it. She handed the driver a large bill, refusing change. She took Kyle's arm and they entered the establishment in style.

The Paradise House contained recreations for all tastes: a bar, a cabaret and a gaming room. At one end of the large central hall a log fire burned in a big stone fireplace and a sleepy bellman sat with his feet up on a settee. The hotel desk was at this end. Out in the center of the room were restaurant tables and a small dance floor. The gaming was separate —Mrs. Bracken never reached it. She made a dash for a slot machine near the front door and began feeding silver dollars into its maw, yanking savagely on the handle. She dominated the machine completely. Almost at once, with a loud clank and a queer, frightening rumble, it spewed out money. Dollars cascaded out of it unstoppably, some of them spilling onto the floor. Kyle was bending to help Mrs. Bracken pick them up when someone pulled his sleeve; he found himself face-to-face with an old prospector, a leathery desert rat of the sort familiar to generations of movie fans. The old bastard's mustache and eyebrows were bleached white and stood out in garish streaks against his sad sunburned face. He had only one eye. With this he winked intimately at Kyle. Seen close up, his eyeball resembled the globes of the world with which elementary schools were once equipped. The blue was the oceans, and the red, coiling veins, the rivers. The white was the land—what there was of it.

"Party acting like they know you, mister."

Alma, sitting at a cabaret table with a group of people, had her hand up, waving. She looked very pretty in a tight-fitting red dress and a small black hat. Kyle waved in return. Well, at least he had found her: that was what counted. Everything else would follow in due course. He started toward her table, feeling as if he had imagined this scene and that in fact it was an illusion, some sort of film he could see projected while at the same time he was taking part in it. To properly carry off his part he must keep his attention firmly fixed on outward things. The sensation was the same as when, having been knocked on the head, one sees double. He understood it, but it put a strain on him nonetheless.

Kyle reached Alma's table. Tall as a tree, handsome and bony, he smiled in friendly style at Alma and the people with her. There was nothing put on about his friendliness. At that moment he had an affection for everyone around him, particularly these people, even Dr. Sotomayer, since they were with Alma and he had found her. The doctor's handsome face seemed to have grown narrower and his beard darker. His lips were compressed.

They had all been drinking but were doing so no longer. An empty champagne bottle was upended in its bucket. Ice had melted in the empty highball glasses. There was a stack of unpaid bar checks on the table. The atmosphere was grim rather than merry. Kyle noted all this in a flash, nodding around as if he were being introduced, although in fact no introductions had been offered.

Alma was putting on lipstick. Unlike the doctor, she was perfectly composed. She paid no further attention to Kyle. She was talking to Sotomayer.

"Kirk," she said, "I'll walk right out of here if you make a scene."

Sotomayer stood up rather sheepishly.

"How do you do, sir?" he said to Kyle, holding out his hand. "I believe we've met . . . at the ranch."

"We have indeed," said Kyle agreeably.

He shook hands with Sotomayer, then with a bald, dark-complexioned fellow, sitting at the end of the table.

"Rudy Perinchio, Mr. Kinsale. We used to be neighbors, ha ha!"

"That was when he lived in Oakland," said a woman at his side. "I didn't even know him then. He was in the real-estate game."

"My wife, Vera," said Perinchio, "twenty-seven years. Now we own this place, joint tenancy. I call it Paradise because that's what it is to me."

"You lived in Oakland?" Kyle said in a tone which, despite his good intentions, did not sound flattering.

"Oakland—Altemira," said Perinchio, "not so far apart, when you see a map, eh, Mr. Kinsale? Fingers Billy," he went on, addressing a thin man across the table from him, "shake hands with Mr. Kinsale, the oil magnate. Fingers Billy Remington, Nevada's outstanding poker artist, until they got wise to him."

"Wise or not, they won't let me play no more. That's for

sure," said Fingers Billy. He bobbed up to shake hands with Kyle, then resumed his seat.

"Not in the casinos," said Mrs. Perinchio. "Not a casino in town where they will let him play. He's burned them all. So now he's a dealer. Is that a laugh?"

Fingers Billy looked remorseful.

"I deal, yes. For Rudy. But a private game is what I like."

"Well, you'll never get me in one. Not with you, you thief," said Mr. Perinchio.

Fingers Billy smiled modestly. He was a deadly pale, small, spindly man in a ruffled cowboy shirt which had plastic cuffs pinned over the sleeves. His eyes had deep sepia smears under them. His fingers were so long they appeared to be built with one joint more than other people's.

A waiter, also in cowboy dress, approached the table.

"All right, folks," he said, "can I bring you something else?"

"Yes, how about that?" said Perinchio heartily. "What will it be? Wine? Highball, Mr. Kinsale? Name it."

Though his tone was cordial he reached forward as he spoke, pushing the unpaid chits toward the center of the table.

"These are on us," said Sotomayer.

He picked up the chits.

Alma groaned.

"Don't, you fool," she said in a low, passionate voice.

She jerked the chits out of Sotomayer's hand, dropping them on the cloth. She leaned forward and spoke into Kyle's ear.

"We're in Tap City," she whispered; "we haven't eaten all day. All we do is sit here and drink."

Tap City! Where did she get expressions like that? The phrase turned Kyle's stomach. It reminded him that there was now a stretch of Alma's life in which she had picked up such weird turns of phrase—a piece of her recent history about which he knew nothing. And it was still going on . . .

In spite of his disgust with this and with the scene in general, Kyle took charge. He took the chits. He pulled some bills out of his pocket haphazardly and gave one, then another to the waiter. "More champagne," he said; "a magnum, if you have it. And . . . whatever else they were drinking . . . Is that all right?" he asked. "Food too, all around. Shall we have menus? Or—you take the order," he said to the waiter. "Anyone for steaks?"

When Alma mentioned food he was reminded that he too hadn't eaten dinner. He was very hungry.

"I'd love a steak," said Alma, "and Vera would too. Wouldn't you, Vera? . . . Vera is Kirk's sister-in-law," she whispered, "that's why we came to this awful place. But they're such cheap people, you wouldn't believe."

"I don't mind," said Vera, "a steak might be nice. How about you, dear?" she inquired of her husband. "Do you care for something?"

"New York, medium rare," said Perinchio promptly. "Tell Constantine, the Kansas City Double A. We got the best meat this side of the border," he said to Kyle. "I'd match it against your ranch meat, with all respect. Or your fine clubs."

The waiter went around the table, asking people how they wanted their steak cooked and writing the answers. He set down an unopened pack of cards. Fingers Billy broke the seal at once and dealt poker hands all around.

"Just so you see what we're talking about," Fingers Billy said, winking at Kyle. "A little demonstration."

"Don't bet with him," said Mrs. Perinchio. She arranged her hand in a split second, making a discard. "Draw, is it? I'll take three."

Fingers Billy dealt her three cards. None of the others had picked up their hands. A silence, heavy and stupefying, fell on the table.

Kyle turned to Sotomayer.

"You and I should have a talk, Doctor."

The doctor jerked his shoulders. The points of his cheekbones glittered above his beard. He worked his lips around as if short of air.

"At your service, sir," he said with drunken dignity. He spoke as if Kyle had challenged him to a duel.

"Rudy," said Kyle to Perinchio, "do you have an office we could use?"

Perinchio was instantly all business.

"My own office," he said. "You can lock the door, be just as private as you like. Francis," he said to a second waiter, who had just set down a huge tray piled with food, "take Mr.

Kinsale in back. You know where the key is. And the doctor too . . . Don't take too long, now fellas," he went on as Sotomayer, immediately acquiescent, rose to follow the waiter; "you got a couple prime steaks here. You don't want they should get cold."

The office was a small, untidy room behind the bandstand, furnished with a large desk, some wooden chairs and a handsome mahogany gun cabinet. A plug-in electric heater supplied warmth, which was minimal. Liquor company art calendars enlivened the walls.

Dr. Sotomayer went straight to the nearest chair. He sat down confidently, as if he rather than Kyle had asked for the interview.

"This is the best way. Man to man, and get it over with. Am I correct?"

"I'll ask the questions, Dr. Sotomayer," Kyle said. His tolerance of the doctor's queer manners was diminishing. Reaching down one hand he took hold of Sotomayer by the collar. He jerked him out of the chair.

"I'd like to know, Doctor, if you or anyone else has tampered with Alma. Surgically. You know what I mean. Answer that at once. We'll take it from there."

"You're . . . choking me, sir."

"Answer the question."

"No . . . one . . . has . . . touched her."

"All right, all right."

He let the doctor slump back. Ignoring him, with a wild expression in his eyes, Kyle strode around the tiny room. So the main point had been settled! His own future, and Alma's, was safe. Now all that remained was dealing with the doctor himself, which as he saw it presented no problem.

Sotomayer struggled with his collar, trying to loosen it. Succeeding in this, he pulled the desk closer to him, as if using it as a protection against an imminent attack. He glared at Kyle with fear and loathing, as a person might who finds himself penned up with a wild animal.

"How and why did you bring Alma here to Reno? If it's true that you brought her."

"I brought her. She wished to terminate her pregnancy."

"You were in favor of this?"

"She didn't ask my opinion."

"Then abortions are not your regular line of trade?"

"I have never performed one. I would not have performed this one."

"Good. But though your own ethics are so lily-white you might not have been above recommending her to some less high-minded sawbones who would do the job, isn't that right, Doctor?"

"I refuse to answer any question put to me in those terms."

"Very well, I'll have to assume an answer—mine! If she wished to terminate her pregnancy and you wouldn't do it, you would have to contact someone who would. Are you a medical doctor?"

"Of course."

"You fell into luck with Dr. Braden, it would seem. You soon discovered that his practice and his lab and his hospital were funded beyond the levels of the most affluent city medical centers. You enjoyed that, didn't you?"

"I was well compensated, yes. I felt glad that Dr. Braden had such strong backing."

"However, you weren't going to spend the rest of your life studying the pathology of Dead Eagle Valley."

"The pathology of Dead Eagle Valley interested me very much."

"But the social life of the neighborhood palled somewhat, didn't it, Sotomayer? Sometime during the recent party at the ranch or more likely the next day, when Alma confided in you, telling you that she was knocked up. She was not happy about it, and you offered to help her. Right?"

"False."

"Then what's the truth?"

"I made no offer. She asked me what could be done, and I told her—"

"That you could arrange it. And by performing this unique and, in fact, illegal service you would be attaching yourself somehow to the money that was funding the clinic. You would be making a personal tie of considerable value."

"You see all human actions in a framework of money, don't you, Mr. Kinsale?"

"It's a convenient framework when no other is at hand."

"It can also be inappropriate. I didn't need that incentive to help Alma. She wanted to end her pregnancy to get away from you. I reckoned this to be a good idea. Now I think so more than ever."

"With all respect, Doctor, that's none of your business."

"She'd never be happy with you," said the doctor calmly, his eyes glinting maliciously above his dark, trim beard.

Kyle sucked in his breath. He turned away, trying to hold on to his temper.

"Be that as it may, Doctor, I think you should take a trip. How would you like to go back to the Sorbonne and do some research? Or . . . wherever you like."

"I should like it very much."

"Good! I suggest that you start at once. How much will it cost?"

"You're planning to pay for it?"

"Yes."

"Why?"

"Let's say because of your sympathy for Alma. Would ten thousand be enough?"

"Enough to pay for several years. But I won't take the money."

"Won't you? We'll see."

Kyle felt in his pockets. He pulled out a large wad of bills, his gambling winnings. He thumbed through this without actually counting it. He estimated it at between three and four thousand dollars. Sitting down at the desk he took out his checkbook and quickly wrote a check for seven thousand more, leaving blank the line for the person to be paid.

"How do you spell your name?"

"Spell it any way you like. It doesn't matter."

Kyle made no reply. He resumed work on the check.

There was a knock on the door. Neither man responded.

Kyle finished the check. He laid it on top of the money.

"You can send up for your suitcase—whatever you have in your room. Please leave at once."

He pushed the check and the pile of bills toward Sotomayer.

The door opened and Alma came in. She came up to the desk with her firm, light step, looking first at Kyle and then at the doctor.

"We're all tired of waiting," she said. Then she saw the money on the table. "What's that for?" she demanded. "My God, have you two been *gambling* in here? Or what?"

Kyle shook his head. For once he could not bring out a word.

"Mr. Kinsale says I should take a trip," said Sotomayer. "What do you think of that?"

"I would say it's up to you."

. Said the doctor: "Actually, I'm inclined to agree with Mr. Kinsale. I shall be going now. I'm sorry the weekend didn't turn out better for you."

"Oh, I think it turned out well enough," said Alma.

"In that case I'm happy."

"You've been very kind," said Alma. "Thank you, Kirk. Thank you for everything."

The doctor took her hand and raised it to his lips in the gallant way he'd learned, perhaps at the Sorbonne.

"I wish you every happiness. And please remember, if there's ever anything I can do I'm at your service."

"I'll remember," Alma said.

Dr. Sotomayer dropped her hand. He kissed her lightly on the cheek, then turned to Kyle.

"Goodbye, Mr. Kinsale," he said. "I won't be needing this."

He tore up the check, then wadded up the money, dropping it on the desk. He turned quickly and left the room, closing the door without a sound.

Alma sat down under the hanging bulb, which poured its naked light into her face.

"It was stupid to offer him money."

"I wanted to speed him on his way."

"I'm so glad he didn't take it. Was it a lot?"

"A fair amount. He could have had it."

"Not if he wanted to keep his self-respect."

"Since when are you so concerned about his self-respect?"

"Kyle," said Alma in a low voice, "if you get angry I'm going to walk out, probably for good. I've had all I can take. I mean it."

"I'm sorry. I don't feel angry. I'm happy. I've been goddamn worried about you."

"You needn't have been. I was perfectly all right."

"Were you? I don't know what you were up to, but Millie had some idea. It's a good thing you changed your mind."

"I didn't change my mind."

"What do you mean?"

"Kirk changed *his* mind. I suppose I'd flirted with him, not that I meant to. I was just trying to be nice to him, or at least nice enough so he'd arrange a . . . curettement or . . . whatever they call it . . ."

"Abortion is what they call it."

"Yes. Disgusting word. He said he **would,** but then he got this great idea, that he'd make an honest woman out of me. He got very boring. So now I'll have to find somebody else to . . . well, to do one."

"Alma," said Kyle at length, "I don't think you mean that."

"Oh, but I do."

"What ever gave you the notion I didn't want a child?"

"I just won't talk about it, Kyle. Now or ever. You asked me, and I told you. I told you how it was, and right away—"

"You said it was a personal affair."

"So it was. And is."

"*Personal!*" Kyle shouted. "Meaning I have nothing to do with it, is that the idea? As if my feelings weren't involved?"

"I wasn't thinking about feelings. I was thinking about love."

"Love. Exactly. I love you; for Christ sake, Alma, what more do you want? I've been going out of my mind. So I got hold of a plane. I walked out on W. R. Hearst right in the middle of the situation."

"Ha! So that's what we're back to—a situation. A situation with dear Mr. Hearst, a situation with dear Alma. That's what you called it when we were in bed at the ranch and you had been dancing with that awful Atlass or Mellis woman, whoever she was."

She broke off. The door opened. Rudy Perinchio appeared, a hostly innkeeper's smile bisecting his gangsterish puss.

"Excuse me, folks," he said genially, "but I got your steaks keeping warm. Are you coming back or will I tell the kitchen to forget them?"

"We're coming back, Rudy," said Kyle. "Serve the steaks and close the door."

4

In every family there are sayings which, because of their absurdity or quotability, or because, like a photograph, they bring back some moment in the past, live on and are repeated until they turn into symbols or codes. Such a quote in the Kinsale household was Kyle's command to Perinchio, snapped out furiously, without thinking, that night in the gambling-house office. Neither Kyle nor Alma ever saw Perinchio again after that night, but at certain times, mocking

Kyle's peremptory way of giving orders, Alma would say, "Serve the steaks and close the door . . ."

At the time neither of them thought it was funny.

The interruption caused by Perinchio had turned them into stone, into salt; they stood staring at each other as if they had been separated for years and had now met again by accident. In a few seconds their feelings swung from quarrelsomeness to desperate need. My God, thought Alma, what's wrong with me, what are we arguing about? She wanted to throw herself into Kyle's arms, but instead of this, frightened of what might happen next, she actually took a step backward. Kyle moved after her. His head hit the hanging bulb and set it swinging on its cord, making their shadows lunge up and down the walls.

Kyle took a deep breath. His expression was peaceful and resolute; calmness filled him, combined with a wonderful sense of well-being. Well, it's over, he thought—the whole ridiculous farce. She's young, that's why it happened; women get confused. I almost lost her. The point is it can never be allowed to happen again. And defying the obscure, unrealistic laws of love of which he knew so little, he returned to practical measures, to the strong, efficient methods by which he had always run his life.

"Alma," he said, "marry me. That's all I want—and no more talk about it. Will you do it?"

"Yes," she said with a look of terror. "Naturally. What do you think?"

"I didn't know."

"Well, I will. *I will.*"

"Then it's settled."

"When, Kyle?"

"Right away. Tonight if possible. If not, then tomorrow. Right here in Reno. No delays. How does that suit you?"

"It suits me, it suits me," she said, bursting into tears.

"Good! Good!"

Locked together now, they lost balance, one or the other slipped on something in the tiny office and they slammed against the wall. The light bulb swung madly. They kissed, the mascara running down Alma's face, a coal-town river of tears. It took some time to clean up so that they could go back to the cabaret table and eat.

Oh, how sweet it was to be alive! Kyle was always conscious of this; sleeping or waking it was the hub of his nervous system, it was what gave him strength, yet he had never felt it as truly as now, now that he had this girl back who somehow had become life itself to him. Did she know that? Did she want to be all that? And what was it exactly that she meant to him, when you came down to it? It didn't matter. He couldn't deal with this question, but it seemed right that she was a California girl, brought up on the same great slant of land as he, shaped by the same suns, the same weather, the same huge blue days and nights. It was enough that she walked the same earth, pronounced her words the same way, the California way, enough that she shared the friendliness and laughter of the same strong, healthy people, a California girl! No other kind would have filled the bill.

5

The justice of the peace turned out to be the one-eyed prospector who had seen Alma waving from her table the night before and had pointed her out to Kyle. Brad Kohlenberg, pilot of the Sikorsky, who had stayed over, was best man; Vera Perinchio attended the bride. The decision to keep family out of it worked both ways: Kyle telephoned Troy and Millie *after* the ceremony; Alma telephoned her parents, likewise after the deed was done, legally and in bang-up fashion.

Alma looked superbly fresh and shapely in a blue dress she had brought with her (For this very occasion? Kyle wondered. You never could tell about women!).

He himself stood big and glistening beside her, making his responses in a deep, quiet voice.

The press was not invited. Nevertheless, elopements make news the world over and somehow the story got into the next day's *San Francisco Chronicle* in a front-page box with a social-page follow-up by Millie Robbins. The *Los Angeles Times* had it on page one, Section Two, with a recap of a previous business-page article describing the Atlass takeover by KinOil. Princess Conchita Pignatelli, in her department in the same paper, reviewed Kyle's genealogy for three generations back, brushed over the bride's, and stated imaginatively that the runaway match had got under way during a party given at the Kinsale ranch in honor of Lord Hector Mellis. The Hearst papers nationwide were out in front with pictures

—Kyle in polo clothes receiving a trophy, and Alma at eighteen, making her debut as Las Madrinas, a Los Angeles social group for marriageable girls. *Time* gave the happy couple a Milestone, identifying Kyle as "hard-riding oil tycoon" and Alma as "dark-haired socialite."

Family comments were diverse—mostly favorable.

"But why did he want to elope?" Luanna said. "We could have given him such a wonderful wedding."

Troy, now getting used to his wife's new social awareness, and far from liking it, corrected her.

"The bride's family is supposed to give the wedding."

"Well, all right. Then a reception or something, an old-fashioned hoedown here at the ranch. I should think he'd have liked that."

"Well, he might," Troy said weighing the idea. "We could still do it, even after Christmas. Why don't you write or phone him and see how he feels about it? If he says yes, then we can go ahead and make plans."

"I'll write," said Luanna. "I want to use my new note paper."

Luanna took Troy's breakfast plate and brought him more coffee. She did not want the servants messing around with breakfast. They could better put in their time cleaning the house. She still fixed this meal for her husband as she had when they were in the oil fields. They ate it alone, in a corner of the dining room.

"How do you feel about it yourself?" she said when she came back, sitting down with her own cup. "Do you think it would be fun, sure enough?"

She had learned to tread carefully when dealing with these two brothers. It was hard to tell when rivalry would flare up, even over the simplest matters.

Troy smiled.

"Let's face it, Kyle likes parties better than I do. But this one should be okay. You're right, we ought to do something. At least make it look as if we like Alma."

"Well, I do like her," said Luanna quickly. "Don't you?"

Troy filled his pipe.

"Good-looking. Great pair of breasts on her."

He winked lewdly at his wife, who made a pantomime of swinging at him.

"Oh, you!" she said. "She's much more than good-looking and you know it. She's absolutely stunning. She's a little young for him but perhaps that's what he needs. And she's smart as can be."

"How can you tell? I didn't talk to her that much."

"I didn't either, but I watched her. She never shows off and she gets along well with people. She won't let herself be pushed around by anyone, not even Kyle. He's lucky to have found her. I hope he appreciates what he's got."

Later in the day Luanna wrote to Kyle and Alma offering to entertain for them. She addressed the letter to the ambassador; it was the first piece of mail the couple received as Mr. and Mrs. The party, however, was never given. He and his wife left at the end of the week for a honeymoon in Hawaii. They were to be gone a month or more. There was no schedule.

Doc and Millie Braden had their say on Sunday, their one day of leisure—Millie on the porch steps, doing accounts; Doc gardening close by in what he called his "weed patch," a bed of wild native shrubs and flowers. Much of what they said had been touched on previously, in other conversations; it was through such repetition that a family topic was gradually polished and worn down, like a sea-rubbed stone, until it fitted comfortably into the flow of their lives.

Millie said, "So what it comes down to is that Kyle found a wife and we lost a doctor."

Doc plunged his trowel into the sweet-smelling, loamy earth.

"Not necessarily related events."

"But of course they're related. Oh, I know Kirk was restless, he might not have stayed here forever. But just to pull up stakes and leave the way he did—it's unheard of. Whatever do you think Kyle said or did to him to make it happen?"

"I regard that as strictly their business."

"You do? Well, I don't. If only for the inconvenience it's put us to—finding a replacement and all. I'd like to ask Kyle for an explanation."

"I'm afraid he wouldn't give it. Let's just say the Lord gives and the Lord takes away. To us mostly he gives, for which be thankful."

"And what prompts this profundity?"

. "Just that as an exchange of family assets we've lost little in Kirk and gained a lot with Alma. Wouldn't you say?"

"Oh, Lord, yes!"

Doc cupped in careful, earthy fingers a damp-rooted clump of wild violets.

"Brother Kyle just may have found a woman to his measure."

PART THREE

PART THREE

CHAPTER ELEVEN

Flash Point (1937)

1

Tomoliko Ushiba, equerry to His Highness, Prince Fumimaro Konoye, telephoned at eleven that morning from the Beverly Wilshire to say that the prince had been delayed. He would arrive for lunch by one-thirty, if that was all right. Kyle took the call himself on his bedroom phone; he said he would look forward to seeing the prince at that time.

He went downstairs to tell Alma about the delay but couldn't find her; a maid who was setting the lunch table said she had gone swimming.

She had indeed. For several moments, looking west into the choppy waves, he couldn't see her at all. When at last he spied her, she was so far out she could have been a permanent fixture of the sea, a buoy or a piece of driftwood, except for the rhythmical glint of arms, white but a different white from the spumy wavetops, as she beat along in her easy, powerful freestyle.

Kyle marveled again at the secret heat supply which enabled Alma to keep alive and joyous in oceans which would have frozen any less thermal creature than a seal. Malibu in March! It was unthinkable! Even in summer, in water temperatures of sixty-five and up, he himself would not have stayed in as long as she did every spring day of her life.

He dismissed out of hand the notion, which he had aberrantly entertained for a moment, of swimming out to meet her. Oh, the day, the sunny air, were warm enough—but those waves . . .

He sat down in the living room, facing the huge sea window, and lit a cigar. When Alma came in they could have a cocktail. It would be nice to have one alone together. Then they could have another with the prince.

The house was part of a cliff. It was not on top of the cliff but built into it in a place, a niche, which one might think had been there always although actually it had been cut out, on an architect's orders, by huge machines. Both the house and the cliff were stone, though different kinds of stone, gracefully and now ineradicably fused. Almost two years in the building (Kyle and Alma had moved in slightly more than a year earlier), it was well designed to survive against the forces which the cliff had contested so long—the Pacific storms, the fangs of time, the lunge of the heavy-shouldered seas. The seas would win in the end, of course, unless the world should end in fire, in which case fire would win, but until some such outcome there was an armistice, however temporary, between the house and the ocean. The high stone crevice in the cliff was a nice place to look out from and the voice of the sea rustled through all the rooms of the house like the whisper of an accomplice rather than an enemy.

The living room was on the top floor, level with the drive. Branching off to right and left were bedrooms, various balconies and passages, the kitchens, the front pantry and the back pantry, the main dining room, the kitchen dining room, a gymnasium, a sauna and a sheltered patio with a great open hearth in it for warmth and for barbecuing. In the patio were rubber trees, monkeypods, cedars and Chinese elms, all in bonsai, the Kinsales having been attracted to the bonsai style during a honeymoon visit to Japan.

Voices issued from the patio.

"Put her down, Linda. You're choking her."

"I am not. She wants to come out."

"She can't come out. I'm going to give her a bath now. Would you like to see her get her bath?"

"No, I wouldn't. She's too filthy."

"That's not a nice way to talk."

Kyle knew what was happening. Linda Kinsale, a precocious two and a half, was trying to drag her sister, Katie, aged four months, over the side of her wooden pen onto the tile floor, where Katie usually landed on her head. It was a recurrent morning incident.

Kyle called to his older daughter, "Come here, honey. You can play with Katie later."

"Wait, Daddy."

A screech from the baby was followed by a tense, not quite audible argument between Linda and Rosalie Love, the nurse. Then Linda marched into the room. She stood looking darkly at her father. She had her mother's black hair and lovely camellia skin tones, but the reddish cast of her brown eyes and, Kyle suspected, her aggressiveness came from the Kinsale side. She wore woolen swim shorts and a tiny halter.

"Can I have lunch with you and Mom?"

"Not today, baby."

"Why not?"

"We have a guest."

"I hate guests. Where's Mom?"

"She went swimming."

Rosalie Love, a medium-size, pretty black woman, stood in the doorway. She had slung the redheaded baby on her hip. She stretched her free hand to grab Linda, who avoided her.

"You come on now, child."

"I'm going to find Mom," said Linda, and was gone.

"She shouldn't go down there by herself, Mr. Kinsale," said Rosalie Love without conviction.

"I'll watch for her."

"You wouldn't ruther I fetch her back up?"

"I can see her from the balcony. I'll watch."

"All right then," said Rosalie. She pulled the baby upright on her breast and went out with her, discontented.

Kyle left his chair. From the west balcony, furnished with iron deck chairs and tables and equipped with a brass-cased captain's glass, he looked down until he saw Linda emerge from the house onto the beach. Alma was closer in now and they would have seen each other.

Kyle returned to the living room. From the teakwood cabinet there he set out glasses, bottles and ice. On the cabinet, in matching frames, were a number of family photos, one of them (taken by a court photographer) showing Alma and himself at tea with the Konoyes in Tokyo, in the Konoyes' garden. It was a nice picture. The garden (the best garden in Tokyo, next to the Emperor's, so it was said) was coming into bloom. Not much of the garden, to be sure, showed in the photograph, but its mood was there, a mood of beauty and happiness, and the people looked gay and as if they were truly enjoying one another's company, which they were. All were dressed in summer clothes, European style, except the princess, who had on formal Japanese court dress. She had put it on, after receiving them in her Paris clothes, to show Alma what it looked like; while he and Konoye had been talking the women apparently had fallen into a discussion about styles and the princess had unexpectedly—and not entirely to her husband's pleasure—gone off to change, taking Alma with her.

That tea had been the last of several meetings with the Konoyes.

Kyle was sorry that Princess Chyoko had not made the present trip with her husband. It would have been pleasant to have had her at today's lunch. Alma would have enjoyed that. Kyle knew that Fumimaro Konoye and his wife, unlike most members of their caste, usually traveled together; the fact that he had not brought Chyoko with him this time indicated that this trip, perhaps, was different in its nature and purposes from some others that the prince had made.

Kyle was the one who had prolonged the honeymoon. Instead of a month in Hawaii they had wandered far and wide. Kyle felt he could afford a holiday; Troy could cover for him, driving over from the Piru field, when need be, to the Los Angeles office. Certainly the Atlass acquisition had helped KinOil. The stock was up several points and seemed set to go higher. Scott Stanfus' letters and cables had been encouraging.

For a while Kyle reveled in his idleness. He swam and partied, ate and drank copiously, and made love to his wife. He even played some polo. They were playing at the Honolulu Club and the Parker Ranch and there was a new grass field on Maui. Pete Baldwin mounted him and Pete's horses were very good, though it was not like having his own. Hawaii was sending a team to the mainland to compete in an upcoming twenty-goal tournament and Pete had invited him to ride with this team. Kyle had been grateful for the suggestion but was tired of the Island group, bored with the drinking, the luaus and the flirtations. There had even been one idiot who had made a pass at Alma, as if taking it for granted that a honeymoon bride would be in such a state of sexual arousal that she would go to bed with anyone. She had soon put him straight on that—but then, when they moved on, heading for other beaches, different luxury hotels, Kyle had been splashing around in the tepid, clear water, a hundred yards away and in full view of the beach, when this native man had walked out of the palms and invited Alma to make love.

The gall of it had been beyond belief.

"What did he say?"

"Something in his own language. Polynesian, I suppose."

"He couldn't have expected you to understand *that*."

"I did though. It was unmistakable."

"He made signs?"

"'Obscene gestures?' No. I was the one who made signs. I pointed to you, swimming out there, and I pointed to my wedding ring."

"He might also have observed that you were pregnant."

"Yes. I'm not sure, but I think that might be what he found so attractive. That or he didn't think it mattered, if I felt like . . . what he wanted. Then he showed himself to me."

"Jesus!"

"Oh, I don't mean he did anything crude. It wasn't like that at all."

"He pulled out his pecker on the beach, and it wasn't crude?"

"I wouldn't have told you if I'd thought you'd be upset. It was just sort of childlike. He took off his loincloth or whatever and when I didn't . . . seem . . . interested . . . he just smiled and put it on again. He seemed very contented with himself."

"I could have made him very discontented. How old was this guy?"

"Not young. His face was young, the way they all look, but he had gray in his hair. He was very well built."

"Apparently."

"Kyle, are you really jealous or are you just pretending? The whole thing was really ridiculous. I suppose it could have been revolting, but it wasn't even that. It was just as if a panel had slid back and we were in some olden time when people behaved like that. Do Balinese women do that, do you think? Do they screw any man who approaches them?"

"I believe they're quite free in their habits."

"It must be confusing when they produce babies."

"Well, keep in mind that you're going to produce one. And next time some amorous stud propositions you just whistle or something. So I'll know."

On the whole, Bali had been fine, but Bora Bora was even better, with its huge lagoon and a tilting wooden hotel straight out of a Joseph Conrad story. The hotel was run by a retired Dutch postmaster and his wife, a young woman who made wonderful seafood crepes, and in the bar the second night Kyle met an island trader, Captain Beckmesser, who played billiards with him after dinner. Captain Beckmesser's two-masted auxiliary cruiser, the *Wilhelmina*, was anchored in the lagoon and Alma wanted Kyle to charter it for the places they were going next until he explained that the *Wilhelmina* was too slow. They had a lot of ocean and a lot of land to cover, so they took the P&O mailboat instead. They took other, smaller boats; they hired shaking, screechy little planes and old cars and once, for a day and a half, they rode mules.

The honeymoon had boiled down to visiting places where there was oil.

There was no question of obtaining concessions, Kyle explained. None were available. He had just wanted to check out these places, to see their production and refining methods, if they refined, which most of them didn't. The Kinsales stayed only a day or two in each place. The hotels were frightful and the weather was getting hot, but with Hector Mellis now about to go on the board of KinOil, cables from his London office moved ahead of the couple. They were met everywhere by executives in grubby linen suits or jeans and the native shirts of whatever country they were in. Then guides took Kyle out to the oil fields while Alma stayed in their room and rang down for ice to cool her bath water. She wrote letters and postcards to people at home and caught up on her diary.

"No woman in the world has ever had a more marvelous time than I am having . . ."

Kyle had saved Tokyo for the last. For once he had arranged no introductions. Like Alma, he had never been in Japan. He had thought it would be fun to keep business to a minimum and explore the city together and Alma agreed. However, it seemed Kyle was not the sort who could long be inconspicuous. Hardly were they in their suite in the Imperial than a person who identified himself as the counselor at the United States Embassy telephoned on behalf of Ambassador

Joseph C. Grew and invited them to dinner on the following night. They were to be in Tokyo four days.

It had been at this dinner at the embassy that they met the Konoyes.

2

Kyle took the photograph from the bar cabinet. He passed a cocktail napkin over its glass frame, then placed it in a better location, on the mantel. If you wished a friend to know that you remembered him it was not well to leave his picture in a dark corner, with a splashed or grubby glass.

Kyle had also another snap of Prince Konoye. Remembering this, he rummaged in a drawer until he found it—a glossy half-page shot clipped out of *Life*. No good without a frame—but there were frames stashed away; Kyle found one that fitted the *Life* candid. He put this product of his handiwork out where, like the other Konoye souvenir, it could be seen.

Voices were audible on the stairway—Alma, chilly and beautiful, up from the beach with Linda on her shoulders. She crouched, dumping the child onto the carpet, then stood up, ignoring Linda's screech, and kissed him. She saw the picture at once.

"My God, are you really going to leave it there?"

"Certainly. Why not?"

"Won't he know we just put it out, for him to see?"

"Even so, he'll be amused. Shows we've been keeping track of him."

"I'm surprised he ever let them take it, the *Life* people. Perhaps he couldn't control them, once they were at the party."

"He could control them all right. He can control as much as any man in Japan."

"Then he must have had a reason."

"He did. In one word, derision."

"Of—the other person?"

"Also maybe of the whole plan for a Berlin-Tokyo agreement, which is still very much in the wind."

"Just the same, it was a strange thing for him to do. Wasn't he making *himself* silly, too?"

"Hard to tell. We'd have to know the mood of the governments then. At that party and at that moment in history—the Japanese government and the German government. If he intended it as a put-down then it was a put-down, and I think he so intended. He has his own way of operating. I respect that."

Alma studied the candid. The shot had been taken at a costume party; the people had on fancy dress or masks and there were streamers and party fixings in the background. Prince Fumimaro Konoye was made up as Hitler—his eyes glary, his mouth open as if in a burst of Sportpalast oratory!

There was the sound of a car outside. Alma quickly set the picture down. She turned toward the door. But the car went on by.

"I'm so glad you liked Konoye," the ambassador had said after that first dinner. "He liked you also, very much. He mentioned that when he rang up this morning to extend this invitation. Now you two can get down to specifics."

"We certainly stayed away from them last night."

"Oh, that's his way," said the ambassador. "Always the personal contact, before anything. After all, what can be accomplished at arm's length? Needless to say, the topic will be oil."

"I should have read up on it."

"Ha, good. Very good indeed. He would appreciate that. He has a tremendous sense of humor. Yes. Ha ha. We're talking now about a popular man, a brilliant and sophisticated man. He's important now but going to be more so. He's had a report on every place you've been since you and Mrs. Kinsale left the Islands."

"He must have had some busy sleuths."

"No, just routine reports. Don't forget, you and Mrs. Kinsale moved through some critical areas, as the Japanese consider them. Their Intelligence establishment is quite efficient."

Kyle had swiveled around so that he could face the ambassador. It had been warm in the limousine and the heaviness of the air was further burdened by the scent of mimosa from a spray in the panel vase. Both Kyle and the ambassador wore linen suits, Grew having for once dispensed with the morning coat, striped trousers and top hat still then in vogue for diplomatic visits, even informal ones such as this.

To further avoid attention by the Tokyo press corps, the car's diplomatic plates had been replaced by civilian ones.

"I'm not sure that I understand his official position. What is it precisely?"

"At the moment, President of the House of Peers. There are three parties now competing for leadership and two of them would be glad to have him head them. But he's still uncommitted."

"And he's friendly to the West?"

"I can't give you a straight answer. Sometimes he seems a man of peace. Then just when you think you have him pegged he'll shift—in the other direction. I'd say in essence he's a liberal and a moderate. He's the Emperor's favorite, and an Imperial relative, a Fujiwara; the kinship of the Fujiwaras with the Imperial family goes back to the dim origins of Japanese mythology. At the same time he's the most Westernized nobleman around. He was dabbling in Marxist theory and writing socialist tracts at a time when an ordinary person would have gone to jail for less. He even considered renouncing his title—emigrating to the United States, if you can believe it. Felt that with us a person would be judged by his abilities, not his lineage."

The ambassador cocked a dark eyebrow at Kyle, and then let it drop again.

"What changed his mind?"

Grew shrugged.

"Prince Kimmochi Saionji talked him out of it. Saionji was the Emperor's tutor. Maker of premiers, they call him. Next to Konoye himself the most popular peer in the country. Getting on to ninety now, I'm afraid—about at the end of the line."

The car was approaching the dragon-topped gates of the Konoye palace in the Azabu section of Tokyo. The gates opened before it. A sentry waved them through. "When you two sit down to tea," said the ambassador, "I shall have a look around the gardens, beautiful this time of year. Try not to stay too long." He dragged a gold watch in an old-fashioned hunter's case out of his vest pocket. "Forty-five minutes should do it, don't you think?"

Forty-five minutes had turned out to be more than was needed. Prince Konoye had been charming, but also business-like. His government, he said, was assessing its energy needs for the next year and beyond the next year—needs which would be in excess of those for comparable periods in the past. Speaking unofficially, the prince had some questions for Kyle: he had read of KinOil's leadership in setting up a consortium of independent oil companies. Was the consortium's product intended for domestic U.S. consumption only or would export be part of the program? If export were possible, Konoye felt that his government could arrange a contract at favorable prices.

And as to ships? Well, as to ships the Mitsubishi Company might deal with that. The Mitsubishis were well supplied with ships.

The prince did not expect a firm commitment from Kyle. Only an opinion, "off the top of your head," as he put it, using one of the new "corporate" expressions in which he took pride.

Kyle had kept nodding and drinking tea. It was an interesting conversation and he gathered several things from it which had not been specifically mentioned. One, for instance, that the Intelligence establishment which served the prince and his associates did not limit its reports to the South Pacific and points west. Konoye was obviously well informed on the recent campaign conducted by the Hearst press to have the United States Department of the Interior stockpile new reserves. No doubt he also knew that a bill to implement such stockpiling, introduced in Congress, had failed to be voted out of committee. KinOil had benefited from the Hearst editorials only to the extent of getting a no-interest government loan for its new pipeline—the one Harry Atlass had dreamed up.

Over the Ming tea service brought in for Kyle (the prince himself had a Scotch on the rocks, Western style), Konoye was saying that if the oil was up for grabs, he wanted it. (He was also saying, without intending to, that he was desperate for it.)

Kyle thought, He will have been to the majors and they will have turned him down. Teagle of Standard and Deterding of Royal Dutch Shell make the world market for all of us. They won't stand for long-term fixed-price commitments—above all, commitments which, if an embargo is ordered on petroleum for Japan, they won't be able to keep.

Kyle said he would make some inquiries.

The prince said that would be splendid.

Through the window the ambassador could be seen in the ancient garden, seated beside a very modern fountain, the jets of which formed the shape of a peacock.

The interview was at an end.

Only at this last moment, when the two men rose to shake hands and separate, had the conversation taken the turn that had made so much difference.

"I believe," Kyle had said, "that you have a son at Princeton."

"Indeed. Fumitaka. You know him?"

"I'm afraid not. But I have heard about him."

"So you have a son there too?"

"A nephew. He and your son are friends—classmates. But Cliff tells me they don't call your son Fumitaka there. They call him Butch."

"You know that too!"

"And more!" said Kyle, smiling. "I know he's a fine golfer, for instance."

"And a miserable student," said the prince, his handsome face alight with pride and affection for his son. "Why, if there is a course within ten miles he won't look at a book."

"The captain of the Princeton golf team doesn't need to look at a book. Your son is also an excellent debater. He and Cliff are both in the debating society."

"And all this you have from letters, from your nephew?"

"Yes. Butch—excuse me, Fumitaka—is one of his best friends."

They had been walking toward the door. But now the prince took Kyle's arm, to restrain him. He looked at him warmly and eagerly.

"How I wish I got such letters. Our young people seldom write intimately to their parents. The outcome of an overritualized society . . ."

"Or just laziness about writing."

"That too. Well, I must tell my wife. How nice that you have heard of him."

"Cliff has been talking of inviting him to visit at our ranch, the family homeplace. My brother and his wife would be delighted to have him. As we would too, either there or at my beach house. Any time at all."

"That is most cordial of you. Well, we must meet again. We must talk some more about these young rebels. They're all rebels, these young people today."

"As we were in our time," said Kyle, knowing from the ambassador that the remark would be accurate for Konoye, whether or not it applied to himself.

"As perhaps we still are!" said the prince, beaming.

He rapped on the glass of the garden window to summon Grew.

Half an hour after Kyle had returned to the Imperial came a dinner invitation from the Konoyes. And from then on, as long as the Kinsales were in Tokyo, the two couples were often together.

3

It was time to get ready for lunch. Kyle shaved and showered. He put on flannel slacks, a blazer and an open shirt. At the last moment before starting downstairs he crossed to his desk and took out a packet of papers in a blue envelope stamped with the KinOil masthead: a report of the shipments of oil to Japan by the new group—California and Orient Petroleum Export.

The arrangement had worked to the advantage of all concerned.

Prince Konoye arrived at one-thirty. A Secret Service operator rode beside the driver of the rented limousine—the usual stonefaced fellow in a bombazine suit. Kyle wondered why that one pistol packer was all the protection that the State Department had offered this notable visitor. The prince would not have wanted a fuss made over him, but it seemed silly for him to take chances; in fact, with all the sword rattling that had been going on it was surprising that the prince had come at all.

He had been in to see Hull, he said; he had talked with the President, though briefly. Konoye's account of this, when Alma asked him what had happened at the meeting, was laconic.

"He made some jokes. He smoked four cigarettes . . ."

"And what did Mr. Hull say?" put in Kyle.

"That he would reflect on the continuation of my country's right to buy oil."

"Mr. Hull likes to reflect. He does it a lot."

"Sometimes it takes him a long time. I also talked to Mr. Ickes."

"There's a real charmer."

"We too have had statesmen like Mr. Ickes. Old admirals, old generals . . ."

"I hope he was polite; he isn't always."

"Polite enough. I had not come for protocol. He said that there was no embargo yet; he would let me know when we must stop buying."

"That's what he says to us—that he'll let us know when to stop selling."

Prince Konoye turned the subject away from oil, as if that had begun to bore him. He was gay at lunch and he looked well but older; there was a set to his face that had not been there in Tokyo. He stooped slightly whereas before he had been ramrod straight. He was tall for a Japanese—almost six feet; Kyle observed again how handsome he was, with his keen, narrow face and well-shaped head—and what good humor he displayed. It should be easy to reach settlements with such a man, he thought, even for those idiots in Washington.

They moved out to the balcony for coffee. The air smelled of the musky, salty kelp that besets Malibu beaches; waves ripped at the shore with a sound like skidding tires. Alma excused herself.

Konoye said, "The Emperor will soon ask me to form a government. I tell you this in confidence. I shall of course obey, but I have never wanted to be prime minister. I am not sure that I am up to it."

"But of course you are! How could a better man be found?"

"Thank you. Such words are heartening, coming from a friend."

It was the first time Konoye had used that term with him.

"I consider you too a friend, Fumimaro. I'm glad that we can work together—that our group has been able to help with your needs. I can assure you, we'll keep on as long as we can."

"Which may not be long. These are bad times. I'm afraid that soon, perhaps before the end of the year, there will be happenings. A flash point. I feel that very keenly."

Konoye broke off. He leaned on the balcony railing, gazing out to sea. Two boys were down there, fishing from a rubber raft. They looked very comfortable and carefree, lying on their bellies on the raft in the afternoon sun.

"Your President," he said, "is concerned with England and with Europe. I suspect he gives the Orient to Mr. Hull as a sop for bypassing him in the affairs of the West. And now Mr. Hull is telling us to withdraw from territory we have occupied since nineteen thirty-one. He tells us as a matter of principle —and he spells out the principles—we are not to do this and not to do that. Is he not a man of very extensive principles?"

"Large ones, a big stock of them."

"I thought so. But when we try to live up to his principles he continues to pile on economic sanctions. This discourages the men of peace, but when the men of war defy his principles or just ignore them, he does nothing. Which encourages the men of war. Do you see what I mean?"

"Clearly."

"After I take office," said Konoye, "I will take these matters out of the hands of those old admirals and old generals—hands with brown spots on them and rheumatic lumps instead of knuckles. I shall need another meeting with President Roosevelt, a serious one that is not for jokes or cigarettes but for the settlement of high affairs. I shall need such a meeting urgently. I say this to you as I have said to to a number of others, Kyle, to politicians and to businessmen, but particularly to businessmen in the oil business, for there is where power lies. If you can help me to see the President at the Head of State level, that will be in the best interests of business and of peace."

The prince left a few minutes later. When he was ready to go, Kyle called down to Alma, who was in the children's room, and she came up to say goodbye. Kyle and Alma stood in their front doorway and watched Konoye drive away in the big rented car with the man in the bombazine suit sitting beside the chauffeur.

Kyle was sure now that war was coming.

Prince Fumimaro Konoye would not get to see the President. You had one shot at that and he'd had his shot. It was too late now, anyway. The war was sure. People would say it was about this or about that but they were the people who didn't understand. Basically it would be like all other wars of modern times. It would be a war about oil.

4

Scott Stanfus sat beside Kyle's desk, balancing a clipboard on his knees. He had the look on his face which meant that he would hold Kyle strictly to the business in hand. Kyle must defend himself against the onslaughts of the redneck dissidents—the aunts, the cousins, the uncles, the remainder-

men from the greasewood hinterlands: the stockholders of
the Kinsale Land and Cattle Company.

True, Kyle did this every year. He had done it so far most
successfully, but this year it would be harder. Scott wanted
Kyle to take the problem seriously. He wanted him to give it
thought before he got his ass in a sling, no matter how boring
the confrontation might be.

Luanna, the squaw lady, was making trouble.

Kyle, of course, knew quite well what Luanna was up to.
He had handled her many times previously. Not rudely;
Kyle's innate courtesy would have prevented that, but he had
told her to behave and made it stick.

This year might be different. She would have the Indians
lined up. Scott Stanfus had been taking a head count. He had
it all down on the clipboard:

Mrs. Paxton Strengle	(Danville)	15	Shares
Judge and Carry Carr	(Merced)	24	”
Epifimia Medows	(Hollister)	40	”
Aguilar Boyette	(Tuolumne)	10	”
Christine and Ned Oman	(Brisbane)	52	”
Clifford Kinsale	(Altemira)	1,000	”
Guadalupe Ortega	(Florence)	12	”
Joven Ortega	(Florence)	60	”
Michael Ortega	(Florence)	5	”
Eva and John Gortish	(Carmel)	155	”

And so on and so forth, for three double-lined pages.

Scott Stanfus was ready for battle. He did not intend for it
to be another Little Bighorn, all those scritching varmints
against the Big White Chief with the beautiful curly locks that
would make such a fabulous scalp after the squaws cut off his
balls.

"I'd like to point out one solution, Mr. Kinsale—quite an
obvious one. I am not sure whether it has been considered
before. You would have information there which I do not
possess."

"Excuse me," said Kyle, picking up the telephone.

"Jock Aughterlonie on line two," said Rose Brady.

Kyle punched the button which changed the line.

"Yes, Jock."

"We gave him a two-minute lick, sunup," said Aughterlonie.

A two-minute lick meant breezing the horse a mile in two

minutes, keeping him in hand. If there had been any question about Aboukir's fitness, Aughterlonie would have mentioned it. But he said nothing.

Kyle felt the surge of well-being which news about his horses always brought him—good news, that is to say: the men around the barns knew better, these days, than to convey any other kind.

"In other words, he's ready."

Aughterlonie's voice rejected optimism. He had a Scotsman's dislike of commitment, above all, on the telephone—an instrument which he distrusted and used as little as possible.

"You can judge for yoursel'," he said dourly. "I been looking for you now, sor, the week past."

"I'll be out this afternoon."

"Verra good then."

Kyle hung up. He turned back reluctantly to Scott Stanfus.

So far today he had accepted—though he could have kept them out simply by advising Rose that he was not to be disturbed—a call from San Pedro, from KinOil's West Coast Manager, Transportation, reporting that the company's ship *Claremont*, inbound from Indonesia, had collided with a foreign freighter, *Khud Saryan*, off Catalina ("Deny fault."); a call from a Midland, Texas, lease broker asking whether KinOil would be interested in a rights purchase in the East Texas fields which had just been made available in probate sale ("Negative."); a call from Armand Hammer, president of Occidental, asking him to speak at the annual banquet of the Petroleum Institute of America ("Okay, if I don't have to follow *you*, Armand—you're too tough."); and a call from Alma saying that Katie had eaten a boiled egg for breakfast and had kept it down. When Katie had had egg in a bottle she had upchucked. Kyle had forgotten about the previous upchuck. Have to pay more attention. An upchuck in Alma's world had approximately the significance of a blazing oil well in Troy Kinsale's.

"The swing vote," said Scott Stanfus, "could be here."

He circled a name on his list, then handed the clipboard to Kyle, who glanced at it absently. He was thinking of what Aughterlonie had said. He wished he had been at the farm to see the trial himself. He loved the early mornings at the farm and especially the workouts of this horse, which Aughterlonie had not even had to name (it was characteristic of his Scotch caution as applied to telephones that he had not done so).

Kyle attended the workouts as often as he could. He had to get out of bed in Malibu at four in the morning and drive forty miles to be in time for them, but it was worth it. Especially it would have been worth it today. Aboukir was the big red stud he had bought from the Aga Khan for a quarter of a million dollars at last fall's auction at Chantilly. Then he had hired Aughterlonie, who had trained for Calumet and the Whitneys, to put him in shape. Kyle planned to enter him in the Santa Anita Handicap.

The 'Cap, no doubt, was what Aughterlonie wished to talk to him about.

Kyle tried to concentrate on the list of names before him.

Scott was quite right—the meeting was important; he knew he should take more interest in it.

Nowadays these meetings were disguised time bombs. The projects and appropriations that came up for discussion would be Land and Cattle Company projects and appropriations. A new half mile of fence for the north hundred. Or a proposition: To interplant the older apricot orchards with pears (said to be the coming thing) or to replace with six-foot Blenheim seedlings? Horseshoes and other blacksmithing supplies: Continue with Altemira Hardware or try to get a better deal from San Jose Iron and Tool? Read the minutes of the last meeting. Election of officers. Once it had all seemed so grand, the big ranch, the land, the bulls that improved the breed, the cows that reproduced the chunky, meaty calves; the purchase of a new truck or van, the rainfall, the slow turn of the earth, the change of the seasons: all so important, so significant until the discovery well changed everything and instead of cows and fruit and grain the shareholders of the Land and Cattle Company became proprietors of an affiliate called KinOil and instead of making deals for thousands of dollars they were making deals for millions or—who really knew?—for billions.

With more to come, much more, forever and ever, amen. It had been hard to realize, but not hard to get used to. For getting used to it the cousins and the aunts and their legatees were quick studies. They picked up that language right away. Packard Super Eights and Cadillac V6 Phaetons and supercharged Duesenberg limos with Parker bodies and four exhaust coils prodding through the sides of the hood and Reo Flying Clouds and Essex Teraplanes and Hups and Hudson Pacemakers. The booze was no gummy dip distilled in a hollow tree; it came straight from the auld sod, you could bet your ass. And when these lucky minions of fortune went down to the bank to pay off poppa's mortgage they sometimes walked out owning the bank.

Then KinOil had gone public.

At this point began an even more interesting era. The capital worth of the company was quadrupled by a combination of a Big Board listing and the placement of nine million shares of the listed stock in the hands of eager buyers. Kyle had foretold all this at the meeting in 1931 when they had agreed to do it. He had made it very clear and they all got the hang of it.

The Land and Cattle Company didn't own KinOil anymore. The Land and Cattle Company just controlled KinOil because its members, in the aggregate, owned twenty-six percent of KinOil's stock.

Kyle hoped that was clear. If it wasn't, all you had to do was raise your hand.

The shareholders of the Land and Cattle Company kept their shares in that company but now they had been dealt shares in KinOil for free, and in a few years these shares had been split many times. A wonderful arrangement, for although the former hundred percent of KinOil owned by the L&CC had shrunk to twenty-six percent it was somehow worth vastly more than it had been before.

You still controlled it, Kyle had said, but the public owned it. They had bought it, but they let you keep it. A bunch of strangers, in other words. Out-of-town people. Those far-off galoots had nipped out their savings and plunked them down. They had lifted the loose floorboard where the bills were laid end to end in mingy packages yellow with mouse shit; they had reached into the cracked teapots; they had written out the savings-bank withdrawal slips. KinOil had needed all that money in order to expand, and the expansion had made everybody rich beyond dreams.

Kyle had said it would happen and by gosh it had. He had stood there under the big trees and told them about it with a smile on his handsome face and his head held the slanty way he had and they had trusted him. They might not have understood the whole of it but they had trusted him and nobody had raised a hand.

They'd all come a far piece since then.

The shareholders of the Land and Cattle Company knew all about the expansion. They knew about the office buildings, the service stations, the tankers, the pipelines, the new wells, the new company acquisitions. They knew about the Hearst-sponsored reserve deal, the Japanese deal, the twenty-million-dollar loan to Turkey. They knew that KinOil stock was a grand stock, but where were the dividends?

They'd whispered that before. Now they were saying it out loud.

Luanna, the squaw lady, had been working the telephone. She had her war paint on.

"Dissent in the L&CC," said Scott Stanfus, and he'd said it over and over. "Dissent could lead to a proxy fight in KinOil, each side bargaining for support from the public share-holders . . ."

Ah, yes. A proxy fight. A misfortune indeed. The worst thing, next to a bankruptcy, that could happen to a corporation. Expensive. Disturbing.

Besides, that fellow in the White House wanted production these days rather than a lot of quibbling about monopolies or malefactors of great wealth, as the other Roosevelt had called *his* oil people.

"I really wish we could spend an evening, Kyle, and go over the whole picture," Scott had said, and Kyle had said he would.

Scott had not formerly used Kyle's first name in addressing him. Nor been encouraged to. That development had come on since the dismissal of Lamar Custis. Scott was treasurer of KinOil now, in line for a vice presidency. Scott had a different look to him. He had gained flesh, the increment that settles on the bones and tissues of a corporate careerist with each well-deserved promotion, but the flesh was not the change. The change was an attitude, an inner hardening. Under the subdued dress style and the bookkeeper's deliberately low-key personality peeped now the lineaments of a hatchet man.

The intercom was flashing. Kyle pressed the switch.

Dan Shannon's Irish tenor voice piped from the speaker.

"We have a table in Perino's, twelve-thirty. Just the two of us, and the other guy."

"Ask Reeves to fill in for me."

"He can't make it. Went down to the port to see about that tanker."

"Well, start without me. I'll join you later."

For Shannon, disciplined in the confidentiality of oil, no person mentioned on the intercom ever had a name. He or she was always "that fella," "that certain lady" or "the other guy." After all, the intercom blatted everything out publicly. You never knew who might be sitting with the boss.

"Okay, sir," said Dan Shannon.

In this instance "the other guy" was Ralph K. Davies, Vice President, Production, Standard Oil of California. The lunch had been set up to determine how much of the crude from the new pipeline Standard would accept for processing at its big refinery. A preliminary meeting. There would be others. Dan was well equipped to handle this one, Kyle decided.

He would drop in, as a courtesy, for dessert and coffee, on his way out to the farm. Lunch was a meal he often skipped.

He turned back to Stanfus.

"Monday night, next week. Down at the beach."

Kyle gave up evenings reluctantly. Evenings were for Alma.

Stanfus stood up, looking at the clipboard. Kyle took off the index of L&CC shareholders and handed the board back; as the treasurer left, Kyle was scanning the list again. His eye ran down the column to the name that Scott had circled, the possible swing vote:

Clifford Kinsale

5

The Rolls was waiting in the restaurant parking lot. Lunch over (he had given less than twenty minutes to it), Kyle settled in the comfort of the back seat for the drive out to the racing farm.

Half an hour of relaxation lay ahead, while Mort did the driving; Kyle had intended napping during this time but found himself wide awake, his mind busy with the suggestion Scott had brought up.

Was there really any chance that Cliff would vote against his parents in the upcoming L&CC meeting?

Of course not—none in the world! There was no division in the family—anyway not yet.

Kyle had a notion Troy did not stand in total sympathy with Luanna's ambitions for him and herself, her new socially conscious airs and her dissatisfaction with the way the company was run.

Having wealth had changed Luanna more than the rest of

them. Was this a self-serving judgment? He did not think so. He himself, for one, had possessed wealth, or at least its accoutrements, long before the oil: the oil had simply enabled him to live his chosen life with the blessings of power and without the need for petty gamesmanship.

Troy, too, was still very much his own person. He had been an oilman before the discovery well and he was an oilman now, only on a bigger scale. He and Kyle each had what they wanted; their rivalries, such as existed, were holdovers from boyhood, the natural competition of brothers stiffened by the jealousies Hub had promoted, almost as if he'd planned it that way, as if he took pleasure in the spectacle of his two sons competing for his favors. Maybe he had, the old son of a bitch.

So—let it be! With a billion dollars, or something close to it, sloshing around in Hub's grave, he and Troy had better things to do than glare at each other across the glut of it.

Odd, though, if Cliff, of whom both were so fond, should hold the scales.

Traffic was thinning out. Moving through the drab section of suburban streets, small bungalows, and little shops, service stations and other small enterprises, Mort swung the big car east at Griffith Park, crossed the river in its dry bed, headed out Burbank Boulevard. One of the new four-engine passenger planes drummed overhead. It skimmed the snarl of high-tension wires (Jesus, when would they get rid of those!) along the road, then settled with amazing lightness on the tarmac near the Lockheed plant.

Bob Gross and those other fellows were expanding Lockheed fast these days. Every time Kyle went by he saw a new factory or a piece of one under construction.

Nothing wrong with the aircraft business that a war wouldn't fix.

War, earthquake and other acts of God. Reeves Thurmond put that phrase into all performance contracts drawn with KinOil as the party of the second part: a catchall defining the conditions under which the company would not be held to perform under the covenants set forth.

War between nations, certainly, you could not do much about, whether or not it had God's approval, but strife between members of a family could be controlled, in fact had to be. Scott Stanfus had been very definite on that score. Kyle had agreed with him; in the warmth and quiet of the car, bearing him toward an afternoon of pleasure, he gave intense concentration to the matter of that thousand shares of voting stock held by his nephew, Cliff Kinsale.

He had thought about that thousand shares before, but never with just this approach. Roughly, in the way Hub's will had been drawn, the estate had fallen into three main parts: one each to Millie, Troy and himself, and a fourth portion split among the cousins (though within those parts, deviously subdivided, various other bequests down to the disposition of "my Parker shotgun, twelve gauge, with silver mounting" and "one pair cuff links, opal; one pair cuff links, silver, with simulated ranch brand"; and "one stock saddle, made by Porters Store, Tucson, Ariz., medium tapered tree").

The thousand shares to Cliff had not been tied in with Troy and Luanna's portion. It had been an island scooped out of the relatives' portion, added in a codicil; a natural action on Hub's part, Cliff being the only grandchild at the time of the will's execution. Helene, to be sure, had been born before Hub's death, but the old man had not got around to altering his will in her behalf.

Stanfus had been trying to figure out just what Cliff's legacy could mean in case of a tight voting contest.

Cliff, a minor, had never voted his own shares. His parents had held his proxy. Born in 1915, he was now past twenty-one; he would vote for himself this year. Could he be persuaded to change sides? Or not vote at all? If he just abstained, and nothing else, it might make all the difference.

No son should turn against a father. Few sons would. Yet Kyle's relationship with Cliff, as it had developed in recent years, had become exceptionally close, almost fatherly. Kyle wondered if Cliff, too, thought of it that way. Kyle himself was quite satisfied to be an affectionate uncle rather than a substitute father, yet that afternoon in Tokyo, when Konoye, speaking of Princeton, had asked, "So you have a son there too?" Kyle had wanted to answer, "Yes . . . a son. Of course I do . . ."

He liked and admired Cliff; loved him, if that was the proper word for the emotion he felt for his good-looking, interesting nephew. Cliff amused him. They got on together. Kyle entertained a certain contempt for blood fathers who had lost touch with their sons, who professed that they could not communicate with them. Nine times out of ten that was the old man's fault, not the kid's.

There was also another element at work here—of which

Kyle was well aware. Cliff filled a void in his life. He was not likely now to have a son of his own. He loved his wife. She had made him the happiest of men. She was the perfect girl for him. But after two daughters in three and a half years, both born by Caesarean section, the medics, including his own brother-in-law, called in as the final arbiter (somewhat to Alma's embarrassment—who wanted a relative peeking up your insides?), had issued an edict: no more babies.

So be it. That was all right with Kyle. Daughters! He hoped he would have sense enough not to make sons out of them. Nor would he make a son out of Cliff. Cliff had a damn good father of his own, but—well, he was a hell of a nephew. A robust and merry and active devil, not inclined to follow either in Troy's footsteps or his uncle's, this kid who had pulled the switch to spud in the discovery well—who'd had to be beaten to get him away from the site when it had seemed at the last that there was no oil down there.

Cliff had had more faith than any of them. He had stuck to his beliefs. He had been that kind of kid. He was that kind of man now—putting in his first year's work for KinOil. Kyle watched as Mort braked the Phantom sharply, then stepped on the gas to get around a stalled brewery truck. In the last respect maybe Cliff was following in his footsteps.

"So Yale wouldn't interest you?" he had asked.

Cliff had come to him soon after the Arc de Rawhide party for H. H. Atlass, saying he wanted to transfer from Berkeley to Princeton at the start of the spring term.

"Ma wouldn't put up with Yale."

Kyle nodded. To Luanna, Yale might represent the sort of snobbery which had put Troy at some real or imagined disadvantage in the family.

"She's against Princeton too," Cliff added quickly. "Dad wouldn't care. He'd let me go wherever I want, but she . . ." He shook his head. "I thought maybe you could talk to her, Unc," he said.

"If your dad can't change her mind, I doubt if I'd have much luck."

"Maybe not. But you've been east, and seems like you've done all right. She can't argue with that. You might think of something that would work," he'd pleaded with an impish smile. Cliff had the big bones and reddish hair, the Kinsale look, the Kinsale skin, the age-resistant, weather-and-perhaps-bullet-proof enamel. He was the only Kinsale who had ever been freckled and the freckles gave him a Huckle-

berry Finn look, especially when he used them to win favor.
He had a slow way of speaking that seemed a natural
component of his gentleness and manliness but he was a devil
just the same. Kyle knew that his nephew was working him
over but he didn't care. Cliff, the Huckleberry bastard, could
melt his heart.

"Well, I'll see what I can do, but don't count on anything."

"I'd appreciate it."

But Luanna had been obdurate.

"Princeton for Clifford? I will not consider it," she said
when Kyle brought up the subject.

"Actually it's quite a good school," Kyle said mildly. If he
was to get anywhere with this he could not afford to rile her.

"Of course it's a good school. He doesn't care about that.
He just wants to be east because of that woman!"

Was he supposed to know about a woman? Rather than
show his ignorance, Kyle asked cautiously, "Are you sure?"

"Of course! The Atlass woman. She's seduced him, the
bitch, and they're having this ridiculous affair. Princeton just
appeals to him because she's in New York most of the time. If
he's in school nearby, then he can get to see her as much as he
wants."

Dede Atlass! So that was it.

He assumed a shocked expression, hoping it would hide his
amusement. He could see before him, like a lantern slide,
Cliff and Dede dancing at the Arc de Rawhide party, Cliff
with his tousled hair and serious freckled face, Dede mashed
against him in her bony, arching way. Ho hum. And then
later the same night, the light in her rooms—the light he had
idly thought might be a Paul Revereish signal for himself!
That must have been where it started . . .

"Disgusting, at her age."

"Oh, I wouldn't quite say that. Classic combination, I
suppose: older lady, young lover."

"A young *rich* lover. Let's not forget that. She's . . . the
lowest sort. Troy checked her reputation. He made a remark
about her which I hesitate to repeat." Kyle waited for a beat
of one while Luanna conquered her hesitation. "He said she's
had enough penises in her to build a picket fence from here to
Vladivostok."

Kyle laughed.

"Sounds like Troy."

"Surely you don't condone her behavior?"

"No, no. But it would be too bad if this affair kept Cliff from changing universities, if he really wants to."

"He doesn't really want to."

"But how can we tell?"

"Get rid of the woman. Then he'll stay in Berkeley."

"I wonder."

Kyle reflected. He could recall, out of his own experience, certain older women who, beside their sexual favors, had helped him gain considerable knowledge of the world's ways, and how to deal with them.

There was, of course, one danger, and Luanna, primed with her own hot urges to move up, to better herself in the family pecking order, had hit on it: the matrimonial hazard. Dede might just have marriage on her mind. Several times the mistress of rich and powerful men, she might feel the time had come to take a rich husband—even a very young one. That would be no good, no good at all.

Cliff's romance might not be in the best interests of the family. That was an aspect which should be looked into.

"Suppose they broke off. Would you be against Princeton then?"

"I don't see why Princeton is any better than Berkeley. But I wouldn't oppose it."

"Let me think about this. Maybe I can help."

Luanna's expression changed. He saw again the straight-thinking, hard-living woman who had seemed so attractive, such a good wife for Troy in other days.

"Oh, I would appreciate that. I wish, I wish you would."

Kyle had Rose Brady run down Dede Atlass' New York address. She had an apartment in one of the best buildings on Park Avenue. Two years' rent had been paid in advance—by Hector Mellis. Kyle wondered whether that gift had been some kind of severance payment.

Hector Mellis was no fool.

On his next business trip east Kyle rang up Dede and asked if he could come around to see her. She showed little surprise at his call—and even less enthusiasm for a visit. Her apartment, she said, was being "redone."

Could they meet somewhere else?

He suggested the bar at the Pierre.

Though he had made a point of being on time, Dede was there ahead of him. She had chosen a corner banquette. She looked very dashing in a belted Persian-lamb coat and a downswept, tight-fitting cloche of matching fur. Her long black gloves lay on the table, beside a frosted martini; she had on several beautiful rings and three diamond bracelets. They made aimless small talk until the waiter had brought Kyle's split of champagne and a bucket to cool it in and she had watched him take his first sip.

She cut through his tactful preambles with contempt.

". . . I won't give him up—if that's what you're driving at."

"I wish you'd reconsider."

"Do you? Well, possibly I've used the wrong word— 'won't.' 'Can't' might be better. I'm no longer in control of . . . the affair, if you want to call it that. You wouldn't understand."

"I'll do my best."

"You don't have much taste for this . . . family errand. Am I right?"

"I volunteered."

"Good for you! *Paterfamilias*, titular head of the clan, and all that. I'm afraid I'll never understand Americans in general, Californians in particular—this applies, I suppose, to myself too. We're all parochial beyond belief."

"It's the frontier spirit."

"Check! Put the wagons in a circle. Then you shoot it out. Don't you see how silly that is? You're not crossing the plains anymore."

"So far no great harm has been done—"

"Perhaps a lot of good. Did you ever think of that?"

"I have. I expressed that idea to Luanna; I told her you might be persuaded to quit while you were still ahead."

"You think I haven't tried?" Tears welled into Dede's eye sockets, rimmed with mascara. She let them course unhindered down her cheeks. Kyle handed her a cocktail napkin. Female dishevelment always made him uneasy—and the show of emotion took him by surprise.

"I told you," she said, "I had a set of rules and I broke them."

Kyle studied her. Her defiance seemed to him as unreal as her emotional outburst of a moment earlier. She was starring in some kind of melodrama—the aging temptress in her last bid for true love.

"Dede," he said, "may I ask you a personal question?"

"We've been pretty personal so far."

"What is your present arrangement with Hector Mellis?"

"There is no arrangement."

"You've both terminated?"

"Yes."

"After a satisfactory . . . settlement?"

"For Hector," said Dede, "heaven doesn't come for free."

"Hector doesn't need heaven for free. That's the advantage of being Lord Mellis of Rutland; he can pay. So could your friend the Earl of Portchester, if I'm properly informed."

"Porchy? Don't be a fool—he never parted with a shilling, just a few trinkets. And . . . things."

She looked absently at the looped bands of diamonds on her thin, slightly hairy arm. Somehow the invocation of vanished loves had put her in a better mood. She signaled for another cocktail.

Kyle said, "I have a friend, a gentleman who works for Standard Oil in Bahrain. He owns a yacht, at present in the harbor at Monaco. How would you like to borrow it for a month?"

"I can't stand yachts. The toilets plug up. And I get seasick."

"This one would charter at a thousand dollars a day—complete with crew, fuel and beverages. And heads that work by electricity, night and day."

"You think you can send me to Monaco, for a lousy thirty thousand dollars—and toilets that will flush?"

"How about fifty? You could go to Mecca and save your soul."

"If I were frigging Turk, I could," she said. She had risen from the bench. Now she sat down again. "Are you joking, or what?"

"I'm trying to save you from embarrassment," said Kyle soberly, "and, as I see it, some needless grief."

Dede Atlass looked at her bracelets. She turned the big one slowly on her wrist. She sat for some time, neither speaking nor moving.

"You're right, you know," she said; "he'll leave me. He'll be nice about it but he'll go; he'll have to. Even in California it was getting bad. That's why I came to New York. He would come to my place and once in a long while we would go out together, to some little dive, but he'd never take me around his friends. Or the dolls they went out with. How could he? I would have looked like his aunt. At least I taught him a few other things."

"He'll always remember."

"Oh, yes, he'll remember. Thanks for trying to be nice, but

you were wrong about the money. I never cared about it; it was just a trophy or something. A prize that made it all worthwhile, because I never cared about the fucking either. Until I fell in love."

"You're doing the right thing."

"Thanks so much. Don't walk out with me. I'll get myself a cab."

She rose, holding up her cheek to be kissed. Her harsh, fashionable perfume enveloped them both for a moment, knotting them together like a rope. She squeezed his hand.

"Have that check at my apartment in the morning or the deal is off."

6

Kyle never mentioned to Troy or Luanna that he had paid Dede. The money had been his private gift to Cliff. Kyle felt he had enough return on it when, with Dede back in London, Cliff proved that proximity to her had not been his only reason for transferring to Princeton.

As time went on there had been other presents, big ones and little ones. The largest, for cash outlay, had been the Bugatti Grand Prix racer which Kyle bought from a San Francisco importer of foreign cars. He had a salesman drive it down to the ranch and deliver it to Cliff a short time before his nephew was to take off for the east, a journey which he had proposed to make by automobile. Cliff appeared delighted with the gift. Kyle didn't find out till a year later that although Cliff had driven the racer across the continent he had never taken it to Princeton but stored it in a garage in Trenton, fifteen miles away.

"It's a swell buggy, just the tops, Unc," he'd said when he made this confession, "but you understand, well, I'm not supposed to drive a buggy like that. Not around campus. I'd get smeared. One fellow from Detroit came in with a Cad Sixteen and he got smeared—just for a Cad! He tried to keep it hidden, had it in a barn down by the lake, but some upperclassmen found out about it. They hot-wired it and took it up on Nassau Street. Drove it through the window of the Baltimore Dairy Lunch and left it there. It was a mess."

"If the Bugatti embarrasses you, sell it."

"Never, Unc. I love it—and it's great for weekends. That's okay—away from Princeton, I mean."

"Reverse snobbism, that's what we used to call that kind of thinking."

"Not even that, Unc," Cliff protested. "It's just that—well, it's different now, back east. Having horses and so forth, the polo thing and so forth, that's out now."

"They don't play polo?"

"Sure they play polo, but they play with the ROTC hides—the remounts for the artillery and cavalry drill units. There aren't more than half a dozen private hides in the barn. But they play all right. They play like hell. I'd play myself," Cliff had added kindly, with a condescension which had made Kyle wince, "if I had time for it."

That Cliff hadn't had time for his nine-goal uncle's favorite pastime or indeed for any sport had not been brought about by his dedication to studying; while never in danger of flunking out, he seldom, in any subject, did much more than pass.

Cliff pursued two urgent but scarcely related interests: journalism and debating. He went out for the college daily, the *Princetonian,* in the only competition held for sophomores, and was elected to the board; in his junior year he joined Whig Hall, and as a senior was a member of the university debating team. Kyle never saw him on the platform but he read the *Princetonian* material which Cliff regularly clipped and sent him and was quite impressed by it. The writing had little spark, though it seemed competent enough, but the range of interests was wide: in a few months Cliff had published interviews with Harry Hopkins, Rexford Tugwell, Alexander Woollcott, Upton Sinclair, Alfred Lunt and other celebrities, few of whom would have put themselves easily at the disposal of a student journalist.

What can that monkey be training himself for? Kyle had wondered.

There seemed some kind of pattern in this, even if all it amounted to was excess energy. A worthwhile boy. An interesting boy. Wherever he's headed, Kyle had added to himself, I'll help.

He had visited Cliff once at Princeton. Once had been enough: that the affection between them had survived this encounter seemed, on hindsight, a singular proof of its durability. The occasion had been a disaster from the start. Kyle, forced to spend some fall days at the KinOil office in Chicago, had suddenly decided to attend a Yale-Princeton football game. He had rounded up Yale friends in half a dozen cities, then got hold of tickets, at scalper's prices, through the Yale Club of New York. He telephoned Cliff that he was coming. Yale classmate Ross Markley, who sat on the board of the Pennsylvania Railroad, had arranged a private car; the trip was slow; there was a good deal of drinking, which continued after the game in the Prospect Street club where Cliff, the designated host, had taken the party as his guests.

Markley's heavy voice boomed through the room.

". . . take a drive through my piece of country; from Wilkes-Barre south, you can find guns in every hayrick. And every cellar. Yes, by God, and I've confirmed this in Washington. They know damn well what's going on. Springfield thirty-aught-sixes, Krag-Jorgensens, saddle carbines, squirrel muskets. The farmers are arming, friends, and one of these days all hell is going to break loose. . . ."

Charlie McGeorge of Youngstown Sheet and Tube winked at Cliff as if to say, "Pay no attention." McGeorge was a trim, sprightly man whose white cap of hair contrasted handsomely with his brown boyish face. He evinced boredom as Ross warmed to his favorite subject: the incipient collapse of the Roosevelt administration.

"Ross," said McGeorge, "the trouble with you is you've got a petty bourgeois mentality."

Kyle smiled, but he felt the attention focused on their group—and Cliff's resulting discomfort. The long, dark-paneled room was festive with postgame cheer; a fire glowed in the big open fireplace but most of the girls had kept on their fur coats, their cheeks still burning from the chill air of the stadium. Their average age was perhaps twenty. This was a Princeton party, a young party, except for his bunch: the flecked and bone-colored heads and portly bodies of corporate power—the Yale grads from the private car.

"Take it easy, Ross," he said.

"Why?" said Markley. "Just because I don't like Commies in government agencies? Go ahead, tell me capitalism is dying. Well, let me tell you something else, there's a man named Black Jack Pershing, General of the Army. I served under him. Only thing *black* about him is his name. Give Jack Pershing a division. Hell, give him a platoon! You wouldn't have to tell him what to do. Just turn him loose. He'd get rid of the Commie bastards in a week."

"Rah, rah," said a sardonic young voice somewhere in the room. "Rah, rah, rah."

Markley turned in his chair.

"May I ask who said that?"

"I did, sir."

A tall young man with very pale, very serious brown eyes rose from a leather couch. He stood facing Markley—a Princetonian young man with button-down shirt and gray J. Press suit—a composed young man, tall and quiet in the spreading silence, paying no attention to the dark-haired girl who was trying to make him sit down.

"I consider that rude, son," said Markley.

Kyle, annoyed now, leaned over and spoke into Markley's ear, but Markley shook his head.

"Rude!" he repeated loudly. He glared around, still not quite pinpointing his adversary.

"I'm sorry, sir," said the young man. "I happened to hear what you said. I don't agree with you that our government is Communistic. My father also served under General Pershing, Black Jack Pershing, as you call him. And my father thinks . . ."

Cliff, who had been working his way toward the young man, kept him from saying anything further; he had his arms on the young man's shoulders and the two of them, standing close together, conducted a low, urgent colloquy, the dark-haired girl joining in, apparently on Cliff's side. In a moment or two the young man resumed his seat beside the girl and the momentarily dampened atmosphere of the bustling, celebrant room picked up again. But the mood was not what it had been before.

Cliff returned to his guests. He drew his uncle aside.

"Jesus, Unc, lots of the fellows in this club *don't mind* Mr. Roosevelt."

"I know."

"Lots of the fellows think he's doing okay. Can't you make Mr. Markley quiet down?"

"I'm trying," Kyle said.

"Where's Peterkin?" asked Malc Lattimer of Batten, Barton.

Peterkin Crouse, Vice President, the Wiston Bank and Trust Company, Baltimore, had started for the john but apparently had not made it. He was located only after a search, asleep under a billiard table. Thus the party, once more complete, was able to adopt Cliff's idea, put forward first to one and then another, that it was time to go, and perhaps past time; at the last minute, however, they were found to be one member short. Fos Vandenberg, a broker, came up missing; Kyle went back for him. Fos had been telling jokes to four puzzled and oppressed young people seated near the service bar, all of whom accepted Kyle's arrival as a deliverance. Fos, who had just built himself a new drink, refused to go along until he had told one more story—the best one of all, he said—which turned out to be long and rambling, distinguished by racism, several unpleasant words, and no point. In the crisp, early-evening air, the lovely towers of the university still showed clear and gentle on the sky as Kyle herded his friends on foot toward the railroad station. It seemed odd to him that a bunch who had been such good company in college should have changed so much, and he was glad to stand by and see them scramble, one after another, up the high step of the car; he turned to say goodbye to his nephew, of whom he was so fond, but Cliff had already left, striding off in the twilight toward his rooms in Harkness Hall.

Cliff had been a good sport about it. In Cliff's correspondence—and he wrote quite often, oftener Kyle suspected than to his parents—he referred to the football Saturday as "Yale fraternity weekend" or "the Prospect Street shoot-out." Cliff had a great sense of humor. During the spring break before his graduation he had come down to the Malibu house. He and Kyle had walked along the beach discussing what he should do when he left college. Cliff said he had something in mind but was not yet ready to talk about it and Kyle said that when he was ready they could get together again. He would support Cliff in any direction he wanted to take. Cliff had seemed grateful for that. Whatever his notion might be, its activation was certainly still a piece down the road. He had promised his father that he would spend one year, his first year out of Princeton, working for KinOil, six months in the field and six months in the office. Then they would see.

Kyle had thought this an excellent idea. He had a feeling that once Cliff got a taste of the oil business he would know he belonged there—hell, he'd been *born* there—but the important thing was to find what he would enjoy doing.

At that time Kyle did not get into the realities concerning KinOil's management, give Cliff a picture of the terrible damage that a family disagreement could lead to, once it got out of hand. (Why, the Kinsales might lose KinOil altogether —wild as that seemed, it could actually happen, once the stockholders in the public section were involved, and the raiders began to close in.)

Later he would make Cliff understand all that. Best not to pressure him, just give him the facts. He would have to find a tactful or at least an inconspicuous way to do it, one that would not tip off his strategy: the power residing in those thousand shares of L&CC stock Cliff held was certainly not hidden from Cliff's parents or from any other L&CC shareholders who might like change at the top. His one advantage at the moment was the assumption by the adversary parties that Cliff's shares would be voted as they always had been in the past, the unlikelihood that anyone would be able to upset this precedent.

Well, someone just might!

As the car moved off the flat valley roads, starting its climb into the Santa Anas, Kyle weighed his next move. He knew where Cliff was working. He could drop by unannounced, as if on some company chore, and chat with him.

Kyle sat up straighter. He leaned forward, looking past his driver's head at the scene now unfolding. Mort had pulled off the macadam onto a narrow dirt track, its banks thick with deer brush, manzanita and native laurel, gray with road dust. A quarter of a mile below, in a sheltered mountain basin, lay the training farm, the enterprise on which for years now he had lavished so much time and money and in which he took such pleasure. It was a pretty scene—the white-painted barns and corral fences, the bright-green fields of alfalfa and permanent pasture and, beyond, the larger, yellowing patches of spring barley. The whole expanse, except the track, was set out in a pattern defined by the huge live oaks—the bigger ones charred on the windward side with the Indian fires. Tuolumnes and Chauchilas had camped in this basin long before Ayala had seen San Francisco harbor or a white man set foot on the continental slope. The faded black scars on the tree trunks came from the fires that the vanished peoples had built when they sheltered here from ancient winter storms.

Some of the barley and a field of volunteer oats had already been cut and a half-dozen racing broodmares with new foals beside them were feeding on the stubble, their hides gleaming in the afternoon light. The training track lay to the east, well away from the stable yard—a three-quarter-mile oval complete with a movable starting gate and a timer's stand.

And in one of the barns stood his great horse, Aboukir.

Kyle had bought the big four-year-old in the September

sales at Chantilly, sight unseen, paying the highest price recorded in the auction.

Aboukir was in his prime, at the best age for racing. Kyle had made a decision about the big horse: he would start him in the 'Cap whether Aughterlonie liked it or not. Not that he minded Aughterlonie's caution—that was the Scots temperament. One had to concede that there was still the unanswered question: How would the horse react to new conditions? Racehorses were capricious—devilishly so. A change of water, now—that might be bad. Different minerals and all. Very well, said Kyle, then they would import Aboukir's water from the reservoirs at Longchamps, the spring water he'd been drinking since he was foaled—and this had been done, hundreds of gallons of the stuff, in aluminum tanks. His hay, too, was what he'd always had—Kyle had paid to have it baled in the Midi and shipped over in the holds of the *Ile de France*.

But—what about American-style racing? In France the races were run clockwise, on grass; at Santa Anita Aboukir would be going counterclockwise, on "turf," or, in other words, packed dirt—actually a slightly faster surface—but would Aboukir take to it? European horses had been known to dog out when they felt the California grit under them, as if they suspected it would hurt their feet.

God, what one put up with to win races . . .

But so far in his workouts Aboukir had been as steady as a parlor car. And his times had been sensational. Aughterlonie liked to talk about "bringing him up to it" and all that. So—fine. Aboukir was up to it now or he'd never be. And there was still time to give him a test race or two, maybe the San Marcos at a mile and a sixteenth. The 'Cap was a mile and a quarter. Aboukir could do either distance handily. He could do two miles. In Europe the trend was all for stamina, the big races mostly longer . . .

Aboukir! Kyle might show Mr. Whitney something with that horse (Cornelius Vanderbilt Whitney had bid against him in the sales); he might show Calumet and the other famous eastern stables something; he might just be the first western owner to win the biggest, the richest of western races.

Kyle spoke to Mort through the speaking tube, telling him to stop the car; he'd seen his trainer waiting for him in the infield paddock, standing with a hot-walker who was holding Aboukir on a lunge line: the big horse liked to frolic after his dinner, rolling and playing in the grass like a colt, then nuzzling the Scot for his reward of carrots. Kyle got out of the car, flipping off a greeting to Aughterlonie, and as he walked toward him his mind went back to his worries about Cliff Kinsale and he suddenly knew how to arrange a meeting, the perfect way: he would invite him to Santa Anita to see the 'Cap. He would invite Troy and Luanna also. If they chose not to come that was their business; certainly there would be no conspiratorial overtones in Cliff's being on hand. That would do it. The box held six: himself and Alma, Doc and Millie, and Cliff. Room for one more. Perhaps Alma could dig up a girl.

Perhaps, after what had happened with Dede, the Kyle Kinsales owed Cliff a girl.

CHAPTER TWELVE

The Graduates

1

The big rip sliced the hill in half. It smashed through the green spring sod, three feet wide, four feet deep. It was a dark brown, a loamy color, like a grave, a strange, sudden scar in the soft, green stretch of the land.

A large machine had dug the ditch. It had piled the excavated earth on the south side of the cut. The pipeline was to be fabricated on the north side.

Once the line had been put together, it would be eased into the ditch and the earth put back. The fescue and filaree and wild rye and volunteer oats would grow over the hump in the ground and the men who had made the cut would go away. After a while it would be hard to tell there was a pipe there at all. Much of the pipe was already in place. It rested lightly on its balks, a long, dark powerful twist of steel. It stretched away farther than the eye could reach in the soft vapor which the sun, though westering now, raised from the range. The pipeline perched gravely on the crisscross piles formed by the balks. These timbers were the size of railroad sleepers, but the pipeline, in its serious composure, made them look spindly.

The pipe was black; the sky above, bright blue; but Cliff saw neither color. For him the world today, as for days on end, was a uniform smoky green—not the green of the hill to the east or the swale in which he was now working, but the crystalline, metallic green of the window in his welding hood. Now and then, for a change of climate, he pushed back this hood. A glorious freedom then resulted; Cliff would take advantage of it by spitting into the ditch or even making some remark to his partner, Ev Evesitch, welding on the opposite side of the pipe. Ev might reply or he might not. Their conversations were not long, in any event. Both men, like all the welders, were paid on a piece basis, long chats interfered with speed, and, aside from the money involved, they took pride in speed. Cliff, who had trained for several weeks in welding school before being allowed on the job, was getting faster. He could lay down almost as good a weld as Ev, who had been a real hummer in his day.

Ev was old now and partially stove-up—lanky, taciturn Slavonian with a gimpy leg and a bushy white mustache, which would have blazed like deer brush if a torch spark ever hit it. Ev was of an age now when he would get grouchy at the end of a ten- or twelve-hour welding day. He did everything sadly; even his speed with his job had something sad and fatalistic about it. When he walked away to piss on the ground he walked sadly and he pissed sadly.

Beside being sad, Ev was mean. The mean old lady he lived with back in some mother-lode town was what made him that way. A fellow on the fill-pass crew had met her and he said she was a real ball-breaker. For the first ten days Cliff had been on the job Ev Evesitch had not said a word to him; when it had been necessary to convey some direction about the weld, Ev had done so with signs. He was better now, though still not hugely communicative.

Ev pushed back his hood and spat, sadly, on his torch—an action which in itself was a command. Ev then lit up a smoke. He stood with his back to Cliff, leaning against the pipe.

Cliff understood. He pushed back his own hood and motioned to his helper, Johnny Ride, a young fellow who had nothing in the world to do but brush off the slag between the passes and see that the generator, on its mule-towed skid, off to one side, was putting out enough juice.

"Turn us up ten amps, Johnny, feels like we're running a little cold."

And Johnny ran over to pass the order.

In the time Cliff had been working on the line the pipe had

come many miles, inching along in its stubborn, dark way, up and down the hills, across the level parts, breaking off at the draws (where it would cross on wooden trestles, to be put in later), then on and on, heading west to the Pacific, to the big refinery at Ventura.

Cliff was pleased with the line. He was content that he was helping to make it and took satisfaction in it for this reason, as one is pleased with anything strong and useful that he had made well. But there was another reason also. This pipeline was to a certain extent *his* line—a family property.

Cliff's identity on the job was well known. He did not brag about it, naturally, but on the other hand there had never been any secret about it. He was down in the time book as Cliff Kinsale, his true name, and everyone on the job knew he was a family person, from the famous family that owned it all—the whole fucking line, as well as the field, the wells, that would put the oil in the line, the gas stations that would peddle it, the tankers that would take it away, even the side boom, the A-frame-counterweighted Cat that brought up the joints from the road to the front end of the pipeline, an extremely rugged machine.

There had been considerable discussion of Cliff's lineage in the pipeline crew. Some thought he was the son of the big boss, the top Kinsale, whoever he might be. Others said he was only the nephew of the big boss, that he had taken up welding because he had made some wrong move and the family had outlawed him. Because of the respect for privacy, however, which was considered comradely among these men of varied pasts and backgrounds, some of whom certainly were happier and fared better in inverse ratio to what was known about them, no one came forward to question him. He was a Kinsale. That was enough. He had become, after his training, in a reasonable time, a fair-to-middling welder, but from the start indeed it had been clear that he was much more than a fair-to-middling man. He was a hell of a strong, likable and intelligent man and the pipeliners accepted him. Some of them even liked him though none buddied with him. He buddied only with Hershel Stepp, the college friend he had brought with him to the job. Stepp was another type entirely. He seemed to care little whether he was accepted or not, so in consequence he was left to himself. Stepp was a tallyman, a job which called for no particular skill except the ability to measure footage. In this capacity he was one of the few salaried employees on the job. The others, except for the side-boom man, the generator man and Crash McConighe, the foreman, were all independent contractors. They were not unionized.

Cliff worked the ditch side of the pipe. That had been his choice, his way of asking for no favor on the basis of being a Kinsale. The first day he had showed up for work he had made the choice. Crash McConighe had put him with Ev, and without any inquiries as to which side Ev liked to work, Cliff had taken his torch over to the ditch side and started in. He had known he wasn't welder enough to be a stringer man, who made the first tack behind the lineup crew; he couldn't weld with the hot-pass crew, the next team up, who put on second weld, the highest-temperature one, then moved on down the line. He was a fill passer, last crew on the weld after most of it was done, with Ev on the other side and Johnny Ride to scrub the weld until all the slag was gone and it shone like the tiara some dowager millionairess might wear to the opera. Johnny Ride was the one person on the job to whom Cliff was socially superior in pipeline terms.

He was careful not to press his superiority.

"Okay?" called Johnny, over at the skid, yelling to make himself heard above the clatter and roar of the generator, and Cliff held up his gloved hand, thumb and index finger forming a circle. He pulled down his hood and resumed welding. In a minute Ev finished his smoke and he too went to work. The sun in the west was down to treetop level, just about quitting time for this time of year.

Back on the hill, Crash McConighe came out of his trailer. He stood there with his thumbs hooked in the armholes of his sheepskin vest and his nose aimed back along the pipe where it disappeared into the scrub. In a minute he would blow his whistle.

This could be the last weld of the day.

Crash put the whistle in his mouth. He looked at his watch once more, then took a deep breath and blew long and hard. Dropping the whistle on its lanyard around his neck he waved his hand. Work was over for the day and also—if you could believe it—for the week.

Saturday night had come at last.

2

The pickup bounced along the country roads, heading for U.S. 101 and the hour-and-a-half drive to Los Angeles.

It was an old pickup, a homemade job, engineered from a Cole sedan by torching off the passenger body and substituting a boxsided flatbed. Owned by KinOil, it was the cheapest and worst vehicle on the pipeline job, used for running errands into neighboring towns, coming out with spare parts for other, better engines and also with mail and medicines and the girlie magazines Crash McConighe read in his trailer. Its small cab was set high up and afforded a fine view of the road. Such a view was needed since the front-wheel alignment was not what it could have been and Cliff, at the wheel, had trouble keeping the leaping jalopy in the proper lane.

The old pickup was the one company perk which he allowed himself. No doubt he could have had others. He had never thought to request them, his aim being to keep himself to what any welder at his skill and wage level would have had. He rode out from his Ventura boardinghouse with other KinOil men; a big Mack Six would fetch them at 7 A.M. and return them to the house at five-thirty. But on weekends Cliff needed a vehicle, and when he asked Crash for the Cole, the foreman had been happy to oblige.

Hersh Stepp, his college buddy, sat beside him on the narrow front seat. Both wore proper clothes for city-going— Cliff a button-down shirt, the suit coat matching his twill pants on a hanger behind his head. Hersh had on a pair of clean jeans and a wool-lined windbreaker. They had gone back to the boardinghouse after leaving the job to change and to get their gear.

Hersh would not be going back to the pipeline job. He had given Crash McConighe notice. He was through as of today.

Coolness met them as they drove out of the valley; ahead were the coastal cities, the limitless ocean, the great road to the south. The air changed from yellow to a frail, feathery lavender; a great horned owl crossed above their lights, one of which, ill-adjusted, pointed at the sky.

Cliff drove with no sign of fatigue, as if this long haul at the end of a hard working day were the greatest pleasure one could imagine. But Hersh, at his side, was nodding.

Cliff's friendship with Hershel Stepp had begun the year both transferred to Princeton from other colleges. It had not been one of those hey-buddy-how's-it-going type of college friendships. Not at all. It had had an unusual beginning. Tod Moran, a fellow from Exeter who lived under Cliff in Harkness, had run into the *Princetonian* offices where Cliff was finishing an assignment one night. Tod told him to get the hell down to the gym. Cliff would laugh himself sick at what was going on down there, said Tod.

Cliff had gone to the gym. It was almost 10 P.M. and the gym was officially closed but tonight someone had a key to the boxing room. That was where the event was taking place, Hershell Stepp *vs.* Wesley Newton, captain of the boxing team and intercollegiate heavyweight champion. They were just about to have at it in the ring. Each had handlers in his corner giving him advice, which Wes Newton did not need. Hersh did. He had never had on boxing gloves in his life. Someone clanged the bell and they met in the middle of the ring and Ducky Pond, the basketball captain, who was refereeing, told them to keep their blows clean, to break when he told them to, and to come out fighting.

It was a scream all right.

Hersh Stepp was by far the bigger of the two. He was enormous, and hopelessly clumsy. He was the only man on campus who wore a beard. His was the beard of an Old Testament prophet, bushy and black. His skin was glistening white. He had thighs like tree trunks and the muscles in his arms, back and shoulders had certainly not been acquired in the work he did to pay his tuition, riding around on a motorbike with a sidecar truck, delivering pressing and laundry from the Student Union. Hersh had worked in steel mills; he had worked in mines. He was by far the oldest man in the sophomore class—two or three years older than Wes, who was a senior—and this fact, combined with his beard, had led to his nickname: The Professor. He was brilliant in discussion groups, out to score. He was also out to win this fight, if it had to be done. He had his mitts up. He had them up like the pictures of John L. Sullivan or J. J. Corbett in old-time fight posters, curling from the elbows in front of his face. He had one foot out ahead of his body and the other behind, stiff as a plank. If someone had shoved him from the side he would have fallen down. Wes, a classic open boxer, with an easy, deceptive style, slid around him, pecking with his left, just letting it float in, so fast you could hardly see it.

Peck peck peck. He did not want to hurt this oaf with the beard. It wasn't a real fight. It was just a gag, Wes knew, but he was a champion, he had to make that clear also.

Cliff was told how the encounter had been developed, a tale which gradually became vague in his mind. Some third person had hoked it up—maybe Tod Moran himself. The Student Union had done something to a suit of Wes's— burned it or lost it. Then, in refusing responsibility, Hersh had made Wes angry. Wes was out to get him, or so Hersh had been told. Hersh would either have to fight or pay for the suit, some idiot challenge like that. The truth was different. The truth was that whoever had thought up the joke (it had not been Wes) was baiting Hersh just *for being Hersh!* It was not anti-Semitism. There was no anti-Semitism in Princeton, everyone knew that. It was just that a person should not wear a beard on campus. He should not be so old. He should not be so ready to talk in class and remember everything he read and argue with the professors. He should not be so big. He should not ride around on a motorcycle with a truck sidecar delivering suits, smiling and nodding at people he did not know and running up flights of stairs with the suits on hangers flopping on his back. If a person was like that, then he should take care not to be Jewish beside; if he neglected this simple precaution, then he laid himself wide open to the application of Princeton's non-anti-Semitism.

Cliff had immediately started rooting for Hershel. To his surprise he was not alone in this. His pal Butch Konoye and at least half of the others showed the same feelings. Several such rooters left when, in the third round of a scheduled four-round fight, Wes's pecking raised a cut over Hersh's left eye. Blood was oozing down his cheek. There was also a lump on his cheekbone and the other eye was not undamaged either. Ducky Pond was looking at Hersh watchfully.

Ducky Pond was quite capable of stopping the fight if Hersh became blinded or something.

As it turned out, he did not have to stop the fight. All he had to do was count ten over Wes Newton while he muttered, "Jesus Christ, get up, goddamn it, Wes, can't you get up?"

This occurred in the fourth round when Hersh fell into a rage. The peck peck pecking was what did it. Hersh lost all control. He ceased regarding the engagement as an entertainment staged for the amusement of the watchers. A wild power entered into him. Hersh's enormous white arms with the steel-mill muscles needed no direction. Hersh just stood flat-footed and let them go to work and when Wes went down he stood over him, failing to understand Ducky Pond, who was pushing him toward a neutral corner. It took Ducky several seconds to accomplish this before he could even begin counting.

Ducky could have counted to a thousand. Wes was not listening.

When Hersh got his clothes on, Cliff invited him uptown. They went to the Nassau Inn and had some beers.

Thus they became friends. Through the rest of their college careers they spent much time in each other's company. They participated in several classes together and later they comprised two-thirds of the three-man university debating team. While there was practically no subject—social, political or philosophical—on which they agreed, they took gleeful and lasting delight in their disputations. They dressed disparately, traveled separately, and vacationed on opposite sides of the nation, yet each, in his own fashion, structured those college years around the leadership—or opposition—of the other. At the graduation ceremonies Troy and Luanna, who had come east for the occasion, met Hershel's stepmother and his father, Mr. Stepp, Sr., who conducted a musical instrument business in Hartford, Connecticut. The meeting passed without incident, but that night, after the senior singing on the steps of Nassau Hall, Cliff and Hersh got away from the old folks. They walked over to the Balt and got some coffee and discussed their summer plans. Cliff had spoken to his father about Hersh. There would be a job for Hersh with KinOil, if Hersh wanted it. It might not pay much but it would surely be better than selling musical instruments on easy monthly payments in Hartford, Connecticut. It would be better than going for a Ph.D. in history, or wandering around the country like a Wobbly taking mill and factory jobs, as Hersh had done before.

Hersh admitted the validity of the proposition. He might want the Ph.D. But it would do no harm to work a little first. It took a bankroll to put letters after your name.

Once more it had been a hot and early spring and the voices singing their farewell to the university on the steps of the old hall were nostalgic in the soft blue evenings. The young voices affirmed loyalties to the past and certainties about the future that seemed fanciful in a world already beginning to burn at the edges.

Cliff and Hersh trained in California. They joined their first pipeline crew in July, a few days after three generals in Africa had risen against the Spanish Republic. By the time the pipeline had crawled across its first small valley General Emilio Mola, in Spain, had established his front along the Carabanchel-Getafé-Valdemoro line. He had cut the Madrid-Valencia road at Arganda and was advancing with four columns on Madrid. He told reporters that when Madrid fell none of the four columns would take it. Madrid would fall to his fifth column, the one inside the city. So said the Fascist general. He filled the reporters' glasses with Pedro Domecq brandy. General Mola had a knack of making catchy statements.

Hersh kept track of the fighting. He had a map on the wall of the boardinghouse room he shared with Cliff and he marked the battle lines with pins as he followed the campaign in the newspapers. He got very excited when he talked about Spain. He had read about the performance of the Abraham Lincoln Brigade. They had beaten back Mola. A newscaster on the radio said that the Abraham Lincoln Brigade had saved Madrid.

One weekend Hersh went to a meeting of the Anti-Nazi League in Hollywood. He listened to several impassioned speeches denouncing the Fascist hordes and to a proclamation expressing unity of purpose with the Partido Obrero de Unificación Marxista.

"I signed up. I'm leaving in two weeks."

Cliff had been lying peacefully in the top bunk of the double-decker, smoking his pipe. He jumped down now and faced his friend.

"You're out of your mind."

Hersh shook his head.

"I thought about it a long time."

He spoke with his face turned sideways, as if shy about revealing this decision that had meant so much to him.

Cliff knew now that what Hersh had said was true and his heart sank. But he still held out against his knowledge.

"All right, if you signed up, where's your passport?"

"What passport? They don't give you a passport for signing up, for Christ sake. Why are you so jazzed up?"

"I just hate to see you get your head shot off in someone else's war."

"It's our war too."

"Sure, *Madrid será la tumba de fascismo.*"

"You bet your ass."

"Okay, but here we don't have *fascismo*. Let them have it and let them get rid of it. It's their problem."

Hersh rejected further argument. He lay down on his bunk and closed his eyes, leaving Cliff to prowl around the room. After a while Hersh said gently, "Why don't you come with me?"

"Because I'm not a Communist."

"What's that got to do with it?"

Hersh's soft, unruffled tone made Cliff ashamed of his roughness. Yes, it would be natural, after all they'd done together, for him to go with Hersh—to go wherever he went, to share what he did, just as Hersh had been sharing this oil-field job.

"Well, are you one or not?"

For the first time Hersh became excited. He jumped up. His fingers flexed as if he wanted to grab Cliff by the throat.

"Let's go back. In Princeton you thought I was a Commie?"

"Not in Princeton. Hell, no, Hersh. Not then, but—"

"But now I've changed, is that it? Now I'm a card carrier! Okay, where would I carry it—in here?" Hersh pulled a stained, crumpled black wallet from his pants pocket, threw it on the table. "Go ahead. Search it. Maybe an FBI guy taught *you* some stuff. Like how to comb out a friend."

"I'm not going to search it."

"Then where's the card? In a tube up my ass?"

"I didn't say you had a card. You could be a Commie without a card."

"Fine! Great! But would it never enter your dumb fucking head that I could sign up to go to Spain *without being a Communist*? Listen, friend, history is being made. Not by Commies, by people—the same kind we got here. People who want a free country, free from Fascist dictators and exploiters. George Washington, was he a Red?"

"He was a landlord. What the Spanish Republicans killed off as soon as they came to power."

"Only the ones who deserved it. What about the Fascist general who put two thousand men, women and children in a bullring at Pamplona and machine-gunned them?"

"We have no proof that happened."

"The papers said it did. Mr. Hearst's papers, your dad's friend."

"My uncle's friend, not my dad's. But that's war, Spanish style."

"Not Spanish. Just the style of Francisco Franco."

"What about that other Francisco? Last name Goya. You took a history-of-art course. Maybe you saw his sketchbook, the one called *Disasters of War*. It wasn't so different then either—for both sides. Show it to your Hollywood friends, particularly the recruitment officer who pushed the enlistment blank at you."

"Nobody pushed an enlistment blank at me," said Hershel Stepp. He sat down at the table, his head in his hands. Weariness had overtaken him, the drain of arguing—the helplessness that arises when one quarrels with a friend.

Cliff walked over to the window and stood there, looking down into the street—the main street of a small California town. The lights on the movie theater were just coming on; Abe Hyman, who owned Hyman's Gent's Locker, was putting up his shutters.

Cliff did not really care anymore. After all, Hersh had been around. He'd known what bullets could do. He'd seen horseback cops cut loose with riot sticks and he'd fought back at them, sent rocks flying at the horses and the men. If Hersh had switched to the Red line you could understand it.

"Don't go," he said.

Hersh looked hard at his friend. While he did not regret his own decision, which was firmly set, he still needed to reconcile Cliff to it.

"I'll tell you what," he said slowly, "I'll think about it. I wouldn't want to take off just like that, you thinking me an anarchist. An old Mustache-Pete-bomb-thrower, huh? I'll examine my intentions and see how they shape up. I will! But you do one thing for me—you come along to a meeting. It's on Saturday night, so we can make it. You meet with these Commies, as you call them, you just come along and see if these people are what you think. Then tell me what you decide. Will you make that deal?"

"Gladly," said Cliff.

So there was still hope! Not much, just a chink in the darkness of Hersh's stubbornness, but still a chance. Maybe he could take Hersh by the collar and pull him through that skinny little hole to safety.

"I'll gladly do it, pal," he repeated. "If they can convince me that the war is as important as you say, the issues all that big, I'll buy a ticket to it myself. They can issue me one of those Crimean War rifles they're using and I'll pack out right beside you. How will that be?"

Without rising from the table, Hersh held out his hand.
And Cliff, rather sheepishly, accepted it.

The test was still ahead. Tonight the meeting would be held
which would decide the argument and perhaps the future of
both disputants.

In Los Angeles, Cliff stopped at a huge house on North
Adams—a Carpenter's Gothic abode, once a grand mansion,
now partitioned into apartments. He got out and Hersh,
grumpily awake at last, let down the tailgate of the pickup
and got out his big tin suitcase. Even looking at that suitcase
you would know what kind of person it belonged to. It was
dented and off-sided, missing a clamp but still serviceable,
willing to go anywhere, but so heavy that only a strong man
could carry it and only a young one would care to. Leather
pads had once been riveted on the corners in order to buffer
the sharp metal edges which could claw like talons, rip like
teeth. The pads had long since disintegrated or been torn
away; only two strong leather straps, fitted by Hersh himself,
kept the ugly box from flying open. A poor man's suitcase—a
loner's receptacle for odds and ends for which he had little
use or fondness but which he drags along to assure himself
that his own life has some sort of pattern, no matter how
confused or mystifying.

Hersh laid hold of the handle. With his body bent into an S
by the drag of the dead weight against his side, he lugged the
case up on the porch of the grand, shabby house, where he set
it down. He stood there beside Cliff looking at the row of
brass tenant mailboxes, each with its bell and its slot for a
name, printed, typed, or handwritten: Ortiz, Chin, Galitsen,
Jennings-Brown, Niemi, and one other.

Cliff was pressing the bell marked Konoye.

3

The weekends in Fumitaka's comfortable apartment had
become a well-established routine. During that winter and
spring of 1937, the visits of the pipeline builders to their
classmate had been as agreeable to the host as to his guests.
There were beds enough for all and the rooms were light and
pleasant, the big windows giving on the trees which the
manorial people of an older day had planted around the
house; there were overstuffed chairs in which one could

lounge at ease and put away a few beers. To the house would come the Sunday *Los Angeles Times* with its eight pages of comics, well designed to lull brains drained by week-long tussling with a welding torch or tallying twenty-two-foot pipe joints; there was the *Evening Herald* and Jimmy Starr's column, the bizarre life of the film colony: Gable Pinched, Cagney Slaps, Garbo Pffts, Leigh Signs, Powell Nixes, Warner Grabs, Zanuck Inks, Thalberg Planes, Cohn Bombs.

Just in case you gave a shit about such doings. Some did.

On days when the sun shone there was the beach. There were girls toasting in tank suits, girls strolling by twos along the tide line. Some would accept invitations to play volleyball or share a Coke or a sandwich or take a ride in Cliff's Bugatti.

The red racing car was garaged a few blocks from the North Adams house. Unused during the week, its twelve-coat paint protected by a dust cover, the Bugatti was a hypnotic toy, potentially aphrodisiac. However, since it was designed for two, and the seats were not large, Fumitaka Konoye could get to the beach in it only by perching between the two larger men, his butt on the folded-down convertible top.

Unlike his tall father, Fumitaka was small, though an average size for a Japanese. He was handsome, like his father, with the same expressive black eyes and readiness to smile. His courses in engineering were not easy and he confessed freely that he had small talent for the subject. When he had time he preferred to paint on silk screens, which he did well. He also composed haiku; these he sent to his family and to friends in Japan. There was a kitchen in the apartment and Fumitaka could cook splendidly; cooking was another of his hobbies, but cooking created a need for cleaning up and it was hard, those weekends, to find cleanup volunteers. There were restaurants of all kinds downtown, the friends often preferring those which catered to a working-class clientele. The food in these was good as well as cheap and they provided a background in which a freckle-faced American, a big Jew and a small, lively Japanese attracted little notice, particularly if two of them had not bothered, as sometimes happened, to change out of their work clothes.

It takes all kinds to make a city.

Tonight Fumitaka had cooked.

It had seemed a good night to do it.

Fumitaka explained this with many quick, lively glances and self-deprecating chuckles. If they would make allowance for his many mistakes! He had cooked only because tonight, as had been arranged, they were all going to the meeting, and since he feared his friends might arrive late for their drive, he had prepared a few dishes. He did not really recommend them. He needed no help. Everything was ready.

Cliff was impressed. The real reason Fumitaka had cooked was for a farewell banquet to Hersh. It was a sad and solemn occasion—the last night, for a long time at least, that they would all be together.

Hersh stashed the horrible tin case in the hall, to have it out of the way, and they all sat down.

The food was delicious, although the host himself ate little. He had eaten earlier, he insisted; through the meal he drank tea and sake and questioned Hersh about tonight's meeting.

"Will they ask us to sign up? Will they try to make soldiers out of us?"

Hersh was defensive. Fumitaka was touching on a delicate area—these ideas with which Hersh had lived so long and on which now he was casting his fate.

"They won't make you do anything, Butch. You won't have to sign up for anything. What are you so scared of?"

"Nothing. I am scared of absolutely nothing, not even these Spanish Fascisti. But I cannot be a soldier now. I have to get one more diploma, you understand."

"You go back to Tokyo they'll make a soldier out of you pretty quick. They need soldiers with diplomas to fight in Manchuria. Ask your father, Butch."

"My father does not approve of Manchuria. He does not want me there. It would ruin my golf handicap."

"In Spain you could play golf with grenades. You make a hole in one every time."

"Wonderful. And what do they call themselves, these grenade golfers we're going to meet tonight?"

"They're known as The Committee for Technical Aid to Spain."

Cliff looked at Hersh to see if he was joking. He had not heard this title before.

"What's 'technical aid'?" he demanded.

Hersh shrugged. "Truckers. Cooks. Ambulance drivers. Field telephone guys. . . ."

"That's what you're going to be, a telephone guy or a cook?"

"They need other kinds too. There'll be some choices. You'll hear all about it. You too, Butch. Just keep an open mind. Write to me and send me rubbers and tobacco."

"No clap medicine?"

"Not if you send the rubbers."

After dinner Hersh went to his box. He took out under-wear and toilet things and made a packet for them out of oilcloth. He checked his passport. He sat at the table for a while writing something. He got a little more stuff out of the case and closed the case again. The stuff he had taken out he put in a paper bag and set it on the mantelpiece.

Cliff and Fumitaka took the dishes off the table and carried them into the kitchen.

"So he's really going?" asked Fumitaka.

"He's absolutely set. I've tried to talk him out of it—might as well be speaking to a rock. Now he's trying to get me in."

"No chance of that, I hope."

"Not a chance in the world. But I said I'd go to the meeting."

"Oh, I'm going too. I'm curious about these people. It's an awful war; he's right about that. The Republicans should win, but somehow you know they're going to lose."

"Not if he can help it."

Before leaving the house Hersh gave each of the others a gift from his brown paper parcel—to Fumitaka a pearl-handled Sheffield-steel knife, obviously one of his prized possessions; to Cliff a half-buckram copy of Machiavelli's *The Prince* with a quotation from the same author on the flyleaf:

"You sow hemlock but you expect ears of corn to grow."

(Is he blaming *me* for what we are?)

The rites of farewell . . .

4

The meeting was held in the basement of a house in the hills, near the crumbling Hollywoodland sign which Kyle Kinsale had been accustomed to see on his way to the Bowl concerts with Alma. The place had once belonged to a silent-picture star who had fallen on hard times; the star had sold it to a screenwriter from New York, a man who wrote dialogue for the "talkies," lines which the star, due to a weak voice, could not deliver properly and so had lost his trade. The star in his good days had been a great one for athletics; to keep fit he had enlarged the cellar into a gymnasium as big as a basket-ball court. Chairs and benches borrowed from an athletic club

covered the floor. The small stage at one end was draped with
the flags of the United States and the Spanish Republic and to
the walls had been affixed large drawings of Lenin, Marx,
John Reed, La Pasionaria, and the Loyalist commander
called El Campesino, as well as signs in many languages:

> Proletarios de Todos Paises! Unansen!
> Proletarier, Aller Länder, Vereinigt Euch!
> Proletaires de Tous Pays, Unissez-vous!
> Proletari di Tutti i Paesi, Unitevi!
> Proletar Juszewszystich Krajow ta Czeiesie!
> Workers of the World, Unite!

Few members of the proletariat were present tonight. The
audience consisted of intellectuals: teachers, writers, actors,
musicians, and painters, with some studio artisans (suspected
as spies) and a few union organizers thrown in for leavening.

This was supposed to be a fund raiser, but the rumor that
certain people present were about to leave for the battle lines
lent tension to the proceedings. It was quite illegal, of course,
to go to Spain to fight. It was also known to be downright
dangerous.

Chairing the proceedings was a stage director fresh from
the east. He was famous for his espousal of liberal causes. He
was a poised, platform-wise man with a fine mellow voice. He
had a statesmanlike nose and a crown of rich black hair which
was getting thin behind. He was attired in exquisite tweeds to
which, as a proletarian touch, he had added a flannel work
shirt; the price of his handmade English shoes, applied to the
cause in hand, would have provided a Republican battery
with ammunition for a month. He spoke movingly and
dramatically of the crisis of the Loyalists, then introduced the
first of the evening's two scheduled speakers, Bonifacio
Cherta, a former minister of the Republican government.

Cherta, a tiny, bent and aging man, crippled with wounds
and arthritis, received a tremendous round of applause. He
sidled bravely up to the lectern, but before he could speak, a
strong Irish voice assailed him from the back of the hall:

"Señor, Your Honor, may I be heard?"

"No, no," shouted the audience.

"I wish to sing a song . . ."

"Sit down, shut up, you clown."

Apparently the interrupter was well known. Cliff caught a

glimpse of a heavy, bald man with a jaw full of large white teeth, which he bared in his struggle to rise. Those around him pushed him back, complaining, in his chair.

Cherta opened his manuscript. He spoke in Spanish, pausing every few sentences to wait for a translator to catch up with him. He stated that since medieval times the people of Spain had lived under conditions which would not be tolerated in the United States for livestock. He explained how, six years earlier, they had overthrown their enemies: the monarchy, the Church, the landlords and the Army. They had got rid of the stupid king. They had taken the education program away from the Jesuits, who had left forty percent of the country illiterate. They had taught the farmers new techniques. They had founded universities and hospitals. They had broken up the great estates of the noblemen, who lived in luxury on the Riviera and in the Paris faubourgs while their tenants starved. They had given the land to those who worked it. They had built factories capable of turning out rifles, cannons and airplanes. They had sworn the Army to loyalty. But the Army had betrayed them. These three generals in Africa . . . and now . . .

"And now all this stands in danger of destruction," said the translator, a tall, severe lady with a British accent and a slight lisp. "All might be plowed under and lost forever were it not for our friends in foreign lands, the loyal freedom fighters who have come rushing to our aid, who have taken up arms for us everywhere in spite of the hypocritical Neutrality Act of Mr. Roosevelt. How can he let our enemies get weapons from abroad? They're doing it, as everyone knows. This neutrality nonsense is a hideous lie. The Italians were sending troops to help Franco three days after he landed in southern Spain. . . ."

The audience loved it; the famous stage director with the handmade shoes and leisure-class voice applauded harder than anyone, the two-thousand-dollar-a-week actors and musicians beating their palms raw.

The British lady helped Cherta back to his seat beside the chairman.

"I want to sing a song . . ."

The Irish patriot was on his feet again. He flailed around him with powerful movements of his thick arms, shoving back those who had silenced him before. A confederate had gone to the piano, where he was fiercely striking chords.

Voices began to hum.

"That's it, now. ALL TOGETHER . . ." yelled the volunteer song leader.

"*¡Qué espontáneo!*" said a Spanish voice near Cliff.

The singing swelled, a torrent of male lament:

> *Early on a Sunday morning*
> *High upon a gallows tree*
> *Kevin Barry gave his young life*
> *For the cause of liberty . . .*

The *espontáneo's* head was thrown back. From deep in his bull throat, from between the rows of teeth which themselves looked like piano keys, billowed the next verse, more and more people now picking it up.

The Irish of Hollywood had apparently turned out in force to show kinship for their brethren in the Jarama Hills.

> *Shoot me like an Irish soldier*
> *Do not hang me like a dog*
> *For I fought for Ireland's freedom*
> *On that bright September morn.*

The singing of the ballad, in which the more dedicated of those present joined at full voice, and the fellow travelers welcomed as a diversion, pulled the meeting together. All participants rose in a standing ovation when a craggy-faced little man with a retreating chin, a veteran of the first battle for Teruel, introduced the evening's recruits and hailed them to the platform. They numbered four: an Italian mechanic, smiling and rugged-looking; a blond dental assistant who had signed on as a medic; an overweight librarian from Los Angeles University; and Hersh.

The Teruel veteran shook hands with each and embraced him, Spanish style; he then presented each with his traveling kit, which included shoulder patches for the uniforms which would be issued in Spain, together with a letter of instruction and a second-class boat ticket. The boat, a Dutch passenger-freighter, the *Zuider See,* would depart San Pedro for Le Havre at 2 A.M. next morning. Rail transportation had been arranged for the recruits from Le Havre to Paris, where they would receive further orders.

How they would get from Paris to the Spanish Front was not specified. Presumably they would scramble over the Pyrenees.

Cliff drove Hersh to the harbor in the Bugatti, Fumitaka as usual sitting perched between them. They left the car in the street outside the pier and walked down to the ship, still three abreast. Hersh was carrying only the kit just issued to him and the things he had tied in his oilcloth parcel; it seemed just as well that he had left his box behind. There would have been scant room for it aboard. All four freedom fighters had been berthed together in a multibunk cabin belowdecks.

The *Zuider See* was a rotor ship, a modern design, but small and dirty. Its superstructure had been damaged, possibly by a storm. One suspected other defects, better concealed. It did not seem likely that such a vessel could get as far as Panama, let alone cross the Atlantic, restless in the spring tempests. A dock crew was loading her with a cargo of lumber and canned goods.

The three graduates stood together on the narrow, dirty deck. The air had become quite cold and neither the ship's lights nor those on the dock shed much illumination. Here, at the last minute, awkwardness possessed them; all three knew in that moment that they would never be together again and the knowledge made it impossible to talk, hard even to look at one another, and when one did look, the others seemed changed, especially Hersh, with his damned beard and his eyes which now seemed like the eyes of a statue, eyes conserving tears of stone.

"Well!" he said.

He put out his hand suddenly and shook hands with Fumitaka, then with Cliff.

"Give 'em hell, old buddy," said Cliff.

"I will," said Hersh sternly.

He stood at the top of the gangway and watched them get off.

Back in Fumitaka's apartment, several weeks later, Cliff had to move Hersh's stupid tin carryall to make room for something else; he had an impulse to look into it, and did; all one had to do was unbuckle the straps, the lock was ready to snap open by itself. On top of the load were some personal things—tools, shapshots (some in frames), underwear, Chinatown souvenirs, et cetera. Underneath were papers which disclosed a different Hersh—not personal papers, far from it! These were pamphlets, printed back as far as four and five years ago, though some were more recent—turned out on little basement presses, by hand, to judge by the looks of them. They were flyers, the kind make to be distributed door

to door or handed out at meetings, setting forth the rights and
wrongs of forgotten causes—a complaint, a strike of elevator
operators, an aircraft factory workers' jurisdictional dispute,
union stuff and nonunion stuff—with letters attached, dittoed
and mimeographed orders from the Hollywood Anti-Nazi
League (a legal body), from the Young Communist League (a
front). There were reports from Hersh himself, signed by
him, written by hand or typed on plain paper or on the
stationery of small hotels in eastern and midwestern towns
and cities, reciting what he had done to carry out the orders
or suggestions and the difficulties he had met with. There was
even a report on his efforts to organize a Communist-
affiliated union among the pipeline workers, an activity which
Cliff, who had got him the job and worked near him every
day, had known nothing about.

The gist of it had been clear. None of the documents were
hardcore evidence of anything except limited, personal activities in this or that special situation, but the body of material,
taken as a whole, pointed overwhelmingly to one conclusion:
Hersh had been a Party member. Much of his thought and
energy, even while he had been in Princeton, had been taken
up with this other work—sweating out the Party line. Hersh a
Communist after all—the kidding about it, and the anger!
Well, for Christ sake. That took some thinking over.

Cliff read the material. Then he packed it away in the tin
valise again, the Medusa's chest of Hersh's past. He set the
snaps and the lock and rebuckled the straps. For some reason
he did not want Fumitaka to see it. Not that Fumitaka would
have cared all that much—it was just that he, Cliff, wanted
Fumitaka to remember Hersh the way he himself had remembered him before he found the stuff. That crazy Hersh! Cliff
could see him that night in the boxing room, raked back in his
absurd, pugilistic posture, facing Wes Newton's peck peck
peck. Hersh with his sidecar full of suits and laundry. Hersh,
big and easy, in his work clothes and field boots, coming
along the pipeline, tallying the joints. Cliff felt neither
disappointment nor animosity because of his discovery but—
though perhaps stupidly—he felt surprise. The discovery
made Hersh almost a stranger; it put him farther away than,
at that moment, he must have been, off somewhere on
Spain's dark and bloody battlefields.

Cliff decided to write Hersh and tell him what he had found
in the tin suitcase. He would ask him to explain why, if he had
been a Commie, he had never told about it. He'd had a right

to be what he wanted. Being what he had been wasn't all that good but neither had it been all that bad. It was just that finding out about it in the way he had found out was weird. He wished he had never opened the box. He wished he had taken out the stupid thing and dropped it in the ocean. He valued Hersh's friendship too much to let such a discovery go unexplained. He would certainly write to Hersh and see if what Hersh said in reply helped to clear the matter up. However, such a letter was a long way from being easy to write. Finally he did get around to touching on it, at least, in a letter which he wrote the following year, describing some changes in his own life. It had been one of the few, the very few letters he had got around to writing Hersh in Spain. Though Hersh had written regularly, or at least as often as he could, this last one was never answered, because by the time Hersh would have received it Hersh was dead.

CHAPTER THIRTEEN

The Main Chance

1

Kyle sat at his great medieval desk in the handsome office in which he had reshaped the family fortunes and brought KinOil to leadership among independent oil companies. Sun streamed through the picture windows—the warm sun of that pleasant, early spring of 1937, its brilliance hardly tinged by the smog which was appearing now on certain days even here in the uptown business section of Los Angeles. The desk, as usual, was piled high with papers, but today these documents were not concerned with petroleum. They were form letters, workout times and wire-service stories bunched together with the handwritten reports of a personal scout, an old-time trainer whom Aughterlonie had hired as a spy to obtain information from rival stables.

The stewards of Santa Anita had just assigned Aboukir the weight he was to carry in the Handicap—128 pounds. It was the top weight in the field next to the 130 posted for the favorite, Rosemont. Kyle felt pleased. He could not imagine why Aughterlonie seemed so dubious. The dour nature of the Scot could be irritating at times.

Kyle circled the official figure with a pencil mark.

"Hell, we've had more than that on him for an early-

315

morning breeze. He won't know he has anything on his back."

"A breeze is na' a race, you know that yersel'."

"He went with four pounds more in the St. Leger—"

"An' cum second," Aughterlonie reminded him glumly.

"—on a slow track, no kind of track at all. He took the Triomphe with a hundred twelve pounds on him."

"He did, sure, but three more strides and he'd of been beat."

Kyle looked once more at his betting chart. Based on the offtrack betting (illegal in the state, but flourishing nevertheless), Aboukir could go in at five or six to one. These odds might shorten somewhat on the day of the race—it was hard to tell—but anyway, the high weight would work in favor of a good price.

Even four or five to one would be just fine.

Kyle was getting down all the money he could, telegraphing wagers to the eastern and Canadian bookies where the odds, for the time being, were a few points higher. He planned to commission some Mexican action also. With enough spread he might get down as much as a hundred thousand in the time still left before the race—enough so that he would not have to fool with the Santa Anita totalizers at all. At the track he could be unconcerned. He could appear to be running the horse for glory alone, like the Whitney or Vanderbilt clans, backing his entry with a conspicuous, sentimental wager in the Turf Club, as if profits were the last thing he had in mind.

Profits were not the last thing he had in mind. He and Scott Stanfus had discussed that subject at some length. A hundred thousand dollars distributed through the betting community at four or five to one could mean a cash return of close to half a million. Not bad! Hell, that would offset much of the huge stable expenses. Not that he'd used company funds. He knew better than that, but there had been times when, coming up short for unforeseen charges, he'd borrowed from KinOil—dipped into the till, as Scott called it—quite heavily. Such sums had always been repaid, but now, with a contest looming in the annual stockholders' meeting, Stanfus had warned him of new dangers. People could ask about his personal expenditures. The stockholders might feel such inquiries relevant in view of the small dividends they were getting. They might draw contrasts between their forced economies and his own kingly lifestyle.

He would weaken their arguments noticeably if he proved that the stable, his largest single expense, paid its own way.

"Five to one!"

Kyle spoke half to himself, jotting figures on a scratch pad, but the trainer caught him up.

"What's gude fa' the odds is na' always gude fa' the horse."

"Right, Jock. So you take care of the horse and let me worry about the odds. What I want to see is Aboukir in the winner's circle with my wife holding his bridle. She's the legal owner, you know."

"We'll gi' her a race to remember, sor," said the trainer heartily.

"Let's do that."

Kyle rose to show the interview was at an end.

The morning was half gone. He had been meaning to call Alma to see if she could lunch with him—they had this meal together at least once a week, she driving in from the beach to meet him—but today he decided against it. She would have to hurry, which would detract from the joy of it. Also, he'd spent enough time today diverting himself. Diversion? Well, that was what it was, of course—everything to do with the breeding and buying and running of horses, filling the gap made in his life when he had phased out of polo.

He buzzed for Rose Brady. It was time for his eleven o'clock break and the one-page digest of the world's news which Rose typed out for him each day: a wonderful time-saver.

DRIVE FOR MADRID CHECKED
Italian Auxiliaries Defeated at Brihuega

Kyle kept up: no one could accuse him of political illiteracy. He knew, through Rose Brady's scrutiny of far horizons, that Benito Mussolini was meeting with Herr Schuschnigg in Vienna, that a food ship had eluded the Fascist blockade, that the Chinese were reinforcing their frontiers, that Herr Hitler was making life miserable for the Jews. He knew this and more just as he would know, when the time came, that the Japanese were moving in force against major Chinese cities and that his friend Konoye had accepted the Emperor's mandate to form a Cabinet.

A world in upheaval. All to be noted and examined with care. Kyle went about this task methodically, and yet

. . . and yet none of these matters were of prime concern to him. He had learned by experience that nations are fragile and that conflicts between them, no matter how bloody, are frivolous phenomena, transitory by nature. Business alone stands firm amid flux.

Kyle fully appreciated his freedom, his ability to isolate himself above events which drastically altered or extinguished the lives of so many others; he thoroughly enjoyed his privileges, though in practice he screened his appreciation behind a facade; as the years passed he had become better and better at it, as at all such exercises. For in truth the politics in which he was involved took place in a nation which appeared on no maps but which embraced all continents and preempted all frontiers, a country whose leaders conferred as equals with dictators, presidents, shaikhs and kings: the global republic of oil.

Kyle's grasp of this subject had not been arrived at in five minutes. He had studied the records. These had not been easy to come by—the petroleum establishment is itself a kind of huge intelligence service, wary of penetration, like all such organizations. Still, there were leaks.

Competition! That had been the root of all the trouble. Everyone had understood this but only Sir Henry Deterding of Royal Dutch Shell had done something about it. Sir Henry had rented Achnacarry Castle in the Scottish Highlands, the seat of the Cameron of Lochiel, and invited there in 1928 for the grouse shooting, and the brown-trout fishing in the loch below, his friends Teagle of Exxon, Sir John Cadman of BP, and Sir John's Man Friday, Hector Mellis; also Messrs. Moffett and Mowinckel of New York (Teagle's advisers) and the jolly huntsman William Larimer Mellon of Gulf.

Cadman had been out of sorts. He was a wretched fly-fisherman and a worse shot; there was also more drinking in the castle than he liked to see when serious issues were up for discussion. Lady Deterding's nieces took a dislike to Teagle's man Riedemann and put ants in his bed. Riedemann came down to breakfast furious and sleepless. Teagle needed all his tact to keep him from leaving right away.

Deterding had bagged the most birds. He also structured the most ideas, starting with the basic rule of all: *"The acceptance by the units (companies) of their present volume of business and their proportion of any increase of production . . ."*

Details of the goings-on at Achnacarry Castle reached Kyle later, at second hand. He had come late into the councils of Big Oil. He could not know and did not know that the original chums at the bird shoot and fish kill were joined thereafter by fifteen other American oil corporations. Nevertheless, like every other independent oilman in the United States at that time, he could and did know that some mechanism had been worked out to limit competition and fix prices and that the agreements arrived at for those items moved effortlessly eastward when the majors turned in that direction for new suppliers. This area had first shown on petroleum maps before World War I, at a time when the discovery that there was oil at Mosul got a British expeditionary force bogged down in a nightmarish campaign in Mesopotamia. Conferees at a meeting convened to draw up a peace treaty turned back to an old concession negotiated by Calouste Gulbenkian, the Armenian entrepreneur with whose sporting son, Nubar, Kyle had ridden to the Quorn Hunt. Calouste Gulbenkian kept five percent of everything even when—after strong arguments by the U.S. State Department—Exxon, Gulf, Texaco and Mobil were later admitted to the venture: the first plunge of American oilmen into this strange land.

No point here either for the participants to fly at one another's throats. Gulbenkian had suggested an understanding: none of the partners was to seek concessions in the former Ottoman Empire except through the "company." Well and good. But what was "the former Ottoman Empire"? Gulbenkian went to the map and drew his idea of what it was with a red crayon: an enormous spheroid bite then christened and forever afterward known as the Red Line Agreement.

A carve-up—but what a masterstroke! All Kyle could do was sniff around the edges, see if there weren't a few holes and pockets that the damned red crayon hadn't looped around. Also there were other countries, other possibilities. Venezuela, for one—and Troy, fully aware of the problem, had been in Mexico buying up what he could from the concessions Cowdray had abandoned, thinking them played out.

KinOil was in the running.

It was expanding. It would keep on that way—but only if Luanna and the other malcontents could be induced to sit down and shut up.

2

Kyle put aside the form sheet he'd been studying when his mind had strayed off; his arm moved out and with his forefinger he touched a statuette on his desk, a small bronze of a racing stallion which looked enough like Aboukir to be his twin. He'd come across this in Paris when he'd gone to arrange for shipping the big racer to California. He picked up the beautiful miniature and hefted it in his hands, looking with admiration at the compact conformation of the animal which the artist had captured so well, the short-coupled back, the deeply muscled hindquarters, the broad chest and dainty tapering forelegs, the elegant, docile head, the sensitive ears . . .

Did Teagle have a horse like that? Did Cadman, the deacon, or Deterding, the stern Dutchman who jumped like a schoolboy whenever his young Russian wife snapped her fingers? Not on your life!

No, he did not envy the men of the majors. Managing their huge companies left them hardly time to eat or sleep, let alone live lives of their own. Such men had power, but they paid a devil's price for it. He could never have settled for what they did; far from letting KinOil wipe him out he looked on it as a projection of himself, a means of fulfillment. And it was only one of several such: his sports interest another, and his happy homelife the best part of all. He wondered how much these pompous, decision-making fellows of the Seven Sisters could cash in for. Most, at the end, had no more to show for all the billions that had passed through their hands than the small nest egg, the poor beggarly million or two in savings on which they retired with their work-related ailments, their neglected hobbies and their little gray kitchen-mice wives to some trim suburban villa to piddle around for a while before they went to the bone pile. Oh, they were the big men of oil, while they lasted; they got the concessions, they fixed the prices, but the independents, the ones who owned their own shops, were the sons of bitches who came down to the finish line in one piece.

The ones who lived!

Pulling a scratch pad toward him, he wrote in a careful, upright hand the list of horses and jockeys as he and

Aughterlonie had disucssed them. Nineteen entries and of these basically three to contend with, the choice of the pack: Rosemont, Seabiscuit, Time Supply.

He prayed for fair weather.

3

The box was full. Troy and Luanna, invited for form's sake, had accepted; he might have known that Luanna would not miss a chance to be present at a conspicuous social function, once she had a way to it. Too bad, since with Doc and Millie and himself and Alma on hand, they lacked a seat for Cliff; after scurrying around to several friends, Kyle found room for him in Hal Roach's box.

Cliff didn't seem unhappy; Kyle had caught a glimpse of him earlier, his head bent to carry on a conversation with Ilona Cape, the English star, also a guest of the Roaches, along with Ernst Lubitsche and another cigar smoker Kyle couldn't quite see, Mervyn LeRoy probably.

Gloria Swanson in black mink. Nothing wrong with mink, but why did she wear orchids to a racetrack? Crosby two rows ahead, with his signature pipe and deerstalker hat. Winthrop Rockefeller, Hugh Blue, Mrs. Leigh Battson, Gene Markey, the Park Avenue version of a racetrack Irishman, always with some star. Raoul Walsh, the one-eyed director who had a horse in the race . . .

You could have fielded a forty-goal polo team from the Turf Club boxes alone: Elmer Boeseke, Cecil Smith, Eric Tyrrell-Martin, all fellows he'd played with. Elmer had asked him point blank if Aboukir was fit and he'd answered rather brusquely, "If he wasn't fit I wouldn't run him."

Alma was finishing a mound of strawberry ice cream; she'd been putting on just a whisper of weight lately, it became her. The fifth race was called but they continued to sit where they were, in the sun on the Turf Club terrace. Alfred Vanderbilt passed, coming up from the enclosure; he nodded and Kyle nodded in return. This was the customary extent of their greetings though they had been introduced several times and saw each other frequently at parties and at the track. It did not occur to Kyle that he was being snubbed but it did occur to him to wish that Mr. Vanderbilt had a horse going against Aboukir. It would be a pleasure to beat him and William du Pont's Rosemont the same day.

Mr. du Pont had not bothered to come out for today's race.

A queer bunch, the eastern racing coterie: C. V. Whitney, with his long neck and his cold, vague eyes, the most standoffish of all. Well, gentlemen, Kyle thought, the time may come, in fact it may come at four o'clock this afternoon —the time for us to settle our accounts.

He felt lucky here. He had come to this place, this wide expanse of sheltered earth, as a little boy when Hub, in one of his more fatherly moods, had brought him south on cattle-buying trips. Old Lucky Baldwin, a crusty prospector type, had owned Santa Anita then, the great ranch from which a piece had been clipped to make the racetrack, the stands, the stables and the parking lots. Hub and Lucky used to sit up late swilling whiskey and bragging what studs they had been in their prime and what cattle deals they'd made. He would hear them cussing and yelling at each other as he went to sleep, and when he woke up in the morning in Lucky Baldwin's house and looked out his window he would always see a long sliver of cloud floating like a fish over the Sierras.

The same slice of cloud was there today. He took it as a good sign.

He touched Alma's hand.

"We'd better go back, honey."

The entries in the fifth race were leaving the track.

4

Aboukir's comfortable routine at the training farm had been rudely interrupted. Three weeks ago he had been trucked to the track and installed in a box stall there with the Kinsale racing colors, black and maroon, painted on the door. A guinea named Pablo, who had taken care of him when he still belonged to the Aga, slept in his stall—and Pinkertons guarded him around the clock. Kyle and Aughterlonie were taking no chances with Aboukir.

Daily the big horse got his early workouts: sometimes a breeze, sometimes a gallop. He worked out in the pitch-dark before dawn, from the backstretch around to the three-quarter pole, to keep him away from the clockers, those harpies, male and female, who stood around with sixteen-power glasses and form sheets and thermoses of hot coffee to time every breath drawn and every stride taken by a contention horse before a big race. The clocker's information was much valued in the betting parlors. The bookies paid for it and the richer of them had their own men out there watching.

Thursday it rained all night. No horses were allowed on the track Friday. Under clearing skies, the maintenance crew went to work raking and mopping, rolling and pummeling the turf, and squeezing moisture off it with a track dryer. Today, Saturday, the chart caller had pronounced the going "good," a condition between "slow" and "fast." No one knew whether or not this would be good for Aboukir. Like Rosemont, the red horse could run on any kind of track.

Oscar Otis in the *Los Angeles Times* picked Rosemont.

Braven Dyer picked Seabiscuit.

Nobody picked Aboukir.

Kyle had been at the draw for post positions. With all the trainers and several of the owners he jammed into the stewards' office Friday morning. He had watched the track commissioner shake the numbers out of his old leather bottle and the chief steward pull the horses' names out of a box. Aboukir had drawn number sixteen. He would not be in the regular starting gate. That had only fourteen stalls in it but there were a few more stalls which could be set up beyond the gate for extra entries. Aboukir, almost on the outside, would have to gain a length for every horse between him and the rail. It would be a race all right. There were no easy-to-beat horses in it, outside of the crazy Sablin and maybe Star Shadow. Well, fine, but Star Shadow had Georgie Woolf up and Georgie could make a plater run like Man o' War. Rushaway, was he a dog? Not with Johnny Longden on him, even at 20 to 1.

Aboukir had passed a restless night. There is usually some partying around the barns at night before a big race and at 1 A.M. an owner and his trainer brought some people down to look at his entry. They did not turn on the stall lights but came through with electric torches, disturbing the horses. Pablo was very angry. He went to his trailer and got his guitar and played several songs to quiet the big stallion. Aboukir's favorite was "Cucurucucu, Paloma," a love song with a fading, falsetto cry in it which Pablo rendered very well.

After listening for half an hour Aboukir folded his long legs and lay down. He had three black-stockinged legs, a color which track people like. There is a tradition that black stockings mean the bones are denser.

Aboukir had other natural designations of good fortune.

The swirls of hair on each side of his huge neck were very pronounced. Such swirls are called the prophet's thumb. When they are clear and deep they signify that a prophet of Allah, god of thoroughbreds and of men, has touched the horse with speed.

Aboukir went to sleep and Pablo also.

At five o'clock the noises of distant partying had become silent but activities began in the barn. Aboukir stood up. His day had begun.

Pablo spoke to the big horse softly in Spanish, the language Aboukir liked best, though he also understood California English, racetrack French, and the dialect spoken by the Ismailian Muslims of Northern India. Pablo gave him a feed of oats, his regular ration on race day. He brushed Aboukir and walked him around the barns for half an hour, counterclockwise, like the track. Aboukir had already proved he did not care whether tracks went clockwise or counterclockwise, whether they were wet or dry, or whether the distances required of him were long or short. Some of his quarter-mile stretches in long races had been clocked at 21.4—which is quarter-horse speed. Or he could run two miles. He had been born to race. He had been trained to win.

Pablo cleaned the straw out of Aboukir's tail. Then he took the stallion to the track blacksmith, Cal Glover, who shod him with new shoes—aluminum racing plates. Aughterlonie came along to watch the shoeing. Plates with calks were available and would have been used if the track had stayed wet but the earth had dried nicely. These were regular plates.

At eleven, at Aughterlonie's orders, Aboukir stood with his forelegs sunk in boots of ice, to tone up his tendons. Then he rested until it was time for Pablo to put on his cooling sheet and take him to the receiving barn where the paddock judge would check him in for the race. The judge had a clipboard chart with Aboukir's identification on it—his height (16.1 hands), his weight (1,150 pounds) and his distinctive markings. There were prints on the chart of the stallion's "night eyes," the whorls on the back of the hocks which serve horses as indestructible I.D., just as fingerprints serve humans.

There must be no doubt that this entry was indeed Aboukir and not some ringer.

Aboukir had been through it all many times. In his wise and aristocratic horse brain he knew what was up. He stood quietly in the ammonia-and-dust-and-horse-piss-smelling barn, his great head high and his stallion eyes tranquil and proud, glad to be Aboukir and to let these people make sure of it once more. He watched the paddock judge give Aughterlonie his number pad. Then he walked sedately and daintily beside Pablo and Aughterlonie to the saddling enclosure where Kyle was waiting for him.

Meanwhile, in the jockey's room, along with Richards, Pollard, James, Corbett, Robertson, Burns, Workman, Gray, Peters, Dotter, Luther, Knapp, Balaski, Woolf, O'Malley, Longden, Richardson, and Young, his rider, Sam Veech, was getting dressed. Veech was a top hand. He had won, in different years, for diverse owners, the Kentucky Derby, the Belmont Stakes, the Withers, and too many stake races to remember. Kyle had him under contract for twenty-five hundred dollars a month, fifty dollars a ride, and ten percent of the winnings. Veech, twenty-eight, looked fifty, his long, sharp face already grooved and gullied with the lines and the old man's wrinkles and the queer bleached pits under the cheekbones which jocks get from the steams and the bakeouts, the castor oil and the jogging that they endure to make the weight, to soak or shit or boil or exercise away those few pounds which one good steak dinner or one lovely lobster thermidor will always put on them, not to mention the baked potatoes and buttery vegetables and oily salad on the side or *profiteroles au chocolat* and the Hennessy or Courvoisier which follow.

Veech was dressed now except for his boots. His valet, Bones Leigh, a black man kneeling in front of him, was pushing these onto his feet. Veech had on his underclothes, his silk shirt, his stock, his vest, and his moleskin breeches, but the boots were the most important and came last. The ritual of getting into them was carefully observed. Bones Leigh spat first into the right one and worked that on, smoothing the soft kangaroo leather up the jockey's calf; then he spat in the left one and did the same with it. To spit in the wrong boot first was as bad as seeing a black cat or throwing a hat onto a bed. It could wreck a day. It could lose you the race. Bones, as good a jockey's valet as Sam Veech was a jockey, would not likely have made such a mistake, but if he had, there would have been just nothing that Veech could have done to make it right. If he had been a Catholic, which he was not, he could have prayed. That was about all unless he could have located a humpbacked man or woman and rubbed that person's hump. Humpbacked people resent having their humps rubbed by superstitious racetrackers but the practice persists because of its supposed benefits.

The room was full of steam. Jockeys from the fifth race were coming in, the silks and moleskins which had been spotless a few minutes earlier now soiled with sweat and the stains left by flying clods of earth. Two jocks were in an argument; one dropped his gear and swung a punch. They went at each other. Abdul the Turk stopped it. He was the masseur, a gigantic man who had once been a wrestler. He had wrestled with Frank Gotch, the Masked Marvel and other great men. His biceps were as big around as the torsos of the little fighters. Abdul picked up both of them. Slinging one under each arm he took them to the showers and dumped them, turning on the cold water. No one paid any attention.

Bones handed Veech his cap and whip. He took from its rack the saddle Veech would use in the 'Cap, and with his tack in his arms Veech got on the scales and weighed in, then went out briskly with Bones behind him.

Aughterlonie was already in the enclosure. Kyle stood with him, waiting for the tack so they could saddle Aboukir. The trainer bent in front of the tall red horse. He stretched first one front leg, then the other, pulling them out to make sure there would be no skin wrinkles under the belly that would bind in the girth. He stood on the horse's near side, Bones on the off; Bones handed him the number pad and the weight pad and Aughterlonie laid them on, first smoothing down the horse's back hairs with his hand, a sensitive, reassuring stroke. The horse turned his head slightly, the great eyes smoldering softly and the breath flowing out of his velvet nostrils. There was moisture in his nostrils but no sweat on his back or flanks as there was with the more nervous horses. Seabiscuit alone, the youngest runner present (he was later to go on to untold glory), equaled Aboukir's composure. Seabiscuit bent over, curving his long thoroughbred neck toward his owner, Mrs. C. K. Howard, who had leaned her head against him. The horse seemed to be concerned for this beautiful brunet woman, as if she were going out to race instead of himself.

Rosemont fussed a little. His jockey, Harry Richards, studied him coldly, tapping his whip against his boot.

Aughterlonie placed the snakeskin saddle on Aboukir's back. He took the undergirth, then the overgirth from Bones and set and tightened them, feeling with his fingers to get just the right amount of tension. Aboukir was cinch-shy. He humped his back as the trainer pulled up on the straps but Aughterlonie said something to him in his Scottish brogue and the horse eased off.

Veech looked from Aughterlonie to Kyle. It was now time for his riding instructions, sometimes given by the owner, sometimes by the trainer. The instructions were a ritual part of the saddling, and like most jockeys Sam Veech knew in advance what they would be. Go out there. Don't try to make the pace, but don't fall too far back. Improve from the first turn on and make your move at the three-eighth pole. Shit like that. Veech listened, nodding his head gravely, paying not the least attention. He had known for days how he would ride this race; he had a plan—but it would all depend on how the horses came out of the gate. You worked the main chance. Knowing what your horse could do was the nub of it, and this horse could do anything.

"Riders up," said the paddock judge.

Aughterlonie made a stirrup of his locked hands. He tossed Veech lightly into the saddle. All the jocks were mounting now and in a moment the horses, with trainers and guineas at their bridles, went out into the walking ring. Here the scene changed totally. In the dimness of the ring, with their long necks and gleaming coats and the huge muscles flexing in their hindquarters, the horses resembled some kind of semi-extinct creatures left over from a previous stage of the earth's evolution, and the people around them, held back only by the low wooden barrier, also seemed bizarre, their faces distorted into masks of excitement and avarice.

The bugle sounded. The scarlet-coated outrider on his buckskin pony led the way into the exit lane. And through the crowd outside went a murmur.

"They're coming out!"

Everyone in the stands and the Turf Club stood up as the horses came out. Down in the infield among the pansy beds, the picnickers who had been lounging all day in the sun, eating and drinking and flirting, rushed over to the rail. Bettors, lined up at the windows, turned to watch as the horses made their ritual parade, walking down as far as the three-eighth pole before they turned and headed back for the quarter-mile chute where the race would begin.

In the box belonging to his uncle's friend Hal Roach, once a producer of slapstick motion pictures, Cliff Kinsale stood up like everyone else. Up to this point in the day he had been enjoying himself hugely. He was delighted with the bright, warm day, the fashionable crowd and the release from his drudgery on the pipeline. The horses interested him the least. He had grown up with horses, he knew all about them, but they had never had any special meaning for him, as they had for Kyle. He did not consider himself a particularly good judge of racers, and though everyone around him was exchanging tips and marking programs, running back and forth to the betting windows, he had not bet a single race. He had money to do it. He had cashed his paycheck, forty-three dollars and fifty cents, and had it all with him. He did not see the sense of whacking it down on some skin that might drop dead in the starting gate and leave him feeling like an ass. He remembered the story his father had told him of how he, Troy, and Kyle as boys had been cleaned out at the Sacramento State Fair. His reaction to that yarn had not been envy of the adventure they'd had but wonder at what fools they must have been. He knew he was not that kind of fool.

"Is there still time to wager?"

Ilona Cape, in the front row of the box, was looking up at him. Her escort, a middle-aged director, had left her to go down to the enclosure.

"Certainly. You can bet until the bell rings."

"Then I will. I'll bet on your uncle's horse. Is that he, the big reddish one?"

"Yes, Aboukir. Would you like me to place the bet for you?"

"Would you?"

"I'll be glad to. How do you want the odds—win, place or show?"

"To win, of course," said Miss Cape coldly.

Fishing in an enormous handbag, she found a gold-mesh purse. The purse had a diamond clasp and her initials on it in gold. She opened it and got out a bill which had been folded and refolded until it was not much bigger than a postage stamp. She kissed it for luck before handing it to Cliff. He was uncertain whether to unfold the bill or wait until he got out of the box. Miss Cape might not want others to see what she was betting. Obviously she could not bet for herself; it would have been impossible for her to get to the windows. A cluster of fans, most of them young, filled the aisle behind the box; they crowded in with notebooks, pictures and pieces of paper in their hands, asking for her autograph. This had happened several times before, during the afternoon; how the fans got past the Turf Club guards nobody knew, but they did, they got in everywhere. Miss Cape patiently signed everything presented to her. She was amazingly good-natured about it.

Well, he thought, that's her line of trade.

He got in line at the fifty-dollar window, wondering what denomination bill she'd given him. He was sure that it would be a thousand-dollar bank note, or at least five hundred. He had never bet that much himself and for effect he waited till it was his turn at the window before unfolding the bill. It was for twenty dollars. Sheepishly he ducked away from the tote clerk and crossed to the ten-dollar window. No reason why she shouldn't bet twenty bucks if that was what she wanted to lay on. She had every right. Still—a lady who earned ten thousand dollars a week for her acting laying twenty singles on a skin's nose! It was silly, somehow. It made her seem different than he'd thought she was.

He stood waiting in the ten-dollar line, holding the bill in his hand. The folds she had made in it had left creases which still showed as did the dab of red from her lips when she kissed it for luck. The bill now had a perfumelike smell, possibly from the lipstick or the handbag rather than her person. The red stain of her lips on the bank-note paper stirred him somehow. He would have liked to mash the lips that had made that stain against his own.

The horses turned in single file in front of the stands, then followed the postilion toward the chutes. Cliff got his two win tickets and left the window. He walked back toward the box and stood in the aisle there, watching Miss Cape, who was still signing autographs. He studied her, wondering what made her appeal to him. She was far from beautiful. He guessed her age at forty-five, about the same age as Dede Atlass, but she was better-looking than Dede. She had a grand figure, full and perfect, with full breasts and long, tapering legs. Even her dark mink coat and the silk dress she wore under it could not hide all that, and had not. Only her face showed her age. Her eyes seemed to have too much white in them. They were glistening, elusive, and sensual; she seldom looked you full in the face but flicked evasive little glances in your general direction, as if afraid to reveal how much you both had in common. Once in a while she let you have it full on, a blazy look that shook you. But also there was something about her, something in those shiny, too pale, slightly bulging eyes which warned you, which said, "I can do this to anyone, old boy, so don't take it personally."

She could be fascinating but she could also be mean.

Perhaps the meanness, the sadistic streak in her, appealed to people more than her sensuality. Audiences sensed it. If she did some horrible thing on the screen they believed it. They knew she would be punished for it and they would enjoy her punishment. But if she escaped punishment they accepted that too. They were willing to go either way with her.

Cliff strolled on down to the box. Miss Cape was there alone, signing for a few final admirers. On an impulse Cliff lined up with these, and as the last one left he held out his race card saying, "Will you autograph this for me, Miss Cape? I just love your pictures."

"Why, how nice of you!" she cried.

She raised her pen dramatically, poised to write. But then, instead of signing on the card, she turned his hand over and wrote on the skin of his hand, pressing down as if she were tattooing him:

With love. Ilona Cape.

"Is that all right?" she asked innocently, dabbing him with one of her flicking, fading glances.

"Beautiful," he said through gritted teeth.

He stared at his hand to see if she'd drawn blood.

She followed his look.

"Don't worry. It will come out."

"I might not want it to come out," he said with his best country-boy smile.

She patted the seat beside her.

"Sit down. Did you place my money?"

"All of it."

She laughed.

"Where you surprised? I never wager—not on horses or anything else. Twenty dollars is a lot for me—four pounds! Good Lord, such extravagance. My business manager would chastise me for it; I shall never let him know. Do you think Aboukir will win?"

"I don't know."

"You're not a bettor?"

"No."

"So," she said mockingly, "not even on the family entry? No nonsense about you, I can see that. I suppose you work. All Americans work, rich or poor alike. They feel it's their duty. Don't you think that's a mistake?"

"Not particularly. I work on a pipeline. I'm a welder."

"Well, that *is* a bit of all right, you know!" she said, exaggerating the British accent which at other times was hardly noticeable.

"Oh, come on, Miss Cape," he wanted to say, "you're overdoing it. I'm not all that young, and I've lived with a woman older than you." But what he said was, "I don't mind it. Just another family project, like Aboukir."

She laughed again, for no real reason, and he heard Dede's kind of wildness in that laugh. Yes, that was it; this woman, who by nature was nothing like Dede, reminded him of Dede: a woman getting on but not used up, a woman accustomed to the ways of men and still needing men. He wondered what sort of terms she'd come to now with her life and her world reputation. This business manager she'd mentioned: who was that and why did she let him control her money? And this other person who had been in the box with her, the thick-necked chap with the gravelly voice and the little bright feathers tucked into his hatband, as if to say he was a sport in spite of his drab gray face and lying drinker's eyes: who was he? Well, it didn't matter. This was the kind of woman to have fun with, the kind he liked. Experienced.

"Oh," she said, "I'm sure your family can use another welder."

And with this she let him have one of her knockdown looks, straight on, and patted his hand. They sat together in the box, smiling at each other. Then there was a shuffle of feet and a stirring of chairs behind them; the others were coming back, Roach and the rest. Cliff had been about to ask her for a date but now the moment was gone, the horses were at the chute, the starters putting them in the gate. The race drove everything else out of his mind.

5

Sablin, the outsider, was acting up. A bony flitch of a nag, long in the barrel and wild in the head, he had no business in the Handicap but the Seagram Stable had lost a better horse to an injury and were starting him anyway. He reared and rolled to the side, almost dumping the jock. An assistant starter had him by the ear. Aboukir, three stalls away, waited for the fuss to be over. Rosemont also was starting outside the regular gate, the blue Foxcatcher silks bright in the sun. A second starter eared the damned Sablin on the off side. The two men, struggling, got him back into his stall. The moment he was in his place the field was off and running.

Kyle had never gone back to his box. From the walking circle he went straight down to the rail in front of the club. He stood with his glasses up to watch the start but quickly lowered them again. He could see well enough and what he saw he liked little. Aboukir had got off badly. The fucking Sablin had impeded the start, not enough for a complaint to the stewards—but enough. Kyle let the glasses hang on their lanyard around his neck. He felt better there at the rail, to be near his horse as Aboukir came by in the melee, running far back, twelfth or thirteenth at best, packed in, biding his time. Now they were opposite the stands, and now the enclosure, and as they went past, Kyle knew, for those few seconds it took them to go the fifty yards, the ferocity of the run, the madness of it, the jammed bodies of the horses, the jocks bent into them, clamped on by their shinbones, the long thoroughbred necks stretched out, the bunched heads with the eerie racing blinkers on them, the surge and smash of it, the rise and fall of hindquarters, the crazy speed. They were there for those seconds, the ground shaking, the deadly hooves cutting clods; nineteen nags bunched in a wild rhythm of unified and desperate intent. Then they were gone, into the turn, beginning to reorder themselves, the sprint horses still making the pace: Time Supply, Special Agent, Indian Broom.

Kyle stood bareheaded, his face keen and tranquil, pushing Aboukir forward with his will. Cliff, catching sight of him there, where he had not expected to see him, thought, Why, he's older! For some reason he had never thought of his uncle as changing—as being vulnerable to age. Yet it had happened, or was about to: the handsome face was heavier now, the neck fuller, the dominant nose more prominent. He was not less handsome than before, perhaps more so, but he was different. Or possibly it was his concentration on the race that give him this new, fateful look. And Cliff, who had always considered that racing was a frivolity for this man, a way of amusing himself, now corrected this. The race might have some significance for Kyle that he had kept secret. Could that be?

Cliff turned back to the track.

The horses were in the backstretch. Small against the ghostly mountains behind, they were strung out, soundless, like an illusion, a tatter of mist or a piece of cloth pulled along there by some force not their own.

"Time Supply," said the race caller on the loudspeaker system, "Special Agent, Indian Broom. And Seabiscuit moving up on the rail . . ."

At Seabiscuit's shoulder was Rosemont. If Aboukir was about to move, he had better do it soon.

Kyle made a resolve—he would not look at the field till they were at the three-quarter pole. He turned and ran up the steps toward his box.

Millie was standing on her chair. Doc had his arm around her hips to steady her. Troy had his glasses on the field but he turned instinctively as he felt his brother jam in beside him. Troy gripped his hand and the feel of Troy's bony, knuckle-mashed fist was warming, reassuring. Troy's voice was yelling in his ear:

"Look! Jesus, here he comes!"

Aboukir was moving at last . . .

Sammy Veech had not been riding well, and knew it. He had almost come unseated, forced to lay back as Sablin swerved coming out of the gate. Aboukir's great early speed had been wasted; all Veech could do was to move with the bunch and watch for holes. Now he was finding them. Firmly, but decorously, like a late commuter in a crowded station, Aboukir passed Boxthorn, Rushaway, Golden Eye and Grand Manitou. Seabiscuit was on the rail, Seabiscuit the horse to beat . . .

"All right, Mother," said Veech; "let's see it now, Ma."

In the cyclone whirl of a race, the vacuum of absolute loneliness around each rider, Veech called all his mounts Ma or Mother; he never knew why. It was a term of endearment, of encouragement with him. A horse knew what it meant. Like most jocks Veech affected to scorn horses, but the truth was he loved every mount he got, if it was any good—some more than others. Aboukir he loved with his whole soul. He would rather have hit his mother than this horse, but they were into the home turn now and he lashed Aboukir twice as hard as he could and turned him loose and Aboukir made a hole in the wind. The noise of the crowd came up to meet them, Special Agent falling back, Don Roberto and Indian Broom long gone, and now there was nothing in front but the wire and the insane swelling crowd noise which bears no resemblance to any other human noise pushing out to meet him and now here was Seabiscuit crowding the rail with

Pollard cramped down on him and something coming up behind.

No jock in his right mind looks back. He does not take that look because if he does he'll see a horse gaining on him. It was enough to beat Seabiscuit in his rail position and Aboukir was doing it, yes, would in one jump more, but then there was this horse out of nowhere in between and the field past the finish line and turning back and the hot-walkers running out to take the bridles and the red light turned on and the word "PHOTO" flashing on the board.

A nose finish.

THE RACE CALLER TELLING THE PEOPLE TO HOLD ON TO THEIR TICKETS.

6

Kyle stood in the box with his arm around his brother, waiting for the photo. No matter what might happen between Troy and himself in the week ahead, they were together now and that was good. He could stand here with Troy, waiting to hear if he had won or lost, as nonchalant as Mr. C. V. Whitney, who owned a fine stable but had not put an entry in the 'Cap, or Mr. William du Pont, who had a horse entered but had not come out. Screw Mr. William du Pont.

"You won, buddy," said Troy. "Why do they need a picture? I saw it with my own eyes!"

That was Troy for you: if the family pride was at stake he would see whatever he wanted.

Kyle smiled at him. At that moment, strangely, he did not care whether he won or lost. It had been a hell of a race. It had been a 'Cap no one would ever forget—three horses, nose and nose at the finish.

Now the crowd was still. The photograph had been developed. In its little metal trolley it was sliding down the wire from the camera booth to the judges' stand.

The numbers went up on the board: Rosemont!

Rosemont had won, the Foxcatcher Farms horse that had come on in the last eighth of a mile.

Seabiscuit and Aboukir in a dead heat for second.

People were rushing to cash in, others tearing up their tickets, one young guy in a watch cap and pea jacket trying to shimmy up into the judges' stand, probably to attack the honorable officials there. A racetrack cop pulled him down.

"It's a lousy deal, Unc. Stinking! I still think we took it."

Cliff gripped Kyle by the shoulders, peering with concern into his face.

"Did you lose much, Unc?"

"Hell, no," said Kyle. "How could I lose? I bet him to place."

CHAPTER FOURTEEN

Home on the Range

1

What a debonair person! What a racetracker—betting his own great running horse to place, shading the risk just that small amount against the breaks of the game. Kyle had seemed completely in character as he told of his wager. He had foreseen just what would happen. He had been detached and practical and so, as usual, he had come out ahead.

Oh, it was all fine, just dandy. Only the catch was—*he hadn't bet that way at all. He had lost more than a hundred thousand dollars on the 'Cap.*

This did not appear until much later, at a time when Cliff—delegated to this task by the family—had gone over Kyle's records for years back. There had been a lot of material, some of it far more startling than the vanished hundred thousand, yet that item, if revealed, would have told so much about Kyle that had never been known, so much that might have made a difference!

Why had he lied? If he'd owned up to his loss he would have been little hurt by the admission; it would have been just one more count, not really a major one, in the docket of personal extravagances which the L&CC stockholders held against him.

Kyle had lied for a different reason. Cliff, thinking about

that day at the track, was sure of his conclusion. Kyle had lied out of sheer arrogance. He had lied because he could never be wrong. He could never be a loser. He must always be a winner—or seem like one. That theory fitted well into the tales Troy had told about Kyle as a boy. As the years passed, however, and the company expanded, this trait of Kyle's had stopped being an attitude. It had become Kyle himself—a Kyle grown larger than life-size, just as the company he controlled had grown larger than life-size, swelling into a monster which nobody, not even Kyle, could keep in hand—the gargantuan implement of power.

So he had lied. He'd had that need to appear more masterful, more brilliant than he was. Cliff came to understand that characteristic in his uncle and to condone it. Kyle was a man of whom he stood in awe while at the same time he retained a great affection for him: it just seemed too bad that Kyle had this hot surge for expansion and aggrandizement, that he couldn't accept a setback or a loss like other people.

Another incident, not long after the Handicap, dramatized this need of Kyle's to win at everything, no matter how. Recently he'd got interested in trap and skeet shooting and set up facilities for these sports near the stables; from casual weekend fun the shoots developed into high-stake betting matches to which he invited some of the best wing shots in the state. A natural marksman, with fine coordination and a deadly eye, Kyle could do well enough against his friends, but the top hands could beat him every time. He was particularly irked by his losses to Harry Sinclair, chairman of Sinclair Oil, a head-on gambler who could score in competition as much by gamesmanship as by marksmanship.

One Sunday, after due publicity, he challenged Sinclair to a private match, five hundred clay birds at a thousand dollars a bird. After a hundred birds, Sinclair was a dozen ahead; Kyle asked if he'd care to double the bet, and Sinclair accepted; no such gambling on a shotgun contest had been heard of, even in the live bird shoots in Reno (live bird shooting was and is illegal in California). Sinclair began to miss. He did particularly badly on the doubles, eight of which, in skeet, are thrown in every twenty-five birds. With the match half over, Sinclair had lost forty thousand dollars. He asked for a delay while he sent to his hotel for new guns. He did no better with these, losing eighty thousand on the match. Cliff, who had been in the party of specially invited spectators, hurried to congratulate his uncle. Kyle winked at him.

"Stick around," he whispered. "I want to show you something."

Kyle took him out to the stable. There, carefully packed away, were baskets full of cast-iron birds, all of them scarred by the pellets of Sinclair's "misses."

Kyle had roared with laughter, and Cliff laughed with him. The two staggered around in the horse-smelling twilight of the stable, punching each other in delight.

"He sent for . . . *new guns*," Kyle gasped. "Did you get that? Hell, he couldn't have broken one of these things with a French seventy-five."

He threw some of the iron targets into the hayloft.

Kyle was happy. He had established his superiority over Sinclair. It made no difference that the implement employed had been chicanery rather than marksmanship.

A week later, in a gesture which appeared (quite falsely) as sporting generosity, he rubbed in his triumph. He laid on a dinner for Sinclair at the California Club. The main course was squab stuffed with wild rice. Everyone was served an edible bird except Sinclair, whose plate held one of the battered iron pigeons from the skeet shoot. Under this curious entrée, in a plastic envelope, was Kyle's check returning Sinclair's lost eighty thousand.

It was all fun, but an uneasy kind of fun. Sinclair had not cared for it. He cashed the check next day. He never spoke to Kyle again.

With such diversions Kyle honed the merciless edge of his will. He had kept and was to keep his will bright and keen, just as he kept and was to keep his body firm and fit. Now once more he depended on his will to give him his way with the stockholders of the Land and Cattle Company; once more his will did not fail him, but this time he couldn't throw unbreakable targets at competing guns. This time he needed help.

He got it from Cliff.

2

The meeting was no friendly family gathering. It had never, perhaps, truly been that, even in Hub's time: there had always been too many temperaments to be dealt with, too many axes to be ground. Yet there had been a peaceful or at least a congenial feeling in the clustering of the people under the big trees, country people who lived much of their lives isolated from one another and were glad, no matter what their disagreements, to see each other again; there had been friendliness in the meetings, the touches of hands and the well-worn jokes which held up so staunchly in the crashing torrent of time.

Of personal appearance:

"Hey, Jess, sure don't seem like you're gittin' any thinner . . ."

"That's right. Arms gittin' weak, like."

"I know what you mean. Don't have strength left to push yourself away from the table ha ha."

Of community affairs:

"You valley folks still got that Paddy priest preachin' judgment and damnation to yer?"

"Honey, he goes on about hellfires till I feel my shoes scorchin' clean through the soles ha ha."

Of social issues:

"That boy from Tulare got the Weebe gal knocked up, you figure?"

"Can't say he has. But if he ain't, she's took to wearin' a money belt under her girdle ha ha."

Such dialogue still went the rounds; the change was in the people themselves. They still talked the same way, but they dressed differently, behaved differently than in the old days. They had been rich now for eleven years—even if not as rich as they felt they had a right to be—and in their march to affluence they had left innocence behind. The women, for instance, still did the family laundry, but now they did it by means of General Electric washers and gas dryers and had seamstresses in to do the mending; they no longer bought their clothes at Hyman's in Hollister or Baughman's in Altemira but at the City of Paris or H. Liebes or Nelli Gaffney in San Francisco and Irene or Adrian or I. Magnin in Los

Angeles, making week-long pilgramages twice a year or more to do so; they lived in bigger houses now, rambling edifices, often built on barren, windy hilltops, the better to expose their grandeur to passersby. Such structures were too splendid to be cleaned by family ministrations. Far better to have the hired help tidy them while the housewives sat in the parlor, a box of Warren Watkins' mixed bonbons or Lowney's peanut brittle handily within reach. They went to the movies often, particularly when a Janet Gaynor-Charles Farrell or a Jeanette MacDonald-Nelson Eddy picture was playing, and if there was no worthwhile movie on, or even if there was, they had their radios, one in every room, the favorite being the big Packard-Bells in the pale wood cabinets, some of which had home-recording devices built into them.

The men were easier with one another than the women. The men talked about the price of spring yearlings. They talked about the rainfall, comparing it to other years. They discussed such matters seriously, with judicious reserve, just as when, in the old days, the worth of beef on the hoof and the amount of water available for crops and orchards had been vital to them, before the black wealth Troy Kinsale had conjured out of the earth set them free from combat with the seasons and the market.

The men clumped at the north end of the lawn. Some sat in the canvas chairs Luanna had put there for them but others just hunkered down on their heels in the style prescribed by tradition for discussions around the edge of corrals, while the branding and dehorning were going on, or after it was finished, or at irrigating or picking times in the 'cots and pears, among the cool green tunnels formed by the trees. They would hunker that way even over in town, particularly near the door of the First National Bank of Altemira at Fifth and San Benito streets. You would not have thought to look at them in their well-washed jeans and Redman boots and tan or blue Windbreakers, the J. C. Penney caps pushed back on their heads, crouching along the wall of the old granite bank, that they were millionaires.

You would not have thought so now either, though one or two new details might have given you a clue. At this meeting, for the first time anybody could remember, professional moneymen were mingling with the cousins and the kissing cousins, the aunts and uncles and assorted other redneck legatees under the shadowy oaks, the locust trees and the big old elms and jacarandas. The relatives had brought CPA's and lawyers with them. The relatives wanted as good advice as Troy and Kyle could get, and were ready to pay whatever it cost. Lupe Stochillo of Danville and her husband, Reuben, had joined with Luanna and the Stoycoves from Yuba City to bring in a man from Price, Waterhouse who would instruct them in their rights, and Labro Kurland, who had bought the Fenton place and paid too much for it, sat on the porch playing gin with a jug-eared, dandified fellow, said to be a partner in a San Francisco law firm.

Seven chauffeur-driven vehicles were parked with the twenty-odd owner-driven ones in the driveway or along the road leading to the barns. Luanna had sent the drivers to eat in the kitchen. They had started a crap game there, much to the annoyance of the new serving staff (Luanna had got rid of the ones Mrs. Crocker had sent down; they had proved too independent for her taste).

Luanna told the serving staff to put up with the drivers.

There was even a reporter present. Paul Smith, editor of the *San Francisco Chronicle*, had got wind in The Pacific Union Club of the struggle looming in the Kinsale Land and Cattle Company. He had come down himself to cover the proceedings. Much public interest would focus on a management change in a small private land company whose members controlled, as an affiliate, a large public oil company.

At quarter to ten on the morning of the meeting, the downstairs manservant placed on the lawn the executive card table used as a lectern for the meetings. This servant was no longer called a butler. Luanna disliked the term because of the first butler, the one whom she had so often caught in the act of staring at her backside. The downstairs manservant knew what to do. He set out on the table a pitcher of spring water, a glass, a gavel and the Book of Minutes. At 10:04 State Assemblyman Polls, formerly sheriff of San Benito County and a shareholder for the past ten years in the L&CC, took his seat as chairman *pro tempore*. Doc, the regular chairman, had disqualified himself today because he wished to bring a motion before the meeting, and Millie, though she stood ready to read the minutes in her role as secretary, had refused to serve as *pro tempore* for the same reason.

Assemblyman Polls called the meeting to order. He requested Millie to read the minutes, which she did, after which, on the regular agenda, came the president's report.

3

The night before the meeting, Cliff had had a dream. He dreamed he was back in grammar school. He was walking along the board sidewalk of Kinsalem, the oil town his father had built in the dunes near Piru. He was on his way to school, struggling to make headway but making little, as so often happens in dreams. He knew he was late because he could hear the kids whooping it up. They were hanging from the bars of the jungle gym and sitting in the branches of the oak tree which sheltered the recess yard. Some had got up on the roof, as they did only when all hell was breaking loose, and they were chanting a song of insult and defiance which they all knew well:

> *Effeedeftee Mr. Rapper*
> *Lost the bell and broke the clapper*

Cliff moaned in sleep as the screech of the voices rang in his head, cruel as the whine of lunatic insects. He knew what was happening and soon, from the fence, he could see it—a sight that always angered him. The kids had stolen the bell. Every so often they did this, to torment F. D. Rapper, the sagging, raging, gentle man who taught the upper four of the eight grades which were housed in the two-room Kinsalem schoolhouse. Mr. Rapper could not see ten feet even with his glasses and these in his agitation he had left inside. He was slopping around the yard, yelling at the kids, threatening them with the rubber hose, stumbling in the dust in his old black shoes, with stuff falling out of his pockets, while there on a fence post, in plain sight, was the bell, where they had put it to taunt him. And now, in the dream, Cliff regained full use of his legs. He leaped lightly over the fence and got the bell, giving it to Mr. Rapper, who thanked him profusely. Mr. Rapper then began to ring the bell, and the kids, obedient to its authority, though they defied the man's, trooped into the schoolhouse. But the strange thing was that as Mr. Rapper stood there ringing the bell he stopped being Mr. Rapper and turned into Kyle.

It was an absolutely senseless dream. There could not have

been two people in the world more unlike than Mr. Rapper and Kyle.

About all he could remember about Mr. Rapper, other than the way the kids tormented him, was that he had loved birds. Sometimes he would give his classes a day off and take them up in the hills. He would ramble along the winding trails, incongruous in his baggy suit in the bright sunshine, but firmer in his speech, younger and more likable there than in the school. He had talked wonderfully about nature. When the other kids had run off, Cliff would be alone with Mr. Rapper and the knowledge and the goodness of the man would come through. Thanks to Mr. Rapper Cliff had kept his own bird list, carefully noting the names of all the birds he'd seen, their plumage, range and nesting habits. Before he was twelve years old he had ninety-six different entries in his notebook under the heading:

BIRDS I HAVE WATCHED

He still had the book, but he'd lost touch with the man who had inspired it. Mr. Rapper had been long gone from the Kinsalem school. Cliff sometimes wondered what had happened to him; it seemed too bad that the old geezer could not have known the influence he'd had on at least one boy's life, perhaps on many others. That must be the fate of teachers, not to know! To feel that what they did had been wasted. It was sad somehow, and Mr. Rapper, in spite of his clownishness, his bad temper, had been sad—vulnerable.

Was that the hookup with the dream? Cliff wondered. That Kyle also was vulnerable? That he was in worse trouble than he admitted? Perhaps that notion, like the dream itself, was preposterous—but perhaps not so preposterous.

Cliff had driven up to the homeranch in Kyle's Phantom, with Alma and the kids and the nurse in back, and Kyle, as he so often liked to be, at the wheel. Kyle had talked to him about the Land and Cattle Company, the harm that could come from a disagreement among the stockholders, and Cliff had realized that Kyle, without coming right out with it, had been bidding for his support at the meeting.

"Maybe we've expanded too fast. That's what some people are saying. I don't agree with them, of course. I'm responsible for the expansion and I'm proud of it. That's my sin in their eyes, of course. Just the same, to an outsider we present a bargain. The book value of our stock is way above market value."

"Do you think my dad wants to sell?"

"No," said Kyle without hesitation, "I don't. He and I haven't always agreed. We don't necessarily agree now, but we've always been able to work things out. Your dad has been . . . under pressure. That's what makes it hard to talk to him. He may feel that he's never had the credit that's been his due."

"Do you think he really feels that, or is someone else trying to make him feel it?" Cliff asked, somewhat surprisingly, and Kyle turned and gave him a quick, hard look, satisfied that his listener was not only keeping up but perhaps thinking ahead of him.

That night the entire family gathered at the ranch, and early in the evening Cliff went to his mother and asked her point-blank whether she had been caucusing to oust Kyle as president of the L&CC.

"Well if I am, dear," she'd said, with a sweetness she affected only when irritated, "I'm afraid it isn't any business of yours."

"It might be, Ma. It just might be everyone's business. Eveyone who has any stock, and I have some, you know."

Luanna turned on him then, anger standing hot in the reddish eyes above her slanty cheekbones.

"Do you for sure now? And who reminded you of that? I know who you've been talking to, Cliff Kinsale, and I've heard enough from that person, and more than enough. You can vote your shares any way you want; we can make do without any favors from you *or* from him."

Oh, if only now he could have gone to his father, if he could have talked to him simply and soberly, laying out the picture as Kyle had laid it out, but—no chance of that! Troy would stick with his wife even though, secretly, he might feel she was wrong. And as always, when he was troubled, Troy was unreachable. He had not come to the ceremonial pre-meeting supper but had gone up to the corral and cut himself out a horse. He had ridden into the hills, his meditation place. Luanna had made no objection. She had even packed him a sandwich to take on his ride, quite satisfied to have him out of the way where he couldn't be swayed by changes of strategy or distraction by last-minute bargaining.

Cliff had gone to Scott Stanfus. He had found him in one of the guesthouse suites, with files and ledgers stacked around him. A fruitwood fire burned in the grate and on the mantel, unopened, stood a bottle of the family bourbon which by custom was supplied to every room in lieu of a carafe of water. Scott would have the KinOil files and records—not the Land and Cattle Company's. Millie would have those. And Millie's and Doc's positions in the coming power struggle had not been defined, though the assumption was that they would stand with Troy.

Scott had been dictating to a secretary; he broke off and sent the secretary away. He poured Cliff a knock of the bourbon. Scott had always felt friendly toward this young man with the easy ways, the broad shoulders—the country boy, the bird watcher, the writer and debater at Princeton, where he had made such odd friends.

"What's on your mind, my friend?"

Cliff, tasting his drink, made a face not related to the whiskey, which was the best, as always. He said, "I don't like the look of things," and Scott said at once, "Neither does anyone else."

"Except my mother," Cliff said frankly. "She's been waiting for this chance. She's been planning for it a long time and she's coming in with the heavy artillery now, wouldn't you say?"

"I would indeed."

Scott studied Cliff. He peered from the thickets of tufty eyebrows, grayer now than they had been but still the best feature of his pale, narrow face. He thought: Does this young fellow know he has the swing vote in his pocket? And if he does, is there any chance he'll vote against his parents?

How Cliff would vote, or how anyone would vote, for that matter, Scott was not ready to predict, but aside from that he knew a good deal about Clifford de Baca Kinsale—enough so that his knowledge would have startled the younger man had it ever been revealed.

Scott had arrived at this information without making the least effort to collect it. The data had sifted down to him in the routine turnover of office activity. Kyle ran his business that way. He kept few secrets from his treasurer. When he took a trip or paid a debt or bought something, the company paid for it. If the outlay was personal he would in due course have Rose Brady write a check, reimbursing the KinOil contingency account, but meanwhile a memo would have passed across the desk of Scott Stanfus and Scott would keep a record of it. He would also note in his excellent memory, if nowhere else, the circumstances of each outlay as they came to light.

Scott Stanfus was a methodical man; it was a principle of his to keep himself informed. He knew of the family disagreement about Cliff's choice of a college and about Kyle's interview with Dede Atlass. He knew about the gift of the Bugatti and the expenses attending the upkeep of that car. He knew about Cliff's weekends to attend debutante parties in New York and Philadelphia and about the disastrous football weekend when the Old Guard had made fools of themselves. He knew about Cliff's interest in debating and in writing for the *Princetonian*. (Scott had even had Cliff's articles photocopied so that Kyle could show them to friends.) It had been Scott who attended to the paper work setting up Cliff's pipeline job and the job for Hersh.

". . . this fellow they're putting up as a new member of the board. Do you know anything about him?"

"The prime facts, yes. If you're interested . . ."

"I am."

"All right." Scott shuffled papers on his tabletop, then pulled one off a spindle. "Here we are. Ready? . . . 'Constable, Harker E., Senior Partner, Constable, Cole and Bragg, 287 Bush Street, San Francisco. Stanford, 1908; Harvard Law, 1911; Psi Upsilon, Phi Beta Kappa, Bohemian Club, Pacific Union Club; Racquet and Tennis Club, New York; Board of Regents, University of California; Trustee, San Francisco Opera. Also director of eleven corporations, including Pacific Gas and Electric, Weyerhaeuser, Utah Construction, Firestone Tire and Rubber, Southern Pacific Railroad and Security-First National.' Not bad for an individual still under fifty-five."

"Great, I'd say. But how is he at running oil companies?"

"Might know more than you think about that. His firm had some of them as clients. Union and Richfield, to name two."

"I should think that would ding him."

"Not at all. His proponents are making it sound like an asset. Look—Stanfus pulled a scratch sheet toward him, started to jot down names—"here's how it stacks up . . ." He held the paper as he wrote so that Cliff could see it.

"Remember, the board, not the stockholders, elects the company officers. If the stockholders' committee, or the dissidents—whatever you want to call them—if they elect Constable then you have a nine- instead of an eight-man board and the decisions will belong to those who put him in.

Thurmond and myself and Shannon will be looking for new jobs. Your father will be president instead of Kyle. It will be a whole new ball game," said Scott Stanfus, smoothing down his aggressive eyebrows with the tips of his thin fingers. "You'll have to make up your mind which side you're on."

Cliff nodded. The slant of his jaw and the lines around his eyes caused him to lose the farm-boy, Huck Finn look, usually so beguiling. He seemed formidable all of a sudden— older than his years.

"That's what I aim to do."

Kyle rosé from his seat in the front row of the group on the spring lawn, in the morning shade of the trees—sixty or seventy people, all told. It was by far the biggest Land and Cattle company meeting ever assembled at the homeranch, due in part to tribal increase but mostly to the outside moneymen who had been assigned a few proxies, just enough to make them eligible to attend, the accountants and the lawyers, the oil production analysts and the estate bailiffs and the rest, seated with the country members.

Kyle smiled at them all.

"I should like to extend a special welcome to the guests we have with us today," he said in his deep, quiet voice. "It's nice to find that our family doings here have become of interest to so many new friends."

He allowed no trace of sarcasm in his tone, but as he paused, repeating the flashing, craggy smile, tilting back the high-crowned Triple-X Stetson just a trifle on his handsome head, a titter went around the gathering. That was Kyle for you! Oh, he was a cool one, easy and nice, as if he were talking to a trustee meeting of the San Benito Saddle Horse Association instead of a crew of angry cousins and their paid hatchet men, out for his blood.

Troy, in the chair next to the one Kyle had vacated when he rose, turned sideways so Luanna wouldn't see him grin. She was right, of course—so justified in many of her contentions, but at the same time Troy wished the issues didn't have to be settled this way. What was there about his family that made it conduct its wars in public? Suddenly he could see in his mind's eye Hub standing where Kyle was now. He remembered how he'd kicked that clod of dirt loose and shredded it up in his fingers, how he'd bullied and cajoled the bunch of them to vote against the oil, which now they wanted more of, an endless spate of it, and the money it brought in.

Hub, gone now twelve years, tough and mean as ever, no
doubt, in that earth that he had put to such good use while he
lived. Well, rest in peace, you mean old bugger, he thought,
and a shaft of regret went through him for the old days when
everything had seemed so much simpler: Hub with his peg leg
up on a stool, talking about the cattle drives . . . Hub riding
herd on all of them.

He glanced sideways at his wife where she sat ramrod stiff,
chunked back as if bolted to the seat of her wicker chair, her
eyes smoldering about the slant of her high cheekbones. This
could be her day.

Kyle put out his hand. He rested it for a moment against
the tree next to him.

"We've had a good year," he said gently, "an excellent
year, really, in the Kinsale Land and Cattle Company. This
year, for instance, we sold the first crop of the two hundred
acres we laid out in walnuts in nineteen and thirty-four, a year
I'll always remember, but not for walnuts. I had the great
fortune to be married in that year . . . Sweetheart, would
you stand up?"

And Alma, in her gleaming dark beauty, with a rebosa
around her shoulders and a high comb, like a Spanish
woman's, in her hair, stood up obediently. She raised her
clasped hands above her head, then spread her arms wide, as
if in a gesture of affection for all. She sat down to a
good-natured spatter of applause, as much of it from the
opposition side as from those backing the administration.

There had been no formal separation of the adversary
groups in the seating.

"For the benefit of our visitors some other introductions
may be in order. My brother, Troy, vice president of the L
and CC. His lovely wife, Luanna . . . Dr. and Mrs. Braden
. . . all principal stockholders in our company. Just so that
you all get the cast of characters right, particularly the
gentlemen of the press. I understand we have one here
today . . . a brilliant person indeed."

And having had each of the family members mentioned rise
for a bow, Kyle pointed to Paul Smith of the *Chronicle*
standing at the back of the gathering.

Everyone craned around to look at him, then settled in
their seats as if at a show.

Kyle cared nothing about Smith. He had pointed him out
just to make his listeners react. He knew that as soon as a
speaker has an audience respond to some command or sugges-

tion he has established a hold over them. He wanted no doubt about his control—he would need all he could get.

He took out a paper Stanfus had had typed for him. Yes, indeed. A good year . . .

Kyle read off the figures. No less than four thousand and some-odd hundred hefty yearlings sold, averaging better than a hundred and ten pounds apiece, at fourteen cents a pound on the hoof. A new well dug to serve recent vineyard plantings, enough acreage in grapes now so that the company could vote on the construction of a winery in the near future. Tonnage of apricots up, too . . . purchase of fertilizer, down . . . new equipment added: a rotobailer . . . a D5 tractor . . .

So much for the ranch. ". . . and for the operation of our affiliate, the KinOil Corporation," Kyle wound up, as if these last items were of the least concern to anyone present, above all himself, "profits of twenty-six million five hundred and thirty-four thousand dollars on gross income of one hundred eighty million three hundred sixty thousand. This represents a dividend of three dollars and ninety cents a share, up seventy cents from the last quarter and a dollar over last year. Thank you all very much."

And with this Assemblyman Polls tapped his gavel.

"The president will take questions."

Assemblyman Polls's career had come on fast since the death of Hub Kinsale and the friendly cooperation with the Kinsale family of Polls (then sheriff of San Benito County) in the unfortunate circumstances surrounding that event.

A man does not rise without effort from a cop's tin star in a remote California county seat to a place in the state's legislative body. Most California legislators are lawyers in private life or if not lawyers then the proprietors of businesses or services which enable them to afford six months a year in Sacramento on the kind of emolument paid by the state; few if any of them welcome the addition to their ranks of a person without wealth, a law degree or even—as in Poll's case—a college degree. Polls had made it though, and if there had been times during his progress to his present position when he had required some help (and there had been such times), he had known where to look for what he needed. He had looked to Kyle, and Kyle had not failed him.

One might have assumed that Assemblyman Polls would have been ready to return tit for tat. The assumption would have been correct. True, a switch in corporate power or in family influence (the same thing, really) might take place today, in which situation Poll's support of Kyle would not be in the assemblyman's best interest. But Polls had faith in Kyle; he did not believe that any such change was coming. As *pro tem* today he did not have great power, but such as he had he used in Kyle's behalf. When the Price, Waterhouse man, voting a proxy of Luanna's, stood up at the same instant as Judge Blaine Gather of Watsonville, a member of the Old Guard, Polls recognized Judge Gather and the Price, Waterhouse man had to sit down.

Judge Gather was a well-known local character, a justice of the peace merciless to traffic violators in his pleasant coastal city but in private life a famous jokester and an ad-lib speaker, much in demand as a toastmaster at weddings and a eulogist at funerals. He was a huge man with an immense torso propped up on little stumpy legs. He needed no collar or tie and never wore either; his dewlap covered the lack of them. He launched into one of his character bits.

"Mr. President, did I hear yew say the company bought a rotobailer?"

"Why, yes, Blaine," said Kyle, rising. "Does that bother you for some reason?"

The audience stirred with delight. Many of them had heard old Blaine do his redneck piece before.

Said someone: "Them rotos never did work, did they?"

Gather's bull voice narrowed to a rustic squeak.

"By God, now. I know all about them contraptions. Bought one myself with soap coupons. Why, did you know that rock scratcher ties the bales with *string?* Wham a hay hook into 'em and they spread out like birdseed. Mout as well try to stack goldfish as make a pile outa them Tootsie Rolls. I'm sure sorry to hear us got stuck with one of them gopher grinders. Ain't there no chance we could swap it for something we could *use?*"

And when Kyle, still playing straight man, said politely, "I don't know, Blaine. Do you have anything to suggest?" Gather replied in his normal foggy tones: "Trade it fer a keg of rifle whiskey an' let's give a hoedown."

Laughter.

A new city man was up now, with others of the same kind. Luanna, leaning forward, yelled into Troy's ear: "Can't you do something about this?"

"Point of order!"

Those on their feet gesticulated angrily, seeking recognition. The shareholders were evenly divided: those backing the administration amused, and showing it; those in opposition impatient and irritated.

"Mr. Chairman . . ."

"The Chair recognizes Dr. Braden."

"Thank you. I move that we proceed with the business of this meeting. Those interested in comedy can get it on the radio."

"Hear, hear . . ."

Voice: "Amos and Andy go on at ten o'clock, and they ain't stockholders."

Second voice: "If they was, they would be screwed . . ."

Laughter.

Polls's gavel whacked the top of the card table, producing a dim clatter rather than a booming sound, but eventually calming down the ruckus.

"The meeting will come to order. The Chair recognizes . . ."

Polls pointed at the stranger who had first risen. "Kindly state your name."

"Julian T. Rich, Mr. Chairman. Price, Waterhouse and Company."

Polls paused while Scott Stanfus, at a separate table, checked the Register of Shareholders for Mr. Rich's eligibility. He nodded to Polls—okay. Rich was voting the proxies for five shares of Luanna's stock.

"I should like to ask Mr. Kyle why we are supplied with circumstantial detail about ranching operations but deprived of information about KinOil, the true focus of interest here. Is this some kind of cover-up?"

"That makes two questions. I'll answer the second one first. It is not a cover-up. As to the first, KinOil may be the focus of your interest, Mr. Rich, but not that of all present. This is the annual meeting of a land and cattle company which has an oil company as an affiliate, not the other way around."

"Nevertheless, sir, the shareholders present at this meeting represent control of KinOil. They are entitled to know why, with a gross of almost two hundred million, KinOil returned a net on capital investment conspicuously lower than that of most oil companies."

"A breakdown of the entire KinOil operation will be supplied to shareholders in the company's annual report at year's end."

"The shareholders have waited patiently each year for that

report, Mr. President, and the equation is always much the
same. An inappropriate amount of earnings is plowed back
each year into acquisitions and expansion."

"Inappropriate in whose opinion, Mr. Rich? Yours or
Price, Waterhouse's?

"KinOil is a growing company and its proper growth, I
would say, should be of as much concern to the shareholders
as the amount of money paid out in dividends."

"Many of them do not seem to think so."

"We will take that into account, sir."

Kyle glanced at Polls, who brought his gavel down.

"The Chair," said Polls, "moves to limit each questioner's
time to two minutes."

"Seconded," said a strong voice from the rear.

The speaker was Cliff.

"Motion passed."

The limitation seemed structured to ease pressures, but
instead it increased them: people crowded to speak, afraid
now that they would be shut off before they'd had their say.

"Mr. President, may we discuss salaries? I have some
figures here on the salaries of chief executives of very large oil
companies: Dr. Deterding of Royal Dutch Shell, a salary in
the three-hundred-thousand-dollar range; Mr. Teagle of Standard, a salary in the two-hundred-thousand-dollar range.
How do you reconcile your own salary as against the lower
salaries paid to executives of companies with many times the
capitalization of KinOil?"

Cliff could not hear Kyle's answer, which was half drowned
by a question from Millie Braden—Millie, of all people!—
asking her brother whether it was true that he spent a quarter
of a million a year on his racing stable! Did she think the
money for the horses was subtracted from what Kyle chipped
in for the slanty-headed sick in Dead Eagle Valley? And Doc,
Doc to whom Kyle had shown nothing but generosity, ever,
sitting with his small gray head bowed, and never a word out
of him!

The questions came from all directions now, the cousins
joining their paid surrogates in getting their licks. The new
contract for oil shipments to Japan, would the government
allow that? The loan to Turkey: had the interest been met?
Why was KinOil borrowing from banks to finance its own
operations when, so recently, it had loaned a huge sum to a
foreign nation, possibly a bankrupt one? Was the Libyan

concession any good? Was it true that Kyle's beach house had cost three hundred thousand? Was KinOil losing money in Mexico? How much had Kyle lost on the Santa Anita Handicap? Why was KinOil buying Greek tankers when American shipyard builders were out of work?

Some of the stupider questions were booed, some ignored, a few withdrawn. Kyle dealt with each on its merits, passing along to Troy or Stanfus those on which he did not have the figures or the technical data. His voice never changed; his manner stayed conciliatory, patient, slightly—ever so slightly —disdainful. Sometimes his hand went out to the big tree beside him, the tree that had shaded the meetings of this company since early in the century—a good strong tree, it would shade many more. Now and then he broke a piece of bark off it, stroking or shredding the bark in his fingers as he answered his accusers—for what else were they? Cliff's anger rose; he even grew angry with Kyle, this man he admired so much. Why didn't he let the idiots have it, tell them what he'd really done for the company, the miracle he'd brought about, taking it from a one-well wildcatter to top status as the biggest, best-organized independent in the state—almost, almost a major!

"Tell them, tell them, Unc," he muttered under his breath. "Give it to the sons of bitches; *tell them!*"

But even as he formulated this wish he knew why Kyle wasn't telling them. He'd done it too often. This scene today, however wrong the thrust of it, however stupid in its pettiness and gadfly annoyance, had been enacted on a lesser scale so many times, almost at every meeting, if you could remember: the same vexations, the same demands over and over—less money plowed back, less expansion, more loot and more and more, so that the hayseed grandees from the backcountry and the little highway gas-and-hamburger towns could buy more of the good life . . .

There'd had to be a day of accounting and this was it.

Cliff saw his mother getting up again.

"I move that the question period be terminated and the meeting opened for a nomination to the board of directors."

"Those in favor of Mrs. Kinsale's first motion? Show of hands will do it. . . . Question period has been terminated. Those in favor of a nomination at this time?" The gavel tapped again. "The meeting is now open for a nomination to the board."

Troy rose.

"I nominate Mr. Harker E. Constable of San Francisco for membership to the board of directors of the Kinsale Land and Cattle Company."

4

Troy, having spoken his piece, sat down. He clasped his strong, square hands in his lap. Then he unclasped them and knocked the fist of one with short, surreptitious punches into the palm of the other. Then he clasped them again. He waited as a man might wait outside a mine where a disaster has taken place and where, to free those trapped down below, rescuers have decided to set off a blast of dynamite. And yet it was not someone else, some other people, but he, he himself who was trapped.

Cliff got up. He stood waiting for recognition, planted like a rock in front of his skimpy funeral-parlor chair while Constable held forth.

Someone, no doubt put up to it in advance, had asked the lawyer to state his qualifications for the board seat and what he proposed to do if he were elected, and he ripped off an unctuous and lawyerly, slick and self-serving speech of admiration for the company, gratefulness for the blah and the blah—the need for reasonable limits to expansion plus the timely and suitable distribution of the blah and the blah-blah. If you did not vote for him for the shape of his Episcopal ears or the set of his striped Racquet Club foulard, Cliff thought, you would surely be supposed to for the way he pronounced certain words, like "schedule" and "anticipation," or the flections of a voice schooled for equal effectiveness in the corridors of power or at cocktail parties where the sandwiches are passed around by lackeys in knee breeches, as in the days of the railroad builders.

Constable sat down with loud appreciation from his backers, and Polls laid the meeting open for discussion; he nodded at Cliff, who thereupon walked down front, his shoulders somewhat slouched—he had never got over some shyness at speaking in public, in spite of his experience as a debater—and the sun bright on his thick red hair. He was careful not to look either at his father or Kyle; he could pretty well tell what they'd be thinking. More than the support or disapproval of the male family members he felt his mother's eyes on him, anger baffled and hot in them. Well, too bad about her . . .

"I guess I'm about the youngest person here. . . . I apologize for butting in and all that, but I want to say I think we're pretty lucky people, we have an oil company to wrangle over. That's fairly unusual, isn't it?"

Laughter, a little clapping. A man's voice: "So far you're right, kid. Now sit down."

Cliff turned in the direction of the voice.

"I will, sir. But may I have my two minutes? Thank you. I guess we're all stockholders here; two minutes isn't much, even at my age. Well, the company—about that I'd like to propose a vote of thanks to my father for drilling the first well and to my uncle for taking it from there. . . . A vote that we can all—"

Polls's gavel tapped, cutting him down in mid-sentence.

"I have heard a note of thanks proposed for Mr. Troy and Mr. Kyle Kinsale. Does anyone wish to second?"

"Hear" . . . "Aye." . . . "Yes, yes," cried several voices, and the gavel came down again.

"Those in favor will please rise," said Polls, and the entire assemblage—some albeit with reluctance—got up.

"Thank you, ladies and gentlemen," said Polls, his expression blank but his coal-bottomed eyes gleaming.

Kyle and Troy were smiling, bowing their thanks. Cliff blinked, pleased but also somewhat startled by the standing ovation, as it seemed, which he had set up. His mother cut in: "Mr. Chairman, the meeting was opened for discussion of the election of a new board member. May we stick to the agenda?" and Cliff said, "Yes, Mother, I intend to. I oppose the election of a new member to the board. Particularly I oppose the election of Mr. Constable to the board. May I give my reasons? All right, I'm not casting aspersion on the character of Mr. Constable. I'm sure he's a distinguished and honorable man and his experience as a lawyer for some big oil companies is very wonderful, but I'd say it was more valuable to him than to us. It's flattering, really, to have a person as well qualified as Mr. Constable even to consider sitting on the board of a small outfit like ours and I'm sure he would not subordinate KinOil's interests to Richfield's—I believe the Richfield corporation is one of his firm's clients. Or Union, and I have great respect for the Union Oil Company, it's one of the best. I'm sure no conflict of interest would ever be allowed to come up, and I say this without the slightest sarcasm. Possibly Mr. Constable would drop Richfield or Union or whatever as clients if he came on our board or maybe he'd resign from his law firm. Or both. He'd do something honorable and right, I'd bet on it. But I just can't help wondering whether, to a man who has the major-company approach, as it were, I wonder whether such a man might not truly and honorably feel that the happiest home for a nice little company like ours might not be in the back yard of one major or the hip pocket of another, provided those majors were in the mood to make an acquisition.

"Now I can't say of my own knowledge that we know of any company which is just now in that mood. I'm new to all this. I've been down working on the pipeline and I've got the blisters to prove it. [Laughter.] But I've heard that statement made by my father; I've heard my uncle say it—'coyotes around a sheep pen' was how he put it, and he ought to know: he's pretty good at making acquisitions himself. We have a lot of things a major wants. We have some of the best oil reserves in California, and I hope we always keep them that way [Clapping, silenced by the speaker.]; we have service stations where we don't have to give away dishes or radios or fireworks to bring in customers [Laughter and clapping.]; so above all we don't want to let a family squabble among some of the people I love best in the world get away from us to the point where the public can step in, because then anything can happen. We have control only as long as we stick together, and not a minute longer. [Clapping and prolonged applause.] And now, sir"—and here he turned in the direction of his original heckler—"now I'll sit down, as you advised me to do in the first place. Probably I should have taken that advice, but anyway—thank you for listening. Thank you all very much."

Clapping, catcalls, boos and more clapping.

Luanna was up, ready to repeat her motion for a vote on Constable. Polls's gavel cut her off at the knees.

"My watch says five minutes to noon and seems like I smell spareribs barbecuing. The meeting stands adjourned for lunch."

Polls's gavel might have done as much to save KinOil for the Kinsales as Cliff's speech, or even more: the Troy Kinsales discussed this point later. Luanna was disgusted with Polls.

"Kyle had him bought and paid for. I should never have let him sit as *pro tem*—never!"

Troy might have reminded her that she'd had nothing to do with the selection. He chose not to, perhaps wisely.

"Cliff did it to you, Mother, not the sheriff—pardon me, assemblyman. Doggone youngster has a golden tongue in his head. How about that piece, about the coyotes sniffing around? That really got to them. It surely did."

"That was Kyle's quote. Cliff even said it was Kyle's, don't you remember?"

"Cliff *said* it though, not Kyle."

Luanna turned away, pride in her son and bitterness at her defeat contending at her heart.

"He could be just too smart for his own good."

Many shared her opinion. Many, around the tables, leaning on their elbows in the family style (the redwood benches had no backs), felt he'd been uppity and brash and said so—his character proved the folly of sending children east to those fancy colleges; he would never have picked up that kind of truck at Berkeley or Stanford, not in a coon's age. But there were a number of cousins, including some of adversary persuasion, who came around to him quietly and shook his hand.

"You made a good talk, son."

The spareribs had helped as much as anything. With them (after Archbishop Xavier Daniel McCaffery had said grace, the archdiocese having become a substantive stockholder in the L&CC, due to stock donations by the faithful through the years) came pepper steaks, prairie oysters, candied sweet potatoes, venison chops, roast quail, julienne beet salad, red beans baked in whiskey and molasses, and apple pie with homemade ice cream—a traditional feast, particularly tasty when preceded and in many instances also washed down with the good brown Kinsale grog. As the meal was ending, Kyle and Troy were seen talking alone at the bottom of the lawn; after a while Kyle beckoned Stanfus over, and Doc Braden, though apparently not invited, joined the group. Assemblyman Polls stayed away. He saw what was going on and if it was what he thought it might be he was not about to stick his legislative nose into it. Instead he had a second helping of everything, letting the lunch break run some forty minutes overtime.

It had been a trying morning.

When Polls reconvened the meeting, Troy asked to present a report. He stated that he had just met with his brother and that they were working on a compromise aimed to satisfy the stockholders who wanted dividends increased.

"How do we know we ain't going to git the runaround all over again?"

Troy turned politely to the interrupter.

"Because you stockholders will be running the show now, Zeke."

"I'll believe that when I see it."

"I think you'll believe it when you hear my next announcement. There will be some changes in the structure of our petroleum interests. Mr. Kyle Kinsale will resign as president of the KinOil Corporation. He will assume the title Vice President, Refining and Marketing. My title will be Vice President, Production. Disbursements for both branches, from the company's revolving funds, will be made by an executive committee elected by the stockholders. Does that sound like a runaround?"

A motion to table the election of a new member to the L&CC board was proposed and passed, albeit by a narrow margin, and the meeting was adjourned.

Cliff went back to the pipeline. He was becoming a better welder day by day and felt proud of what he could do, but the work was not much fun anymore without Hersh there to argue with and get mad at. The weather was hot and the dry Santa Ana winds made skins rough and tempers brittle. The sun rose earlier every day and hung in the sky longer every evening; it pounded down on the darkly stretching pipeline with fierce yellow hammers, heating it up so that if you touched it with your bare skin after 9 A.M. it took your hide off.

The line had now inched down from the foothills with their greenery, their random springs and cool little veils of moisture; it had pushed out onto the dry rangeland near the sea. Clumps of sage and greasewood clung to the draws; everything else was grass, an ocean of pale-tan grass, such as the

De Bacas and the other Spaniards must have found when they tramped wearily north along this coast, treading out the track which they named, in their grandiose, preposterous style, *El Camino Real,* The King's Highway. It was all valuable land, fenced and cross-fenced; the company had needed a complicated easement in order to cross it legally. There were rules to be observed: gates and fence gaps to be closed, cattle to be protected, roads and firebreaks to be restored, if damaged, to their original condition.

The lessor of the easement was the Kinsale Land and Cattle Company. The lessee was its affiliate, KinOil, a California corporation.

CHAPTER FIFTEEN

Starring Ilona Cape . . .

1

The gloom of the stage pressed down upon the small lighted space where the people were jammed together. On them it forced the weight of its vast brown shadows, sharpening the lights into a feverish core, as hot and incandescent as the eye of a Fourth of July sparkler.

The shadows were piled all around. They towered into the ceiling, slouching on the catwalks there. They lapped out to the sides, obscuring pieces of forgotten scenery, scrims, goboes, various types of lights on stands, and machines, not now employed, for making mist, rain, wind and snow.

The air smelled dry and musty.

Only in the set itself, the lighted pinpoint, was there any action. Here life went on, it is true; it went on feverishly but at a queer, arrested pace, as if the participants were struggling against the effects of a gas.

"Would you try it once more, dear?" said a man's voice, and Ilona Cape's voice—that wonderful voice which you would have recognized anywhere but which, hearing it now, you realized belonged only here, in a tiny place on which lights were trained, among the piled brown shadows—said, "Of course, Sam. But from the top, Sam? Do you mean from the top?" and the man's voice said, "Yes, if you don't mind, dear. From the top, dear," and Ilona Cape turned and walked carefully back to some chalk marks on the floor.

Standing in the marks, but with her back to the man called Sam, she beckoned to someone outside the furnace eye of the lights and at once a young man wearing a baseball cap and an open sport shirt appeared beside her, handing her a script, which he held open for her.

"My glasses, for Christ sake," she said.

The young man handed her a pair of glasses and Miss Cape put them on. She looked intensely at the script. She studied it, holding it close to her eyes, for perhaps thirty seconds. Then she handed it back. She took off the glasses and gave them to the young man, who walked rapidly away. Ilona Cape turned around. She looked down at the chalk marks and put her feet squarely into them. She arranged herself inwardly, into her role, holding her spine, her legs and her shoulders differently, making her eyes, her mouth and her mind alien, altering them so that they became someone else's, those of the character in the script.

She looked dutifully in the direction of the man named Sam and nodded.

"Jimmy?" said Sam.

"Ready," said another voice.

"Roll 'em," said a third voice, and the big Mitchell camera, in its blimp of asbestos padding, began to whir softly.

The company was in its fifth day of shooting United Artists' film D612, *Low Man Out*, a Walter Wanger production, directed by Sam Wood, starring Ilona Cape, George Brent, costarring Oscar Homolka, with Una Merkel, Walter Brennan and Ben Edwards, and introducing Carrie Drew as Zan.

Before commencement of photography the company had rehearsed for a time with another director—a procedure far from unusual. Although he had not attended the rehearsals, there had also been another cameraman, one of less repute than James Wong Howe, the Young Chinese ASC man now in charge.

Surely these replacements would be good for the picture. Everyone was convinced of that. The results would prove themselves as time went on. For the present, however—except for the presence of the new director and cameraman themselves—the only alteration was the placement of a new canvas chair in the area behind the camera reserved for members of the cast whose names had been in on that day's call sheet and for such executives as might drop in.

The chair had "Mr. Kinsale" stenciled on it. And in this chair, from 9 A.M. to 6 P.M. daily, except for meal breaks, sat Cliff Kinsale.

He had been coming to the set now for a week and he had enjoyed every minute of his visits except for the first day, when he had come uninvited. There had been no special chair for him that day. He had crept in, trying not to trip over the wires and cables which littered the floor; then after edging around, this way and that, he had found an inconspicuous place to stand, where he could see what was going on. He had spoken to no one except the guard at the door of the sound stage, who had let him in, but in spite of his efforts to be unnoticed, he had created a disturbance.

Ilona Cape had broken off the scene.

"This is supposed to be a closed set," she had said with emphasis.

"It *is* closed, dear," said the director, the poor fellow who was later replaced.

"I think not, darling," said Ilona Cape, "or, if it is, then who is that person over there? I can't go on until he leaves."

She pointed dramatically at Cliff in his corner. Then she retired to her trailer, placed on the sound stage to serve her as a temporary dressing room, and lay down.

An assistant director approached Cliff. They exchanged a few words, after which the assistant knocked deferentially on the trailer door.

"We're ready, Miss Cape."

"Did you throw that person off?"

"No, ma'am. He has a pass from Mr. Goldwyn's office."

"Mr. Goldwyn can't pass fuckers onto my set."

"I guess this one doesn't know that."

"Then I'll tell him."

Ilona Cape left her trailer. She crossed to where Cliff was standing, large and uneasy, still half sheltered behind a scrim.

"I hear you have a pass from Mr. Goldwyn. May I see it? Thank you!" She took the small slip of paper from him, tearing it into pieces which she dropped onto the floor. She then looked at him for the first time.

"Oh, it's you," she said. "Why didn't you send in your name, you fool?" . . . *You'll have to leave at once, this instant,"* she said, raising her voice so it could be heard clearly by all present. *"This set is closed to visitors. . . .* Go to my dressing room, ground floor on the left, in the New Building. We'll be breaking for lunch soon. You can wait there."

With a movement of inexpressible scorn she turned her back on him and walked away.

The dressing room billowed with light. It contained white walls, a white desk and a large amount of white furniture, all overstuffed and billowing, as if aerated for flotation in case of an accident at sea. On one wall was a life-sized nude portrait of Miss Cape, hauntingly beautiful except that an arctic horizon extended from the ventral cavity into the genitals where a dogsled was breaking through the ice. The picture was painted on the plaster of the wall, a signed original by Salvador Dali.

A stout, elderly woman typist worked in a corner, an electric fan whipping back and forth beside her; the draft thus created lifted one of her papers and dumped it at Cliff's feet.

ILONA CAPE'S NATIONAL ANIMAL FAN CLUB

Dear Epiphermia Snipe and all Grafton, Iowa, members:

How darling of you all to name your nanny goat after me! But what do you mean she has trouble eating? Has she indigestion? Possibly she should see a veterinary, but first you might try giving her a little warm molasses followed by . . .

Lunch was carried over from the commissary on two trays, Miss Cape undertipping the Filipino steward who brought it. She took off her shoes and opened a bottle of white wine.

"Your uncle's horse was second in that race, wasn't he? All I know is I lost twenty dollars, but— Don't laugh! You should have come to see me right away. I almost forgot about you. This place is a madhouse; that's why I closed the set. I never close a set, not even for rehearsal. We're in a public business, aren't we? I closed this set because I detest the picture. It will be bad enough without letting people see it while it's being made. When I signed on for it I thought Mr. Goldwyn would produce it, the old devil. He talked me into it, then he lost faith in it and . . . Walter Wanger! Can you imagine? He went to Dartmouth, darling. He brings me copies of *The Virginia Quarterly!*"

She pantomimed with puckish artistry a man who might have gone to Dartmouth, who would read and give away *The Virginia Quarterly*.

"Too bad," Cliff said.

Stuffing himself with endive salad, vichyssoise, pressed duck, he wondered what college a producer should have attended, what magazines he should be reading to produce *Low Man Out* with Ilona Cape and George Brent.

"Mr. Goldwyn would have got me someone bloody decent. Edmund Goulding—he's so wonderful with women. Or Sam Wood. At the *very least* Sam Wood. Sam is a mechanic, but he's nice. I would have accepted him. Also I asked, I begged for another cameraman, not this lout we have. A Greek, for God's sake. I saw his last picture, the one with Norma Shearer. She was the only individual he bothered to light. She looked as if she were working with an all-Negro cast."

"What cameraman would you like?"

"Lucien Ballard. He's number one, definitely—for me, for my kind of face. Does that sound dreadful? At my age, the best is none too good."

Cliff had not thought of an actress as someone with technical problems or stress relationships such as might occur in the oil business. He had not been to many movies, but when he did go, when the giant faces of beautiful women, magnified to thirty times life size, filled the screen—when they wept or whispered or made love—it had always seemed to him that all this happened naturally, that little planning had been necessary to bring it all about. It was only a very slight disillusionment, however, to discover that he had been wrong, naïve. The movie business was a business after all, like any other. That was easy to understand. Movies created a make-believe life but were not, in themselves, make-believe. The women of course were real enough. And yet . . . and yet this woman, now, with her golden skin and her strong, poised back, with her great violet eyes enlarged by makeup until they could smash you to bits, confuse you completely with their flicking, secret knowledge of you and your base intentions— who could imagine that a woman like this would be wrought up about trivialities: directors, cameramen . . . or who was standing in the shadows on a sound stage?

She wasn't English either. That came out during lunch. She'd grown up in South Africa . . . "on the veldt." Then why English? A publicity story, never contradicted.

But—the veldt!

"Oh, don't doubt it," she'd said, reading his thoughts. "I'm a bush woman. I can drive six horses at a gallop, hitched to a spring wagon. There's a scene similar to that in this picture and I won't let them double me. You'll see!"

She stuck out her long, snaky tongue, licked the corner of a napkin with it to remove a spot of French dressing which had fallen on her costume.

Hmmm. A woman from the veldt then, if you were to believe it—not married at the moment (Cliff had checked that earlier); a timid gambler, a meager tipper (Cliff stuck a few extra dollars on the lunch tray, for the nice little steward), but a woman in command of her own life and many contiguous lives.

She was quite nice to a girl who brought in some costume sketches during lunch.

"Wonderful. Are the designs yours, your own?"

"Oh, yes. Do you really think they have the right mood, the twenties?"

"Perfect. You must get credit on the screen."

The girl seemed shaken.

"Oh, I'm afraid not. Only Miss Head gets credit in our department."

"I shall speak to Miss Head. Your name will be on the screen. I make you that promise."

She smiled, and the girl went out with the sketches clutched to her breast and her head in the clouds.

"Make a note," said Miss Cape to the stout secretary, who had continued her typing throughout lunch, and the secretary, without looking up, said, "I already have."

Dessert and coffee came in, also a large, youngish man with a big briefcase and a very gentle, confidential manner. He held papers for Miss Cape, his client, to look at, holding them and the pen for her to sign with, almost fondling these objects with his broad, sunburned fingers as he hunkered on the floor beside her chair. He was a business manager and the papers had to do with a boat Miss Cape was buying.

"But why shouldn't it be registered in my name, Jackson? I don't understand," she said.

"It's a new rule they have."

"What new rule?"

"Federal law. No alien can own a boat of more than a limited waterline, overall. Just a formality—we can get around it when you sign this."

"But this puts the boat in your name."

"Only in an affidavit in the customhouse. I'll give you back an unrecorded deed. That is your safeguard."

"Jackson, I don't need a safeguard. If I can't buy this boat without putting it in your name I'm not going to buy the fucking boat."

"That dear lad has been stealing from me," said Ilona as they strolled back to the set. "I'm not quite sure yet, but as soon as I can pin it down—too bad!"

"What will you do?"

"Throw him right in the pokey. I hate cheats."

The guard at the door of the sound stage had his chair tilted back against the wall. He was reading the *Police Gazette*. On staples in the wall over his head hung the sign "CLOSED SET."

Ilona Cape removed her arm from Cliff's and turned to face him.

"I can't ask you to come in, I've made such a fuss about keeping people out. But you must visit me when we're further along. Meantime, you must meet Mr. Wanger. I'll arrange a little dinner. He's fascinated by the oil business. But then everyone is, aren't they, darling? We didn't get to that, did we? But I did enjoy our lunch. . . ."

Her hand was on his chest, the white fiber of her eyes giving him a cool, veldt-raised, Old Vic-schooled goodbye. And also by way of goodbye, with some hello in it too, she ran her hand firmly down the middle of his body to the place where his crotch began and just a few inches farther. Then she turned and entered the sound stage where the director she detested and the cameraman she considered worthless would be waiting. The heavy door closed behind her. The guard still had his chair tilted back against the wall.

Cliff went to a pay phone and called Kyle's office.

"Hello, Unc," he said, "who do we know at United Artists—do we have any connections over there?"

2

Thus after due lapse of time, major photography began on UA film D612, the first day of actual shooting having been set back a little "to allow the company to rehearse longer," as the Wanger Unit press release stated. On that day—confirming certain rumors circulated on the lot, the gossip grapevine of a motion-picture studio being by tradition one of the world's most sensitive—the rehearsal director had disappeared and in his place was a famous person, Sam Wood, a brisk, middle-aged man who looked like a country lawyer, which at one point in his life he had been. Behind the camera was James Wong Howe, the youthful Chinese who had once been a flyweight boxer in San Francisco.

On that day also the chair with Cliff's name was placed on the stage.

In a meeting between Cliff and Mr. Wanger held in the latter's office it had come to light that there was room for an additional investment in *Low Man Out*. KinOil was not represented—the two hundred thousand dollars Cliff put in had been a bank loan he obtained by hypothecating some of his L&CC stock.

Now, in the shadowy space in front of the sparkler core of light, a seating pattern developed, ritualistically adhered to, day after day: Mr. Wood and the script supervisor up front in their proper places, Cliff in his chair, and Carrie Drew, the youngest actress in the cast, in a random seat with no name on it.

Miss Drew always seemed to be there. She was a tall, brown-haired young woman with a pretty nose which turned up slightly at the end. She would wear a light terry-cloth wrapper over whatever costume the script called for, and the collar of the wrapper was stained with makeup. She always had a script with her and sometimes a novel as well; it was too dark to read comfortably on the set but she would read at lunchtime, in the commissary. The novel was always the same: *Anthony Adverse*, by Hervey Allen.

Miss Drew watched with rapt attention everything that happened on the set. She came and went alone and refused the advances of the young crew members who tried to flirt with her. She had worked in the Provincetown Playhouse and in one long-running Broadway play. Her part in *Low Man Out* was her first major film role. It was a good one.

Cliff did not know when or how he got the idea that Carrie Drew had a crush on him. He might have been wrong—he had not focused on the notion; he was not even sure that it appealed to him. When he did focus on the notion he concluded that he might have got it because at the times when he and Carrie had held conversations she had carefully avoided the subject everyone else was so ready to explore, namely, his relationship with Ilona Cape.

Or his assumed relationship. For—perhaps inevitably—certain assumptions were made, some of which were a long way from being wrong while others were downright ridiculous. One of the more ridiculous ones was the assumption that having invested in a picture starring a woman you were taking to bed you would be eager for investments in other pictures even without the woman. Cliff quickly found that he was the possessor of a formidable reputation, born as it were overnight and at first underground but rapidly surfacing, so that before *Low Man Out* had been shooting two weeks, William Wilkerson, in his column in *The Hollywood Reporter,* a trade paper which Mr. Wilkerson also owned, referred to Cliff Kinsale as "possibly the new Howard Hughes." Mr. Wilkerson also called Cliff and Ilona, in combination, a "new two," a designation which had some relevance since by this time they had in fact been in carnal contact frequently and pleasurably although they had not appeared publicly, anywhere, in each other's company.

Bankers, front-money men, promoters and lawyers wrote, telephoned and laid in wait for Cliff to present him with propositions. The command echelon of the William Morris office took him to lunch. Tiny men all—the biggest of the three hardly more than five feet tall—they swarmed out of an enormous black limousine into the front banquette at Romanoff's restaurant. One spent the meal writing figures on a menu; another (who suffered from ulcers) furnished, along with every dish he ate, the medical reasons why his stomach would reject it. The third presented the deal. They wanted Cliff to back a film featuring Palenberg's Trained Bears. Cliff declined. Undismayed, and cordial as ever, the agents suggested a game of gin rummy.

What is love? Cliff had seldom asked himself that question. His first and only serious relationship with a woman had been with Dede Atlass and Dede had not talked about love at all. She had taken the position that if he gave her pleasure and she pleasured him that was all the love they needed; they had come together on even terms, striking a balance between their ages. Their parting had been less equitable: Dede had been bitter, he himself relieved. He had looked forward to new adventures, not realizing that Dede had robbed these of excitement in advance by spoiling him: here he was, starting with a new woman in the pattern Dede had made him at home with—older woman, younger man.

Ilona Cape, to be sure, was nothing like Dede. Ilona was committed to pleasing people. She devoted all her force, her practicality to that end, manipulating the professionals around her in the service of Those Others, the unseen horde of adoring, anonymous faces and throbbing hearts, the international audience which had made her a star. For herself, she held back only the small, terribly precious portion of life that was left over after she had paid her dues Out There. She was soft where Dede had been hard—Dede, who cared nothing about people, only about money, about power. Dede had understood money and power; she had learned about them from men. Ilona did not even understand the power which was genuinely hers, the power of pleasing just by being herself. Even in sex she felt an obligation to perform, in the dramatic sense: the set might be closed, but someone had sneaked in . . . her lover!

The first time she and Cliff made love Ilona forgot this duty. In a grand moment of oblivion she turned herself loose. They were in her trailer where Cliff had been waiting to take her home. She had sent her maid away, stayed late after work for a newspaper interview.

They started against the wall, which did not work; with her girdle down around her ankles when he reached for her, she could not get her thighs apart. Tramping on the bustle and pantaloons, the lacy underskirt of the three-thousand-dollar dress she had been taking off, grinding it all into the white rug, they slammed sideways onto the couch. The girdle hung on, a faltering chastity belt, then—oh, how blessedly—ripped apart, dropped off, and he was into her, albeit at an angle that made it hard to move, let alone ejaculate, both of them hurting, moaning, one of her big beautiful thighs hoisted back over the end of the couch, the other clamped around him, a deep-fleshed, golden hook, well designed to hold him where he was as long as she cared to keep him there.

She made him pull out of her and for some time sucked and licked him, talking to his penis as if it were a person.

"Don't you dare come yet, you red-eyed devil . . ."

They finished on the floor; he on top again, her back arched, her ass on the desecrated costume, her head thrashing from side to side to side as Cliff delivered himself at last.

He felt happy but slightly let down. He had never fucked a star before. He was not sure what he had expected, when you thought of the thousands of guys around the world who jerked off, imagining they were banging Ilona Cape; it was very much like fucking your basic, sexy woman of forty.

Or so he thought. He was soon to be disillusioned.

Back at her house in Benedict Canyon, after some stingers and a miserable supper which Ilona herself whacked out of the icebox, she said suddenly, "Which of my films did you like the best?"

Cliff looked blank. Throughout their courtship, such as it had been, he had tried to hide the fact that he had never seen *any* of her films.

He groped for some clue. An advertisement? The memory of a six-sheet, in the studio dining room, saved him.

"The one where you took a bath in the rain barrel."

"Oh, the one with *Gable*. Everyone remembers that scene —where he came over and looked right down *into* the barrel? Oh, my God. In some states they had to cut out that part. Would you like me to do that scene for you?"

"I'd love it."

"Well, I'll do it, but we have to have a candle—it was at night, you know, they didn't have electricity in the Old West. I may have some candles somewhere . . ."

Candles were located; one was cut in half so that, on a fundament of melted wax, it could be stuck onto the washbasin. Cliff, entrusted with this job, noticed prior tracings of wax on the basin. He wondered if the rain-barrel scene had been reprised here for other guests, but put the thought out of his mind as indecent.

Ilona let the bubble-foam come up high to simulate, in the bathtub, the sides of the rain barrel. She scrubbed herself from top to bottom, she posed entrancingly, she soaped and giggled. After she had sluiced off she let Cliff dry her, something Gable had not done—at least not in the film. Once she was dry on the outside—and also, as he found to his surprise, in spite of the vigorous pantomime, on the inside too—they got into her large, rented four-poster and made love once more.

During succeeding weeks of their romance (it extended through the summer, well past the ten-week shooting schedule of *Low Man Out*), the great, billowy bed did duty for sets or locations of other long-gone, well-remembered hits: the voyageurs' canoe in *Home on the Mississippi*, the lighthouse in *The Sky Is Burning*. Sometimes, if the fantasy invoked at the moment meshed with her mood, or some physical evocation, Ilona would experience the jolting, implacable throes that had coursed through her on the night of their first union;

often, though, these were absent. She would simulate orgasm
—or neither experience nor simulate anything, but just give
herself up meekly and wantonly while Cliff made free of her.
She would get up at five, leaving a note in the kitchen or
written in soap on the bathroom mirror: *"I love you."*

Five A.M., a six o'clock call at Hairdressing. Six P.M., the
wrapup, then the rushes. If a coal mine or an automobile
factory had inflicted such a schedule on its workers the unions
would have closed it down. A hard life! People would put up
with a lot for twenty thousand dollars a week. . . .

Love got better when photography was over. At last Cliff
and Ilona could go out together, dine at fashionable restaurants, dance at El Sarape, the Macambo or the Grove. Cliff
became skillful at fending off the fans who rushed up for
autographs, holding out stubs of pencils, scraps of paper. As
the escort of a famous woman he learned certain responsibili-
ties. He would bring the Bugatti up to the back door of places
she wished to leave without being noticed; he would write
down messages, take her cat to the vet, buy eggs and milk,
pick up the cleaning. He refused, however, to buy in when
her agent, the Brigadier, whom he was to meet later, offered
him half her contract for two hundred thousand dollars.

"An opportunity, my young friend, which will not knock
again," the Brigadier said.

Cliff explained modestly that he was in another line of
trade.

3

But was he, though? He wasn't working, not at anything.
From the day he made his last weld on the pipeline he had cut
himself off from oil, even from thinking about it.

He had been making other plans. The Kinsale clan's first
access to these occurred on a September day when his father,
visiting the Los Angeles office, invited him to lunch. They
met at the Jonathan Club. Troy was in the bar, drinking with a
square-set man whom he introduced as Captain Rieber. The
Captain had small, hard blue eyes and spoke with a Norwegian accent.

"I am your fadder's first boss in the oil business," he said as
he shook hands with Cliff.

"Not true, son," said Troy cheerfully. "When I worked for

him he was skippering a broken-down tanker, the worst ship in any ocean. He was a mean old Captain Ahab."

"This Ahab, he was a Norsky?"

"He was a whaler."

Rieber flipped a square brown hand.

"With whales I don't bodder. Bat a nice little company like you got, that I like. Someday you're comin' with Rieber."

"Not yet, Cap," said Troy. "We're not for sale."

"Someday you want a good safe port."

Troy told him that when that day came, he'd let him know. But he inquired, rather deferentially, "Will you join us for lunch, Cap?"

Rieber shook his head.

"Thanks, but you got this fine young man. Aalzzo I got a smart aleck coming here from Houston; he's selling service stations."

"I'll buy them if you don't," said Troy.

"We see what the price is, afen a couple drinks. I let you know." He offered Cliff his hand. "Don't let your fadder put nothing over on you. On my ship, he's playing cards in the fo'c'sle. He's stealing money from my crew."

The Captain raised a finger, signaling for another whiskey, which was instantly set before him. Cliff, whose martini had just been poured, had to carry it with him to the dining room, his father leading the way.

"This Rieber," Cliff said as they sat down, "he's really trying to buy KinOil?"

Troy shrugged.

"I gather you know who he is."

"Who doesn't?"

Torkild Rieber, the tanker captain who had risen to become chairman of Texaco, rated with the toughest and the most powerful men in oil.

"He's like a kid in a candy store," Troy said. "He'll buy anything that's shiny and goes for a nickel."

"We'd never sell out to him, would we?"

"Not while I have anything to say about it. But I didn't pull you in here, son, to talk about oil."

Now it comes, Cliff thought; Ma's been working him over: "Get your boy out of the movie business." But the meal turned out to be more pleasant than he had foreseen. Troy was tactful in expressing the hope—withheld until the entrée had been served and eaten—that Cliff's dealings in the cinema should by now have run their course.

His father put this forward as his own wish, though confessing that Luanna had concurred.

"Now, son," he said, "I know you're using your stock for collateral. Doc Giannini at the Bank of America—he's A. P.'s brother, handles all the movie deals—called me, on account it was L and CC stock. So I said, 'Hell, it's the boy's stock to do with as he likes,' and he said, 'That's what I thought you'd say, sir; I just wanted to make sure.' They're good people over at the B of A."

"Dad," said Cliff, "it's a good movie. You'll like it, when it comes out."

"I'll bet I will."

"Mr. Thurmond read the contracts. He said they were okay."

"Good, fine. Now, son," said Troy, "you know I don't gossip. I don't even listen to gossip. So if you've got something going on the side, that's all right too. I have no objection. I never messed around much myself. Your uncle did, of course, and he seemed to enjoy it. It's a matter of how much time you have to waste."

"Thanks, Dad," said Cliff.

"But hold on, son. I hear they're calling you the new Howard Hughes. We don't need a new Howard Hughes. A new Noah Dietrich—that we could use. Noah always was the one, ran Hughes Tool after the old man passed on. Noah was the one we dealt with. He made us the bit we used drilling Cliff Kinsale Number One, your own well. Young Howard, he was off in the clouds. Airplanes and, yes, movies and I don't know what all. Smart and so forth, no denying that but . . . you're not aiming to be one of those, are you, kiddo? You level with me now."

"No, I'm not, Dad."

"Fine! I should hope not. But what's the next step? You have anything in mind?"

"I think so," said Cliff. His somber young eyes blinked warily in their grooves of bone. He was not sure if this was the time to expose what he had decided on.

Yes, he thought, he would spring it. He had nothing much to lose. After all, he could do as he liked; his one compunction was the risk of hurting his father, this man whose solidity had been like an oak tree full of sheltering leaves spread above them all, through now so many years. In some ways, in the last stages of his growing up, he had been closer, more temperamentally compatible with his uncle, but he loved his father deeply—the strength of him, the simplicity and fullness of him, the strong lines of his face, the thick frosted hair that clung to his head like a tight gray cap.

His father had now turned, after meal-long restraint, to the matter of petroleum production.

". . . don't forget, we've got twenty-two percent of current resources under lease in Mexico and all hell is breaking loose there. I'll have to go down and see what I can do. Want to make the trip with me? You might get a kick out of it."

Cliff avoided his father's eyes. He fiddled with the tableware, his freckles darkening as they always did when he was under stress.

"Dad, I'll go anywhere you want, but I don't want a job with KinOil. Anyway not now. I've put in time for the company ever since Princeton and now I should have the right to choose my next move. Do I have that right?"

"You do, son."

"I want to go into politics."

PART FOUR

. . . and Introducing Carrie Drew

1

It was his decision, his own, but he had not arrived at it without help. His counselors had been his two best friends, Butch Konoye and Hersh Stepp; true, both were far away—Butch in Tokyo, Hersh in Spain—but he invoked their presence, constructing an imaginary dialogue in which they could take part. He put his proposition to them *in absentia*, as it were, taking a fix from their letters, such different letters, just as the two were such different men, yet in net context both relating to a single subject, the world's predicament at that moment in history.

In Japan, Butch Konoye, lighthearted companion of Princeton days, was writing about war. His letters, gay at first, were slightly mocking as he described the war fever gripping Tokyo. ". . . flags on all the buildings, and official cars flying through the streets." His father, at the end of June, had been asked to form a Cabinet, "the moment we have all been waiting for . . ." But as the summer wore on the mockery smoked away, the tune became clearer; Cliff detected criticism of the elder Konoye, implied at first, then openly expressed in the letters which came through to the United States by diplomatic pouch, evading the scrutiny of the recent strict Japanese censorship. "I am a dutiful son, I hope; my God, in our family that's taken for granted, but sometimes I wish the new Prime Minister (i.e., Poppa, I must get used to his official title) weren't so set on his role as a man of peace. War is sad and gruesome, we all know, but there are times when it's necessary for a nation's future. Even the most humble people feel that here; soldiers are everywhere and civilians who see them in the streets often bow to them out of sheer excitement and respect. You will soon read of important events which I suppose I had better not mention. . . ."

History moved ahead of the letter; by the time Cliff received it Japanese forces were already striking deep into mainland China.

Sometimes, after several successive nights at Ilona's house, Cliff would make a special trip to the North Adams Street apartment to see if there was any mail. He had taken the apartment over when Butch, a month after Hersh's departure, took off himself, though in the opposite direction. Was he heading also for an opposite political pole?

It was weird to think of Hersh freezing his ass off in the Jarama Hills, fighting for the freedom of a people with whom he had no ethnic connection, while Butch, a statesman's son, was buying the Fascist line in Tokyo. "Policy can be shaped from below, by the young as well as the hidebound conservatives who are afraid to hear guns go off. One can be a terrorist and still be pure in heart. . . ."

Hersh, meanwhile, was requesting "a few pairs of warm socks and a lighter that will work. . . ."

The letters were ties with a warm, friendly past which now seemed far away, receding at an unruly pace; answering them, he tried to make his own activities appear romantic and delightful, and in the old scale of values they were so, beyond any doubt, and yet . . . he felt embarrassed, as if what he was doing, the sort of life he led, had somehow become old-fashioned, in poor taste.

Hersh and Butch, though now set on such different paths, were his true friends, his pals for life. Yet changes had been taking place in both, and in the world at large, at an incredible speed. Not much time had gone by since he and Butch had left Hersh in San Pedro, looking sternly, grandly down from the dirty deck of the S.S. *Zuider See*, but now everything was different. It was as if his friends, leaving a party, had been swept away by a hurricane, off into the dark, while he had stayed behind, sipping champagne and prancing around to music they had long since ceased to hear.

There were different kinds of realities. There was the

reality of the small, hot lighted space on the big sound stage where the movie people brought some private dream to life and there was the reality of Hersh dropping potshots into the forward positions of the Fascist General Mola and there were those other realities, the corpses in the streets of Nanking, the 14-inch guns from Krupp, the people of captured Chinese cities bowing on the sidewalks to the Japanese soldiers who had been raping their women and burning their houses.

What changed wasn't the realities. It was the values you attached to them.

Was there one set of values for the United States and another for the rest of the world? Many people said this was true. Many people felt Americans had designed their own house and paid the mortgage when they sent the Redcoats packing.

Fortress America, protected by two oceans. The idea was impressive. Cliff was no crusader with an iron ass like Hersh or the golfing descendant of mythological gods like Butch Konoye, but he wanted a piece of the action, on whatever terms were then available. He'd seen the male members of his family drive for what they wanted: Kyle for power and more power, Troy for oil and more oil. He couldn't settle for either of those targets. Neither accumulation nor aggrandizement appealed to him; democracy did. Maybe that was what the noise was all about. Maybe if he could get a place, even a small one, in government, he would make himself heard, he could hold up his head as a man of his times . . . in the face of news from other lands which had also been free but which history had now betrayed.

2

Low Man Out finished on schedule and a wrap party was held on the set on the evening of the last day of shooting. There was catered food and a combo for dancing. Mr. Wanger paid for everything. He was very happy with the picture. Ilona gave Sam Wood a pair of diamond cuff links and James Wong Howe a ruby money clip. She had a present of some kind for every member of the cast and crew; she had sent her secretary out at the last minute with a shopping list—a burst of generosity made possible by a loan from Cliff, Ilona having been too busy to get to the bank. She had a wonderful time at the party and danced with everyone, including the grips and juicers, the propmen, the greensman, the sound man, the technical adviser, the camera team, and the people from Costume, Casting, Set Design and Music. When Mr. Wanger banged on a champagne glass and toasted Ilona as "a doll to work with" she kissed him and laid up a toast of her own, to the company at large, ". . . all you darlings who have made this film such a wonderful and heartwarming experience for me and one which I will remember forever. . . ."

She left at dawn the next morning. Cliff drove her to the airport, Ilona holding his hand all the way to Burbank. It was their first separation but it could not be helped. The Brigadier was coming to New York. Off and on there had always been some chatter about this individual, the Brigadier. He was an old duck with some British Army connection, which was in England about like being a Kentucky Colonel in Kentucky, as Cliff understood it. The Brigadier handled Ilona's affairs in England and worldwide except in the USA, where she was handled by the Old Sport. Ilona had once mentioned offhandedly that at one time she had had a tiny little thing going with the Brigadier, but it had amounted to practically nothing except that it got her out of her marriage to her first husband, Sir Montague Trevor-Gore, K.C. She'd had dreadful rows with Sir Montague and actually at times had feared for her life but she had not known how to get away from him. As a barrister and by no means an obscure one, he knew all the ins and outs of the laws of Court and he had assured her that divorce, besides its destructive effect on her career, was legally impossible.

Ilona had been young and, as she confessed, naïve; she had believed Sir Montague until the Brigadier made clear to her that he had been talking nonsense.

As it turned out, the case had never been called up because, as luck would have it, Sir Montague Trevor-Gore had dropped dead one day leaving the Carlton Club, where he had lunched.

That had been a bad time for the Brigadier. He'd had to answer all sorts of questions. Autopsy had revealed that Sir Montague had not died of a heart attack, as had first been assumed, but of a blow delivered to the back of his head with a blunt instrument some days or perhaps merely some hours earlier: a delayed concussion, as it was called.

"So you see, my sweet," Ilona had said when she told Cliff about this, "life *can* imitate Agatha Christie, that wise old bitch. I once did *The Ashcroft Murders* at the Drury Lane with dear Aubrey Smith, bless his heart. Sheer heaven!"

The Brigadier had been completely cleared. His reason for coming to New York now was that the British Gaumont people would be there; he had crossed on the *Ile de France* with Alexander Korda. Korda had a script with him in which he planned to star Bette Davis but the Brigadier was trying to make him sign Ilona instead. First, of course, Ilona had to read it. If she liked it, she could sit down and discuss it with Sir Alex across a table—always far, far better than across an ocean. Then they could see. She would have an excellent chance to get the part, especially since in the distant past she had had, she admitted whimsically, a small thing going with Sir Alex, even tinier and less actually a thing than the one with the Brigadier.

"And if I like the story, darling, they want Leslie Howard for the other star. Don't you adore him? That Scarlet Pimpernel smile . . ."

And with a magical contortion of mouth, eyes and teeth she transformed herself into a young leading man, devilish and debonair.

"Ilona Cape," she said in Leslie Howard's stylish, reedy voice, "you are a talented old bitch!"

From New York she telephoned at least once a day, sometimes oftener. Cliff had to submit a schedule of the times he would be at his own apartment and those others when he would be "looking after things" at Benedict Canyon. One morning, going to the studio to pick up some stills, he got a call from her there.

She sounded happy and businesslike.

"They're previewing *Low Man Out* tonight in Inglewood. Had you heard?"

"No, I hadn't. Are you sure?"

"Absolutely, Angel. It's a sneak."

"What theater?"

"The Forum."

And Cliff, who had not been listening to film chatter for three months without learning something, said at once, "But that's a Warner theater."

"That may be *why* they're doing it; nobody outside of the working staff is supposed to be there, possibly not even Walter. The Brig got word from someone in the New York exchange."

"They could have invited you and me, wouldn't you think?"

"Oh, *never*, sweet one. Not me. I'm *cast*, and cast *never* goes to previews, only to premieres. And not you, you're only *money*. They haven't heard about all your other marvelous qualities and attributes. Do you still love me?"

"Madly."

"Good darling. You must go to that preview and tell me *everything*."

"You mean, whether they laugh in the wrong places or . . ."

He'd intended a joke, but she said rather irritably, "They won't laugh in the wrong places or cry in the wrong places. This is a good picture, my dear. I've never been more sure of anything. I merely want a report. Make them let you see the cards."

"The cards?"

"At this kind of preview the p.r. people will hand out cards for the audience to fill out. Just a sort of questionnaire, but important. So don't forget."

"I won't."

"Make notes. And call me the minute you get home. Must rush now. By-eee."

"Goodbye, honey," Cliff said, but the telephone had already gone dead. He slowly replaced the receiver on its hook. The stout secretary who typed the answers to the fan letters cocked her eyebrow at him, her thick fingers still flying. She typed:

Dear Brother Julian and Little Nicolette:
    I am glad to hear your salamander is still eating so well, but I suggest you stop feeding him houseflies. Flies are fine for turtles, which can eat anything, but sometimes flies drag their feet through flypaper which is poison, and then . . .

3

Cliff dropped off the stills in the mail room, then strolled over to the commissary. All the tables were taken, but Carrie Drew, lunching alone, waved to him and he joined her. They had sometimes eaten together during progress of *Low Man Out*, teaming up on days when Ilona had some other appointment or, as she sometimes did, elected to skip lunch and nap instead.

Today Carrie looked radiant. She had discarded the bathrobe with the brown-stained collar for a belted silk suit which showed off her figure. Her face was scrubbed clean of makeup and her burnished-looking, heavy brown hair was pulled back in a ponytail. She had been posing for publicity pictures. She was excited because Sam Wood had telephoned her to say he had seen the rough cut and was pleased with her work. Mr. Wanger also was pleased.

"They're trying to get me an interview with Hedda Hopper for the *Times*. That's never happened before. It all depends on how my scene goes over."

Cliff remembered that Carrie had played a rather long scene with Ilona on one of the last days of shooting but he had not paid much attention to it, his concern centering rather on the scenes Ilona played with George Brent. Ilona had once mentioned having a tiny, tiny thing with Brent.

Carrie cued him in.

"The scene where I let her know that I've found out about her—about her murderous ways. We did it in one take and the crew applauded. Don't you remember?"

"Of course," said Cliff vaguely. "Great. Just great."

"Well, anyway," said Carrie, "Mr. Wood seems to think so. Are you going to the sneak?"

"I thought that was a secret."

"A sneak is not a *sneak*. There are no secrets on a movie lot. God, I wish I could go."

"Why don't you?"

"Can't. There will be a man from Publicity at the door to keep people out, everyone without a special pass. Did they send you one?"

"No, but I can sure as hell get one!"

"If you do, would you do me a great favor? Call me later and tell me how it went over—the whole picture, but especially . . . you know, *my scene*." Cliff began to laugh, and she turned on him in mock ferocity. "You bastard. I know what you're laughing at. You're doing the same thing for Ilona. Isn't that right?"

"It is."

"Well, I don't care. Call me, no matter how late it is."

And she had written her number for him.

They left together after lunch, walking back arm in arm to the gallery where she was working. Their small complicity had nurtured a companionable feeling—one begun, as it seemed now, some time before, during those earlier noon-time dates which had not really been dates but just the happenstance of being thrown together and finding that it was easy to talk to each other. Both had grown up in small California towns, though in such widely separated and contrasting portions of the state that the two places might as well have been in different nations: he in Kinsalem, the oil town his father had built in the dunes of Piru with its two-room elementary school, its wooden sidewalks, company shops and small chain department store; Carrie, in a lumber village in the Cascades. She had a mountain look to her, a different way of walking and talking, of looking at you sternly and hopefully while she composed her thoughts before speaking. She was nothing at all like the surfing girls, the beach kids he'd come down to see while working on the pipeline—worlds apart, too, from the eastern debutantes at New York and Philadelphia parties and Princeton proms. Compared to the latter she seemed almost too "nice"—deliberately wholesome, well arranged. Always the book under her arm. Fine. But did it always have to be *Anthony Adverse?* Even as compared with such high-living women as Dede and Ilona she would not be uninteresting—this he had decided early in their slight acquaintance: . . . there was also that easy feeling with her. Cliff wondered what it would have been like to walk to school with a girl like this, having the guys whistle at you and pretending not to notice. Was that what he had missed, growing up?

They sat in the still gallery, waiting for the photographer to come back from his own lunch. On the tables and around the walls, stuck in here and there among the blowups of Ilona and Brent, were experimental shots of Carrie—the stuff she had recently been posing for. Most of these showed her as Zan—direct, highly effective production stills. Carrie could not have been cast in a feature of this kind if she had not been photogenic as well as competent—but she was more than photogenic, she was blazingly beautiful. Cliff had not previously realized what the camera was telling him; he looked around with approval, bypassing only some cheesecake shots in which the photographer had taken Carrie in a low-cut leg-slashed costume that was neither her own nor a costume for the picture, in attitudes which neither she nor any woman in her senses would ever have assumed.

Carrie tipped one of these to get a better light on it.

"We worked hard on this one."

"I'll bet."

"You don't like it?"

"Pull 'em in like watermelon sugar."

"I don't like it either, but at least it's a change of pace. I suppose that's what acting means. That you can change yourself. I'm not really the perpetual Girl Next Door, though my parts have made me seem that way."

"You do it very well."

"Of course. There's only one role I'm better at: the Happy Young Hausfrau. You know? The Lace-Curtain Kid—"

"—In the checked apron. Washing the new china, bought by saving soap wrappers and cereal boxtops."

"Exactly. Well, I played that one in real life for almost a year. It was the hardest work I ever did but I was letter-perfect in it—till I found I had an understudy who was even better."

"You were married?"

"Not really. Just pretending. I told you it was a role, didn't I? But I tried. Oh, my, what good make-believe I made."

"What happened?"

"I stopped pretending. But it's a dull story."

"Doesn't sound that way to me!"

"It would, if you knew the details. This person was . . . well, older. Quite a lot older and quite famous. You bet! A Great Person of The Theahtah! Do you really want to hear this?"

"Yes."

"Well, I'm not sure I want to talk about it, even now, and it was—when was it? Year before last, at least. I had a walk-on in a play at the Provincetown one summer and I worshiped this person from afar, then not so far. At the end of the season we left together and we shared, if one calls it that, this ducky apartment on MacDougal Street, Greenwich Village, New York City. Did you ever hear of MacDougal Street? Lots of talent there, my friend."

"For sure, if you lived there."

"Flattery will get you anything your heart desires. But I left, you see. Wrote a note and flounced out when the lace curtains started to look dingy. That took place about the time I could cook two helpings of lamb chops, and then find myself eating them alone."

"He got tired of lamb chops?"

"No, he loved them except when he could dine at Pavillon

or the Colony or Twenty-One. Perhaps they tasted better there, particularly if the lady took the check. I wrote him a goodbye note and left it on the toilet seat. I went to see Jed Harris, my former producer, and told him I needed a job, and Jed had nothing for me but he rang up somebody at Paramount. I was working a week later and hating it. I even considered going back to the Eminence of The Theahtah. Fortunately, I rejected the idea. Story of my life . . ."

For some time now the still photographer, entering without either Cliff or Carrie paying heed, had been moving around the large untidy gallery, fussing with his equipment.

"Miss Drew . . ." he said into the sudden silence.

Cliff continued to ignore him.

"Look, Carrie," he said, "all these rules about the preview, that's all bullshit. You can be there, rules or no rules, because I'll take you. I'd enjoy it. . . ." And Carrie, who had seated herself in front of a makeup mirror, turned her head and smiled for him, her beautiful, wide-lipped smile—once more the Girl Next Door.

"Hey, Art," she said, addressing the photographer, "what time will I get out of here?"

4

Studio publicity men liked, and perhaps still like, to preview pictures at The Forum. It is a convenient place—not so far away that a long drive is needed to reach it, but still well apart from those local areas where the production of motion pictures is the chief concern of life. Its audiences are supposed to represent a true cross section of opinion, the tastes of that great faceless wad of Middle Americans who, in the long run, determine the success or failure of all films. Again and again these Inglewood folk, out there on Manchester Boulevard—shopkeepers, small householders and service people—have upheld this theory: their reaction in the theater itself and their comments later jotted on the question cards provided for that purpose have borne it out with an uncanny consistency. Only the most cynical surmise the truth—that the Forum crowd has acquired its expertise simply *because* it sees so many new films and knows, while watching them, that it will be asked about them afterward.

During the preview of *Low Man Out* they succumbed, nevertheless. Once the images began to spin over their heads onto the enormous screen they yielded themselves up, surrendered their beings to the magic which danced on a dusty beam of light. They sat enthralled and their faces, row on row, could one have looked back at them from behind the screen, were the faces of bewitchment.

Several rows of center seating had been roped off for the studio people; Cliff's passes admitted him to these. Carrie, still not quite confident of his influence with the person at the door, had improvised a sort of disguise—a pair of enormous dark glasses and a man's black Borsalino, which she wore slanted over one eye in the manner popularized by Edward G. Robinson in *Little Caesar*.

produced by
WALTER WANGER

directed by
SAM WOOD

When the cast names—hers among them—began to run, her body jerked as if an electric current had been applied to it. After that she was very quiet.

The story itself was quite good, forerunner of a cycle of psychological westerns which were later to be all the mode. It presented several innovations, in itself a difficult feat for this genre: first, the emphasis on female deviousness rather than male action to move the plot forward; second, the casting of a British star, Ilona (here supposedly an Irishwoman, mysteriously transplanted to the Canadian Northwest), as one of the two principals. Having taken George Brent from his wife, Ilona set him to rob a bank; to hide her own participation in his deed, she drove out alone to his wilderness hideout and brought him back, dead, in a buckboard pulled by a four-horse team which, as she had told Cliff she would, she drove herself. Only Carrie, the town's young schoolteacher, sensed a double crime. She revealed her knowledge in a confrontation with the older woman—the climactic moment which Carrie had referred to earlier as *"my scene."*

Sometimes at The Forum, audiences interrupted key scenes with applause; when that happened it did not necessarily mean that either the scene or the picture was successful—often, merely that the viewers felt the actors had bid for recognition and experienced some obligation to give it to them. It was different when an audience was really engrossed.

Then they kept quiet till the scene was over; they wanted to see how it came out. They did so with *Low Man Out;* when the applause started, nothing else could be heard for some time.

The reel or so of film which followed was anticlimactic but still fairly gripping and above all obligatory: the details of how Ilona came by her comeuppance. Carrie, on the screen, took little part in the proceedings. When the lights came on she was shaking; she gripped Cliff's hand with icy fingers. She broke loose from the handful of fans who, recognizing her in spite of the dark glasses and the man's headgear, crowded in for autographs—the first of her life.

"Get the cards. I'll be out in the car."

Already a tight, nervous group was gathering in the tiny office of the theater's manager—Mr. Wood, along with his famous production designer, William Cameron Menzies; the studio publicity boss, Jock Lawrence; the cutter, Hans Praeger; the assistant cutter; a young executive from Mr. Wanger's office, an older one from United Artists. There was little conversation, there was the tautness, the awkwardness of people constricted too long, and here still confined to a space too small for them. They had a hit. That much they knew. The only questions left were which of its qualities made it one and what were its dimensions. At the last minute Walter Wanger wandered in—a well-built, graying man with a pipe thrust into his belt like a side arm.

"Where were you sitting, Walter?" asked Sam Wood.

"Way in the back. I *bought* a seat."

"You should have more confidence, Walter," said Wood sternly.

Menzies turned his back.

Jock Lawrence smiled. He, like Wanger, had an Ivy League air about him. His good humor seemed part of his professional stance. Throughout the evening he had kept smiling at everyone.

From time to time publicity staffers entered, bringing small packets of preview cards. They had been handing out the cards both before and after the showing. Preview goers accepted them readily, some conniving to get more than one. They stood in the lobby and in the aisles or lounged on the seats, filling out the cards.

> How would you rate the film you just saw?
> Excellent   Good   Fair   Poor

Which female performer did you like best?
Which male performer did you like best?
What impressed you most about the film?
What other comments do you wish to make?

A new climate expanded in the tiny office. Tension dissolved; a vigilant jubilation appeared in the faces of those present as they passed the cards from one to another. Sometimes a person would seize another by the arm to point out some statistic.

"Hey, look at this—twenty-one cards, eighteen Excellents. . . ."

". . . seven out of eleven, only one Fair, no Poors. . . ."

"I have some Excellents underlined three times, exclamation mark!"

"Jock," said Wanger, "did you pay for those?"

"No, I came early and filled them out myself."

"Some press agent we got," said Wood; "he thinks of everything."

"Just as long as you're happy," said Lawrence meekly.

Menzies held up a clutch of cards.

"The kid—that Carrie Drew."

"Yes, the kid," said Wanger. "I'm pleased about that. Not that Ilona did badly. She did very well, but the kid—"

"Oh, they always like Ilona," said Sam Wood.

He winked at Hans Praeger. The two of them had spent several hours earlier that day splicing in additional close-ups of Carrie Drew.

"Who is Carrie's agent, Sam?" said Wanger. "Do you remember?"

"Leland Hayward," said Wood. "Would you like his home number?"

Wanger seemed surprised by the question, but rallied his composure.

"Yes, as a matter of fact . . . unless it's too late to call."

"Not for Leland. He's up all night, nursing his ulcers."

Wood looked up the number in his pocket phone book and Wanger dialed it. Evidently Hayward or someone who could reach him answered; Wanger pulled the phone into a corner of the room and began talking rapidly, his hand cupped around the mouthpiece.

"Long-term contract coming up," said Menzies *sotto voce*.

Cliff drew Lawrence aside.

"Jock, could I borrow some of the cards? Just a sampling? I'll get them back to you tomorrow."

"Ho," said Lawrence. He looked darkly at Cliff, then smiled his Ivy League smile, as if putting a seal on private deductions. "What time?"

"Any time you say."

Lawrence began sorting through a packet of the cards. "Against all the rules, my friend," he said. He slipped the cards into the pocket of Cliff's sport coat. "Noon will be okay. Don't lose them."

Carrie had the dash lights on. She was stretched out as far as the Bugatti's bucket seat permitted, her hands clasped in her lap and her eyes closed. She didn't move as Cliff slipped in beside her.

"Just tell me in one word, good or bad?"

"Good. Wonderful."

"Oh, my God. For me or the picture?"

"Both. But mostly you."

"You're not kidding?"

"Hell, no. I have the cards." He started the engine. "Wanger is calling your agent; he was on the phone with him when I left."

"Now I know you're lying."

"All right, call Leland when you get home. Ask him yourself."

He gunned the engine, moving out into Manchester Boulevard, almost empty at this hour.

"If you're making this up I'll kill you."

"Fine, but meanwhile you can look at these."

He dropped the cards into her lap. Carrie's hands closed around them. Once more she shut her eyes. Cliff, as he drove, glanced at her from time to time, but her posture never changed, the long, round throat stretched back, the hands holding the slim packet of cards with a queer possessive curve of her wrists, as if contact with them in itself provided some vast reassurance.

"Aren't you going to read them?"

"Not till we get home."

"So you believe me after all."

"I'm just beginning to. I'm not a quick study. . . . Do you want to come in and telephone?"

Cliff's head jerked around. The evening's activity had driven from his mind his promise to tell Ilona about the preview.

"You don't mind?"

"Not at all. I'm happy for her too. You must tell her how wonderful she is. Without her we wouldn't have had a picture; we'd have had nothing at all—even if she is a complete bitch."

"I'll tell her."

5

Carrie's apartment was a small new walk-up in Westwood, overlooking the UCLA campus. The furniture had evidently come with the lease. It was characterless, spotless and functional. A pile of magazines on the sofa and some feminine undies drying on the back of a chair provided the only evidence of human occupation, except for the books— quite a lot of books and scripts, the scripts in covers scrawled with pencilings, with turned-down pages and with notes clipped to them.

The books were all over—on the floor, the sofa, even on a kitchen shelf intended for groceries. *Anthony Adverse,* as might be expected, had the place of honor in the center of the cocktail table, but when Cliff picked it up the cover came loose in his hand. There was another book inside it.

Carrie cleared desk space for the cards.

"Are you allergic to dogs?"

"Good God, no."

Cliff looked around once more. There were no dogs.

Carrie said, "Frankly, I have this animal. So many people are allergic, it seems, at least in California. Wait . . ."

She went out, leaving the door open into the apartment house hallway. There were distant voices and a moment later a young Irish setter bounded into the room and leaped into Cliff's chest. Carrie followed him in.

"Down, Trey. Behave yourself. Heel!" she said without much conviction.

The setter obeyed none of these commands. He frisked around on the floor, sniffing at his mistress's shoes and legs.

"The lady on the top floor sits him when I'm away. Now I'm afraid I have to take him out, just for a minute or two. Then—"

"Will he go with me?"

"Of course. He goes with anybody but . . . you will?

Honestly? Oh, that would be marvelous, then I can look at these. You don't know how I've been dying to."

She sat down at once and began reading.

"A leash?" Cliff asked. In spite of his bravado he was not sure what one did, walking a dog in Westwood. Was there a fine, as in some places, for do-do on the pavement?

"Hanging behind the front door," said Carrie without turning.

Down he went, Trey tugging at his arm, down the stairs and out into the quiet, fog-smelling streets of a university town, between the little lawns, the neat, well-tended hedges of the middle-sized, middle-class houses. Urgent, furtive breezes ruffled Trey's golden-red coat, secret odors stimulated his tracker's brain; he made darting movements here and there, pulling his attendant along with him. Cliff wondered how he had got into this. Probably the compulsive power of the Girl-Next-Door strain in Carrie had turned him temporarily into the Boy Next Door, the individual who watched her comings and goings, who brought in mail, milk, papers flung onto the porch, who cut the grass and, well, walked the dog.

A large gulf seemed to stretch between his present servitude and Carrie's bed, if that was where he was heading.

Carrie had finished reading. She was sitting there at the desk holding the cards, her hands, her wrists strained around them.

"Well," he said, "do you believe it now?"

"I don't know. I keep going over and over them. Did you pick this bunch specially, just to show me?"

"The rest were the same. Favorite performer, female: quote, the girl who played Zan, unquote; quote, Miss Drew, unquote; Miss Carrie, Carrie Drew, the young schoolteacher, the young woman who loved Danny Conners, Miss Drew. Quote quote quote. So forth and so on. . . ."

"Ilona got a lot of good ones too," Carrie said briskly, her eyes hard and her cheeks burning—saying it firmly, once and for all, to get it out of the way. "She got almost as many, very near . . ."

"'Almost,'" he mimicked.

"I know." She pushed the cards into the light, stared at them savagely and intensely one more time. She brushed her fingers through them—long strong woman's fingers, squarish at the ends.

"They're used to her," she suggested. "I'm a novelty. A new face. Couldn't that be part of it?"

"New wouldn't be enough—it has to be a certain kind of new, I guess. She's been a star for twenty years. Now you're also a star. It's as simple as that."

"A *star!*"

Her voice made a shape, a sound out of the word that gave it a new status.

"Yes. That's why Wanger rang up Leland Hayward. Leland Hayward doesn't go to sleep it seems. He stays up because he has ulcers."

"I don't like him having ulcers, he is such a darling man. I hope Mr. Wanger didn't wake him."

"I don't think he did."

"He can be crude at times, Mr. Wanger. He's a good producer though. I was glad to work for him. Do you think the picture will be a hit?"

"Of course. They're all sure it will be a hit. That's what they were saying when I left, and I don't think they'll change their minds."

"All right. But don't get angry about it. Are you angry, darling?"

The endearment, the first term of its kind, passed unnoticed by both of them. For some time now—some hours—they had been living with a mood in which such terms had been possible, in which they had not occurred, but had they occurred, they would not have been intrusive.

"Hell, no."

"Well, I don't want you to be. It's been a wonderful day, a wonderful evening. One of the best of my whole life. I think perhaps absolutely the best. Definitely. I'm just trying to take it all in, what it means to me. I'm trying to get it all straight."

"I know."

"I didn't especially *mind* my own performance. I really liked parts of it. But it's getting late and before it gets any later you'd better do what you promised."

Cliff looked blank.

"Call Ilona," Carrie said sharply.

"Oh, Jesus—"

"Now don't tell me you forgot."

"I'll call her in good time."

"Do it now. You can use this telephone. I'll go in the bedroom."

"You can stay right where you are."

"All right, then."

She spoke as if a most important issue had been settled; an

act agreed on that would somehow set Cliff free—liberate
him from another woman, who until she was removed, stood
as a hazard in Carrie's life, on her day of triumph.

"Here . . ." she said, handing him the telephone.

Cliff looked sleepy, as he always did when puzzled. He
understood perfectly this gambit of Carrie's but was unsure
what to do about it. If he placed the call, it would be hard
not to make a fool of himself; if he refused, he was sure to.
He juggled the instrument in his big freckled hands as if
it were slippery or, at the moment, had become too hot to
hold. . . .

After all, it was almost 3 A.M. in New York. Wouldn't that
do as an excuse?

He started to say something of the kind . . . and then, after
a queer creaky warning, the telephone *rang*. It jingled, then it
went off like a bomb, almost in his ear. Even Carrie seemed
startled. Cliff looked at her helplessly. His first thought
was—Ilona. Somehow she had heard, had learned already
that he'd taken Carrie to the preview—hadn't Carrie herself
said there were no secrets at the studio? Someone had tipped
off Ilona, and she had then assumed that he . . .

The thing rang a second time! Carrie snatched it from him.

"Hello," she said.

Cliff leaned forward, then relaxed. What was happening
was not good, but it was better than what he had imagined.
He could not hear the words at the other end but the voice
wasn't Ilona's, it was a man's.

"Oh, *hello*," Carrie was saying. "No, it's *not* too late, no
not at all. . . . Why, yes . . . yes, it was. . . . That's right.
. . . They really said that? . . . Oh, my God. . . . Well,
yes . . . I did think so . . . it really . . . Well, I don't know,
but it did . . . it really did seem that . . . Yes, well, that's nice
to hear. . . . Oh, yes, incredibly, I just don't know how I feel
I think my head is going to . . . fly into space. . . . The cards,
yes." Here she listened without saying anything for quite a
while except for a laugh—a low, soft repeated laugh, too
intimate for Cliff's taste. "No, no absolutely. You were *sweet*
to call. I do appreciate it and . . . and René"—this with much
urgency—"René, *listen*. I signed autographs, several *autographs!* Can you imagine? Ha ha! Thank you so much. Yes,
yes it was . . . sweet of you, and I do . . . Well, thank you
once more. I hope so. . . . Thank you, René. Goodbye. . . ."

She hung up. For a minute or more she sat without moving,

her hands pressed against her cheeks, looking at the telephone.

Cliff cleared his throat.

"A distant admirer, I gather."

She nodded vaguely. Damn actresses, damn them all. He tried again.

"News travels fast, I gather."

Her head came around, the eyes no longer fitting in it properly because tears distorted them, formed odd, glistening bulges which, as he watched, tipped out onto her cheeks. He handed her his handkerchief.

"You seem to be gathering a lot," she said.

"I suppose I should have gone into the . . . uh . . . bedroom. After all, you offered to for me."

"I'm glad you stayed. I suppose one of the United Artist people told him there had been a preview. He's been doing something for United Artists. Always the Great Person of The Theahtah. Letting you know he knows what's going on."

"The fellow who got sick of lamb chops?"

"He didn't get sick of lamb chops, *I* got sick of lamb chops. It could have been a call from anybody. He was congratulating me and I was thanking him. He can never upset me again as long as he lives."

Cliff leaned forward. He kissed her lightly on the lips.

Carrie shivered.

"No," she said, "I'm half out of my mind tonight; I wouldn't know what was going on."

"Yes, you would."

Carrie got up. She took a step away, looking at him severely, her wild shining hair tumbled around her head like a scoop of burning wires and her beautiful face stained with tears. The dog, drowsing in the corner, twitched in his sleep.

"You're getting out of here, Buster."

6

He didn't call Ilona. It was late, he was tired, and by New York time, daybreak, for God's sake—an evil, an impossible hour to ring someone up.

Ilona called him herself later in the day, apologetic. She had been out with friends the night before. Had he telephoned? She was so sorry to have missed him, she had left instructions that . . .

And how had the preview gone?

Splendid, he said, a hit. The cards? The cards had been . . . fabulous.

She was coming back in two days. "Just the minute I get one last thing settled. Oh, I've such good news for you. But you must wait, wait till I see you. Alex is with me now, he and the Brigadier. Would you like to say hello to Alex? He's heard all about you. . . ."

Certainly, Cliff would say hello. But who in hell was Alex? It would not, he knew, be in good taste to ask. That would only prove you were stupid. One did not use last names in Ilona's crowd. One spoke of Lynn and Alfred, and of Kit, Helen, Jed, Sam, Thornton, Lillian, Toots, Sherm, Ron, Darryl, and so on. One was supposed to *know*.

Call him *sir*, the only possible cover-up.

"Hello, sir."

"Hello, Mr. Kinsale," said the pleasant, measured voice, "this is Alexander Korda speaking. Congratulations on your film. I hope we shall meet before long."

His film. Cliff hadn't exactly thought of it that way, had not yet adapted to the group metaphor by which any member of a group engaged in a film project might lay claim to the whole. But from that time forward he caught on rapidly.

Next evening he took Carrie to dinner in an out-of-the-way Italian restaurant, misty with ferns hanging from the ceiling, where loud Caruso records were played. Even here someone came up to congratulate him—a portly bald-headed chap with a drunken woman on his arm.

"Motion-picture banking has long needed some new blood."

Cliff thanked him. He would have enjoyed the compliment more if the speaker had not brought in blood. He preferred not to see the relevance of that, assuming there was any.

Ilona arrived by plane later in the week. Cliff met her with a hired limousine, sending the chauffeur to collect the luggage —fourteen pieces; the man came back to get money for the overweight charges, billed through for collection on arrival. Cliff had got used to this type of minor shakedown, but he thought that in the present situation the Brigadier, who was escorting Ilona, might have looked after it; that would have been better manners. It all depended, he supposed, on the Brigadier's role in Ilona's life.

Cliff waited for this to clarify. It never did.

"Not that he disliked the Brigadier. Liking or disliking—

either would have been hard to get on with. The Brigadier gave you no chance to maneuver. He kept his center firm, but poised for withdrawal, his flanks well covered. He betrayed no intimacies and if he gave Ilona orders or took them from her he was never caught at it. Once, once only, during a conference in his suite at the Beverly Hills Hotel, when Cliff saw his head jerking in such an odd way that it seemed possible he was having a fit; apparently, though, the jerking was a signal of some kind, for when the Brigadier walked out on the balcony Ilona followed him. The Brigadier stood with his back to the French door, which he had closed behind him; through the glass, Ilona could be seen at a three-quarter angle, talking rapidly, her face showing signs of strain. The Brigadier shook his head. Ilona spun away from him. She went to the railing of ornamental iron which protected the balcony from the drop below and struck her hand against it twice. When she turned back toward the window her mouth had a queer set to it but she had regained her composure. Both returned to their places inside and resumed the conversation as if nothing had happened.

One afternoon Cliff found the Brigadier asleep on a sofa at Benedict Canyon, a long, hairy man with a cleft chin and a high-bridged, crooked nose. He slept in his customary dress —a well-cut, crumpled blue blazer worn with gray flannel slacks and evening pumps. One pump had slipped off onto the floor, next to a half-filled brandy glass. Ilona was upstairs, in her bath. She had evidently heard the front door, to which Cliff had a key; she called to him to come up.

On the whole, the Brigadier was seldom at the canyon house. He was busy seeing people, putting together what Ilona referred to as The Deal. One gathered that for the Brigadier, a deal was itself an art form. He was constantly in touch with his London office by cable, with New York by telephone. He was charming to headwaiters. Often, in the evening, he, Cliff and Ilona dined together as a threesome; when Cliff became bored with this arrangement Ilona did her best to calm him.

"We mustn't hurt his feelings," she insisted. "He's terribly sensitive. After all, it won't last long. He expects everything to be signed by week's end."

"Well, whatever gets signed, it won't be a dinner check. Not by him."

"He has been naughty about that; he's really impracti-

cal in little ways. But in the long run you'll find him help
ful."

Cliff suspected that he himself rather than the Brigadier
was supplying help. He had already agreed that half his
percentage in *Low Man Out* could be used to cross
collateralize the Korda film in which Ilona would be starred
as a bookkeeping entry in his balance with United Artists, the
credit would cost him nothing and might eventually produce a
profit. More than this, he privately decided, he would not do.
He still liked Ilona; she had opened a new phase of life for
him, but their relationship had changed. They made love less
often than before, and when they did, their joinings resembled a pornographic waxworks which had somehow come
alive and was in danger of being closed by the police.

He had been courting Carrie on the side and getting
nowhere. Now she had gone to visit her father in the northern
hamlet where she had been raised and where he taught
something in a small state college. Cliff wondered whether it
was this parent who had advised her to conceal books of an
intellectual content—such as *Man's Fate,* by André Malraux
in French—between the covers of *Anthony Adverse.*

One day Ilona said, "The Brigadier wants to have lunch
with you."

"But we were with him last night."

"This is about The Deal—the final stage of it. He wants to
speak to you about it *à deux.* I'm sure he'll pay for the lunch."

Apparently the Brig had forgotten that it was to be a lunch
for two. He had brought along a motion-picture lawyer, a
small, jug-eared man with a gravel voice and a strong
handshake. This person had made his start, as he shortly
informed Cliff, as a criminal prosecutor in Chicago.

"We sent them to the pen, my friend," he said. "We got
threats, but shit on threats. We sent 'em up in droves."

The Brigadier nodded approval.

"Harry and I were together late," he said gently, "and
again this morning. Can you outline the gist of it, Harry?
Your reservations."

"Not reservations," said the lawyer firmly. "I had some
but that's in the past. What we have now is urgency"—he
fixed Cliff with a shaft from his tiny, metal-bottomed eyes: the
look which had squelched of old the gun toters, the hoods—
"the need for a new element."

The Brigadier was ordering crab Louis.

"What element is that?" asked Cliff.

"A little nugget of cash . . ."

Slashing at the porterhouse steak, the lawyer explained the function of the nugget: it would "balance the budget." Other credits have been promised, matching the amount of deferments for salaries and services, i.e., sums to be paid later, out of theater revenue.

"*Pari passu*," said Harry. "That's how it comes out. Everyone equal, after the bank is paid, of course. Barclays of London and B of A in a joint venture. Impossible without names like Sir Alexander's and Miss Cape's."

"The nugget, Harry," prompted the Brigadier.

"Exactly," said the lawyer. "Sir Alex has his part up. We've been on with him all day. Forty thousand pounds from him, two hundred thousand clams from you, and away we go."

Cliff signed for the food but withheld the nugget. To obtain it, Harry had explained, all that was needed was to sell his estimated *Low Man* profits for the sum stipulated. A buyer had been found—a Count Sangiacomo, an Italian utility mogul who admired Ilona.

Cliff pointed out that he had offered to roll over half of his *Low Man* percentage, not all of it—a reminder which was seen as neither relevant nor generous.

"But, Sweets," said Ilona, when they were alone, "the Brigadier is most upset. I practically promised him you'd do it. Why did you change your mind? It's not like you at all."

"I offered credit. Now he wants cash."

"Count Sangiacomo will give you the cash."

"If I let him buy my points for half their worth."

"Why are you so suspicious, darling? He's a man of honor, and extremely rich. He has no reason to take advantage of you."

"Then let him put in the money himself. I'll keep my piece of *Low Man*, he'll have the Korda picture and we'll both be satisfied. What's wrong with that?"

"Merely that I can't stand Count Sangiacomo. He once made a foul proposal to me. I don't wish to be associated with him."

"Ilona," said Cliff, "you're making this too complicated."

The remark annoyed Ilona, and they quarreled. She called him next morning to make up. She and the Brigadier had dined with the Count and the Count was definitely pledged to some kind of investment, though how much was not yet clear.

The Count had invited them all to his ranch in Nevada. Cliff could be included in the party, if he wished to come. He declined with thanks.

"I'm through with the whole bunch of them," he told Carrie.

"And I don't believe you!" Carrie screamed at him.

He had not even been sure that she was at home, that she had come back from her trip. She had gone for a week but stayed three; another had gone by since his split with Ilona. Thinking about Carrie, he had driven past her apartment, seen a light and rung the bell. Carrie was there, her suitcases still unpacked, her dog still not reclaimed from the lady upstairs. She had a lovely tan. She seemed overjoyed to see him but informed him, without asking him to sit down, that she had decided they should stop seeing each other.

"But why, what's wrong, for God's sake?" he asked, his lips dry, his voice coming out in a croak. "What is there to break off? We were just getting off the ground—"

"We were not getting off anything. It would never work. That's why I left, to be sure—and now I know, I know absolutely now I could get into something I can't handle and I'm not going to do it. You might as well get that through your head."

"Honey," he said, "we never talked about this. There was never any need to talk about it."

"There isn't now either. It's a played-out movie theme—the starlet and the producer."

"You're not a starlet, you're a star—or will be. And I'm not a producer. Just because I had some dollars in a film, does that make me some kind of leper or—"

"I didn't say there was anything wrong with it. I just said it was a script that I didn't want to be in. Also—what was that delightful item in New York—"

"What item? What the hell do you mean?"

"I brought it along just in case you felt like ignoring it. Winchell's column . . ."

She searched in her purse, brought out a bit of paper crudely ripped from a newspaper column.

". . . Cliff, youngest of the Kinsale clan (California oil), will back a second pic for cinelovely Ilona Cape . . ."

"It's not true."

"You questioning our Walter, the soothsayer?"

"You're damn right. I know who planted it, but it's a lie.

First I agreed to a limited investment. They kept pressing me for more, so I pulled out."

That was when she told him she didn't believe him. She screeched at him, her face wild, her mouth pulled into the weird, dramatic shape it had taken when she played her big scene in *Low Man Out.*

". . . if you had to buy yourself a whore there are a lot cheaper ones—and better actresses . . ."

"Carrie, there was never any secret about Ilona and me. It was just one of those things, never much; God, now that I think of it— But at least—"

"Ah, now it comes out."

"—at least you knew—"

"But I didn't know you'd have a *second time around;* you never said it would go on *forever.* You and your cinelovely! I could throw up and if you want to know—"

"Carrie! Sweetheart—"

"—I think I just may. *Why, Cliff?* Just tell me that—and no more—"

"Tell you what?"

"Why you kept on—and even now you're probably lying, you're probably still seeing her. A murderess. She and that manager of hers killed her first husband; they beat his head in. Everybody knows that. . . . Let me go."

Her voice shredded away as his arms went around her. She resisted physically, carrying on at first as if calisthenics could redress an argument long ago decided against her. Slowly, suspiciously, as if surrendering a treasure, she gave up wildness, lay still, quiet as a game bird, too young to fly, picked up in the field; he could feel her heart beating, see the high, fair color burning in her face. Her lips, stunned or paralyzed, were cold, forbidding, slowly softening, opening in a kind of blessed decrepitude, her tongue lolling into his mouth, her thighs, her breasts pressed against him as if to be separated from him now, even for a second, would cost her life.

7

She loved baseball and knew how to keep a box score. She and Cliff went to see the Hollywood Angels play the Seals at Gilmore Stadium. They listened to the eastern big-league games on the radio, betting against each other; when Hank

Leiber singled off Hadley in the second inning of the fourth game of the Series with McCarthy and Harry Danning scoring right behind him, she choked on one of the hog dogs she'd fixed so that, eating them, it would seem as if they were really at the game. Next to hot dogs she liked hamburgers made with pickles, onions, and relish; Coca-Colas, thick shakes, ice-cream cones, and chop suey. She hated to cook almost as much as she disliked going to expensive restaurants. They dined mostly in drive-ins and bowling-alley coffee shops. She taught Cliff to bowl and was delighted when, after two lessons, he beat her. She would not make love during her period, had cramps then and would sew in the evening; she had rented a sewing machine in her apartment and used it to make Cliff a shirt. She washed his clothes and her own by hand, in the kitchen sink; she was a poor horsewoman but enjoyed camping; she could cast a fly and read omnivorously, mostly in the bathtub. Among the books she talked about, those with which Cliff was familiar, were *The Waste Land, As I Lay Dying, Lives of a Bengal Lancer, Gulliver's Travels, Twelve Against the Gods, Das Kapital, Oliver Twist, The Royal Road to Romance, Ethan Frome,* and the plays of Sean O'Casey. There were still a lot of film scripts. Agents were sending many now—a dozen a week; sometimes she would glance through them and throw them out.

"They should send them to Leland, not me. When it's time for me to do something he'll pick it. He gets paid for that."

Cliff's first house present was a box of flea powder, a joint gift to her and the setter, Trey. Fleas would not touch Cliff. They would touch Carrie. Then she would squirm and scratch when she should have been lying quietly beside him in bed. He had a struggle keeping Trey from his former sleeping place on the foot of Carrie's bed. Victorious in this, he made amends by walking the pooch in the evening, the two of them weaving an erratic pattern through the demon smells of Westwood Village, Trey twisting and turning and pissing and Cliff looking forward to fucking Trey's mistress.

Any bunch of notes on Carrie Drew supplied material congruous with the Girl-Next-Door concept; her screen and stage work suggested the same idea and United Artists flacks were not busy polishing and refining it for public presentation preceding the release of *Low Man Out.*

Sexually, her behavior called for quite another metaphor. Like all worthwhile, high-strung women she was changeable, passionate, gross, inventive, conquerable and somewhat secretly (if the truth were known) inhibited. She would wash herself and stride over to the bed proudly and carelessly, like some white jungle queen, but not white exactly, just in the loins and across the breasts, where the material she'd used for sunbathing during her trip home had left strips: brief, grafted vestments. The light must be adjusted with care, a towel over the shade. Not too much, not too little . . . but enough to turn her hair, so brown by day, into a bonfire, to summon flecks of madness, sand grains in the water-clear blue of her irises, her face wary, waiting.

"You goat! Don't be in such a hurry . . ."

Touch her and her thighs would open, her broad, thin pelvis rise, spread as if pulled by wires, wet, foaming . . .

Don't touch her. She would let you know the right time. Not yours yet. This could be for anyone at all, maybe the old bastard in Greenwich Village, the Great Person of The Theatah whom at all costs you must keep from getting in bed with you.

No place for him at all in the congress of these nice young people, though of course he was at hand, as was Dede, as was Ilona, their Dionysian masks leering from the shadows, the essential decor.

Carrie laughed. She pushed his arm away, then put his fingers in her mouth. Lying on her side, hip now raised, still jungle queenish, she pushed her hand on down his flat, muscled, freckled body like a carpenter smoothing down a plank he is about to slice into strips.

"I love you, darling."

Loud sucking noises as her lips, so innocent, so virginal, worked over the glistening, blood-engorged tip of his cock, her fingers squeezing him judiciously, estimating what to do next . . .

The first ejaculation into the vagina: fireworks on shipboard.

Licking her wetness, honey-sweet, gunpowder-musky, he waited for the tug on his ear, signal that she wanted him topside. This time much longer, beginning to be—Jesus!—too long?

"Do you want me to stop?"

"Oh, God, no . . . don't ever . . ."

Other codes to be learned in Westwood, in the Indian summer of 1937, World Series time past and gone; fingers against his shoulders; squeezing or tapping "Slow down!" Then at last, at the outer rim of a distant seascape, the twitches of lightning, the first spasms, her hands on his buttocks.

She was so sweet. They took a pack trip to the High Sierra, rented twin sleeping bags from the pack outfit at Badger Pass—there was no double sleeping bag. They made do with the two singles and shivered all night till they got the idea of building a pine-bough bed and lying on it with a tarp spread out, both bags opened and laid over them. Huge granite spaces supplied air preserved intact from the earth's original issue. Carrie cast tiny flies for golden trout. Only two weeks left now before she had to start a publicity tour for *Low Man Out*.

Back in Westwood, they put on their best clothes to spend a long weekend with Kyle and Alma at the beach.

8

Cliff hadn't told his uncle that Carrie was an actress. Her name, to be sure, was beginning to be known, but the Kyle Kinsales might not be following show business closely enough to have heard of her. Cliff wanted to see how they would react to her as a person, without advance billing.

They reacted well, as he'd thought they would.

After lunch, the second day of their visit, Kyle took him out on the "flying bridge" to tell him how attractive he thought she was.

"Your taste is improving. She has a great quality—sort of gal you should have met at high-school age. Kept you out of a peck of trouble . . ."

"You're on target, Unc—dead on. Exactly how she seemed to me. . . . Now let me tell you what she really is— Hollywood's next big star, the best young dramatic actress on the scene."

"And beautiful besides."

"They'll call attention to that too."

"Not that they had to call your attention to it," said Kyle dryly, "but I like her. So does Alma, for whatever that's worth, and Alma doesn't like many women."

Lighting one of his small cigars he studied Cliff through the smoke, wondering how serious his nephew was about this Carrie Drew. Somewhat, surely—she was the first girl he'd brought to the beach house, ever.

An actress—well! Maybe it had been a mistake to praise

her. He had always stayed away from actresses himself. They got too much admiration. That kind of thing could turn a woman's head.

Kyle looked over the balcony rail at the beach where Alma was building a sand castle with Linda while Carrie, with little Katie on her shoulders, jogged in and out of the chilly, mild-mannered surf, making the child giggle with delight. Family tableau, Pacific style—you would have thought the two women were the same age, as far as looks went: how much difference was there really? He would guess about five years.

Feeling his eyes on her, Alma looked up and waved and Kyle waved back. She seemed to get better-looking all the time. No woman, not even this girl of Cliff's, with her lithe brown body and blaze of hair and her serious, proper manners, could compare with Alma. No woman in the world. Good thing *she* wasn't an actress, that would never have worked.

He was glad when, at dinner, Cliff said he didn't plan to continue in the motion-picture business. Alma too glanced approvingly at Cliff over the candles, their flames steady in the unseasonably windless air—they were dining in the patio on the landward side of the big house.

An odd sort of constraint had settled on this dinner, as if getting to know one another had produced self-consciousness —a certain stiffness—rather than, as one would have expected, the reverse.

"Oh, I don't think he means he'll stop forever, Mr. Kinsale," Carrie said, her eyes on Cliff. "There are always chiselers who lie in wait for anyone with money to invest—but there are good propositions too."

"Cliff might have another notion in his head," said Kyle. "Has he talked to you about politics?"

Cliff smiled at Carrie.

"Kyle wants you to understand that I'm an idiot to dabble in entertainments or run for office. Where I belong is out on a rig. Isn't that right, Uncle?"

"Now I never said that, and you know it. Never even implied it, did I, Carrie?"

"If you did," said Carrie, "it must have gone over my head."

"Not much goes over your head, dear," said Kyle. "Not much at all."

9

Weekends at the Malibu house, formerly leisurely, had changed since the last meeting of the Land and Cattle Company's shareholders. Whereas once the family had slept late, now they were up early; Kyle, at least, had to be, or so he said, and with him up and about, scant encouragement was offered others to lie abed. Cars began arriving as early as eight in the morning, corporate limousines and rental jobs, hacks and station wagons and the smaller, older models driven by lackeys and henchmen of one kind or another in such numbers that Da Costa, the second chauffeur (he drove for Alma and the children), was put in the courtyard at peak hours to supervise parking. Inside, in Kyle's study, now transformed into an office, two secretaries worked, one for appointments, the other for typing and filing, just as in the KinOil Building during the week, although not of course the same girls.

Rose Brady didn't come in. Saturdays she took off, Sundays she went to Mass—an implacable routine which nothing and on one, not even Kyle, not even the most dire emergency, could disrupt. But Rose had carefully chosen the girls who did come to the beach; she had picked them and drilled them and only then, when she was certain of their skills and confident of their discretion (a basic requirement for any employee of the Kinsale family), had she sent them along for Kyle's weekends. After that she washed her hands of them just as she washed her hands of the activities in which they had been hired to assist, "that Malibu stuff," as she termed it—not pejoratively. Rose, loyal through and through, would never discredit, verbally or otherwise, anything Kyle chose to do. But—how would you define what went on there, in the beach house, now, on days consecrated (one of them by the Lord Himself) and ordinarily devoted to other uses. It had no definition, really; it was business but it wasn't oil, it was this and that and Himself only knew what, it was different kinds of gimcrackery that Kyle had got into under the lash of necessity, the need, in spite of his great holdings and lofty station, or perhaps in some mysterious way because of them, to add one dollar to another.

Rose Brady held herself aloof. She did not like any of it but

406

she was not going to be disturbed by it; after all, it might be a passing phase in the life of this man to whom her own existence, silently, inflexibly, was offered up. It might pass. But once it became, as it seemed, permanent, self-perpetuating, she was moved to make a novena for Kyle; clutching her missal with the medals of her favorite saints dripping from the spine of it on broken-neck ribbons, Andrew and Teresa, the good Giles and Francis of the birds and flowers, fearless Boniface and raging, righteous Patrick, she knelt on the cold stones of the Good Shepherd and prayed that he might be delivered from evil. Long had God's favor shone on him and still, as it seemed, poured down bounteously, yet in her heart Rose Brady sensed that all was not well with Kyle Kinsale.

"Well, my boy, I'll tell you why I'm doing this," Kyle had said when Cliff came up to his rooms that morning. "Our shareholders in their wisdom have cut me off at the boot tops. Oh, I'll bounce back—but it's not easy to survive on half a million a year when I spend again as much. I've developed a project of my own to take up the slack. Make no mistake—I still work as hard as ever for KinOil. I confine this other matter to my spare time. Here, take a look."

And leading Cliff into an anteroom he showed him a row of filing cases, each bearing, above its alphabetized drawers, the logo: PETROCHEMICAL CORPORATION OF CALIFORNIA.

In the same manner with which Cliff had become familiar when his uncle pointed out the virtues of a new racehorse, Kyle described his corporation acquisition.

He had recently bought up, at a modest price, a medium-sized Midwestern company manufacturing petrochemical products, synthetic rubber, cosmetics and building materials. Kyle and two or three associates had moved the company to California, greatly expanding it and providing a new plant for it in Oakland. Its principal assets, aside from factory machinery, were its beneficial deal with KinOil for petroleum by-products, and its patents. Over one such patent the great German chemical consortium I. G. Farbenindustrie had brought suit, but Kyle and his fellow directors felt that the Farbenindustrie claims would not stand the test of U.S. courts, so Petrochem had gone right on producing output with its own version of the patents, duly and properly registered.

". . . someday we may be able to build a city, clothe all the people in it and supply their drugs, furniture, transportation, and some of their food out of oil residues which a few years ago we were throwing away . . ."

Cliff was impressed, yet it seemed too bad that his uncle, who had always been so keen to enjoy life, should now, at the peak of his success, be working twelve hours a day with no days off. That might be the American way but it never had been the California or the Kinsale way—not that he'd ever heard of. Perhaps it was only a passing phase for Kyle—a test to show the Land and Cattle Company stockholders that he could keep up his lordly spending in spite of their efforts to curtail him.

But Cliff had come up to the office today with a problem of his own.

"I'm not a 'new Howard Hughes'—Dad's already had me on the mat for that—the cockeyed label some reporter hung on me. Movies—they were a one-shot deal for me. But I am serious about politics. I'd like to go in that direction. At one time you seemed ready to help me. I was wondering if you'd changed your mind."

"Not at all."

Cliff pushed his hand through his red thatch of hair, some of his tension leaving him.

"That's good to hear."

"Alma and I have talked about it. And I've talked with your father. We all think that's where you may belong—ultimately, that is. It's a long road and it's a tough road."

"Oh, I know that."

"I'm glad you do. You were laying the foundations in Princeton—the newspaper work, the debating. It was all to the good. I'd be lying if I let you think we didn't have some contacts. We've got IOU's we can call in for collection just as soon as some current business is out of the way."

Kyle finished with a quick, hard glance at his ambitious nephew.

Cliff's ear picked up the loaded phrase unerringly.

"What current business do you mean?"

Kyle lit a cigar. He walked up and down the long, sun-shot room, weighing his next speech.

"You had lunch with your father not long ago. Did he mention Mexico to you?"

Cliff nodded. "Yes, he did." He tried to remember what had been said.

"But he didn't go into specifics?"

"No. All he said was that he was going down there. Wanted to know if I'd like to come along. I said I would but that I didn't want a job with KinOil. That was about where it ended."

"I see. Well, there's trouble at our Tampico base there. Troy knew it when he met with you. I thought he might have gone into it more thoroughly."

"You know how Dad is. Never says too much."

"Sometimes not enough. He hasn't been feeling well. He wouldn't stay in Mexico five minutes if it weren't for this trouble with Cárdenas, the president. He's making outrageous demands, always with the threat that if we don't concede he'll nationalize the oil—all of it. That's the new politics, Latin style. Pretty hard for your dad to run the Pánuco field and negotiate for survival at the same time."

"In other words, he needs someone with him."

"Absolutely. That's why I asked you for the weekend, to lay it out for you." A secretary entered, glided swiftly to Kyle's desk and laid a message under his eyes. He wrote something on it and she went away. He turned back to Cliff, his face somber, his eyes hooded. "When you come down to it, it's not a question of whether or not you want to go. It's a question of how soon can you leave."

CHAPTER SEVENTEEN

The Train from Jiquilpán

1

The flames licked and clawed at the base of the smoke column. They chewed at it as if the smoke rather than the jet of oil below it were what they wanted to destroy. Sometimes they would disappear entirely. They would go into hiding only to pop out again, more savage than ever, in some new place. They attacked fiercely, jumping from side to side; with sharp little mouths they nipped like wolves, like foxes at the haunches, the underbelly of the smoke. Meanwhile, the column, with its unstoppable life, its monumental frame, ignored them; it piled into the sky, making a new, horrible sky of its own; it wobbled on its vast underpinnings; it would not be downed; it gained rather than lost strength, waiting for night, for the wide black night of Mexico to come down over it so that it could show its true power, so that it could make free of earth and heaven and ravage both equally.

The well had been burning now for ten days, a good stout well at the northeast end of KinOil's Chorreras field: a monster, Boca Riza 56.

For a square mile around it the land was bare. Everything was gone—rigs, roads, equipment, huts, pipes, vehicles. Emergency crews had removed what was movable. The fire had incinerated the rest.

Troy and Marshall Borland, the company field manager, standing on a small, wheeled platform, watched the latest effort to put out the fire. The platform was protected by an asbestos screen. It was located two hundred yards from the flames, but even here the heat was scarcely bearable. Troy and Borland wore asbestos-covered fire hats, with tinted glass visors; through the protected apertures they could see three figures tramping across the scorched ground, straight at the fire. All three—young, strong Mexican fire fighters, trained in KinOil's disaster school at Tampico—had been supplied with asbestos suits, manufactured by the Johns-Manville company. The suits were thick and cumbersome and the three attackers shambled forward clumsily, erratically, trailing wires behind them. Each man carried a fifty-pound dynamite pack, all three packs lined with the positive and negative electrodes to which the wires were attached. The packs too had their housings of asbestos, but in spite of such precautions there was always a chance that the heat would ignite the charges before the fire fighters reached their objective—an iron stand located fifty yards from the burning hole.

Nothing was certain. That was why these fire fighters were paid golden time, Mexican scale, for the jobs they had. There might also be a bonus. They were brave fellows. If they succeeded in their plan, they would be big men in the El Bolívar in Tampico that night and for many nights following. If on the other hand the packs went up prematurely, then what was left of the *hombrecitos* in the asbestos suits would be laid to rest, presumably together, in the company cemetary alongside the Chijol Canal.

That was the business in hand.

The attackers laid their bundles on the stand. Then they turned and shambled back, possibly believing they were running, along the lanes formed by the wires they had laid. Near the executive observation platform they jumped into a trench and immediately a third man, somewhere nearby, pushed the plunger of a detonator. A magnificent explosion followed—a Fourth of July bang to end all bangs; a squirt of adobe dirt leaped up, almost as high as the smoke, and presto—there was no more smoke, no more little snarling, flaming fox mouths, nothing! It was a miracle. From around the circle of a scorched earth a frail, queer sound went up—a cheer, or something like it—and now it became perceptible that field workers of all sorts and stations had come to see the show and spread themselves around. They jumped up, they embraced one another, they capered like imps in their happiness and excitement, and they raised this queer, insect-like sound of joy.

In the trench the *hombrecitos,* in their strange clothes, grinned behind their masks; they whacked one another on the back but they did not stop watching, over the top of the trench, the place where the charge had gone off and where there was now this big hole. And on the executive platform Tony Kinsale and Marshall Borland also watched, their faces keen and tired, expectant and wary. They watched and they waited. This period at hand, this uneasy, empty aftermath of daring rather than the Fourth of July cannon cracker was the moment of truth. For it was all very well to puff out a burning well with a big noise as a child might puff out a birthday candle but that didn't always end the situation.

The monster might have gone underground. It was a devious as well as implacable monster and it had strange ways.

Troy looked at his watch. He had punched the stop hand at the moment of explosion. One, two, three, four minutes went by—a good, healthy lull, a stretch of time that was almost into the start of the positive cycle, ten minutes of extinguishment being calculated as positive, as a salvage accomplished, unlikely to be reversed.

Six, seven, eight minutes . . .

"From the sides of the circle the watchers began edging forward. With small steps, like burglars, with wild, smeared faces, their long-nosed, high-cheekboned Indian mugs, dirtied by their work and by the cloudburst of dynamited earth, they crept onto the scene, farther and farther, claiming victory, pushing out so that by being there they could identify themselves with it.

Then from the sidelines a motorcycle lurched out, a person of authority standing up in a sidecar, waving them back.

This person, whoever he was, must have known what he was doing.

For now it happened—a wisp, an upward trickle that was not dust but . . . smoke, and then, Christ, a yellow tongue, and then . . . more smoke, more tongues, more ravening mouths . . . and up, into the softly darkening air, into the tropic twilight with a roar, out of the very hole dug by the dynamite to do away with it, the fire returned.

The monster was still alive. It had just been playing games. The well was burning again . . .

Troy took off his iron hat. His body was soaked in sweat, not all of it from the heated air. Lately he'd been suffering onset symptoms of the malaria he'd contacted here during an earlier visit. The sweats at night and the chill nothing could warm. He wanted to get in some dry clothes.

"Okay, Marsh," he said quietly to his field manager, "let's get out of here."

2

The trip of less than ten miles was made in two shifts—a Ford bus to the railhead, then a gasoline-powered railcar to the refinery, the tank assembly and the cluster of low tin-roofed buildings that made up KinOil's Chorreras headquarters. There had been a road, quite recently, a decent macadam-topped highway clear through the marshes, but the summer rains had flooded it out. Troy privately blamed Selby Clay, superintendent of Tampico operations, for the failure, but had refrained from saying so.

Things went wrong anywhere. They went wrong more in Mexico than anywhere else—but lately they had been going wrong more often in Mexico than ever before.

Selby Clay could not be responsible for all of it but he might sure as hell be responsible for some of it. Troy had made up his mind to check on that.

Selby Clay was waiting for them now. He had come up the Pánuco River from Tampico in one of the company's seagoing launches. He had been appointed to bring with him another passenger scheduled to arrive at Tampico that morning from Los Angeles.

"Where's Cliff?" demanded Troy, disappointment heavy in him. He had been looking forward all day to seeing his son.

"Plane was late," said Clay, "but he's on it. My wife's going in to pick him up—he'll be at the house by the time we finish here."

Troy nodded.

"Good. That's fine then. I assume that Mr. Rubio and Mr. Avila are here?" And being told that the gentlemen were indeed present—Betty, Selby Clay's secretary, had put them in the small conference room—Troy demanded a cup of tea.

"And three five-grain quinine pills, if you have them," he added, conscious again of his sweat-soaked shirt and under-things, clammy cold against his skin. He had brought up a small suitcase from Tampico but that, naturally, was in his quarters; he took Borland aside, asked him with urgency, as a special favor, to pick up the suitcase, bring it to the staff building at once, and Borland hastened off to comply.

Troy jammed down the quinine with three swallows of scalding tea, then took his cup into the room where Clay had preceded him and where the others waited to begin the meeting.

When my clothes get here, Troy thought, I'll excuse myself and change. By God, if I'm still cold then I'll wrap up in a blanket. Or go home and go to bed.

Far off, still, but deep inside him, like the chill from a vault, he felt the attack lying in ambush. Only a lot of heat—heat and determination—could still scare it off.

He shook hands with Rubio and Avila and took his place at the end of the table.

Cortés Rubio, a compact, swarthy man of middle age, was the most influential private lawyer in Mexico. He was a graduate of the University of Texas and held a degree in economics as well as in law. At present he had as his clients five major oil companies, correlating their efforts to prevent the expropriation which President Cárdenas had been threatening for some time now.

"We must keep," he would say at some point in every meeting, in his strong, guttural voice, "a united front. Do not hold *him* lightly. Do not make that mistake!" And then he would point upward with a stubby, hairy finger, indicating the ceiling or perhaps actually the realms above, as if Lázaro Cárdenes, the former revolutionist from Jiquilpán de Juárez, Michoacán, had already taken his place among the religious deities whom his regime so strongly disavowed. "We must stand together. Otherwise I guarantee nothing, nothing! I must make this clear."

Now, gripping Troy Kinsale's hand warmly, keeping his hold on it longer than anybody normally would, he said at once, "I am so sorry to hear that the blast was not successful, the fire is still burning. What bad luck!"

And with this he produced, like a conjuring trick, his quick, hard smile.

"Well, we're trying, counselor," Troy said.

He turned to accept the chilly paw of Rafael Avila, a tall man with a sorrowful, monkish face and an ill-fitting black hairpiece.

"But surely," said Avila gallantly, "Mr. Kinsale will soon prevail. He has dealt with such incidents before."

He obviously intended the remark as flattery, but Troy caught him up on it.

"I have, Rafael, but never so many so close together."

Troy glanced across the table at Selby Clay, but for the moment Selby refused a reaction. He sat looking vacantly at the tabletop, his young face parchmenty with the dryness of five years in a tropical climate. He had never, when you came down to it, been worth much. Perhaps if he'd taken a firmer stand at the start . . . but they were all in trouble now.

"There have been just too many accidents, if that's what you want to call them. I call them sabotage."

Rubio nodded sympathetically but Avila flipped a bony arm in disavowal.

"You have proof, I suppose?"

"So far we have witchcraft. We have a boatload of fourteen-inch casing that kicks away its balks. We have gate valves that open by themselves and dump sixty thousand barrels of crude into the Pánuco River. We have bailers that blow up through crown blocks and we have wells that blast off and burn for weeks. It's not the events that are wrong, it's the percentages. Both you gentlemen work with major companies. What increase in accidents have those companies been getting lately, may I ask, eh, Rafael?"

Avila's long, pitted face reflected pain at the question. It seemed, his expression indicated, unfair. He would not know these things, had not actually been, for some time now, connected with labor, with operational problems in the field. And he too, from the depths of his being, opposed expropriation. Why not? Opposing expropriation was rapidly making Rafael Avila a millionaire.

"I am afraid," he said softly, "I would not have those figures, Señor Kinsale. Sabotage is not a tool of negotiation. It is not in any sense to be condoned."

"Good, I'll remember that."

Some of Troy's tea had slopped over into the saucer. He poured it back, but now it was cold; he signaled Betty, who had entered to say something to Selby Clay, that he would like another, hotter cup. The quinine must be taking effect, he felt definitely better; he waved Borland away when he saw him peering through a crack in the door, no doubt with the change of clothes at hand.

To Betty Manton he said, aside, "Leave word at Mr. Clay's house to have my son call me the minute he arrives. You may interrupt me for that call, but nothing else. Except maybe a pill—another quinine."

"Mr. Kinsale, you just had fifteen grains," said Betty with the presumption of long acquaintanceship. "But all right," she agreed, feeling Troy's steely glare, "if you insist."

"I do," said Troy, conscious of the ringing in his ears, the return of life to the pit of his stomach and grateful for both. He turned back to Rubio, who had moved into his usual spiel about a united front.

". . . I have an appointment this week with General Hay, Secretary for Foreign Affairs. Señor Eduardo Suárez of the Department of Finance will also be present. Both are well aware that one-sixth of the national income of Mexico derives from the nation's share of oil production. Any interruption of that might be catastrophic both to the economy of Mexico and to the regime of Lázaro Cárdenas."

"The United States will not let it happen," Avila said.

"And how would they stop it señor?" said Selby Clay in his mild, reasonable way.

"They have ways," said Avila darkly. "Mexico is familiar with them. Mexico remembers how, not many years ago, the man who is now your ambassador here sent an American fleet to Veracruz. Occupied it for some time. And for far less reason than we have at issue now."

"What about you, Señor Rubio? Do you agree that a grab of our industry could bring armed intervention?" Troy asked.

Rubio shrugged his chunky shoulders.

"Only under . . . the grossest provocation. An incident of some kind. But—"

"Such incidents have come about," said Avila dourly. "They have come about with frequency."

"Gentlemen," said Troy, "Josephus Daniels isn't Secretary of the Navy now. He's a diplomat and a good one; he is not about to call in the Marines. Señor Rubio," he said, turning to the attorney, "if you come to me with any reasonable compromise my company will go along with it, but I can't and won't delegate you to represent KinOil in the current negotiations. We may have reached the point where it's every man for himself and devil takes the hindmost. And now, gentlemen," he concluded, rising, "if you'll excuse me . . . thank you both for dropping in."

3

"Son," said Troy when he had supplied Cliff with a boiled-down version of the afternoon's events, "there's nothing in God's world as arrogant as an oil company that has been making too much money in a foreign country for too long. BP and Royal Dutch and some of the other big ones have me on their shit list. They have me written down as a traitor because I won't fight for the old contracts. Well, I won't, so screw 'em."

"That'll be tough, won't it? If I know their ways . . ."

"Yup, it will be tough. But I've got one advantage they lack. I know Cárdenas is going to expropriate. They can't bring themselves to recognize that." Troy struck a kitchen match and laid it to his pipe. "I'll tell you something, son—this is between you and me. My aim is to get out of Mexico with my skin in one piece and a refund in my pocket for the equipment we're leaving behind. Just that much—but not much less. Does that make sense to you?"

"It surely does, if we can get away with it."

"Well, that's the plan."

Father and son were stretched out in comfortable canvas chairs on the porch of the VIP residence. Brandy and coffee were at hand, the lights turned low to limit insect interest and the screens reinforced with mosquito netting. Troy had changed into tropical white linen; Cliff wore flannels, an open shirt and native huaraches. With his powerful young body, his red hair and fresh skin he looked like someone minted in another world, designed for other uses than the tough, older man who sat with him, so different were they—yet linked with the family resemblances that stamped all their breed: the angle of a head; the tone, the rhythm of a phrase or a question.

Cliff was deep in thought, weighing his father's projected course of action.

"We'll still have the unions to deal with," he said slowly. "The sabotage and so forth."

"That's not the unions. It's just one more way the majors are using to make us toe the line."

Cliff looked up sharply.

"The fires and the other stuff—they're inside jobs?"

"They have to be."

"Meaning you have your suspicions."

"Boiled down to one—our host tonight."

"Christ, Dad."

"I know. It's not a nice idea."

"Well, with all respect to you I don't believe it," Cliff said flatly. "He just didn't strike me as that sort of guy."

"He doesn't strike anyone as that sort of guy. But the stakes are high, if he were open to a bribe. He's been here five years and he knows he'll never make it to the top. And he's not paid very much."

"You could always pay him more."

Troy laughed. The solutions of the young! When, in an older time, he'd made that sort of remark to his own father, Hub would have batted his ears down.

"Not now. Not even if I'm wrong. Things are moving too fast. There'll be a decision about the Cárdenas grab within sixty days, maybe less. You're going to be busy, partner. I'll have to spend a lot of time in Mexico City and for some of those negotiations I'll want you with me. When you're down here in the field you'll still be working under Selby Clay. So just keep your eyes and ears open."

Cliff stared at a yellow spot in the brown gloom—the glow of his father's pipe.

"I'll work with him," he said. "I'll try to learn the job, if that's why you want me here. But as long as he's my boss I won't spy on him. Not unless I catch him shoving a wrench through a sheavewheel guard. Or setting fire to a gas tank."

Troy—secretly approving, and amused—told his son truculently that he'd do as he was ordered. "I wired Kyle today to send us the best fire-fighting crew he could locate. Maybe those two fellas, the ones who did the job on the big blowout at Kinsalem, when you were in high school. I couldn't rightly think of their names. Might not be around anymore, the kind of work they do."

"Hell, I know their names," said Cliff promptly. "Alexander was one. Oliver was the other, wasn't he? G. E. Oliver—they called him Porky."

"You're right, by God. Ford Alexander and Porky Oliver. How could I forget that? Must be getting old."

"You're too ornery to get old," said Cliff brashly, pleased with his father's praise—if praise this was meant to be.

"They came from Taft, if I'm not mistaken."

"That's right," Cliff confirmed. "Both of them. Fearless sons of bitches. You let Helene and me come out and watch; Mom wouldn't come—she was afraid they'd burn up, I guess. Oh, I'd never forget those guys."

"I'll send Kyle another wire. I'll mention the names. Maybe he can get hold of them. These Mexicans today, they had guts all right, but they couldn't get the job done. Didn't go at it the right way. Oliver and Alexander."

And Troy, tapping out his pipe, at peace with himself and the world, now that the malaria had been scared off, thought quietly, You'll do, my young friend; you'll be all right down here. You've got an oilman's head on you.

They had dined, two hours earlier, in a highly civilized manner, for an oil-field dinner. Cliff was surprised now to find Troy suspicious of the man who had provided it.

Selby Clay's house at Chorreras was the handsomest and largest of four executive houses, all more or less similar, lining a rise above the Pánuco River. All had neat little gardens in front of them, laid out in purple squares of bougainvillea and blooming reseda, roses and calendula; to the rear were patios and porches from which one had a view of the river where it joined the Chijol Canal. To the north, behind an eight-foot chain-link enclosure, topped with barbed wire, was the company compound—tanks, rigs, storage buildings, sheds and offices; to the south the workers' villages clustered in jungle clearings—roofs of palm, plantain and oil-drum tin pounded flat, winding streets of dark-brown earth. A thoroughly pastoral scene.

Selby Clay's young wife, Justine, circling with a frosted pitcher of margaritas, saw Cliff looking down at it and stopped beside him.

"Pretty, isn't it?"

"Delightful. You must have the best back-yard view in Mexico."

"I often tell myself that. But I've been over there, and that may have spoiled it for me. It doesn't smell as nice as it looks. From here you can see the skeleton dogs on the prowl or the sick kids wrapped in rags and covered with flies."

"We're being blamed for some of that, I hear."

"Of course. And we've promised to do such wonders: the

sick leave with pay, the medic stuff and the twenty pounds of ice per family per day. The unions have been quite explicit about it all. But no one mentions that a roustabout can go there to see a girl or drink in a cantina and disappear without a sound, without a ripple. His shoes may show up on the beach and his knife next year, in the back of some *campesino*. But his bones will stay in Chorreras."

And with this Mrs. Selby Clay refilled his glass and moved away—a small, dark-haired woman with a pretty figure and a mobile, mocking mouth. That a sharp tongue lived in that mouth she proved again later when the talk returned to the inevitable subject, the endangered continuity of American and British oil leases.

"We have no chance with them."

The remark, heard in a silence, out of context, was a non sequitur, and her husband, from his end of the table, tried tactfully to get the conversation back on its tracks. He said that the table was not discussing the outcome of a horse race or a prizefight.

"We've had talks, you know—no actual confrontation. And if I have my way there'll never be one."

Justine, for her part, made no reply; she just turned to Cliff—she'd put him on her left—and pulled down the lower lid of her left eye with her forefinger.

Cliff laughed. As general talk resumed, he leaned toward her.

"I'm inclined to agree with Selby. I'm new here, I know— but haven't we always done pretty well when it came to trading?"

"Too well, too long. That's what they realize and we don't, we smart gringos. I'm *not* new here, you see; I went to the University of Mexico, in San Angel, to study mining engineering. My father's trade. I never practiced it; I got married instead. And Dad was killed in the Sangre de Cristo Mountains, bringing in a payroll. He always said he could trade hell out of a Mexican until you got to the end of the line and then you lost . . . because he knew you were at the end of the line and you didn't."

"You would have no reason to love Mexicans."

"True, but I love them. They're the most engaging, unpredictable people in the world. What I can't stand is Mexico— the land itself. It's soaked in blood. It was soaked and seeped in it for thousands of years before Cortés came ashore and introduced European styles in massacre."

"And burned his ships."

"Well, I haven't burned mine. No thank you. I don't need a country dedicated to the cult of death: skulls, skeletons, mummies, human sacrifices, bullfights—"

"Bullfights and human sacrifices are hardly the same thing."

"They are exactly the same thing. Whether bull or man dies or both the death worshipers go home satisfied with their outing. It is the national myth, the spirit of the land. And there's the Day of the Dead, November second, when the ghosts themselves come back: the hell-Christmas of the most death-oriented culture in the world. Wait and see; the oil confrontation—which is what it is, no matter what Selby says—will end in bloodshed. It's the last straw. I'm going home as soon as it's settled. And if Selby wants to stay he can feel free to."

Cliff saw his father, seated opposite, angling his head as if trying to hear Justine while he carried on his own talk on the other side. Had he turned against Selby, suspected him of disloyalty, or worse, because Selby's wife hated Mexico? Absurd—there could be no connection. Cliff wondered what the real root of dissatisfaction was: rumors circulated by Marsh Borland? Marsh was the type Troy liked and understood; Selby might be too overeducated, too oblique to suit him. But Cliff, on leaving, with the company car at the door to take him and his father up the hill, thanked his host warmly and sincerely for an interesting evening. He felt drawn to Selby, a man closer to his own generation than to Troy's—a person whose problems were not confined to the oil business.

Early that morning Troy, with chattering teeth, woke Cliff and sent him in search of blankets, hot drinks, a heating pad. Troy had come down with the attack of malaria which he had, the day before, so confidently dismissed. He lay ill for three days and nights, then on the fourth morning he got up, pale and still shaky, but purged of fever. President Cárdenas, he'd been informed by telegram from the central office, would be visiting San Luis Potosí at week's end and it was Troy's intention, well or sick, to see him. He would take Cliff with him. They left Chorreras at dawn, in the launch *Adelita*, then went on by automobile from Tampico on the riprap road recently finished through the marshes to the north. Beer, blankets, a hamper of food and a thermos of coffee were packed in. Behind them, against the pure violet sky, the blowout well burned like a gigantic, evil candle.

Carlos Mendez, Cárdenas' private secretary (he had previously served as his campaign manager), had made a suggestion about the presidential train.

"You should have an engine behind as well as in front, *mi presidente.*" Such a rear guard, he explained, would deter hostile individuals from packing a railcar with TNT and turning it loose from behind to catch the train and blow it off the tracks: a favorite guerrilla trick.

"I need no second engine," said Cárdenas. "I have no enemies."

The story, however apocryphal, was in the same vein as some recent presidential decrees. Cárdenas, for example, had ordered the National Telegraph Company to accept free of charge, for an hour a day, the messages of anyone who wished to communicate with him. A current joke had it that each day Méndez would bring in a list of what was happening in the republic, for the president's decisions.

"The peso is falling."

"Tell the treasurer."

"The crops are failing."

"Tell the minister of agriculture."

"The railroads are bankrupt."

"Tell communications."

Then Cárdenas opened a telegram which read, "My cow died, my burro died, my sow was stolen, my baby is sick.—Pedro Juan, town of Huitzlipituzco."

"Order my train at once," said the president. "I am leaving for Huitzlipituzco."

"This man," wired Frank Kluckhohn, *The New York Times* correspondent, "is the best thing that has happened to Mexicans since they shot Maximilian."

Many agreed—not all. Not the European backers of the Foreign Club, an elite gambling establishment in Mexico City. Cárdenas had turned it into an orphanage. Not the Stalinist clique. Cárdenas had given asylum to Trotsky, after seven major countries had refused him. Not the Junkers representative, Baron Hans Heinrich von Holleuffer, brother-in-law of Count Wolf von Helldorf, the Berlin police chief and a close friend of Chancellor Adolf Hitler's. Cárdenas refused to trade oil for Junkers planes.

And not, conspicuously, General Saturnino Cedillo, formerly a supporter, who had now reverted, in San Luis Potosí, to old-style revolutionary hostilities.

The long, olive train with the wide gold lettering on its cars pulled into San Luis Potosí early one morning. The plaza was full of people including widows of the revolution, amputee guitar players, unfrocked priests, disappointed agrarians, the old, the young, the crippled and the curious, with their attendant animals, plus a solid leavening of Cedillista soldiers, suppliers and camp followers. Vendors of tortillas and cactus candy and paper toys were circulating as usual and the shops were open for business—*por las buenas,* as one said, meaning nicely, as it should be one—but there were distractions. Someone had brought in the body of an unpopular official, believed to have cheated in land distribution and hanged in consequence, and strung him up again outside a shoe store (Mexico having more shoes stores per street than any other nation) with a sign on him, borrowed from an adjacent flophouse:

SUPLICAMOS QUIETUD
EN BENEFICIO DE LOS
QUE YA DESCANSAN

President Lázaro Cárdenas got off the train. Alone he walked up the street and into the plaza, the tall figure, with the sloping shoulders and barrel body, moving slowly, the red mouth slightly open under the heavy, close-trimmed mustache, the pear-shaped head tilted back, the pudgy, pale hands waving, left and right. He walked into the courthouse and sat down. There, as was his habit on such trips, he sat all day, and again the next day, listening to complaints, arbitrating disputes, having his secretaries take down lists of what was needed: a new well, a new roof for the school, the need for a proper veterinary, more beds in the hospital. And for this visit he inaugurated a startling program: he ordered forty large haciendas which had partly escaped distribution to be cut up now and handed out to applicants, first come, first served.

From that day General Cedillo's soldiers began to melt away. When later he was taken in the hills and killed there were only twelve followers with him.

Troy Kinsale and his son Cliff waited for the train at Calcas Riza, a tiny hamlet, the next stop on the line. The president was working in his office. The car, which contained his desk and its fittings, was equipped also with his private shortwave sending and receiving sets and his comfortable bedroom; in other cars were suites for his staff, the traveling kitchen, the guards' quarters, the meeting rooms. There was even a car for vehicles and a car for horses to be used for the mountain trails, the jungle tracks where gasoline engines were of no use.

The train was indeed a fine one in every respect, a modern implement by which the president could keep watch over the domain entrusted to him; he had designed it himself and spent much of his time in it. Indeed, it may have seemed to him that all his life, in a sense, had been a journey in this train, or a phantom one just like it, a trip on the endless track that led from Jiquilpán, a village like any one of thousands he had known, through the vast and shattered country, the wars, the service of the generals, each in his day—old, bearded Holy Moses Carranza, now long gone; one-armed veteran Obregón, of whom it was said that when his severed arm was found it lay palm up, twitching for a bribe; Calles, Indian-faced ex-bartender, street fighter, ruthless killer. A long *viaje*: Lázaro Cárdenas had got his first commission at eighteen when, serving as a village jailer, he liberated his solitary prisoner and ran away with him to join the revolution. His next duty had been in the oil fields. He knew much about the oil fields. He knew much about Mexico, much about men and women, little about economics. Ramón Beteta, his most trusted aide, would take care of economics. If Ramón made mistakes they would be Lázaro's mistakes. That was how one governed, accepting the mistakes as one accepted the task of trying to do for Mexico in six years what in other lands had taken two hundred.

Six years, and the curtain came down. The Constitution permitted no re-election. It was a wise restriction. Meanwhile, in this office, in the National Palace and in his house in Chapultepec there was one rule of precedence: the barefoot and ragged first.

Lázaro Cárdenas felt the long train stop. He turned from his desk, pushed up the bottom of the stiff green canvas window shade. He saw the two gringos standing by the tracks, the old, thick-shouldered one and the young one with the crest of flaming red hair and the sensitive face. Ramón, tall and elegant, was greeting them, welcoming them with the charm he used so well.

Newspapers had been put aboard the train during the night. The president rang for them. Then, while he read the papers and drank coffee, he switched on the intercom which permitted him to hear what was being said in the conference car. The *Norte Americanos*—one should not think of them as gringos—were speaking of the escalation of demands of the workers as presented to the Court of Conciliation and the other courts and reviewing boards, all the way up to the Supreme Court of Mexico.

". . . and in each case," the older gringo, no, Americano, was saying, "the arbitrating body has doubled or tripled what was originally asked: the sick pay, the death benefits, the hospital conditions, the government's share."

"That seems unfair to you, of course," said Ramón Beteta sympathetically.

But the old one said surprisingly, "Not really, Señor Beteta. The chance for escalation came because the companies refused to pay, when they referred the demands to a higher authority. They should have paid what was originally asked. Then the problem would have ended."

"Mr. Kinsale," said Ramón heartily, "I concur in your opinion. I commend you for it."

Said the old one, "Thank you, señor, but I ask no credit. KinOil, as you know, is by definition an independent oil company. We were not party to the contract drawn between the unions and the major companies, before the crisis. We operated, of course, under its terms, but I do not feel bound on that account to negotiate on a collective basis."

"I see," said Ramón Beteta quietly. His tone was both respectful and expectant. He waited, and Lázaro Cárdenas, on his intercom hookup, also listened intently, setting his coffee cup down softly in its saucer.

The younger American was saying something which did not come over the hookup—apparently a low-voiced reminder to the older one, who whispered something in return. Then to Beteta: "We are convinced, though they are not, Señor Beteta, that your president has now lost patience. That, in short, expropriation is certain. I should like, in strictest confidence, your comment on this conclusion. It is most important to our company—to the considerations which brought us to ask for this meeting."

At this request, an unusual one, there was a pause, a silence on the humming line of the intercom which endured for several beats. The president could imagine Beteta, his bony, attractive face screwed up in thought, staring at the old one with his sharp blue eyes. At length Beteta said, "I might say then that your guess is closer to the truth than theirs. Beyond that I cannot go."

Cárdenas, in his sealed compartment, brought his hands together silently, as if applauding. Well, he thought, Ramón took care of that one.

Oh, he would give Ramón hell for his indiscretion, the presumptuous young *chingado*. But not too much hell, for this, obviously, was what they had been waiting for, not only he and Ramón but the Labor Board, the Foreign Office, the Department of the Interior—the first break in the solid front of the oil companies.

These Americans had come to make a deal!

The president pushed his tray away, let the newspapers slip to the floor. He shucked off the loud silk pajamas which his wife had bought for him at Sanborns since it was not suitable for a nation's chief executive to sleep naked or sit that way at his desk, no matter what he might do at home; he put on a clean, embroidered cotton shirt in the native style, some rawhide sandals and a pair of white peon breeches of canvas, with a belt of hemp. Thus attired he padded through the train to the conference room, which he entered without knocking; he stood stiffly, his greenish eyes veiled, as Beteta, not in the least startled by his entry, introduced him to the Americans, Mr. Troy Kinsale and his son, Clifford—leasers, through the family company, of great oil fields on the Pánuco.

"*Muchísimo gusto, señores,*" said the president, and then in English: "It is no longer early, and I think none of us has eaten. Let me offer you some breakfast."

CHAPTER EIGHTEEN

Ciudad de México

1

Ford Alexander and Porky Oliver, the fire fighters from California, arrived at Chorreras by plane, launch and railcar, and were taken out to see the blaze at Boca Riza 56. They ordered tunnels to be dug, approaching the fire at a sharp, converging angle. Once more dynamite was laid in, this time at the ends of the tunnels, and the wires were run to detonators outside. The chunk of earth thus lifted and dumped onto the flames did the job for Anderson and Oliver. In a space of ten seconds Boca Riza 56 was just an evil-smelling, oozy hump in the ground.

The casing, of course, would still be there. It could be dug out and hooked into the pipeline and the twenty thousand barrels which had been burning daily would then be disciplined to flow into the tanks prepared for it, down by the Pánuco.

Staffers who had gathered to watch the taming of the blowout well went back to the KinOil field office and toasted the occasion in good brown U.S. whiskey and sour-sweet Guadalajara champagne. It was a happy day, although Troy was surprised and none too pleased to find that Frank Kluckhohn, head of *The New York Times* Bureau in Mexico City, and Betty Kirk, a large, sharp-eyed lady from *The*

427

Christian Science Monitor, had flown in to be on hand. They had come, he felt, for something more than the scheduled happening, the type of event which, if it drew attention from the press at all, would have attracted no one more important than César Torres, the plump, seedy chap who wrote weekly *Cosas de Petróleo* for *El Heraldo*.

His guess was right. He soon found himself being interviewed.

"They had me wriggling like a garden worm on a trout hook," Troy said furiously, when the company car had driven off with the reporters. "Who leaked the story?"

"What story, boss?"

Marsh Borland's seamy face showed puzzlement. He had been the only KinOil staffer present at the interview.

"You know fucking well what story."

"You went to meet a person in the government, that's all we knew."

"That could have been enough."

"They might not even have heard that much. They might just have been guessing."

"They didn't act as if they were guessing," Troy said, somewhat less truculently.

He pushed a button and spoke into the office intercom.

"Selby, could you come in here?"

"It wasn't Selby. I can tell you that right now," said Borland. "You might as well figure it was Cliff."

"It wasn't Cliff."

"I'm sure. But Cliff was with you. He knows whom you talked to, nobody else does. By the way, where is he now?"

"He went up to Mexico City. Some girl friend of his is flying in."

"Well, he'd better not talk to his girl friend," said Borland with a grin. "Women. They're the worst."

"Cliff wouldn't talk," said Troy heavily. He was in no mood for jesting.

Both men turned as Selby Clay entered, his youthful, prematurely lined face smiling and composed.

"Alexander and Oliver picked up their checks," he said. "They were delighted with the bonus. Wanted to come in and thank you personally, but you were tied up with the reporters."

"I'll say we were," said Borland.

Clay's glance moved to the formidable figure of Troy, seated behind the desk, his head lowered, his hands clasped in front of him.

If the hostility of the boss's attitude came through to him, Selby Clay managed to seem unaware of it. He's a smooth article all right, Troy thought. He could not have said why, aside from his suspicions of an information leak, the man irritated him so much—his three-piece seersucker suits, his neckties and initialed cuff links, his air of imperturbability.

"At least we got the blowoff mended," Selby said.

He picked out a chair and sat down in it.

"We did," said Troy. "A first-class job, all the way down the line—but that's not what interested our newspaper friends. They were on to something else, another activity entirely. I'm trying to pin down what they may have heard."

"Oh?" said Selby Clay.

He spoke with complete casualness, his eyes fixed on the raised toe of a handsomely boned English boot.

"They seem to think that KinOil has a deal on—that we're going to take a cash settlement to get out of Mexico."

"It's the logical solution," said Clay coolly.

"Right," said Troy. "Meanwhile, get this—if there's any chance of getting paid for what we leave here, when and if we pull out, the field must be operational. I don't want any more barbecued Indian roustabouts. I don't want any more gate valves opening without the touch of human hands."

"You were talking to the right man about it a few days ago. I thought Avila would flip when you asked him if other companies were suffering the same way we are. They're not."

"So how are they getting to us?"

Selby's glance moved from Troy to Marsh then back again.

"There's a strong-arm man around from Tamaulipas, Brolio Camba. He sent us a couple of ragged-ass *bandidos* a month ago, before you came in. They wanted a payoff. I refused."

"You did right. I know about Camba. He's a small-timer."

"Well, he gave himself a battlefield promotion; he's a general now."

Troy swung around to face Borland.

"The majors have been paying off to this bum?"

Marsh nodded.

"He's their agent on a regular retainer to work us over. Or so I heard."

"Who told you, some gal in the Bolívar?"

"The Suprema," said Marsh without expression. "I quit going to the Bolívar."

"I'd like better information than the whorehouse overnight line."

Said Borland, "Why don't we slip Camba some *mordida* and see what happens? We don't have much to lose."

Troy aimed his pipestem at Selby Clay.

"Do you go along with that?"

"To a limited amount—twenty or thirty thousand pesos, maybe. It's not a bad idea."

Troy's graying head came down over his locked, lumpy knuckles.

"I wouldn't pay twenty thousand pesos to drop Camba into a tank of hot oil—and El Zopilote with him. Ten years ago, when things were rough, we didn't give—and in those days *mordida* was a way of life. They all paid, all of them except us. Kyle and I talked it over, we decided we'd do it the hard way. We'd give top wages in the field and nothing for shakedowns. I'm not about to break that rule now that we're within a hop or two of getting out. I want you to lay on more security. Get it out of Veracruz or San Luis if you can, at least some guys with no local connections. Put guns on them. Hang more lights on the rigs and tanks; fire up at night until this place looks like a country fairgrounds. Let it be known that we're not paying . . . we're keeping this field in full operation unless and until the time comes when we decide to leave."

The docket of defensive orders, easy enough to carry out in California, difficult or impossible in Tampico, ended at length; when Selby had left the room Troy said reflectively, "Was I too rough with him?"

"Maybe I like him better than you do."

"He just doesn't smell right to me. That offhand air of his."

"I know. But he's been in there; he's been trying."

"That wife of his."

"Oh, yes."

"She's not a happy lady. She hates Mexico."

"She just hates Chorreras."

"When a lady wants to move, her husband automatically steps into a danger area. You start wondering if you can still trust him. Why didn't he tell me about Camba sooner?"

"I could have told you about Camba. I guess neither one of us thought it was important, not until I picked up that scuttle in the Suprema."

"You better stay out of the Suprema."

"Whatever you say."

"I mean it. The chips are down now, and I want you where nothing can happen to you. I'm going up to the Ciudad tomorrow and stay until *El Presidente* has some papers ready for me to sign."

2

With a crash like a brass concert chord, the daily 4 P.M. rain slammed onto the tin-and-tile roof of the airport. Cliff, standing behind an iron girder, saw the three *señores* come in from the ramp where they had left their limousine, all three in dark suits and white shirts, gray or black ties, *muy correcto*, the one in the striped pants obviously in charge. Raindrops beaded his shoulders and stuck like tears to his oiled black hair. He lit a cigarette.

A flash of lightning glazed the tarmac where United's flight from Los Angeles had just set down, an hour and twenty minutes late.

Cliff had been early. The telegram, relayed over the Western Union tie line to KinOil's Chorreras headquarters, had said to meet her "if you can," and had given the date, time and flight number. "Love," she had said. Well, all right, but the photographers had been there ahead of him and even farther ahead of the reception committee in the dark suits.

Striped Pants was now intently watching the deplaning passengers. In the huge vault of the airport, smelling of urine, burned gasoline and the wild, clean rain, a pariah dog with crippled hindquarters slunk past and a wasted child with an angelic face stood before Cliff, selling camellias on a tray.

"No, gracias, chica."

The child calmly handed him a flower. It had a large, rusted pin through it.

"Para su novia, señor."

He bought the flower. It would be idiotic, of course, to walk up to Carrie, to kiss her, embrace her, with a half-dead, soiled camillia in his hand, possibly ripping her at the same time with the stiletto-sized pin, yet . . . yet perhaps it was just the thing to do. Excitement filled him. Carrie had arrived. She was already here, less than a hundred feet away, though as yet he couldn't see her. He took a few steps from behind his girder, tossing into a trash can the newspapers he has passed the time reading.

Excelsior had Carrie's picture on the front page, one of the gallery shots he'd seen at the studio the day of their first date.

La simpatiquísima y encantadora Carrie Drew, *notable artista del cine, ahora se encuentra entre nosotros. Pronto habremos de verla en una película sensational, EL MAS BAJO PIERDE, en el teatro METROPOLITAN.*

Battered by the torrents, holding coats over their heads, the last passengers staggered down the ramp. A tall girl in a traveling suit of black, gray and orange, with a huge three-cornered hat, waved to somebody and a flashbulb winked, coinciding with another burst of lightning. Carrie! Cliff turned up his collar. He rushed forward but—*chingar,* Striped Pants was there ahead of him. Striped Pants was kissing her hand, pressing into her arms a bouquet of long-stemmed roses, big enough for a Derby winner, which till then had been invisible. Striped Pants took her arm, stood with her for another picture, that asshole.

A porter pushing a dolly laden with some very impressive luggage sloshed in out of the rain and headed for the vehicle ramp.

Carrie had seen him at last. She was waving again, this time—there could be no doubt about it—specifically at him. Not only waving—she was pointing to the porter, making signs, largely intranslatable, but Cliff got the idea: he was to head off the luggage. The photographers were leaving. Carrie walked in with Striped Pants and his two flankers. She seemed to be explaining something which required emphatic gestures, affording Striped Pants little pleasure: very decorously, very much a man of large affairs, conscious of the importance of his mission with the *artista encantadora,* he gave way. The flankers shook hands, Striped Pants shook hands, ventured— a sophisticate in the protocol of public welcomes—a kiss on the cheek. Then he and black suits retreated, made their exit to the big blue car visible through the windows, streaming with water.

"Hello, darling," said Carrie. "Were you waiting long? I'm so sorry."

"Not long at all," said Cliff.

The porter had waited. Carrie handed him the winner's

circle bunch of superb roses. Then she was in Cliff's arms, her lips on his. The porter, with Latin courtesy, looked away as they embraced stiffly, self-consciously, once more strangers. Could that happen in—how long was it?—less than three weeks? She was pale; she was taller, hideously remote—she didn't even look like the same Carrie with the long, tanned legs and the burnished hair, the person he had driven back to the walk-up apartment in Westwood after their weekend at Kyle's.

She took the roses from the porter. She dropped them, ribbons and all, into the same receptacle where Cliff had tossed the papers announcing her arrival.

"What's that?"

"Compliments of United Artists."

She had noticed for the first time the camellia with its soiled, drooping petals.

"Welcome to Mexico."

"Wonderful. I love camellias."

Heedless of danger, she jammed the lethal pin through the blouse of her multicolored, flamboyantly cut traveling suit— the sort of suit a person of her type and taste should not, Cliff thought, be caught dead in: the suit, by Jesus, of a star!

With a radiant, assured look, more like the real Carrie he remembered, she took his arm and matched her steps to his. A blink of harsh light brought them up; one of the photographers had evidently stuck around. Cliff turned angrily, but the offender, a tiny, shabby person in a raincoat and visored cap, was already halfway out the door with his exclusive.

"Pay no attention," Carrie said. "That's how they make their living. Do you have a car?"

He had a car, indeed he had: one of the chartered limousines which KinOil kept on call in every city where the company maintained major offices, a car fully the equal of, if not better than, that of the United Artists deputation which had been so unceremoniously shuffled off. With the Louis Vuitton luggage locked in the trunk and the Lilly Daché hatbox riding up front with the driver, Cliff and Carrie settled in the deep cushions of the back seat—holding hands, to be sure, kissing now and then, to be sure, but undergoing as it were a decompression period, each recuperating from separate perils, secret distractions.

Carrie explained the coup by which she had arranged her Mexican trip. She had agreed—although no such requirement was in her new contract—to visit a number of U.S. cities for personal appearances on condition that the company throw in a gala opening in Mexico City.

"They've only done that three or four times in the last ten years, and then for pictures that had some special Latin appeal. But they're doing it for *Low Man Out*. How's that?"

"A beautiful idea."

"It's our opening, yours and mine. Even if we're the only people in the theater, which we may very well be for all anybody ever heard of me in Mexico City."

"Leave it to the fellow in the striped pants. He'll have a crowd as if Dolores Del Rio and Cantinflas were playing a double bill. By the way, I checked your reservations. They put you at the Reforma. It's a good hotel but not for us. Not if we want to be a little private."

"So, where are we going? I'm sure you have a place picked out."

"I do. Don't worry about it."

The hotel Cliff had selected, for use during those hours when Carrie would not be on public display, was the Geneve, on the Avenida Londres, a small, spick-and-span hostelry which catered to what was left of the Mexican elite, to family visitors from South America and to the overflow personnel from various European embassies. You could converse in English with the maître d'hôtel, the desk clerks or the head porter—otherwise, French, Portuguese or even German would serve you adequately. The cocktail bar was a tangled jungle where tropical plants, separating the booths, had proliferated into an impenetrable maze, offering easier passage to a machete than a cocktail shaker, and where the barmen had been trained to distinguish between the drink requests of the guests and the parody screams of the parrots and mynas, concealed in ferny cages, satirizing the accents of the patrons. Carrie and Cliff shared a pitcher of margaritas, after which, upstairs, in the suite which consisted of a bedroom registered in his name, another bedroom registered in her name, and a living room registered in nobody's name, she opened the Louis Vuitton bags, dumping their contents on the floor, the chairs, the tables, and the carpet—a tweed-and-ermine suit by Schiaparelli, straight, clinging couture dresses made by Chanel and Mainbocher which closed and opened by the back or the side with a new kind of instant fastener called a "zip," never used before. There were draped and folded silk jerseys by Balenciaga and by the smashing, yet still Establishment couturier Vionnet, who dressed Madame

Martinez de Hoz, the arbitress of world couture. There was also an enormous flask of perfume from Marcel Rochas which Carrie instructed Cliff to put out in the hall for the chambermaid to take away—"Because it's not my kind of smell and will stink everything up. I can't convince those idiots at the studio that I can't and won't use perfume. Why should they care? Nothing smells on the screen except bad dialogue."

"At least you won't suffer from that. But how about the rest of this stuff, was it all for free?"

"Not a dime's worth—not even the phony jewels from Dufy. Dali designed them—yes, dear Salvador, the ex-lover of your ex-friend Madame Cape, as who hasn't been? Half of all this is on loan, rushed over after being worn in the spring Paris shows by sweaty mannequins and the rest deducted from my future salary. I'd love to wear leather pants, boots and spurs to the grand opening here—after all, *Low Man* is a western, isn't it? But wait—I have to show you all my new stills. We can paper the walls with them."

And from an Hermès pigskin portfolio she spread out for him a stunning sweep of theatrical studies by Steichen, Hoyningen-Huene, Horst, Man Ray and Cecil Beaton. All the photographs differed widely in style, but each photographer, with his individual response to her beauty, had caught her essential quality—dramatically, ineradicably American; that above all . . .

Cliff had phoned down for more margaritas, also for hot coffee, rolls, chicken sandwiches: he was dying of hunger himself and was sure Carrie must feel the same. To his surprise she paid little attention to the food. She was busy taking off her clothes—her multicolored "film star" outfit—to model this or that masterpiece of her new wardrobe, even if only by holding it up, smoothing it against her creamy skin, and for this purpose, when skin was necessary, she shed underthings as well, until she was standing naked. One of her new treasures, which she seemed to regard as a huge joke, was an eerie "uplift bra" of a sort Cliff had never imagined, much less seen—hell, the damn thing had a piece of wire in it! Wire, as if for a cattle fence—as if Carrie's lovely breasts, with the nipples which seemed to point ever so slightly out to the side, instead of straight at you, couldn't have held up a real fence by the sheer strength of their curves.

"Darling, you'll never believe this, but Howard Hughes designed this contraption—the same man whose company rents drill bits to your dad."

"He must be a pervert."

"Not necessarily. He just likes women's breasts."

"I do too, but I'll take them in the natural state."

"You mean like this?"

And stooping over the big chair in which he was sprawled, watching the one-woman fashion show which had seemed to go on unendingly, she seized one of her breasts in both her hands and pushed it into his mouth as hard as she could, then pulled it out and repeated the performance with the other breast. Both nipples were soon fiery red. They jutted out like small, tough rods. Cliff licked them and bit them. She moaned as he pinched them, squeezing them hard between thumb and forefinger. He well knew her tastes with respect to such treatment—she had, more than most women, a masochistic satisfaction in having her breasts tormented, especially when she had provoked the performance herself—but when he tried to pull her down into his lap she resisted, at first playfully, then half angrily, jamming a strong white knee into his groin until he let go of her.

"Christ, what's the matter?"

"I haven't had my bath."

"Baths are for later."

He had his cock out, giving it a rub or two himself both to provoke her voyeurism and to restore the engorgement which the whack with her knee had cut down. She pushed his hand away, replacing it with her own. Mesmerized, she ran her own fingers lightly up and down the shaft, then squeezed. A single drop of moisture oozed out of the red tip, above the veins which were now standing out as if they would burst. She bent down and licked off the drop, then went back to rubbing him as if his tool were some kind of toy. At the same time she studied him suspiciously.

"It's bigger than it used to be."

"You've forgotten, that's all."

"I haven't forgotten anything, not the slightest thing that ever happened," she said fiercely, her long, strong fingers, which looked thin against his swollen penis, never stopping their hard, sliding pulse. "Have you been fucking someone else?"

"Hell, no."

"Because if you have, I'll kill her."

"You're nuts!"

"I mean it."

"Christ, I haven't even played with myself."

"Well, I've played with *myself*, every day. Sometimes oftener."

"Shut up, Carrie."

He'd always suspected—been sure in fact, though for no reason that he could have proved—that she, his true love, masturbated. He had learned this from previous instructresses, highly informed sources, all. Yes, indeed, they did it, all of them, the sexy ones—and what good were the others, if there were any such?—they did it in devious ways, which sometimes they would talk about and sometimes not, they did it with or without artificial aids. It didn't matter; one accepted it. The notion, in fact, could even be exciting, stimulating to himself, a male; yet at this moment, in his wild desire for Carrie, the idea was divisive, it had no place in the scene.

He grabbed her buttocks, pulling her off the floor, intending to carry her over to the great, old-fashioned, canopied bed, to get inside her, but her own thoughts worked ahead of his; she sprang up, scissoring her legs around his belly, trying to reach down with her hand, to take hold of him and get him in her cunt—an awkward project.

They stood there locked helplessly, heavily together; they swayed, staggered. As she forced herself lower on him, almost tripping him, they collapsed onto the bed, supported at last by the blessings of mattresses, springs, sheets, but Carrie still insisting on sexual dominance, playing with him, flirting with him, as it might be called, more than even Ilona had ever done, or Dede at the height of her erotic fancies. Carrie turned him on his back, spread herself with her fingers so that, astride him, she slid up and down, his cock against her clitoris—this itself no maidenly little bulb now but a wet, solid chunk of feverish flesh, red and inflamed.

Straddling and rubbing this secret place on him, her vaginal lips open, she worked up his body, inch by inch, up to his face, touching his extended, slavering tongue, then pulling away, then rubbing herself on it, on his mouth, lightly, then in a fury, a passion that dumped out vaginal fluid in a Niagara, a spout with more than a few squirts of wine inextricably mixed with it. And even while she was still coming, knowing that his time was ripe, that one more instant of fooling around would spoil it, she moved down, twisted onto her back, pulled him in to screw her in hard, fast strokes which seemed as if they would never stop.

Throughout these acrobatics neither of them had spoken nor had there been any sounds other than the delicious ones of the sucking and fucking. She wiped his face off with the pillowcase and herself, between the legs, with the sheet.

"Oh, that was nice," she said, and lapsed instantly, silently into deep sleep, her face as pure as a newly consecrated nun's.

They stayed in the Hotel Geneve ten days, which comprised most of Carrie's allotted time in Mexico City; during this period they made love often—daily, in fact, with the rare exceptions when Carrie had become too tired by her public activities to be interested—and the physical side of their love had never been as wonderful, as rewarding to Cliff—and he was sure to her also—in satisfaction, inventiveness and pleasure. Yet there was something lacking, some quality, so frail and far away that it could hardly be brought to mind, though it had once been there, been stronger, thrilling—a reality very much a part of their lives, of their happiness in the early days in the Westwood apartment, the days when they'd gone to the ball games, when he'd been sent out to walk Trey along the quiet, leafy streets, when they had played hooky from studio appointments, raided cheap restaurants for dreadful food, swum at twilight on chilly beaches, argued about books and people or just lay on the couch, holding hands. It took Cliff a long time to figure out what was different now, what was gone, if anything—or was he just making this up, wasn't their closeness, the whole captivating game still really the same, only better, richer, more exciting, more perfect? It took him a long time and when he did figure it out he pushed the answer to the back of his mind. There were many explanations for it, for so slight a matter—actually one that could change in an instant, and was of no real consequence anyway, though its absence, once it was clear, bothered him somewhat. Their love now had a different tempo, as if some factory rheostat had taken it over and speeded it up and in that speed had been lost—despite passion and closeness—whatever had been there before. They now had a love that was better than ever but it was a love without contentment.

Contentment, for Christ's sweet sake. And what was that, might one ask. Was it a ticket to the bullfights, was it a diamond ring or a piece of candy that you'd dropped in the street, so that you had to go scouring around for it? They had this ten days—not *his* ten days, Carrie's ten days—she was the one who'd arranged them, paid a price for them, brought off this dazzling coup to bring them together. The tenderness was there; it just wasn't sticking out all over as it had been, and beside which . . . well, beside which the Girl-Next-Door identity and all that crap might indeed be just his own devising, out of some childish need. If you were coming two or three times a day as hard as you could, in one way or another, with a beautiful girl you were mad about, and who was demonstrably mad about you, then you were sure as hell getting some contentment somewhere along the line. There were also nights when it was there, when it would take hold of them just as in what he now thought of as the Early Days. There were times when she didn't have to go to a filming or a newspaper or radio interview or a reception or some other public function (always with himself, of course, her loyal escort, tagging along as anonymously as possible, by mutual arrangement, since from the point of view of the guys in the striped pants it was obviously contraindicated for the *artista encantadora* to appear immediately with a conspicuous lover, particularly, a large, young American oilman with a famous name). Much, much better, for the studio, to have her a public virgin, no matter what she might be in private—at least until after the premiere.

Only an idiot would fail to understand that.

Cliff, being by no means an idiot, cooperated as much as he could despite news leaks now and then: syndicated gossip notes from wire-service stringers and random flash shots like the one the sneaky Joe with the Graflex had grabbed as they were leaving the airport.

There were the nights and the afternoons of magic and privacy—sometimes whole days which belonged to them alone, when they could eat, unrecognized, in the good German restaurant, Belinghausen, almost across the street from the hotel, or one of their other favorites, Prendes, downtown, or the old, excellent Café Suizo, or Boca del Rio, with its enormous bar and sawdust floor, where fresh fish and seafood were hauled in by truckload daily, none of it to be cooked—for no cooking was allowed at the Boca del Rio—but where you could stand at the bar and stuff yourself on Guaymas shrimp and delicious pink clams and all sorts of ceviches. After eating, if a walk was on your mind, you could stroll arm in arm along streets named for poets or great cities; you could visit Chapultepec or rent a boat and drift around on Lake Xochilmilco. Not too many such nights or days but enough. Then it would be back: the easiness, the sense of belonging to each other that he'd never had with any other woman, the feeling that had made him think very deeply and seriously about his life with Carrie and what should be done about it.

There was also, of course, the formality of introducing her to his father.

Troy was staying at the Ritz, which he liked because it was the Ritz, and also because his friend Juan Belmonte stayed there. But this time he was not drinking at the bar with bullfighters, had any been available. He was much on the move and also at some pains to keep the scope of his activities in low profile.

It spoke well for the quality of the security with which Cárdenas (who walked abroad so boldly!) had privately surrounded himself that not one hint of the current negotiations or even of the boarding of the train by the two Americans at a lonely whistle stop, shortly after dawn one recent morning, had appeared in the press.

There was talk, to be sure. But then, there was always talk. . . .

Troy and Cliff chatted on the telephone daily. They made a lunch date, for which Carrie got all dressed up—Christ, Cliff thought, if she would only go back to saddle shoes and sweaters, how much clearer Troy would see her!—but Troy had to break the date. He didn't meet Carrie till the night of her triumph—the grand opening of *Low Man Out* at the Cine Metropolitan.

The men in the striped pants did a superb job. They designed the occasion in the best Hollywood style of the era, a manner and a cachet internationally recognized long before the term "art deco" had been coined.

Sid Grauman, at his peak, could not have done it better at

the Chinese or the Pantages. Hundred-food beams from studio sun arcs, powered by portable generators, slashed at one another above Calle 16 Septiembre while fans in improvised bleachers cheered the arrival of people in evening dress, easily imagined to be celebrities (several of them actually were) as they sashayed across strips of dusty red carpet to say a few words on the loudspeaker. Mariachis played in the lobby, and as the houselights dimmed, a large percentage of the audience (provided with free tickets and carefully drilled) applauded as Ilona Cape's and George Brent's names, with which they were familiar, and Carrie Drew's, which they had been told about, segued onto the screen.

Spanish subtitles had been provided for those whose English was not up to the demands of western argot, including many, one assumed, whose native tongue *was* English. Everyone loved the picture, and the local critics, who had seen it that afternoon at a private screening, were gratified to feel that the glowing terms in which they had prematurely adorned it would not make them seem ridiculous when they appeared in print the next day. How could you go wrong with a western, anyway? The favorite screen character of Latin America of that year, in many audience polls, was Gilbert Rowland as the Cisco Kid.

Later there was a party at El Patio, for the guests who counted. El Patio was the best cabaret in Mexico City and the most expensive. It was one of the few places of elite entertainment which *El Presidente* had not turned into a charitable institution of some sort. He knew, even though the knowledge was not to his taste, that the rich had to have some place to spend their money. The rich were always with you, like the generals—the latter often qualifying under both terms.

There were also the unions. These were run by Señor Toledano, who usually avoided public appearances at events sponsored by foreigners, particularly gringos. He had, nevertheless, turned out for the United Artists party. The significance of this was not lost on those members of the oil community who also attended, nor on the press.

Lombardo Toledano was a slender, wiry man with a small, gaunt face which somehow suggested a high degree of suppressed violence. He looked and at times behaved a good deal like Paul Joseph Goebbels of Germany, then also much in the news. His presence at the party meant that if it was true, as rumored, that a deal was in the making between

KinOil and Cárdenas, it would have labor's blessing. Any resistance still at hand would come, not from him or even El Zopilote, but from the oil companies themselves.

Troy watched the union boss as he moved around the stylized, festive room, never staying long in one place but pausing here for a handshake, waving there to someone across the room, moving aside for a short talk at the bar or the acceptance of a glass which he would later put down untasted—always on the go, covering a specified piece of territory.

One such area was Troy's table—an unexpected visit. Troy felt a touch on his arm—and there was the spindly body next to his chair, the intense, veiled eyes looked into his.

"Señor Kinsale! I am enjoying your fiesta."

"Ah, Señor Toledano. I'm afraid the party is not mine, but it was kind of you to come."

Cliff and Selby Clay, who had flown up with his wife for the opening, had got to their feet, and Troy performed the introductions. Toledano bent over Carrie's hand with a grace not learned in labor halls.

"My congratulations. Our newest, our most brilliant star!"

Then he was gone, dissolving into the general scene. Later he sat down with Diego Rivera and a beautiful red-haired woman—perhaps his date, perhaps Rivera's—at a table specially placed for them at the edge of the dance floor. He stayed until the lights went down and a cast of dancers in ancient feathered costumes performed foclórico numbers which brought down the house. When the lights came up again his chair was empty. But the deal, Troy thought—the deal is solid now.

To Cliff, who drank more than he should have that evening, the event passed in a hazy, happy blur.

He had enjoyed the premiere. It had had style, and *Low Man Out* seemed better with subtitles. You could still hear the dialogue, of course, but the Spanish words somehow made it scan better. The press-pass section of the audience, from its seats on the side, clapped vociferously for Carrie's smallest scenes, which made her furious—"How idiotic! And how phony! I'm going to leave." . . . but she didn't leave. And Cliff didn't mind the applause. It was . . . Latin, *simpático* . . .

The party was still going full blast. Cliff ordered more margaritas but found that he had been left to drink them himself: Justine Clay was dancing with her husband, looking quite as if they belonged together, while near them, slowly circling the room, Troy Kinsale led Carrie Drew through a 1924-Altemira-California version of the fox-trot, his bone-colored head on a level with her burnished, blazy brown one, his seamy face wreathed in smiles.

It was a wonderful evening, a triumph for all concerned, but yet . . . but yet, across the mountains, beyond some pieces of jungle, some chunks of malaria-ridden, crocodile-infested swamps, there beside a sea terminal filled with tank ships were the oil fields where the lights on the rigs burned all night and the security guards patrolled and the membrane between raw violence and this elegance and ease, visible on every hand tonight, the skin between life and death, as Justine Clay had once observed, was thinner than in other places. Cliff wished devoutly that he could be somewhere else, that Troy could be somewhere else and the whole bitter business settled. He wished that they weren't both fated and dedicated to the rules of the game which prescribed that they stay on for five or ten more million. What difference did it make? He would hang in there. He had been born and bred and schooled to hang in there and get what was coming, what was due or could be itemized, inventoried, demanded and paid as proper whether due or not; he would do his part . . . but he could hardly wait for the moment to pick up his chips and walk away from the table—walk away, then run, rush to plunge himself into a different way of spending his strength and his purpose, of engaging in a different kind of life altogether, and one which promised so much more reward for body and soul and—who could tell?—perhaps for Carrie's body and soul as well.

4

Cliff and Carrie had now been at the Geneve eight days. There were two days left. That had been the time agreed on both with the striped-pants group in Mexico City and the heavyweight decision makers up north. There were other things for her to do. She had suddenly become that most fascinating of acquirements in the ratings of a motion-picture company's assets—"a property"—a generic term that applied about equal weight to a piece of real estate, a book, a play, an additional technical process or a human being.

Carrie's apprenticeship had made her aware of the significance of being a property. She had adjusted to the idea. She did not hold it lightly but she understood that its force was more than rhetorical. Its gravitational authority was set forth in legal language in a multipage covenant which she had signed, being well apprised of everything in it, the small print as well as the large, and which, if its specified option periods ran their full length, as no doubt they would, she would have to abide by for the next seven years. Even at the age of twenty-two, seven years could be seen to be a formidable portion of a person's lifetime. Carrie was aware of this too. She was determined that being a property would not also prevent her from being a person, a transformation she had seen happen to other properties, and she had acted accordingly; with the help of a sympathetic and powerful agent she had seen to it that the covenant contained certain clauses with respect to her rights as a human being, certain escape hatches out of which she could from time to time emerge and shed the accoutrements of being a property and go back to being herself and doing whatever she wanted to do.

She tried to explain all this to Cliff. She was not sure, from what followed, that he understood, but she really tried. She did it on the next to the last night they were at the Geneve, after they'd dined at Belinghausen and were walking in the fall dusk of the Colonia Azurez. The last two days had been very nice—perfect, in fact. Carrie had no more interviews to submit to, and the easy feeling of the Westwood days had revived as if it had never been interrupted—those days when the preview cards from The Forum had glinted in their minds more like the candles on a birthday cake than the edicts of an unseen, all-powerful senate, commanding them to a new way of life.

"Darling," said Carrie on this night, "I know it's silly, but I have to tell you something. I haven't mentioned it before, but I've been thinking about it a lot. I have the right to do a play. It's in my contract."

"Fine," said Cliff, "what's wrong with that?"

"There's nothing wrong with it," said Carrie. "That is, it's rather nice. I've only done one good play, and I had a tiny part. I think I could do a real part now and I might be all right."

The subject of plays had come up before, Carrie expressing her preference for them vis-à-vis a motion picture and Cliff in general concurring, without paying much attention. Nor was he paying much attention now.

"Why, I think you'd be great, honey. You'd knock 'em dead. Why not?"

He paused in the green shadow of a jacaranda tree to kiss her lightly on the lips, but though she responded, Carrie was not to be interrupted.

"Well, I do feel I would be all right, and it's a lovely play. Jed Harris is producing it. He's probably the best producer in New York. He takes chances and he does wonderful things. He got in touch with Leland. Can you imagine that? The lead! I'd have to read for him, of course. I'd have to do that right away, as soon as I got back. That was one thing I wanted to talk to you about. I don't think you understand about plays. They're different from pictures."

"So what else?"

"Separations. I would have to sign on for the run of the play. That's what they call it. It could be just wonderful or it could be perfectly awful. Nobody has a clue."

"You mean the play could flop?"

"It could, yes. There's no way to tell. It could be a rehearsal in Hartford, then a week's tryout in Boston or Philadelphia and two weeks in New York and a closing notice—goodbye, you dear people, I'll see you all later. I'd still have my Hollywood contract, and Hollywood actresses—of which I'm not yet really a certified, blue-ribbon one by any means—are proverbially supposed to bomb out in the theater. I'd go back to California and everyone would forget the whole thing. But remember—the play could be a hit. It could run for two years. That's not usual, but it happens. With Jed's—Mr. Harris'—plays it happens quite a lot. And *after* New York there are road companies. My contract has something in it about road companies. Usually with a hit play a star has to do at least one road company, so there goes another six months. So, when would I see you?"

"In between, I guess."

"In between what? Six evening performances a week, plus two matinees, plus interviews and stuff. You tell me about the in betweens."

They strolled on, still arm in arm, to the end of the Calle

Edgar Allan Poe. Good ole Poe, not to be forgotten, and above all now:

> *Thou wouldst be loved? Then let thy heart*
> *From its present path part not . . .*

"You do want to do the play, though," he said. "You want to do it a hell of a lot. Am I right?"

"It's a lovely play."

"So how can I decide for you? What do I know about plays?"

"You know about us," said Carrie in a low voice. "I'll do whatever you say. And whatever you say to do I'll love it."

"Well, now, there's a proposition," said Cliff slowly.

They turned away from Calle Edgar Allan Poe. "I can't decide for you," said Cliff at length. "You know that."

He spoke firmly, although at this point, in possession of all the facts, the problem that had seemed no problem at all when first mentioned now thoroughly confused him.

"I've been worrying about it," she said in a hardly audible voice.

Cliff squeezed her arm. "Nothing to worry about," he said gallantly. "After all, you're an actress."

"That's part of it."

And Cliff, peering at her with his flashing, tender eyes, in the shift of shadows, said, "What else is there?"

"You and me—that's what else. That's the only *real* part."

"We'll be all right."

They walked on again. Carrie said, "There *is* one thing that might work for us, outside of our loving each other and all that. Some men would hate what I do—my career, quote unquote. How I detest that term! But you *like* my being an actress. That's why I'm even considering this play."

"I think I could start *not* liking it. I may be starting right now."

"Oh, no, you're not. You couldn't love an ordinary kind of woman. I don't mean I'm bragging—do I sound as if I was bragging?"

"Not yet."

"Darling, this is the truth and we both know it. You have to have a special kind of girl. If I wasn't an actress or at least *something* special you never would have given me a second look. Maybe not even a first look. I *am* an actress and you like it and you want me to be the best actress I can be. That's why it may be all right for me to do the play—if you say so."

"Well, I haven't said so," Cliff said harshly, suddenly annoyed. What did she mean she had to be a *special* person? She was putting him into some kind of class or category—limited as to choice of mates or playmates.

"Then I'll turn it down," said Carrie decisively.

"Of course you won't turn it down. We'll manage somehow."

An older couple, walking arm in arm, passed them in the opposite direction, and Carrie and Cliff stood aside for them. And in the enforced pause thus created, a lump formed in Cliff's throat and in the lump a toad took shape and jumped out of his mouth—mottled body and side-bulging eyes and all. Cliff did not recognize the nature of the creature though he would wish later he had kept it within him. But there it was, right out in plain sight in all its lumpiness and ugliness.

"I think we will," he said. "I think we'd have to. *Even if we were married* these situations would come up. We'd deal with them. You go ahead and tell Harris you'll do it. Let's forget about him."

"All right, dear," said Carrie.

The toad, it appeared, had been that clause—*"even if we were married . . ."* This was not defined until the following afternoon, not until the critical hour when he was driving her to the airport, she back once more in star's accoutrements—a trench coat from Fenwick's made of silver lamé and Ferragamo handmade shoes with wedge-shaped soles, the first ever seen, although by no means the last, the Vuitton luggage and the Daché hatbox all in place again—and refusing to let him get out of the car at the airport in the goodbye rain which, like the welcome rain ten days earlier, had arrived exactly on schedule. Carrie had wept all the way to the airport—not at all because they were parting temporarily. She had wept because of those words he'd used—that evil clause, *"even if we were married . . ."*

A toad! A toad if ever there was one because, as she explained it, she had felt privately *that they were, in effect, married;* she had never felt otherwise, or at least not since coming to Mexico.

Somehow, she had assumed, she had concluded, crazy as it was—and she was most emphatic, most reasonable in asserting that it *had* been crazy, idiotic—that he felt the same way.

Well, he hadn't—he didn't. She had given him power over their joint destinies, and his power, for good or evil, she could not now rescind. He had told her to do the play so she would do it, much as she loved him, and they would both abide by the outcome. She kissed tragically, but without passion, her lips salty with tears. They sat desperately, silently in the big car while she repaired her makeup.

Striped Pants and his two aides, *muy correcto,* were waiting in the lobby. One of them, carrying a large umbrella, escorted her to the boarding platform.

That walk on the Calle Edgar Allan Poe seemed suddenly a long time ago.

Cliff didn't wait to see the DC–3 take off. If Carrie had to do a play she had to do a play.

They would make it work. They would make it work no matter what she did.

That same day he got out of the Geneve and moved in with Troy at the Ritz.

5

Cliff knew what had happened to him. He had been taken over the hurdles. That was what had happened. He had been made to leap, willy-nilly, through fiery hoops like a circus horse, laying back his ears, closing his eyes, seared—no matter how high he leaped—with sizzling flames of emotion, entirely new to him.

Oh, he did not accuse Carrie. The game she had played had been impromptu, he was sure of that. It generated from no venal strategies like the wiles of Ilona.

Carrie was a different sort of woman. Carrie was real. Their love was real. Women, naturally, were up to all kinds of tricks, but Carrie's moves were basic, instinctual.

While not given by nature to prolonged sessions of introspection, Cliff could now see clearly the true meaning of the conversation on the Calle Edgar Allan Poe. While they strolled and chatted Carrie had been asking—no, demanding —a judgment from him but precisely, as he saw it now, the opposite of the decision she had seemed to require. Without a whisper, without a sign of her true desires in the matter, she had been inviting him, begging him, if the truth were known, to forbid her to do the play.

That was the proposition she had laid before him, slightly disguised. Had he been too stupid to realize it? Had he pulled back at the last fateful moment because of some instinct of his own, his reluctance to take over her life, as it were—to hand down a suggestion that would make him forever responsible for *whatever came next*, in short, for the whole future, *their* future?

"A play? For Christ sake, no, darling, forget it. Why, it's absurd. Two years of this and that, and directors and matinees and separations? Tell them you're sorry. Impossible!"

Those were to have been his lines. By them, or some far less forceful, less dramatic speech, he could have swung the whole bloody turn his way. Only thus could he have lived up to the secret inner commitment on her part, finally exposed with such torrents of tears, that she felt "as if we were already married . . ."

Crap! He was not buying that at all. She had no right to ask him to take over. He was not ready for that yet. He might never be. The very thought of it gave him the shivers.

She had become an actress on her own. He'd had nothing to do with that. She'd tried out her wings and by some wild coincidence, a thousand-to-one chance, she had soared straight to the top. Well, let her perch there a while. Let her breathe the rarefied air up there, he would breathe his own kind of air. Then they would find some point where the two climates mixed, where both could survive and their love flourish.

She didn't have to be a stage actress. What was wrong with making movies? A movie took six or seven, at the most ten, weeks, with many days and every evening off: a manageable schedule, even for two people in love. Far, far from the mad hysteria of a play, as she had defined it.

At least, with her gone, he could get back to his normal activities. He plunged into the crisis of the KinOil company's exodus from Mexico.

Cliff made himself as useful as he could. He kept in touch with Chorreras by telephone and found himself, in the capacity of a secret courier, constantly traveling back and forth between the *Ciudad* and the Pánuco field by company plane. But even while occupied with all this he was by no means his usual, carefree self. Certain phrases that Carrie had used kept coming back to him, though he had cared little for them, finding them puzzling, also possibly untrue, at the time they were uttered.

"You couldn't love an ordinary kind of woman. . . ."

What a thing to say! Fiendish—especially coming from a woman who was not only beautiful and intelligent and loving but who could see into your soul!

"If I wasn't an actress . . . you never would have given me a second look. . . ."

Yet . . . yet she had not said it meanly—not at all! Not even as if she resented it, rather as if she accepted it as an ordinary fact, one familiar to both of them and easily lived with. Could it be that what made it so hateful was . . . a certain disgusting content of truth?

There were times, looking back, when he tested that truth, bringing the past before his eyes with special focus on the women in it.

Take Dede Atlass, for instance. Dede had been by no means his first girl, but certainly the first who had deeply appealed to him. Dede! He had quite fond memories of her. Surely she had been no beaut—somewhat of a rag of skin and bone, yet so charming, such a great lay, and above all so much fun. She'd had all those assets but also one other: she had been the mistress of not only one but several rich and famous men. She had not been at all the type who would condescend to date a college boy: regarded in that frame of reference she had certainly been "special," in the terms of Carrie's definition. You had to grant her that.

But suppose one left Dede. Should one then pass on to Ilona Cape?

Well, the less said about Ilona the better, with her constant need for large, impossible sums of money for new films— Ilona with her fading reputation, her seedy Brigadier and her dead ex-husband with the crunched-in skull. But Ilona—yes, Ilona rated the definition "special" all right.

Carrie had scored there again. Not that he'd let her get away with it. He wouldn't. He'd confront her with it, make her see how far his feelings for these vanished, scrubbed-out women differed from the way he felt about her, Carrie, his true love. What right had she to cast the past in his teeth anyway, as if it mattered now?

Special women, for God's sake.

Cliff made a resolve: when this Mexican ruckus was over,

he might just go to New York and get back into the matter of Carrie's play. Maybe a play was the last thing she ought to do.

He missed her. She hadn't been gone three days and already he missed her desperately. A cure for that, however, was at hand. He soon had other things to think about.

CHAPTER NINETEEN

A Message at the Ritz

1

Frank Kluckhohn had finished lunch. He was seated at his customary corner table in the Prendes, his favorite restaurant, yesterday's airmailed copy of *The New York Times* propped against an empty bottle of Pouilly-Fuissé. He poured a second cup of coffee into which he added a little of the excellent brandy of Pedro Domecq. He enjoyed the Prendes, the bustle of it, the excellent food service, the glisten of the heavy, gleaming tableware, even the feel of the thick linen napkin as the waiter unfolded it for him and spread it on his lap. In the evening one could dine here elegantly, in the presence of women, but at lunch Prendes was largely a meeting place for men—officials from the National Palace, executives from the banks and commercial houses of the downtown area, members of the consular corps and the sporting world—the sort of people who were news sources. Sometimes Frank Kluckhohn came to Prendes to catch up with some specific person, someone best seen informally, in a public atmosphere where their meeting could obviously occur just by chance: catching sight of his quarry across the room Frank would hold up thumb and forefinger, pressed almost but not quite together in the Mexican signal which means *"momentito,"* knowing that the individual thus invited would later drop by his table. Then, of course, there were always the others, those who came without being summoned. Those with news of their own to suggest for Frank's daily wire, or those trying to find out something not yet in the wire, or if in it, not sufficiently clarified.

The New York Times was read in Mexico City. It reached subscribers two, sometimes three, days late, even coming as it did by plane, but what of that? It was not a politically controlled medium; it spoke with the voice of the great world as well as, specifically, that of the giant nation to the north whose affairs, particularly in these crucial times, were so closely interwoven with those of the *Ciudad*. It was read indeed, and in offices and national departments whose bosses were not fluent in English, a morning digest was often prepared by a secretary who was.

Today there had been an unusual number of table visitors. Frank treated all with courtesy, even the nuisances; a nuisance today might be a news source tomorrow, and it was easier as well as more pleasant to accumulate obligations rather than to be standoffish. A reporter prospers by collecting IOU's.

Frank would see a face approaching down an aisle of tables, a smile of greeting at the ready, or he would feel the touch of a hand on his shoulder and look up, sometimes to be confronted with an individual he could hardly identify. No matter. Frank Kluckhohn would make the conventional, aborted pantomime of rising; he would gesture to the empty chair opposite and permit a modicum of small talk. Today, it seemed, the chat always led to the same subject: an article which appeared on the business page of the issue which had reached the Federal District that morning. The story had been pretty routine. It had rehashed the latest developments in the long-drawn-out negotiations for new oil-production contracts, much of the material familiar by now even to those who were not petroleum insiders, but it had concluded with an attention grabber:

. . . a large independent oil company may soon quit-claim its subsoil holdings in Tampico in return for purchase by the Mexican government of its surface installations for a sum in the eight-million-dollar range. Only conditions: none of current equipment can be

removed and field must be delivered with production at
its present level.

Frank Kluckhohn put down his coffee cup. A new table-
hopper had settled into the empty chair. Kluckhohn studied
without pleasure the scarecrow frame, black hairpiece and
long, beaky face of Rafael Avila, El Zopilote.

"Con permiso . . ."

"Claro!"

Kluckhohn ignored Avila's presumption in seating himself
first and asking permission afterward.

"Copita?"

With a hostly gesture he pushed the brandy bottle in
Avila's direction. Already a waiter was setting down an extra
glass. Avila accepted the drink. He lit a cigar, blowing the
smoke carefully away from Kluckhohn. Actually, judged by
his own terms, he was trying to be polite.

"Señor Kluckhohn, I have a bit of news for you."

The reporter answered, "You know my need for news,
señor."

"You jest, señor. You are the best-informed man in the
city, as everyone knows. However, your article today . . ."

El Zopilote passed his hand over his eyes.

"It surprised you?"

"It shocked me. And I was not alone. Only a few weeks
ago I talked with Mr. Troy Kinsale. At that time he made no
hint of such a deal."

"I have not mentioned Mr. Troy Kinsale."

"Ai, but the reference was clear. One can only hope that
for once your information is not as accurate as usual."

Kluckhohn signaled for more coffee. He had been enjoying
himself until now, but the presence of his visitor, the seedy,
black spread of him, corrupted his pleasure.

"What is it, in short, that you want to tell me, Rafael?"

Rafael Avila's long, yellow face twitched with some undeci-
pherable emotion. He pushed his beak across the table until it
was almost in Kluckhohn's cup.

"That the deal as you told of it will never take place."

Kluckhohn pointed across the room.

"Troy Kinsale is right over there. Why don't you tell him
yourself?"

"I wished only to set the record straight. So that your
brilliant reputation for consistency can be maintained."

"Well, thank you, Rafael. I will remember your kindness."

Kluckhohn turned his chair slightly sideways, as if to bring the confrontation to an end. Taking the hint, El Zopilote rose, but remained for a moment bent over the table—cloaking it with his dark, disheveled shape.

"You will write another item, then?"

"Not until I hear more evidence, Rafael."

"You shall have it, you shall have it."

El Zopilote made a queer, lifting movement with his sleeve, which was so long that it hung down to his knuckles. He seemed about to offer his hand and then, as if in fear that it would be refused, he patted Kluckhohn lightly on the shoulder.

"Always a pleasure to chat with you, my dear señor," he said as he moved off.

At that moment, in the agreeable, busy hubbub of the restaurant, Cliff and Troy were lunching with a group that included Scott Stanfus (he had flown down for the inventory taking) together with his opposite number in the staff of the Mexican Department of the Interior. On hand also were several lawyers—in deals like this, as Troy remarked, you had lawyers coming out of your ears. Everyone was eating hugely—the *carne asada*, the roast goat in hot *mole* sauce, the *cabrillo a la plancha*. Now, as the meal ended, notebooks and ledgers made their appearance, patched strategically among the wine bottles, the glasses, the plates of sweets, fruit and dessert. In spite of the business being done on and around its periphery, it was a merry table, a good group; ordinarily such a conspicuous and well-placed gathering would have been visited or greeted by the government and corporate people coming and going nearby. But today the atmosphere was one of isolation. Pitor DeWilde, for instance, of Royal Dutch Shell, found them all invisible; Sir Linfoot Beckton of BP, with whom Troy had often sat for postlunch cribbage games (the current fad), walked past with a spectral nod and the leanest of smiles.

"I guess we haven't won the door prize for popularity today," Cliff said into his father's ear as they stood at the checkroom, waiting for their hats behind a paunchy Gulf executive who, like the Exxon people, had not seemed aware of their existence.

Troy was lighting his pipe.

"Have to thank Kluckhohn for that."

They walked out into the mild, dusty air of the Calle 16 Septiembre.

"Will this goddamn newspaper item really do much harm?"

Troy dropped money into a beggar's cup. He was conscientious about beggars.

"So it will be a little tougher now, that's all."

"I saw Kluckhohn inside."

"I was careful not to go near him."

"Oh, I know. We don't want to confirm his story, even if he didn't name us. I wonder what his source was, that's all."

"He gets around."

"I'll say he does."

"To tell you the truth," said Troy, "we're lucky to have kept it under wraps so far. There's always someone with a big mouth."

"Maybe that little *rubia* in Beteta's office—the one with the good shape. They all give her a play—the newspaper guys."

"It doesn't matter too much. In two weeks I wouldn't have given a shit."

The satisfying facade of the Ritz loomed up at the bottom of the street. Troy was heading toward his siesta: an excellent habit, the siesta, especially when you'd finished lunch at 4 P.M. and might go back to work again from eight till midnight.

Troy Kinsale was mistaken. He got no siesta that day. When he and Cliff reached their suite they could see a white envelope protruding under the door, indicating that the desk clerk had a message for them.

Frank Kluckhohn also had a communication waiting: an AP flimsy his office teletype operator had stuck on his desk spindle during the lunch break. It was the usual mix of morning news developed during the last six hours in a nation of thirty-one million people, over a third of them Indians, stretching from the Atlantic to the Pacific and from the Rio Grande to the Golfo de Tehuantepec: a school bus had gone over a cliff at Atzcapotzalco; former agrarian workers had burned down a bank in Tlaxco; a lady, already the mother of sixteen, had given birth to quintuplets in Torreón, three of them alive; General Camacho, formerly a governor and a champion polo player, had been mentioned by Lázaro Cárdenas as his possible successor (a straw, Kluckhohn thought, to test the wind); and a refinery was on fire in the KinOil field near the Pánuco River.

Kluckhohn crumpled the dispatch and dropped it in his wastebasket. None of it was worth putting on the Overnight to Times Square. He did, however, have a story: an interview he'd picked up at Prendes, cornering DeWilde and Sir Linfoot at the same time; a rare stroke of luck! Both men were informed and important, Sir Linfoot exceptionally articulate for an executive in a trade not noted for its trend toward public confidences. Pitting one man against the other, Kluckhohn had extracted a new angle on the expropriation question, the only real news coming out of Mexico these days.

What these gentlemen feared, he gathered—if this madness of Cárdenas really became an actuality—was that it might start a chain reaction.

Venezuela! What about that? President Gómez had always been cooperative, not the type to fuss about ice machines to cool the drinks of oil-field roustabouts or hospitals where they could go when they were sick. But now old Gómez was out and there was a new fellow at the state-house in Caracas— Eleázar López Contreras, a miserable bastard. He was opting for new royalties—a fifty-fifty split. It gave one the jitters.

Then—good God! The Middle East, the Kuwaitis, the Iraqis, the Iranians: if the infection spread, there was only one weapon left to use: boycott. The world would be put on notice. Not a barrel, not a drop of expropriated oil would be merchandised by the companies which owned, if you cared to go into it, all the merchandising facilities there were. Let Whitehall scream its loudest, let hysterics burst from Tokyo and Unter den Linden—not a drop, not a soupçon of the precious petrol would be carried in the ships of these companies, the only available bottoms afloat. . . .

Not even for military uses!

Kluckhohn finished his article. He gave it to the teletype girl. Then he went back into his office and locked the door.

Well, nothing had, perhaps indeed nothing could have been done, yet in retrospect Frank Kluckhohn had an odd feeling about that day. He was not sure how General Camba had come into what happened later and he was not comfortable about it; he was not even sure that he himself had done the right thing. He wrote the news as it came to him. It was possible, though perhaps not likely, that the tragic entrapment which took place shortly thereafter in the KinOil fields was the work of a grudge-animated betrayer, an outsider, and that General Camba, for his role in it, had acted on his own.

2

A company car, one of the twenty-year-old Peerless stretch-outs used only in the field, had stopped near the jetty; as the launch pulled toward the landing float, Troy and Cliff could see Selby Clay standing there, a slim figure in his usual slightly wrinkled seersucker clothes. The deckhand forward secured the bow, then ran back to take the stern painter from the steersman who doubled as engineer.

Selby shook hands with composure, but he looked bad—ill, really. His complexion was greenish and there were dark pouches under his eyes. The man never did have any stamina, Troy reflected. To the northwest, smoke from the burning refinery smeared the immaculate tropic sky.

"I'm sorry to leave you with all this mess." Selby addressed his words to Troy and Cliff impartially.

"Leave us?" said Troy. "What do you mean?"

"My severance, as agreed between us a month ago. Termination as of yesterday—nine A.M., to be exact. Justine left last week. I've already stayed over a day."

His gesture, deliberately sardonic, took in the smoke.

"I ought to break you in half," said Troy.

Selby did not seem to hear. The deckhand, at a nod from him, loaded his luggage aboard the launch—a huge old portmanteau and some lighter stuff.

Cliff felt less angry than disgusted. For an oilman to leave during a field emergency was unheard of! Incredible! In that moment his secret support dissolved, his feeling that Selby had been getting a raw deal. So Troy, with his more sharply honed instincts, had been right about the bastard all along.

Now there seemed a strong possibility that Troy would throw a punch. Cliff took hold of his father's arm. "Come on, Dad. Let's go." But Troy's attention stayed fixed.

"You're not only through at KinOil, you're through in the oil business," he told Selby. "I'll see to that. I give you my word."

Selby's mouth twitched—not with fear but with the pleasure he felt in his own reply.

"I've already accepted another job, a far better one. Sorry about that too. And what," he finished, "makes me particularly regret leaving just now is that you're another hand short beside myself. Marsh isn't at the field either. . . . Goodbye, Cliff."

He offered his hand and Cliff, in spite of himself, took it. "Goodbye."

As Selby stepped aboard the launch, the bowman cast off, the steersman holding the stern against the rubber fender just long enough for the current to head the craft out into the slow, coiling water, always with an iridescent skim of oil on it. The engine was already turning over; the steersman gave it a full throttle and the launch headed downstream, toward Tampico, the sea terminal and the airport.

Selby Clay had taken a chair amidships. He never looked back.

"He's got to be lying about Marsh," Troy said.

"Well, we'll sure as hell find out."

They got into the stretchout. A company guard sat beside the driver. He carried a side arm and a Savage 30-30 carbine. Another guard, similarly armed, rode in the last of the stretchout's four seats. They started up the rutted road into the field.

Troy addressed the driver.

"Donde está el Señor Borland?"

"Raptado, señor."

Cliff looked at his father. The word was not familiar.

"Kidnapped," Troy translated grimly.

"Do you believe it?"

"You're damn right I believe it. If Camba could break through our security and set fire to a refinery he could sure as hell snatch anyone around. The fire might have been a diversion—that's just sabotage. There's money in kidnapping."

The west gate into the plant stood wide open. It was a stout gate of double-layer chain link reinforced by X-braces. Something had bent the middle braces at the point where they crossed, enough to permit passage of a vehicle, if that was what had struck it. The burning refinery was located a half mile farther on. This was protected by a second chain-link barrier, topped with electrified barbed wire. The gates here had not been damaged at all. They too were open. Inside, the plant fire-fighting apparatus was in action, an asbestos-suited crew pouring chemicals at high pressure into the flames. On a tall metal crane, the field fire chief, Bob Northglen, struggled with a nozzle that directed the chemicals at the same target. The fire had been burning for twenty hours, but was now under control. No gas-propelled column rose into the sky as it would have in a drill blowout. The refinery itself was a ruin—a grotesque coil of twisted, blackened pipes, girders and fittings, but all flow of crude had been shut off for some time; what burned now was disintegrated metal detritus plus seepage from the tanks that had blown nearby. The smoke was white where the chemicals hit it, but coal-black above; it coiled on the ground, struggling to rise but constantly falling back. The men with the hoses wore masks, crouching as low as they could.

At headquarters, the walls had been blackened by the smoke and the windows had been blown in but the office was in operation. Betty Manton, with a raincoat hanging unbuttoned over a soot-smeared white blouse and skirt, wearily sorted papers that had scattered when the explosion dumped the filing cabinets.

The telephone rang—that too, amazingly, was in working order. Betty turned to answer it.

"Wait," she said, then shouted, "Wait! *Espéreme!* He's here now. He just came in. . . ."

She hung up.

"Some individual calling from Tampico—English-speaking, cultured voice. Asks for you, and I tell him you're expected. But the last of couple of times he hangs up as soon as he hears my voice. It's kind of spooky, like some other things around here. . . . Hello, Cliff."

"Hello, Betty," said Cliff.

Betty Manton looked around for a chair. She failed to find one close enough; she sat down on the floor, her back against the wall.

"Oh, Jesus Christ," she said.

She began soundlessly to weep, the tears pouring unchecked down her smudged face.

"I suppose you heard about Marsh Borland?"

"I did—about five minutes ago."

"I saw it all," said Betty, "every bit of it. First there was the goddamn explosion and then . . . oh, Jesus Christ . . ."

"Take it easy."

"They snatched him. They beat him, and I saw it. I was in my room and Christ—the refinery! It went off like a bomb; it threw me out of bed. I thought, well, another fire, and I ran outside. The cars were there already, Camba and his bunch, and they had him. He was fighting them, the goddamn fool, but what else could he do? They had him and they slugged him; they beat on him as if he was . . . wasn't human . . . oh, my God . . . and then they drove away in their ratty old cars. They'll kill him, the bastards, yelling and shooting their pistols in the air . . . Bob Northglen shot one of them . . ."

"Kill him?"

"No. Doc Travis has him in the infirmary. I wish he *were* dead, though. I'd have been glad to kill him with my own hands."

"Many of our guys hurt?"

"Six, one critical. Blown off a catwalk. And one guard, the only one that stuck. The rest, all those Indian cops you had Selby hire—you remember? 'Stick badges and guns on them,' you said."

"Yeah, what happened to them?"

"They just disappeared, into the swamps or down the Pánuco, badges, guns, and all. And they left the gates unlocked. Oh, they'd been told what to do all right."

"They had *keys?*"

"No, only Marsh and Selby had those. But they got hold of some someplace."

Marsh and Selby!

Cliff turned and spat through a blast-shattered window. It wasn't hard to believe Selby had passed a key to the saboteurs, his farewell gift to KinOil!

"I want to talk to that hombre in the infirmary."

"All right. But I'll have to get Juniel Herrera to come over then. He's the only one who can speak this man's dialect— he's one of the river people, never learned Spanish *or* English."

"Get him then, on the double."

And with this Troy strode out of the office, with Cliff a pace behind him. They left Betty on the phone once more, calling Accounting for Herrera, a junior clerk there.

The infirmary, a large, well-equipped one by field standards of that time, was a low tin-roofed building in a corner of the headquarters quadrangle. Long-bladed electric breeze-makers revolved slowly in the ceiling; insectproof tents protected the dozen or more beds, eight of them occupied. Dr. Manual Travis and his Scottish nurse, Sheila McCreary, were working on a patient—a small, bearded roustabout with second-degree burns; the doctor acknowledged Troy's arrival with a motion of his head but kept on at his job.

Troy and Cliff moved between the double line of beds, Troy stopping for a few words with a patient, a shop foreman, who was not under sedation.

Attached to the foot of each bed, a clipboard record supplied data on the bed's incumbent. Troy took guidance from these, stopping at the last bed in the east row.

The man here looked about sixty years old. He was beardless and gray-haired with high cheekbones, a shrunken mouth and the usual pointy Indian head. The arms sticking out of his hospital gown were long in proportion to his body, laced with an intricate weave of muscles—paddling muscles, hauling muscles. Not the sort seen in a white man. He looked up at Troy with his calm, captive eyes, then scornfully closed his eyes again, shutting out with indifference and hauteur a world without hope. He pretended to sleep.

"Is he badly hurt?"

Manuel Travis, who had come up soundlessly on his rubber-soled shoes, made an equivocal gesture. He put a thermometer in the patient's mouth and started taking his pulse.

The clipboard for this patient read:

NAME—UNKNOWN.
PAYROLL NUMBER—NOT EMPLOYED BY KINOIL.
TYPE EMPLOYMENT—(BLANK)
INJURY—GUNSHOT WOUNDS (TWO).
WAS INJURY INCURRED ON THE JOB? (BLANK)
TREATMENT—SURGICAL.
MEDICATION—ORAL SULFUR, 15 MM. DAILY.
MORPH. AS NEEDED.

"Where was he hit?" Troy asked.

"Left buttock, flesh wound. Bullet went clear through. Second shot—I'm assuming it was the second, the one in the ass wouldn't have knocked him off the car—grazed the femur. Thighbone to you. Shattered it where it articulates with the tibia. I've set it."

Manuel Travis, alert and chubby, KinOil's field physician, had become through practice expert in burns, in concussions and internal injuries due to falls, explosions, and general carelessness, also to VD of every common type in males, to malaria and to the sorts of emphysematous lung damage that results from exposure to gasoline fumes. He had dealt frequently with knife cuts and dysentery, less often with bullet penetrations though, when such occurrences came to his attention, he felt well qualified to treat them. He looked at the thermometer, then shook it down and handed it to the nurse.

"Hundred and one," he said, "pulse eighty-six. Blood pressure probably low, we'll check. But he's not a very sick Indian," he finished to Troy, "if that's what you wished to know, sir."

"Can he travel?"

"Yes. Unless he has to ride a horse or sit in a boat."

"He'll be riding in a pickup, on a stretcher. With a mat on it or whatever you want. You can be with him. In fact, I want you there. All he'll have to do is look at the country and point out a route."

"Yes, sir," said Dr. Travis. "When did you wish to start?"

"In about an hour. Will that give you time enough?"

"I'll be ready."

Betty Manton was coming down the aisle between the beds. With her was a fragile, handsome little fellow in his twenties. He wore a Hawaiian sport shirt and the brand of chinos that were sold at the company store. His oiled hair was combed in a cowlick and he sported a thin, Gable-style mustache.

"This in Juniel Herrera," Betty said to Troy. "And there's a call for you from Tampico. I had it transferred here, line two in Travis' office."

"I'll take it in a minute." Troy turned to the accountant. "I hear you can speak the river talk."

"*Es mi idioma, señor,*" said the clerk.

"Fine. Then you talk to this *compadre* here in the bed. Tell him we know that General Camba has a hideout someplace thataway"—and he pointed westerly—"in the high ground, out toward Posa de Fiero. We want him to show us the way in. Make it very clear. That's what he has to do."

In Travis' office he picked up the telephone.

"Ah, Mr. Kinsale," said the voice, "I have been trying to reach you since early on. I have an important message for you."

It was a man's voice—not American, but not English either—the sort of international voice that was coming into style about this time. Its pitch was that of a drawing room or a café at the best level, confident and conversational.

"As you must know, sir, General Camba is holding your executive, Mr. Marshall Borland. I'm afraid the purpose of the seizure is extortion—a ransom operation. I am not personally in contact with General Camba but I have a friend who is. I have been called in as amicus curiae, as it were—a sort of go-between."

"I understand," said Troy.

"Thank you," said the voice. "The fact is, I have been delegated to tell you that Mr. Borland is completely safe. He is in excellent health and sends you his best wishes. The price fixed for his release is two hundred thousand pesos, payable in cash within three days. The arrangements can be made through me and they are not too distressful, really not distressful at all. Would you care to hear them?"

"Go ahead."

"If you, my dear sir, or anyone delegated by you will inquire at the desk of the Imperial Hotel you or he may pick up a letter. It will be in English, addressed simply to the KinOil Corporation. It will contain full instructions on where the money is to be left and all that. I think I can assure you that Mr. Borland will be freed the moment the sum mentioned has been paid. He will be set at liberty here in Tampico. The Imperial is already holding a suite for him."

"That's dandy," said Troy. "But suppose we don't lay down two hundred thousand pesos for Mr. Borland, what happens then?"

"I couldn't say, sir," said the voice, shaded now with well-bred regret, "I'm afraid I have not discussed that alternative. I have simply passed along the information that I was instructed to give. I must ring off now. Thank you, Mr. Kinsale. Goodbye, sir."

"Goodbye, cocksucker," said Troy.

Back in the ward, Herrera had finished his conversation with the captive, who asked for a cigarette. Herrera hand-rolled one for him, lit it and put it in his mouth.

"Did you tell him what he has to do?"

"He says he cannot, señor."

"Why not?"

"He says the road is very difficult. He doesn't think he can remember it."

Troy pointed out the window toward the smoldering refinery.

"Hoist him up a little. I want him to look out there."

Troy smiled in paternal style at the captured man as Herrera, assisted by the nurse, raised him up. The Indian grimaced as weight came onto his injured buttock. The nurse looked reproachfully at Troy, who ignored her. He addressed Herrera.

"Tell him to take a good look at that crane, where Bob is spraying with the chem hose. Tell him we'll hoist him up on that and hang him in the smoke until his memory improves."

Herrera nodded. He spoke in quick gutturals to the prisoner. The old man listened quietly. He looked once, without interest, at the crane, then turned his resigned burning gaze on Troy.

"He says it makes no difference to him," Herrera translated. "If he takes you to the hideout, General Camba will kill him anyway."

"Tell him we will protect him from General Camba. Tell him I give him my word for that. A guarantee."

The accountant seemed at a loss.

"*En mi idioma,* there is no word for guarantee."

"Tell him if he remembers the trail correctly he can live a long time."

Troy turned to Betty Manton. During the exchanges between Troy and Herrera she had been taking notes. One did not know, in a situation like this, what one might be asked to remember.

"Call down to Personnel. See if they can rustle up eight or ten guys in the bunkhouse who want to take a trip with me. Tell them they'll be provided with weapons. There's some danger attached—we're going to bring back Mr. Marsh Borland."

Betty Manton snapped her notebook shut. "Those guys in the bunkhouses now have just come off the early tour." She pronounced the last word "tower"—the universal diction of the oil business. "They'll be exhausted!" she said. "Some of them have been up for two nights."

"Just do what I say, Betty," Troy said testily. "I want the commissary to pack enough cold stuff for a dozen men, two meals. I'll arrange for the vehicles myself. You got all that? Cliff and I are going to get something to eat."

"Just a moment, Mr. Kinsale," the nurse cut in. "Do you intend to take this patient with you?"

"Yes, I do."

"Then," said Nurse McCreary, "you are an unspeakably cruel man."

Troy stared at her, seeing her for the first time as a person rather than a medical accessory: a tall, furious, well-shaped woman with dark hair and dark-blue eyes blazing with anger. She spoke with a touch of a burr.

"He's been shot in two places," said Nurse McCreary; "he shouldna be moved. Dr. Travis knows that. This mun is in great pain."

"We'll do what we can to alleviate his pain, nurse," said Troy. "Have his medications ready to take along. Thank you very much."

As Troy and Cliff sat over a quick meal of beer and sandwiches, served in the executive dining room, Troy said, "My, what a wildcat *she* is!"

"She still might be right."

"Now, son," said Troy placidly, "we've got a job to do, that's all."

"But why? It seems ridiculous, going in with our own guys. What are we, vigilantes?"

"We've got to get Marsh. We don't have much time."

"Kidnapping is against the law, isn't it? Well, let them send us some law, let them send us some troops, some Federales. *Then* we can go after Marsh."

Troy finished his beer. He signaled the steward for another.

"Cárdenas is on his train someplace. And Beteta with him."

"So General Hay can get in touch with them by short-wave."

"Okay. Then *they* try to contact Veracruz. From Veracruz, to get Federales to Tampico by boat, let along up here, will take two days, maybe more. And Camba has friends on the outside."

"How do you know?"

Troy told him about the call from Tampico—the ransom demand.

"That call had to be planned *before* Marsh was grabbed or the refinery touched off. Camba's a *bandido,* he's on the run, in the hills. He has no way of getting in touch with Tampico, not in a matter of hours. He can't pick up a telephone. It was all set ahead of time, I'm telling you—the kidnapping *and* the fire. Plus which, the call coming from Tampico would project that Marsh is being held in Tampico—bullshit! Dead or alive now, he's with Camba. We're just lucky that we've got this ass-shot Indian to take up to him, and that's what we're going to do."

The steward brought Troy's second beer and a plate of cold

peeled *camarones,* to be dipped in a green *salsa.* Troy fell to with a good appetite.

To Cliff, it all still seemed sheer madness, a design borrowed from another day, an earlier time. He himself would obey. He would take his part, whatever that might be, because he too was conditioned in a certain way—he could not defy his father even when he disapproved of him. But he had no stomach for it. He would go, but he would give anything if, just this one time, he could be excused.

The cars set out in early afternoon. The lead car was a Dodge wagon equipped with a winch installed behind the front bumper. The winch operated off the drive shaft, on a special gear. The wagon had long proved handy getting through the boggy places in the field, the sumps from oil spills and such. The thin but strong steel cable could be carried forward by hand and affixed to some firm stationary object. Then the motor would start cranking the winch, pulling the vehicle through any kind of mess you would be likely to encounter.

Saturnino drove. With him in the front seat, a tight fit, sat Troy and, on the outside, a young rigger, Dude Kelly, as rifleman guard. The back seat had been folded down to make room for a cot and a mattress on which lay the wounded man who was to serve as guide. Doc Travis and Herrera, the interpreter, rode with the patient.

Behind the wagon, a heavy-duty White six-wheeler truck carried twelve field men—the shock troops of this curious invasion force. The men, many as tired as Betty had said, were in high spirits. They were well supplied with food and ammunition and weapons from the field armory, mostly Savage carbines with a few new Winchester 30-06's and some ancient cut-down Krag-Jorgensens. For good cheer the detail had brought some booze along, but this was largely consumed in the first hour or two of the trip, after which the jokes and horseplay in the big, panel-sided truck cooled down, and many of the men stretched out, as best they could, to doze.

Cliff rode in the last car—a Ford pickup in which was stored extra gasoline, most of the food and water, and some additional medical supplies. Bob Northglen alternated with him at the wheel. Apparently still fresh and strong in spite of his work on the firefighting crane, Bob was one of the older field hands and an ex-soldier. Like Cliff, he took a dim view of the current expedition but, trained to do what was needed, he kept his thoughts to himself except to say, "We'll need a bit of luck."

At first the trail of Camba's force was easy to follow. By the nature of the tracks it was clear that the kidnappers had been driving ancient vehicles—ten- or fifteen-year-old army trucks or troop carriers, probably, bought cheap or stolen from military pools. The old-fashioned narrow tires cut deep into the marshy ground near the Pánuco. Beyond, on the higher ground, riprap road would lead you on buoyantly, then dip without warning into swales and hollows in which almost any kind of wheeled thing could bog down. The ground grew firmer as the trail swung north and westward, finally emerging from the jungle onto a mesa. Here the going was still rough but the tracks were clearer. A few early stars appeared in the stretched arc of the sky. The caravan kept moving.

Twilight came slowly, night suddenly. A new, pitchy substance filled the great horizon, which, only a few moments before, had been clear, luminous air.

In a few seconds everything had changed, even the thoughts of the men in the wobbling little cars and trucks; the feeling in their souls was no longer the same. The enormous night of Mexico engulfed them all. It bent its implacable will upon them. It pressed down on the tiny mesa where, in some unknown cul-de-sac, a crazy *pistolero* was holding a man prisoner. Who could tell? The cars struggled on, snaking around obstacles which loomed up with strange, distorted faces like the mummers at a carnival—clumps of cholla or saguaro, boulders tossed down randomly, no one knew how. And the lights, the lights of the cars, so impressive and efficient when a vehicle is rolling down a well-kept road, bearing its passengers to a pleasant tavern or a meeting with friends, suddenly seemed spindly and diminished, not at all equal to the demands being made on them, the requirements that they must fulfill, absolutely without question . . . for without the lights, then there was nothing but the night.

The wounded man in the Dodge wagon still acted as guide. That was all bullshit about his not being able to remember the trail. He remembered very well; he remembered everything. He had asked for a compass. He was guiding as best he might, but he was tired now and his fever was higher. Dr. Travis injected another ampule of morphine. The man's pain must be held at acceptable levels but he could not, except for brief intervals, be allowed to sleep. Dr. Travis had counted on the sulfa to control the infection inevitably associated with gun-shot wounds, but even too much sulfa . . .

He decided he would withhold all further medications for the time being.

The expedition had now reached a place on the mesa where the going smoothed out. Brush and cactus fell away, the wheels of the vehicles moved freely, as if along a man-made track. The guide, more sensitive than others to the nature of the terrain, since the reduction in the jolting eased his discomfort, was the first to notice this. He ordered the car to stop and asked to be raised on his pallet. Herrera, with the doctor helping, lifted him a little; he stared for a while into the blackness on all sides, then motioned to go ahead again. This happened several times. Troy looked questioningly at Travis. Was the poor fellow delirious? But the doctor shook his head. There was really nothing for it now but to let the captive have his way.

Some sore of heavy shape, an escarpment, dark against the faint luminosity of the sky, loomed on one side of the trail. The guide ordered another halt. He seemed excited. He jabbered away in his queer gutturals with Herrera. He looked again at the compass in the beam of Travis' flashlight. He seemed to be making some new demand.

Herrera turned to Troy.

"He says it is very dangerous now. Camba will have posted lookouts. He says we should go no farther. He says we should camp here and wait for daylight."

Troy studied the shrunken brown guide, his bandages soiled with the dust of the trip. The little man's eyes looked quite mad.

"Tell him no, I don't like it. When we stop we turn into targets. Sitting ducks. Tell him we are going ahead."

Herrera conversed briefly with the prisoner. Then he turned back to Troy. "He says in that case he wants to get out. He wants us to put him down and leave him here."

"He'd be dead by morning, wouldn't he?"

"I guess he doesn't care."

"Well, we can't leave him. He's just trying to pull some shit on us."

He studied the escarpment. It had a queer point, or beak, to it. Yes, there could be a hideout back in there, in some scoop of volcanic tumble.

He pulled a shell into the chamber of his Savage.

"Go ahead," he told Saturnino. "But go slow."

Once more the cars advanced. Cliff, in the pickup, the third vehicle in line, woke from a doze. His head came up as Bob Northglen, driving, turned on the lights, which he had cut during the last halt, to save the battery. The escarpment was dead ahead. Would there be an opening in it where the trail could enter? Certainly, with its outlandish beak, it had a queer foreboding look, dim as it was . . . and then, abruptly, it was brightly lit! An immense burst of blinding light illuminated the rock walls, the jutting overhang; a fraction of a second later, the ground shook, an explosion rocked the earth, tossed the big truck, just ahead, sideways on the trail; it banged Cliff's head against the window of the pickup but he saw . . . unbelievable . . . the Dodge on fire, coming apart in the sky, off the ground, a ball of fire with body parts, people, shoots of flame spilling out of it, whizzing off, separating, settling, still on fire, in the dirt, on the mesa, burning and burning there. Oh, Jesus Christ.

Cliff got out, fell over a cholla, ran forward, cactus splinters in his legs and body, past the White, with men getting out of it, forward on the trail to the flames, the smell of burning metal and incinerated flesh, the pieces on the ground, in the rocks and the cactus, Troy there, Troy's body there on fire, Troy's body with one side of it gone, one side and his head—that gone or part of it—and Cliff kneeling beside Troy, trying to beat out with his hands the flames of explosive and blown gasoline which still, in spite of all that he could do, consumed the half-beheaded body, the crushed, smoldering and dismembered body of Troy Kinsale.

PART FIVE

PART FIVE

CHAPTER TWENTY

The Collection

1

January 30, 1940, was a bad night for an art opening but everyone had come; there was a crush at the doors. Parking boys yelled at one another, jumping in and out of owner-driven vehicles, many of them old and humble ones, not the sort you would expect to see at a fashionable event.

Kyle had insisted that this evening should belong to the public: the first view of his collection at the Palace of the Legion of Honor.

A grand affair! But—who could have foreseen such a storm? There were not enough doormen-escorts; also they were having trouble with their umbrellas. They sloshed up and down the red carpet which had been laid for the occasion but was now as soaked and slippery as the pavement on each side of it and across the broad terrace along which the winds hurled themselves recklessly and the raindrops spurted like bullets.

Inside—blessed contrast—decorum prevailed. Here there was warmth and the music of a string quartet. Here Kyle and Alma circulated, greeting people, chatting with them in the anteroom or at the buffet, but always, at some appropriate moment, sending them along into the gallery where the crowd moved slowly clockwise, experiencing the glory that expands the air, that penetrates the soul—the climate generated only by first-class, famous works of art.

The Selim Karkar Collection—soon to be known as the Kyle Kinsale Collection—was unique, in some ways the most impressive assemblage of paintings ever presented in San Francisco, or possibly anywhere else, except once—the time this identical exhibit had been seen in Paris, in the Boulevard des Capucines, in April 1874.

Until that date the painters represented in the collection had been known, somewhat pejoratively, as the Intransigents. However, during the exhibit some Parisian critic—possibly Louis Leroy—had found a new name for them: the Impressionists!

Well, times had changed; prices and reputations with them. Possibly in 1874 the show at the Boulevard des Capucines could have been picked up for a hundred thousand dollars. Tonight the price tag was closer to twelve million.

Kyle had decided to come up with it. He would let nothing stand in his way.

Even the figure gave him satisfaction. He liked big figures. They—like the pictures themselves, like racehorses, beautiful houses and cars, like lovely women and famous friends—were an adornment of life. You dealt with them, lived with them, possessed them and showed them off, that is, if you lived the way a proper man should live: a man who wished to be a figure of his times and had the means to be.

Of all Californians, only Hearst, the old man, had behaved that way; Hearst had wielded power, he had gloried in beauty, he had lived and still lived to the full. Kyle, beside enjoying the publisher's friendship, had liked and admired and even imitated him, up to a point—but he had long ago recognized Hearst's weakness, the flaw in his status as a true California Medici: Hearst was an accumulator rather than a collector. To accumulate took money but it did not take taste. Hearst had wound up with a pile of expensive junk, with warehouses bulging with armor, châteaux, furniture, costumes, even churches, forts, bridges and whole villages. . . . Kyle could not see the point of it.

To take your place as a collector you must seek out and then possess the beautiful, the unique and . . . the unobtainable. And that was exactly what he had done.

His own introduction to paintings had come early during his first forays into France and England in the '20s and '30s. He had picked up a few good pictures then, the Mondrians and Klees now in his Los Angeles office and the Malibu house; he had added other items since—always carefully selected, prestige works; as time went on his taste veered away from the "neoplasticism" which had first intrigued him to the deeper, blander harmonies of the Impressionist School favored by his friend Nubar Gulbenkian.

Nubar had known about art. He had learned from his father, Calouste, an outstanding collector. Calouste Gulbenkian, the richest man in Europe, was as shrewd in his art dealing as he had been in finding oil. He had explored the Middle East, optioning leases which later yielded him a steady five percent on the total production of the earth's richest petroleum areas. He was celebrated as the only man who had worsted the famous dealer Sir Joseph (later Lord) Duveen in a trade.

Kyle had met Duveen several times in Paris, at Calouste's suite in the Ritz. He had not been impressed by him. Duveen was eminently a man of the world, but his polish, his clipped mustache and infectious, ringing laugh had—to Kyle—the smarmy slickness of a California oil-lease salesman. There was no denying, however, the effect he had produced on many rich Americans. Henry Frick, J. P. Morgan the Elder, P. A. B. Widener, Collis Huntington, George J. Gould, Andrew Carnegie and Andrew Mellon had spent millions buying art from him. In their eyes a picture seemed to acquire authenticity not because it was a Velázquez, a Frans Hals or a van Leyden but because it was—or had been—a Duveen. When they hesitated over a purchase, Duveen's clincher—a statement that could not be applied to the stables, mansions, yachts and other expensive addenda with which such customers established their elitism—was always the same: "There is no upkeep."

In those days Selim Karkar had been one of Duveen's staffers. He had worked in the London gallery with a few other youngish men whom Duveen kept around. The staff people were all well bred but not necessarily intelligent. It was an advantage to them not to know too much about the stock. Duveen never let them sell anything. They were waxy-faced, soft-stepping fellows who could take the customers around to see the poorer stuff, but they must never mention price. They wore cutaways and wing-tip collars; they might be Americans but it was a requirement that they should not speak like Americans. Duveen had fired one of them for saying "Okay" instead of "Yes, indeed, sir" when receiving an order.

Selim Karkar—actually a Libyan, though born and raised in Merced, California, less than a hundred miles from Altemira—had been miserable working in that gallery, but he had learned a lot there; when Lord Duveen died (in 1939, one year before Kyle's exhibition) Karkar struck out on his own. He had a customer in mind.

He's ready, Karkar said to himself.

He was using a phrase picked up from Duveen. He had perceived that Kyle had reached the point where the only further extension possible for his fame and fullness was the acquirement of art. But what sort of art? No Titians for him, no Fragonards, no subtly restored Ghirlandaios or refurbished Mantegnas.

Selim Karkar knew, from the international sales records, exactly what pictures Kyle already owned. Kyle was a leader of the new wave in sport, in finance, in everything. What one brought him must be daring and unique as well as beautiful: something that would interest the press. Karkar put his mind and his connections to work. With a war going on, even though most of his dealings took place in the U.S. (a country which still considered itself at peace), the plan seemed impossible at first; but if the shipping problem could be overcome (and there were ways of doing it), war conditions, in a freakish way, could help him: dealers and private owners, even museums, were desperate to get their possessions out of Europe. And so, little by little, Karkar had brought his inspiration into being, had reconstructed—not completely, of course, no one could have done that, but still to a remarkable degree—that epoch-making 1874 show where the Impressionists had first burst upon the world in all their splendor.

Dealers had the smallest part in it. The museums and private owners must be induced to loan, and had been. Karkar had set his price. Step by step, he had involved Kyle's interest, then his hunger for acquisition, finally his will—the most powerful personal will of his state and of his era—By the time Kyle had decided to sponsor a special exhibition he already looked on the collection as his own. People came up to congratulate him—they were not sure for what, but obviously this turnout, on such a dreadful night, meant a triumph of some sort.

Kyle accepted their felicitations grandly. He had added to

his costume, in the style he often chose for great occasions, the western touch which became him so well, a pair of hand-tooled kangaroo-hide stock boots. These, worn with his Poole dinner jacket and a frilled shirt with black pearl studs, raised his heels three inches off the tiles, giving him almost a giant stature. The extra height was set off by the weight he had been putting on the last few years—not flabby, and of it; he still rode whenever he could, he also swam, two or three times a week, in the pool at the Pacific Union Club, but . . . there was just more of him now, that was what it was . . . and that there should be more was somehow quite appropriate, tonight more than ever. His handsome head tilted, his eyes angled just to one side of the person he was greeting, he reflected the traditional, now almost Medici-like Kinsale look; he shed it, benevolently, on the George Camerons, who had just pushed their way through the jam—nice, bald George, publisher and co-owner, through his wife's inheritance, of *The San Francisco Chronicle*, sure to see that the collection got the write-up it deserved. Kyle bent to kiss Mrs. Kenneth Monteagle, then shooed her and Kenneth and the Robert Watt Millers along to where their culture, already passable, could be quickened by the treasures on the gallery walls. Mrs. W. P. Roth, greatest horsewoman of her day, waved to him with a bold, impudent look, as if to say, "Wouldn't we both be more comfortable in a stable?" but as she approached, he drifted off; she would be sure to talk about her new tandem driving team.

Alma had the William Wallace Meins in tow. Trust Alma to do her part, there was no one like her. . . .

One of Kyle's large, pale hands flicked out, nipped a scoop of champagne from a passing tray; holding this, and without a pause, he placed his free arm around a stout, handsome lady who had just come in and stood near the umbrella rack, dusting raindrops from her dyed black hair.

"I was afraid you'd drowned in the flood."

"Well, I was a fool to come out in it, I can tell you that."

Kyle knocked back his champagne. He pushed the empty glass into a convenient flowerpot. Spendidly, at a ritualistic pace, he escorted Mrs. Alma Spreckels into the gallery. She, of all people, was the one he had hoped to see tonight: without her the evening would have lacked a certain tone. She and her husband Adolph had *built* this museum, for one thing—built it and sumptuously presented it to San Francisco and then (Kyle tried to remember the story) when Adolph died and Alma had wanted to bury him in the Legion of Honor the Board of Supervisors had refused to allow it. Outrageous! If she had wanted to plant Adolph in the middle of the Civic Center the city should have been only too grateful.

"I'd just like to see, Kyle Kinsale, if you have any taste. I know that wife of yours has. I'm just not so sure about *you.*"

"Let's start with this Degas."

Mrs. Spreckels leaned forward, trying to read the card beside the picture.

"What is it called?"

"Washerwoman."

"She looks as if she needed a wash herself."

"That might have been Degas' idea. We've got his *Dancing Girl* too."

"I know the one. Her leg is out of joint. Otherwise I'd have bought it myself, years ago when I bought my Rodins."

"Well, here's Manet's *Olympia*. At least she's all in one piece."

"Who sold you that floozie?"

"Selim Karkar, my dealer. He used to work for Duveen."

"Duveen was the biggest crook of all."

"At least let me show you the Cézannes."

He was never sure when Alma was joking and when she wasn't.

"Don't you really like the show?"

She squeezed his arm as they edged through the crowd.

"Baby, what kind of fool do you take me for? It's magnificent—the most incredible thing I've ever seen. If you give all this to the city, people will forgive you for everything —even the prices in your damn gas stations."

Kyle winked at her.

"We're making a slash next week—half a cent per gallon less. And we clean your windshield."

2

From a corner of the softly lighted, overcrowded room, Scott Stanfus watched the proceedings with a cynical eye. It might be all very well to bring Cézanne's *House of the Hanged Man* back from Europe and hang it smack dab alongside Monet's

Luncheon and Renoir's *Harvesters*—all this bother and expense to re-create an art event that had first happened sixty-five years ago and drawn bad notices.

Scott Stanfus had little taste for art. He could see its value as a public relations ploy but even that could come too high; the half-cent-a-gallon cut in gas at the pump was more significant to him than what some long-dead critic had said about these pictures or what the *Chronicle* or the *Examiner* might say about them in the morning. If Kyle went through with his insane idea of buying the collection and then building, as he'd threatened, a public edifice to house it, Stanfus would have to rustle up the money. That was always the job that fell to him, and for once he didn't know how he was going to do it. He was at the end of his rope.

Scott Stanfus had not, like Kyle, put on weight as he put on years. Once plump and cheerful, with a kind of Hardy Boys, go-get-'em optimism and drive about him, he had grown sharper, dryer, and tougher. He had married well. Since the time when Kyle had shifted the center of his action northward, Scott had bought a house in San Mateo and had joined the Menlo Circus Club and The Family. In the two years since Troy Kinsale's death he had made amazing gains; he was treasurer of KinOil with a seat on the board. He was also treasurer of Kyle's struggling, debt-ridden operation, Petrochemical Corporation of California. For his salaried duties he was well paid, but you didn't get rich, not as rich as Scott was, on a salary; for that you needed shares of private ventures—stock options, bonuses. These Scott Stanfus had obtained. He had earned them for special services; for the promotion of new credit lines when the old ones were stretched too thin; for caucusing behind the scenes, before stockholders' meetings, when some issue vital to Kyle's activities was up for discussion. He had earned them for quiet entrepreneurship which could detect, from the rhythm of the marketplace, when a young, thrusting company was ripe for acquisition or a tottering but still respected one vulnerable for a raid. Above all, he serviced a magic, perhaps nonexistent cache from which unexpected disbursements, usually in the form of drafts on European or eastern banks, must be met— "immediately," Kyle's cables would order if the transaction was, for him, a routine sort; "instantly" if it was a true emergency.

Scott Stanfus' expertise in the navigation of corporate

bookkeeping had been won, as Ben Hur got his strength, at the galley oar. He had begun by being dependable. Now he was indispensable. He was also a rogue. He had slipped into this role by imperceptible degrees; he would have been amazed had he ever stopped to realize how much of his life it had become and how good he was at it.

Every international personality with a taste for imperial living and a talent for bravura gestures needs a rogue in front of him to make the arrangements. Without such a henchman, either trained to order or bought ready-made, the personality is forced into actions which fall below his station but which a proper rogue can perform without diminishment and in fact with heightened stature. Scott was Kyle's rogue. He managed somehow to keep an enormous cash flow available even though KinOil, like all U.S. oil companies, was embarrassed with inventories which had been growing year by year—the worst glut since Depression days, and no place to go with it—tanks slurping over, dividends way down. It seemed to Scott Stanfus that Kyle insisted, out of sheer perversity, on expanding his expenditures at the particular moments when his income was at its lowest. Not enough that the costs of the racing stable had jumped from half a million a year to nearly twice that—Kyle and Alma had suddenly decided that the Malibu place was no longer suitable for a year-round residence; they had to buy, for close to another million, one of the largest, most magnificent houses in San Francisco for their winter use. Here, of course, they entertained expansively; they contributed generously to the Opera and the Ballet—the most direct method for new people, even a family bearing a famous California name, to announce their presence among the San Francisco elite. All this, over and above formal and hopefully productive investments in new, individually owned ventures which so far had failed to return much—as in fact, they had not been expected to—forced the enlargement of credit lines already sweating at the seams. So far, Scott Stanfus had risen magnificently to these various challenges.

He had kept paper moving between various corporate accounts and Kyle's personal exchequer without more than a momentary halt or hitch, a forfeited payment date or a sudden margin call. Only lately, in this damned art project, had his heart failed him. It seemed sheer madness—an extravagance unmatched even by the wildest flyer of Hearst's or of the great eastern families that patronized painting, sculpture and such. Insanity, as far as Scott could see—until his eye fell on Kyle in conversation with a big man whom Scott recognized instantly, as indeed who did not. A towering man, almost as tall as Kyle himself, even in his raised heels—a graying, slightly balding man with a small shoe-brush mustache and heavy-lidded but shrewd, lively, snapping eyes. A cloakroom attendant, who had brought this person his coat and hat, stood quietly by and the big man's party was also waiting—his small, plump wife in a long, dark mink coat; his bald-headed son and the son's wife plus an honor guard of henchmen, Bank of America upper-level staffers. With the backing, like a claque, of the storm beating against the doors, Kyle and A. P. Giannini parted with an Italian-style embrace.

Scott Stanfus was still in the alcove when Kyle turned back to it.

"I never thought he'd come."

"I did," said Kyle. "That misunderstanding—it's all blown over now."

The "misunderstanding" had happened when Harker E. Constable—finally confirmed as a member of KinOil's board —had replaced Bank of America with Wells Fargo as "lead bank" for KinOil.

"There's still the Petrochem loan."

"We'll take care of it. If they want collateral we'll put it up, that's all. Excuse me . . ."

He stood for a few moments on the edge of the crowd, which was not thinning out, accepting thanks of departing art viewers, shaking hands, kissing cheeks, escorting certain individuals as far as the door, and Scott Stanfus, his purse keeper, followed along at his elbow.

"*What* collateral, may I ask?" he inquired during a lull in the farewells.

"The Turkish nines. What else?"

"I don't like it."

Kyle's powerful hand closed around Scott's arm, a squeeze of conspiratorial gusto.

"A. P. wants us back in his corral—that's the main thing. Nothing else counts, don't you see? He doesn't give a damn about painting—opera is all he likes! Do you think he came here tonight to look at Renoirs and Matisses? My friend, our problems are solved."

"I hope you're right."

"I know goddamn well I'm right. We'll take care of the

Petrochem thing and we'll come out with enough on top to buy this collection, just as I planned—maybe even build a place to put it in. The Kinsale Gallery!"

"You have a site all picked out, I suppose."

Scott's sarcasm passed unnoticed.

"A. P. will be with us all the way. We'll have our permanent collection and we'll bring in guest collections, special exhibitions from all over the world. Believe me, Scott," Kyle finished, his heavy, handsome face alight. "Tonight may be the best thing that's happened to us for a long, long time!"

3

Amadeo Peter Giannini was at this time sixty-nine years old. He was still a bull of a man, with a powerful neck, a barrel body and immense, thick legs; in his bank at 300 Montgomery Street, he disdained the elevators, dashing up and down stairs, appearing unannounced to employees. In the hallways, if displeased, he seized men by their coats. He banged them against the walls, yelling at them in a fearful voice, but there were other times when he whispered, when he prowled on light feet like a hunter, poking into things. He was still as full of stealth, craft and shrewdness as when he had founded this bank at the turn of the century.

Fame had come to A. P. Giannini in the glare of San Francisco's worst catastrophe—the 1906 earthquake and fire. He had got three hundred thousand dollars out of the city in the vegetable cart he had used when, before his banking days, he had brought produce in from the country to sell in the markets. Two days later, sensing anarchy in a city without funds, he brought the money back. He put a plank across two boxes, nailed up a sign: "Bank of Italy." He accepted notes of hand from anyone he trusted, and from many whom he didn't. He cashed checks on any San Francisco bank. Most of the loans were repaid; few of the checks proved worthless. A. P. Giannini had rescued the city's credit. He had established himself forever as its outstanding man of money.

A. P.'s son Mario was now president of the bank. A. P. had kicked himself into the kind of title he despised—"Honorary." He was now honorary chairman of the board but he still came to work every day. In this capacity he had seen the file on the Petrochem loan, to which Mario had clipped a memo saying, "What shall we do about this?"

Only this morning A. P. had reviewed the file, then sent it along to a bright young fellow in the Loan Department, a certain Lent Tatum, recently recruited from the Mellon Bank of Pittsburgh. A. P. wrote across the file: "Mr. Kinsale will be coming in. See what you can work out with him."

4

Lent Tatum was happy with his job at 300 Montgomery Street. It represented an important promotion for him. He had been chosen because he had an enviable record of dealing with a particularly sensitive area of banking—the handling of distressed corporate loans.

Lent took a folder out of a small, unobtrusive filing cabinet, one of the few pieces of true office equipment to be seen in the charming and sophisticated room. He opened it, and while chatting with Kyle about unrelated topics he ran his eye over the folder's contents, as if to refresh his memory.

The folder contained all the elements of a first-class disaster.

The trouble involved Kyle's new company, Petrochem. For starters, Petrochem had borrowed ten million dollars on a short-term six percent loan from Bank of America. Kyle had co-signed the note. In the thirty months which had passed since then neither interest nor principal had been repaid; however, because of Kyle's personal credit as guarantor, the loan had been rolled over twice, each time for several million more. With each new roll over, the back interest and the back principal payments had been brought up to date but last time only after serious criticism by the Loan Committee and over the objection of the loan supervisor, Lent Tatum's immediate superior. Petrochem had excellent prospects and Kyle was indeed a valued customer, but it was time to put the loan on a rational repayment basis. The most obvious way (Lent touched very lightly on this) and of course the usual one would have been to collateralize the loan with the stock of the borrowing entity itself had it not been that in the present case the stock of a company engaged in a manufacturing operation which as yet showed no profit did not meet the bank's collateral standards.

Lent Tatum was hopeful that Kyle had some solution to propose; Kyle did. Kyle suggested putting up the Turkish nine percent bonds acquired along with an oil lease when KinOil had made its loan to Mustapha Kemal's government. A good many Turkish lire had come off the presses since then, but Petrochem's willingness to adjust at the going rate of exchange would certainly fix that.

Lent rang his bank's Foreign Department to obtain figures on the lira vis-à-vis the dollar. The loaded question was to what extent would Kyle collateralize the Petrochem loan with these lire. Lent Tatum leaned back in his chair, his attractive face toughening as he calculated what the Loan Committee would consider satisfactory. Sixty percent, over and above back payments of principal still due and outstanding plus unpaid interest, might be acceptable; seventy or seventy-five percent would be excellent.

"One hundred percent," said Kyle.

"Indeed!" said Lent Tatum. "Then that's firm?"

"Firm," said Kyle, "but we'd appreciate a little more on top."

Tatum nodded. He'd expected something of this sort. He glanced down at his scratch pad, then up at Kyle. He turned on the contagious bonhomie that had taken him so far at the Mellon Bank.

"I'll do the very best I can."

The weather worsened. In Europe, the winter was the coldest in a hundred years. One was torn to imagine the ordeal of the hardy Finns, on their skis, with rifles from the Krupp works slung across their backs, gliding through the mountains in the white storm gear that made them invisible, killing Russians.

In the United States, the isolationists held their ground. They defended to the last man the principle that nations which had defaulted on previous debts should receive no military aid. An Englishman who had been a guest at the White House infuriated many congressmen. He had suggested that the United States send fifty old destroyers to help out the English Navy. The British Embassy advised him to leave Washington at once.

Lent Tatum had accrued some vacation time. During an ordinary year he would have spent it in Europe, taking along his tall, pretty wife, but obviously this was not an ordinary year. Lent made reservations at the Royal Hawaiian. He put off departure only so as to be on hand when Petrochem made delivery of the promised collateral. Sometimes undue delays occurred between an agreement to post securities and their actual arrival at the bank; there were even occasions, in institutions less efficiently managed then the Bank of America, when the securities never arrived at all.

When a week had passed since his talk with Kyle Kinsale he rang up Scott Stanfus at KinOil to suggest delivery. Scott accepted the reminder gracefully, and sure enough, next day the Turkish nine percenters came along. The driver of the Loomis truck double-parked on Montgomery Street while the guards took the sealed canvas sacks upstairs. The guards waited at the reception counter in the Corporate Loan Department for someone to sign for the sacks. Two signatures were needed on the receipts fastened to the lead seals on the sacks, two people had to witness the delivery of the sacks, two people had to be present while the sacks were opened, two people had to count the contents, verifying each other's count, and two people, each with a separate key, had to take the sacks down to one of the collateral rooms, the great storage closets situated in the main vault, entirely separate from the vaults where customers had their safety-deposit boxes. The main vault required separate entry procedures. A fifty-seven-ton steel door, made in Germany, guarded its contents. The door closed at night and opened in the morning by the operation of an electric time clock.

Dual custody, as practiced in most banks, is a proper safeguard, but it can involve inconvenience. The Loomis men had arrived a few minutes after twelve, noon, when most of the people in the Corporate Loan Department had gone to lunch. Lent Tatum, who had been sitting with his door open, saw them at the counter and came out himself to accept delivery. He looked up and down the rows of desks in the open portion of the room to see who could serve to share custody with him. Only one clerk was still there working—an older person, Marcellino Giannini, a distant cousin of A. P.'s. Marcellino had worked for the bank for thirty years. Lent beckoned him over. He and Marcellino took the sacks to Lent's office and opened them. The bonds were in there all right—high-denomination bearer bonds handsomely engraved on stiff parchmenty paper with the likeness of a military man with a sweeping black mustache, probably Kemal Atatürk himself, emblazoned on them. The bonds were in ten-thousand-, fifty-thousand-, and hundred-thousand-lira denominations. Marcellino and Lent Tatum went to work at once, counting them and checking each other's count. Marcellino did all this faster and better than Lent, his superior, who was bored with the task. Marcellino, on the other hand, relished it. He had been, at various stages of his life, a teller, a cashier, and once, in Italy, before he leaped across an ocean and a continent, a bank executive—the president of the tiny bank in the village of Favale di Malvaro, where he and A. P. Giannini had been born. Marcellino loved the feel that came when paper of high valuation passed through his fingers. He especially admired the character of these Turkish papers—the weight of them, the authority of their gloss and stiffness. Even when nearly all had been counted and registered and packaged to be taken down to a collateral room he picked up one bond from the top of the last pile, snapped it between his strong, gnarled hands—an act of tribute or of leave-taking. A random act entirely, but after it had happened and the bond had been restored to its place on the pile, Marcellino noticed something on Lent Tatum's desk—a small, perfect circle of paper, no bigger than a British ha'penny or an Italian soldo. By all odds it was a tiny thing indeed—nothing at all which would attract attention except that it had not been there before. Marcellino was sure of that. He moistened a finger and placed it on the little white dot, to pick it up. He showed it to Lent, holding it that way on his fingertip, but Lent was already starting for the door with his share of the packaged bonds. Lent did not react. Marcellino, as he afterward related, deduced from this that Lent had already noticed the little white dot, that he knew where it had come from or considered it of no importance. Marcellino picked up his own load of bonds and followed Lent. But he put the tiny dab of paper in a change purse, and the change purse in his pocket.

Down into the bowels of the bank went the two men. The vault custodian let them into the high security area. Here each, with his separate key, unlocked the door of a collateral room and, again with separate keys, unlocked the wired cage, on the appropriate shelf, which would contain the bonds: a job well done. Lent, whose lunch had been delayed an hour or more by all this, hurried off to the University Club. Two days later he left for his postponed sojourn in Hawaii. Marcellino Giannini stayed on the job. The matter of that tiny, round dab of paper lived in his mind, however, and after due reflection, Marcellino Giannini did something about it. His investigations were rapid; they required no more than a few days, mostly on the telephone, but included one return to the collateral room, where he was accompanied by an executive of the Corporate Loan Department, so as to effect dual custody. When he had everything pieced together and was sure of his conclusions, Marcellino called his cousin, A. P., on the office telephone. It was the first time, during his thirty years at the bank, that he had done so.

"Amadeo," he said, "this is Marcellino. *Buon giorno.*"

"*Buon giorno,* Marcellino," said A. P. as briskly as if they chatted this way every day of the week, "what can I do for you?"

"I should like to see you, Amadeo," said Marcellino. "I have something to tell you."

Marcellino had chosen to speak in Italian.

"Then come up," said A. P. "You know where I am."

"I shall come immediately."

"Good," said A. P. "*Ciao,* Marcellino."

"*Ciao,*" said Marcellino.

Thus was begun the destruction of Kyle Kinsale.

5

Only two categories of people, when speaking to A. P. Giannini, called him by his first name, Amadeo: Mrs. A. P. Giannini for one, and for two, anyone born in Favale di Malvaro. Marcellino Giannini was the oldest of those thus born who still worked for the bank. Marcellino had achieved his importance later, but from the first he had been a man of whom much was expected—more, in fact, than from A. P. Marcellino had been the first person in Favale de Malvaro to learn English. He had studied it with the priest who taught at the parish school. The priest could read English well but he could not pronounce it and the pronunciation stuck in Marcellino's palate also. He had learned from the priest and he spoke like the priest and he never improved much even after he had accepted the job which A. P. wrote to offer him. His trouble with the language had impeded his rise in A. P.'s bank. That was too bad, because as far as knowing how a bank worked, nobody knew more than Marcellino.

Marcellino had gone to the files. He had got out the financial statement submitted by Petrochem when that corporation had first applied for a loan from the Bank of America, and the additional statements filed when the original loan had

been rolled over. He noted that Petrochem had loans outstanding with other banks, not located in California, but the
distant location of these banks made no difference to Marcellino: the Corporate Loan Department had a list of the loan
officers of all major banks, together with their telephone
numbers. Banking cannot be conducted without an inter-
change of information, often of a confidential nature. Marcellino understood this very well. While he did not know
personally the loan officers with whom he wished to speak—
as Lent Tatum, for instance, or his other superiors would have
known them—he was quite aware that no executive of any
bank, anywhere, was going to refuse a call from Mr. Giannini
of the Bank of America in San Francisco. Naturally, he had
himself announced that way. Once he had the relevant
executive on the line he identified himself immediately as
Marcellino Giannini but by that time it made no difference,
he was still a Giannini, and the information was supplied.

Sometimes, in cases where Petrochem had put up collateral, the lender banks had to check the records, but when the
executives of these banks called back it usually turned out
that some, at least, of the collateral had been the stout
Turkish nine percenters.

In his thorough fashion Marcellino looked over the annual
financial statements of KinOil in the Corporate Loan Department's files. Some went back many years. Most of the loans
involved had long since been paid off but a few were still
outstanding and collateralized and some of the collateral, on
review, turned out again to be the Turkish bonds: bearer
bonds, as originally issued—negotiable by the person in
possession of them—so that no change in registration had
ever been necessary.

Marcellino now had some evidence to back up his hunch.
But he needed more. He had to know the total amount of the
issue at the time it was first offered. Moody's publishing
service had a figure. Moody's also informed him that the
broker for this issue in the United States had been Lazard
Frères of New York. Marcellino called Lazard Frères and
Lazard Frères confirmed Moody's figure. The Treasury of
Turkey, without reference to the oil lease which had been the
bonus inducing KinOil to become the sole taker of the issue,
had put out twenty million dollars of the bonds.

Here, into broad daylight, out of the shadows and dust of
the collateral rooms in the vaults of famous banks—where

(except for the periodic spot checks of bank examiners, superficial at best) securities, good and bad, lowly and high-born, often sleep their profitable sleep for years on end—here emerged the stunner: the discrepancy that Marcellino's instinct had driven him to hunt down.

Petrochem—or KinOil and Petrochem together—had hocked more Turkish nines than Turkey had ever put out, six or seven million dollars more, if Marcellino's figures were right!

What did you make of that?

Much, Marcellino thought, could be made of it.

Marcellino drew up an accounting sheet. He was good at accounting, he'd had a lifetime's practice. The sheet made clear that either Moody's and Lazard Frères and the reporting banks were wrong or that, by some secret and hitherto unknown kind of fiscal copulation, the Turkish nine percenters had been reproducing themselves even while they were lying stashed away.

The accounting sheet was the first document that Marcellino, during his thirty years at the bank, had ever personally handed to his cousin, Amadeo Peter Giannini. Marcellino gave it to him as soon as he was seated, at A. P.'s invitation, beside the great man's desk. He sat quietly and watched as A. P. ran his eyes over it. In spite of their kinship, the two men showed little likeness. Marcellino Giannini was small and gnarled. Few men in Favale di Malvaro grew up tall, broad, thick and kingly like A. P. There was something in the water or the soil at Favale di Malvaro, or perhaps merely the stunting, endless farm work in the stony hillside patches, begun early in life, when young bones were not yet fully formed, that brought on arthritis. The old people and many of the young ones did not walk straight or stand upright. They stooped or bent to one side. Their legs bowed. Their necks thrust forward. They were peasants; they were poor. They looked with awe and wonder at a person like Amadeo Peter, one who could hold his head high and stride over the earth as if he had on magic boots. Even without his wealth and prowess A. P. would have been a marvel, coming from Favale di Malvaro.

Marcellino had felt that his own appearance belied the powers, the forces within him. He had longed for a chance when he could put those powers, that force to use.

Now the time had come.

A. P. took in the accounting sheet in one swooping glance. He understood from this one glance exactly what was in it and all that it meant. Nevertheless, he read it again. He read it very slowly and a harsh line appeared in his forehead, between his black, secret, heavy-lidded eyes. He laid the sheet on his desk and he looked at Marcellino, knowing that more was to be forthcoming. This was evident because Marcellino had brought with him another person, a junior executive from the Corporate Loan Department. The principle of dual custody had made necessary the presence of this second person. He and Marcellino had visited the collateral room and taken something out of it, duly authorized and signed for with both their names. They had brought one of the Turkish nine percenters with them in a plain twelve-by-fourteen-inch envelope with a tag on it showing that its contents belonged in a certain collateral consignment. The junior executive, not fully apprised of the meaning of his visit to the honorary chairman, but playing his ritualized part, handed Marcellino the envelope and Marcellino took the bond out of it and gave the bond to A. P., his cousin. When A. P. had looked at the bond, Marcellino, after asking permission, left his seat and came around to A. P.'s side. He gently took the Turkish bond from A. P.'s fingers and laid it on the large green desk blotter, beside the accounting sheet. Seen thus, against the green below, a small, round aperture appeared in the left upper corner of the bond, at the end of the space where the value of the bond was designated in Turkish lire. Quickly then, with the confidence of a conjurer performing a trick he had done many times before, Marcellino took his change purse out of his pocket. From his purse he removed a piece of paper, the identical round white dot he had picked up when he and Lent Tatum had been registering the bonds for consignment as collateral. Once more moistening a fingertip he put the little paper dot into the hole in the bond. It fitted perfectly, exactly as it had when some gluey substance had held it there, before Marcellino's handling of the bond, the snap he had exerted, had dislodged it. With the dot in place, and one or two other slight changes, and hey, presto! A ten-thousand-lire bond became a hundred-thousand-lire bond. It was an interesting trick.

A. P. Giannini nodded. He put up two fingers and rubbed them across his bristly mustache.

"Capisco," he said. "Grazie, cugino."

"Di niente, cugino," said Marcellino.

The interview was over. From now on the matter was out of Marcellino's hands. He stepped back as A. P. Giannini rose from his chair.

A. P.'s heavy face lightened with cordiality, and he shook hands gravely and respectfully with Marcellino Giannini, his cousin from Favale di Malvaro.

CHAPTER TWENTY-ONE

The House in the Brush

1

From that moment Marcellino never knew what happened. The machinery of the huge bank, for which he had worked so long and helped just now in such alert, hardheaded fashion, swung into action. It went forward in sealed conference rooms, in legal chambers where sat the great, fierce *gumbas* of the hundred-thousand-a-year class, the *consiglieri* who looked after A. P.'s interests. A. P. had clamped down. He had invoked the code of confidentiality without which no bank can conduct its business let alone one still in thrall to the inflexible will of its founder.

Not a word leaked out. No mention of the odd little hole in the Turkish nine percenter to the muckraking press, ever avid to drum up a circus out of far less intriguing episodes. After all, how could you tell, without the most elaborate, sophisticated inquiry, how many of the bonds had suffered tampering, how many, in spite of all, might not be genuine? Other banks, the most formidable in the nation, had accepted these bonds as genuine; an international investment house of the very first order had underwritten them.

All this must be weighed before a true accounting could be made.

Recompense would follow; punishment would fall where it

should, rather than on the bank's two million five hundred thousand depositors, who had not deserved it, let alone the uncounted millions of depositors in the other famous banks which did business with Petrochem. What was at stake was confidence, that faith on which stands planted the whole architecture of finance capital. For every banker knows that in the sealed boxes and envelopes of the armored collateral rooms are certain interlopers, pieces of illegitimate paper, stolen or crafted, which have been accepted at face value by qualified borrowers and which still serve, in their anonymity, like crashers at a party, to support the orderly flow of affairs.

Naturally, outside the bank there were certain repercussions.

Cliff Kinsale, for instance, couldn't understand why Harker E. Constable had requested—ordered, in effect—a meeting of the board of the L&CC.

Odd that Constable could issue such requests, such orders now, when earlier there had been so much opposition just to having him around, in any capacity, but the fact was that he could. Harker E. Constable had been quick to seize upon two opportunities, both the handiwork of death. After the demise of a cousin, Monsignor Eduardo de Baca Pons, one of the elder Church officials and the representative of the archdiocese's interests in the L&CC, Luanna, with Troy and Cliff away and Kyle busy with Petrochem, had met no serious objection when she proposed Constable to fill the vacancy; and after Troy's disaster in Mexico, Constable had vaulted higher. By custom, the chairman of the L&CC also held the chairmanship of KinOil. Constable had obtained the third chair within months of his election to the board; he had maneuvered his way to the second while Cliff was still in Mexico.

The current meeting was to be at the ranch, apparently for privacy. Either that or to ensure that Doc and Millie would attend, since both, as they grew older, had shown a distaste for traveling.

But the ranch, in midwinter! Nothing could have been more inconvenient.

"Couldn't we wait till the annual meeting?" Cliff asked.

"I'm afraid not, old boy," said Constable. He spoke casually, in his round, lawyerly tones, but there was an imperiousness about him that Cliff found exasperating. He knew Constable had disliked him ever since his original effort—successful at the time—to keep him off the board. Too bad he couldn't have stayed off permanently!

"In other words, this is some kind of emergency."

In the history of the Land and Cattle Company, much of its business seemed to fall into this category. Cliff could remember, from his earliest boyhood, the tall, tough-skinned men shouting on the lawn, under the big trees, the women mostly silent, not quite understanding, rather frightened—all except his mother. His mother had not been silent and she had understood very well everything that happened. Lately, he had worried about her living there alone on the ranch. Women, he thought, suffered more than men from loneliness —a different condition entirely from solitude, which could be enjoyed. At least he could see how she was holding up. He wondered if once more she was in league with Constable . . . or even whether there was a further relationship. But he put this thought out of his head.

"I'd say that was an understatement, if anything," said Constable evenly.

Cliff sighed.

"All right, I'll be there. When do you want me?"

And Constable, in his quiet dominating way, suggested a day and hour. Cliff said these would be all right.

Since Troy's death, he had been living an interim sort of life in a big rented house in Brentwood.

The house itself was an interim sort of house, hardly a habitation at all, when considered as a proper place for people to live. This was its unique quality, that true, ordinary life had never gone on in it, perhaps, or at least not to the extent of giving its tenants, whoever they had been, a sense of relationship with it. Various people had sojourned in it, most of them connected in some way with the motion-picture business, but other people also, some famous, some merely rich. One person, perhaps more, had died mysteriously in it; there had been a police investigation. Photographs were on record in newspaper libraries. "Canyon Mansion Probe . . ."

It was a big house, tiles, its grounds sprawling over an acre or more, surrounded with brushy slopes, dry as tinder, which caught fire from time to time and burned down other, far more beautiful, more lavish houses, but not this one.

This one, in its brutish, concrete way, could survive anything—an earthquake, a bombing. It was there to stay. A baby had once drowned in its pool, where deer, at dawn, stole out of the amazing brush to drink.

Cigar smoke hung in the curtains. Cliff sent them to be cleaned. They came back, wrapped in cellophane, the cigar smoke still murmurous in them, like the record of a half-heard conversation. Cliff bought new curtains. He had rented the place fully furnished. Servants came with it, if one wished, but Cliff refused them; possibly they were responsible for the cigar-smoke smell, the spider-shaped crack, carelessly spackled and already flaking, on the pantry wall. He got in a whole new staff—cook, driver, butler, upstairs maid, cook's helper, gardener, and a union projectionist who reported on call, when Cliff ran a film. He slept in a big room in which, during the night, the furniture seemed to rearrange itself so that in the morning, groping his way out for a nude splash in the pool, he bumped into it.

Every day he drove from this house to the KinOil Building and worked eight or ten hours, using Kyle's office there since Kyle, taken up with the international scene, the strange stalemated war and his personal extravagances, had moved largely now to San Francisco.

An interim life! He would leave it as soon as possible. He was making plans to get out, get into the political scene in California, but for the present he was stuck here, a prisoner in the big bedeviled house balancing in the brush between two worlds, the busy city down below and the lonely trail on a small mesa near Tampico, where Troy had died.

Cliff had come back from Mexico emotionally and physically drained. He had stayed there nearly three months after the disaster on the mesa—gone back grimly, after bringing his father's body home for burial, or those parts of it which could be collected. The Rosary had been held in St. Francis Xavier Church in Altemira and Troy's casket had slipped down slowly on its canvas straps to repose beside Hub's. The Mass had been nice, everyone said, though performed with fewer trimmings than the one for Hub. Kyle had written out a check for ten thousand dollars for the archdiocese—a most generous gesture; he had given the envelope to Cliff to hand to the bishop. The weather had been miserable, rain oozing from the umbrellas of the mourners; when His Eminence reached for some earth to drop onto the coffin he came up with a handful of mud.

Cliff started back to Tampico that same night. There had still been a lot to do. The field inventory was completed and the government's check received late in February; on March 18, 1938, Cárdenas expropriated all foreign leases, as had been expected. KinOil had been one of two U.S. companies which came out with cash. The other was Sinclair. Both had settled for the cost of their surface installations, properly estimated and promptly paid for. During all those final weeks, in the last adjustments, the endless commuting between Mexico City and the Pánuco, the man working at Cliff's side—his one link with the past—had been Marsh Borland. Marsh had been released unharmed in Tampico, after being held for several days, although the ransom demanded by the "voice" on the telephone had never been paid. So the whole, sad crazy trek into the jungle and up onto the mesa and the deaths of the six men in the booby-trapped lead car—the wounded guide; Herrera, the translator; Dr. Travis; Saturnino, the driver; Dude Kelly, the armed guard; and Troy—all in vain! All unnecessary! If only . . . but Cliff, by determined and repeated efforts, had taught himself to keep such speculations, and in fact all the happenings of that fearful night, out of his waking thoughts. Bad enough that sometimes, in spite of all his struggle to push them away, they entered his dreams.

Carrie had written him a letter of condolence. It had been a warm, sweet letter, full of shock, horror and sympathy. He had written her in return. He had also talked to her several times on the telephone, on the buzzing and perpetually delayed and interrupted international circuits of that time. She had sounded all right. She had sounded like Carrie and yet also in some way, possibly due to the circuits, not like Carrie. She had told him about her work. She had gone into the play which they had talked about as they walked on the Calle Edgar Allan Poe. It had been a wonderful play, she said; it had been most unfair that it had failed. Something had gone wrong. Cliff had not quite understood what, on the buzzing line. The producer had interfered with the director or the director had not understood what a wonderful play it was, or had been. Anyway it had closed and Carrie, in New Haven, had been unhappy about it; to Cliff it seemed that she was weeping but he had not been sure, the connection that night had been particularly bad.

He would go to New York. He decided that instantly. He said he would leave in the morning but she told him firmly not to do so. She would explain why. She would call him tomorrow. Or she might not call him. She might write him a letter. Yes, a letter . . . no, she had not changed. She loved him, but she had been . . . thinking.

"What do you mean, thinking?" he shouted. "Thinking about what, for Christ sake?"

"Please don't shout," she said, "I can hear you perfectly, darling. I've been thinking about us. I want you to come to New York but not until I've written the letter. I've been too exhausted to write it but I will now."

"Oh, a kiss-off letter, is that it?" he said furiously. "Is that what I'm supposed to wait for? Well, no thanks."

"Darling," said Carrie sweetly, "I'm talking on a public telephone and there are just certain things I can't say and I won't. I've told you I haven't written the letter but it would not be in any sense a kiss-off letter, in your lovely phrase. It's something I've given a lot of thought to. I adore you and I'd love to go on talking to you but there are other people waiting to use this phone so I have to stop."

"Marry me!" yelled Cliff. *"Listen, Carrie . . ."*

She had already hung up. He could hear the money she had been putting into the coin box slide down to the bottom. Then the line went dead.

The letter came all right. It was a legibly written, logically reasoned letter, written in her firm handwriting on the stationery of the Algonquin Hotel. She wrote that she had been working very, very hard, and sometimes hard work changed a person's perspective. It might help one see certain things more clearly or it might make one confused. She felt confused. She had been wondering whether two people in such different and demanding businesses could make a success of life together.

A kiss-off, just as he had thought.

The letter infuriated him. In Mexico, he could see now, he might have been stupid, from her point of view. She had been way out ahead of him emotionally on this life-together proposition. Now he had caught up! He knew that if ever two people had been shaped to be the male and female parts of a whole, he and Carrie were those people. He had not caught on to that in Mexico and since then she had lost track of it. Also there was probably some character in the acting company who had been trying to get her in bed. That was no doubt what she meant when she said she was confused. First he thought of calling her to clear this up. Then he decided not to. Nothing of this nature would be cleared up on the telephone. It would be cleared up when she was in his arms and they were making love. For the same reason, it would be ridiculous to answer her letter. She must have known how he'd react to that. He would go to New York at once. He was in Los Angeles, picking up some city clothes and attending to some last chores in the office when he read in *The Hollywood Reporter* that Carrie Drew, United Artists star, and Patrick Millage, actor, had been married in the apartment of Jed Harris, producer of a play in which both had recently appeared.

Cliff wired to congratulate her. Assuming that now she would set up housekeeping as she had once before, as she'd told him, with the Great Person of The Theatah from Provincetown—had that person been anything like this Patrick Millage?—he ordered a silver serving dish from Shreve's in San Francisco. Carrie wrote prettily to thank him. The letter, like her previous effort, the kiss-off, was written from the Algonquin or at least on the notepaper provided there. She and Pat had not found an apartment yet but they were looking for one. They wanted to have a real home of their own. When she found one she would let him know the address and he must come to dinner. She knew he would like Pat. She was anxious for them to meet.

Cliff did not share her eagerness for such a confrontation. He did, nevertheless, meet Mr. Millage—once. The incident took place by chance. Cliff had gone to the Beverly Hills Hotel for an appointment with Lester Pearce of Midland Oil, who had flown in for a conference. He was leaving Pearce's cottage, walking toward the Polo Lounge, when he saw a couple ahead of him, going in the same direction. The girl was Carrie. There was no mistaking the flame of her burnished hair, the set of her hips and back. Cliff crossed a small piece of lawn. He came up from behind, shuffling his feet so as not to startle her, and touched her lightly; when she turned, he put his arm around her.

"Don't I know this girl?"

"Oh, my God! Cliff! Cliff Kinsale! I don't believe it."

He kissed her on the cheek and then, because she moved her face so as to make it happen, on the mouth.

"Cliff, this is Pat—my husband. Pat Millage. Pat . . . Cliff."

"Glad to meet you, sir," said Cliff.

"Hello there," said Pat Millage.

They shook hands. Cliff waited until they were in motion again, this time as a threesome, cramped on the narrow walkway, before he looked down—the obligatory look to confirm what he had felt when her so-familiar body, thicker, heavier now, where one did not want it to be thick or heavy, had touched him as they kissed. She was at least six months pregnant.

"You never came to see us," said Carrie accusingly. "You sent that lovely dish and I wrote to give you our address but you never came. Shame on you!"

"I know, I know. I haven't been east at all lately. And we've been busy as hell."

She had never actually given him the address.

"I suppose the oil business is riding high these days."

"Well, no. It should be but— Well, we've got troubles. I won't bore you with them."

"You poor man!" said Carrie, laughing. "How I pity you! Don't you feel that way, Pat?"

"One has to," said Pat Millage.

He was not quite as tall as Carrie, well built and muscular, though he looked a little flabby. He was blond and he had a handsome, sunburned face. He looked adoringly at Carrie, grateful to be included in the conversation.

Actors, Cliff thought.

"Are you here to do a movie?"

She patted her belly complacently.

"With this? Good Lord, no. But Patrick is. A war thing. He rather likes it, don't you dear?" She turned back to Cliff, not waiting for an answer. "Pat's been in the Army—British —but he's changed citizenship. If it weren't for that he'd be back there now, fighting."

"Should be, I suppose," said Millage. "May still go. Have to see what happens next."

Effortlessly, his face pulled itself into a lean, soldierly vigilance.

Actors!

Could they have lunch? Cliff said he'd lunched. Were they at the hotel? They were at the hotel. He'd call, he said. He never did, somehow, nor did he hear whether Millage had reported for duty under the auspices of Warner Brothers or Buckingham Palace. He did not meet Patrick Millage again, but he did read, in Louella Parsons' column a few months later, that Carrie had borne a son, Christopher Millage, weight eight pounds. She would soon resume her film career.

That had been the last time he'd seen Carrie until tonight, when, after a fashion, he'd be seeing her again: tonight he was running one of her pictures.

2

The guests for the private showing in his projection room numbered twenty: a mix of oil and film people, with the latter in preponderance; after all, they were far and away the most amusing, and they entertained him in their turn. Several of the contacts he'd formed during the making of *Low Man Out* had settled into durable, pleasant friendships.

Then there were also the others—the agents and money-men, the executive entrepreneurs—who could never be convinced that he had really left show business. No one ever did, no one with Cliff's kind of money. He might fake indifference, but some day the right script, or the right woman, would lure him back.

"You keep on," one of them told him blandly. "It's like gold fever—you keep looking for that one big bonanza."

"I don't need a bonanza. All I wanted was some fun."

"We can supply that too."

"See me in a couple of years."

What he would want from the motion-picture business, in a couple of years, was not entertainment but—if his plans went through—political support: a source of campaign funds, and a propaganda machine which, even if used sparingly, could swing any California election, promulgate or defeat any ballot measure, make or unmake any candidate.

Ilona Cape had gone back to England. He had lost touch with her entirely, but there had been others, even after Carrie—enough to provide a steady flow of women through the big house in the brush, above the spread of the city. There had been a time when he'd brought women up there: actresses and starlets, since these were the most available, but others too: good-looking, idle women, some of them rich in their own right, others recently divorced and living on alimony. A few, inevitably, were shopping for a husband, but a larger percentage simply wanted "romance"—a special kind of lovemaking in which certain rules must be observed, the proper opening of doors and lighting of cigarettes, the right tables at Ciro's or Romanoff's or Chasen's or the Trocadero or La Conga. Once you had gone through the courtship stage (in some cases a week or even more) they took their clothes off happily. If the dress was an evening dress it might have the new zip fasteners like Carrie's wardrobe in Mexico City. Irene had been using them in Beverly Hills. Lady Honor Chanon of London was known to be partial to such fasteners.

You could help with these, of course. At times you had to, they were hard to reach. Best, though, to keep your mitts off the girdle. She could wriggle out of that alone. It would go on the chair next to the bed, its elastic shrinking it curiously and a rubbery smell rising from it. Then the decorous trip to the bathroom for makeup removal and the insertion of the diaphragm or whatever; or perhaps just a routine check to make sure it hadn't sloshed around. Some of these ladies were surprisingly adept, once in bed, at what they had come to do, and after breakfast by the pool, if the weather suited, you would go to the car to fetch the suitcase (so much better to think ahead!) containing the daytime outfit. New makeup then, of course.

In Paris, with the Huns safely hemmed off by the Maginot Line, Coco Chanel had introduced white eyelids and green eyelashes. . . .

There were coffee and nightcaps in the den for those who wished to stay and talk about the film; later, Cliff walked out to the parking area with the Leland Haywards and the Fondas.

"Pretty good, I thought," said Hayward. "Carrie is maturing. Not quite the right part for her, but she got away with it."

"She can get away with anything," said Mrs. Fonda.

"No, she can't," said Maggie Hayward. "She can't at all; she just does a certain kind of part very well. She has a range of about this size . . ."

She held up two fingers to show the size.

"Why, Maggie," said Hayward, "I thought you adored Carrie."

"I do adore her. But the part just wasn't right. What do you think, Hank?" she said to Fonda. "Do you think it was right for Carrie?"

"I don't think it was right at all," said Fonda. "But I liked the picture."

"It was an interesting picture and she was damn good in it," said Hayward staunchly. He could be quite free with criticism of his clients' work, but only if the client was present. In this case the host was present. He put his arm around Cliff's shoulders.

"Don't let Maggie fool you, we all enjoyed it very much."

"I did, for one," said Cliff.

"We all did, Cliff," said Mrs. Fonda.

"Oh, let's stop being so polite," said Maggie Hayward. "I know just what Carrie did. She got impatient, having the baby and all. She was tired of sitting around, so she took the first thing that came along. I know exactly how she felt."

"The baby—yes, of course," said Mrs. Fonda. "How's that marriage going, Leland? I heard something. I've forgotten what."

"I heard nothing," said her husband quickly, "nothing at all."

He looked sternly at Mrs. Fonda, as did Hayward. It was possible that Mrs. Fonda did not remember, or did not care, that Carrie Drew had once been, rather publicly, Cliff's girl. Or possibly it was because she *did* remember that she'd made the remark, testing Cliff's reaction rather than the response of the person addressed. At all events, to most of those standing beside the Hayward car, the question did not seem well chosen.

Hayward answered Mrs. Fonda with a gesture—the equivocal swivel of a hand that could mean "this way and that" or "tell you later."

Mrs. Fonda was already in the car. She waved goodbye to Cliff from the back seat. Cliff kissed Maggie Hayward's cheek.

"Don't pay any attention to me," she said, squeezing his hand as he helped her into the car. "When I talk like that about a part it always means I would have liked it for myself. I would have loved this one."

"You would have been marvelous in it, darling. Absolutely marvelous," said Hayward without conviction.

He shook hands with Cliff and got into the car, pulling down one of the jump seats. Fonda got into the back, between the two beautiful women, and Cliff shut the door. They were the last of his guests to leave. He stood looking after them with his hand raised, watching the big car as the driver took it down the pea-gravel drive between the walls of brush.

Cliff walked slowly back into the empty house. The oakwood fire in the living room had sunk into a bed of brightorange coals; the air was heavy with post-party staleness. Cliff emptied ashtrays, gathered glasses on a tray. His man, no doubt in bed by now, would normally attend to all this in the morning, but the small cleanup chores provided something to do, an excuse not to go upstairs.

He had expected to sit through Carrie's film impersonally, and indeed he had—but in a strangely disturbing way: it had been as if, able to step backward in time, he had been forced by the changes in her to reprise their past, their passion and their lost chances, through the jaded eyes of a voyeur.

He searched the room for a pipe, found one he wanted and sat down with it by the fading fire. He knew well, better than anyone else—better than Hayward, who had seen but refused to admit it, or his wife, Margaret Sullavan, who had so quickly proclaimed it—what had been wrong with Carrie's performance.

It was very simple. She had been too old for the part.

Could one be too old for anything at twenty-five? He had never thought of that, but there you were; they had all sensed it. He wondered if they had also sensed his own reaction to it—not that he cared.

Physically, Carrie—or at least the buoyant image of her on the screen—could still thrill him. She was as earthy, as natural, as beautiful as ever. What had changed, aged, had not been her body but her spirit. Something had gone wrong there, her feeling for a role she could once have understood in all its nuances. It had been a very good role. It had taken her away from the Girl-Next-Door image she'd projected in *Low Man Out;* it had been a role capable of bringing out the flash and deviltry of the real Carrie.

In the film tonight she had played the daughter of a rich, attractive man—a painter—with two mistresses: one, coarse, pretty and promiscuous, who had no chance for a long-term relationship; the other, an elegant, older woman who wanted to marry him. Eager to keep him for herself, Carrie had conspired with the trivial mistress against the scheming, eligible one, and in the end got rid of both of them. The mood was light, the screenplay clearly designed to keep it that way, the erotic thrust of the plot always present, never stressed. Yet Carrie had missed the lightness, worked too hard for the laughs, made the scenes with her father, her feeling for him, tense instead of joyous; she had colored the twin conspiracies with the women as a little shabby, a little sad. Had it been the director's fault? Some of it, no doubt—but this director was a man of talent, famous for his touch with just this kind of material. Also, what director could put Carrie down, send her off in one direction when she wanted to move in another? The

youth of her, the blaze and the verve of her hadn't reached
the screen. It was as if she had grown a skin over them, to
choke them off. Or as if life had done this to her.

Cliff's pipe had gone out. He poked a splinter of kindling
into the coals, took a light from it. That queer wiggle of the
fingers Hayward had made when Mrs. Fonda asked him about
Carrie's marriage! What about that? There was nothing to
prevent him, Cliff, from calling Hayward, asking him point-
blank whether Carrie and Millage were having trouble, but
somehow this was not the sort of thing one asked Hayward
about a girl who was also a client of his; you picked up that
kind of gossip from the columnists. Or found out for yourself.

Cliff tapped out his last pipe. He took his tray of glasses to
the butler's pantry and turned out the downstairs lights.

CHAPTER TWENTY-TWO

The Embezzler

1

The ranch landing field on the top flat was no longer composed of bumpy, steamrolled adobe but of tarmac, installed by contractors who had built Mills Field in San Francisco. Landing should have been easy, but the Coast Guard weather bureau had reported gusts of storm velocity. Paul Mantz, a movie pilot who flew KinOil's DC-3 when the regular man was off duty, circled the field twice, then spoke to Cliff on the intercom.

"It's dicey down there."

"It's always that way."

"Sure you don't want to go into Altemira? A lot less wind, that much lower."

"All right, if we have to. But we're late already."

The angle of Mantz's head expressed protest. And this man had flown a De Havilland through a railroad tunnel with less than twenty feet total wing clearance for a film! There was no one more cautious, Cliff reflected, than a stunt flyer on a private charter flight.

Mantz brought down the big plane into the gale, the leeside wing all but brushing the station wagon in which a ranch hand waited to drive Cliff down the hill. Cliff left the hand to help Mantz secure the plane; he drove the wagon down himself.

Half a dozen cars were parked in the pea gravel, under the big trees that surrounded the house; he could see through the window, as he passed under the porte cochere, that the meeting had already begun. Whatever "emergency" Mr. Constable had cooked up for today, he was wasting no time getting at it; the lawyer's voice came through to him from the grouping of chairs at the far end of the big living room.

". . . breakdown right here, for anyone wishing copies."

Millie Braden, seated with Doc on a couch against the wall, was making notes. Cliff chose a chair next to his mother. She reached to squeeze his hand—a welcome of a sort—but never took her eyes from Constable. A secretary had set up a stenotype machine; she penciled something on her ribbon of paper, already cluttered with strange symbols. Cliff nodded at Dan Shannon and Reeves Thurmond: the Old Guard was here in force—these two now based, at Kyle's behest, in San Francisco. An attractive, stylishly dressed man, with an eastern or foreign quality about him, took a question from Thurmond, and it was soon evident that this youngish man with his intense blue eyes and thatch of light-brown hair—this stranger, rather than Constable—was running the meeting.

"Who's that?" Cliff whispered to Luanna.

"Tatum, Bank of America. Shush! . . .Why weren't you here on time?"

Cliff muttered something about lousy flying weather. And as if in confirmation of his words the great eucalyptus by the driveway sent a limb crashing down. The elms were thrashing as if pulled by wires.

". . . vital to obtain . . ."

"You are quite right, of course."

"Then why," said Reeves Thurmond, his manner quite as circumspect as Tatum's, yielding nothing here to him or anyone, as yet, "can't a complete accounting be supplied? After all," he added dryly, "KinOil and Petrochem have the advantage, if such it can be called, of a joint treasurer, Scott Stanfus."

"He's gone," said Constable.

"You're not serious?"

"I wish I weren't. His telephone has been disconnected. His bank accounts are closed. His house is up for sale. Likewise his automobile, on consignment with the dealer who sold it to him. We have information that he has been moving money into a numbered Swiss account; money in quite large amounts."

"Incredible!"

"Not really," said Tatum, "not in this type of situation. Although I realize," he added in a mollifying tone to Thurmond, "I quite realize it must come as a shock to you. A person you have dealt with through the years."

"Dealt with!" interrupted Shannon. "Jesus, he was just an accountant—got to be treasurer at KinOil five or six years ago when we moved him up to replace another thief."

"Easy, Dan," said Thurmond. "Lamar Custis wasn't a real hard-ass thief . . . excuse me, Luanna. Just a market rigger. An over-sharp—"

"*Thief!*" Shannon finished for him. "Do you think Stanfus has left the country?"

Constable shrugged.

"Wherever he went, he took his family with him. We won't see him again—not without extradition proceedings, or I miss my guess."

Shannon said blandly, "If you're talking extradition then you're talking about charges—a whole hell of a mess."

"Exactly," said Tatum. "At the moment, I have no interest in the whereabouts of Mr. Stanfus. If he has explanations to make, let him make them to you. Or let him keep silent. So far as the bank is concerned there is no assumption of fraud or of intent to commit fraud on the part of anyone. I should like to make that clear."

He looked around, drawing all present into the spell of his brightness, his frankness.

"Our common ground here seems to be that both the bank and KinOil Corporation are creditors of Petrochem—a situation complicated in our case by some unacceptable collateral tendered by Petrochem to secure a loan. Hopefully, between us we can find a way to replace the bad collateral with good collateral, as soon as possible. It's as simple as that. And the means to effect that replacement . . . the means, of course, are at hand, once the details are worked out."

"In other words," said Constable glumly, "another loan from KinOil to Petrochem."

Tatum nodded. "Certainly that would be the most direct approach. KinOil might, in lieu of that, choose to absorb Petrochem and dissolve it. Or recapitalize it. I don't put those options forward as suggestions—merely as possibilities. We're not going by the book here, as a bank examiner might—as he would have to, I suppose, if the matter came to his attention."

There was no mistaking the premonitory tilt, the faint beaky shadow of a threat in Mr. Tatum's last phrase, airily, brightly uttered though it was. For, obviously, the way the matter might come to a bank examiner's attention would be if the bank called it to his attention. In which case quite a different sequence of events would take place than those alternatives just mentioned.

Reeves Thurmond cleared his throat.

"I should like to commend you, sir, for your goodwill, and the bank for its cooperation."

Tatum smiled his thanks, but Constable cut in.

"Do you make that commendation, Reeves, as a stockholder in Petrochem or as board member and chief counsel for KinOil?"

"I make it," said Thurmond heavily, "in both those capacities. Is there something wrong with that?"

"Not as long as you make clear which side of the table you're on. You can't be in two places at once."

"Gentlemen," said Tatum, "let's take it that we all stand together. I've discussed this with Mr. A. P. Giannini, and that is his hope—that divisiveness will not creep in, corporate divisiveness or any other kind. Banking, as he sees it, is a family affair, and there are few families with which the Bank of America has had a longer or, if one may say so, happier relationship than with the Kinsale family. Here we have two Kinsale companies, technically separate, to be sure, but still interlocking at the board level and, of course, at the executive level also."

The last reference obviously applied to Kyle—conspicuous, in the time-hallowed phrase, by his absence. Cliff, trying to get his bearings, and annoyed at Constable for not briefing him better on the telephone, wondered why Kyle, since his new company was in some kind of jam, had chosen to stay away. It did not then occur to him that Constable had been careful not to invite him. Constable had never, face-to-face, been able to stand up to Kyle—not even at that critical meeting two years and a half ago when Luanna had first nominated him for the board.

A young Mexican girl came in carrying a heavy silver tray with a silver coffeepot and a number of cups on it. Also spoons, cream in an elegant silver pitcher, cookies, and whatever else was needed for a conference break. Leaving the girl to pour, Luanna fetched a cup for herself and another for Cliff. She led Cliff over to a table near the wall, the same ormolu table at which, when Hub had been dying, two bill collectors had been sitting.

"That fellow from the bank is an idiot."

"He seemed all right to me."

"He never told you the nub of it."

Luanna's mouth had the queer, wry twist it got when something bad had happened which suited her taste. She leaned over, speaking into his ear. "Kyle stuck A. P. Giannini with a bunch of phony bonds."

"Mother, that's ridiculous."

"I agree. But it's happened."

"Well, if it has, Kyle didn't know about it. Maybe Scott Stanfus . . . if it's true that he's disappeared . . ."

"He most certainly has. But don't let's start making him the fall guy."

"The bank seems ready to. If we're to believe Mr. Tatum."

"The bank wants the bonds redeemed. They don't give a hoot where the money comes from, and the likeliest place to get it is from us. And the worst of it is, we'll have to fork out. Even Harker recognizes that."

So it's Harker now, is it? Cliff thought. He took stock of his mother. She had much of her old spirit back, the verve and the mean-eyed Indian heat that had gone out of her when Troy was killed.

"But, God, Mother, surely Uncle Kyle has enough money of his own to—"

"We don't know. He's chucked in eight million developing Petrochem, lots of it borrowed."

"But his other assets . . ."

"What assets? The horses? Who wants them? There's a war on, dear, and racers are no good for pulling gun limbers."

"The art collection—that's no drop in the bucket."

"An art collection that's been taken on consignment. And he's also contracted for a huge gallery to put it in, and he plans to give the whole kaboodle to the city of San Francisco. Nobody spends money like that—not the du Ponts, not the Rockefellers. Fraud and embezzlement, false certificates . . ."

"Tatum never said they were false."

"He said they were unacceptable. But the bank accepted them. So why are they throwing them out if there's nothing wrong with them? Naturally, if you spend insanely, fraud's the next thing on the program. He'd break us all if we'd let him and he's getting worse. Spending! It's some kind of a disease; it takes hold of certain people. Even your father couldn't control him. 'Kyle!' he would say. 'Kyle just . . .' and he'd throw up his hands, telling me the latest crazy extravagance."

"Mother, Dad never understood . . ."

"The hell he didn't. He—"

". . . what it took to build KinOil from a one-strike independent company to what it is today. And I mean it *took* spending, it *took* extravagance. Kyle and Dad were close, closer than you ever want to admit. It was only in a few ways that they—"

"Yes. A few ways, goddamn important ways. Honey, in *lots* of ways they hated each other's guts. Had, ever since they were boys. I lived with all that love and a lot of that hate. I lived with it for years, and I *still* couldn't handle it. *Or* Kyle. Nothing could convince him, then or now, that the laws other people live by have the slightest meaning for him. Did you know he tried to screw me once?"

"Mother . . ."

"Well, he did. His brother's wife, the brother whom you say he loved so much. Not that he had more than a passing whim for me. He didn't. It was just . . . one more of his kingly notions!"

"Kingly, for Christ sake . . ."

"Yes, kingly. 'Take what I want because I'm in the mood. Take it—the money, the women, anything. It all belongs to me.' That's how he figured. Well, it didn't work. It was the morning Cliff Kinsale Number One came in. We'd just got home, after driving out to the gusher. Your dad sat down in the parlor, went off fast asleep. I was in the bedroom. Well! . . . I never told anyone. Not till now."

"You mean he actually . . ."

"I mean he *tried."*

Luanna pushed her fists under her cheekbones, narrowing the naturally tilted eyes. Her lips thickened, moistened, as if avid for the memory she was presenting as so evil.

" 'Oh, no, you don't,' I said. 'I've got a pistol here. You just come one step nearer and I'll blow that thing of yours clean off. It won't grow back,' I said. I didn't have a pistol, but there was one in the closet. I was scared to death we'd wake up Troy. . . . We both had oil all over us—"

"Then something *did* happen."

Up to this point Cliff had suspected that Luanna, with her jealousy of Kyle, plus her fury about the current dilemma, had been making all this up . . . but now he wondered. Had the antagonism between Luanna and Kyle through the years really been her jealousy, as he'd thought it was, or had it been rage, the frustration of sexual betrayal? The copulation of two bodies stained and slithery with oil: a brother's wife, the cuckolded husband asleep in the next room.

"*Nothing*. Never! Only just enough to . . . make him go away. So finally he did. Troy would have killed him. I wouldn't have blamed him. You never knew that, did you? Never thought your wonderful, princely, money-crazy uncle would do something like that. Or," she corrected herself quickly, "I mean, that he'd try. So all through the years Troy worked, he drilled wells, he built a town. You grew up in the town, out in the dunes, in Piru. And Kyle played polo. He raced horses. He bought pictures. He screwed women. He traveled around with kings and dukes and spent the money. And now we have to make good for him. It makes me sick. It makes me want to vomit."

Luanna wiped her mouth. She took a few sips of her coffee, now grown cold, as if literally to keep her stomach from upheaving.

Cliff sat with his hands on the shiny little table and his head bowed over them. Then he jerked his body upright.

"I have to talk to Tatum."

Luanna looked over her shoulder at the group around the fireplace.

"Well, you'd better hurry then. Looks as if he's just about to go."

2

As Cliff stood in the granite entry of Kyle's great San Francisco house, he felt it would be quite appropriate—even to be expected—if the manservant who had just taken stock of him through the peephole in the massive, iron-banded double doors would presently open those doors and throw him into the street.

He had come on no proper errand. He had in his pocket a letter—a crazy kind of letter: not a request, which could be rejected or at least argued about; not even an order, which of course no one had authority to give except the stockholders, none of whom had even heard about this letter.

Harker E. Constable had dictated it. He'd had his secretary, the stenotypist lady whom he'd brought to the meeting at the ranch, write it up on a plain sheet of typing paper. It was addressed to him, Harker E. Constable, at KinOil's San Francisco office, and all it said was that, for personal reasons, *Kyle Kinsale resigned as chairman of the board of KinOil*, the great corporation he had co-founded.

The resignation was to take effect as of the date the letter was received. That was all there was to it, except the signature. It was to be signed by Kyle.

Naturally, the letter could have been sent by mail. Either that or a hired messenger could have brought it around. Neither of these courses had been followed because Cliff had volunteered. He'd made up his mind even while Constable was still dictating and the lady was typing. He could do it. There was no one else who could.

He was not doing Constable's bidding. He hated Constable. He hated the letter, the outcome of the discussion which, after Tatum took his leave, had dragged on that windy morning into the lunch hour and past it. "One thing we've never done," Millie had said, "is wash our dirty linen in public. We're not going to start now."

She had glanced over at her husband, grayer and thinner but spryer, if anything, than in the old days—the way small-boned, busy doctors get as they grow older, watching what they eat and such, and rushing around. And Dr. Braden, sitting by the fire, warming the medical circulation as he weighed the corporate opinion, nodded. Yes, the resignation. He supposed it had to be.

Dirty linen! Cliff couldn't look at his mother. Millie and Doc, proud of their work, the fame of the Braden-Kinsale Clinic, its research in a special field—viral-related diseases of the spine. Out-of-state, even foreign-country patients now augmented the practice which had started with the slope heads in the valley—those, and the poor stiff bones in the mission graves.

No dirty linen there to bury. And no scandal to be tolerated, even one of such remote connection as these mysterious collateralized bonds.

The linen Millie had in mind, no doubt, was the old fable about Grandpa Hub and the orchard girl, once such a solemn secret. Cliff hadn't heard it until he was in his teens, on a camping trip with Troy, who, after a good day's shoot and a few straight slugs, had revealed it as the deer liver was broiling, first exacting an oath that not a word of it must ever be passed on.

Kyle had smoothed out that situation. Kyle the leader, the trailblazer, now considered such a villain. That he had also been the protagonist of a successful or an attempted sexual assault in a small wooden house, two bodies lubricated with primordial squirtings of the oil shortly to make the family's fortune—this, as Cliff thought about it, took on increasingly the aspects of a masturbatory daydream, a cabin fantasy of Luanna's: some revenge for a sex life which, as Troy's visits home grew more infrequent, had been less than what her Indian heart felt suitable.

Constable had his way. From the first (Cliff was convinced), that had been his objective: to get Kyle out . . . scrub his image from the company he had made great. Constable, dutiful, well-paid lackey of the eastern money which all too often stretched its muscles across the continent.

Constable had dictated the letter and Cliff had said, "Give it to me. I'll take it to him."

The eye vanished from the peephole. The servant opened the door.

"Mr. Kinsale is expecting you, sir."

The servant crossed the hall. He pressed the button for the elevator which the old-time railroad tycoon who had built the house had put in when his legs got spindly. His railroad still worked better than ever but he had some trouble with his joints.

The servant got into the elevator with Cliff. There wasn't much room but they could make it up if both stood straight.

The servant pressed the button for the fourth floor.

"He's in the aviary, sir," he said.

"Thank you," said Cliff.

He had been in the aviary before. At the top of the house, it too a creation of the railroad tycoon. It had fallen into disrepair before Kyle's purchase of the place, but Kyle had restored it. He had made it even better than before. Above the great circular cage of gilt wires which filled the center of the room he had put a sky of azure glass which revolved electrically, timed to the spin of the earth, so that the placement of the artificial stars and the planets, in their clockwork heavens, corresponded exactly to the actual unseen cosmos hung in space.

The technician who had installed the mechanism had assured Kyle that the correlation had a beneficent effect on the birds. He himself, he said, had been a bird watcher.

"They are sensitive creatures," he said. "They feel everything that is happening—even much that is about to happen."

"Do you believe that?" Cliff had asked his uncle when Kyle had repeated the man's remark to him.

Cliff had put the question lightly. He knew that Kyle, like Troy—and most of the world's oilmen, for that matter—was superstitious. It was hard not to be, in a business in which the enormous stakes at issue hang on a turn of chance.

Kyle had answered seriously.

"Well, I don't know. This house survived the aught-six earthquake and fire; they say the birds in this room went quite mad hours before it struck. Raised a hell of a fuss. It's all in the old man's log."

Apparently he was referring to the railroad tycoon.

The elevator opened directly into the aviary. Cliff, entering, wondered if the birds' perceptions of approaching crises would enable them to sense the letter in his pocket. But they were singularly quiet.

Kyle had his back to him. He stood looking down through the big windows at the city and the harbor. At one pier, so close it seemed as if one could have tossed a pebble onto it, a white Norwegian freighter had just cast off; it was backing into the ebb tide while another, flying the Greek flag, stood by to load. There was a vessel for every slip, ships flying the flags of the whole world; every kind of ship—except a tanker!

Kyle did not turn, but he had heard him; he had a hand up, beckoning him over, and as Cliff came up beside him his uncle put an arm around his shoulder—a rare gesture of affection. (Christ, did Kyle know? Was it he, not the birds, who could read the future? Was he forgiving him in advance? Or just making it impossible for him to do what he had come to do?)

Kyle was the first to break the spell. He thumped Cliff on the back, more in his usual style of greeting, then lounged over to a wide upholstered window seat. Here he stretched out his long legs, his feet encased in English velvet pumps with gold stitching.

"Funny, how I remember, I mean the way certain things will . . . pop into my mind. I was just thinking— But to hell with it. Must be senility coming on."

"Senility, in *you?* Come on, Uncle Kyle."

"Well, maybe not quite yet, not yet," said Kyle with

satisfaction. He flexed his powerful shoulders, feeling in the pocket of his robe—gold corded, to match his pumps—for his cigar case. "Yes, we'll try to stall old age awhile, though I think I know of certain parties, certain individuals, who would, well, wouldn't mind seeing me go belly up.

"Matter of fact," Kyle said, "I was thinking about you, when you were a kid. A snot-nosed little shaver, you used to come up to the homeranch with your mom and dad. First thing you'd do, you wouldn't even wait to eat. Grub might be on the stove or sitting on the table but you'd just grab hold of a legbone or a biscuit and you'd light out for the corral. You had this *grulla* mare you liked, good-looking three-year-old about three-quarters broke. Your mom didn't much care for you to ride her, didn't think you were quite ready for her, but your dad said leave you go. Worst that could happen was you'd get bucked off a few times and have some of the smart-ass shaken out of you. Not that you were smart-ass, for a kid your age. You were just sick of that oil town. You wanted to get out on the range and sniff some fresh air. You remember that little mare?"

"I sure as hell do," said Cliff. "Queen Nicette. We called her Queenie. Queen Nicette was her book name. She had some breeding in her. And a great way of going."

"Queenie, yes. You brought her along just perfectly. Rode her in the finished-stock-horse class in the San Benito show one year. Took second with her, didn't you? As I recall . . ."

Cliff laughed. Suddenly he was relieved, carefree, living again that day on the infield of the horse-show track, spinning the *grulla* in front of the judges, three turns right, three turns left, then straighten out, dash thirty yards, slide-stop her, spin three right again, three left, dash back, slide-stop. . . .

"I enjoyed her, all right. She was a sweetheart."

"Yes, indeed. And you never knew it better than one other day. We'd all turned out to gather cattle. You peeled off to head out a stray. Then I heard you cussing. Some dumb hand, pulling down a fence, had dumped about fifty coils of old wire in a little draw and the brush had grown up and covered it. You'd jumped the *grulla* right into the middle of the coils."

"Oh, year, sure—that time!" Cliff's mind flinched from the memory. He tried to change the subject. "But, Unc—"

But Kyle kept right on with his train of thought.

"That little mare just took about one hop out of sheer terror. Then she stood still. She stood still, up to her belly in barbs, shivering, trying to keep from tearing herself to pieces.

Oh, she was a smart one, that little *grulla.* I couldn't do a thing. If I'd started down to help it might only spook her. I saw you slide off, get right down into the wire yourself. You had cutters on the saddle and you went to work; must have taken you an hour to cut her clear. Then we both tried to lead her out. She couldn't take a step. She'd cut one front tendon pretty near clean through and the other almost as bad. 'All right, now,' I said, 'I'll stay with her. You take my horse, go back to the barn and get the trailer. We'll pull her out of here.' But you wouldn't have any part of it. You knew she'd have to be destroyed. You loved that *grulla,* well, about as much as I ever saw a boy love a horse, but what you did . . . you took my saddle gun. You asked me not to look—*me!* . . . Well, listen to me rambling on. The things that come to mind!"

Cliff was silent. The scene, one of the most painful of his growing up, was as clear as if an hour old: the look in the *grulla's* eyes before he bandaged them with his bandanna. Some animals, some dogs and horses, had that quality: the *you-ness* in them, the sharing of life with you and the knowledge of life and death. . . .

But there was more to this than just reminiscing.

"Why did you remind me about that, Uncle Kyle?" he asked at length.

"I was puzzled about that myself . . . why I thought of it. Then as I was talking, just now . . . it came to me. You wouldn't delegate?"

Cliff was truly puzzled. He took a small cigar from his uncle's case, lying on the wall seat; he lit up and for a few minutes neither spoke; Kyle, usually so articulate, feeling softly, gingerly, for the right words.

"I mean, if something had to be done to Queenie you were not about to let some other person do it. It would be an *intimate* thing, between you and the *grulla.* You wouldn't let some other person mess it up. Don't tell me that's not true, because I know I'm right. There's mercy in you, son, *but let me say this."* And here Kyle's voice, so slow and groping, turned into a rasp. "This shit today is a whole hell of a lot different from being the *end* of anything. A terminus—of *me,* for example—"

"Oh, Jesus, Uncle Kyle—"

"The *grulla* was one thing. I'm something else." Kyle's head came up heavily, against the bright background of the window. "I appreciate *your* action. If someone had to bring it, you goddamn well took care of *that*—it wasn't going to be one of *them*. I thank you, Clifford; what you did was *right*. It had to be done, so you did it and I'm grateful. Now you can give me the letter."

So he's talked to Constable, Cliff thought. A vast relief took hold of him. Naturally, Kyle would call. He'd heard about the meeting. He, Cliff, should have thought of that, knowing Kyle's ways . . . what he might have doubted was that Kyle would condescend to speak to Constable at all.

Slowly Cliff took the letter out of his pocket and handed it over.

Constable had addressed it in his own hand:

> *Mr. Kyle Kinsale*
> *Chairman of the Board*
> *The KinOil Corporation*
> *San Francisco, California*

Kyle tore the unopened envelope, letter and all, twice across. He dropped the pieces on the floor.

"Why, the stupid son of a bitch," he said. "The hit man from the Racquet Club, New York City. Thinks all he has to do is write a letter and I'm out. Well, he can just think that through again. And Luanna and Millie, and Doc too! They owe me their asses, every one of them. Phony bonds, he told me. 'Tampered or falsified securities.' I'm quoting his exact words. He must have said them at the meeting, too. You were there. Isn't that what he said?"

"It is, Uncle Kyle. It's just what he said."

"His exact words, now? Because I want to know."

"Well, I don't know about 'phony.' I'm not sure he used that word. But 'tampered,' yes, he said that all right. Bad collateral, unacceptable. Mr. Tatum was there too, for the bank."

"Sure—the official executioner. Let me wriggle for a while, kneeling on the block. Likable chap, Lent Tatum, lately of the Mellon Bank, giving the ax a few last licks with the sharpening stone. A grand chap, didn't you think? Knows his job, does he ever. And all for a few dollars' worth of paper that might have been fussed with. They're checking on it now, got an expert working on it. The rest is genuine, they know. Two, three million of the bad, at most I put out more than that in *tips!*"

Kyle had risen from the window seat. He strode up and

down the room, burly in the gold-trimmed robe. His face was grim, his wide, flexible mouth curved in scorn.

"Petrochem isn't KinOil, son. They know that. And it will just take a hell of a lot more muscle than they have now to get me out, as they'll discover shortly. Reeves Thurmond has precedents going way back—not that we'll ever go to court. Last thing anybody wants. A. P. Giannini told me that himself."

Kyle tamped out the stub of his cigar. He stood still, staring out the window.

"But, Uncle Kyle," said Cliff, "how did it happen in the first place—I mean the bonds that had been fussed with. Scott Stanfus—was he the one?"

"Stanfus? *Scott Stanfus?*"

Something even in the sound of the name seized Kyle as humorous. He repeated it again, incredulously, as if it had surfaced in his mind from some immense distance, from a cloudy, a hardly discernible past. "Scott . . . well, I never would have believed it now. But . . . that's it. You hit it on the nail. The poor fool! The poor misguided loyal idiot! He did it, you know. I can hardly get hold of it myself."

Cliff leaned forward, his face toward the window, his back to the great cage. So now the truth was coming out at last.

"There is such a thing, my boy, as being just *too* loyal. That was Scott, all the way down the line. 'Hey, Mr. Treasurer,' I'd say—I called him that sometimes, he gloried in the title—'Mr. Treasurer, I'm short this month.' Well, I'd be buying stuff in Texas, maybe some old leases; no one thought they were worth a hoot, but we'd buy them cheap and sometimes, by God, they'd prove up."

"Why, sure, sure, Uncle Kyle. I remember when we did that."

When he spoke with Kyle, the second person singular had a tendency to upgrade to the first person plural: "you" became "we," so strong was Cliff's identification with his uncle.

"That was in the early days, right after we'd given the boot to that crook, Lamar Custis. 'Mr. Treasurer,' I'd say, 'I hate to inconvenience you, but you're in charge of credit, so get busy. Come up with some do-re-me! Three-quarters of a million, half a million. We've got empty saddles around here,' I'd tell him. And he'd jump. He'd get it. He'd do anything for me; he'd hock his soul . . ."

"I wish his soul was all he'd hocked."

Kyle sniffed and snorted, in his old way, but this time he didn't laugh.

"Take the collection—did you ever see anything like it? Did *anyone* in this fair city? Mrs. Spreckels, she's spent ten dollars on art for every two I've spent. And she never saw anything like it."

"Well, you spent enough."

"I did, I did. Used to laugh at her, though. When she'd come to dinner, I'd have an extra glass at her plate. One for her wine, the other for her teeth. She had a removable rack, always complained they hurt her, so she'd take them out after she'd eaten. But Scott, now. He'd get the money. I can't hold it against him that he lined his own pockets at the same time; but could I criticize what he did for his own benefit if I didn't notice what he'd do for mine?"

"But for sure, Uncle Kyle, you never authorized—"

"Never!"

"But did you, yourself, ever actually see the bonds, these Turkish things, that the bank says were falsified?"

Kyle held up his hand, as if in court.

"Oh, they offered to show them to me—Tatum rang up personally—but why should I get down to their level? I declined with thanks. 'You're very kind,' I told him, 'but I have no experience in these affairs.'"

"I guess he had to accept that all right."

"From what I hear the job done with the paper must have been a bit crude. The superscription where the lira sum was written out in Turkish was all right. They'd used some sort of chemical on that. It was the arithmetical portion that— But look, my boy, why waste our time discussing it? You've brought the letter, and I thank you. Now you can take back *my* message. Will you do that?"

"Of course, Uncle Kyle. Anything you say."

"Good! Well, this is my reply. It's short, you can carry it verbally. Tell Constable I shall continue as chairman of KinOil unless removed by action of the stockholders, as provided in the bylaws."

"'As provided in the bylaws.' I'll tell him."

"I'll fight to the end. I'll make them all eat humble pie."

"Fine, Uncle Kyle."

"The work of a trusted accountant, who, unfortunately, had less than his proper share of ethics."

"Right!"

"And trivial—though that may seem a strong word. . . . It will all be taken care of. Trust me for that."

Cliff got to his feet. He stood facing his uncle, and Kyle, from his great height, put his hands on Cliff's shoulders, at the same time peering slantingly, inquisitively into his face, as if to say, hell, how are you taking all this? Do you believe me or not?

"Goodbye, Uncle Kyle. I'll tell them."

"I know you will. Goodbye, Cliff, my boy—and thank you, thank you."

And with his arm around his nephew, Kyle walked with him across the room.

The door of the elevator slid shut; Kyle found a chair and sat down in it. He stared glumly at the birds. There were birds there in the cage of all sizes and colorings, native and tropical ones, small birds, mostly the kind that thrived in captivity, or at least did not destroy themselves in it. Most of them, as the bright-blue and golden day waned outside, sat quietly on the perches or ledges provided for them; occasionally one would warble or chatter, then a small bunch would take flight: as if in obedience to a secret command, they would circle around the cage a time or two, under their intricate electric heavens. Something in their subdued animation, the play of their bright wings, like a stirring of leaves, usually beguiled Kyle and calmed his thoughts, but today, though he watched, he was hardly aware of them.

He was sorry he had let Cliff go. How stupid to send him off, commission him with a message to Constable . . . or to other people whom he, Kyle, no longer cared about, who no longer seemed, in spite of all the bonds of kinship, to have any bearing on his life. Troy was dead; Troy, who had taken so much of the world's warmth away with him—what was left centered now on his, Kyle's own family, his wife, Alma, and the children. For years he had seen little of Dr. Braden or Millie. The KinOil Foundation, a nonprofit depository for free-floating corporate funds, still sent regular checks to the clinic—tax-deductible support always greatfully acknowledged—but this was very different from a personal contact: he and Millie had certainly grown apart. Family interests separated them, dramatized in the critical stockholders' meeting when she had supported Constable against him. As for the country cousins, for them he had never entertained much more than a sardonic contempt. A bunch of sodbusters and apple knockers. How could you identify with rednecks who, without effort on their part, had been pulling down, collectively, millions a year in dividends?

Indirectly, with their constant screeching and complaining about the size of these same dividends, they had brought him to the damned embarrassment in which he found himself.

Worse than embarrassment. He must face up to that—a deadly trap!

Up and down the room he strode, around and around the gilded cage. A trap! And yet he'd tried, while Cliff was with him, to make light of it: a situation that he still had power to control. Power, indeed, had become a way of life to him, a condition as natural and necessary as the ability to draw his breath; he had used it grandly, bestowed it where he wished. Ah, what a thing it was, this power over events, over people; how it had made everything exciting and worthwhile! And how stupid, drab and meaningless were the prospects in the world outside, and in his soul within, if it was snatched away.

Kyle stopped his pacing. He stood still. His feet, in their elegant pumps, were spread apart for extra bracing, yet his body, wavered; he felt ill in some queer, hardly detectable yet dreadful way. He had to tighten his muscles against this queer feeling. He had to brace himself for balance as if resisting the roll of a ship's deck.

A trap! And no one's fault but his own that he was caught in it. Oh, how he wished it all could have been the way he'd made it seem to Cliff. He couldn't tell now why he'd done that part—why he'd improvised, apparently rambling on but really thinking hard, inventing a marvelous structure, ingeniously and rapidly, for Cliff's sake. For it had been absolutely necessary at that moment to retain Cliff's admiration, Cliff's good opinion of him. He had always wanted a son so much—not that he blamed Alma for her failure to supply one; it was not her fault. The girls were sweet too, adorable, and growing more so all the time, but—they weren't sons. Cliff was the nearest approximation of a son that he would ever have, a fine boy, one whom he loved and who returned his love, he was sure of that. Cliff had come himself, he had brought the letter, he would let no one else bring it—and for that reason alone, if no other, for those few last minutes that they were to have together before everything changed, it had been obligatory to convince Cliff that all was still as it had been. And yet—and here was the strangest part!—every second that he had been talking to Cliff he had longed beyond

measure to shed all shams and strip off all disguises, to let
Cliff know what was really in the wind, and how, in all
likelihood, it would turn out. Instead, he had used all his
forces of persuasion to make Cliff accept a false version of the
events in hand; he had sent him away convinced that this
great Uncle Kyle of his, as usual, was quite all right and
would come out on top . . . and he would have this to believe
in for a few days longer.

He, Kyle, had done the very same business to Alma too.
She didn't have a doubt in the world.

The feeling of weakness or self-disgust, so rare with him,
had passed. He caught sight of himself in a wall mirror, his
face creased with heavy lines, his hair mussed and his eyes
with a stupid, baffled look in them that he hated; he knew it
so well from seeing it in the eyes of other men who had come
up against him, the loser's look. He forced calmness into his
thoughts, feeling in his pocket for a comb; not finding one, he
pushed at the long, gray-stranded hair with his fingers, doing
it little good.

But to hell with it! He tightened his velvet belt and turned
back to the window. A wide, tender wash of ocean dusk was
sweeping into the port and the city and the lights were coming
on in the houses on the hills below and in the streets; here the
room was shadowy, only the gilt cage managing to suck into
its net a little spin of light. The birds inside were showing
more activity now. It might be their feeding time, or perhaps
they were used to having less darkness around. Kyle paid no
attention to them. Although strength was trickling back to
him, his depression grew stronger too: a black wave of misery
in his mind. Now and then, all his life, he had been subject to
such fits; they would fall on him as mysteriously as they would
leave. But he had dreaded them. Only movement, action and
excitement would stave them off, defeat the coldness that
signaled their onset, the chill in his body, particularly for
some reason in his lips.

And now—now, goddamn it all—such a fit was coming
back. It was swelling up inside him. His lips. His lips were
starting to . . . feel cold. He pressed them together, chewed
them, even, but it did no good. A door opened within him, a
corridor into a bare, blank and awful place he had always kept
closed but that now, because of the unexpectedness of the fit,
had sprung open. The bad feeling he had defeated a moment
ago rushed into him again, this time with such force that his

knees buckled and he had to grab the nearest chair and sit down in it.

Irresistible, implacable, the force slammed him backward through time. He was in a room . . . a room at the ranch; he was a boy, he was kneeling on the floor, he was struggling, bending forward, he was weeping and at the same time, at his wit's end, trying to do something he didn't know how to do but that must somehow be done. He was with his mother, he . . . had pulled her from somewhere. She was lying on the floor—that was it—and the coldness . . . came from her, from her lips against which his own lips were pressed! Oh, God . . .

Even in the blackness of his soul, which had a somewhat stupefying effect, like a drug, one of those truth serums which, he'd heard, made the past come clear, he marveled at the scene. It seemed incredible that it had ever happened, yet it had. He had brought his mother there. He had . . . taken her from where she had been, among the dresses with their smell, their sweet breath and presence of her, of herself, and he . . . he had pulled her out and tried to breathe life back into her. He had never heard of what is now called mouth-to-mouth resuscitation, he had not the slightest clue that it would work, he had come by the idea naturally. It had been the only thing to do but it hadn't worked and after a while he had given up; despair had seized him and he had got out of that room, all of a sudden, even with his mother lying there, he could hardly get out fast enough.

Kyle got up. He had made no decision to act, but he acted decisively. He stepped onto the window seat and stood there while he undid the complicated catches of the window above it. He then opened the window and stepped onto the window ledge. A blast of chilly air rushed at him but he hardly noticed it. He stood calmly on the ledge, perfectly balanced and in full possession of himself and all his faculties. He looked down gravely at the pattern of lights outlining the streets, the houses and the port. He was untroubled. The one thing that bothered him was the birds. They had set up a fearful fuss. They were squawking and yammering, hopping around on their perches and flying from place to place. Some of them, in their stupidity, seemed to have lost their senses. They gave out cries entirely different from their usual sounds. Flying, they collided in the air and tumbled to the floor of the cage.

Kyle glared at them angrily. Then he turned back to the abyss of resolution within him and the gulf of peace opening before him. He took hold of the sides of the window and braced himself for a leap.

At this moment there was audible the slight mechanical whir, then the click as the elevator of the crippled railroadman arrived at the floor. Alma stepped out, calling to him in her deep, soft voice. Then she saw him. Her breath sucked in. All strength went out of her. She caught hold of the cage to steady herself.

"Kyle!"

Kyle hesitated. Then he stepped carefully through the window. He put one foot behind him. He located the window seat, then stepped down onto it and from the window seat onto the floor. He went to his wife, who had slipped down beside the cage, and raised her in his arms.

"What's the matter with you?" he demanded brusquely.

"With *me?*" she cried. *"With me?* Kyle . . . *Kyle! . . ."*

"Jesus, honey, it's all right. Don't take on so."

Alma just shook her head. She couldn't speak.

Kyle got his arms under her. He lifted her. He took her body, a dead weight, and carried her to a chair. Once more he was reminded, reminded horribly, of dragging his mother's body out of the closet—but no matter. This was not a day of good memories, or happy omens. He sat Alma down in the chair and bent over her.

"Rest a minute, then you'll be all right," he commanded. His voice sounded just as usual.

Alma was gasping. It was still impossible for her to speak.

"Kyle," she brought out at last, "I saw you. I—"

"Saw me?" he snapped. "Of course you saw me."

"There!"

But instead of turning her head toward the window she bent it in the opposite direction, as if not to reprise what she had seen . . . as if Kyle might be still there, in two places at once. Or as if he would, somehow, always be *there*. . . .

"Oh, my God, Kyle. Oh, my God, oh, my God."

She choked.

"Alma!" Kyle said firmly. "Stop dithering."

"Please, Kyle."

"Please what?"

"Don't . . . pretend anymore. I love you but I'm getting so that I . . . don't understand you anymore."

"Nonsense. We've always understood each other. Always *will.*"

"Kyle, honey," she begged, "all I ask is— Oh, Kyle . . . *I saw you.* Honey, *I saw you there!*"

Kyle, beside her chair, reached over. His heavy face was gentle. He put out a hand, touched her cheek gently, compassionately. Now her tears were flowing fast, her breath coming and going in gasps. Kyle took a silk handkerchief out of his breast pocket and handed it to her.

"I know what you saw, but—*don't be absurd.* I . . . get up there quite often. Yes! You—I quite understand. You would have no way of knowing, but that happens to be true. Looks risky, I suppose, but that's just the thrill of it. Such a grand way to look out at the city. Get a breath of air. I—"

"Kyle! Stop! Stop it, I say."

Kyle stared at her. He had never heard her speak in just this way—her voice lost and hopeless, commanding him (and she never commanded!) but really pleading, like a child begging for an end to punishment—her body crumpled in the chair, her hands pressed to her face.

"What is it?" he said stupidly. "What's come over you?"

She shook her head. She tried to bring out words that wouldn't come.

"I . . . don't care. I don't care, don't care, don't care whatever it is that made you . . . that's been bothering you so much. I don't care, it wouldn't matter. Nothing would matter if you'd only talk to me, if you'd only tell me . . . what it is. I know it must be . . . awful, but . . . I don't care. *What I can't stand is being shut out.* I can't stand the lies, the awful lying when . . . we used to be so close. Can't you feel that, the way you've shut me out? I can't stand it. I can't stand being alone. If I lost you—"

"You won't lose me," he said brusquely.

Alma lifted her dark head. She turned her face to him, smudged and streaked with tears and makeup, and twisted with such pain that it looked like another face entirely— someone he didn't know.

"Won't I?" she said. "How can I know? Just now you were going to . . . just now you were LEAVING ME," she screamed. "LEAVING ME ALONE! I saw you there, I saw what you were going to do. COWARD! LIAR! FILTHY LIAR! Oh, Kyle . . ."

"Alma, I'm no coward. I may not have told you everything, but that doesn't mean . . . that anything is different . . . between us.''

With the handkerchief he had given her she dabbed at her face, as if trying with these automatic, socially dictated movements to grasp some measure of sanity or sense in what he had said.

"If there's still love, then how could you do it, how could you have thought of it? If there's love I don't see how a person . . . how anyone could do what you—"

"I WASN'T GOING TO DO ANYTHING," he yelled with sudden fury. "CAN'T YOU GET THAT THROUGH YOUR HEAD?"

She shrank back from him—not from his anger, but with a shrinking in the core of her being.

"I saw you, Kyle," she said softly and hopelessly. "I saw you with my own eyes, standing there. And even about this you lie to me!"

They sat long, talking, at first harshly, then more and more gently, more carefully with each other, in the dim room lighted only by the glow of the city reflected against the windows, the one which had been opened now securely locked again. Kyle, driven at last to speak frankly, told her—not all, of course, but something—about his predicament, inventing, since it was his license and habit to invent, a plan for survival, a vague scheme for getting out of it all. Downstairs, the puzzled servants waited for them to come down to dinner.

The great cage glittered in the darkened air. The birds were quiet now, settling themselves for the night. In their clockwork sky the constellations moved, presenting—unnoticed by those whose destiny they might be charting—the pattern observed so often from the homeranch: Orion rising, Altair and Vega going west.

CHAPTER TWENTY-THREE

A Walk on the Beach

1

"He trusted the wrong people," said Cliff.

"He trusted nobody," said Alma sharply. "Do you think he didn't know what Scott Stanfus was up to? He knew every minute of the time. He would tell Scott to get money or credit for him and Scott would do it. Kyle had no interest in *how*. Scott came and went when Kyle told him to."

"He seems to be gone for sure."

"Kyle knows all about that too. He knew Scott was feathering his own nest; he just didn't care. So when the time came to shut up shop Kyle gave the word—and goodbye Scott. Kyle would deny that, of course; he'd lie about it. The lying—that is what I can't stand."

She leaned toward Cliff. They were at the corner table at Perino's in Los Angeles—the table which the maître d'hôtel always reserved for the people from KinOil.

A waiter whisked away the plates of the first course—Cliff's oysters, Alma's vichyssoise. Entrées appeared.

"I just don't understand it."

"You don't? It's very simple. It's what happens when a person spends a million dollars more a year than he's taking in."

"But with his salary as chairman. And his dividends—"

"What dividends? Last year there were hardly any—and he *hated* being chairman. As president *and* chairman he could move money in and out of KinOil any way he wanted, but Constable stopped all that. Constable was out to get him from the first."

"Well, we're not going to let him."

He spoke firmly, but Alma held to her own train of thought.

"That stupid petrochemical company, that was supposed to fix everything. The collection! The goddamn house in San Francisco. How I missed the beach, my own beach house that he promised me and gave to me. You'll never know."

"Petrochem will be okay in the long run."

"Well, the run is getting too long for me. Do you know how I found out about the patent suit? I answered the telephone at home and took a cable. It was a coded cable, but I went down to the office and I got the company code. I never told him."

"Alma, it's not his life. It's only money."

"You're so wrong."

Wine was served, a château-bottled Beaujolais, hard to come by now.

"He has these terrifying moods," she said, "these black, despairing moods. He's had them ever since he was a boy; he told me about that on one of our first dates. I never paid much attention to them, not until I began to connect them with his gambling."

"What do you mean?"

"If he felt low or . . . just disturbed . . . he'd gamble, take some crazy risk. Not necessarily in business. Aboukir! He told everyone he'd bet Aboukir to place, do you remember? In the Handicap? Well, he had him to win; it was weeks before he could pay off the bookies. The first time we took a trip—we went to Mexico so we could spend a few whole nights together—he got up, he left me alone in bed so he could go out gambling."

The passion with which Alma brought out this confession was so fierce, and she so beautiful, that Cliff raised his napkin to cover a grin.

"He likes to be ahead of the game," he said mildly.

"A lovely way to put it!"

"Alma," said Cliff, "he has to resign, that's all. That's the first step. If he refuses, nothing can be done for him. The stockholders will force him out; Constable will see to that. It's not a question of the . . . altered bonds. He had no right, as chairman, to authorize, or Stanfus, as treasurer, to issue a loan of that size to Petrochem without the consent of the board. That's all the authority the stockholders need, and believe me they'll use it."

"But if he resigns?"

"Then what would be the sense of raising a big stink to get him out?"

Alma looked at the dish in front of her, her attention drawn to it because a waiter was starting to take it away. She waved him off. She tasted the chicken, then began to eat. She devoured her meal rapidly, ravenously, cold though it must have been, washing it down with gulps of wine. Cliff watched her, amazed. It was hard to understand the ways of women. He wondered what had passed between them that had so restored her appetite for food, and perhaps for life as well.

When the *coq au vin* was gone she broke a roll and mopped up the sauce. Then with a sigh she pushed the plate away.

"I trust you, Cliff," she said in a low voice, her big, soft eyes bathing him in darkness, in softness, the warmth of her large, lovely body penetrating him like the heat of some glorious oven.

"You can, believe me."

"I know I can. I know you'll do what you say. No one else could do it, but you can."

"I'll try."

"And you'll succeed. We'll get him out of this. You can give me another letter like the one he tore up. I'll make him sign it. I don't know how yet, but I will."

"As soon as you do, I can go to work."

"Done, it's a bargain. But now that it's settled and I've made a pig of myself, eating all this food and getting about half drunk, I'll tell you something else, the most dreadful part of all. The other day, the day you came, after you'd left, he was about to . . . do away with himself."

"Jesus Christ! You're sure?"

"Do you think I'd tell you if I weren't? I went up there, to the damned aviary—I don't even want to think of it. He was— He was going to— You're the only person I've told, and I have a reason for telling you, so please listen."

"Go on."

"This Petrochem thing isn't going to work. He'll be *stripped!* Mrs. Spreckels may take the collection. Or some museum. And the stable— Well, even the Aga Khan is selling his stables. He's living in Geneva; he's broke now, he says, but he doesn't care. Kyle has to have something to do, otherwise—"

"You think he'll slip back. I mean, get one of those moods you've mentioned?"

"Yes."

"I don't."

"You didn't see . . . *what almost happened.*"

"I wouldn't worry."

"How can you say that?"

"Because I know him too. He's a charger. He'll find a way back. I'm sure of it."

Feeling the woman's fear, Cliff had tried to be encouraging. But as he said this he sincerely meant it. Kyle was not a man easily beaten.

"You say he'll be stripped," he went on. "That's absurd, Alma. He's had—well, call it an accident—it can all blow over. He has all kinds of connections, he's an absolute genius at making deals."

"But how can I trust him?"

"I don't care if you trust him, others will. You'll see. He understands the uses of power."

"But I feel so helpless. If there was only something I could do."

"Love him. Stay close to him. That's what you can do."

"Oh, I'll always do that. But, Cliff, answer this truthfully—"

"I'm being truthful."

"I know. But . . . do you think he'll try . . . to do something terrible again?"

"Absolutely not."

"It scares me so."

"Don't be scared, and don't worry. It's going to be all right."

"Oh, I hope so."

"It will be. I know it."

"He loves you, Cliff. He admires you so much. You keep in touch with him too."

"I will."

"Call him. He gets so bored with my . . . keeping track of him. But if he's ever out of my sight, I start to feel . . . I don't know . . ."

"When you feel like that, call *me*. I'll remind you of what I've said. He'll make a comeback. Just give him time."

"Well, you've made me feel better anyway. Can I really call you?"

"Anytime, day or night. But *don't worry.*"

The conversation drifted off to other subjects. They sat long over the meal; Cliff felt the chill of his own "interim life" warmed and challenged by the earthy, pulsing power of this dark-haired woman, so little older than himself. He envied his uncle, who, lucky in all things, until his current debacle, was luckiest of all in having such a wife.

Cliff pored over the ledger sheets, the records brought to him by Reeves Thurmond and others who had served Kyle through the expensive, luckless venture at Petrochem. An accountant, signed on from Price, Waterhouse for special duty, pointed out the salient mistakes; he and Cliff sat together at the great desk Kyle had used in the Los Angeles office, the drill bit of the discovery well enshrined on it in its teakwood stand.

The accountant shook his head—an expert in the soiled arithmetic of corporate disaster.

"The timing was bad," he said.

Would the bank allow more time?

Cliff corresponded with A. P. Giannini.

A paper manufacturer from the Jeffries Banknote Company, Los Angeles, checked the Turkish collateral to see how much of it had been worked over. A Treasury man could have done the checking just as well or better—and for free—but once you called in the T-men you had to let the cat out of the bag.

There had been only one real mistake: extravagance. This had never let up from the mid-twenties. By the time KinOil went public in the early thirties Kyle's personal fortune could not have been estimated at much less than twenty million; he had whittled away at it in a manner so proficient and at the same time so subtle that, even now, the pattern of deficit spending was blurred. Some years the racing stable had broken even; once (the year Aboukir came into his own!) it had made money. There was no doubt of the immense value of the art collection; the house in San Francisco stood in Alma's name. Even while he had been stalling off Petrochem's creditors Kyle had set up a revocable five-million-dollar trust for Alma and the girls, then dismantled it within a year. Always at war with his shrewdness, his genius for spending in the interests of sport and grandeur was insatiable: attached to one balance sheet, little of it in black ink, was the incredible notation: *"Hold reserve of $160,000 to bid for Whitney stallion Sir Beetle if offered at spring auction."*

Kyle's letter of resignation, as chairman of KinOil, came through at the end of the month.

2

Cliff parked his car in a slot bulldozed out of the hill where the one-lane driveway ended and the path began. There was not room for more than two or three cars; the person or persons who lived above would not be expecting many visitors. He locked the car, from force of habit—who would molest it here?—and for a moment or two stood looking down at the ocean, a luminous half circle of blue-green with the Little Sur Lighthouse, tiny as a piece of chalk, stuck on its rim. The sun, behind clouds, was low. It would be gone in an hour.

He turned away and started climbing, his city shoes slipping on the packed shale: a steep way up. Growth hemmed him in, wild laurel, scrub fir and Monterey cypress, slanted and twisted by the northwest winds. Tucked in against a heavy granite outcropping, the house had found a way to stay out of the blow. It had done well here; its redwood had weathered to sea color, cloud color, but with a sheen rather of the sea than the clouds: it sucked in both sea and sky; it clung hard to its judicious niche. The path curved around to one side but the deck in front had a flight of steps and Cliff chose these.

"Hey, anybody home?" he called, halfway up.

His voice, outrageous here, had a flat, betraying sound to it—a violation of the peace. He crossed the deck and pushed back big glass doors, a faint sound to them, to their effortless slide, like skis in snowpack.

No one was home. You could tell by the feel of the air. On the floor were some of the bulky, comfortable wooden toys that people give to very little children. A Mexican tile fireplace, a Mexican or Guatemalan knitted spread on a big couch, also obviously used as a bed, Chianti flasks with candles in them, a brass ship's telescope, and a big built-in radio, probably with shortwave capability, in the corner, with notebooks and papers scattered around. Coffee mugs with today's or last week's dregs in them, one on a table, one on the hearth.

Two coffee mugs?

Cliff—reckless invader, incipient violator—had taken only two or three steps into the cool, sea-breathing room; he backed out, closed the big doors, went down the steps, down to the path, then around on the path to the proper door, the one with a sheep bell hanging on it, on a thong, for a knocker. This door would not be locked either, but he did not try it.

The door had a broad, convenient threshold, adzed out of a single redwood log; here he sat down and leaned back, more at ease now that the house and some of the things in it were no longer merely imagined but known. It won't be long now, he thought: the last sunrays, with final whirling pinwheel beams, had dipped out over China. She was coming up the path. She was carrying a little boy. She had him in a kind of sling on her back, like a papoose. Her walk, even with the weight on her back, hadn't changed, the calm straightness of her, the turn of her hips, the stride of her long, strong legs.

Another person, a woman, smaller, stockier, walked behind—slipping still farther back out of alarm or shyness when she saw Cliff.

"Hello dear," said Carrie, "have you been here long?"

"Not long. Maybe half an hour."

"Good," she said. She gave him her cheek to kiss, then turned to introduce him to the other woman. Jean Stuart, her name was: a dark-haired woman with a handsome, clenched face which lightened warmly when she smiled.

"So now," said Carrie with a grand air, "you must meet my son Christopher. Christopher, this is Cliff."

"Hello, Christopher," said Cliff.

Christopher said nothing. He looked sleepily at Cliff with burnished chestnut eyes.

Carrie took a key on a silver chain from around her neck and opened the door: so it had been locked after all! She turned on the lights.

"First," she said, "Christopher must have his supper. And we must all have a drink."

"I'll start the grub," said Jean Stuart.

She disappeared into a galley-sized kitchen.

Cliff watched Carrie deftly swing the child off her back, lay him down and pull the outdoor clothes off his dimpled, squirming shape. The kid has taken over. She's a mommy now, he thought—so be it! Better by far a kid than a new man.

But once Christopher was fed and bedded and the drinks made, the fire lit, the lighthouse beam winking below on the sea's edge, they were heavy with each other where once they had been light. There was something wrong with Carrie's eyelids when she looked at him, as if they had pins through them. She had turned off the blaze. She had been glad to get his note, she said. Leland Hayward had called first, asking permission to give out her RFD box number. Had there really been a story in Louella's column? Oh, yes, Cliff assured her, Louella had given her a Sunday feature: total exhaustion following bad reactions to a sneak of her last picture and the separation from Pat Millage. Reconciliation still hoped for. Picture being recut. Millage, apparently, just cut.

"Louella says you've become a hermit, you're turning down scripts."

"She always takes the producers' side. Leland thinks I've gone crazy."

"No, he says you've growing pains. An affliction that hits young actresses when they're not pleased with themselves."

"Or have bombed out twice in a row—after one hit."

"Everybody bombs after the first hit. You just had bad material."

"For the films, yes. But not the play," she said, the damned pins out of the eyelids at last and the voice clear and ringing. "The play was good. It should have been all right."

"I missed that. But I ran the pictures. You were fine in *Sister of the Groom.*"

"You're still hustling movies?"

"No, I just happen to rent a house with a projection room."

"Oh, and a pool and a tennis court and starlets and—"

"You know it. The gloomiest goddamn place you ever saw."

Carrie laughed.

"What's so funny?"

"The gloom, I suppose, that surrounds young, handsome oil tycoons. In large rented houses."

"Thanks. But I'm getting out of the oil business too."

"I'll believe that when I see it."

"We talked about it before."

"We talked about a lot of things."

"No," he said. "We didn't talk enough."

She moved to the fireplace. She stood there looking at him seriously, her legs apart, her inner being wrapped in a chill no fireplace was going to warm.

"I wrote you," she said. "I wrote you about your father. I was so terribly sorry. I'm afraid it was a lousy letter."

"No. It was a sweet letter. Comforting. Thank you. I wrote you too, didn't I?"

She nodded, her eyelids down again, her attention elsewhere. From the kitchen could be heard the sounds of Jean Stuart washing the dinner dishes: Jeanie, for short, the hairdresser-secretary-companion. An indispensable person, Carrie said. Cliff could well see how, in this lonely place, a paid companion would be a necessity.

Cliff got up. In one stride he had his arms around her, he pulled her up against him. This and the smell of her hair, her toilet water and her body started an erection to which she responded by moving one hip slightly sideways, so that it would no longer be in contact with her.

"No, sweetheart."

"We never split up," he said. "We never quarreled even. What was it? What went wrong?"

"It's a boring story, I'll tell you if you like. Only not now, please?"

Cliff dropped his arms. He might as well have been embracing a section of drill shaft. He resumed his seat; Jean Stuart, the indispensable, and now really working at it, returned, drying her hands on a clean dish towel, always a prime badge of indispensability.

"Well," she said cheerily, "that's done. Anyone for more coffee?"

"Not for me, dear," said Carrie.

"Well, it's there if you want it."

From a bag hanging on the back of a chair she removed a long gray piece of knitting and began to knit along a row of it with nimble dexterity and quiet menace. Madame Defarge of the Redwoods.

"Cliff was just saying he may get out of the oil business," Carrie said.

Jeanie's needles continued to fly.

"I thought that was the business everybody wanted to be in!"

"I thought so too," said Carrie. She turned to Cliff as if

picking up a conversation interrupted by Jean's entry. "What do you plan to do, Cliff, if you do get out? You must have something in mind."

"I do," said Cliff. "I'm hoping to run for the state assembly."

"Why, I think that's wonderful," said Carrie. "Don't you, Jeanie?"

"I do indeed," said Jeanie. "Great. Just great."

Her fingers flew. The long gray garment, or whatever it was, so fast being added to, trailed from her lap onto the floor.

3

Next morning, after breakfast and the ritual of cleaning, bathing, powdering, and feeding Christopher, the knitwear had an hour to extend itself still farther. Jean stayed in the cabin.

Carrie and Cliff walked on the beach. She said quietly that she had made some mistakes.

"Was I one of them?"

He spoke without sarcasm. He just wanted to know.

"Of course not," she said, "you were wonderful. You weren't a mistake at all and neither was Patrick. I wish you'd got to know him. You would have liked each other."

"I'm sure," said Cliff.

Naturally, he thought. We would have been pals right off. You always like a fellow who is fucking your true love, and not only that, but has got her pregnant and married her.

"At least," he said, "you have something to show for Patrick."

"Oh, no," said Carrie, "Christopher is yours. I thought you knew."

He caught her arm and pulled her around so hard that she fell in the sand.

She bunched her legs under her and got up awkwardly, angrily, refusing the hand he instantly held out to help her.

"That wasn't necessary."

"I'm sorry."

"Forget it."

"How in the hell would you think I knew?"

She walked on ahead, silent, hostile, then turned back. Her bandanna had come off when she fell; she found it. She stood in the wind, shaking it out. In the sea light there were lines that gave her face a different look than he remembered. He hadn't noticed them the night before—lines for Patrick Millage or for Christopher Millage. Not for him.

She put the bandanna around her blowing hair and tied it in the back. "I thought we'd been together long enough so you'd know something about *me*."

"I would think I did. I think I do."

"Then you might have known that I wouldn't leave you and jump straight into bed with another man. As much in love with you as I was."

"I might have known that. Or assumed it. But you could also have picked up a telephone."

They walked on, the mild, bleak wind pulling at their hair and clothes, the spume of the long Pacific rollers nibbling at their feet.

"I could have," she said. "Or I could have just written you a postcard, 'Darling, I'm knocked up, come and make an honest woman out of me.' I'm sure I was stupid but I couldn't write that or go into it on the telephone connected to a drill rig or something. I know, in fact, that I was ridiculous, I was so charged up. Just so long as you understand."

"I don't."

"I'm sorry."

"For Christ sake, quit saying you're sorry. *Help me*."

"Oh, Cliff, oh, honey. I'm trying. That's what I'm trying to do, to help you. It's all right. It's all perfectly all right now; it's all under control. Why do you refuse to see that?"

He stood still, his face pulled aslant by the sea wind and his confusion. Would a woman lie about something like this? Would Carrie lie? What would be the point of it? Well, the point of it would be . . . But he couldn't surface this thought: the real father, in a pinch, substituted for the legal father.

"You knew in Mexico then."

"I *suspected* in Mexico."

"That night we walked on Edgar Allan Poe—"

"Yes."

Once more he pulled her around. He hit her with his open hand and with the back of his hand.

One blow caught the side of her head, the other her face, where a blotch appeared.

She did not move. His legs gave out. He sank down on the sand, his arms around her hips.

"Let go of me, you bastard."

He let go. Losing his balance, he flipped back on his haunches. They stared at each other with hate.

"What I'm trying to say," she said coldly, "is that it was only partly my fault. Too many things happened to me, too fast—you. You were one, the biggest one. And being a star. Being pregnant was the least of it, but it was the part I couldn't handle. I put a proposition to myself and you were the answer. I wanted to be with you. I blew up my hopes— one pinprick and *pow*. Do you see what I mean?"

"No."

"Okay, well . . . that night. I told you about the play."

"You wanted me to tell you not to do it."

"Yes. Exactly. So you *did* understand."

"Only later . . . After you'd written me those kiss-off letters."

"I'd decided not to put a shotgun to your head. Marry the woman, little man. When did one of those ever turn out right? I wish you'd get up."

Cliff hunched forward. He got up, unsteady, like a fighter after taking an eight count. She, the woman, was the stronger. It was as if she, not he, had delivered the blows.

"Millage sold you a bill of goods, that's all."

"Patrick never sold me anything. We were together a lot and I told him. I told him also that I'd never have an abortion. I'd go away and . . . have Christopher. Well, he put some sense into my head."

"So he could screw you."

"I can't blame him for that either. We're good friends. We'll always be good friends."

"Where have I heard that before?"

"Not from me, anyway. What he said was true. A private person, even in this day and age, might get away with it—having a baby outside marriage. Not a public person. Not a star. And since I am a star," she said quietly, "I did what I did. I know I should share Christopher with you. I hope I can someday, but right now I won't. He's part of the peace I've found, living here. Sometimes they send me scripts and I read them, mostly trash. If I find something I really want to do I'll do it. I'll have to be careful though, very, very careful that it's the right thing—or that could be an interruption too."

"Of the peace?"

She nodded.

"It's a phony peace, Carrie."

"Oh, no, it's not. Perhaps I shouldn't expect you to

understand *that*. But I'm glad you've seen Christopher; I want you to be friends. I want you to be wonderful friends, and someday I want him to know. But not yet. You asked me to help you, and I've tried to, but do that for me."

"All right."

Walking along beside her, loving her, hating her, caved in on himself, he said he would do anything she wished. They followed their own footsteps up the winter beach, crossing Highway 1 where the dirt road started into the redwoods, to the cabin. When they got to the path from the parking area, Jean, the indispensable, was ringing a bell, calling them to lunch.

Cliff spent one more night, rolled in a blanket on the big couch in front of the fire. Twice he got up and tiptoed into the kitchen to find a bottle and make himself a drink. He slept little, and that fitfully. Once he went into the den that had been fixed to serve as a nursery and looked for a long time at the sleeping baby there. He left before the women were up in the morning.

There were certain odds to overcome, certain pressures, terrible ones, unseen in the move of that clear stream, Time, but enough to rip your hand off should you be so unwise as to insert a finger in its shining, shifting surface. . . .

The thirty-foot enlargements of Carrie's face for all the world to see, projected onto screens in every city, town and hamlet on the earth's surface: that did something. The three or four thousand fan letters a day, or some such number, processed by some ladies in a studio cubbyhole, at Carrie's expense: that did something. The midget agents piling out of the long black limousines, the piles of worthless scripts, one of which might by some mad chance be a masterpiece, so that all must be read: that did something. The charming voices on the telephone, with a million or five million dollars hanging on the outcome of the conversation . . . *that did something!*

"And since I am a star . . ." she'd said on the beach, a plain statement of fact, no ego involved. That was what she was. She'd been one from the moment the people at the sneak preview at The Forum turned in their cards, but she hadn't really known it. She had been a star in Mexico, and partly known it, been afraid of it, begged him, without really coming out with her petition, for a word that would command her to set it all aside.

He couldn't have said that word. He had loved her to

madness, but he couldn't take charge of her life. They had
never talked about marriage. That too would have been a
betrayal, just a different kind of one.

They hadn't been ready. Marriage, like sudden death, was
for others.

A star! Lovely idol of the silver screen, now living in
seclusion. Jesus, what a crock!

He'd been with Ilona Cape. He should have known what a
star was. He hadn't been able to connect the concept with
Carrie. He did now, but the hell of it was he wanted her and
needed her more than ever; she, his love, she and her phony
peace, won no doubt with great difficulty but quite impossible, due to the way the world was made, for her to maintain.
And this peace of hers, this charmed oasis in the little secret
house above the great wintry seas, was in fact a total cop out.
It was flight, for Carrie the equivalent of his own loveless life
in the Brentwood canyon, surrounded by brush and plagued
by whores.

At least now he had one advantage: he had a spy in her
camp, a curly-headed, chestnut-eyed infiltrator, Christopher.
Christopher, product of his and all the Kinsale genes, back to
his great-grandpappy, the devious dockside auctioneer, and
beyond. Christopher—trained and toughened in the spy
school of his, Cliff's, own testicles, of his own soul—would be
working for him. With Christopher to head the operation, he
would get Carrie back. It was inevitable. He had first
observed the terrain. Next would come the assault. All one
needed was a proper plan.

Meanwhile in San Francisco, A. P. Giannini passed word
along that he would like to chat with Harker E. Constable.
The visit was a friendly one. Shortly afterward the Bank of
America replaced Wells Fargo as the lead bank for the KinOil
Corporation.

CHAPTER TWENTY-FOUR

Rites of Passage

1

Cliff and his tall, handsome uncle checked their coats and hats together at the coatroom near the entrance to the Palm Court of the Palace Hotel. Adolph, the maître d'hôtel, was already beckoning. He escorted them down the center aisle, under the famous glass dome, to the special table, located halfway along, where the gentlemen were already seated.

This was the Cabinet Table. The men who lunched together at this board ran the state. They were Republicans. A Democrat at their repasts would have been as welcome as a bluetick coonhound at a White House wedding. They held no organized conclaves, kept no minutes of their talks; they handed down their decisions with a quiet word or two—a caucus, measured now and then by a name or a few figures scribbled in pencil on one of the Palm Court's thick, gleaming tablecloths. Solid men, all of them. Down at the end, in his usual chair, J. F. Neylan, lawyer for the Hearst interests, a broad, thick gold watch chain, such as Lamar Custis had once affected, crossing his vest. That is what he would have called the garment in question—a vest, not a waistcoat.

J. F. Neylan could not, single-handedly, elect anyone to office, but no one in California held office if J. F. Neylan was against him. Clarence Lindner down there near him—a responsible person, a keen strategist. Bartley Crum, corporation counselor, with a broiled filet and a half bottle of Châteauneuf-du-Pape; the food here was as good as you could get. Paul Smith, editor of the *Chronicle*. Young for this group, a provisional member, but esteemed as a comer. Once Smith had brought along a columnist even younger than himself, fellow from Sacramento named Herb Caen. This chap's bearing was acceptable, but the table regarded him with suspicion; he was beginning to be identified as Mr. San Francisco, a fictional, know-it-all character, who appeared sometimes in his columns.

Kyle never sat here as a regular member but he had been welcomed from time to time, like other distinguished Californians, as a guest.

Politics, not finance, was the concern of the Cabinet; Kyle bore a great name. Never mind the rumors of recent crisis which had oozed like gas from certain boardrooms, a certain bank. Anyone who lived on the extraordinary scale Kyle had chosen for himself would have his ups and downs. He was a person to be reckoned with, whether as chairman of an oil company or as a private entrepreneur; if now he wanted a political future for this attractive nephew of his, son of the brother who had died so tragically—well, if that was in his mind, so be it: they were happy to meet the young man. They would estimate him, judge whether he would shape up for the long pull. There was no quick road, where he was headed; he would know that himself, if he was any good.

It was worth a look.

Cliff felt the weight of the scrutiny, its decisiveness. Kyle had briefed him. His unconcern was genuine. He might need these men but they also needed candidates: this was not a one-way street. He ate his lunch and chatted with them amiably enough. He had expected some questioning about state issues, even got some answers ready; he could have saved himself the trouble. It was not his views but his personality that was being evaluated; the Cabinet, schooled in the uses of power, assumed that anyone brought to its attention shared its coloration, its entrenchment, or wished to; if he didn't he would be brought around—or dumped.

Time enough for all that, later on.

It was a rather dull lunch.

Paul Smith had to get back to work. He went off early but at leavetaking came around the table to shake hands with Cliff. The rest dawdled over coffee. Brandy was offered;

Crum and Lindner accepted. Kyle lit a cigar; he was obviously enjoying himself. When the group rose, Neylan drew Kyle aside. Cliff went on ahead to get the coats.

"He wants you to see James Musatti," Kyle said as they crossed Market Street, heading toward Montgomery.

"Who's Musatti?"

"Top man at the second level. He'll talk over your plans with you. Introduce you to Artie Samish. Maybe a few others."

"Just another checkpoint I have to pass?"

"No, you just passed the only one that matters. They liked you—I could tell. Neylan said so, straight out. That's why he stopped me, to tell me that, but he takes it step by step. That's his way."

"Which may not be my way. All I want from those gentlemen is a start. I don't want to be their errand boy. Sooner or later they'll have to find that out."

"Then better later than sooner. This was step number one. Musatti is step number two. After that we'll see."

"Whatever you say, Uncle Kyle. And thanks for the lunch."

"Don't mention it. I owed you that—if only for the one you bought Alma in Los Angeles. You were a real help to her." They entered the elevator, falling silent as others jammed in with them.

Cliff felt surprised. Though he and his uncle had been together in the past week, this was the first time Kyle had spoken of the meeting in Perino's. Cliff himself had been careful not to mention it. It would have embarrassed him to acknowledge to this man, who must at all costs be a conqueror, that he, Cliff, knew of his inner desperation, that Alma had told him of that moment when Kyle had been ready to give up.

Kyle was different now, stronger. Today at lunch he had seemed much like his old self, proud and easy, projecting his will and charm on the group in the Palm Court. But as they paused in the foyer of the KinOil suite, separating for the afternoon's chores, Cliff noticed once more the new lines in his uncle's face, the weave of red veins in the eyeballs, usually so clear and healthful, the slight trembling of the broad, muscular hands. I wonder if he's going to pull through, he thought—but almost instantly with this reflection came another, more urgent one: He must, he has to, not only for his own sake but for all of us.

Cliff had promised Alma he would try to help Kyle find some road back. And here, instead of giving help, he was asking for it; and Kyle, as could be expected, was giving it, using his place and influence to get him started.

Kyle moved off down the hall to the big corner office which was still his—at least temporarily.

2

Everything in the office was as usual: the same brilliant art, the comfortable chair groupings, the thick carpet, the big windows, the case of polo trophies, the snapshots of sport and travel. Everything was as usual but nothing was as usual; the familiar objects no longer seemed to belong to him; they had a new fragility about them, like things put in a hotel suite to make it more livable but which would soon be set at the disposal of some other guest. And there was another oddity about the room: its corners no longer appeared as angles; they were rounded off, as if some force were pulling them toward the center, closing them in to stifle his words and thoughts or even . . . to crush the life out of him!

Kyle sat down at his desk. He closed his eyes, pushing back with his spirit against this weird sense of confinement, of entrapment. There was no entrapment here. He was free to come and go; in fact, if the truth were known, the real intent which had recently come into the bustling organization of which this office was a part, though not perhaps a true part any longer, had not been to keep him here but to get him out.

Last week, for instance, a change had been made in the door lettering. Whereas before the letters had spelled out "THE CHAIRMAN," now they said simply "MR. KYLE KINSALE."

Someone had ordered it—pointless to inquire whom. A workman had come around and made the change. He'd had certain tools with him, also a box or a bag of brass letters, a whole alphabet, with duplicates. He could put any name or designation on a door that anybody wanted. He had come around in the evening, after everyone had left, or early in the morning, and had done what he was told.

So that's it, thought Kyle when he saw the job. You've started, have you?

He was not addressing the workman, but Harker E.

Constable. He flung many speeches at Constable these days—not aloud, of course, but in his mind.

Well, go to it, full speed ahead, he said to himself. You may be the one to go ass over tip, not me. Did you ever think of that?

Harker E. Constable had probably not thought of it—nor would Kyle's question, since it was silent, have prompted him to do so. Kyle had not, in actual fact, spoken a word to him since the day he had handed in his resignation.

Constable, or the forces he controlled, kept nibbling away. No longer did the weekly reports of company activities—known at KinOil as "the yellow sheet"—come to Kyle's desk. Rose Brady had to go out and borrow a copy from some other office. As for Rose, she herself was another sore spot. Kyle had brought her up from Los Angeles when he'd transferred his activities north. The San Francisco office manager had found an apartment for her on Telegraph Hill and the company had been paying the rent. Now Kyle had received a note from the new treasurer, Scott Stanfus' replacement, saying that the rent had been discontinued. Then a few days later came another memo: did Kyle want Rose Brady kept on the KinOil payroll? If so, the treasurer suggested that Kyle could reimburse KinOil for her salary.

Kyle recognized his options here: he could reimburse KinOil or pay Rose personally—or do without a secretary. He said he would pay Rose personally.

I know what you're up to, you bastard.

The petty annoyances only served to make him fight back. Constable's cleverness was the kind he despised. Kyle had been dealing with such well-bred, frozen-faced mannequins from prep school onward, smug little pygmies scuttling around in their club ties and their handmade shoes. Naturally, he regretted the carelessness, the overreaching on his part that had given Constable his advantage—surely a temporary one. All he feared was the black moods. These he had held off: they had not visited him again since that one evening, at the top of the house, when he . . . but even the memory of that was blurred.

Alma still worried. She wanted him to call her several times a day just to be sure everything was all right; she'd contrive reasons why he had to make the calls. Understanding her, loving her, he tried to comply, but it was a nuisance, calling so much about invented trifles: an errand she'd asked him to do on his way downtown, a doctor's appointment . . . something! Once, when he'd been in a meeting, and Rose had the afternoon off, he hadn't called and Alma hadn't been able to reach him. She'd come storming down to the office, terrified, and they'd quarreled. . . .

Kyle lit a cigar. He went over the notes he'd jotted down for this afternoon's meeting: he'd sent Reeves Thurmond to make some inquiries, asked Dan Shannon to come in. It was only a few weeks now until the general stockholders' meeting of the KinOil Corporation.

The intercom buzzed, the receptionist ringing to tell him Thurmond was on his way in. Kyle got up. He wanted to shake off the lethargy, be on his feet when the lawyer arrived. From the desk to the windows he strode, then back, from the windows to the door. Again he felt the pressure, the corners pushing in; he could almost sense their weight on his body, his chest; he made a queer movement with his hands in front of him, a picking or peeling motion, as if trying to get rid of this weight or threat or whatever it was. He was conscious of the movement—it was silly, ridiculous—and it brought back a memory. Once, during a polo game in Santa Barbara, one of the players, a good friend, had spilled; he'd gone over his mount's head and the pony, somersaulting, had broken the man's back. Kyle got into the ambulance with his friend; during the ride he had noticed the hurt man making the kind of gestures he himself was making now, when the walls seemed too close—the picking at his chest. Did all people who were hurt or . . . done for, in some way . . . feel that closure, that weight on them almost like a . . . presence? Did they all try to push it off with these aimless, doomed movements?

He must stop it—at once, he commanded himself. Others would notice. They would draw bad conclusions, wrong ones. He might have been out of touch for a time but he was back in control again, in complete possession of himself. He was ready to turn the tables on Mr. Harker E. Constable or anyone else who stood in his way.

Thurmond came in, then Shannon, the keen, blade-thin Irish fixer with the ulcer grooves in his cheeks and the handshake like a wrestler's. Rose brought them coffee; they waited to find out why they'd been summoned here.

There was a knock on the door. Marsh Borland entered. He crossed to Kyle's desk and put a folder on it, then pulled a chair around—Marsh, the field boss, always vaguely ill at ease in city clothes, with office people.

They were ready now—rump honor guard of an exiled leader. They had contracts. They had years of honorable service to their credit. The lowest-salaried man in the group —Borland—made fifty thousand a year, but all three of them could be liquidated once Constable took over, and they knew it. This was the first time they had been together since A. P. Giannini had blown the whistle.

They were here to find out if The Man had anything left for them; if he didn't they had better look for new pastures.

Kyle opened Marsh's folder. He glanced through it as if its contents were already familiar; he nodded his thanks to Marsh, then laid the folder aside.

He turned to Thurmond.

"Have you heard anything more from Lazard Frères?"

The conference lasted two hours. On the whole, Kyle felt it had gone well. Now at last he could ring Alma. He planned this call in the morning, when the chauffeur had driven him downtown. The call, at an hour when she would be waiting for it, then the ride home together was one of the ways he allayed her nervousness.

Waiting now, he took a turn up and down the room. Only a few lights were on—the wall brackets, the multicolored Tiffany lampshade over the desk. Outside, the foghorns were blowing, the mist heavy as an upended marble column over the invisible water, but the dusk a clear, limpid azure in the street below. He opened Marsh's folder, a sardonic twist curving his lips. He had not really wanted the report; he knew the grievous figures almost by heart. There was more here too, little of it good: the field geologist's memo, for instance, the "absence of the lagoonal phase in tertiary sediment"—an ill augury. So be it: the Turkish border lease land, thrown in as a bonus by Kemal when KinOil had given him his loan, would now be well established as worthless. The word would go out.

You didn't get the kind of deal he wanted by showing your hole card.

Oh, he thought, striding up and down the carpet, how could he have been so upset, so stupidly cast down by the fiasco with the Turkish nines? That trouble with the Bank of America seemed a thousand years ago. He would never, as long as he lived, stick his neck out so stupidly again.

Preposterous! Yet the incident, awful as it had seemed at the time, had its humorous aspects. Nobody had ever suspected that for a while, long before any alterations had been worked in the bonds, Scott Stanfus had found a place in Istanbul, the printshop where the original issue had been run off. Scott paid the craftsmen there to print some more, with sequential serial numbers, from the original plates! Was that counterfeiting? An unpleasant word, a courtroomy word; he remembered how Scott's face had seemed to shred apart the day he, Kyle, told him he had better take the first plane out of town.

"But . . . but, sir . . . Mr. Kinsale," he'd stammered. "I only did what you . . . that is, I felt we'd agreed that—"

"We agreed on nothing," Kyle had said sternly. "I hope you've been socking it away in that Swiss bank account. You're going to need it. Now get out."

No more of that, not ever again. There'd be, in a better-controlled project, no need for it.

The phone rang. Kyle picked it up. The doorman on the Montgomery Street side informed him that Mrs. Kinsale had driven up, that she was parked in the white zone, waiting.

"I'll be right down," he said.

CHAPTER TWENTY-FIVE

A Monstrous Force

1

North went the great highway, through the farm cities of the upper Sacramento Valley—Chico, Red Bluff, Redding—then east in the long foothill climb to high ranchland. It was April, 1940—some two months since the Cabinet's scrutiny of Cliff in the Palm Court. Already he was on the campaign trail. Everywhere there were meetings: service clubs to be addressed at lunch or breakfast—the Rotary, the Elks, the Lions; coffee-break stops at lumber mills and farm co-op offices; faculty gatherings at high schools, where the teachers, critical and polite, met courteously, curiously, to hear what this young fellow had to say. Country bartenders, polishing glasses in the beery nub of a gray afternoon, looked surprised to find a large hand held out to them and a deep, youthful voice saying, "I'm Cliff Kinsale. Glad to meet you."

He was barnstorming, out in the boonies where it could do no harm and just might do a lot of good. Not for himself— much too soon for that; he had to do his party footwork first. An election year, a Presidential coming up. Wendell Willkie was the Cabinet's choice to unseat FDR with his evasive but hell-bent intention to get the USA into the shit storm in Europe in spite of his lip service to peace and the opposition counseling of such stout, proven senators as Borah of Idaho

(Teapot Dome), Nye of North Dakota (the Neutrality Law), Vandenberg of Michigan (against the draft). Nor could one overlook the well-loved, the impatient, ornery, opinionated, perpetual senior statesman Hiram Johnson, California's own, who had got the state out of hock to the Southern Pacific Railroad and who now accused the Squire of "meddling internationally where it is none of our concern."

Besides, who ever heard of a President running for a third term?

Willkie had come on late. He'd been a Democrat, a delegate to the 1932 convention that had nominated FDR in the first place. Now he was against him. He had switched parties. Now from coast to coast his slow Indiana voice was telling his "fellow Amuricans" what he thought about Big Government. He was against that too.

He had a chance. Shop-front headquarters for him, financed by the Cabinet and their good friends, were springing up all over. Cliff called on them. He talked to the lady volunteers. He left bundles of leaflets and kits for house-to-house vote gathering. He gave them boxes full of tin badges stamped with Wendell's honest, handsome, Hoosier face. The primary would be along before you knew it and then, who could tell?

The Kinsale name had weight. It also reeked of oil and that, some places, was a dirty word; he would just have to see what he could do. No show of wealth, no accoutrements of power. That was to be avoided. Andy Karsh, a saturnine, dark-haired professional from the prestigious firm of Whitaker and Baxter, campaign managers, rode along with him, shared the driving and did most of the drinking. They moved in a two-year-old Hupmobile Skylark, a medium-priced car, a little dirty, a little battered. No use looking too spiffy; it gave the wrong impression. When they stopped for gas at KinOil stations Karsh, who carried party cash, would pay the bill in full. He would go take a leak, then smoke cigarettes, patiently self-effacing, while Cliff passed the time of day with the pump attendant.

"I'm Cliff Kinsale. Glad to meet you."

South again. A loop over bad roads into the mother-lode country, the first Americanized part of the great state, where, before the bright trickle of gold had shown in the mountain tailings, John Charles Frémont, the Pathfinder, and his guide, Kit Carson, pathless and hungry, had been rescued by an expedition from Sutter's Fort. Down the Sierra slope to Sacramento, then in milder weather to Fresno, biggest of the six counties usually lumped together as the San Joaquin Valley, a huge, incredibly abundant pocket of rich soil and perpetually troubled farmers: cotton, cottonseed, barley, rice, citrus, alfalfa, Thompson grapevines.

A sudden burst of warmth had brought out the almond blossoms. Crows perched in the white trees like monks at a First Communion.

Cliff passed the time of day at crossroads stores which were also post offices and gas stations. He stalked in boldly, a wired bell shivering somewhere at his entry. Smells of rope here, smells of dry goods and fruit, tobacco and sheep's wool and last year's prunings burning for heat in the potbellied stove. Men came up to him who had worked for his father or his grandfather. Cliff told them about Willkie, the corporation lawyer who, on the airwaves, sounded like a farmer, like one of their own. He *was* a farmer, Cliff said— farmed in Indiana. Willkie *understood*. He would continue subsidies; he wouldn't leave them in the lurch. By no means . . .

He was getting down now into Democratic purlieus: hostile turf. Shell-hard hands contacted his hands gingerly; eyes appraised him, suspicious behind dime-store glasses. Cliff explained about the ballot: for the Presidential primary, there would be only one name on the Republican side: Gerald L. Seawell. He would put together Mr. Willkie's slate.

Cliff sat on vine-clustered porches, stood on the platform in Grange halls; he talked in Modesto to the American Legion; to a potluck supper of the Oakdale PTA. He arrived with a good shine on hand-stitched, hand-tooled stockman's boots such as Hub had worn and Kyle sometimes affected; he set down his ten-gallon hat beside his chair. He was not comfortable in the costume. It had not been his choice. Mr. James

Musatti, guiding light of the State Chamber of Commerce, boss—or as near a boss as anyone could be since Hiram Johnson had cleansed the state's political structure—of the Republican organization, under the Palm Court Cabinet, had made the decision.

"Look, you went to Princeton, didn't you?"

"Yes, sir."

"I heard so. Well, you don't *sound* like Princeton. You don't want to *look* like that."

"Mr. Musatti, I went to grade school in Kinsalem, the oil town my father built. I went to high school in Bakersfield. Won't any of that show?"

"Not in what you got on it won't."

James Musatti looked without favor at Cliff's brown Shetland suit, tailored for him by Eddie Schmidt, who also made clothes for Clark Gable and Spencer Tracy. The fine cloth enlarged Cliff's already broad shoulders with padding. There were pleats in the pants. It was no good.

Musatti smoothed his formidable eyebrows.

"Haven't you got some ranch clothes?"

"Not anymore. I've been living in Brentwood."

"I heard about that too. The movie stuff and all that. For this campaign that's out. Or if it comes up, just soft-pedal it. We'll think of something. . . ."

Mr. Musatti gave thought. He leaned back in his chair, his hands locked behind his dark head, graying at the temples.

He buzzed his secretary. "Didn't we have a Sears, Roebuck catalogue around here at one time? . . . I see. Well, if you can't find it, send someone over to the store and pick one up."

Cliff had rejected the Sears, Roebuck line. If ranch dress if must be, then it would be the best. He got himself outfitted at a store on Vineland Avenue, near Studio City, which made garments for the western stars. He had grown too far away from the ranch scene to dress it now—but he understood the political pragmatism of the right clothing. Republicans, so long in total control of the state, were now an endangered species. So if a certain identifiable imprint was needed to make him acceptable, he would take on that guise. After all, it was no masquerade. He had been east, but he was no Easterner. He had invested in a movie, but he was no Hollywoodian. The farther he went in the hinterlands or circulated in the cities and the hamlets the more he felt that these were his people, that he could hear their views and respond to them and they could listen to his pitch and know that he spoke their language.

The oil was an accident. It had not changed anything. He was a Californian, and proud of it; that should be enough, but there was a further richness that he had discovered from his travels and his talks, the touch of hands, the faces of the people. At first they disturbed him with their rural wariness toward all strangers, interlopers in the turn of days so quiet in their seasonal spin, their neighborliness.

He might be some kind of gilded scalawag. What was he after? Was it really votes? What was his connection, truly, with the green-and-gold KinOil stations, where you chunked your money in for gas, for fuel oil, for drums of tractor grease.

At best, he thought, trying to catch his image as it flicked through their eyes, he was some kind of crown prince, heir of a hidden dynasty, sent among them, half disguised, by the big robbers, the social and financial elite who ran everything. Gently, patiently—since each little clump of them had its small differences from the last bunch—he flicked away at this impression till he could feel it come off in his fingers like the skin of a peanut that covers the meat, under the hard outer shell. He worked it off, and before long came contact, laughter and warmth . . . and even something like affection, like trust. "Stop by," they'd say, "when you're out this way again, mister. Stop by the house, the one with the yellow window boxes, on your way out of town. . . ."

The warmth was welcome. It helped him keep off the chill that had beset him since his visit to Carrie. She had given love, then in some strange manner taken it away—a rejection which had not eased with time. Not to be wanted was puzzling and hurtful—not to be needed was even worse. What was he to do with the energy bursting from him, the happiness that filled him when people responded to his presence? Here, unexpectedly, was the answer: the country faces turned with a weathered gravity to hear what he had to say, the people coming to his meetings from five or fifty miles around, waiting later to tell him their problems, as if he were in truth holding office instead of campaigning to help another man hold one someday:

. . . the damaged road that the county supervisors had promised to pave and never had.

. . . the next rodeo, come Fourth of July: Would he give out the prizes for the bucking-horse contests?

. . . the Fish and Game Commission: What was the matter with those donkeys? Did they know that people followed the State Hatchery trucks down to the streams and dipped out the fingerling trout with buckets and garbage-can lids?

The crowds grew. That was the surprising part. The voices on the farm telephone lines moved ahead of him so that a lunch group figured for a couple of dozen suddenly expanded to twice that and more tables had to be set up, sometimes extemporized out of planks and sawhorses.

How they wanted someone outside their isolated, latched-off little corners of the great state—someone they could believe in. A change had taken place in the climate of the meetings. He was no longer a curiosity. He was a hope. He just might be . . . one of them, the attentiveness of him, the thatch of red hair and the slow friendly eyes, the refusal to be taken in by freaks or chatterboxes.

He took notes on the grievances. He would write a letter, do what he could. He withheld promises but his young voice rang with a quality they hadn't heard before. He said Mr. Willkie was concerned about them, but they suspected that the concerned person was this big young fellow, never mind the Hoosier candidate. This one would do to take along.

The crowds grew and the warmth pushed out. It was a palpable thing, a sustenance. And as the welcome expanded —the ease and the thrust of it—so did his confidence. How great it would be to run on his own, to embrace the trust they were so ready to give in their hard-shell yet tremulous fashion, to go up front for them, to stride boldly, when the time came, into the purlieus of those men at the Cabinet Table and . . . *represent these others!* Who knew where such an adventure could lead?

For now it was good just to be with them, from day to day, from town to town. What had begun as a trial run had turned into one of his most rewarding experiences. From the depths of his own misery he had risen to an amazing discovery: he had found what he wanted to do with his life.

"I'll be back," he'd say at the end of his talks. "I'll be here again, and I'll come to see you." And when they clustered around at the end of his talks, shaking his hand, punching his arm to make sure he was for real, they'd say, "Don't forgit, now. We'll be watching for you."

It was a great feeling. For certain spells during the long days of driving and talking, he could get Carrie out of his mind, then a latch would lift or a door flip open and she'd be back again.

3

He had wanted to call her, but he had resisted. That crazy, terrible walk on the beach: he could not have behaved worse; he would have given anything to have that hour or even a fraction of it to live over, but if he had he did not know, even now, what he would have done differently. He had been rough—out of control, out of his mind almost. But she—what about her craziness? What about the insanity of packing herself and the baby off into that cranny in the cliffs? It was a flight from all sense.

"I know I should share Christopher with you . . . but right now I won't."

Had any woman ever made a madder statement? But above all a woman like Carrie, whose whole life had been giving, had been sharing: even—perhaps especially—her acting. Giving, opening herself to delight, to a world that rushed to possess, to embrace her.

". . . the peace I've found . . ." she'd said.

It might seem like peace, he'd argued, agonized but confident later that evening by the fire in the redwood cabin. It might seem good, but only because she'd had so much strain, such confusion. Certainly he'd let her have it, if she wanted; he'd go away, since that seemed her wish. But they had to talk again. They had to settle things.

"Darling," she'd said, the term of affection itself a cruelty in its new context, "I love to talk to you, at any time. I love your voice, and the way you look but we really have nothing to talk about and I *have* settled things. I wish you'd believe that. It would make everything so much easier."

Madness! That kid with his chestnut eyes and the mop of reddish hair, the spy in her camp, sound asleep in the next room, knowing nothing of the way his parents were apportioning his fate.

It would all be changed. He had gone away confident he could accomplish that. Carrie was playing some kind of aberrant game with him, but she was still his girl, his one love, he could bring her around in the long run. But now, with weeks gone by, there seemed a lunatic finality about this "settlement." He had written her about the work he was doing, sent her his itinerary so that she could answer, and before he left San Francisco she had written in return, briefly and bleakly, thanking him, wishing him well . . . and that was all.

4

He thought of her, curled up on that huge sofa with a storm beating on the great sea-looking window, reading. Trash, she'd said about the scripts. Well, they probably were, and she'd probably do one to please some agent, some sweet-talking producer.

The tour swung through Orange County, a huge portion of it owned by one family, the Irvines. Cattle and citrus country, with a sprinkling of thriving resort cities on the coast and the great naval base at San Diego: solid, golden ground, Republican to the core. Young Tom Kuchel ran things here. He might even chair the Republican delegation to Philadelphia if he could beat out ex-Governor Merriam.

Cliff wrote Carrie that he'd be meeting a group at Hartnell College in Salinas in mid-March. She should see what kind of politician he was becoming, just one time. The college was only an hour's drive from Big Sur. Wouldn't she come?

He didn't hear from her.

He had been looking forward to the Hartnell College appearance. It would be different from the sort of work he had been doing—a discussion group rather than a vote solicitation. Three Democrats and three Republicans were scheduled to participate: on his side, State Assemblyman Polls, long a family friend and KinOil stockholder, and a young political science teacher, Roger Hellman, who had been in high school with Cliff and now taught at Hartnell.

The meeting had been Roger's idea.

Opposing them sat three prominent local Democrats: the chairman of the Annual Rodeo Committee, the mayor, and a popular physician and rancher, Dr. Reeves of San Juan Bautista. The issue of debate was the President's proposed third term. The public as well as the Hartnell faculty and students had been invited to attend; Cliff, from the wings of the auditorium, watched the audience come trooping in.

Roger tapped him on the arm, and Cliff tried to fix his mind on the job in hand. His disappointment, he realized, wasn't sensible; there was no reason to expect that in her present frame of mind—her withdrawal and her queer, new, hurt and hurting kind of arrogance and distance—Carrie would pay the least attention to his invitation.

The dean of the college introduced him; he took a bow to a polite rustle of applause. . . .

The discussion was lively. He pushed himself to enter in. He had done well, he felt; in the coffee and cake session which wound up the evening he circulated nimbly, balanced a plate and cup, chatted with the people who came surging around. He was standing thus, his mind at ease and his depression lifting, looking out through an open doorway at a black marble panther. A Hartnell person was a Panther, just as a Princetonian was a Tiger in the reverse anthropomorphism which turns campuses into zoos. There beside the panther was Carrie. She had on some kind of bulky, unbecoming jacket which had changed her shape. Her face was turned aside; he had recognized her by her hat, the same black Borsalino she had worn to the sneak preview. She was standing there alone beside the gleaming marble beast, waiting. Cliff excused himself from the group around him. He got a fresh cup of coffee and went out to the panther. He handed the cup to Carrie, who merely nodded thanks, still bundled up in herself, in her private concerns and the ugly, bulky jacket.

"Well," he said, shaking as if with a coffee jag, "where were *you?*"

"In the back," she said, "behind a post. I came early."

"I looked for you early."

"I saw you looking. Why are you shivering?"

"I'm shivering, for Christ sake, because it's cold out here. Don't you want to come inside?"

"Not really."

"Well, there isn't any other place."

"All right then, but only for a minute."

She walked ahead of him through the open door. They stood in a corner, she unbuttoning the jacket, he holding her cup while she did this. The ladies with whom he had been discoursing, getting in some licks for Willkie—wives of faculty, wives of civic leaders—turned their backs.

"You were awfully good."

"Really?"

"Absolutely."

Suddenly he was eager for her praise.

"I thought it was all right. Rather friendly, not pressured. The way politics should be and never is."

She sipped her coffee, weighing this.

"There *was* pressure—antagonism. Lots of it, but it was understated. *You* were understated. Perhaps that's why I thought you were so good, but I'm not sure I liked it."

"What do you mean?"

"That shirt. The pants and all. The cowboy look. What's that supposed to be?"

"It's a costume. Wouldn't it make you vote for Willkie?"

"I'm not sure. But those ladies will vote." She glanced at the group he had just left. "They'd do anything you told them to. I watched them through the door."

"They're returning your interest right now." He took her empty cup. "Frankly, I can do without them."

"I want to talk to you," she said, "but just to say this. I may have been a bit of a shit about Christopher. Not that there was any excuse for *your* actions."

"No excuse! At this point in our relationship, when you suddenly tell me that he, that you . . ."

"We've been through all that."

Oh, what a wary, wild thing she'd turned into!

She said, "I thought I'd made it clear—we have no relationship."

"Oh, yes, we do. We'll always have a relationship, goddamn it, especially with . . . Christopher on the scene."

He took her arm, steered her through the quadrangle, where the panther's blank eyes and coiled body gleamed down at them, into the street.

Carrie unlocked the door of a small car standing at the curb but did not get in. She leaned back against the car, looking up at him.

"I said I'd been a shit. I've been seeing a psychologist, a person who has helped me so much, and he said to hold on to my peace at all costs. He's right, but I have a firmer hold on it than he knows. I won't lose it if . . . we alter the arrangement about Christopher."

"We had an arrangement?"

"That you couldn't see him. He may need you. I'm going to make a film."

"I see."

"It's a very good film!"

She spoke hotly, as if to defend herself against her own intention.

"I'm sure."

"I've waited a long time for a good film."

"And the shrink approves?"

"I haven't discussed it with him."

"But you will."

"I may not. I still make some decisions for myself."

"Of course. And Millage. He approves?"

"Spare the sarcasm. Patrick is in England. He's with a group that's entertaining the Home Guard—the troops. He's doing something about the war, which seems to be more than you and I are doing."

"Carrie, don't make the film."

She stared at him, appalled.

"Why do you say that?"

"Because—it's not *right*."

"With reference to what?"

"Once you told me you were going to do a play, that night in Mexico City. You wanted me to tell you not to do it, didn't you?"

"Yes, I think that's what I wanted."

"But I didn't. I had no right to make that kind of decision for you."

"But now you do? Now you have rights that you didn't have then?"

"Now I know what it means to be apart from you. You know it too—you alone with that girl and our baby in that shack in Big Sur. Peace it may be, but it's not a life."

"I needed it. Now I'm leaving it. What's wrong with that?"

"Nothing. Only don't make the film. Marry me, Carrie."

"*I won't listen to this!*"

She was bending over, opening the car door. He pulled her up, turned her around to face him; he put his arms around her body in the stupid, absurd jacket.

"Please," she said.

She opened the car door. She had left her purse on the seat and from the purse she took a paper and handed it to him.

"There," she said, "that's the Big Sur number. When we

move you'll be referred to a new number. So call me. You can come and see Christopher while I'm working."

"Carrie," he said. He had to stick his head inside the car now, since she had gone around to the driver's side. "Listen to me. Let's go uptown. Let's have one drink together and talk about this."

"Some other time," she said. "Call us. I have to get back now. And shut the door."

Since he didn't seem to hear the last command, she reached across the seat. She shut the door herself, he pulling back just in time to keep from being decapitated.

She drove off.

Cliff went back into the assembly room, where the crowd was now thinner.

Karsh approached him.

"Wasn't that Carrie Drew?"

"Yes. Why?"

"People have been asking."

"Tell them it was Carrie and she's gone."

"I've got an idea," said Karsh, "one that could sure as hell help this campaign."

"Fine," said Cliff. He headed for the buffet. He was shivering again. He needed coffee, and after coffee some strong drink. Karsh was still tagging along.

"You know all these movie actresses, and the actors. You've lived with them; they're your friends. We should stage a rally: Claudette Colbert, Carole Lombard, Jean Arthur. And some guys: Clark Gable, Tyrone Power. A Willkie rally, preconvention. Hell, we could put that in the Hollywood Bowl."

"It's too cold in the Bowl."

"I mean when the weather's warmer."

"Most of the people down there are Democrats."

"Not all of them, for Christ sake. Adolphe Menjou. He wears *knickers* to play golf. Would a Democrat do that? Ronald Colman. No guy who looks like Ronald Colman could be a Democrat."

"Ronald Colman is English. I don't think he votes."

"To hell with him then. Gary Cooper!" Karsh's eyes took on a visionary glow. "William Powell. Myrna Loy. Jimmy Cagney. With people like that we could fill the fucking Bowl."

Cliff moved away from him. His coffee was cold, the place was almost empty. His mind was on Carrie, driving home to

Big Sur on the great highway cut into the face of the cliffs. She had come and she had gone, leaving no cheer behind.

"I didn't mean to smart off about your 'peace,'" he wrote her later that month. "I think I know what you mean by it. You worked hard to arrive as an actress and you've had success, you really scored."

He could see her in memory, sitting beside him in the Bugatti, her hands folded with that childish, yearning curve around the stack of preview cards she held in her lap—the cards that would mean letters set in lights soon on the marquees of theaters all over the world.

You had a lot of joy in acting. You didn't realize success could turn that joy into a commodity. It became a many-million-dollar asset for anyone who could package it. So your telephone started ringing and never stopped. You had Leland Hayward up in front, and you had the contract with Wanger, but even that combination could be penetrated. Worst of all, maybe, you had me and what we might call The Situation. Maybe you had good and honorable reasons for not telling me that you were pregnant, but, sweet Jesus, don't you think I had a right to know?

Carrie, honey, when I saw you last week I got the shakes. That's why I was shivering, not with the cold. I'd been afraid you weren't coming to the meeting. At least you did that much. Thank you for that, and for what you said about Christopher.

I love you as much as ever—no, more than ever. I don't hold blame against you for anything you did. Now you've got your 'peace,' as you call it, but peace is wholeness, isn't it? I feel as if all that divides us is a thin little curtain, but when I try to pull it down I get all tangled up in it. Or it chokes me, like smoke. I think about it but I never get the right words to say and maybe these aren't the right ones, but we never needed such a hell of a lot of words, we knew how we felt. You know how I feel now. Please answer this. I love you, dearest. Write or call me. At least we ought to talk some more—

Carrie wrote back—not as soon as Cliff had hoped, but she wrote. She used the stationery of the Hayward-Deverich

Agency, a stiff, expensive kind of office paper, 9200 Wilshire Boulevard.

> Dear Cliff: I loved your letter and will always keep it. You have a wonderful feeling for life and for a women. [She had actually written it that way, "for a women," then she had partially crossed out the *e* before the *n* and tried to make an *a* out of it before she went on.] As I've told you many times, I love many things about you. In many ways you are the most wonderful person I have ever known, but I don't think people can go back. I hate the expression "missed the boat . . ." but that's what we did. It was probably more my fault than yours. Frankly, if I were to give anyone a second chance it should be Patrick, who was so nice to me when nobody else knew. [She had crossed out "cared" and written "knew."] But I'm afraid even that would be "going back," which can't be done.
>
> So I'm going ahead with my acting, as hard as I can. The script is *even better* now—Robert Sherwood will rewrite some scenes—and William Wyler is going to direct. (This isn't confirmed yet, so don't say anything to anybody. I admire Mr. Wyler so much, I'm absolutely thrilled to be working with him and also terrified, he's such a perfectionist. But sometimes I work best when people are demanding!)
>
> You didn't get an answer at Big Sur because we were all down here in Beverly Hills. For the moment we are in the penthouse in the Beverly Wilshire (what grandeur!), that is, Christopher and myself. We are looking for a less grand, less expensive place, but central to the studios. Jean has gone back to close up the Big Sur house. . . .

It was quite a friendly letter, its friendliness part and parcel of its finality. All passion was spent—even the anger that had made them yell and strike at each other that day on the beach under the cliff, the lust to destroy what love they'd had.

Carrie was gone. The classic way to cure himself of her would be to work up a grudge for the wrongs she had laid on him, her rush to spill her own dilemma into the care of another man, but even this he could not do. Best just to start some kind of ordered life himself. He would give up the damned house in the brush and move down to someplace more civilized. He would plan Christopher's future, he alone: a boy would naturally gravitate to his father. He had a long way to go with Christopher.

5

The end of his barnstorming trip came on a raw, windy afternoon at a small steel factory in South Los Angeles. He and Karsh stood outside the factory gates, waiting for the five o'clock whistle. A young p.r. man from KinOil's Wilshire Boulevard office had driven them out in a company station wagon. Leaflets had been circulated in the area for several days announcing the talk, and there had been several evening spots on local radio.

The whistle blew right on the minute and the gates opened; some of the workers crossed immediately to the parking lot and got into their cars, many of them pooling, but a few dozen hung around. Cliff put on his handshaking act, introducing himself to as many as he could, then he climbed onto the tailgate of the wagon and went into his spiel. He told the group what Willkie would do for the country if elected.

Smog whirled around him and his listeners, the sultry reek of the cold gusts compounded by blowoff from the Bessemer chimneys behind them and the stink of nitrous oxides from the utility compound farther up the block. Across the street a huge rubber factory added its flux to a mix that stung the eyes and throat and made it hard to get a word out of the constricted larynx.

"It's a disgrace," Cliff shouted hoarsely. "This kind of thing will not be permitted. With a new Administration . . ."

The last daylight, bouncing from the soiled, yellowish factory windows, gave his face a bizarre, almost diabolic cast.

". . . degradation of our cities . . . long-needed cleanup . . . men in Washington who *understand* the God-given right to clean air . . . get rid of filth forever . . . Wendell Lewis Willkie . . ."

Karsh handed out the campaign literature, the buttons, the instructions for delegate voting, struggling with the usual complication—the fact that Mr. Willkie's name would not actually appear on the primary ballot.

The crowd fragmented in the chemical twilight, drifting off

to homes not yet cleansed by Republican enterprise. Cliff wanted coffee and the KinOil rep. Priestley, located a greasy-spoon café; the proprietor, who had been putting up his closing sign, turned it to read "Open" as the station wagon parked in front. Cliff and his entourage marched in like hoods bent on a stickup; they took a table in the rear. While they were ordering, Cliff pulled napkins out of a half-empty container and wiped his face with them. The paper came away smoke-gray.

"It's a wonder people can survive down here."

"Some don't, I guess," said Karsh.

"But plenty do," put in Priestley. As a liaison with the public, high or low, he took a professionally optimistic tone.

"They make top money."

"No amount of money would be worth it," Cliff said. "Who owns that fucking steel plant anyway?"

An odd silence fell.

"I have to take a leak," Karsh said abruptly. He pushed back his chair and walked away.

Priestley blew on his coffee to cool it. Then he raised his head. His eyes met Cliff's squarely.

"You do, Mr. Kinsale."

"You're nuts."

"No, sir," said Priestley firmly, "Manchester Smelting and Casting. KinOil bought it while you and your dad were in Mexico. Plan was to retool it for pipe casting, but I guess that never went through. You own it all right—or we do, as you might say."

Cliff put milk and sugar in his coffee. He stirred the mixture slowly, staring out into the street. When Karsh rejoined the table Cliff turned on him with repressed fury.

"Why wasn't I told?"

"Told what, Cliff?"

"That KinOil owns that steel plant."

Karsh glared at Priestley, who looked at the floor.

"You knew, didn't you?" Cliff persisted.

"Yes, sir," said Karsh meekly. It was the first time in their two-week barnstorming trip together that Karsh had called him "sir."

"But you didn't think it was worth mentioning?"

"I didn't think it was relevant."

"So you let me make an asshole out of myself."

"You were not an asshole, Mr. Kinsale," said Priestley soothingly. "None of those workers knew. I don't believe anybody in that company knows you own it. Only the executives, maybe, and they weren't there."

"They listened to you, Cliff," said Karsh. "They liked what you said."

"The hell they did."

"You made a great impression," said Priestley, "a wonderful impression. Didn't you have that feeling?" he finished, turning to Karsh.

"All the way," said Karsh.

"Cut the bullshit," Cliff said. "They knew. Some of them did, anyway. They'll pass the word around. I was a prime, grade-A, blue-ribbon asshole, and I don't care for that. I don't care for that at all."

The café proprietor approached the table. He was a Greek. By stipulation all proprietors of cafés of a certain type in the United States are Greek regardless of their passport nationalities.

"Closin' op pretty soon, no hurry."

Cliff put down a five-dollar bill for the three coffees. He told the Greek to keep the change. Then from force of habit, he shook hands with him.

On the drive back to Beverly Hills in the station wagon he reviewed his embarrassment about the steel plant. He decided to request the board to put it up for sale. If it meant a loss for KinOil, that was just too bad. Losses and gains were the vocabulary of businessmen and he had had his bellyful of business. Fron now on his business would be the people.

6

Cliff had a seat when the State Central Committee met in Sacramento and voted Leo E. Anderson to lead its delegation instead of ex-Governor Merriam, who had counted on the job. Merriam stalked out of the hall with his bald dome flaming red.

Verdun fell. Guderian's XIX Panzer Corps and Hoth's XV flanked the Maginot Line, its troglodyte garrison manning pop-up gun turrets which pointed east but could not be reversed to point west. The French government moved from Paris to Tours, from Tours to Bordeaux. Reynaud asked Roosevelt for "clouds of planes," and President Church of the Carnegie Institute posted a reward of one million dollars for the capture of Adolf Hitler. General Weygand, marching from Beirut to defend the Iraq pipeline (which had not been attacked), was summoned home, and in Philadelphia, His Eminence, Cardinal Dougherty, Prince of the Church, in his scarlet robes, paced portentously into a blue spotlight and invited divine guidance for the Republicans assembled at their Presidential convention.

As each roll call of the states was taken, Willkie floor leaders hustled around trying to get delegates to switch their votes from Dewey, the crime buster, from sourpuss Robert Taft or mean old Vandenberg. Kansas and Michigan swung to Willkie on the fifth ballot and he was ready for the grand slam on the sixth. It was sweltering hot. Cliff jumped down into the arena and helped Rolly Marvin, the 220-pound mayor of Syracuse, grab the New York banner from five Dewey men who were hanging on to it tooth and nail. Rolly belted one in the stomach and Cliff threw a headlock on another; they got the banner free and then Cliff ran back to the California delegation, where he belonged, and they started the victory parade around Convention Hall.

It was crazy and splendid, wonderful, this American circus in which voters cast their ballots for lists of electors instead of directly for a President, with no constitutional redress should the electors violate their pledge: it was a hootenanny, back-woods range-and-river kind of politicking—the sweating, the drinking and hollering, the drum thumping, the badges and the paper hats, the solemn count, the sonorous names of the great states resounding from the platform, their banners and shields draped from the roof and stuck to the walls between mad-eyed gold spread eagles and gray elephants with American flags curled in their rolled-up trunks.

". . . join me . . . help me . . . you Republicans! The cause is great! We cannot fail . . ." cried the nominee in his hoarse, urgent voice, his great shaggy head rearing up there, champion of free enterprise: Wendell Lewis Willkie said he would give back to the people the government which the New Dealers had been stealing away. But, oh, Jesus Christ, why did he have to say "you Republicans!" Did he still think he was a Democrat? Could he really beat the smarmy bastard in the White House?

The *Ile de France* sailed for England from New York with crated Lockheed fighter planes lashed to her decks.

An era was ending—the short, restless and bedeviled interlude between two major wars. Cliff had been born into this uneasy gap in history; his life stretched through its entire span.

Back at his Philadelphia hotel, he found a message:

> I am in Suite 218. Call me when you come in, no matter how late. Most important. Alma Kinsale.

Clipped to the note was an advertisement by The Superior Oil Company of Houston, Texas, tendering sixty-four dollars a share for twenty-five percent of all outstanding KinOil Common: twenty points above the market.

Twenty-five percent would be more than enough to give Superior control of KinOil.

7

The Grand Ballroom of the Palace Hotel resembled in no way Convention Hall in Philadelphia from which Cliff had so lately come; one could not compare the two, one could only note the differences. In Philadelphia the great auditorium had been stifling, smoky, fetid—swept by savage but changeable emotions and charged with the jungle ferocity of history in the making.

Here, in the ballroom, there was decorum, but there was also terror. Money was the issue—a far more frightening thing than leadership. Here the walls were gold and white, the parquet floor as slick as a dowager's pince-nez; here one did not talk, one whispered; one did not walk, one sidled: a finger would beckon at the end of an aisle and a person would rise, would wiggle out. The chairs were spindly, the stage removable, the middle-aged faces feral and well preserved, stamped with an implacable anxiety.

For here, too, decision was being made.

Cliff had not planned to attend. After all, that night in Philadelphia he had told Alma to vote his proxies. He was out of it now—out of KinOil, or soon would be. He was in another line of work.

"I should think Kyle could handle it. Even if he's not on the board anymore, he's a stockholder—a big one. Hell, a lot of shareholders still believe in him; they'll do whatever he suggests."

"What you don't seem to understand," Alma snapped, "is

that Kyle doesn't give a shit. Anymore than you seem to. He brought this on; he laid us wide-open for a takeover, just by that one crazy thing he did. Now he's in Portugal, on his way to Istanbul, and we've got to pick up the pieces."

The "crazy thing," it appeared, hadn't been Kyle's posting of dubious collateral with Mr. Giannini—his resignation and Constable's assumption of power in KinOil had effectively smoothed out that contretemps. Kyle's immediate sin had been that he had gone to Constable and made a deal with him: he had traded control of Petrochem, his ailing company, with its plant, its inventory, patents and all other assets, for the Turkish oil lease KinOil had acquired when it made its loan to Kemal Atatürk in the thirties. For Kyle, the Turkish lease was to be his comeback. For Constable, the attraction of the trade was Petrochem's eight-million-dollar tax-loss carryforward. Such a shelter would be of considerable advantage in KinOil's year-to-year operations, but Constable had not been slow to see that it also made KinOil a target for acquisition by another company. Either way, the situation dealt him a promotional opportunity.

"Alma," said Cliff, "I wouldn't pick up anything—except the money on the table. A twenty-point spread—that could interest the cousins and the aunts."

"And others," said Reeves Thurmond, "a lot of others. This isn't Kinsale Land and Cattle voting under the trees at the homeranch. This is KinOil, a public company with seventeen thousand stockholders, ripe for the picking."

Thurmond had come east with Alma. He participated in the midnight conference, the dishes handed around from a room-service spirit oven in Alma's suite; apparently the plan was to go on to New York, where the big money was, in some last-ditch attempt to keep KinOil for the Kinsales.

Alma had wanted Cliff to help with the presentation to the Wall Streeters. After all, he'd gone to Princeton with some of them—or their lineal descendants.

"Don't you see?" she said, her eyes blazing. "We have to stop Constable before he runs off with everything. Even your mother realizes that now—the horrible mistake we made, taking him on in the first place. You were against it at the time, when you were hardly out of college. I remember your speech at the meeting."

"He got in though."

Thurmond swung his leonine head to face Alma.

"This young man has been around petroleum since he was in knee britches. I don't think he wants to sever his connection with it. Maybe he just doesn't understand the game plan. Would you like," he said to Cliff, "for me to enlarge on that—to explain what can be done, right now?"

"If it's your plan, Reeves, I'm sure it's a good one, but I don't see why my family has to keep pumping oil. The time may have come for us to take our money and walk away."

"And 'if that be treason, make the most of it,'" quoted Thurmond. "So that's it, eh?"

"That's it."

"Which is the most disgusting thing I've ever heard," said Alma. She pushed back her chair and walked to the window. A silence fell, during which the waiter collected his dishes and table and left the room.

"I'm sorry, Alma."

"Don't apologize. Just go back to your politics. We'll do without you. We'll hang on somehow."

"I'm sure you will, but before you have a fit about it, stop and ask yourself just what oil really did for us, for the family. After all, you married into it, but we, at least I, grew up with it, as Reeves just mentioned. I spudded in the discovery well, but what does the rest of the record say? That we got rich?"

"You sure as hell did," said Thurmond softly. "You got rich, and it wasn't bad, was it?"

"No, it wasn't and isn't. But we were rich before. Not crazy *big* rich, but maybe rich enough. We had land, we had a lot of land—the best you could find anywhere. My grandpappy, they say, wanted to keep it that way—just land; maybe he had a point there, but I pulled the switch, as no one has ever let me forget. Grandpappy was dead and couldn't object, at which point a lot of hard-working California rednecks didn't have to work anymore. A monstrous force had come out of the ground and made work unnecessary."

"Nobody worked harder than your dad, Cliff," said Alma. Calmer now, she returned to her chair, lovely in a soft negligee which clung to the opulent curves of her body. "You were with him," she said; "you ought to know."

"He was an oilman, Cliff," said Thurmond.

"Yes, he was," said Cliff, "and he died running an oil field we were going to abandon. We couldn't locate much of his body in the dark, but next morning we found most of it and put it in a bag. He was an oilman and that was what oil did for him. Uncle Kyle—I don't think you could really call him an oilman. He was . . . is . . . a gamesman, an internationalist, but he was all that before oil came along. What he got out of oil was the illusion that he was some kind of Aga Khan and Medici combined. Plus that he owned a money-printing machine he could use any way he liked."

Thurmond said slowly, "A monstrous force. Yes. That could be what it is. Risk is involved, physical and, I suppose, moral; a lot of risk. But what, may I ask—regarding this power—what are we supposed to do now that we are threatened—or blessed, if one goes by your notions—by the loss of it? Are we supposed to start running scared?"

Alma leaned forward.

"I think all this talk is ridiculous. Oil is where we've always been and where we are now. It's been pretty good to you, Cliff. Don't give yourself any fancy airs about that."

Cliff rubbed his lips. An inner pain contracted his flesh, made him look thinner, older. Perhaps, after all, he hadn't lost Carrie because of his job. His failure to respond to her needs might have had some other cause than his distraction by professional crises. It might have been due just to his own nature, his stupidity—or even hers. Perhaps it would have happened anyway. . . .

"But I know this," he said aloud, addressing both Thurmond and Alma, "from here in I'm going to run my life the way I want to, or as near as I can. I've said you can vote my shares. That's as far as I'll go to beat Constable and keep KinOil. We may all be best served by losing it. So you"—and here his glance took in both his listeners, the angry dark-haired woman and the formidable old attorney—"go ahead with your game plan, but count me out."

8

They had gone ahead. The present meeting was the direct outcome of their efforts. It had been called into session under a bylaw in the KinOil articles of incorporation which provided that a special meeting of the shareholders could be ordered at any time (1) by the board or (2) by a petition signed by one hundred or more shareholders. With Kyle off the board, Alma and Thurmond had no chance there. They had collected the hundred signatures.

It was KinOil's first special meeting; it was also the biggest meeting of any kind in the company's history. Ordinarily at the regular annual meeting (scheduled to take place in three weeks, had the rebel group been willing to wait that long) not more than a couple of hundred of the company's vast body of shareholders attended: for this more than twelve hundred were already on hand, voting God only knew how many absentee proxies. More kept arriving. The young lady from the hotel's catering department, in charge of the affair, sent for additional chairs.

Harker E. Constable called for order just as the bell in Grace Cathedral, high on Nob Hill, boomed two o'clock. He looked trim and fit as usual in his maroon-and-blue club tie and a gray pinstripe suit, but for once he was in control of neither himself nor the situation; if the truth were known he felt ill and dizzy. He should, he knew, have forestalled this despicable sortie by the rebel group; he should have stopped them in their tracks. He should have called a special meeting himself, or had the board do it—the board which, since Kyle's debacle, had been doing just what he told it to. He might have been able to ram through Superior's tender—such a tempting offer and so much to everyone's advantage. He had even outlined mentally the language he would have used, perhaps from this same podium, to congratulate the shareholders on their action and to accept, for his own part, the board seat and in all likelihood the executive post which would have been his by right in the new, combined corporate entity. His glance swept over his listeners—the aging, carefully tended, often surgically improved faces of the rich, the only type of audience Harker E. Constable ever had occasion to address.

"Ladies and gentlemen! As you are all aware, two corporations have recently shown interest in acquiring our company. First, Superior Oil of Texas submitted a tender to buy twenty-five percent of our voting Common at what seemed to many of us a beneficial price.

"This, like all such offers, contains one condition: a deadline date. If, by this date, Superior has not acquired the stipulated amount of stock, Superior retains the right to rescind the sale of shares submitted under the terms of the offer.

"The deadline falls due next week. We are still taking

count. It is, however, clear that to date Superior has not acquired the twenty-five percent which limits the offer. Those shareholders who have already deposited their shares in the escrow opened by Superior Oil in the First National Bank of Houston still retain their voting rights in those shares and thus may, of course, vote them at this meeting.

"All of you, I am sure, have received by now the statement put forward by the Texaco Company with headquarters in the Chrysler Building, New York City. This proposal does not present a cash tender but is in essence an offer for a tax-free exchange of stock on a basis of two shares of Texaco Preferred for three shares of KinOil Common. There is no limit on this offer. Texaco will make the exchange for all the KinOil stock outstanding.

"Ladies and gentlemen, the business before this meeting— the first special meeting of the KinOil Corporation ever called under Section Four, Article Two of our bylaws—is the consideration of the Texaco bid. For this reason, as your chairman, I have dispensed with a reading of the minutes of the last meeting and all other customary items of agenda. I respectfully address your attention to the Texaco Company's statement."

Harker E. Constable took a sip of water. During the course of his speech his dizziness and the ache in his guts had gone away. Who knew? If he made an impartial presentation, and the shareholders accepted the Texaco deal, he might still be part of the package.

"There are, I am sure, some of you who received that statement too recently to give it proper study, some perhaps who never laid eyes on it until they picked it up just now at the door. In view of this I may remind you that if you have already filled out a proxy but wish to change your vote, or have failed to fill one out but wish to vote now, you may ask for a ballot and one will be brought to you. Should any shareholder wish to address the meeting, to speak either for or against the proposal laid before us by the Texaco Company, he may indicate his intention and an usher will bring him a microphone so that he can be heard.

"One person present, though not a shareholder, has already asked permission to speak. I refer to Captain Torkild Rieber, Texaco's chairman. Captain Rieber's address will be of limited duration and due to the urgency of the matter under discussion the chair sees no reason to deny his request.

It has allotted Captain Rieber ten minutes. Ladies and gentlemen, Captain Torkild Rieber."

Rieber heaved himself up. He had been sitting in a row near the front, between Dr. Braden and Millie, and directly ahead of Alma, Luanna and Reeves Thurmond, all of whom joined to start the applause as the stocky man made for the rostrum. He shook hands perfunctorily with Constable, who surrendered the lectern to him, then Rieber favored the audience with a smile which seemed to expose more than the usual number of teeth, square and yellowish. His thick gray hair was parted in the fashion of an older day, straight up the middle.

Cliff, planning to leave early, had not sat with the family group. He had chosen a place in the rear, near an exit, and as Rieber's chesty Norwegian-accented voice boomed into the loudspeaker system, a memory came back: the day when his father had introduced him to this man as ". . . the Captain Ahab I worked for when he was skippering a broken-down tanker," and Rieber, denying that he was—or ever had been—an Ahab, had added something about KinOil coming into "a good safe port" whenever Troy had a mind for that.

Even then, Cliff thought, he must have been putting muscle on Dad, trying to merge with us or buy us out. That's what they had been talking about before I showed up.

That had been—how long was it? Just about three years ago.

Alma could have known nothing about such discussions between Troy and Rieber. Thurmond might have, but Cliff doubted it. He wondered what clue had taken them to Texaco, to tough old Cap. Was it the coincidence that Troy, as a young man, had served on a Rieber ship?

Cliff found out later that, leaving Philadelphia, the two had tried Standard of Indiana, the Mellons of Gulf and then Richfield, the latter traditionally long on sales outlets and short on product. Every company they'd contacted had been interested but Rieber had come up with the best offer.

"Mr. Constable, he has been too kind to me," Rieber was saying. "If he does his duty, he throws me out of here. Never have I been a KinOil shareholder. Now I wish I was. How rich I would be then!"

The shareholders laughed. Rieber could afford his joke. He was said to have packed away a bigger personal fortune than any major oil company executive except the top Rockefeller echelons; such at least was the gossip in Houston, his home base, and throughout the sprawling oil industry everywhere.

"Captain" Rieber had retained his seagoing title from his tanker days. He had first come to Texas as a mate aboard a damaged ship bringing crude from Port Arthur. Joe Cullinan, founder of Texaco, had taken a liking to him, put him in charge of the company fleet, then pushed him to the top. Like Cowdray, Deterding, Teagle and most, in fact, of the pioneer oilmen, Rieber had great daring. He had built a 260-mile pipeline across the Andes to carry Colombian oil to the sea. He had bought half of Socal's interest in the Bahrain and Saudi Arabian concessions—the greatest jackpot in history. The world was his market—politics a nebulous area in which men lacking in a true grasp of affairs sometimes interfered, usually to their own detriment, in the distribution of the commodity by which nations lived or died. Certain of his ships, consigned to "neutral ports"—what was this "neutral"?—changed course mysteriously in midpassage. President Roosevelt was furious; plaster-puss Biddle threatened to indict. "For what?" said Rieber agreeably, showing his large set of teeth. "For conspiracy, sir," said Biddle coldly. Rieber said there had been no conspiracy. During carefree Manhattan evenings, sitting at his favorite table in the 21 Club, chatting with such regulars as Quentin Reynolds, Westbrook Pegler, John O'Hara or Noel Busch, the Captain described his harassments. He gave an amusing imitation of Biddle. The Attorney General was not amused. Rieber's expense accounts were checked. Was that certain jolly lawyer, much entertained by Texaco, in fact the agent of a foreign power? Federal investigators said he was. The lawyer, declared *non grata,* left on a Japanese ship. Texaco shareholders were now as little amused as the lawmen. The stock was falling. Rieber might have to resign. He admitted one mistake: "Maybe I talk too much. . . ."

Cliff, prompted by the Texaco statement, had filled himself in on much of this. He could see how the KinOil deal might, in the clutch, be as important to Rieber as to KinOil—a face-saver.

He paid close attention as the Captain in clear-cut sentences, compacted with his Nordic twang, outlined his salient points: The trade would transfer all of KinOil's rights and assets to Texaco while still leaving KinOil with a degree of autonomy, its identity perpetuated in new nomenclature,

"Texaco-KinOil." The affiliate, though wholly owned, would keep its West Coast offices. Three KinOil nominees would be invited to fill vacancies on Texaco's board.

Dollar comparables to Superior Oil's tender had been worked out by Kuhn, Loeb and Company, an international banking house: by this analysis KinOil shareholders would be getting seventy-four dollars per share, ten dollars more than the figure should they elect to go with Superior.

Constable, on the platform, looked at his watch.

"Two minutes, Captain Rieber."

"Thank you, sir," said Rieber, unruffled. And to his listeners: "Now I come to the best part: taxes. *No taxes*. I am not lying to you: if I tell one lie about taxes you sue me for every dollar I got and the government besides throws me in jail."

He looked around the hall, searching for someone who might be used forensically, in the fragment of time left him, to dramatize this all-important point.

"You, sir," he said, pointing to a burly bald man in the left rear section of the hall. "You, mister—yes, I thank you," as the bald shareholder, as if levitated by a magician, rose to his feet. "Maybe you had your KinOil stock some time?"

And then as the big man, now somehow turned into a collaborator, nodded vigorously, Rieber went on.

"You excuse the question. I don't want to mess into your personal business. But how long, how many years you had that stock? Can I ask you that?"

The man matched Rieber's timing with his own. He hitched up his pants; he put up a large liver-spotted hand and scratched his naked dome. Chuckles rose from the Kinsale relatives, those who in past years had attended the old, so much less formal meetings under the spread greenery of the homeranch. They were in for a treat now, and knew it, after all this dull talk about shares and tenders and such like. Possibly Rieber had been conscious for some time of heavy throat clearings and subdued but audible expressions of approval coming from the section of the hall where he had chosen the big bald fellow now up on his feet—either that or by sheer accident he had picked out of the herd the renowned Judge Blaine Gather, court jester of so many Land and Cattle Company meetings.

Old Blaine could give the Cap as good a show as he dished out, and more to boot.

"Captain Rieber," said the judge, "my pappy give me my stock when I was just a shaver. I was so skinny I was afraid I'd fall through the outhouse hole."

The elegant city and suburban shareholders glared at the speaker with utter revulsion but the country elements roared with laughter.

Constable banged the gavel, but Rieber went on suavely.

"So you've held it, let's say, thirty years?"

"Thirty years and three months. My tax for the tender would be six hundred and eighty thousand dollars. I feel bad when I give some driver a five-dollar fine. What have I done to git fined six hundred and eighty thousand dollars?"

Laughter and clapping.

"Time's up, Captain Rieber," said Constable.

He shook hands with the Texaco chairman, who returned to his seat. The byplay with the judge, however raucous, had got over Rieber's point—the enormous government levies on the profits of a sale to Superior.

A dozen people had their hands up now, some asking for ballots, some for recognition from the chair. Ushers came down the aisles, trailing microphones on long cords. Constable kept order as best he could, finally allotting time in which speeches could be heard—each to have a three-minute limit—with a recess to follow in which ballots could be filled out. Three secretaries, seated at the door, would record the new filings.

Cliff left the ballroom and went down to the Pied Piper Bar; after ordering a drink he spread out the Texaco statement. It was a fine presentation—too bad it couldn't have come earlier. He could see that in many ways the Texaco proposal was of more advantage to the shareholders than Superior's, but he doubted that, in spite of all this last-minute push, the KinOil folk would see it that way. Texaco was a major—dreaded monster!—part and parcel of the huge world consortium against which the smaller companies waged a perpetual contest for survival. Superior, now—there you had just another independent, though a slightly larger one than KinOil. In all likelihood the tender offer would come closer to what the family, at least, really wanted—a "defensive sale" which still presented some aspects of a merger.

Too bad. Rieber's rough-spun personality had its own kind of appeal, and there was the remote personal link with the past—only Luanna and possibly Kyle would have known of Troy's service aboard the Captain's tanker in days gone by.

He ordered another whiskey and was taking his first sip of it when a bellboy came through the bar paging him for the telephone.

His mother was calling him from the ballroom.

"Somehow I thought that's where you'd be."

"Well, I'm sober, if that's what's worrying you."

"Why would it? You never drink, dear, but you can now. You can get as drunk as you like. We're going with Texaco."

So his calculations had been wrong. He could hardly believe his ears, but managed to bring out the appropriate words.

"Great. Congratulations."

"Thanks. But there's still a lot you don't know. Will you please come back here now, as fast as you can?"

Cliff remembered the tone: it was the same Luanna had used in his boyhood, yelling through the door or a window of a little house on an oil-town street, calling him in to supper.

"Whatever you say, Ma."

He put money on the table, left his unfinished drink and hurried out; he hadn't gone far when he saw Alma coming toward him.

"Did Luanna get hold of you?"

"She did. She sounds as if she's riding high."

"She has a right to. The shareholders just voted: she's going on the board and so is Doc Braden."

"What about Constable?"

"He's out."

"How does she like that?"

"Good riddance. You're the one she's worried about now."

"Why me?"

Alma took his arm. She pulled him into an alcove near a serving pantry. Waiters hurried past them, carrying trays of drinks and food.

"Listen, honey. She wants to ask you something. I hope you'll do it—for her sake, for all of us. It could make such a difference."

"What, for Christ sake?"

Four men carrying a banquet table forced them together. Her eyes searched his.

"She's been talking to Rieber. He'll take you on as vice president in charge of production."

"For Texaco? There are twenty guys ahead of me for that."

"Of the Texaco-KinOil affiliate. He wants an answer right away. He's flying east tonight, and the Texaco board will have to confirm you. They're meeting next week. Cliff, dear," she went on hurriedly, as resistance hardened his face, "I know how you feel about the oil business—you've made that very clear. Listen this one time! It could mean a lot, having one executive in the family. Kyle would like it, I know he would."

"I've put in my time, Alma."

"Oh, I know that. Only—try to keep an open mind? Until you've listened to her? I know you two haven't always got along, but this time . . ."

She broke off. A group of musicians, carrying their instruments, followed a hotel official into the banquet hall.

"It's a vice presidency, Cliff."

"Yes, Alma."

"Well, at least I've spoken my piece. . . . Cliff?"

He said nothing, tall beside her, looking down at her with that angle of the head and body that they all had, the Kinsales—so infuriating when they they used it in disagreement.

She turned away, moving down the corridor ahead of him with her light, quick step, her back stiff with annoyance.

The ballroom was almost empty. Men in coveralls were taking down the platform, others stacking the gold chairs. Doc Braden and Millie stood in a group with Luanna and Constable, who seemed to be taking his leave. He bowed over Luanna's hand in courtly style, then turned his heel and stalked out of the room without a glance at the others present.

Luanna came up to Cliff and kissed him.

"You *have* been drinking, shame on you. But perhaps we all should join you. Shall we open some champagne? Aren't you happy?"

"If the deal is what you want, Mother."

"Well, it's not what I planned, but it's . . . splendid. Naturally I'm sorry for poor Harker. He worked so hard on that Superior Oil thing."

"Too bad."

"Oh, I know you never liked him, so let's not talk about *that*."

"I opposed him to ward off what's happened now—a takeover by a major."

"Darling, it's not a takeover. Besides, things change—and they've changed terribly, for all of us. Do you think we could have struggled along without Troy *or* Kyle? Don't be absurd.

At least, thank God, we don't have to struggle along without *you*."

"But you will, Mother."

Luanna looked reproachfully at Alma, as much as to say, "Didn't you persuade him?"—and Cliff realized that Alma's sales pitch in the corridor must have been concocted between the two women.

"If you mean this job with Rieber," he said, "I can't take it. I'm starting a different life. You know that, Mother, and Alma knows it. So what are we talking about?"

"Not politics, I hope," said Luanna, her eyes pulling into slits above the Cherokee cheekbones.

"Mom," said Cliff, "I've just been a delegate to the Republican convention. I'm running for the state assembly in the fall—unless by that time I'm wearing a uniform. Either way, that's politics—whether you like it or not."

"I don't like it a bit. Not that you'd care."

Millie winked at Cliff over Doc's shoulder.

"I would, Mom. And I do," said Cliff. He put his hands on her shoulders, trying to draw her close—to ward off one of her furies, if that was what was coming.

"No, no," she said fiercely. "You *have* been good but you've been flighty too." She jerked away.

"You're going on twenty-seven years old now, son, and you have to settle down. So don't you," she said, her eyes blazing in their deep slits and her voice rising, "stick up your nose at a man like Cap Rieber offering you the vice presidency of a great company, right at his side. Don't you dare! Because he's upstairs now, up in his suite packing his bags. He has to catch a plane. He wants to know your decision. Go up, son, go up there now and tell him your real answer."

"What your mother means," said Doc, deadpan, "is she'd like a Kinsale man with Texaco, looking after her interests. In an executive post—"

"Don't you put words in my mouth, you country saw-bones," said Luanna. "I know how to talk to my own son."

"Excuse *me*, Your Highness," said Doc.

"I know what hurt this boy," said Luanna. "He was just like his father; he had a deep feeling for it, for the substance in the ground. That day when we bailed and bailed and it wouldn't rise in the pipe, he just *knew*. He wouldn't leave; he wanted to stay there. His father had to go after him. He had to catch him and drag him away. He hit him. That's what I mean—that's what Troy never should have done. Troy, the truest, most wonderful man who ever walked the earth and the most loving father and husband. It was the only time he ever raised his hand to Cliff except some little whack on the ass when Cliff freshed off. And Cliff was the one who pitied him. I remember the very words he used. I could never forget. 'I'm sorry for your trouble, Dad,' that was what he said."

"Mom, I *was* sorry. I didn't mind his hitting me. Hell, I'd forgotten all about it."

"But the blow was unfair, son. Troy knew it. You worked, of course; you have oil in your blood, but you never had your heart in it after that. The blow was what turned you away. So don't deny it, dear," she cried, turning the full force of herself back to Cliff, who had been standing idly by, used to these outbursts of old, knowing they would pass. "The blow did it. And Troy didn't understand. Little did he think you'd be the one to pick up his poor body, all busted apart, that awful night in Mexico."

She stood before him, fierce and frail, quaking in all her Indian bones with hope that her ploy would have its aimed effect, that it would pull him down, this big, calm, handsome son with the reddish cast to him, just as she had, that it would reduce him at least temporarily to a boyhood stature that she could control.

Just so he would do her bidding!

For once he didn't know what to do or what to say. Certainly he remembered the wild day when the discovery well at first had refused all wooing. He remembered his father's trapped anger and discouragement—the people leaving, the Bakersfield mayor and all, and his resistance, and the slap. It was all so far away now, the people so small, reduced by distance, yet so clear: shapes in an old photograph that one would have to take to someone older, wiser, and ask, Was that really my pa? Was that me? Was that where we were?

And then at dawn, the house heaving, he falling out of bed, running outdoors, seeing the great black monstrous plume of the blowoff filling the tender sky . . .

He took his mother in his arms. He could feel her heart beating—she had grown so thin! He wondered if it could be true about the fits she said came over her.

"Now you just take it easy, Ma," he said. "You'll be all right, you'll see. You don't need me now—but I'll be watching, I'll be taking care. I'm most grateful to Captain Rieber for his offer of a job for me."

"Grateful?"

"Yes, Ma. I surely am. I'll go upstairs right now and explain to him why I can't take it."

9

"So he walked away," said Millie. "How wonderful!"

"You didn't think he would?"

"I didn't know if any of us would or could."

"You and I don't have to. We aren't hooked."

"We may be hooked more than you think. I don't know what we'll do with all this new stock. Is it really worth as much as they said?"

"More, probably," said Doc.

They were driving to Dead Eagle Valley, he at the wheel of the Auburn, the lights of the Camino Real flicking past.

Millie said, "I hate to think of her racketing around in that big house all by herself."

"So do I. Maybe we should get over to see her more."

"We should, but you know we won't."

"Some Sunday we could. Or a holiday."

"Or the L and CC meetings," said Millie. "Do you suppose we'll still have them now?"

"Of course we'll have them. They're for the land, and the land is home."

"Not anymore. And not for a long time." And then, with one of the effortless changes of subject which both were used to, Millie said, "Maybe now she'll get Helena back from that Swiss university to keep her company."

Doc snorted. He pulled out to pass a hay truck. For a moment the sweet fragrance of alfalfa blocked out the gas swirls of the highway.

"If the school has worked, Helene will be a lady now."

"Are you implying that our sister-in-law is *not* a lady?"

"No. But I'd want to see her diploma."

Millie laughed.

"I loved it when you called her 'Your Highness.'"

"Did you happen to hear what she called me?"

"I'd rather not remember."

A silence fell. Millie watched her husband's profile, outlined by passing headlights; she could tell by the angle of his chin when he was getting tired.

"I'll drive pretty soon," she said.

"Wait till Gilroy. We'll get gas there, and we can switch."

"Yes. And you can stretch out in the back seat and nap."

"I just might," said Doc. "This country sawbones has had a long day."

CHAPTER TWENTY-SIX

The View from Jedda del Beshri

1

Kyle woke that morning (fall, 1940) with the same charged feeling that he'd had in California on the days of major polo games. It was, of course, to be that kind of day—a horse day. Also an oil day. Never forget that part of it, the oil part. He was very positive about the oil this time. No doubt of it at all.

The rig was a vertical black line in a five-hundred-mile circle of naked sand. It had moved three times in fifteen months, from the original concession to Bagga, then from Bagga to Ishriva, and from Ishriva to Jedda del Beshri. In Bagga and Ishriva it had left dry holes behind. After each move, the holes had been plugged. The walking dunes of the sand quickly covered the places where they had been.

Whenever the rig moved there had been pain. New money had been raised. Kyle got the money for Bagga from a consortium of Lazard Frères and certain English bankers after he had abandoned the first site, on the Turkish-Syrian border. He had gone to London with empty pockets which were soon filled when his Armenian friend Nubar Gulbenkian had come up with pounds sterling. When the pounds had shredded into another dry hole Kyle entered into a joint venture with Texaco and BP for one more try, in Syria.

The formations at Jedda del Beshri were very good. British

De Havillands had flown in heavy-duty blowout prevention equipment and Glubb Pasha and his men had come up from H3 to guard the site until Major Gooch was in a dicey spot, down at T1, the only pumping station on the Tripoli pipeline inside Iraqi territory.

T2, T3 and T4 were all in Syria. Beyond T4 the pipeline reached the edge of the desert, at Homs, and between T3 and T4 lay the oasis of Palmyra where the French had built a resort, the Hotel Zenobia; the attractions there were a bartender expert in making pink gins and a few bedraggled Algerian whores. One could also ride by camel or donkeycart to Queen Zenobia's famous walled city with its theater, baths, palace, orchards and great stone colonnades, most of them still standing. Emperor Aurelian had captured Palmyra in A.D. 272 and led Queen Zenobia in chains to Rome; more recently, over the long-buried Roman road, the Free French and the British had been shooting up the Vichy French garrisons; at Sanamein, for instance, Colonel Collet's *groupement* had lost a quarter of its Circassian horsemen, trying to cross the Nahr-el-Awai against enemy machine guns. Further east, the genial and popular General Legentilhomme, peeking out of his solid stone headquarters, had been pinked in the shoulder by a ricochet.

In Libya, General Rodolfo Graziani was bogged down— done for!

Kyle got over to the Hotel Zenobia whenever he could but for the last week he had been living at the rig, sharing quarters with Marsh Borland. Marsh shared also his own positive views about Jedda del Beshri. All day yesterday, to clear the line, he had been letting mud and oil squirt into the sump and the raw, seminal smell of the oil was present in the air along with the fragrance of the coffee, fresh brewed in the British mess, which Trooper Pennyman had just brought in.

Trooper Pennyman was Kyle's batman, detailed to his service by courtesy of Glubb Pasha. He had entered without a sound but Kyle would have known of his presence even without the coffee smell; the opening of the tent flap had sent a ferocious beam of yellow light splintering into the tiny mirror at which Kyle stood shaving. Kyle wiped his face. He sat down in a canvas chair and stretched out his legs so that Trooper Pennyman could pull on his boots. Then he attacked his breakfast—Irish bacon, jam and bully beef, hard biscuit and a pitcher of hot camel milk. The British did well by themselves and their friends, but just because Glubb Pasha, who had served half his life in the desert and spoke faultless, courtly Arabic in several dialects and would eat sheep's eyes swimming in pale tan broth when offered them, or any other stomach-retching native dish—just because he liked camel milk did everyone have to like it?

Kyle didn't, but he dumped it copiously into the good coffee. He had given up drinking his coffee black. It no longer agreed with him that way and could create a churning that would only add to the tight-gutted feeling one experienced on this kind of day, a horse day, an oil day.

He had been thinking, as he shaved, of another such day, the long-ago Sunday when he had played polo against the Argentines and Glenn Laufer, husband of the charming Marjorie (what ever had happened to her, bless her heart?); he had been remembering the wager he'd made privately, betting with himself, that if his team won that game the oil would come in. And it had. By God, it surely had!

He smeared good English gooseberry jam on the jaw-breaking biscuit.

Today he would make no such wager. Today he would not win in the horse games. There was no way he could beat the devilish, agile, young Arabs at their own pastimes. No way in the world, any more than he could wear a *burnous* and headgear and disguise himself as one of them. No one could do that either. There were too many subtleties about the costume, details conveying origin, tribal affiliation, rank—he didn't even believe T. E. Lawrence had done it, no matter what the books said.

He would not win, but he would compete. That would be enough. And it would be a lot.

That bygone morning, at Del Monte, Troy had wired: *"This is the day they give babies away."*

He smiled at the memory—but it was hard, even now, to get used to a world without Troy.

He pushed the tray away and rose. "No bets today," he said to Trooper Pennyman, who had been waiting patiently for him to finish breakfast. Trooper Pennyman wouldn't know what he meant but he could look as if he did. Trooper Pennyman knew the score. His long, narrow face was burned to the red color of the Devon earth from which he sprang. He was a good man to take along.

"The goddamn oil is sure," Kyle said. "This time you can bank on it."

"You're quite right, sir," said Trooper Pennyman.

He held up a sleeveless polo shirt so Kyle could pull it over his head. From outside, a pounding of horses' hoofs shook the tent, followed by a burst of musketry. Kyle had his arms through his shirt. He pulled it down and tucked it into the top of his breeches.

"I gather that the Amir has arrived."

"Yes, sir," said Trooper Pennyman, "last night, past midnight. He's all settled in now, trim and cozy, sir."

The Amir had visited the site before. He had come to witness spudding-in. That had been two months earlier. There had been no games or speeches in his honor, as there would be today, but the drill crew had soon got more than they cared for of his tribesmen's antics, circulating on their small wild mounts, armed with French, German and British rifles and sidearms which they fired incessantly at nothing in particular. The senseless consumption of ammunition was their favorite amusement, outside of horse games.

They were a damned nuisance.

Some of them had stayed to work in camel transport and do odd jobs around the rig; they were good at such things, and at riding patrol, but there was a saying at the rig, you never owned an Arab, you only rented him. He'd disappear whenever the mood pleased him and you could assume he'd gone to work for the Vichies.

Kyle took his pith helmet—another gift from Glubb Pasha—and went outside. He stood in the blazingly bright but still cool morning air, looking about. During the night a city of black tents had sprung up around the rig. There was an area for camels and another for the Amir's war mares and a tent garage for his gun-cars—they would have become unusable if left in the midday sun.

The Amir's tent was in the center of the compound—a billowy, oblong structure, made of black-dyed, tightly woven sheep's wool. It was a beastly heavy thing to transport, but now that piston engines had multiplied on the desert the local shaikhs and minor rulers traveled in style.

Another volley split in the air, at a greater distance now—the palace guard still out for their morning canter.

From the direction of the rig came the sound of hammering. That would be Marsh and his men putting in the separator, a device which looked like an exaggerated version of a housewife's washing machine. The men were hooking it up to the line through which later today the oil would flow. The separator would leach off the gas. You never knew until the separator was working and the oil being piped out how much oil you had or how much gas. That was the problem for today. All you knew was the thickness of the formation. Kyle had an impulse to go over to the control shack and take one more look at the Schlumberger strips that Marsh had pinned up there. These strips recorded the passage of a low-voltage current which had been injected through the formation. All of them showed a beautiful, crazy wobble where the current was diverted by the presence of a non-conductor—the petroleum.

Marsh had run several tests to make sure, and the wobble had always been there. It made Kyle feel fine to look at it. He'd done it a lot; he decided that, in fact, he'd done it enough. The accuracy of the tests would be proved or disproved later today. First would come the horse games, then the banquet. For several days now the arrangements for the games had been ready—the mud wall built for the dash-and-stop exercise, the lances placed in the ground for the turning game, and the race track staked out. Kyle still felt, as he had earlier, the pre-game tension, the tightness and the absurd weariness, the sense of unpreparedness for the task in hand. He knew from experience that somehow these feelings would go away after a while; nevertheless he longed —as before those riding games of quite another sort—for good Tip Morrisey, for the bottle of oatmeal water, for the flask of brandy to be used in emergencies, in Tip's hip pocket. Well, too bad—Tip wasn't around, so to hell with that.

The best way, no doubt, to get over his funk would be to go and look at his horses.

He set off on foot for the stable compound.

2

"I'm sure it's good for you to be riding so much," Alma had written, "but some of these Arab acrobatics, or whatever they are, sound dangerous! I've stood for a lot, but I don't think I could stand for your being hurt just for some crazy horse game. You say they've been playing these games for thousands of years, but *you* haven't. Please, darling, bear that in mind . . ."

Oh, she was a worrier—but only at long distance. What she had to do herself, at home, she'd done with courage and dispatch. She'd attended to everything—the selling of the San

Francisco house, the long, involved dealing with Selim Harkar about the art collection, the sudden, unaccustomed economies which the new explorations and his own departure for the Middle East had forced on her. His credit in the marketplace had been suddenly nonexistent; the trickle he'd been able to raise on personal notes had gone into the new venture and his expenses in setting it up. There'd been a period—she'd touched on this lightly, as if afraid it might anger him—when her family had helped her out.

Well, that was done with now; their troubles would be over as of today. Best of all, they would soon be together again. It had often seemed to Kyle as if that moment would never come.

They'd met only once in fifteen months: a mad ten-day rendezvous in London, in the middle of the bombings. The logistics of that—the priorities for her tirp, the timing of it with his own—would have been impossible without Texaco's power in Washington, plus some help from Cap Rieber. They'd brought it off, they'd honeymooned once more, this time with the German bombers droning overhead, the sirens screaming and the Londoners, when not jammed together in some underground cover, doggedly going about their usual affairs.

They'd stayed at the Savoy, in a suite overlooking the Thames; they'd stretched out deliciously in old-fashioned, seven-foot bathtubs, made love in big clean feathery beds, dined sumptuously in the Grill where, when Parliament was sitting (and it often sat around the clock) the Prime Minister would drop in for a late snack: the hunched, chubby, baldheaded figure who had given England back her glory, who had thundered to his enemies, "We will never surrender . . ."

Ten incredible days—an excursion into a fantasy of terror and splendor. Kyle thought of those days as among the happiest of his life. Back at the drill site, he missed Alma more than ever, but now with the renewed conviction that she would never fail him, no matter what, or he her. The black and bitter mood which had once, for a few moments, made life intolerable—an alien condition—would not bother him ever again. Not even if this roll of the dice went against him. And it would not go against him. The oil was sure.

"No bets today, I don't need them," he said aloud, this time with even less comprehension on the part of his listener than when he had made the same statement to Trooper Pennyman. His Number One groom, Rizah, understood about ten words of English, Kyle, the same amount of Arabic. They communicated by sign language and extrasensory perception.

It was unusual for master and groom to visit her so early. Something out of the ordinary must be afoot today. Mahroosa knew this even while she turned her handsome head toward Kyle, nuzzling him for the dates he always carried in his pocket for her. These men would make demands of her. There were always demands, of different kinds. Well, all right. She was ready. She accepted what Allah sent. Abdul Sadan, who trained horses for King Ibn Saud, had taught her well. She had been Glubb Pasha's mare and she had put up with him, but she liked Kyle better than Glubb; though Kyle was heavier than Glubb he dealt with her lightly. He had hands of silk. He gave her the dates and she chewed them easily since she had no bit in her mouth, she wore only a headstall. Rizah had not yet brought out the ring-bit or the *mariqe*, the light saddle she would wear. She chewed the dates and nuzzled for more. She rolled her eyes softly and stamped her delicate forelegs as if to test the strength of them, first one and then the other.

Mahroosa was a purebred mare of the Saqlawi type, a strain renowned for its beauty. She was a faultless creamy white all over except for the matching black stockings on her hindlegs and a slight feathering of darker tones across her powerful rump. She was four years old, the best age for war or for games. Like all purebred Arabs she had great width of brow and behind the brow the large equine brainpan which makes the Arab more intelligent than other breeds. Because of the width of the brow her large, softly burning eyes were set far out at the sides of her splendid head. With this placement of the eyes Mahroosa could look behind her without bothering to turn her head—or so it seemed. Her head had the exaggerated taper seen in medieval paintings and drawings depicting the war mares and stallions of famous kings and shaikhs; it not only tapered but was slightly scooped or dished, ending in a tiny muzzle which, as the saying went, you could fit in a cup. Kyle had paid Glubb a smashing sum for her—Glubb claiming he was only selling the mare to encourage Kyle's interest in desert riding, but standing hard on his price just the same. Kyle felt he had never made a better investment. He loved Mahroosa like a daughter or a mistress. He was proud to be her master. His aim today was not to do anything stupid, not to shift his weight badly in the game or give some other wrong signal that would spoil her performance. She would know what to do at all times and do it well unless he made some mistake. He ran his hands over her pasterns, more as a form of caress than to feel for the heat of an injury since there was no injury; Mahroosa was perfect in every respect. He discussed briefly with Rizah the tack he wanted used, then let the groom lead the mare off for a short walk to limber her up before it was time to begin.

Khalif, the Number Two groom, held his stallion, Dahman, waiting for inspection in his turn. Dahman was wearing nothing, no headstall, not even a camel's-hair lead rope. Khalif kept him in place by dropping one arm casually over his great stallion neck. Khalif alone could control him that way; Kyle, though on good terms with the horse, had no such power over him until he mounted; then, due to much practice over the past weeks, he had no fears. Dahman was of the Kuhhaylan type of Arab, the strength type. His color was dark bay, the color of roasted coffee, but he was also a *mukhawaze*—a horse with four white stockings "as if he had run through a river," in the Arab phrase. In a language which contains over one thousand words and idioms applying solely to horses and horsemanship (perhaps not strange for a race whose survival for thousands of years has depended on horses and the skills of handling them) there was another term also for Dahman: *khatan*, "the Bridegroom" (a stallion which has been marked as a future breeding-stud by clipping the tip of his right ear). Not that Dahman, so far, had been bred: to have used him thus would have made him unmanageable on the field where mares were competing. Like Mahroosa, he too had been perfectly trained. He could run and turn, rear and spin like the legendary winged sexless steed of the prophet Mohammed which had the head of an angel and the face of a peacock. Kyle would need some such mount to do well in the wall-game, the most dangerous and taxing of today's exercises. Dahman came close. He would wear the big, upholstered war saddle, but it would still not be easy to stay with him. Kyle fed him, too, dates, and Dahman jerked his head high and sucked in the sand-and-smoke, tree-and-camel-dung smell of the desert through his kingly nostrils.

When he brought his head down again, Kyle spoke to him reassuringly in English, telling him only what Dahman already knew well—that they had a job to do together; then he patted him and left him to the care of Khalif and his own devices.

Servants were laying out carpets for the spectators to sit on outside the Amir's tent; down at the rig the hammering went on.

Glubb Pasha was nowhere to be seen. Probably he was still snoozing. He would not be riding today. Though an excellent horseman he had never drilled himself in the Arab exercises. Kyle understood this: Glubb had a fine sense of elitism. As the British authority in the area he could do nothing that would impair his dignity.

Kyle's funk was dissolving but his drowsiness remained. Could there be time for a short nap before everything started? Perhaps—just barely. He went off to his tent where Trooper Pennyman had put everything shipshape.

"Call me in forty-five minutes," Kyle commanded.

Trooper Pennyman waved off a half-salute and went out of the tent, closing the flap carefully behind him.

Kyle took off his helmet. He drank some water, then a nip of brandy. He lay down on his cot and crossed his booted legs. He fell instantly asleep.

3

The Amir came out of his tent at two o'clock. He sat down in a camp chair, British style, to witness the games. On his left sat the elders of his court, the old warriors who composed his entourage. They had ridden with him for years, in the desert raids that followed the Great War. They had seen many shaikhs rise to power for a while and then go under. They had stood firm. They sustained the Amir and still protected him night and day, for no one knew when an enemy might strike, even with Glubb Pasha at hand and an oil well, it was said, about to come in.

The elders were stern, lean old men with dark skins, gray beards, and faces like falcons or foxes. They would be judges at the games. They would confirm or refute the decisions of the judge on the field.

On the Amir's right sat Glubb Pasha. With him were three

staff officers. All, like Glubb, wore khaki fatigues, pith helmets and full decorations. Out of courtesy to the Amir they refrained from smoking. To a Moslem, the use of tobacco is a deadly sin, in a class with murder or adultery— worse indeed than putting the left hand in a dish of food in order to convey some to one's mouth. One ate with the right hand. But the eating would be done later.

Marsh and his crew, finished with their morning's work, had a spectator section to themselves.

Kyle lingered to watch the first part of today's drill. This consisted in a mad dressage by the Amir's cavalry: the horsemen rode in at top speed, firing their rifles into the air as was their stupid custom. They formed into columns of two abreast, crisscrossing in an intricate, serpentine pattern in which each man controlled his mount by leg signals alone, never touching the reins. To Kyle the riders looked like brigands of the lowest sort, which in a sense they were, but they were also passionately religious, supremely fatalistic and completely fearless. Their horsemanship was perfect and their mounts beyond compare. After the drill they rode away with more shooting and yelling, and the British staff and the elders rose to salute them, the Amir alone remaining seated.

Kyle left to warm up Mahroosa for the lance game.

Rizah had been holding the mare in what shade he could find, behind the Amir's tent. She was calm and playful, only the slightest hint of sweat darkening her creamy coat. Kyle figure-eighted her gently while he waited for the other competitors, several British officers among them, to line up. He nodded a greeting to the youngest rider present, a very handsome, beardless, long-legged boy of seventeen, the Amir's youngest son, Jelou. Kyle had met Jelou during the Amir's first visit and liked him but he had not known that he was going to compete. Would his presence make a problem for the judges? Kyle hoped not: the Amir took pride in demonstrating his impartiality. He had once had another of his sons publicly whipped for killing a tribesman's cow.

Aha! The field judge lining them up now—twenty-one horsemen, facing the three rows of lances. Off go the first three, weaving through the rows, circling each lance three times right, three times left, down to the end and then back again, at the last lance swinging out of the saddle low enough to rip off the clump of ostrich feathers tied where the lance pierces the sand. Tight, tight circles now, or you'll be hanging there with grit in your mouth and the horse out from under you . . .

Crack! A lance broken; the rider disqualified—too bad, he'd been in front. . . .

Time out!

The field judge lowers his arm. Out go three more, the winner this time a heavyset, older bedouin, forty if a day, maybe fifty.

So there was a chance for the old buggers after all. Kyle brought Mahroosa up to the starting line—he'd be going in the next set, Jelou in the lane alongside. Mahroosa takes off like the wind, round the first lance, changing leads, round the second, third, fourth, fifth, Kyle hooking a spur over the saddle to stay with her, sweeping out wide, fast and low, grabbing for the damned clump of feathers.

Missed! Back to the barn, lady—sorry and all that, but at least we were in there, we put on a show.

He rode slowly off—the Amir, Pasha's staff and even the elders giving him a hand. What the hell, he thought, is a jackass of my age doing out here, riding against a seventeen-year-old Arab on his own turf?

Better just get the mare into a cooling-sheet, have a rammer for myself and pull my dumb, middle-aged guts together for the wall-game, the one that divides the men from the boys.

The wall-game was an exercise in stopping. Just that—no more, no less—but a kind of stopping that could kill you and the horse both, or one or the other separately, and make no mistake about it. You turned your nag loose. That was the nub of it. You went full out down a staked lane toward a piece of wall. Then you stopped. You did not take up on the bit, the reins had to be slack. All you did was shift your weight to the rear—your mount did the stopping for you, a slide-stop, rearing as he shoved his hind legs under him. That was the trick of it, and the requirement—that you stop with him upright, flush against the fucking wall.

Nor were you through yet, even if you made the stop in perfect form. On that reared-back mount you had to face about and salute the judges before you let the forelegs come down.

Dahman could do it. He'd been doing it for years and he was famous for it. Also here today you had another favorable factor: the wall was a simulation. Instead of the solid masonry you'd have been up against in some old-time caliph's castle or crusaders' fort, you faced a wall of mud bricks covered over with a piece of tenting cloth. You could knock it over, if you chose to be inept, and you'd probably come through.

A better idea, brother: just don't knock it over!

Only six starters this time: Jelou and the old guy who had come in second in the lance exercise; also a pair of wizened, undersized tribesmen on mounts that looked fit to fall down, plus one new man—a noble of some kind, broad shoulders and tiny waist, gold bangles on his arms, an ugly, scimitar-nosed puss on him.

The British officers were not entered. This kind of drill was not learned at Sandhurst.

The judge's signal—go! The race, the slide-stops! Perfect! Those two desert buddies know what they're doing. Only one thing wrong, the black paws the wall, loses his balance on the turn, touches his front feet to the ground before his rider can get him up again! No good; so—a score for the cross-breed with the golden mane and tale.

Next pair: scimitar-nose against the old bugger, the pudgy courtier. Old bugger crashes, comes down heavily on his well-padded ass but is up again in a flash, running after his horse as it trots away from him, unhurt, the reins dangling. The Amir is amused, the judges laughing. It seems the old bugger is some kind of relative of the Amir, a kissing cousin. The judges respect his guts, sportsmanship being very big with them. They give him a hand . . .

Last pair: Kyle versus Jelou. A mismatch if ever there was one. Jelou has just won the lance-game. And he is the Amir's *son!* In a close decision the falcon-faced and fox-faced judges might think of that.

Bookmakers, had there been any around, wouldn't be making Kyle the favorite.

"Line up, gentlemen," says the field judge. Or the equivalent of that in Arabic. He sits calm and solid on a brown gelding no bigger than a donkey. Servants are brushing out the shallow trench used as a starting line.

Go!

Jelou off smoothly on a fine, short-coupled gray; Kyle fighting Dahman who, usually composed as a judge, takes it into his head to reach for the sky.

Jelou and the gray are already four lengths down their lane.

Speed counts in the judging, it's not everything but . . . Jesus! What's got into the shit-head stallion? Kyle has him on the ground at last—feels the great muscles surge under him.

Dahman knows the moment better than he. NOW! Sit back—the movement of an inch, two inches. That's enough. Dahman's haunches tense, the hind legs go under, the front feet spring up, up against the wall, seeming to touch but not quite touching, the great neck coiled, the muzzle down, the brow lined with the chest, and Kyle vertical also, flattened on the stud's back.

So far, so good.

Jelou—now where is he? Kyle can see out of the corner of his eye the prince's gray mare rearing, still in the air . . . WHAT?

Something is wrong. For the gray is there all right but . . . she's *riderless* . . . Jelou . . . *where in hell is Jelou? . . . Only one place he can be . . .*

Dahman is taking his first powerful bound toward the finish line. Kyle brings him up, Dahman fighting the ring-bit, Dahman knowing he and his rider have the game won, feeling Kyle must have gone mad to be checking him now. . . .

Kyle relentlessly turns him back.

Prince Jelou is on the ground. He's prostrate under the hoofs of his mare. And the mare, incredibly, is still erect, still dancing, turning and turning on her hind legs in the reared position, the saddle half off, pulled to one side and empty, the stirrups swinging, the dust rising. Jelou down there somewhere, a lump in the sand, helpless as the hoofs strike downward.

Spectators are running out.

Kyle snatches at the gray's loose reins . . . misses them . . . then has them, the gray hitting at him with both front feet. He pulls her off the fallen man.

The field judge on his pony reaches Jelou, kneels beside him. And now others. They make a litter out of lances and a *burnu;* they carry him off. . . .

"He was a fool to ride that mare, you know," said Glubb Pasha. "His father told him not to."

"Why, was something wrong with her?"

"She'd been trained as a dancing mare."

"A dancing mare?" said Kyle.

He and Glubb were sitting next to each other at the banquet in the Amir's tent—Jelou, not much the worse for wear, a few places down. The battalion doctor had examined him: two broken ribs, some bruises, a kick in the head that could have been a fracture but the doctor didn't think so. The kick was what had immobilized him, knocking him unconscious so that he hadn't rolled away from the hoofs.

". . . they dance *on* a man. Or seem to. They work with the dervishes—*dayyars:* a religious show. In fact the word dervish stems from another Arab word: *darwish.*"

"You mean fakirs?"

"Not exactly. Holy men, really. They put themselves into a trance and the mares dance on them. Can't hurt them, since they have Allah's protection. I suppose the trick must be that the weight is off the hoof that strikes the man. *Dayyars* command great respect. They are chosen of Allah. Jelou may have thought the horse was blessed."

Glubb watched a servant pour tea into a tiny cup from a spout held three feet above it. Spilling even one drop would have been a breach of etiquette. No drop was spilled. Glubb Pasha raised the cup to his lips. You drank a lot of tea in the interminable course of a long meal during which no alcohol was served.

"By the way, the Amir appreciates what you did, pulling the nag off his son. He wants to do something to show his gratitude. He asked me what I thought you'd like."

"What did you tell him?"

"Never mind. You'll find out in due course."

The servants were passing small sweet pastries made of barley, dates and ground locusts. Glubb Pasha helped himself copiously. He had a stomach of iron.

The Amir's gift turned out to be a hunting falcon, the creature closest to the Amir's heart: closest, that is—as he set forth in his presentation speech—next to the son who had been preserved for him today by Kyle's prompt action. The gift was not enough by any means to encompass the feelings it represented, but the Amir begged Kyle to accept it in the spirit of eternal brotherly esteem and respect. All this, translated by Glubb's ADC, a tall subaltern with an earnest, schoolboyish manner, brought a great round of applause. The Amir himself placed the hooded bird on Kyle's wrist and Kyle, who had been beaten hands down by Scimitar Nose in the finals of the wall-game, thought with pleasure, so I am getting a prize after all.

The Amir and his guests rose from the banquet table toward evening, replete now and ready for the ceremonies still to come. The Amir's gun-cars were lined up outside and the more important guests got into them, others mounting their horses or proceeding on foot; after all, the distance from the Amir's tent down to the rig was only a few hundred yards. The working lights blazed up and down the derrick as if this were to be just a night of drilling like any other.

Kyle always enjoyed the desert most as twilight fell. Then a new softness smoothed away the menace which coarsened these alien spaces by day. New contours appeared in it then, erotic in the softly spreading duskiness, the secret curves and odors that had been withheld or hidden from the sun. The desert then was like a naked woman, dusky, deep-bosomed, a woman drowsy and passionate who had put off an unbecoming robe to embrace you and take you into herself with a spell which would last forever—yes, a proud and loving woman like his Alma.

The dusk was clear and windless. It piled high into the sky above the rig, dwarfing the group assembled down below.

Everything was in place. Trust Marsh for that. The blowout prevention equipment had been tested—it would hold. The separator had been properly installed and a good smell of oil came from the sump. They were home free now—into a field? Surely there was a field down there, a huge subterranean reservoir—or so at least you could assume for now. And keep your fingers crossed.

Marsh tapped Glubb Pasha on the arm. This was the moment of truth. Glubb Pasha mounted the small platform, draped with a beat-up Union Jack and some red-white-and-blue stuff that was supposed to represent the Stars and Stripes. Glubb introduced Kyle, and his own remarks, a rehash of what he'd said at the banquet, wound up with a call on the Amir. Never one to hang back in such circumstances, the Amir almost leaped onto the dais. He launched at once into a lively speech. This time no arrangements had been made for translation, but when he finished all present clapped furiously. Marsh Borland raised an arm, signaled to Kyle, and Kyle escorted the Amir off the platform and around the rig to the main T-valve. They had rehearsed this piece of business several times, so the Amir knew what to do. He turned the big valve counter-clockwise and with a shudder and a heave and then a solid, even throb from eleven thousand feet down, the oil flowed through the new line which would take it to T3, and from there through the old 24-inch to Homs and the tanker anchorages in the Mediterranean, and the war.